HOLLYWOOD SOUND . . .

'Boys, meet my new friend, Mr Leslie Buckingham
– from London, England . . . and New York City,'
Solomon said, glancing down at a handsomely
engraved calling card, 'Uh – he's from the
headquarters office of what is called the Alleffects
Company, Limited, of America. How does that
sound?' Introduction completed, Solomon let out
his breath, then continued.

'While you both were being entertained by
Thomas Edison in Philadelphia, Mr Buckingham
came to our theatre to show us something his
company with the fancy name says is going to
revolutionise this whole business! A shame it
wasn't yesterday, maybe you could have saved
taking the trip.'

Ham was hopping up and down with eagerness to
speak, and broke in on his father.

'Sound! Sound . . . to go with the pictures . . . And
Mr Buckingham has all his things right here with
him . . . the Alleffects machine, and I helped him
move it up on our stage. Wait till you hear what it
does! It's all set up inside and he brought a special
reel of film and for free he's going to demonstrate
for our first show tonight!'

The Dream Factory

JACK WARNER, JR

SPHERE BOOKS LIMITED
London and Sydney

First published in Great Britain by
Sphere Books Ltd 1985
30–32 Gray's Inn Road, London WC1X 8JL
Copyright © 1982 by Jack Warner, Jr.

This is a work of fiction. The characters, incidents,
places and dialogues are products of the author's
imagination and are not to be construed as real. The
author's use of names of actual persons, living or
dead, is incidental to the purposes of the plot and is
not intended to change the entirely fictional character of the work.

TRADE
MARK

Set in 9/9½ pt Compugraphic Mallard

Printed and bound in Great Britain by
Collins, Glasgow.

To my wife
Barbara
for her encouragement
and invaluable help.

And with special appreciation to
Carole Baron, Arthur and Richard Pine and
Irma Rogell.

Besser a mensh und nicht a Yid, oder a Yid und nicht a mensh.

Better to be a decent human and not a Jew, than a Jew and not a decent human.

– Yiddish saying

Part One

CHAPTER ONE

'Deuce!' shouted the man with the worried eyes and the callused hand as he bit into a thick hamburger sandwich, which squirted rich brown juice and a slice of tomato out onto the court surface. The defending net player raced back, stepped on the tomato and came crashing down on the seat of his white shorts. Two spectators – a doctor and an attorney – droppe their food and ran from the sidelines to the fallen player, but he bravely smiled and struggled back to his feet unaided. The two men returned to their seats, minus either patient or client, and glumly continued eating their food.

A very angry voice roared from the far court, and all heads turned toward its source.

'Goddammit, Sandy! How many times do I have to tell you not to eat where somebody will slip on the crap you drop and break their neck – or their ass!' Ham Robbins was outraged today at many things: hamburgers, tomatoes, tennis *shnorrers* and Sandy Nichols. That close call just now to a stinking personal-injury suit, and the insurance complications sure to follow, made him squeeze his racket handle almost one size smaller. Not one word, though, of sympathy for the recovered player, who scraped tomato off his shoe and dust from his shorts. This was the fourth time Ham's idiot doubles partner had thrown them back into deuce when they had game, set and match in their pockets. The fact that he was playing with a member of the United States Davis Cup team was beside the point, as was the continual poaching by Ham into his harried partner's territory. Time after time his partner would line up a sure-kill smash shot into their opponents' court: then Ham raced across the midline from his side, leaped high in the air and batted the ball into the net, over the ivy-shrouded fence or at the hamburger-eating beer drinkers watching from the sideline guest house.

It was the usual Sunday afternoon tennis game at Ham Robbins' place. The magnificent court with its cushioned seats overlooking the playing area had its usual assortment of excellent players, a few fair ones and several nonplaying spectators who knew precisely when and for whom to cheer. These last were drawn by the food and drink and the possibilities for business. Ham ran these Sunday matches much as he did a picture being shot out at the studio. Sandy Nichols, the juice dripper, was a former internationally seeded player now on the studio's publicity department payroll. His real job, though, had nothing to do with the studio. Outwardly a happy, smiling man, Sandy was fast developing into a top-seeded worrier of world class. With a damp towel he mopped up the small mess he had made on the court surface, wishing he were in Forest Hills instead of being headed for Forest Lawn. Sandy was casting director for these Sunday entertainments at Ham Robbins' perfectly groomed courts and was expected to line up the best players available in the Los Angeles area, one of the tennis capitals of the world, and invite them to play up here on Sierra View Drive. This was not too difficult, as the court had a reputation for physical beauty and general quality of play. The food and drink and company were excellent, and it was a welcome relief from the grind of the tennis tour. The part making Sandy so increasingly upset was having to tactfully explain to each new visiting tennis star that his doubles partner, or occasional opponent, would be their host. Ham Robbins was to win enough of the games to make him believe it was because of his superior backhand, smashing forehand, devastating service and all-around skill at net. Though Ham was a fairly capable player for his age, weight and build, he was not half as good as the contrived victories and his ego made him appear.

Now and again things went all wrong in spite of Sandy's tact, when a new player in town forgot himself and won too often or by too wide a margin or, worst of all, smashed a fast drive into the body of their host. Then Sandy would scratch the overachiever's name off the list and he would never again taste the famed Robbins hamburgers or quaff the chilled draft beer on a lovely Beverly Hills Sunday afternoon.

A few studio executives and an occasional agent with an important client being wooed for a film might be among the guests. These people never needed Sandy to tell them who was going to win. They could look good – but never too good – and if Sandy matched them with or against the Chief, they knew their roles perfectly and the game that was

4

expected of them. Any business talk must be deferred until
the playing on the courts was over. There would be plenty of
time later for the other games they all played so well – negotiations, anticipations and recriminations.

Usually when the tennis was done there would be a buffet
dinner up in the party room, and then came the screening of a
new picture in the theater that filled the basement of Ham's
mansion overlooking the tennis court and swimming pool.
Now and then a top-rated woman player might be invited, but
except for a pretty young starlet or two sitting around as
living decorations with their cute behinds stretching skin-
tight tennis shorts, the near absence of women and of a
hostess went almost unnoticed. Everybody sensed there was
someone up there on the second floor of the house whose
name was Nita Kobbins and that she was Ham's wife – but
very few of the tennis players or the others had seen her for
many years, and it seemed almost as though she existed in
some other place in another time.

The sun dipped behind the palm trees and the court lights
were put on. Ham, who was letting others play after the
disastrous last set, pulled a wristwatch from his pocket,
checked the time and jumped to his feet. He looked trim and
much younger than his years. All those hours on the massage
table, in the steam room and chasing after tennis balls paid
off as he stood there, face flushed and pulse speeding from
his exercise. The players stopped their rally and came over
to their host, who stood by the net post.

'All of you keep playing as long as you want. Sandy, watch
everything, and this time remember to turn off the court
lights when you leave. Make sure you lock up the bar. The
damned gardeners are stealing my Scotch and getting so
loaded they leave the lawn sprinklers on all night!'

Sandy made the fatal error of trying to crack a joke.

'Chief – I'd hate to have either your water bill or your
Scotch bill!'

Ham was not amused, and fixed Sandy with a piercing
look.

'Keep your mind on the tennis, Sandy. I handle the smart
cracks around here, and don't forget it. Sorry, folks, no
screening tonight. I promised to show up at some kind of a
banquet at the Palladium in a couple of hours. Can you beat
it, I'm getting a cockamamy award as 'Hollywood Humanitarian of the Year!' Either somebody has a hell of a sense of
humor or he's trying to con me for a job. What the shit – it's

5

all in a day's work. Some bastards cooked up this crap – and like a shmuck I went along with it, and now it's too late to back out. Well – the tennis was good, so the day hasn't been a total loss! Good-bye, and Sandy will let you know who's coming back next Sunday. Don't forget what I told you about turning the lights off, Sandy, unless you want to be playing in somebody else's court!'

He shook the sweaty hand of the lean young Davis Cupper, waved at the other players and freeloaders, then again at Sandy, whose tensions began to ease now that the session was ending. A dark heavyset man, known simply as the Greek, appeared silently, and Ham walked with him off the court and across the lawn to the pool house. For nearly fifteen minutes he lay naked on a massage table while the Greek's magic hands soothed away the ache of old muscles in rebellion. Half awake, he walked into a shower and soaked in the comforting warm water, gasping as the spray turned into an ice-needled finale. He dried off with the Greek's help and pulled on fresh underwear and socks. With a soft terry cloth robe wrapped around his shoulders to keep off the evening chill, he went out again onto the lawn.

Ham briskly went up a flight of stone-paved steps cut in the side of the hill, following a path softly lit by lamps set in the low hedges. A gentle rise in the ground led him through the magnificent formal rose gardens surrounding the house. Several paces behind walked an armed security guard, one of the two studio police always on duty roaming the estate grounds. They reached the house, where the guard unlocked a side door leading into the basement screening room and bar, and Ham went inside as the door was swung shut and locked behind him.

Nita Robbins, once fairly well known to certain small-time casting directors and agents of doubtful reputation as Nita de Valle, was a vivid argument against ageing. Now a heavy smoking, hollow-cheeked woman, her once inviting curves and seductively soft voice had become all sharp points and angles. Once-bright hair of an incredible redness was now a frizzled mass of tight henna-rinsed curls, and she wore baggy, shapeless, garish patterned dresses that might have been left behind by some long departed cook.

The most memorable and disconcerting thing about her were still those piercing deep brown eyes that seemed to reach out and hold tightly to whatever person or object fell within their range. Now she sat staring down at a large chart of the planets, which was unrolled and held down with weights to cover the big round table in the middle of her bedroom. A wispy little man wearing a loose-fitting open-collared shirt sat across from her and nervously scribbled on pads, made tiny notes on the charts, sighed and showed signs of deep distress. He spoke in just above a whisper, with a chain-smoker's rasp.

'Are you absolutely positive as to the date and time of his birth? There could be an inconsistency . . . some of these people lie about such things just to get a license or job. It looks as bad as it could possibly be, Mrs. Robbins. Keep him away!' He coughed with the dry anguish of a smoker forbidden to smoke.

She reached across the table to pull the notes closer. Her piercing dark eyes covered the page in an instant. There still were remnants of the deep throaty promise in her voice that Ham had once found so attractive and compelling.

'That fucking agency knows damn well that when I ask for people they are to give me full and complete information . . . and that means exact dates and everything else I must know . . . everything . . . everything! I cannot trust them. This one will never work out! Every sign is in direct conflict with me. They should never, absolutely never, have sent his man here! I don't care if he has the best references in the world or was chauffeur for the Duchess of Kent! My God . . . look at his signs and the way they oppose mine! It's insufferable! Tomorrow I'll phone and give them absolute hell for wasting our valuable time on him. Now give me the other card.'

Except for the round pool of light on which the table seemed to float like a wooden island, the room was almost black, with tiny spotlights beaming down from the ceiling on the litter of charts, graphs, books and scraps of paper. Outside the darkness of this heavily curtained and paneled bedroom on the second floor of the magnificent house was a glorious estate with gardens, sweeping lawns, fountains, pools and waterfalls that kept five full-time gardeners busy, but the woman leaning over her cluttered table rarely ventured beyond these walls. Her few excursions into the world outside were usually to visit a variety of doctors who dreaded her appointments and to an occasional clinic happy enough to see her money, happier to see her leave. A long-ago bit actress, or perhaps an extra with far more ambition than talent, she seemed sick in ways difficult even for specialists to describe. Once she had a bright and sensual beauty that, like her flaming red hair, stood out in a crowd scene. Now she avoided all but the very few people she felt she could trust – until they failed her, as they always did. Then she made a search for others whose horoscopes, she hoped, would not have the hidden errors and omissions that her former astrologers must have missed spotting, costing her so much in emotional exhaustion. There had been one frightening meeting with a psychoanalyst recommended by someone no longer a friend. The session ended almost before it began when she fled in terror at the probing questions she could answer to nobody, perhaps not even to herself. And so she sought comfort in the stars, planets and galaxies, where she could ask all the questions and receive only sure and comforting answers, except occasionally when they concerned her hired help.

Ham silently walked down the deeply carpeted hall from his rooms at the other end of the house, where he slept and dressed. He and Nita had not shared a bed or bedroom since a time and a night he tried not to remember. Now he opened the door to Nita's suite and stepped into the foyer, hidden in the darkness. He watched the woman as she sat utterly consumed with her mystic business. She was not joining him on this night he was to be honored, and he felt a sad satisfaction that once again they would go their separate ways.

Over the years, almost without his fully realizing what was happening, Nita had driven away most of his old friends, alienated every member of his family and built higher and higher walls behind which he had to come and join her if he felt the need. The need was now gone and instead had become a habit. At least, he thought, he was not the prisoner she had made of herself and could come and go freely through the massive bronze gates that sealed off the estate from the street and the world.

What once had seemed only to be a possessive jealousy of the man she had taken away from another woman had in time become a kind of sickness of revenge and other symptoms as she guided him with his half-willing compliance away from brothers, sisters, son and all those old friends left back in the swamps of yesterdays. Now, having gained everything she had fought so hard to possess, losing only her youth, beauty and tranquillity, she had become infatuated with astrology, numerology, supernatural things beyond comprehension, the seers and all those leeches who lived off the fears, supersti-

8

tions, hates and memories of rich idle women growing old, fat and frightened.

She picked up the phone and called the housekeeper downstairs.

'Mrs. Burke, send the new chauffeur away immediately! I'll call the agency tomorrow morning for someone else. Get him out of this house at once!' Soon all the bad vibrations she could sense coming upstairs would fade away.

Ham watched this display and remained another few moments in the darkness beside the half-open door. He was immaculate in his tux, and the good clean smell of shaving lotion filled his nostrils. Again he looked at Nita and the astrologer bent over the new sets of figures on the housekeeper, a most important member of this household, whose charts must be kept absolutely current. Housekeepers arrived and departed so rapidly in this place that their charts were constantly being drawn, redrawn, revised and abandoned. The woman downstairs must be known in every phase, cusp and curve or one of the rocks on which this house stood might crumble.

Perhaps Nita sensed that her husband stood nearby in the darkened room, but she would not have bothered to look even if he had moved into the light. What she was doing was much too important. He would have to get his ass kissed by all those fools without any help from her.

Why in the name of God, Ham thought, had he ever allowed her to come back here after his people found her that night up in Beverly Glen with . . . Forget it! Blot it out! What good did it do to remember now? He had been a stupid fool to let her come crawling back into his life, pleading and crying . . . but he was damned then and damned now if he would ever let his dear sisters – and the memory of his brothers and parents – have their smug satisfaction with those words he hated more than any others in the whole world: 'We told you so!'

Slowly he shook his head to clear away the memories. It was too late now. There she sat with her asshole astrologer and their charts, reading the stars as though she could find all the answers in outer space, when the problems were right down here on earth. A fool married to a fool taken back by a fool!

'Humanitarian . . . Humanitarian of the Year . . . That's what they're going to call me tonight – along with a lot of other things! Who the hell is kidding who!' he muttered to himself as he looked over his wife's head at the shriveled

9

little man, whose straggly beard brushed the big curling chart. Ham's silent conversation with himself continued.

'Ha . . . I wonder if that phony runt can horoscope some of those shitty pictures we've been putting out lately before we spend our money and tell us if they're bombs or Oscars . . . My God – I'm being taken in too!'

Deep inside he felt everybody at the Palladium tonight would secretly be laughing at him. The ghosts of his brothers, his sisters . . . Momma . . . Poppa . . . all of them, all laughing somewhere at little Chaim Rabinowitz, the *pisher* with the plaque saying he was something they damn well knew he was not. Hamilton J. Robbins – Hollywood Humanitarian of the Year! Laughing at him the way the whole town had laughed at poor old Louie B. Mayer after he had lost all his power and they gave him something called the Big Brother Award. Ham remembered joining in that laughter, and tonight it was going to be his turn. Louie was laughing someplace too, damn him!

He was hit by a sudden painful cramp deep in his gut and grabbed at his stomach with both hands for an agonizing moment. The pain passed quickly, and as he turned to leave the room a great bubble of gas left him, with the roar of small thunder. He went on through the door, closing it behind him. Nita and the astrologer started and turned in alarm at the noise, but the door was closed, the corner was dark and only the fetid odor remained.

The black Bentley waited in the circular drive, which swept around the Spanish fountain in the forecourt. The motor idled softly and the studio driver held the door open for Ham, who came out of the house, stepped into the car and slid behind the wheel. He hated having anybody else drive him, and whenever possible the foot on the pedal and the hands on the steering wheel were his. The driver ran around the back and got up front beside him. Ham quickly had the big car around the circle, down the hill, past the pool and the deserted tennis court. He turned his head slightly to make certain that all the lights had been put out, then brought the car to a stop as they reached the guard who stood beside the massive closed gates. The two bronze portals were over ten feet high, so it was not possible for casual passersby or tourists to peer into the estate and violate the privacy of those inside. Pressure on a button sent out a signal from the car that started the gate sections moving, and they silently slid apart on their tracks. He waved at the guard, then drove through and with another push on the button closed the gates, sealing off nearly everything he had left behind. Some thoughts of what was still up there in the darkened bedroom came through the gates with him and could not be blocked by the pushing of buttons.

He drove down the short stretch of Sierra View Drive, then swept on through dark side streets to Laurelwood. This was just across a hill from the Pickfair estate, where Ham and his brand-new bride, the stunning dark actress with those hypnotic eyes, had been royally entertained by Mary and Doug . . . or was it Buddy? When was that . . . centuries ago?

The car moved down the hill through the narrow residential streets dimly lit by an occasional lamp, as though Beverly Hills had secrets to keep in the dark. Suddenly they burst into an intersection and were on North Beverly Drive, a wide and well-lighted street, where Ham turned left to Coldwater Canyon, going past a fire station that in any other place could have been mistaken for a private home. Five minutes later he had left the Canyon and was following the rising twists and turns of Lago Vista Drive.

High above the city like a lovely blue jewel in a setting of green hills was a small body of water called Lake Franklin. A part of the Beverly Hills reservoir system, it was practically unknown to most of those who drank or flushed its contents. A few homes had been built above the little lake, and Ham pulled up to one near the end of the short street. A man stood alone beside a parked sports car and shielded his eyes from the approaching headlights.

'Hi, Chief, right on the dot. Shall I get her?' The voice had the kind of lilt only someone born and raised in Dublin could use with such ease. George O'Neill had a rather special job of great value to Ham. He was urbane, entertaining and, above all else, discreet. Though publicly a part of the studio, George, like Sandy Nichols, was privately in the direct employ of Ham Robbins, who relied on him for very special services – absolute loyalty, discretion and availability at any hour.

Ham sat for a moment behind the wheel, his mind elsewhere, then realized he had been spoken to.

'Yeah . . . okay, George. Tell her to move her ass.' He unclenched his tense hands from the wheel and waited. O'Neill walked up the path to the front door, which swung wide before he reached it, letting a broad beam of light come

11

out into the night, and with it a very well built beautiful young woman of perhaps twenty-five blonde years. She pulled the door shut, turned the key and walked with O'Neill to the waiting Bentley. The rear door was held open and the girl, her full mink coat, and George all got inside. The door was closed and the studio driver returned to his seat beside Ham, who turned as much as he could, tilting his head back so the girl could lean forward and give him a kiss on the cheek to show some affection, but not enough to smear her lipstick or muss her hair. That would all come later.

'How in hell did I ever let myself get talked into this fucking evening!' Ham said to the two in the backseat, who returned no answers because they had none. He got the car moving in a tight turn, coming again to Coldwater, then on to the Sunset Boulevard intersection. He might have thought of a few answers of his own to the unanswered question, but was too busy watching for the light to change so he could make the left turn that would put them on their way toward Hollywood and what was waiting there at the Palladium.

The girl in the backseat had one great quality in addition to the superb body that she knew how to use so well. When she had nothing to say, she kept her beautiful mouth shut. This was something Ham appreciated. Too much of his time was spent around people who filled his ears and wasted his time with worthless chatter, always asking for something. He was finding more of his old pleasures with this girl and her considerate silence. One thing he enjoyed about her – she was full of tricks in bed that made him feel young again for a few hours – almost as young as he was the first night with Nita, who used to have some pretty good tricks of her own. He gripped the wheel in suddenly remembered anger at thoughts of the woman in the dark bedroom who made him feel that for all his power and masculinity, he was hopelessly enmeshed in a trap they had built together.

The car left Beverly Hills to enter the neon-stained Sunset Strip with its senseless sensual billboards stuck high on the violated buildings. They all seemed to blatantly advertise sex-soaked, electronic-noise-making groups bearing weird names concocted by lobotomized louts. Ham felt a sense of personal outrage at what he saw until he remembered his own company had gone into the record business less than two years before – somewhat against his better judgment after meeting some of the peculiar people in this odd business. Now those noisemaking perverts with all their youth,

12

energy, drugs and sex were earning beautiful profits for Robbins International. He smiled and relaxed a little, pointing up at one of the gaudy spangled billboards, then spoke to the man in the backseat, who as usual was at full attention.

'Hey, George, look at those potheads up there. They're making us a potful! If that's the kind of shit that sells, that's the kind of shit we'll give 'em!' He laughed, cynical at how simple it had become to switch motives and morals where profits were concerned. 'Maybe in a few years our company can open up a hearing-aid division and be all ready when the dumb kids buying all those records grow up and find that goddamn loud music has ruined their ears!' The others in the car smiled, though they didn't quite understand what he was talking about – the usual penalty for mixing private thoughts with public conversation. Never mind, though, if he was pleased about something, so were they.

There was a red stoplight ahead, but Ham saw no other cars and drove on, leaving the Strip and passing Schwab's Pharmacy on Crescent Heights. Now they were in Hollywood.

'Another couple of miles and the damn thing will begin. This is all I needed to ruin a perfectly good Sunday! Say – you should have been the terrific pratfall some guy took on the court today . . . like something out of one of my old one-reel comedies!' There was silence for a few blocks, and then the blonde finally had something to say in her surprisingly deep voice:

'I hope there's a bar near the door. George, you've got to get me something to drink the minute we get there!'

Up ahead on Sunset Boulevard powerful searchlights crisscrossed the sky, and Ham wondered how much the studio's electric department was spending on all this old-fashioned carnival hoopla. What the hell – it went with what people expected. The traffic had gotten heavier, and they were stuck in back of a big freight truck. The stink of diesel exhaust made him cough, and he thought of his father, Solomon . . . Sol Rabinowitz. He could never remember seeing the old man without his Camel cigarettes, fingers stained mahogany brown; his rasping cough was the very last thing Ham ever heard come from his father's lips. Poppa . . . What would Poppa have thought of his little *pisher*, Chaim the Humanitarian, tonight? The truck rumbled away, and Ham swung the Bentley around to get as far as possible from the stench, all the time drawing closer to the lights in the sky over the Palladium.

'Chief, the best spot to drop us would be a left turn on Argyle right after you cross Vine, then you can swing into the parking lot in back,' said O'Neill, leaning forward. Ham nodded and kept his eyes on the lighted sky and the traffic ahead. He crossed the wide boulevard, turned left at the first street and pulled over to stop in front of a fire hydrant. O'Neill and the blonde got out of the car. Now George would begin the job he was paid to do. He was The Beard – the man who took another man's woman to public places so a charade for fools could be played out.

The blonde stood on the sidewalk and looked back at Ham; then, holding tightly to George's arm, she walked with him from the corner to vanish in the crowd and flashing lights outside the Palladium's Sunset Boulevard entrance. The Bentley slowly pulled forward to join a long line of cars threading their way into the rear parking lot. Ham looked up at the spangled sky, where a few stubborn stars still competed with the searchlights. Other kinds of stars were getting out of their cars up ahead in the line, and he thought he saw Gary Cooper and Marlene Dietrich struggling through the waiting crowd of press photographers and television news crews. It was hard enough to handle stars like those when you ran a big studio, Ham thought, but that dear wife of his with her astrology crap was letting the stars handle her – and him too, if she could manage it. Getting him to change decisions, meetings, friends . . . ideas . . . dump his family . . . everything dictated by those fucking charts of hers and the leeches who sucked away his money to pump her full of all that nonsense. God! How many years had he gone along with it? . . . Too many . . . too damn many!

The long line of cars approaching the rear entrance of the Palladium slowly moved forward, then stopped again. Ham relaxed his tight grip on the wheel and looked down at the softly glowing speedometer dial.

The numbers climbing up from zero past one hundred and twenty held his attention, and he thought of all the years passing by like so many miles an hour when he raced the car down Sunset Boulevard. You were ten years old and then suddenly you were fifteen, married at just past twenty and then the father of a son before the moving needle on time's dashboard had even reached twenty-two. A boy . . . a son . . . his and Irene's. The numbers under the steering wheel shimmered in the dark.

A polite honk from the impatient Rolls-Royce in back and he moved his car forward, looking up from the speedometer to his whitened knuckles on the wheel.

His son was no kid anymore. My God . . . where did the time go? He was nearly forty-nine already, with children of his own. He worked with some independent production company over at Paramount, and from what Ham heard he was doing quite well. Ham was certain he had told his secretary to send his son an invitation for his evening. It might do him some good to see all these people honoring his father as a humanitarian, regardless of what he might still think of him. As he eased the car forward in line he wondered if he would see any of his family in the crowd doing him honor tonight. Maybe his son and daughter-in-law might show up. So many of his family, though, had gone where invitations could never reach them.

'Mr. Robbins, Chief! Come with me and let your driver park the car over in that space we've been holding.' Charlie Freeman of the studio's publicity department had been waiting since early morning to see that foul-ups were held to the normal minimum. For a worried half-hour or more he had been standing outside looking for Ham, who, thank God, wasn't as late as usual. With all the bars inside crowded to the walls, nobody had cared about delays except the press, which liked early getaways, and the television people, who had to be back at their stations for the evening newscasts.

As Ham was convoyed through the crowd, hands were thrust out at him to be shaken. Charlie pushed ahead like a good blocker making space for the ball carrier, and soon they were through the door and into the big lobby, where people clustered around the several bars, emptying glasses almost as quickly as the overworked bartenders filled and refilled them.

'Charlie. A double Scotch . . . right away!' ordered Ham, and in a moment Charlie had pressed a cold glass into his boss's hand and watched him pour the reviving liquid down his throat. Across the crowded lobby the blonde and The Beard stood in front of another bar. The girl sent a wide smile over the rim of her glass, making Ham desperately wish it was hours from now and he was in her bed, finding old pleasures in her young body. Another swallow went down and almost at once a refill was pressed into his hand.

'Charlie,' Ham said, 'how the hell did I ever get conned into

15

a thing like this? At least it can only last so long, and if the Scotch holds out, I guess I can too.'

Charlie smiled to himself. He knew damn well how Ham had been conned into this thing, since he himself had been the con artist, and for what he saw as the very best of reasons: survival. Rumors had been flying all over the lot that the ax was poised and pink slips were coming out of Personnel and he would be among the first of the casualties. It was a law of the industry . . . whenever production dropped off and overheads had to be trimmed, the last hired in Publicity was the first fired. The answer was simple for a clever fellow like Charlie Freeman. If there was no work, make work, and do it so that you become absolutely indispensable to whatever it is you invent. His boss, Fred Simms, head of the studio's publicity department, was back in the New York home office rebuilding a failing advertising campaign for a multi-million dollar bomb that was going to lose double its cost, so fortunately he wasn't available for consultation or approval. Fred's assistant was Herman Bradley, an ineffectual pencil-pushing office manager whom Charlie manipulated with ease. He walked down the hall from his office with fragmented beginnings of the con job in his head and pushed through the door.

'Herman, something just came across my desk that has to get to the Chief. Something that's going to happen in less than a month! It's a terrific honor for him and the whole studio. He'll really go for it – but we've got to move right now! Since Fred won't be back for another week or more, you'll have to set up an appointment for me with Mr. Robbins soon as you can. I'm not kidding – this really is important, and can't wait even a day!' Herman was a fat round carbon copy of his boss, but lacking his brains and shrewdness, and he tended to take too much on faith alone, so he phoned the Chief's office, spoke with Bob Silver, the Chief's executive secretary, and came up with an appointment for Charlie at five-thirty that same day.

For the next three hours Charlie was on the phone, working with the best airbrush man in the art department and going through his private loose-leaf book filled with the names and numbers of people who owed him favors. He made it to Ham Robbins' outer office in plenty of time for his appointment. At six-fifteen he was still sitting in front of Bob Silver's desk holding tightly to a bulging envelope and somehow thinking of himself as being pregnant in the doctor's waiting room. In a certain sense he was pregnant – with an idea conceived in haste and about to be delivered right on Ham Robbins' big black desk. He hoped the kid would survive – and if he did, so would he!

'Charlie, you're not trying to sell the Old Man a screenplay, for God's sake!' Bob said as he looked over his naked desktop at the envelope clutched on the waiting lap. 'I hope it's something good for a change. The crap they're turning out at the Writer's Building and the junk the New York office has been buying just about has the company on the ropes.'

'No, no – this isn't a script, honest. It's something I know the Chief's going to like very much. I wish it was a screenplay – but that really isn't my racket,' Charlie answered, trying to keep his voice cool and calm. He glanced at his wristwatch. A loud buzzer went off in a box on Bob's desk and made him jump. The executive secretary flipped a switch on the intercom and the metallic voice of Ham Robbins rasped through the room.

'Bob, bring your book and take some notes on retakes and added scenes for that turkey I just ran.'

'Mr. Robbins,' Bob softly said to the box, 'Charlie Freeman of Publicity has been waiting to see you. Says he has something quite important – do you want him to wait?' For a moment there was a humming silence, then the voice from the box.

'Send him in now and let the notes wait until later.'

'Go right in, Charlie. Mr. Robbins is expecting you,' Bob said, as though he alone had heard the intercom, which filled the room with sound.

Charlie rose from the long couch on which he had spent nearly an hour and looked through the large picture window running the length of the opposite wall. There were the rows of silent dark stages, now softly lit by the last rays of the setting sun. The stark block buildings seemed bathed in a lovely shade of pink. Charlie swallowed nervously, remembering that was the same color of the termination slip he was sure would soon hit his desk if there was about to be a stillbirth. He straightened his tie, hugged his envelope tightly and went through the inner door to walk the length of a long anteroom, down three steps and a right turn finally into the spacious inner office.

The Chief sat at the far end of the room behind a wide ebony desk wondering what he had to see that was so damn important at this hour. His eyes still ached from all the bad film he had just screened, and he squinted slightly as the vaguely familiar young man approached on the long walk that had cowed so many others before him.

'I know you . . . you're with Fred Simms in Publicity. . . . What can't wait!' It was not a question – it was a command, followed immediately by 'Sit down . . . er . . . Freeman, isn't it?'

Charlie sat, slid the envelope over between his thigh and the side of the chair and answered the Chief.

'Yessir, Mr. Robbins, Charlie Freeman. Mr. Simms will be in New York the rest of this week and part of next –'

'You're telling me something I damn well know and it pains my ass why he's in New York!' Ham said in an unhappy voice. 'We have to redo a complete advertising campaign cooked up by a fancy Madison Avenue outfit on a super-stinker of a feature nobody will book! All right – just what is it you want!'

Charlie tasted bile but forced it down and continued.

'Something came up just this afternoon and I felt you should know about it right away since it concerns you personally.' This in his regained unflappable public relations voice.

'All right, all right, I haven't got time to waste! What is it – ferchrisakes!' Ham's impatience and anger filled the room, and Charlie put the big envelope on the desk and pulled out the beautiful rendering that he had a genius with an airbrush make up during the past few hours. It was done magnificently with flashy metallic ink, the inscription in crisp black accents, all set against a rich velvety blue background. Dignity, pride and importance seemed to radiate from the drawing, which Charlie propped up on the desk against a lamp, where it was bathed in exactly the right kind of light. Ham tilted back in his high-backed chair, reached into his pocket for a pair of half-glasses and read the inscription.

The office was dead silent except for the soft hum of a clock and the dull thud of Charlie's heart, which only he could hear. Ham looked over his glasses at Charlie, then slowly read aloud from the airbrushed rendering.

'HOLLYWOOD HUMANITARIAN OF THE YEAR – HAMILTON J. ROBBINS.'

He stopped and looked up again at the man across the desk, then continued reading silently until he came to the final lines that he voiced in tones of disbelief and disgust.

'Given in Gratitude and Heartfelt Appreciation by the Members of the George Spelvin Club, Hollywood, California . . .'

Ham pulled off his glasses, set the big card down on his desk and fixed Charlie with a cold stare.

'Humanitarian of the Year! What absolute shit! Who dreamed up that fucking nonsense and exactly what's behind it? I know that Spelvin Club bunch . . . a card room full of old has-beens promoting a free feed and some bucks! Come on, young man . . . I've been around too long to be taken in by crap like this. What's the real story behind it?'

Charlie was positive the Chief would hear the tympani solo his heart was performing.

'Mr. Robbins, it's quite important to all those people. The George Spelvin Club wants to honor one of the real leaders of our industry in which they too are pioneers and veterans, just like you. It's something never given to anybody else before.' Charlie kept it coming fast, his mind racing his mouth. He was laying out the copy as rapidly as it was being manufactured in his mind, without mentioning the phone job he had done on those poor old guys at the Spelvin Club. The Chief would never hear about the selling job he did on some pretty savvy show people, who finally went along with the promise of some money for their emergency fund, some good national publicity – and laughs. Even old actors like to see their names spelled right – and often – so in those crucial telephone hours Charlie convinced them to buy something he now hoped he could sell to The Humanitarian himself.

'Mr. Robbins, most of these people have been in the business as long as you and your late brothers . . . This truly comes from their hearts!'

Ham wasn't listening. He had his glasses back on and was rereading the inscription on the artwork. The second reading was still asinine, then the next time merely stupid, and when he went over it again one last time it began to take on a kind of truth, a realness he could feel and almost believe. A showman all these years, he was used to baiting hooks to catch suckers and could admire the flow and content of what would be on the silver plaque. That word 'Humanitarian,' though, bothered him. As far as he was concerned it meant a soft touch with a soft head who'd die for some other slob – and Ham Robbins was nobody's slob! He looked up at Charlie and spoke again, this time with a voice suddenly more soft and relaxed.

'Are you damn certain those old bastards want to give me *that*? I know the whole bunch, and I'll bet I've hired and fired

19

just about every one of the bums. Hell – they'd rather hit me over the head with a chunk of silver than present me with it!'

'No . . . No, Mr. Robbins!' Charlie insisted, the sweat now pouring down from armpit to waist and a pink-slip vision growing ever more real in his mind. He struggled to appear cool and keep the words coming. 'They're dead serious . . . They've done a lot already on this and have to know right away if you'll accept because it's gone as far as it can without your okay. They've already contacted most of the top names in the business – people from all the other companies and TV and the press – and the whole thing is the kind of public relations I've heard you say so many times our business needs to counter so much of the junk that goes out. Mr. Robbins . . . they're real high on this, and if you give the go-ahead I'll help them on some details like getting the best place for it and coordinating the program with their committee. They'll put the best entertainment together . . . the biggest names . . . already have lots of commitments, and there will be a terrific show we can turn into a TV special for lots of extra mileage. They've already approached people from all over the industry, and everybody, absolutely everybody, is one hundred percent enthused! Now all it needs is your approval.' It was absolutely amazing how easily truth could be bent, twisted and hammered into new shapes.

'What's it going to cost us – in hard dollars and cents? What do we have to lay out for this great honor, young man . . . It could be a bundle!' said Ham, back to his old sharp voice.

'Mr. Robbins,' replied Charlie, reading fast from the Tele-Prompter of his mind in his deep-from-the-heart serious voice, 'this shouldn't cost the company a penny, unless we put out for a few tables, which I recommend. Even that's a charity donation, since the Spelvin Club plans to use any overage from the evening for their emergency fund.'

A decision came even quicker than Charlie had hoped. Ham closed his eyes a moment, perhaps had a vision himself of that glorious piece of silver hanging on a wall in a certain room.

'Okay, kid . . . Charlie. Go ahead – only don't let it cost the company anything! Hell, maybe we should spring for a few seats . . . say forty or fifty . . . charge it to studio overhead. If it's a tax break for charity, make it a hundred and forty, a nice round number. The accountants will love that, and it always looks good in the annual report to the goddamn

20

stockholders, who wouldn't piss on a humanitarian unless he paid dividends and split four for one every year!'

Charlie felt his armpits turn off the sweat, and for the first time he relaxed and leaned back in his chair.

'It sounds fine, Charlie. You're doing a good job. Now stay right on top of it and get a daily report to Bob Silver how it's coming together so I'll know everything that's happening.'

Anxious to get out while he was ahead, Charlie stood up, collected the artwork and slid it back into the envelope, then reached across the desk to shake hands with Ham. He turned to take the long walk to the turn left, the three steps and then down the long anteroom to the door. Again he passed the picture window, and saw that all the sound stages were now completely dark except for the streetlights. With the final setting of the sun, the pink glow that earlier had bathed the studio was completely gone. Charlie softly closed the door behind him, and smiled all the way back to his office.

Now, three months later, Ham Robbins looked down into his glass and saw only half-melted lumps of ice. Faces loomed up and hands kept pushing out to be grasped and shaken. The evening had yet to get under way and already he was sick and tired of it. Some unheard signal reached all the lobby bars, shutting off the liquid flow, and the Palladium lights flickered on and off, then on again.

'Mr. Robbins . . . we're to go over to the far corner with all the guests seated at the head table, then all go inside together after everybody else is at their tables,' Charlie said as Ham shoved the empty glass at him.

'Another Scotch and then I'll go with you.'

Charlie scurried to the nearest bar, where he convinced them to pour just one more for the guest of honor. With the shutting down of the bars and the flinging open of the bank of doors to the main room, the crowds were forced to leave the lobby and drift in to find their tables.

All the inhabitants of the main table were corralled over to one side by Charlie and his helpers to await their entrance cue. It came with a roll of drums and playing of 'The Stars and Stripes Forever.' Charlie had failed to get the orchestra to play 'Hail to the Chief,' since that was strictly reserved for somebody else who had been invited to attend tonight but very conveniently had made arrangements to be in Paris or Geneva. Well, the president of the Motion Picture Producers and Distributors Association showed up, so what the hell.

The entourage, with Ham in the lead, majestically walked down the wide center aisle between the packed tables to the dais and riser, where there was a long table of honor facing all the others. Ham looked around at the decorations, which in spite of the property department's best efforts still looked like Early Paradise Ballroom.

He was aware of a small wave of applause at the group's entrance, nothing uproarious but good solid sound. For some reason he found he was listening for the laughter, jeers and derision he remembered from that night they gave Louie Mayer his Big Brother Award. Louie's face was pale when he came into the hall, but by the time they got him to his seat his cheeks and forehead were bright red and large tears were rolling down to his chin and dripping on his formal shirtfront. Everyone agreed it was an eloquent display of emotion, but Ham knew better and he waited for the humiliation, which never came. Only a very few negative comments drifted down from some of the old throats way up at the rear balcony tables, where most of the Spelvin Club members had been stuck for their free dinner. By the time the last little jeer lost to the applause, the orchestra had completed its imitation of Sousa and the only noise was that of a thousand behinds settling down on a thousand chairs.

Ham looked around the audience as the Marine Corps Reserve color guard moved into position and the orchestra struck up the national anthem. He rose to his feet with the others and tried to sing the words he never could remember. The raised main table looked down on all those on the crowded floor and he saw a mass of faces he knew, many of which he hoped he could avoid later on. They were mostly from the industry, press and television, and all the companies who lived off the studios and found it good business to be here.

All of those upturned faces at floor tables looking up at him and the ones high up on the narrow balcony staring down. He swept them with his eyes, searching the whole room for one face – his son. Each time he saw somebody he knew very well he paused and then kept looking, seeking and not finding. The little bastard! He must deliberately be staying away. A wave of nausea and anger gripped him, and he clutched at the table edge for support. Would this damn song never end! At last '. . . and the home of the brave' burst confidently from the thousand throats, letting him sit down heavily in his chair. He held tightly to his half-empty glass with one hand,

22

massaged a sudden stomach cramp with the other, grateful for the clamor of voices, which covered a noise he could not suppress as the pain in his gut passed out into the open.

Why the hell had he even expected his son to show up at a Humanitarian Award for the father whose humanity he knew so damn well after all these years? Once again he swept the great noisy hall with his eyes, seeing only familiar strangers. He had hoped, though . . . he had hoped, just as Poppa had hoped for him long ago when he was little Chaim Rabinowitz . . . before Hamilton J. Robbins, Hollywood Humanitarian of the year, had even been born.

'Ladies . . . Ladies and Gentlemen!' boomed the amplified voice of Georgie Jessel, the most available Master of Ceremonies Charlie had been able to tie down for the evening. 'I beg of you, Ladies and Gentlemen, some attention and a little silence so we can get going with this wonderful event!'

Each table had become its own banquet and every guest was the speaker of the evening, all talking at once. The orchestra rolled its drums, blasted one fanfare on top of another and built a pyramid of ignored chords. Georgie cajoled, pleaded and begged until finally little islands of silence sprang up and spread throughout the room. At last there was only the voice of Jessel, so electronically overwhelming that Ham thought he was at the funeral of all mankind, with Georgie delivering the ultimate eulogy.

'I ask you to rise while Rabbi Edgar Magnin, a great friend of our guest of honor and practically everyone in this room, delivers the benediction . . . Rabbi . . .'

The rabbi stepped to the podium, nodded with dignity to Ham and in his rich voice pronounced the ancient words, the Hebrew from his lips going not into God's ear just yet but into microphones carrying it through amplifiers and out of the great speakers hung on the walls. Ham found himself saying them along with the rabbi. There are some things a little boy never forgets and a grown man always remembers. These were the words he remembered from the lips of his father . . . from Poppa. He held tightly to the edge of the table and looked down into his half-empty glass of Scotch. The words were pressed into his ears by the amplifiers and the amplified voice of Rabbi Magnin seemed to become the voice of another man . . . the words still the same, but the voice that of Solomon Rabinowitz reciting the prayers and blessings before the Sabbath meal, with Momma and all the family around the big table in the kitchen.

Ham thought of things so overpowering they drove away the words roaring at him from the speakers up on the wall.

Poppa . . . Poppa . . . if you were alive would you be here with your Chaim . . . or someplace else with all the others laughing at The Humanitarian . . . laughing at your son? I would want you here with me tonight, Poppa, like I want my son . . . my only son. Why are you all someplace else?

Spoken in silence, the words were as real to Ham as the benediction from Rabbi Magnin, who had reached the final amen and was seating himself with the thousand others. Ham's eyes remained tightly closed, and he held on to the back of his chair with both hands.

Chaim remained standing, and when at last he opened his eyes, he saw that his father and brothers all were seated and Momma and the girls were serving the food. He pulled out his chair and quietly took his place at the table.

Part Two

Part Two

CHAPTER TWO

Solomon Rabinowitz was a tall, powerfully built man with a
sweeping black moustache. It was nearly twenty years since
he had fled Russia to escape the Tsar's recruiting parties,
sent into the great rural ghetto called the Pale to seek out
strapping young Jewish farmers for impressment into army
labor battalions. Solomon left behind his young wife, Esther,
and their two little children – Rivka, who would one day be
called Ruth, and Moishe, who would become Maurice, then
Maurie when they all were in the New World.

Traveling by night with other young men of the village
where their families had lived, farmed and worshiped for
more than two centuries, he crossed one border after
another, finally arriving at the great port of Hamburg. Here
Solomon bartered Esther's precious silver dowry candle-
sticks, which she had given him for just that purpose, and
took steerage passage to America.

Packed below decks with hundreds of men on tiers of
bunks, Solomon listened to the dreams of the dreamers, the
chants of the pious and the retching of those made deathly ill
by the ship's motion. At last the still waters of New York
harbor brought the dreamers back to reality, the pious to
prayers of thanksgiving, and nervous comfort to those who
thought their souls might follow their stomachs into the
Atlantic. The ship slowly passed an island not far off the tip
of Manhattan, and Solomon stood at the rail looking at the
half-finished base for some great monument that was to
stand on the fragment of land sticking up above the water.
The immigrants looked in awe at the vast jumble of granite
blocks and the heaps of crates stacked in long open sheds
surrounding what might have been the half-built pyramid for
a pharaoh.

'Look, gentlemen,' said one of the Hamburg Line's officers,
'Prussia defeated France in a war and so the crazy French-
men, who lost their own liberty, sent a gift to the people of

27

America and they call it "Liberty Enlightening the World." There it is – all inside those boxes, where it will stay because nobody in this great country cares enough to have a place ready to put it. Welcome, gentlemen, to your new homeland!'

And so Solomon came to America, where a doctor thumped his chest, listened to his heart, peered into his eyes, ears and throat and then passed him down the line to where an Irish-American immigration officer, himself not here long from the old country, entered an approximate translation of his name on an entry certificate. Solomon picked up the precious piece of paper, left the confused babble of Castle Garden Immigration Center and soon was lost in teeming lower New York.

After nearly two years of hard work in kosher meat markets and slaughterhouses, where all his farm training and religious upbringing were put to use, Solomon was able to send for Esther and the two children. Not so very different from the story of thousands of other families coming to this Golden Land in the late nineteenth century. The growth and prosperity of America came about in good part because of the new blood and fresh minds coming to its shores, acting as a great national stimulant.

The Rabinowitz family adjusted quickly to their new life, grew in numbers, wandered from crowded New York to upstate Albany, then to Rochester, where an official of the Hebrew Immigrant Aid Society told Solomon that the growing Jewish community in Harrisburg, Pennsylvania, desperately needed someone who knew ritual slaughter and butchering. Soon the family found themselves in that lovely rural city, where in time the memory of cossacks sweeping through a pillaged countryside was more and more a fading nightmare. Here a pious man of blameless character, repute and skill could make a good living providing meat for the tables of those who followed the age-old rules and traditions.

During their second winter in Harrisburg a terrible snowstorm, like billions of little white cossacks, swept down from the Great Lakes bringing misery to a thousand or more square miles of Ohio, Pennsylvania and Maryland. In a single day the sky turned from bright blue to leaden black as threatening clouds jostled each other for position over the city. A thin dusting of first snow lay on the streets, and horse-drawn wagons, drays and cabs pulled into warm protected stables to take shelter from the coming storm. One wagon, though, did not leave the street. An aged gray vehicle with high enclosed back, it had long ago delivered merchandise from a fine department store, but now on its side was roughly painted RABINOWITZ & SONS, KOSHER MEATS – 264 GRANT AVENUE. A wheezing old brown horse, which had also seen better days, pulled the creaking wagon, and high up on an exposed bench in the cold air sat Solomon Rabinowitz holding the leather reins firmly in his strong butcher's hands. He looked up at the black clouds and flicked the reins to hurry the old horse as they passed down Grant Avenue. Sitting up on the bench with him was his next to youngest son, Lou, eleven years of age, tousled hair covered by a cap pulled down almost to his ears. The blanket over his legs was shared with his father, and the bitter cold brought tears to their eyes as they looked up and down the street.

The wagon pulled up to the front of Ginsburg's Clothing Emporium and Sol saw the owner, an old friend, shrugging his shoulders and locking the door as he gave up on the rest of this unpromising day.

'Hey, Ginsburg! Nathan! Have you seen my little boy, Chaim?'

The merchant squinted up at him, looked down the street, then back through the front window into his locked store.

'No, Sol. He comes in and out bothering me and my customers, but today he has spared me the pleasure of his company. What a *boychik* you've got with that Chaim . . . good luck you'll need with that one!' He hurried off as a gust of wind stirred the gutter papers, blowing them high up toward the roof.

'Lou,' said Solomon, 'where does that brother of yours go at this time of day?'

The boy thought for a moment, then said, 'Poppa, I think he's been doing some work for Mr. Johnson at the portrait place right near here on West Main.'

Sol looked down at his son.

'Portrait place . . . Chaim's no painter! What does he do in a portrait place?' They were moving up the street now, with snow blowing even harder and scraps of paper swooping in the chill wind up and between the buildings.

Lou laughed. 'Poppa, not painted portraits. Mr. Johnson has one of those camera studios where you sit down and they make photograph pictures of you. Chaim has been sweeping up and Mr. Johnson pays him to keep the place clean.'

'Ha!' grumbled Solomon. 'Clean for Mr. Johnson – but for his Momma his part of the room at home looks like the back of our butcher shop!'

They reached the curb of a nondescript storefront over which hung the proud black and gold sign ELITE PHOTOGRAPHIC STUDIO – J. JOHNSON, PROP. Just then the front door flew open and a young boy with a too-long over-coat flapping around him and a wide smile on his happy face shot out of the studio, helped along by the strong right arm and knee of J. Johnson himself. A happy bright voice came from the happy face.

'But, Mr. Johnson – I only thought you would want me to make sure the camera was working right – and who else could I photograph in an empty studio but myself?'

Mr. Johnson yelled over the growing noise of the wind, 'Kid, don't you ever come back here until you pay me for all those damn pictures you shot of yourself – and stop conning me for two bits pay to do a penny's worth of work!' The big front door slammed shut.

The little boy scooped up his cap and in one swinging motion hoisted himself up on the wagon to sit beside his brother and father on the bench. The smile never left his face.

'Look at the pictures I got of me today!'

Solomon shrugged his shoulders as much as his heavy overcoat would allow and, unsmiling, took the strips of pictures, saying to his youngest and wildest son, 'Chaim, a butcher like me you'll never be ... an honest tradesman – never! Maybe, God forbid, you should be an actor ... or at least do some dancing on the streets so you should make some honest money!' He guided the old horse in a wide turn to head the wagon in the opposite direction.

'Poppa – dancing – dancing I like, but singing I want to do most of all! Please – let me take some singing lessons and I'll bring home lots of money and be famous!' came the reply from the little boy, who had pulled most of his head deep into the collar of the overcoat handed down from his bigger brother.

Solomon looked over Lou's head and down at Chaim.

'A singer – hah! The only Singer we need in our house is a machine so your sisters can help their Momma sew up all the rips you boys put in your clothes! A singer yet ... a calamity! Better you should volunteer for the cossacks!'

'Poppa – Poppa! Watch out for the horsecar!' yelled the errant prodigal, and the father held tightly to the reins as their aged horse took them slowly around the dimly seen car, which had suddenly loomed up out of the growing storm. They passed over a bridge and down another wide street toward

30

the sounds of bells and steam whistles signaling the arrival of the Pittsburgh express at the Harrisburg railroad station.

Chaim stood up on the bench, trying to see through the swirling snow toward where the station should be. He could barely make out the cluster of wagons, drays and cabs, and suddenly they almost walked into a disabled horseless carriage, its motor dead as the sun of last summer. The driver, some draymen and a sweating, swearing police constable shoved and heaved to clear the inert machine out of the way. With their wagon stalled in the long line of traffic, Solomon relaxed his hands and looked at Chaim.

'Singing lessons! Lessons you want . . . ha! What happened with the Hebrew lessons? The *melamed* couldn't get you to learn even a word. Singing! My son – you're not even going to have a Bar Mitzva . . . *then* you could have been singing for everybody! But no . . . with you life is a song and a dance and a strip of funny pictures, and your Momma and your sisters give you anything you want . . . and when your older brothers and your father try to tell you your responsibilities, you give a smile and a joke and . . .'

The broken-down automobile was out of the way and the column started up once again and they were in the crush of wagons and cabs pulling up to the front of the station.

The passenger entrance had almost vanished behind a curtain of steadily falling snow that hid all detail. Solomon peered into the white void, then called over to Lou and Chaim.

'Boys, get over to the sidewalk and look for a young man we are calling for. His name is Birnbaum . . . from New York. Just go in and shout as loud as you can, "Birnbaum! Birnbaum!" I'll wait right out here for you to bring him.'

The boys climbed down, felt their way between horses, wagons and cabs, sank deep into something covered by snow. After wiping their fouled shoes reasonably clean on the curb, they plunged into the growing mob of porters, passengers and baggage building up under the slight protection of the marquee at the passenger entrance.

Off to one side of the mass of people a young man was vainly trying to get a porter to help collect the cases and rolls of material dumped around him by the baggage handlers. He looked out toward the invisible street, his panic growing as he saw only the sheet of falling snow. The two little boys pushing and shoving their way through and under the crowd were quite invisible to the young man with all the baggage.

31

'Are you Mr. Birnbaum from –' called Lou to a man, who vanished into the storm without looking back.

Chaim caught another man by the sleeve. 'You gotta be Mr. Birnbaum from New York, please?'

'I'm not Birnbaum from anyplace! Let go of me!'

A great booming voice rang out over all the hubbub, the thundering of Solomon Rabinowitz somewhere out in the storm as he stood up on the wagon bench, sounding like a shofar, the ritual ram's horn calling the ancients to battle.

'Birnbaum! *Birnbaum!* From New York . . . *Birnbaum!*'

The young man, who had given up finding a porter, sat deep in his pile of cases, crates, rolls of fabric and a barrel and was hit full force by the trumpeting of his name from out of the storm. His despondency vanished and he turned toward the hidden voice and shouted back as loudly as he could:

'That's me! That's *me!* . . . Birnbaum . . . *Birnbaum!*'

He looked wildly for the man behind the clarion sound, but the curtain of swirling snow kept him from seeing who it was out there shouting his name in the storm.

He grabbed at a box here, a case there, all the time keeping up a screaming conversation with the invisible shofar someplace out past the white curtain.

'I'm Birnbaum! Here I am . . . Find me! For God's sake . . . *find me!*'

From under the legs of surrounding passengers, as though passing through a living tunnel, came a small boy quickly followed by another. Shapeless in their overcoats and pulled-down caps, they appeared to Birnbaum as miniature messiahs when the first came up and said, 'Mr. Birnbaum . . . Our Poppa is here for you. He's over by the curb with our wagon. We're here to help you get your things there.'

The young man let out a great sigh of relief. He and the boys lifted a crate and a roll of the material up and through the crowd around the door. With much shoving and pushing they made their way to the curb, where Solomon calmly awaited them, directing the boys to get the box into the rear of the wagon.

'Birnbaum . . . Hello. I'm Solomon Rabinowitz. Rabbi Wolfsohn told me we'd find you here . . . so get all your things inside the wagon and we will go to our house and get something hot inside you so you can sit down and tell us all about New York . . .'

Chaim looked up at his father, then over at his brother.

'Lou – come on, I'm starved! You heard Poppa . . . get the stuff into the wagon and we'll go home. You can listen about New York – I'll listen to Momma's matzo ball soup and the chicken!' The two boys dove back into the crowd, thinning out now as wagons, cabs and drays took on their loads, and soon, with Birnbaum's nervous help, they had all the baggage beside the wagon. As the boys heaved up a case onto the tailgate, Birnbaum cried out as though wounded.

'Wait! Wait . . . handle that box like it was glass! See what it says on the top and side . . . "Fragile!" Like you could break what's inside just by breathing heavy on it!'

The boys, who had never before heard such a fancy word as 'fragile' for such things, let Birnbaum help them ease this largest and heaviest case up through the open rear door of the wagon.

Solomon, holding the loose reins and relaxing high up on the wagon bench, turned to look back, saying, 'Chaim, Lou – listen to the man. He's come a long way, so don't smash whatever he's got in his case. Now have you got everything inside?'

Birnbaum looked into the wagon, then pulled back and shouted at the boys. 'The rolls of material . . . the barrel! They're not here. We must have left them. Come quick before some momzer takes them!'

Another trip and at last everything really was inside the wagon, where there remained just enough room for the little boy to squeeze through the rear doors, close them behind him and carefully work his way to the front, where he could look through the small opening up at the two men, with Lou crushed between them on the bench. Lou leaned forward with his head down as far as it would go to look at his little brother safe inside from the fury of the storm.

'Next time, Chaim, you get to sit here and freeze – remember that!'

Solomon clucked at the old horse, and they slowly pulled away from the curb and swung around, heading directly into the storm.

With his great sweeping moustache glistening with snow, which also built up on his bushy eyebrows, Solomon had almost the look of an ancient Hebrew prophet, although the beard was missing, a concession on his part to being a citizen of this new land – also a realistic act ever since he had nearly chopped off most of it when it got involved with the dismemberment of a steer in the butcher's shop.

33

'So, Birnbaum,' said Solomon, turning to face the chilled young man. 'So – is there a Mrs. Birnbaum?'

Chaim pulled his cap up from his ears and pushed himself up a little through the opening under the bench to better hear the conversation from his cozy nest inside.

Birnbaum looked ahead into the mantle of falling snow.

'Oh yes . . . my mother . . . in New York . . . Well – really the Bronx. She and my father live with my sister and younger brother. He's still in school and she's studying to be a –'

Chaim pushed his head out between the dangling legs as far as he could and yelled, 'Poppa wants to know, are you married or aren't you married!'

The young man jumped with alarm and surprise at the sudden little voice from below.

'Oh . . . oh . . . *that* Mrs. Birnbaum . . . No, I haven't met her yet. One day I am sure I shall, but now I'm single.'

Chaim pushed even farther through the opening so he could be heard by all three up top.

'Poppa! We've got a bachelor boarder at last! Now Momma and Ruth and Miriam will be happy!'

'Ruth! Miriam? Who . . . who . . . who are they?' said Birnbaum, turning to Solomon as sudden beads of sweat popped out in the narrow space between his hat and his eyebrows, even though he sat in the full blast of the cold wind.

'Never mind, Mr. Birnbaum . . . you'll be meeting all of them in just a little while,' answered Solomon, and he twisted down, trying to face the little boy, who still looked up between their legs from inside the wagon.

'Chaim – *schweig still!*'

A very small voice, almost unheard over the growing storm, came up from the little figure.

'Poppa – I don't like the name Chaim. People laugh at it . . . the kids on the block make fun of me. Can't I change it? The fellows all call me Ham.'

Solomon almost exploded, and bent over even lower, trying to look his son in the eye.

'A seller of kosher meat with a Ham for a son! An idiot for a son is what I have! Chaim you were born, Chaim you will stay!'

'Poppa,' came back the little voice from down at their feet, 'Poppa, maybe . . . maybe Hamilton instead?'

Poppa pretended not to hear – but to himself he said, '*Nu?* Hamilton . . . Hamilton Rabinowitz . . . not very kosher . . .

but very fancy and maybe very American . . . like Rivka turning into Ruth and Moishe becomes Maurie. Well, things change . . . and so maybe do names.'

He shouted down through the storm noise to the little boy, 'All right, Hamilton, my son. I will ask your Momma.'

The small voice spoke again, but so low that the three up on the bench could not hear. 'Thank you, Poppa . . . but it's gonna be Ham, whatever you say!'

CHAPTER THREE

They pulled up at exactly the right place, even though nothing was visible an arm's length away. The wagon was directly in front of the Rabinowitz house, all two floors of it, square and solid, with more comfort than style. A big wooden building for a big family, with more than enough room for parents, two sisters, three brothers and space for a boarder to bring in some extra money now and then. For a while now there would be such a boarder, thanks to Rabbi Wolfsohn, whose cousin in the Bronx had written that a young man named Birnbaum would arrive in Harrisburg on this day. Not only was he very available, but he also had good prospects in some new line of business not made quite clear. This was enough to know, and the rabbi alerted Solomon Rabinowitz, father of two marriageable daughters, thus proving himself not only a student of the Talmud, but also a master of timing.

'The Eskimos should take over Harrisburg, and welcome to it!' shouted Solomon over the noise of the wind at the young man seated next to him. 'Dog sleds will be the only way to travel if this storm keeps up.' Fortunately, their horse was as wise as he was ancient, and as long as he was headed toward his stable, he could find the way unaided in any weather.

Solomon climbed down to the ground, stamped his feet to get the chilled blood flowing, then handed the reins up to Lou. Chaim scrambled out through the narrow opening under the seat and jumped over the side of the wagon to scoot off to the house. Birnbaum slowly descended and stood on his frozen feet as Solomon swept his arms wide to indicate the general location of his house, dimly seen through the heavy snowfall. A lone gas lamp flickered on the sidewalk with futile illumination of blurred outlines.

'Welcome to our home, Mr. Birnbaum. Now get inside and the boys and I will bring in your things.'

'Thank you, but I should help with the cases. What's inside could break if you're not real careful and lift things wrong,' the young man answered in an anxious voice.

Lou tied the reins to the lamppost, got down and went around to the back of the wagon, then swung the rear doors wide and lowered the tailgate. He had one case almost out when Birnbaum rushed around to help lower it to the snowy street. Together they carried it to the house and up a few steps to the porch, where Solomon held the front door wide open and shouted inside, 'We're here! We're cold – and we're hungry!'

Ham was already standing in front of the roaring fireplace warming himself. His mother came from the kitchen and wiped her hands on her apron. As Solomon was about to introduce the boarder to Esther, Ham piped up in a louder than usual voice, 'Momma, this is Mr. Birnbaum. He's an unmarried bachelor from New York! Where's Ruth and Miriam?'

The mother, a large woman with hints of gray in her tightly curled black hair, waved in annoyance with her son.

'*Sha!* Chaim . . . for a minute be quiet!' Then to Birnbaum, who stood quietly beside Solomon in the doorway feeling for a dry handkerchief to mop his suddenly damp forehead, 'Mr. Birnbaum, Rabbi Wolfsohn has told us all about you. Welcome, welcome!' She took the young man by his hand and drew him into the warm house, firmly shutting the front door behind him. The young man wondered just what it was the rabbi had told them about him and if being taken into a house full of unmarried daughters was the rabbi's way of making business for himself. His handkerchief was completely soggy.

Ham pulled on his cap, hitched up his flapping overcoat and joined Lou out by the wagon in front, where they lifted the remaining boxes and rolls of material carefully over the snow-covered walk, up the three porch steps and into the front hall, piling them in a small heap beside the staircase leading up to the second floor.

'Quick, Birnbaum, up to your room . . . the second door to the right,' said Solomon, waving toward the stairs. 'If you want the toilet, it's in the backyard right outside that door. Nothing fancy, a little house you can't miss . . . but in the morning you had better get there ahead of Chaim. When he is in there first, the rest of us wait an hour!'

'Poppa!' said the little boy from beside the barrel in the hall. 'I only get in there first so I can light the oil stove and have it nice and warm for the rest of you.'

'You sit in there so long just to keep the rest of us waiting and waiting!' said Lou, who obviously had suffered long and often waiting for his turn in the freezing cold outside.

'Chaim!' Solomon said firmly. 'From now on you will kindly permit Mr. Birnbaum to use the outhouse first – unless what you have is a genuine emergency – then later when we are all through you can go inside, lock the door and be alone for as long as you like . . . unless one of us should have an emergency.' The subject was closed, and the boys picked up some of the smaller cases and started up the stairs.

Ruth and Miriam had stayed in the kitchen making the final preparations for dinner, but managed to peek through the partly opened door to the front hall. Their mother heard them whispering, pulled the door open and grabbed each girl by an elbow, pulling them out with her.

'Ruth, say hello to our new boarder. Mr. Birnbaum from New York City . . .'

'The Bronx,' said the young man, a tremble in his voice.

'Bronx-Schmonx,' replied Momma, and she plunged into her soft-sell matchmaker sales talk. 'Such a bright, cheerful girl. Kind and good and almost as fine a cook as her Momma . . . so wonderful with children she is . . . Ruth, say hello to the young man!'

Ruth pulled loose and vanished through the door back into the kitchen to stir the bubbling soup, which most conveniently had picked then to boil over. Momma at once began a new approach with her remaining daughter, Miriam, who stepped forward to softly shake the hand of the boarder before turning to rush after her sister into the kitchen, where both girls giggled as they stirred. Poppa stood there, sure he could have done it all much better, but Momma went right on.

'Lovely, lovely girls – but bashful and nothing at all like their brothers, especially Chaim, who hasn't been quiet since the midwife slapped his behind!'

Momma stopped and fixed the young man with her best potential-mother-in-law gaze, and Solomon, who could sense the panic in a steer being led to slaughter or a bachelor to the altar, came to Birnbaum's rescue for the moment.

'Enough already about the girls! So now, Birnbaum, you know us all except Maurie, my oldest boy. He's like you – on the road, selling – only he sells meat . . . lard and hides for the Armour Company . . . So it's not kosher – but we're in America now . . . it's a living . . . and anyhow he wouldn't listen to me!'

When Lou and Ham came down the stairs for another load of boxes, they were filled with curiosity.

'What's in that barrel, Mr. Birnbaum, and all those rolls of black cloth?'

'Uh . . . well, it's something very interesting and later . . . uh – I'll . . .' Birnbaum said haltingly as he tried to move past the boys over to the part of his baggage bearing the FRAGILE warning labels. Solomon followed him and looked down at the bulky object.

'You look like a salesman and you travel like a salesman. What is it you are selling?' Solomon asked the boarder.

'Could we get it all up to my room and later on I can tell you about it. It's kind of complicated and maybe I have to explain it better to you,' Birnbaum said, ill at ease and eager to get off alone in the outhouse sanctuary he hoped would be available to him when he needed it – which was going to be very soon!

Solomon put his arms around the barrel and lifted it, surprised at how light it was. He started to carry it up the stairs. Lou picked up a valise and Ham lifted a long roll of tightly wrapped black fabric and put it on his small shoulder. He scurried around the others, already on their way up, and they followed him upstairs. Ham reached the landing and turned to shout down to his mother in the hall below.

'The soup, Momma . . . it smells good and I'm really starved!' Then he turned back and swung the long roll into a lamp on the wall, which knocked it off his shoulder. The roll bounced into the heavy banister, split open with a loud popping noise and spilled out a great width of black cloth. The heavy part of the roll started down the staircase, bounding over the heads of the small procession still coming up behind him. Birnbaum, hanging on tightly to the box, leaned out as far as he could to avoid the spreading cloth as it billowed past him, then over Lou and the valise. Solomon was halfway up the stairs, carrying the barrel in a bear hug. He let it drop with a thud, and it bumped and thumped down the stairs, pursued by the spreading black cloth, which whipped to an end just as the rolling barrel smashed into the wall beside the front door.

The top flew off the barrel and long coils of something black and sinuous sprang out onto the floor. Esther and the girls ran out from the kitchen when they heard the noise and stood watching in horror. She saw the long black strips pouring out and slithering close to her feet. With her soup ladle the mother flailed away in defense of her daughters as

39

she herded them back out of the hall and into the kitchen. She gave a piercing scream as some of the black stuff pursued her and wrapped around an ankle.

'Vay iz mir! Snakes he has in the barrel!'

Birnbaum too screamed, from midway up the stairs, and threw himself recklessly down and over the spreading dark fabric, which covered Solomon and Lou like a long black tent. The stricken boarder slid all the way on the wide strip of cloth down to the hall floor, where he clutched at the long shining strips, which grew and grew as they poured out of the barrel. The boarder frantically reached out, trying to stuff back as much as he could, his mouth working in horror when he saw the blazing fireplace just beyond some of the curling strips. At last most of it was crammed back into the container as Lou and Solomon fought their way down the last of the stairs and crawled out from under the fabric. Ham stood at the top of the staircase, his mouth hanging wide open, silent for once as he watched all the havoc he had wrought.

'Good God! Mr. Rabinowitz . . .' the shaken Birnbaum managed to say. 'Do you know what happens when celluloid catches fire?'

Solomon was quick to regain his composure and came over to the unnerved young man, who still trembled, and helped him finish packing the last of the stuff back into the barrel.

'So, Birnbaum, maybe if I know better what is this celluloid I can answer your question.'

Ham popped out from under the end of the black cloth on the stairs and came over to look down into the barrel.

'Poppa, everyone knows celluloid is what collars are made from. Mr. Johnson wears one all the time, and so does the cantor – even under his board!'

Lou too had come over to peer at the black strips, now safely in their barrel. He was fascinated and picked up a loop, which he held up to a lamp.

'Poppa – look! See what's on this!'

Before Solomon could take the black strip from Lou, Esther Rabinowitz hit the side of the soup pot with her ladle.

'Come, Solomon, boys, girls . . . Mr. Birnbaum with your snakes in the barrel . . . Enough foolishness. It is time now to make the blessings and light the candles . . . then we shall eat.'

Solomon looked up at the great sheet of black cloth draped over his staircase, then at the few remaining boxes and at the barrel in the hall.

'Get everything rolled up and into the boarder's room!' he roared at the boys. 'Momma says dinner is ready, and if you don't want another calamity should hit Harrisburg tonight, you all will be ready to eat in five minutes!'

The storm outside grew more violent and great gusts of wind-driven snow beat against the wooden house. The two girls helped their mother put food on the table, candles already placed for the ritual blessing. The boys rolled up the black cloth and got it and the rest of the baggage upstairs, washed their hands and faces and made a pass at combing their hair. At last Solomon sat at the head of the table, Birnbaum at his right looking through cracks in the shuttered windows at what he could see of the storm raging outside, then over at the two unmarried daughters bringing food to the table. Ham kicked Lou under the table, Miriam told Lou to stop complaining and Esther lit the candles, bowed her head and recited the age-old blessing.

It was silent except for the noise of wind outside and the murmur of the blessing within. Birnbaum looked deep into the bowl that soon would hold his soup, then up over Esther's shoulder to see both daughters looking directly at him, and he wondered how long, dear God, how long the storm would last.

Two weeks of good food and terrible weather and the recitation of countless blessings, none of which seemed effective, had taken their toll on poor Birnbaum, who now was twelve pounds heavier and fourteen days poorer. Customers who would have been buying tickets for the show in the rented store were all marooned inside their houses waiting for an end to the soft white plague that was destroying him. How he would ever manage to pay for his room and board caused him constant worry, from which the only escape seemed to be eating and sleeping. Ham still beat him to the out-house each morning, and it seemed to take hours for it to get heated and for Ham finally to emerge.

Birnbaum sat alone in his room, looking out the window at the furious snowflakes falling in a white curtain that blotted out the deserted streets. With a soft cloth he polished the big lens and its shining brass tube. Over by his bed stood the large case filled with the mysterious machine he had carried with such care so far from home to make his name and fortune. He cleaned and oiled it every day but never had the heart to put it all together because he knew the sight would depress him too much.

Lou and Ham came in and sat on the bed, watching the young man at his melancholy task as he rubbed the piece of glass like a failed Aladdin waiting for a genie who would never come. Lou broke the silence.

'Please, Mr. Birnbaum, you've never really explained whatever that thing is to us. Please put it all together and show us what it is and how it works.'

Birnbaum sighed, pulled his gaze away from the fatal landscape outside and turned to the two boys.

'Well . . . I really didn't want to get it all together until I had it set up for a regular show . . . but now it looks like this storm will go on forever and I'm stuck here . . . All right, boys, come here and I'll show it to you. This glass is a lens and the tube it's in slides into the machine in front of the gate and the film is pulled . . . Here, let's get it all out of the case and up where we can see it.'

With the boy's help, he lifted the collection of shining gears, wheels, copper and brass up out of the box and set it carefully down on the floor. After turning the empty case on end, they gently lifted up the machine to rest on the platform it made so it was at just the right height, and then he opened the side to show them the gleaming parts inside. Soon he had the carbide lamp filled with white powder from a square tin box and, after putting water into a little tank, worked the pressure pump so that there was a sound of gurgling and hissing. He hung the lamp assembly on its brackets in the machine and struck a match to light the gas coming out of the vent, just as Ham pushed the barrel right alongside the machine. Lou gasped as he shoved the smaller boy and the barrel back almost to the wall.

'Hey! You wanna blow us all up and burn the whole house down!' Lou screamed at his shaken brother.

Ham managed a half-smile and launched into a complicated excuse, but his voice faded as Birnbaum put the big wooden-handled crank in the side of the Edison Kinetoscope, DeLuxe Traveling Model AA, and, as the light built up to full intensity, reached over to pull the film barrel gently alongside.

'Be very sure you have the head-end . . . that's the front end of the film, hanging here over the side of the barrel. Use this little nail to hold it by a sprocket hole so you can find it.' The head-end of the 'black snake' that had so frightened Momma and the girls was pulled up from the coiled mass in the barrel. As he threaded it through the various slots, gates, loopings and geared rollers, he explained each move to the closely watching boys.

Birnbaum was finally ready. He stood back from the machine, depressed still but immensely proud of the shining assembly and what he knew it could do if only given the chance.

'Ham, get the roll of black cloth off the bed and hang it over the windows to shut out the light.'

While Ham was doing his assigned job, Birnbaum picked up a folded white sheet and with Lou's help carefully tucked it over several pictures and the molding on the far wall.

Behind them the half-open door swung a bit wider as Ruth and Miriam, who had been sweeping the upstairs hall, peeked into the darkened room, then silently slipped in to stand quietly by the back wall and watch what was happening. The boarder gave the crank a turn. The shutter opened, gears clicked and metal claws poked into the sprocket holes to move the film forward one frame. As the round shutter turned open, for an instant the sheet hanging on the wall was illuminated with the scratched blank nothingness of a clear frame of film. The crank was turned several more times and the brightness of the screen gave way to a jumble of blurs, which came into focus with a series of jerks as Birnbaum twisted the long lens tube with his free hand, and then suddenly they were looking at a busy city street filled not with snow, but with crowds of lively active people, horses pulling wagons and carriages, men striding, women walking, children running ... movement ... movement ... a miracle!

Ruth and Miriam let out little screams, which so startled Birnbaum that he jumped up and stopped turning the big crank. The wall went dead dark.

'Ha ... uh ... what ... Girls!' Again he was utterly lost when confronted by Ruth and Miriam, but managed a weak smile and turned the crank again, turning the white sheet back into a city street. Far off in the background appeared a rising cloud of steam and a cluster of white dots, which quickly turned into a team of great white horses pulling a big fire engine that belched heavy clouds from its boiler. The charging images that filled the screen seemed about to gallop right into the bedroom. Again the girls squealed in fear and delight. Lou jumped up and down with uncontrolled excitement.

'Look ... look how they're all moving ... the fire engine and all those people! Mr. Birnbaum – how do you do it?'

43

The girls stopped squeaking and chattering in wonder at the moving images, but found it impossible to remain quiet. Ruth was first to speak, in a voice filled with excitement.

'Oh – what a wonderful thing . . . I can't wait to tell Momma and Poppa . . . Please, Mr. Birnbaum, keep turning the crank!'

With the reactions from his brother and sisters filling the room, Ham was unnaturally silent. He watched the projected scene for a moment, then turned his head not to observe the action up on the screen but to watch the excited little audience looking up at the magic moving shadows that were – yet were not. Ham was looking for more than shadows on a sheet – he was watching what they did to the people watching them.

The fire engine passed off the screen, to be followed immediately by another, which careened around the far corner. This shining engine was pulled by a team of sweating black horses and there were firemen in black leather helmets clinging to platforms on its sides and rear. Up beside the driver, who held tightly to a great collection of reins and shouted at the team as he cracked a long whip, sat a white-helmeted man who held a long rope fastened to a big brass bell high up on the fire engine.

All this excitement was happening in an almost silent bedroom with only the click-clack of the projector and the tiny hiss and acrid smell of the carbide gas, but in the minds of the little audience there was clearly imagined and heard the thunder of hooves, noises of hissing steam from the boilers, shouts of warning from the heroes in helmets and the clanging of the bell screaming in a voice of brass that help was on the way.

Clouds of steam and dust filled the screen when abruptly the tail end of the film passed through the gate and only a dazzling white glare remained, followed quickly by darkness as the shutter closed and the crank stopped turning. Now the only sound was that of breath being let out by the excited brothers and sisters and the echo of a sigh from Birnbaum, mourning the free screening of his treasure for this nonpaying audience. Lou pleaded for another show, and this time, with Birnbaum closely watching and instructing him, he was allowed to thread up the projector, pump and adjust the lamp and, with the turning of the big crank, set everything in motion.

Ruth slipped out of the room and quickly returned with

44

Solomon and Esther, who joined their girls against the back wall to see the fire engines race around the corner, down the street and almost right into the room, then out of the scene.

'Dear God!' said Esther in a voice she could hardly recognize as her own. 'I can smell the smoke and feel the heat from the fire! Quick – is my wall safe?'

'Momma ... Momma ... relax ... They're only shadows on a sheet,' said Solomon the realist, although he was moved with deep inner excitement at what he was seeing. 'Birnbaum ... how did you get all of that into your barrel? Please – can we see more?' Solomon had become almost as excited as his wife and children, but tried to hold most of it in. He could restrain himself no longer. 'Birnbaum – please! Isn't there more?'

The boarder had more than fire engines in his barrel. He reached deep down and came up with another head-end of film. Soon the family gazed with renewed wonder on street scenes of Paris and saw carriages crossing the Seine River bridges. Not quite the blood-tingling excitement of the fire engines, but to have a wall of their room come to life and show moving images of people in a city thousands of miles away far across the ocean seemed truly some kind of a miracle.

When at last it was all over the boys took down the cloth from the windows and the white sheet was folded back on the bed. Birnbaum turned off the gas valve, removed the lamp assembly and, after releasing the remaining air pressure, put it on a table near the window to cool. He looked out at the ever-growing heaps of snow with another deep sigh of resignation.

Solomon insisted on being shown the insides of the wonderful machine. Lou opened and shut the film gates and lifted the sprocket gears to show his father how beautifully the projector had been constructed.

'Whoever thought of this must be a genius!' said Solomon.

'Well – a lot of people really put ideas together to make pictures that move,' said Birnbaum. 'Thomas Edison gets most of the credit, though, because he took all of those ideas, added some better ones of his own and did something about it.' Ham stood as close to his father as he could and listened intently. His mind was working and he knew that he too could take ideas and do something with them. Lou, of course, was interested mainly in the beauty of the machinery and how it worked and did what it did. Momma and the girls were impatient to get out of the house and tell all their friends about the miracle they had seen in their boarder's bedroom. Now if only that damn storm would go back to where it had come from!

Ham walked over to where the white sheet had been hung on the wall. He kept looking at the faded wallpaper and in his mind he was sitting up there on the seat of the fire engine, smiling into a camera as he magnificently raced the great black team past, snapping the reins, cracking the long whip, pulling on the bell cord, feeding the steaming boiler, holding the power of life and death over horse and man, and perhaps even setting the fire they were going to himself so he would have a place to direct all of this wonderful exciting commotion.

The Kinetoscope went back into its case, but the dreams it had created stayed alive and would not go to sleep as the house settled down and another day ended.

Ham lay wide awake in his bed in the dark room he shared with Lou, whose head was still filled with the clack of gears and the bittersweet smell of the carbide lamp.

'Lou – Lou . . . you awake?' came from Ham, breaking in on his brother's gleaming vision of the glorious projection machine.

'Yeah. How can I get to sleep after what we saw? Ham, that was *something!* I want to find out everything I can about it and . . . and . . .'

Ham sat up in his bed and broke in.

'Lou, did you see how those fire engines *moved!* Nothing like the magic lantern or the slides in Mr. Johnson's studio. They really moved . . . and all those people in the street!'

Lou, seeing in his mind only the beautifully intricate workings of the machine, answered back across the dark room, 'Yeah – it was lovely, lovely . . . the way the shutter opens at just the right time . . . so one picture gets its shadow on the screen and then it closes so the screen goes dark so fast you can't even see when the next picture is pulled down and the shutter opens again just right and there's a brand-new square there exactly when it should be . . . I've just gotta find out more about how it works and how they make those films and . . .'

Ham was annoyed with his brother's infatuation with gears, shutters and shadows. He whispered loudly, hoping his parents were asleep by now, but eager to tell Lou his feelings.

46

'What I think is so great is the things you see up there on the sheet ... the *moving* things ... the street and all the people and the fire engines all moving ... and how you can go from a city right here in Pennsylvania across the ocean to a place like Paris ... or maybe London ... even to Pittsburgh! You think you're really there yourself! Lou ... maybe we can get one of those machines and some film ourselves and ...'

The older boy was sitting up in his bed now, and his enthusiasm matched Ham's.

'Take it easy, kid – those things must cost plenty. It could be maybe three hundred dollars ... that's a fortune! Where would we dig up that kind of *mazuma*?'

Silence filled the room, which seemed almost lit up by the flashing ideas and thoughts of the two boys. Lou broke the silence.

'Ham – we're gonna talk to Poppa tomorrow. Maybe he can help us on this. Say – if Mr. Birnbaum can get people to pay money for tickets when there's no snowstorm just to see fire engines and Paris, France, maybe we can do it too ... So now shut up for a while so we can get some sleep and in the morning think of what we can say to Poppa.'

'All right ... all right,' answered Ham, but he stayed wide awake for hours dreaming with his eyes open as he saw himself selling tickets, calling out to the long, long lines of people waiting to see the magic shadows and throwing money at him to see the wonders on the wall – and as he drove the fire engines past the camera for perhaps the fifteenth time, his projector handle slowed down, the shutter of his mind came to a gradual halt and the screen, with a last fitful flicker, went dark and he was asleep.

CHAPTER FOUR

The next morning began as always. The last asleep and the
first awake, Ham once again locked himself inside the outhouse so he could sit, meditate – and completely tie up the
normal routine of the entire household.

'Chaim! Didn't you listen when I told you that always the
boarder goes first?' shouted Solomon through the door when
he found himself barred.

Lou stood in back of his father in the cold yard and grumbled
about having to hold himself in every morning while his
younger brother monopolized the privy. Solomon turned to
him.

'Go see if Mr. Birnbaum is up yet. Apologize for your
brother's bad manners and tell him he can have the toilet in
just a minute.'

Wishing they had a second outhouse in the yard, Lou went
back into the house, certain the boarder must be wide awake
from all the shouting. The boarder's door was ajar, and after a
gentle knock he pushed it open and stuck his head inside. The
bed was neatly made, the curtains were pulled back, showing
the softly falling snow still coming down and blurring the landscape, but Birnbaum was not in his room. Lou stepped inside
and looked in every corner, opened a clothes closet, peered
under the bed and behind the chair, then saw the Kinetoscope
case, the film barrel and rolls of black cloth. Everything but
the valise was still in its place – except the boarder, who was
nowhere to be seen. Lou ran back to his father, who was shaking his youngest son, finally emerged from the outhouse and
very busy making excuses for locking everybody out.

Lou cut in on the heated father-and-son discussion.

'Poppa . . . Mr. Birnbaum isn't upstairs!'

'So go downstairs. Maybe he is getting himself breakfast
since Chaim here wouldn't let him go to the toilet!' and again
he glared at his son, whose small voice could barely be heard
answering.

48

'Please, Poppa . . . Ham, not Chaim . . . and if you had just knocked a couple of times on the door I would have finished what I was doing and come out.' He went on, but nobody listened.

Lou ran down the stairs and soon was back again after having gone through the entire house and finding no sign of Birnbaum.

'Come on, boys. Let's see what's going on,' said Solomon, leading them all back into the boarder's room.

On top of the projector case lay a small piece of paper, which Lou had overlooked. Solomon read it aloud.

' "Dear Mr. and Mrs. Rabinowitz . . . I am sorry to leave you like this – but I am running out of money and the storm has made it impossible for me to earn anything. I have just enough left to buy a ticket home and I am leaving you my Kinetoscope and the film so please sell it maybe to pay for my room and board. Please forgive me and I will never forget you or Harrisburg." ' It was signed in a defeated scrawl, 'Samuel Birnbaum.'

The father read it again, this time to himself, then called downstairs to his wife.

'Esther . . . Mr. Birnbaum has gone. Here, a message he has left . . . What shall we do?'

'Don't stand there making talk!' said Momma after she had come up the stairs and listened as Poppa read Birnbaum's last words. 'Chaim, Lou, put on your coats and heavy shoes and find him . . . Such a nice young man. Quick – get outside and look!' She already sensed that they had lost not only a boarder, but worse yet – a possible son-in-law!

The boys bundled up, wrapping mufflers around their faces so only their eyes peered out, pulled down caps to cover their ears and set off in search of the vanished boarder. Soon they were back, stamping snow off their shoes and slapping arms to warm up their chilled hands.

'Poppa . . . only some tracks in the snow headed toward the bridge. We heard the train whistle and I'm sure he's left town by now,' Lou told his parents, while Ham bit at his frozen lips and dripped on the floor.

Momma went back to the room and pulled the sheets off the bed.

'Now we have a projection machine and no boarder. He could have stayed . . . who cares if he couldn't pay us . . . such a nice young man . . . and maybe . . .' Esther drifted on with the imagined hope that maybe Birnbaum just might have

49

worked out for one of her girls, but she realized they would have to settle for the Kinetoscope and the barrel of film and wait for somebody else on another train another day. She sighed a little and called over to her sons.

'Boys, get all this stuff out of the room. Before your brother Maurie comes home again we might still have another boarder, God willing . . . so make everything tidy!'

'As soon as the storm ends and we can move around again I'll see if Lefkowitz will buy that machine for the brass and copper . . . maybe we won't lose too much on the nice young man from the Bronx,' said Solomon, and the boys looked over at their father in alarm. Sell his wonderful Kinetoscope for scrap metal – never! They would have to talk about that later, as their father went down the hall and slammed the bedroom door shut behind him.

Lou and Ham carried the big case, the barrel and the rolls of material down the hall to their room. They opened the big box after gently setting it on its end so the projector could be lifted out and looked at. Lou pumped up the lamp and adjusted the mirror. They dragged over the barrel of film and found the head-end, which the older boy carefully threaded up just as he remembered Birnbaum doing the night before. Ham again hung up the sheet and covered the windows, and now, with the big wood-handled crank in place, Lou brought the wall alive with the familiar street scene. They watched the fire engines race toward them again and again until they almost seemed to be going in circles. Lou stopped turning the crank and turned to his brother.

'We just can't let Poppa sell this – we *have* to do something with it!' He stood back to look at the wonderful shining machine and reached out almost tenderly to touch the warm side as though it were a living thing. Ham walked over to the window and took down the long black cloth. He looked out at the big vacant lot next door. The snow had almost stopped, the black clouds were slowly moving on to other places and fragments of sunshine broke through to light up parts of the city. The storm and Birnbaum both were leaving Harrisburg, but something remained behind that would change this house and the people who lived here.

With the coming of dawn next day it was as though a siege had been lifted from the beleaguered city. Now only the snowdrift barricades of the departed enemy remained, and in a few hours these were breached by battalions of men armed with shovels and brushes loading a procession of wagons. Soon the narrow paths down streets were widened into lanes, and by afternoon they again were busy thoroughfares echoing to the sound of hooves, creaking wheels and the occasional snarl of a gasoline motor.

Solomon and his two sons helped clear the street in front of the house, and when he learned that the way was open to the kosher slaughterhouse on the edge of the city, he had Lou go to the stable and hitch up the horse to their wagon. The three wedged themselves up on the bench and set off down the sparkling roads to pick up a full load of meat for the hungry customers who would soon be descending on the shop. During the trip their wagon passed the scrap metal yard belonging to Meyer Lefkowitz, and Solomon was reminded of the collection of copper, brass and glass left behind by the departed boarder.

'Boys – first thing tomorrow you pack up that machinery so we can see what Lefkowitz will give us for it.'

'Poppa!' Lou cried out as though mortally wounded. 'Poppa – that isn't scrap! It's a beautiful Kinetoscope and you *can't* sell it! You can't! I already know a lot about it and how it works and some way Ham and I can use it to make more money than Mr. Lefkowitz will *ever* give you for scrap!'

'Please, listen to Lou, Poppa – please!' Ham piped up, and Solomon smiled, then gave a great laugh as the wagon pulled up to the rear alley door of their shop.

'All right, all right, so if in one week you figure out how to make what we lost on the boarder – fine. You can keep the machine. If not, well . . . Lefkowitz owes me some favors, and you boys can do more good helping me cut up meat and selling to customers. Now – unload the wagon!'

Soon everything from the back of the wagon was stored in the ice locker or laid out on block tables, where Solomon's strong right arm and flashing knives, saw and cleaver cut sides of beef into saleable portions for the customers already filing into the shop. Ham swept up the damp sawdust from the floor and spread a fresh dry layer while Lou ran around helping his father with orders.

With more and more customers coming into the shop, Solomon sent Lou and Ham back to the slaughterhouse across town with enough money to reload the old wagon. On their way they once more passed the Lefkowitz scrap metal yard, and Lou let the reins go slack as he turned his head toward the dismal collection of rusting pipes, stoves, beams and other refuse waiting to be broken up. His heart seemed suddenly as heavy as one of those lumps of metal lying out there in the snowdrift-spotted yard.

'Ham – a whole day's nearly gone by and we haven't done a thing about the Kinetoscope. Poppa gave us only one week to get back what the boarder cost him, and if we don't – it's good-bye projector.'

'Look, Lou . . . Wasn't Mr. Birnbaum going to rent some place to show his films and sell tickets to people? Couldn't we do that too? First we find a room someplace we can make dark and then get some tickets to sell and maybe some cards to put around the neighborhood . . . Ruth and Miriam can help us. We only run it after the shop is closed late afternoon to get started and then –'

He would have run on and on, but his brother managed at last to squeeze into the conversation.

'Wait a minute, Ham. Finding a place means putting out some money, which we haven't got – or at least making promises maybe we can't even keep . . .' Lou thought a minute, snapped the reins to speed up the slow walk of the old horse and then with a broad smile said, 'Chaim – promises we can make and keep . . . we'll give it a try . . . we'll do it somehow!'

'Lou, please . . . please . . .' came the aggrieved reply, 'please . . . I'm *Ham* – not Chaim!'

The wagon came down Grant Avenue, then turned as Lou guided it into the alley between the rows of buildings. They reached the back door and started throwing the sides of meat onto a small wheeled cart, which they pushed inside to where Solomon was sharpening the knives and cleavers while customers impatiently called out orders and raked over the heaps of gossip that had piled up during the long storm. Lou took the horse up the street to the stable while Ham swept the sawdust thrown down earlier and replaced it with a fresh supply.

On his way back to the shop, Lou stopped at every storefront and looked through the display windows. He crossed back and forth from one side of the street to the other, skipping around puddles of mud, water and horse droppings to look at anything he thought might have some promise, but there were no empty stores, and his dejection increased the closer he got to the butcher shop. Just as he was about to squeeze through the small knot of customers standing outside the front door, a large van drew up at the curb and a full-bearded, bare-armed teamster leaned out to shout down at Lou.

'Son – where is . . .' He paused to squint at a wrinkled scrap of paper held with the reins in his grimy hands. 'Where in hell is the Feinberg and Weinstein Tailor Shop? It says here Grant Avenue . . . it should be right here . . . but it ain't!'

Lou looked up at the man and his helper and pointed farther down the row of shops.

'It's right there. I'll go ahead and show you. They don't have a sign where you can see it, so you have to know where to look.' He skirted the few customers still waiting to get into his father's shop, and with the van pulled by a team of husky draft horses slowly following him down the mudfilled street, he guided them four doors down to the tailor shop.

Feinberg the tailor darted out of the door when he saw the big van draw up in front. The man was distraught, and with good reason. With his late partner Herman Weinstein only recently placed beneath a memorial marker at Mount Zion five miles out of town, Feinberg fully expected to follow him there soon if he failed to get rid of the bolts of cloth, the sewing machines and the other fixtures the van had come to pick up so he could pay off his clamoring creditors.

'Take it! Take it all! And if you got room, take me too!' the harassed tailor cried out, and, leaving his front door wide open, he ran off down the street and out of business.

For a while Lou stood and watched the two men loading the van; then he walked back to the butcher's shop to help out for a few minutes. Soon he was out in the street again to see the last of the tailor shop being emptied and the van pulling away. As the final customer departed from Solomon's store with a bundle of prime brisket under her arm, the father and his boys began cleaning things up. Lou emptied the last of the old sawdust into a box and motioned to Ham to follow him outside into the street while their father was busy inside the storage room.

It was getting dark and gas lamps were being lit one by one, so the boys could look into the new emptiness of what had been the tailor shop but was now only three stripped walls, a glassed-in front and a set of big open doors, which the boys pulled shut after stepping inside. They stood in the barely lit gloom with the flickering of the streetlamps coming through the wide front windows. Without a word, they looked at the long narrow space, the height up to the ceiling and the expanse of timbered flooring now bare of its carpet. Then they turned for a moment to look wide-eyed at each other and ran out of the empty store back to their father's shop, bursting with that same tremendous excitement first felt when the fire engines careened around the corner on the wall of their house.

The boys tried again and again to tell Solomon about the vacant store down the street, but he told them to keep quiet and help clean up. By the time that was done, the only thing on his mind was getting them all home for Momma's dinner, which already must be getting cold. The boys knew from experience how unwise it would be to bring up any other subject until that one had been disposed of and all stomachs concerned were full.

Since they were all too tired from the hard day's work to walk home, they took the horsecar, which let them off a block from their house. Momma was waiting for them on the porch and she was very excited. She came down to the sidewalk the moment she saw them and almost screamed, 'He's home, Poppa . . . boys . . . He's home! Maurie is up in his room! Be quiet . . . he's sound asleep!' she shouted, and pulled them all with her up the three stairs, across the narrow porch and through the open door.

They all rushed up the stairs and into what had for a while been the boarder's room. Here they found Maurie, oldest of Solomon and Esther's children, stretched out sound asleep and fully dressed on the bed. The noise of the family awakened him, and inbetween yawns he told them that more than three months on the road selling meat, lard and hides for Armour and Company had been quite enough.

'All I want to do is sleep for a week, eat all I can of Momma's cooking and help you, Poppa, and the boys once in a while at the shop if there's no heavy lifting.'

Within an hour Maurie almost wished he was back on the road in Allentown, Scranton or Steubenville or even down in Mennonite country in those two towns with the wonderful names of Blue Ball and Intercourse. His younger brothers overwhelmed him with a barrage of pleas and words like sprocket gears, calcium lamps, Kinetoscope, dark curtains, shutters and many others Lou remembered from the departed Birnbaum.

'Maurie, you've gotta convince Poppa to get us the empty tailor shop down the street for a couple of weeks or longer so we can set up the Kinetoscope and sell people tickets and make a lot of money!' they poured into the sleepy ears of their older brother.

'Wait a minute . . . hold it, fellows! I know something about these things. I went to one of those shows in Scranton and heard plenty more about it in other places. You'd be insane to play with that dangerous stuff! Film is just like dynamite – it's even made of the same things, I think. One spark and wham! . . . you go right through the wall, and lucky if you only get killed! Momma and Poppa would never forgive me for encouraging you.'

Lou persisted and Ham echoed his pleas, so finally Maurie, outnumbered and outvoiced, shut them off by promising to look at the wonderful machine later after dinner – and if he was at all impressed by it and their knowledge of its operation, well, maybe . . . that is, if it wasn't going to cost anybody money or be a dangerous risk . . . well, perhaps . . . he might . . . *might*, mind you . . . talk with their father about it and save the damn thing from the Lefkowitz scrapyard.

The family sat at dinner listening to Maurie tell stories of life on the road, and Solomon laughed as his oldest son told of each triumph of salesmanship or about a competitor out-witted. He and a salesman from Swift and Company, their great rival, had both moved in on a big market in Wilkes-Barre, each trying to take an account from the other, each positive it was his – only to have a shrewd little Greek named Spyros something-or-other from a tiny packinghouse nobody had ever heard of move right in and walk away with it all.

Solomon laughed. 'Remember, smart Jewish boys get smarter when they have Greeks or Armenians for teachers! If your friend Spyros ever comes by my shop I'm going to give him an order and thank him for giving my son Maurie a good lesson in salesmanship and for teaching him never to take anything for final!' Sol wiped soup off his moustache and let loose a contented sigh of joy at having the family all home again.

Now Lou spoke up in a voice strangely tight and small.

'Maurie – the shop . . . the tailor shop . . . remember . . .'

Big brother Maurie thought a moment and gave Lou a blank look.

'Tailor shop . . . what tailor – oh yes, now I remember. Lou, didn't I say first I wanted to see the . . . but I guess I have no choice.' Then he turned to their father.

'Poppa, Lou and Chaim . . . I mean Ham . . . have this idea . . . Maybe it's worth something, maybe not. You know me, I don't jump at something until I know all about it – but if I'm here to help you and the boys out, maybe it might work. Lou told me about that Kinetoscope thing. While I was in Scranton last month I saw just what the boys here were telling me about. Some men put up tents and another group took over empty stores and they sold tickets and filled both places up. It's hard to believe, but people will pay good money to see anything new – even if it's only shadows on a screen.'

Ham and Lou broke in eagerly.

'See, Poppa, what did we tell you? Give us a chance . . . please!'

Maurie waved an impatient hand at the boys, trying to shut them up.

'You'd think people had never seen teams pulling fire engines down streets before, the way they acted. They screamed and hollered, and one guy even got up and ran out of the place and –'

Ham broke in almost with a wail.

'Fire engines! They had fire engines on their Kinetoscope! Lou, if fire engines is all they're showing, what can we do that's gonna be different? You just can't see fire engines and nothing else!'

He seemed to have completely forgotten how he had loved that shadow parade so like a merry-go-round as he and Lou had the steaming engines dashing around and around the corner and down the street again and again. Young as he was, Ham knew from his street knowledge that people wanted novelty – something different, something new, a lift from the dull pattern of just living out their hard routine lives.

Maurie spoke with the mature voice of reason and years.

'Listen, when you start something you use what you have – then, if it works, later you look for something new to add when you've succeeded. Don't worry if they have fire engines on every screen in Ohio, Pennsylvania and Maryland. The one place they don't have them right now is here in Harrisburg. Later on if what you have gets you started and pays off, then you get something different. Meantime, Poppa, what about that empty tailor shop up the street from your place? Who's the landlord and can we see him tomorrow and do some selling of something besides lard, hides and meat?'

Both Ham and Lou thought their big brother Maurie was one of the greatest men in the entire world – after their

56

father, when Solomon said:

'Feinberg is out of business and Weinstein, *alav ha-sholom*, is out in Mount Zion . . . so now the store is owned by . . .' He thought a few minutes. 'Owned by . . . ah . . . by Lapidus the undertaker, who right now is in New York for the Hebrew Immigrant Aid Society . . . A good man, Lapidus – for when we're alive and perhaps later too . . . and Mrs. Lapidus, Sophie, lets the oldest son, Isadore, run things when the father is away . . . and Isadore –'

'Sol,' interrupted Esther as she again filled their plates, 'Sol, to the point, please. Enough family history from Lapidus. The empty store he owns is what the boys want to know about; not a long *megillah* about out good friend Lapidus, who we should never live to see as customers!'

'Momma – always to the point. The empty store shouldn't be a problem,' said Solomon. 'Tomorrow I visit our friend Sophie Lapidus – take her a nice bag of fresh kidneys, tell her what a good job her man is doing for Immigrant Aid . . . tell her my boys want to borrow the empty tailor store for a few weeks . . . maybe for no rent, just to keep it looking busy . . . maybe a small percentage from profits if the tickets sell . . . better yet, just a pass for her and the boy and the husband when he returns. Then Sophie will call her son Isadore in from his undertaking work and he will wipe his hands – which I will try not to shake, even though I am usually very polite – and he will say, "Anything you want, Momma," because he is a good son, even though he works in a business I would never want for a boy of mine . . . but of course necessary until maybe someday man should become immortal . . . we should only live so long!'

Before Sol could launch into a Talmudic discourse on man's chances for life eternal, Maurie said, 'All right then, it's as good as settled. Now, Lou, and you, Chaim, get that Kinetoscope thing put together here and let me see if you know what you're doing well enough so people in Harrisburg will pay their good money to see it.'

When finally all the family sat in the darkened front room and Lou turned the big crank in the side of the machine, Maurie looked up at the illuminated sheet as it sprang into life. Under his breath, unheard over the clacking of the machine and the hiss of the carbide, he sighed deeply.

'Good God almighty! Fire engines again! I just can't get away from them. Well – maybe old P. T. Barnum was right after all . . . there's a nickel for every slot, and for every slot there's some yokel who can't wait to stick his five cents in to see anything that's different. Fire engines! Doesn't anything else *ever* happen!'

CHAPTER FIVE

The dust flew up in Ham's face as he slashed at the floor with a longhandled broom. Ruth called over to Miriam, 'Look at him work! His own room at home should be so clean!'

The boy with the broom pretended not to hear his sisters' comments as they watched him help turn a tailor shop into something else. Lou had whitewashed the big glass windows facing the street after both boys cleaned them thoroughly, with the girls working just as hard with mops, brushes and buckets borrowed from home. When the old walls were as clean as they ever would be and the timber floor had been swept clear of the past, they were ready to set up the room.

Maurie and Lou waited for Poppa's shop to close, then went to their house with the horse and wagon to collect the most important things of all. They brought them back to the former tailor shop, where the others waited, and Ham helped his brothers carry the cases and barrel inside. The boys carefully lifted the shining Kinetoscope up on its box at one end of the long room and then they all stood back in admiration of what to them was a thing of true beauty. Lou looked around and sensed something was wrong.

'This thing makes such a damned racket when it's running that the audience is going to think real fire engines are coming in through the front doors. We have to do something about it.' A few minutes of thought and Lou figured he might have an answer.

'Look, we put up some kind of a wall right here and the projector will be in its own little room. If we get lots of old blankets to hang inside, then they could soak up most of the noise.' Lou didn't realize he had just become the first acoustic engineer in Harrisburg.

Maurie brightened. 'Yeah – if a blanket soaks up water and keeps out cold air, then there's no reason why it shouldn't do the same thing for noise. It's worth a try.'

After pacing off dimensions, he and Lou devised a kind of

59

wall made of scrap wood strips covered with blankets that Ham ran home to borrow from the extra supply in Momma's storage closet. He hoped next winter would be warmer than the one they were having now. Little openings were cut in the blanket wall for the lens to shoot light through and for a peephole to help them check focus on the screen.

While all this was going on, Solomon, who had secured the tailor shop for the three passes, was across the street with Lapidus, the returned land-lord-undertaker. Now he worked out arrangements for borrowing the long wooden benches and some of the folding chairs used in the undertaking establishment so the customers watching the pictures wouldn't get splinters in their behinds from the floor. Of course, if there was a funeral then all the seats and benches must be rushed back to the undertaker. Solomon silently prayed that the entire Jewish community of Harrisburg would enjoy good health and long life.

Early next day they put up their screen, four of the largest available sheets, also borrowed from Momma, who had washed and bleached them as white as possible. They were raised up and fastened against the far wall, where they reached almost from floor to ceiling. Stretched tight with only a few wrinkles showing, they dominated the end of the store. The room still was not quite dark enough, so Ham and Lou climbed up on some of the borrowed benches that Maurie had just carried in and tacked up Birnbaum's dark cloths over the whitewashed front windows. Now there was enough gloom inside to clearly see images on the white sheets when Lou turned the big crank and the shadows flickered.

Ham wasn't too interested now in technical matters and kept strangely silent as his brothers set up the projector, made all the adjustments and finally found the right place to set the machine and focus the lens so the image completely filled the screen. Something very important was missing, and he suddenly realized what it was.

'This place has to have a name!' Ham shouted over to his brothers and sisters. 'People gotta know we're here and it isn't the tailor shop anymore!'

Maurie cleared some of the dust from his throat.

'Say – the place I saw in Scranton was called the Bijou, whatever that means. Sounds like a fancy French word and it's got real class!' He frowned with sudden worry. 'Uh-oh . . . suppose it's one of those dirty French words and somebody finds out. Then we'll have some real problems!'

The two girls came right in on cue with giggles, but Ruth ran over to the small pile of books. She pulled out a dictionary, flipped the pages, looked down a long list of words and came up with a broad smile and good news.

'Don't worry, it isn't a dirty word at all. Listen . . . under common foreign words . . . "French: bijou – a gem . . . a jewel . . . sometimes the box a jewel or jewelry is kept in." '
She looked up from her book and around the long dark room, cluttered with benches, chairs, bits and pieces of wood and blankets. 'This sure isn't any Jewel Box you have – it looks more like a Junk Box or somebody's bad dream!'

Ham yelled at the top of his lungs, 'Hey, that's it! Bijou Dream Nickelodeon. How's that for our name?'

Since they all agreed it was his idea, and a good one, Ham was sent to get materials for a sign to go up over the front door. Within an hour he returned with a long flat piece of wood, two cans of paint, he hoped of colors that would attract attention, plus some fuzzy brushes, all 'borrowed' from shops in the area whose owners probably wouldn't miss them for a few days, if ever.

With a pencil stub Maurie drew outlines of the letters on the wood, and Ham went out again to borrow some more paint while Lou started to fill in the background. Soon the name was blocked in and the paint began to dry. Ham went out once more to borrow a smaller brush while Lou continued touching up the letters. Very soon the entire sign was done and the long piece of wood was propped against the side wall.

The girls stood back to read the words, the strange one in French, the others in more familiar English.

Miriam sniffed at Ruth. 'I don't care what your book says, I'll just bet it's some dirty French word!'

'So who'll know?' answered Ruth. 'Learning English is enough of a job for most people around here – but what's more important is how much it's going to cost them to get inside the Bee-Joo Dream.'

'A nickel,' Maurie answered, 'just like the place in Scranton that I saw. Now let's make another sign that says "Admission – Five Cents." '

The signs were done and left to dry while the boys went back up the street to work with their father in his shop and the girls walked home to help their mother prepare dinner.

Next day, after several hours spent helping unload, prepare and store meat, Lou and Ham carried the rest of the benches and chairs across the street from the Lapidus Undertaking Parlor into the former tailor shop, which was about to undergo its reincarnation. The boys pulled out the long wooden sign, which now was completely dry, and carried it through the front door into the street. They stacked two of the benches and with a good deal of perilous stretching managed to get up high enough to nail the ends of the sign into position right over the front door. Ruth and Miriam stood down on the sidewalk and steadied the teetering benches, all the time cautioning their brothers to be careful and not break their necks. When the last nail had been hammered, the girls helped the boys down to the ground, and in another minute they had fastened the smaller ADMISSION – FIVE CENTS sign on the column to the left of the open front door. they crossed the street to stand on the opposite sidewalk and look over at THE BIJOU DREAM – NICKELODEON.

A giddy wave of excitement, pride and joy almost engulfed them. It was a feeling they might often experience in the years ahead, but this was a special first moment – theirs alone, never again to be equaled.

A bearded old man wearing a long, shiny black coat and a broad-brimmed hat slowly walked by and stopped in front of the little group. He looked over at the sign and then back at the young people standing beside him.

'Aha! Another synagogue is opening?' He squinted through thick glasses that gave him the appearance of a squat black owl. 'Of course already perhaps we have enough synagogues here, but another shouldn't hurt.'

Lou, Ham and their sisters looked at the old man in wonderment.

'Wha . . . what do you mean, a new synagogue?' Lou asked in disbelief.

'Young man, look what says the sign . . . 'Be a Jew . . . Dream!' Don't we all do that? Sometimes for us it is a way to clear the head for important thoughts. A good name . . . it should be a good synagogue.' The old man smiled at the young people, ducked his head in a little bow and slowly continued his walk up the street.

The two boys looked at each other in dismay. Ruth broke out in a wide smile and hit her brothers on the arm.

'Bijou Dream it stays! See how it gets attention – even if it's not for the right reason. Come on, let's go back. Soon it's time for people to come by with their nickels – then we really see what happens.'

62

Lou mumbled to himself as they crossed the street.

'Be a Jew ... Dream ... Who figures that from a little jewel box comes such a mix-up ... but maybe it does mean something good. Ham ... Chaim! Quit dreaming ... come on, let's put the benches in line and the film in the projector ... we're in business!'

It was almost dusk, and a slight chill remained in the air. Few people were out on the street. Some wagons and buggies passed the Bijou Dream, slowing down only slightly as the occupants looked over at the new and unfamiliar addition to Grant Avenue. Some people walking past the entrance also paused, stood back and tried to read the strange words, then went on their way. Lou had the two front doors swung wide open, and light streamed out to reinforce the glow coming from the gas lamp on the sidewalk. Solomon drew up with the delivery wagon to unload Maurie and the girls, as well as the dinner Momma had wrapped for the two boys, who hadn't been home yet and were working so hard.

'All right, now what do you do with this new business of yours so you get people to come inside?' Solomon asked Maurie as they tied the horse to the gas lamp pole just down the street.

'First we have to make people notice us,' Maurie replied. 'Something maybe like posters around the whole neighborhood and a banner out in front. That sign we made is all right but it's too small, and unless we just want to run pictures for ourselves, well – we're going to have to make some real noise in Harrisburg.'

Ham lit the lamps by the front doors while inside Lou pumped up the carbide lamp after checking the water level in the tank and polishing the mirror. The benches and chairs, all in straight rows, were clean but very empty as the girls trimmed the lamps running down the walls of the long narrow room. Maurie took his position beside the open front doors, his pocket full of change borrowed from his father; on a little ledge fastened to the wall beside him was an empty cigar box ready for the expected admissions. Tickets would have to be printed later. More carriages and a farm wagon came down the street, and the drivers reined in their horses at the sight of the new Bijou Dream.

Now the far end of the store lit up as Lou turned the big crank and checked focus by sliding the brass-encased lens back and forth. The few men who had gathered out front on the sidewalk and some of the curious people up on their rigs peered through the open doors to get a better look at what was going on inside. Maurie turned to see the open gap behind him, and was about to pull the blanket curtain closed when he realized that he would have to lure people inside. A free peek might be worth a dozen admissions. He shrugged his shoulders and stood there patiently waiting.

A few more wagons, buggies and pedestrians came along the street, and some paused in front of the little theater, trying to make out the strange new words over the door and the even stranger things they sensed going on inside.

'What's happening here, Sol?' one of them asked. It was Kravetz the pharmacist, the most curious, gifted and active neighborhood gossip. Dispensing pills and rumors was the great pleasure of his life, and now there was something brand new for him to investigate.

'For a nickel, Kravetz, you will find out,' answered his friend Solomon. 'But since you happen to be the very first person to ask, you will come in to be my guest. If you enjoy yourself and like what it is you see, give the boys here a nickel on your way out . . . tell all your customers and your family and friends. But if you don't like, keep your nickel and also keep shut your mouth – if that is at all possible!'

Said with a smile from a friend, it was accepted with a smile, and Kravetz entered to seat himself on the best-positioned middle bench, the first customer – or rather, the first guest.

Maurie's face registered acute shock at his father's benevolence.

'Poppa! You can't just invite everyone in – not tonight, Poppa!'

'Moishe, I can and I have. We want an audience . . . so Kravetz is a good beginning with his loud mouth. If worst should come to worst, I will pay his nickel.' Solomon chuckled. 'Maurie . . . Moishe, my son – you remind me of when you were a little boy at Passover asking why tonight was different from any other night. Now you see . . . it is very different!'

The father recognized a whole group of old friends from the shul who had collected outside the front door. He stepped outside, shook hands all around and invited them all to come in as his guests. Maurie uttered stricken objections in a hoarse whisper to Solomon, who took him aside.

'My boy, don't worry so much. These gentlemen are my

guests, and later tonight they will tell their families and their friends what they saw here. Tomorrow they will go to work or to visit or to *shul* and they will talk and talk and talk. From now on they will pay to come inside – and their friends and their families! Moishe, to catch a customer, give first a sample – then make a sale!' Solomon broke away and briskly walked up the street to greet with open arms and an invitation more old friends he had seen walking toward the nickelodeon. He brought them back and grandly ushered them all through the open door, past his red-faced son, and saw them to their seats.

'Poppa, we don't need a *minyan*. This isn't the high holidays,' said Maurie as his father shuttled back and forth to collect more old friends he had spotted standing outside.

Solomon smiled at his eldest offspring and soon had several rows filled up in the long narrow room. He told Ruth and Miriam to lower the wall lamps, and as he passed the opening to the little room where Ham and Lou stood beside the projection machine, he leaned inside, saying, 'Begin the show, boys. We have inside at least eighteen guests waiting – my friends ... Nearly *two minyans* ... enough to start. Crank the machine, Chaim!'

The boy went over to the Kinetoscope and cranked.

The screen lit up with the street scene and the flurry of fire engines. The men on the benches gasped, and one even got to his feet in wordless panic, then laughed nervously and sat down. It seemed that every jaw of every person in the room dropped open at the same time, and the gasp of intaken breath could be heard even over the muffled click-clacking of the projection machine. A miracle was being presented and accepted, and excitement swept back and forth across the narrow room almost like something with a life of its own as the images up on the screen seemed to come right down into the audience.

A couple of the men had already seen the moving picture peep shows at carnivals or in large cities like Pittsburgh or New York, but this was altogether different. Now they shared a thrilling experience with all the other people right around them, not looking all alone down in a box, but here in a room and it was there big as life! It was as though they had all been lifted out of this little place and were standing together in a street in another town and time, as heroes on steaming chariots roared past to rescue the victims of unseen disaster. Soon the views of Paris held them entranced, although with lessened heartbeats and excitement, and some pointed out landmarks or familiar places remembered from long ago when they were young and had passed through that lovely city of light and dreams. Suddenly the show ended with a flash of white as the tail of the film passed through the gate. Ham stopped turning the crank and the shutter blade closed to cut off the bright beam.

Maurie and the girls turned up the inside lamps while Lou and Ham, sweating heavily in the tiny cubicle, fished out the head-end of film from the barrel, turned off the hissing lamp, added more water to the tank and pumped up pressure for the next showing.

From the audience arose a babble of voices – pleasure, wonder, astonishment – but not a movement of rising or going to the front door. They all sat, eyes glistening with excitement, and while they waited they talked.

'Poppa!' Maurie whispered loudly as he pulled Solomon's sleeve. 'How do we get them to leave so we can get another audience in and run the picture again? They were your guests only for one show, weren't they?'

Solomon turned to him. 'My boy, you don't invite guests out – you invite them only in. So if they want to stay, it is a compliment to the host. Let them stay, and then when they go home they tell their families, and wherever they go tomorrow, they go to work for us. Right now to be our guests is our payment to them for what they will do for us . . . and we pay them with pleasure. Such a small price for what it brings us back. Be patient, my son.'

Lou looked out again from the hot little room, whose blanket walls kept most of the noise and all of the heat trapped inside. When he saw the same men on the benches and chairs, he and Ham went over to their father and Maurie by the front door. They looked down into the empty cigar box, then out at the street, deserted except for horses and wagons tied to the curb posts.

'Poppa,' said Ham in a tight little voice, 'couldn't you invite the horses inside too? Then we'd have a bigger audience.'

'What do we do, Poppa, if it's all a big flop?' Lou sighed.

Solomon reached over to put a big hand on his son's shoulder.

'We run it again for my friends . . . maybe a couple more times we run . . . then we say good night to everybody very politely and let them go home to talk – and tomorrow to talk some more. Then when we open these doors, watch the people

66

fill this cigar box to the top with nickels. Tonight is a kind of
. . . a kind of *mitzva*, a good deed – for them and for us too.
Nothing has been lost. Tomorrow . . . tomorrow . . . *that* is
the beginning!'

Lou again looked in at the eighteen or nineteen men chattering in the little hall still so full of empty space. He and Ham
returned to their small blanket-linked room, and as the lamps
again were turned down, they started up the projector. The
audience immediately was stricken with silence, and whole
new waves of excitement built up, no less intense than the
first time, as again they lived the scenes on the big white
screen. Solomon stood in the back hugely enjoying the pleasure of his guests. Maurie leaned in utter dejection on the
front doorpost, jingling his pocketful of unused change in a
sad metallic dirge.

The image flickered a moment, and Solomon stuck his head
through the blanketed door.

'Keep cranking . . . keep cranking, Chaim! They love
it – they love it!'

The boy kept cranking and cranking. Pains shot up his arm.

The Bijou Dream had come to Harrisburg.

67

CHAPTER SIX

The street sweepers came just before dawn and were closely followed by the refuse wagons collecting the heaps of manure and garbage donated to the city by its horse and human population. Working their way slowly down the street came men carrying short ladders, which they climbed to turn off the gaslights, no longer needed with the departure of night. Tradespeople yawned as they unlocked their shops, and finally, with clattering feet and gasping breath, came Lou and Ham, who had run all the way from their house to the alley behind the butcher shop.

They let themselves in and swept out the remnants of yesterday's meat scraps and old sawdust, then sprinkled water and fresh wood shaving on the floor. At any moment they expected the arrival of their father and older brother with the loaded wagon from the slaughterhouse, so everything had to be ready – or else!

Lou left his broom several times to open the front door and look outside. All he saw was the length of Grant Avenue stretching itself awake under the brightening sky. Delivery wagons rattled down the cobblestones; the early cries of a street vendor sounded as he tuned up for the day ahead. A mailman came out of one store and entered another, and a police constable followed him to get in out of the chill morning air as the street and all of Harrisburg slowly came alive.

The clopping sound of hooves came closer, and the slap-slap of worn harness and the screeching of wooden brake blocks on metal wheel bands announced the wagon's arrival at the rear alley door. Solomon shouted for his sons to come out and help carry the load inside, where meat hooks, chopping tables and storage lockers waited.

By eight-thirty all was ready, and Ham wiped his forehead with a damp sleeve as he walked to the front of the shop and pulled the door open to let in the first customers. He stood there looking out through the door for a long moment, then

68

turned to scream in a high excited voice, 'Poppa . . . Lou . . . Maurie! Come here quick! Look what's happening outside!'

Before the others could respond, Ham raced to the back of the shop, grabbed his father by an arm and pulled him up front, closely followed by his brothers asking what kind of calamity could have struck Grant Avenue so early in the morning. They all burst through the door and collided with a jabbering line of men, women and children standing three and four abreast on the sidewalk, blocking all foot traffic and stretching in a ragged line from the corner, past the Rabinowitz Kosher Butcher Shop and the two neighboring stores, and ending at the closed doors of the Bijou Dream Nickelodeon.

Solomon threw his arms around Maurie, then grabbed the other two boys.

'See, see! What did I tell you last night! Don't keep all these nice people standing out here on the cold street! Get busy!'

They politely shoved and pushed their way through the swarm of people, and Solomon nodded all the way to his friends and their families standing in line. Finally they reached Kravetz the pharmacist and his wife, three sons, daughters-in-law and an assortment of grandchildren, aunts and uncles, and the locked front doors of the Bijou Dream. Maurie quickly removed the padlock and took his place at the side of the entrance next to the empty cigar box, which soon began to jingle with the pleasant sound of falling coins. He called over to his father, who stood greeting the customers.

'Poppa, one sign we forgot to make – the hours we are open. Eight-thirty is just too early to open if we have to get things going first at the butcher shop!'

'*Sha*, Maurie,' answered Solomon. 'Don't make any limits to success – not yet, anyhow!'

Lou and Ham raced from one lamp to the other, striking matches and trimming wicks until the dark little auditorium grew light enough for the line of people to find seats on the benches and chairs.

Inside the blanket-curtained room they wiped the dust of the night off the big lens with a not-too-clean handkerchief, poured water into the tank from a coffee can, added calcium, then fiercely pumped up the air pressure until a reassuring hiss was heard in the lamp housing. Solomon ran back to lock up his shop for a little while, then returned to the nickelodeon. He looked into the room where Lou and Ham worked over the projection machine, urging them to hurry on with the show since the place was filled and a whole new line was forming out on the street. His eyes glistened with pride in his boys, who pumped and pushed the machine into position until they too were glistening with the sweat pouring down their faces. Ham reached into the barrel for the head-end of film which somehow had slipped off its nail. His father and brother heard him use words they had never before heard come from him as the perforated strip slithered through his damp fingers and lost itself deep down inside the crowded barrel.

The audience sat in the semidarkness, families calling out to friends across the room, men with voices grown hoarse from talking too much and telling of things they had seen the night before in this very place. Nearly everybody felt a little guilty not being at work, in school or at *schul* – but that was something for thinking about another time. Miracles didn't happen every day, now was now, and it was important to be here in this place to see . . . to see what? Nothing at all was happening. There was nothing to see except a white square on a dark wall, and already they had sat on these hard benches and chairs for more than fifteen minutes.

A late miracle was no miracle at all! Already the morning was passing, nothing was happening and what were they getting for their nickels and dimes except sore bottoms! The happy babble of excitement was turning into an angry murmur of annoyance and impatience. Feet and hands softly began a rhythmic stamping and clapping.

Maurie left the front door, stuck the coin-filled cigar box under his arm and rushed over to join Solomon at the opening to the projection room.

'My God! Lou . . . Ham . . . The place is filled with people . . . our friends and customers . . . their families . . . and you're playing games in a barrel! Soon there's going to be a riot . . . Come on! Start the show!'

Neither of the sweating, swearing boys inside could hear too clearly with their heads almost lost inside the overturned film barrel. They pulled out great lengths in their frenzied search for the head-end so they could thread it up in the waiting Kinetoscope. Loops of film flowed out over the floor, and Lou emerged to nervously push the growing mass away from the projector and its hot lamp housing. Tears of anger and frustration crowded the sweat from Ham's eyes as he scrambled through the heaped film, pulling it through his wet fingers, feeling for an end that never came – for the beginning he could not find.

With a cry of joy he jumped up, holding the squared-off tip of film, which Lou snatched away and started on its path through the machine. Ham set the barrel right side up and gently put the heap of film back inside.

The handle was turned and a beam of light stabbed out through the hole in the blanket as the images appeared on the big white screen at the end of the now silent room. Again the mass intake of breath . . . the shared gasp, and they all were standing in an unknown city watching little dots off in the distance coming closer and close as they turned into fire engines.

Solomon watched a moment, then turned and ran down the street to his shop, remembering he too had waiting customers, who needed food for their stomachs, if not for their eyes. In the cold brisk air outside on Grant Avenue another line of people already pressed forward to the doors, where Maurie and Ruth held them back while inside the long narrow room Paris, France, flickered on the wall. Suddenly the image faltered, there was a cutting off of the light beam and for a moment the screen went dark, and in the little projection room Lou cried out in pain.

'Chaim! . . . Ham . . . I've got a terrible cramp in any arm! I can't turn the crank . . .'

The younger boy grabbed the faltering crank handle from his anguished brother and, using both his small hands, kept it turning. Lou sat down on the floor, eyes tightly closed, and rubbed his aching arm as pain was written across his face. In the outside room the carriages continued to cross the river and go on to the boulevards. Ham turned the big crank with a kind of furious pride that clearly said, 'Look – I can do anything anybody else here can do – only better!' By the time the film ran out, Lou could again move his arm as his muscles unknotted, but Ham kept right on turning even after the film had gone through and there was nothing else to show.

Maurie and Solomon faced the new crowd at the door and asked each other how they were going to get rid of the audience still inside, who had forgotten their sore bottoms and their impatience and were chattering excitedly about the sights just seen and the emotions they had experienced. They made absolutely no move to leave, and in desperation Maurie turned to his father.

'Poppa, would it hurt if one of us should yell "Fire"?'

At last the old audience departed and the new one entered. This was repeated again and again in the two and a half weeks that followed.

Although the Bijou Dream Nickelodeon was not a resounding success like the nearby steel mills and other great ventures, it was a solidly modest achievement that put almost four hundred and twenty-five dollars in the doorside cigar box. Not only was Birnbaum's debt fully paid, there was a substantial profit. The Lefkowitz junkyard would have to look elsewhere for its brass, copper and glass.

The film was only film, though, and after so many trips through the machine it began to break again and again. Lou managed to fasten it together each time, thanks to his natural aptitude and the instructions he found with the little film repair kit in the Kinetoscope case. Soon though he was splicing the splices and patching the patches, managing to keep one repair ahead of the next break and be ready for the next showing.

It was Maurie who finally got fed up with the never-ending procession of fire engines, French carriages and film breaks. When he began to make inquiries about other pictures that might be available, he kept running into a dead end called the Motion Picture Patents Company, a trust that saw to it that the only films available were their films, at their prices, plus license fees for every picture projected on their machines. If the Patents Company learned what was going on in a former tailor shop in Harrisburg, Pennsylvania, it would end the entire operation, so Maurie went on the road again – this time, though, for himself and his brothers. He contacted owners of other storefront nickelodeons in Pittsburgh, Steubenville, Youngstown and Scranton, but found no answers and no films to replace the rapidly deteriorating saga of the fearless firefighters and the Parisian tour.

Maurie had been on the road for nearly a week when the big problems began. Ruth had replaced him at the front door taking coins, and she turned the lamps low before each show as the audience filled the room and found places. Inside the cramped projection room Ham wiped off the lens, pumped up the lamp and watched Lou mend the latest break in the film and inspect those splices still holding from past shows.

The audience settled back to enjoy the moments of magic, the beam of light came alive and there was a click-clack of gears as Lou got the machine moving. Just then, Hyman Lapidus came running as fast as he could from the funeral parlor across the street, closely followed by his son Isadore. They came right up to Ruth at the front door, who was happy

72

to see their kindly landlord, whose passes were always good at the Bijou Dream.

'Welcome, Mr. Lapidus, Isadore. You're just in time for the show.'

'Show? Show! Who's got time for a show!' Lapidus senior snapped. 'My bright son here forgets entirely our benches and chairs we have borrowed to you and we are taking back for a service now before it should be sundown!' He jabbed a finger at his chagrined son. 'This shlemiel lets the whole family and their friends stand. Only the late Mrs. Schneiderman, may she rest in peace, is lying down comfortable! If I do brag a little, she has never looked so good! Now quick – the chairs and benches go back, and maybe if we tell a little fib to the rabbi that it's an hour earlier than it really is, he won't be too upset. Come, my clever son who ruins his father's business – get at least the benches back!'

Ruth's mouth opened but no words came out. Lapidus and son pushed past her and through the narrow curtained opening into the larger room. Each gripped the end of the last bench in the back row and gave a pull. There was a series of soft thuds as six silent people who had been seated were suddenly dropped to the floor. Their eyes never left the moving shadows up on the far wall, though now all they could see was the top half of the screen, with clouds of steam and dust from the fire engines.

Lou kept the big crank turning but Ham left the projection room to see what was going on. Ruth motioned to him and whispered in his ear what was happening, and with a shrug of his shoulders they both approached the next bench in line. Ruth muttered an embarrassed apology and the seated patrons half stood as the bench was pulled out from under them. Then they too settled down on the floor, still watching the action on the screen as though nothing unusual had happened.

Lapidus and Isadore dashed back from their place of business to grab more benches, this time stacking one on top of another, leaving a dozen more customers seated on the floor. They ran past Ruth and Ham on their return trip, dodging wagons and buggies and going back into the theater for another load.

As they reentered, Ham stopped a moment, saying, 'Ruth, how would it be if we put up a big sign in front saying "Standing Room Only"?'

Ruth gave him a look and shoved him into the long room. 'Chaim – grab a bench!'

73

Soon the entire audience was seated on the floor, but not one person had left and every eye continued to look up in fascination at the screen. Lou cranked on for another round of fire engines. He got the Parisians across the Seine just as the last tired splice gave way and the taut film wrapped itself around the sprocket drive, to be chewed into brittle fragments that became tightly wedged in the gears and other machinery inside the box. The crank came to a jarring halt in Lou's blistered hand, with the shutter stuck fast in the open position. Now the only shadow on the bright screen was the greatly enlarged one of a lone moth that had fluttered in from outside to suddenly become a celebrity for a moment. Lou quickly shut off the gas valve, the screen went black and the moth returned to its obscurity.

Just then Solomon came down the street from the butcher shop. He went through the open doors and looked into the darkened interior with what looked like a human carpet seated on the floor. Ruth and Ham returned from their final trip to the funeral parlor and joined their father in the back of the long room while the people on the floor, many of them repeat customers used to delays, patiently awaited the early resumption of the show and chatted amiably among themselves.

All alone in the stuffy projection room, Lou stood back from the dead machine, whose vital parts were frozen tight by the broken pieces of film. This was no ordinary delay – this was absolute disaster! He stuck his head out the door opening and motioned to Solomon and Ham, who crowded into the little room. He showed them what had happened.

'Look – I can't get anything to move. We're in real trouble!'

'A calamity!' said Solomon. He shook his head.

Outside the audience continued their gossip as they awaited the return of light and shadow to the screen. Solomon well knew how easily patience could change to anger and shouting. With his ability to come up with what usually was the best thing to do in moments of crisis, he turned to Lou.

'Quick – while Ruth and I make the lamps brighter, you get down in front of the screen and introduce to the audience your little brother Chaim ... Ham ... the singer of sweet music. Tell our friends for a special treat – this show only, at no extra charge, he will make for them some music like never before they have heard. Hurry – before anything more

74

should happen, get out and announce your brother the singer!'

With deep gloom and a sense of impending disaster, Lou listened to the low hum of voices from the audience. He hesitated; then, taking a deep breath, he began to step around the people, delicately threading his way toward the darkened screen. Solomon and Ruth squeezed past customers along the side walls, turning up the wall lamps so that gradually the room grew brighter. Ham cleared his throat, easily at first, then with increased nervousness and tension, which grew quickly into a tiny knot that he knew would stop all the notes from finding their way out of his mouth. A wide smile fixed itself on his face as he followed Lou down through the crowded room. Forced over toward the side wall, he bumped into his father, who grasped his arm and leaned over to whisper, 'Chaim – Ham ... Remember how you told me you wanted more than anything else to sing? Well, go ahead. Sing, and maybe something can be done to give all these people a show they paid for.'

'Poppa, maybe I could dance a little too,' Ham whispered back. Then, with a gentle push from his father, he found himself standing next to his brother in the front of the room. Lou nervously raised his hand for attention. The noisy room went almost silent as Lou, sweat beading his upper lip, spoke in a strained voice.

'Ladies and Gentlemen ... uh ... We are having a little delay with the pictures, and while we wait the Bijou Dream is pleased to present for you something special and extra.' He stopped a moment, wondering how he could break it to all these people. 'Uh ... For your entertainment our own Chaim ... er, Ham Rabinowitz ... the Nightingale of Grant Avenue ... will sing for a little while before the next showing. Thank you.' He scrambled back to the front door, hoping to be out of range before the Nightingale began his song.

Ham's high little-boy's voice cracked slightly as he pushed the first reluctant notes past the knot in his throat. After the first few quavers had trickled out, the words came with more confidence and volume, and he closed his eyes tightly to concentrate on the sound he was pouring into the room.

'You made me what I am today ...'

The sad, accusing lyrics kept coming as Ham thought only of what this lament of a lover's distress must be doing to his audience.

'I hope you're satisfied ...'

75

For all of Solomon's fears, the audience was very considerate. They made almost no noise as they rose from the floor, shook their heads as though to clear away the disbelief, then filed out of the Bijou Dream past the apologetic Solomon Rabinowitz, who quickly grew tired of shrugging.

At last Ham reached the end of his plaintive melody.

'That's the curse of an aching heart . . .' He opened his eyes and bowed with a triumphant little flourish.

The room was now completely empty except for Yetta, the deaf-mute, who lived over the hardware store with two blind cats and a voiceless parrot. She sat all alone in the middle of the room and stared at him with her watery blue eyes, clutching tightly at her worn purse. Very slowly, and with much cracking of her aged joints, she rose from the floor, gave the boy a sweet smile, then came forward to hand him a small piece of sticky candy from a twisted paper bag. She turned and slowly limped out of the theater to the street as Ham stood alone in front of the screen, putting the candy in his mouth. For a happy few minutes he had had an audience all his own, and one day there would be others and they would stay and they would listen to him!

A whistle from Lou, a little cheer from Ruth and a loud shout from Solomon, all standing in the back of the room.

'Thank you, thank you, my son! A famous singer you may never become – but for emptying a theater in an emergency you have a great gift. A real star! Now, Mr. Nightingale, come and help your brother with this mess, and tomorrow we decide what happens with your Bijou Dream.'

Tomorrow. Tomorrow there would still be Solomon Rabinowitz and Sons, sellers of kosher meats – but the Bijou Dream without film was a body without blood and soon would be another vacant store awaiting its next tenant.

CHAPTER SEVEN

As though atoning for the terrible snowstorms of winter, summer brought heat that soon grew almost unbearable. Ham sought refuge in the meat storage locker of the butcher shop, where big chunks of ice rested beneath layers of insulating sawdust. Maurie, back full time helping his father in the shop, had to haul his youngest brother out whenever he was needed. The daily delivery of ice was the only part of the long hot day the younger boys enjoyed, and they tried to stretch it out as long as possible.

One afternoon Ham waited until the street was in shade, then walked up the street to look at the shop that for a while had been the Bijou Dream. It had become a luggage and handbag store, and all evidence of its recent glorious past had vanished. He slowly walked back to his father's shop and went into the meat locker, where he found Lou holding a long loop of beef intestine, imagining it to be a strip of film and the side of meat on its hook a projection machine waiting to be threaded up. 'No use,' Lou sighed. It was still just beef guts, and there was no new film anyplace where he could get his hands on it. Even Maurie had given in to the power of the Film Trust, returning home empty-handed more than a month before from his unsuccessful search for new pictures.

Solomon sent the two boys on trips to the slaughter house, where they loaded the old wagon, then let their horse slowly take them back through the summer-scorched fields. Setting out just after dawn, they usually managed to begin the return trip in the cool of early morning, and they had the road almost to themselves.

On one hot summer morning, as a swarm of bothersome gnats and flies buzzed around the loaded wagon, Lou waved his long whip as usual but had little success in driving off the annoying bugs. Ham dozed beside his brother on the bench, and the horse flicked his sparse tail and tossed his weary head in a futile attempt to discourage the insects. Except for

77

the clop-clop of hooves, the buzz of flies and the chirp of crickets, it was one of those warm dull mornings that leave almost no impression and are rarely recalled when grown men remember the days of their youth.

Over the buzz and hum around the wagon could be heard another sound, which steadily grew in volume and had a strange growling pitch, louder and louder with sputtering pauses. Lou swung around to look back down the road, expecting to see one of the new motor-driven carriages that were spreading like the plague, frightening everybody or being towed by a reliable horse to the nearest blacksmith for repairs.

He shaded his eyes and looked far down the dirt road, which lost itself in the stubble of the fields, but he could see nothing that resembled a motor vehicle. The buzzing continued to grow and soon was louder even than the drone of the insects circling them. Ham stirred in his sleep, then came fully awake as Lou's sharp elbow jammed into his ribs.

'Hey! What are you doing!' he shouted at Lou, who had scrambled up to stand on the bench so he could stretch full height and look across the wide field to a sloping hill that cut off the view of whatever was coming closer and closer, sounding like all the locusts in all the world.

Suddenly, an airborne machine, like a great wounded butterfly, its two delicate outstretched wings quivering and shaking, careened up over the crest. It staggered in the air about fifteen feet above the ground, then with a renewed roar flew down the slope and over the wide field, lurching in an erratic course over the shimmering expanse of stubble straight at the wagon and the terror-stricken horse and the frightened boys.

The noise grew louder and louder and seemed to be coming from a small engine set somewhere in the machine between the outstretched trembling wings. It swooped down, then bounced up for a moment when the buzzing roar cut off dead and the two twirling sticks hanging between the wings shuddered and were still. Then came a series of frenzied popping noises, over which Lou and Ham could hear a loud human voice shouting at them.

'Get out of the way! I'm putting down on the road . . . right in front of you . . . Be careful!' With a loud crunch the machine flopped down on the edge of the field and skidded into a ditch not more than ten yards in front of the old horse, who lifted his straggly tail and shook all over as he added a

78

contribution to the debris spread on the road.

A young man wearing a cap with its peak pointing backward, badly wrinkled tight pants and a high-buttoned sweater over a striped shirt rose from a prone position on the lower wing. He pulled goggles off over his cap, hung them on one of the short sticks he had been holding to guide the machine, shook his head and walked unsteadily down the road to where Lou still stood up on the bench and Ham sat in rare utter silence, his mouth hanging wide open. The horse lowered his trembling tail, and the gnats and flies moved away to inspect what he had left for them on the road.

'I'm sorry I scared you, but I ran out of fuel and I'm lucky to get down in one piece,' the tall young man said. 'Just where the hell in Pennsylvania am I?'

Lou was the first to find his tongue. 'Harrisburg's straight down this road about six miles – and over there's the Susquehanna River,' he said, pointing east.

'My Lord!' the young man said, pulling off his cap and scratching a balding head. 'I'm way off course. At least I'm in the right state – but I'm supposed to be miles south of here! Could your horse help me get my flying machine out of that ditch?'

The poor horse could barely move himself and the wagon, and shook all over as though at any moment he might lie down in the ditch beside the stricken machine.

Lou hopped to the ground and was all over the wings and fuselage, asking questions, looking at the little engine and inspecting the chain drive leading from it up over gear wheels to the two sticks of wood to make them spin.

'What are those things?' Lou asked, pointing at the pieces of delicately curved wood.

'Well, my brother and I call them airscrews and they're very much like propellers on a boat – only these pull our machine through the air.'

'How does it stay up?' Ham had found his voice again. 'Do you use a balloon or a kite?'

'No, no – all the air passing over the wings creates a lifting action, and as long as those airscrews keep turning and pulling us through the air, everything's just fine. Now you just saw what happens when everything goes wrong. Now, can you give me a lift into town so I can come back with some fuel for the motor and a few tools to repair the controls and get up in the air again? We've got another week or two of cross-country testing, and then my brother Wilbur and I have to be

79

in Washington to demonstrate our aeroplane to the Army.'

Lou had tugged at his cap, turning it all the way around until the bill stuck straight back. He slipped the pair of goggles over his eyes and lay on his stomach on the center of the bottom wing, holding the two guiding sticks in his hands and making loud buzzing noises as in his imagination he roared down the road and swooped up into the bright blue sky. Ham brought him back to earth with a loud shout, reminding him they had to get back to the shop before all the meat spoiled in the heat. Lou reluctantly got up from the flying machine and came back to the wagon, where he helped their guest climb up on the bench.

The boys felt terribly old-fashioned now, moving on the ground at the snail speed of the old horse while knowing that back there in the ditch, waiting to again gloriously soar into the sky like a great dragonfly, was something more important maybe than the Kinetoscope or anything else Ham and Lou could think of.

'Boys, there's a whole new age coming, and man is going to fly into it . . . unless his motor quits and he winds up in a ditch!' Their guest laughed and pointed ahead as they came around a bend in the road. 'Here, let me off up at that blacksmith shop. Many thanks for the lift. I'm really sorry I scared you and your horse so much. I'll certainly try never to let it happen again. Let me write down your names and addresses so the next time Wilbur or I are near Harrisburg we can give you a ride in our flying machine and we'll all be even.'

They pulled over to the side of the road and Orville Wright jumped down to the ground. Lou snapped the reins and the horse began to move as they both turned on the bench to wave good-bye until the road made another turn and the exciting young stranger was lost to sight.

After such a stirring event, the rest of summer was a tremendous letdown for both boys. Everybody listened at least five times to their telling and retelling of the adventure with the flying machine that chased them all the way from the slaughterhouse to Grant Avenue, and after a while they ran out of listeners.

The heat of summer and all of its boredom vanished when Maurie returned from a weekend trip he had quietly taken alone to chase down an interesting rumor. Now it was a rumor no longer, and he was back late Sunday night with news for the family.

'Poppa, boys,' Maurie said, 'I think I've got us something

good. I know none of us has ever gotten the Bijou Dream out of our minds, and when I heard about a brand-new nickelodeon that closed before it could open because the partners got in some kind of a fight, I thought I would look into the situation. I kept it strictly to myself until I found out more. It's in a wonderful location, just twenty miles from here in the town of York. That's right on the road to Baltimore, and it's a growing community. The theater's beautifully equipped, there's some film there already and plenty of advertising posters we could use, even an old piano that can make music for Ruth when Ham sings, and a brand-new projection machine, a big one, with one of the new electric arc lights. The seats would belong to us – and not to an undertaker! I found that we can buy more film from an importer who's got offices in Philadelphia and gets pictures from places where the Trust can't stop him. York is right in the center of thousands of people earning plenty of money and ready to spend lots of it at a nickelodeon!' He ran out of breath and words at the same time and looked around at the others with a big smile.

'So – what have you done about it, my boy?' asked Solomon, almost knowing the answer before he heard it.

'It's ours!' Maurie said. 'I gave two hundred dollars to tie it up and we take over anytime within a week and the creditors will give us up to six months to pay off the rest out of profits. We should be able to do it easy – look how well we did with the Bijou Dream until we ran out of film.'

'Aha!' said Solomon. 'Nothing you get for nothing . . . how much is the rest?'

'A thousand five hundred dollars, more or less,' answered Maurie, 'and I think it will be less since all they want is to be bailed out of their investment.'

'These men are either very charitable, very stupid, or very kind – but it sounds good and I approve!' the father said, smiling broadly. 'But what's this about getting bailed out? Is this a boat you've taken over, or a nickelodeon?'

Lou laughed. 'It's called the Bandbox, but for luck I think we should change it to the Bijou Dream.'

Already Lou was mentally threading up the new projector and wondering how an electric arc light worked. Ham tried to remember just where York was located and wondered if the Nightingale of Grant Avenue could sing as well in this new showplace. He hoped the film would never break, but if it ever should, he would be ready!

It was much too late that day to take the road south to York,

81

and anyhow Momma insisted they all have a good hot meal and a night of sleep before embarking on this new adventure. The meal was easy to dispose of, thanks to Momma's skill in the kitchen and the usual healthy family appetites. A night of sleep was something else again. Long after the last apple dumpling had entered upon its final journey, Lou, Ham, Maurie and Solomon lay awake in their rooms, not from indigestion, but from anticipation. Esther and her daughters of course slept well, having had little time to think of this new craziness. Their evening had been filled with cooking, serving and cleaning up, so that they were the first asleep and first up the next morning to feed the adventurers and get them on their way.

Lou and Ham piled some clothing in a battered old bag and rolled up some blankets so they could stay the next night in York and take care of whatever needed to be cleaned, adjusted or changed by the proud new owners of the failed Bandbox. The horse was fed and harnessed by sunrise, and as soon as the boys, their father and the luggage were all aboard, the wagon pulled away from the front of their house. The hooves sounded a hollow clip-clop on the empty street, and the lettering on the side of the wagon, RABINOWITZ & SONS, KOSHER MEATS, could scarcely be made out in the dim light of dawn. Solomon hoped he could get back in time to take care of his customers, who were going to wonder why the shop was closed most of the day. A few turns, crossing the Susquehanna and railroad tracks, and they were on the York road.

Though their hearts were racing, the old horse pulling them was much too wise and too aged to move any faster than was absolutely necessary. Solomon held the reins loosely in his hands amd smiled at the impatience of Ham and Lou.

'Boys, where we are going has been there for a long time. It will still be there when we arrive, so sit back and admire the scenery.'

An hour and a half, which seemed like an entire day, passed and they came to their destination. A thriving town, York was not too different from Harrisburg, which of course had the advantage of being the state capital. One very special thing York did have, though, was the Bandbox, the only theater in town, open or closed. Solomon guided the wagon down Main Street to the front of the theater, which looked rather plain and dowdy at first. It truly looked like the furniture store it had been before its change of life. A sweeping arch framed two sets of double doors standing on either side of a small glassed-in box office with its tiny round window. No need here for empty cigar boxes. This was a real theater with most of the trimmings, and all it needed was some fancying up, an audience and the balance of the promised purchase price in the next six months.

The boys piled out of the wagon while Solomon tied the horse to a post. Maurie dug up the keys to the front doors and they all went inside to admire the long dark hall with its blank white screen at the far end. No pieced-together sheets here; it was a professional job entirely.

'All right, my boys, now turn this empty place into something you will be proud of!' Solomon said, with complete satisfaction at what he saw and at what he was certain it could be.

Lou headed right for the projection room, which was solidly built with thick soundproof walls and filled with the kind of machinery that kept him dreaming wide awake at night. Ham found a broom and some old towels and, after sweeping out the entire room, whisked the cloth over the rows of seats, which were firmly bolted to the floor. Nobody, customer or undertaker, was going to move these seats from the premises. Best of all were the cases of film Lou found up in the projection room closet. They held sixteen reels of film, each with a running time of about ten minutes, and he was grateful that there would be no more haphazard barrels with wandering head- and tail-ends.

The films were all from France, some the work of a genius named Georges Méliès. He used his camera in most original ways and had the great advantage, along with Louis Lumière and the Pathé Company, of being thousands of miles and an ocean away from the Film Trust, which tried with no success to bar their films from American theaters.

This time a professional sign painter was hired to turn the Bandbox into the Bijou Dream and to make two lovely boards for the side columns bearing the simple legend ADMISSION ALWAYS FIVE CENTS, and another panel of gold letters on a blue background promising REFINED ENTERTAINMENT FOR LADIES, GENTLEMEN, AND CHILDREN.

In one week, when the theater reopened under its new management, the audiences trooped in from the rough hard outside world to the wonderful, welcome escape from reality they found in the Bijou Dream.

CHAPTER EIGHT

There is an old American tradition: Never leave well enough alone. The new Bijou Dream was more than holding its own in spite of some problems in getting new films as the old ones wore out their sprocket holes and their welcome. Fire engines still occasionally raced across the screen, as did chariots, locomotives, elephants, zebras, comedians and anything else that would move. Sarah Bernhardt, the immortal French actress, appeared as Queen Elizabeth in a daringly long film, and for more than a month they ran a classic of the time, *The Great Train Robbery* starring Bronco Billy Anderson. Great artists of stage, opera and vaudeville presented their shadows, mouthed songs, dialogue and jokes. But always something was missing. Except for the muffled noise of the projector, there was an absolute absence of sound. This seemed to be the ideal medium for a totally deaf audience.

With her brothers' encouragement, Ruth worked up enough nerve to leave the box office and approach the aged piano beside the screen. Although her talents were limited, the tinkling music helped make the illusion almost real, and it was even better when a hired musician was brought in on those evenings she had schoolwork to do. Now and then Ham was called to sing and empty the house in a hurry if the customers persisted in remaining seated after the show had ended, but essentially it was a silent art. The viewer had to imagine the sounds that had been there when the camera recorded the event.

It was a situation made to order for inventive minds, and many nickelodeons became testing laboratories for a multitude of hopeful inventors attempting to break the silence barrier – who instead too often broke themselves and the cooperating theaters.

Thomas Edison himself had grand ideas from the very first for synchronizing the sounds produced by his phonograph to the Kinetoscope so the shadows could speak, sing and roar. It seemed the Wizard of Menlo Park would succeed in everything else but this.

One day the Bijou Dream received a notice from Edison's company that there would be a demonstration of his new Kinetophone system in Philadelphia and they were invited to view and hear this new wonder, which would revolutionize the whole business. Maurie showed the intriguing notice to his brothers.

'This may be a whole new thing, and even though we're not really on speaking terms with Edison or the Trust, we can't afford to miss it. I'll go there for a day with Lou and we'll see if it's worth anything.'

'How about me?' said Ham, feeling left out. 'I'd like to see if they can make sounds come out with the pictures. Maybe someday I could even be in a picture and sing and dance . . . and –'

'Kid, you stay right here with Ruth and Miriam and clean out the theater and scatter handbills for our new program. That's important too. The place looks like a mess and you have to sweep out all the junk the customers leave behind. There's just no other time to do it. Don't worry, we'll be back before the evening show,' Maurie said to his younger brother, who again felt he was being left out just because it was his bad luck to be the last born.

Maurie and Lou caught the early train and before noon were in a Philadelphia theater waiting for the demonstration to begin. As soon as the lights dimmed, Lou quietly left his seat and went around the side of the screen to see what was going on behind the scenes. Two of Edison's technicians had set up an oversized phonograph speaker horn directly against the back of the screen, where it was unseen by the audience out front. On a table was the rest of the equipment brought from the Edison laboratories in New Jersey, the very latest concert phonograph, its spring fully wound and the black wax cylinder held motionless by the index finger of the chief technician. He looked across the stage at his assistant, who peered around the far side of the darkened screen up at the projection room in the rear wall of the auditorium.

A flicker of light came through the projection port and the screen was illuminated. It was the old familiar railroad yard with tracks stretching far out in the background and vanishing into a roundhouse and sidings. Another flash of light from the projection room, this time from a red signal lamp – the cue! The assistant waved over to the technician, who released his finger from the wax cylinder, which started to rotate. The needle was attached to an acoustical box connected by a large flexible tube to the big wooden speaker horn. Amplified scratchy sounds came through the back of the screen and could be heard in the center of the first two or three rows of the theater.

A big black locomotive came closer and closer on the screen. Something that possibly might be a steam engine could barely be heard. At first the chugging and chuffing, blended with the tinny sound of a bell, was almost inaudible under the loud, pervasive scratchy noise amplified by the speaker horn. Then the sound grew louder and could be heard as far back as the fifth row. Things were improving! The rest of the audience still sat waiting for the miracle, which seemed to be lost somewhere down in front.

What should have been the screeching sound of brakes came out like the dying squeals of a stuck baby pig. Laughter came from the audience, and was the first sound actually heard throughout the house. A jet steam squirted out of the train whistle and the audience leaned forward, listening to the terrible silence. There was not a sound, the laughter having died away as the audience strained to hear Mr. Edison's modern miracle of sound motion pictures. It was only after the steam jet had completely vanished that a high-pitched bleat like that of a scalded heifer was heard by the fortunate front five rows.

Lou still stood in the wings, watching as the agitated technician and his helper quickly took the equipment apart, stuffed it into boxes and made a rush for the stage door just ahead of the irate manager, who wanted to give them a personal message to deliver to Thomas Alva Edison. He had moved too slowly. They were gone.

The trip back to York seemed to pass in no time, so busy were Maurie and Lou in talking about the locomotive that squealed and the silent steam whistle. When the engine pulling their car let go with a blast at a crossing. Maurie said, 'See, that's how it's supposed to sound. Edison knows all about electricity, but he has plenty to learn about noise and pleasing an audience!'

Just before evening they reached York and the Bijou Dream to find Solomon, Ham, Ruth and Miriam in front of the theater talking with a distinguished gentleman whose clothing was as impeccable as his British accent.

'Boys, meet my new friend, Mr. Leslie Buckingham – from London, England . . . and New York City,' Solomon said, glancing down at a handsomely engraved calling card. 'Uh – he's from the headquarters office of what is called the Alleffects Company, Limited, of America. How does that sound!' Introduction completed, Solomon let out his breath, then continued.

'While you both were being entertained by Thomas Edison in Philadelphia, Mr. Buckingham came to our theater to show us something his company with the fancy name says is going to revolutionize this whole business! A shame it wasn't yesterday, maybe you could have saved taking the trip.'

Ham was hopping up and down with eagerness to speak, and broke in on his father.

'Sound! Sound . . . to go with the pictures . . . And Mr. Buckingham has all his things right here with him . . . the Alleffects machine, and I helped him move it up on our stage. Wait till you hear what it does! It's all set up inside and he brought a special reel of film and for free he's going to demonstrate for our first show tonight!'

Maurie looked at Lou and they both looked at Solomon.

'Poppa!' Maurie said in a loud voice. 'We haven't told you yet what happened today in Philadelphia! Sound from Thomas Edison it was . . . and maybe it revolutionized the business too – the walk-out-and-get-your-money-back business!'

Leslie Buckingham was used to resistance, and had the gift of glibness to overcome almost any argument.

'My dear gentlemen, and you, my dear young ladies' – this to Ruth and Miriam, who stood fascinated by the suave London accent – 'the Alleffects equipment, whose manufacturer and distributor I am honored to represent, is a proven thing. It is entirely self-contained and you control it – not the other way around, as with Mr. Edison's Kinetophone system, which has yet to be proven. I assure you this is the wave of the future, if you will – the sound wave of the future. My company has chosen your Bijou Dream especially to demonstrate the miracle of Alleffects. I am certain that after this demonstration you will share with your customers, you will immediately want to join all those other theater owners who have purchased this device. Do not cheat yourselves out of this opportunity – it may never come again!'

Ruth was entranced, as was her sister, and she nudged Maurie.

'Give it a chance. If it sounds half as good as he says it is we should hear it.' What she really wanted to hear was more of the delicious British accent.

Maurie looked over at Solomon, who nodded in agreement with his daughter. Then he turned to Lou, who was willing to try anything new. The first customers for the evening show were lining up, so Ruth hurried inside to begin selling tickets.

'All right, we'll go along with it for this show, but Ruth better stay pretty close to the piano just in case anything goes wrong, and I'll have another reel of film all ready to put on. Come on, hurry up, everybody – we've got less than fifteen minutes until the show starts.'

Buckingham gave the demonstration reel of film to Lou, who took it into the projection room. Maurie and Ruth supervised ticket sales, and the house began to fill up with customers, busy with their usual before-show gossip.

Ham was behind the screen with Buckingham, who wheeled a large upright metal and wood box over to center stage. He unlocked the two front panels and swung them wide to reveal brackets, shelves and hooks holding gongs, bellows, birdcalls, whistles, ratchets, sheets of tin, and all manner of mechanical noisemaking devices. A shielded oil lamp set on one door illuminated an open cue book. Buckingham stood back, waving his arms with pride at the equipment.

'Behold, my young friend, the greatest marvel of mechanics since the invention of the motion picture itself – the All-effects machine. Now stand beside me so I can instruct you in its use, and I will call upon your help, so be sure to –'

He was cut short by Maurie, who had come through the audience to stand before the screen on the narrow stage apron and make an announcement in the same hesitant voice he might have used to introduce the Nightingale of Grant Avenue.

'Uh . . . Ladies and Gentlemen . . . uh . . . The Bijou Dream has something very special for you before we run our regular show. You are about to see – and hear – moving pictures presented by the Alleffects Company of New York City. Please remain silent throughout this film so you can hear everything!' He cleared his throat, wondering if there was more to say, realized he had said it all, and made a quick exit through the expectant packed house to the rear of the lobby, where he grimly looked at his father and mopped his drenched forehead.

The lights were lowered, Lou pulled the switch and the show began when the electric motor took over the job of pulling the special demonstration film through the projector in front of the bright electric arc light. The show began and it was Philadelphia all over again, only without the Edison name to give it some semblance of class.

The noisemakers were easily heard throughout the entire auditorium, but poor Leslie Buckingham had the evil fortune to have chosen Ham as his assistant. Following the cue sheet and synchronizing sound effects with the images he saw in reverse up on the screen, Buckingham got off two loud thunderclaps with the hanging tin sheet, three dogs barking with hand-squeezed bulb, and a well-placed group of birdcalls. When it came time to fire the blank shells from the pistol during a battle scene, he glanced down at his cue sheet, realized he only had two arms and hoarsely whispered to Ham, 'Quick – hit the Chinese temple gong with that hammer! Now! Hit it *now!*'

Ham was enthralled with the reverse pictures on the screen and all the sound and fury backstage. He grabbed the heavy padded hammer and swung it like baseball bat. He missed the gong completely and smashed the hammerhead into the side of the wheeled Alleffects cabinet. It was just enough of a blow to get the big wheeled box started on its way.

The building had been erected on the side of a hill by an addled architect, and everything still had a slight tilt, including the narrow stage. The cabinet, with Ham's innocent encouragement, followed gravity's law and rolled massively past Buckingham, who had his hands full of noisemakers. Picking up speed, the Alleffects cabinet smashed into the left wall of the theater, where it produced tremendous sounds synchronized to nothing that Lou was projecting on the screen. The slant of the wall and floor then caused the big cabinet to bounce back and begin to roll off the riser platform. Suddenly the bewildered audience, ears numbed from so much sound, saw the advancing monster cabinet as it tore through the lower part of the screen and attacked them. This sudden apparition had nothing to do with the promised wonder of the century, and, screaming sound effects of their own making, the first two rows of spectators jumped to their feet. They turned in terror and climbed over the backs of their chairs, retreating into the laps of the customers sitting behind them just in time to escape the final crash of the behemoth as it smashed down on the front seats and let go its final overwhelming death rattles of thunder, chimes, bells, bellows and gongs.

Maurie and Lou stood by the main door refunding money to the departing customers, who delivered scathing remarks along with their outstretched palms.

'Come back tomorrow, please,' Maurie pleaded with each one as he left. 'Tomorrow it will be pictures only, and maybe for a special treat Ham will sing something special between shows.'

'I've had enough trouble today,' said one disgusted patron. 'Please don't make it any worse!'

Solomon stood on the sidewalk trying to catch the audience as they passed with their refunds, telling each in quick confidence, so as not to be overheard by his sons, to come back next evening as his personal guest, free admission, and everything would be absolutely wonderful. All he received was a series of black looks and some replies he hoped Ruth didn't hear from the box office.

Ham helped Leslie Buckingham clean up the debris and load it on a wagon hired to get him on his way to the depot and back to the Alleffects office in New York. Buckingham, suave seller of sounds, was completely silent and in deep depression all the way to the station. Finally he looked over at the upset boy by his side.

'Mr. Rabinowitz – Ham . . . my dear boy. May I make a most serious suggestion to you at this crucial point in your career. If anybody ever comes to you and asks you to become even remotely connected with anything to do with sound for moving pictures, run away, young man, run away just as fast as your legs can carry you!'

He sighed deeply and then, as they reached the railroad station and stopped at the freight platform, looked at the battered Alleffects cabinet.

'Good Lord in heaven, what will I tell them at the office? Nobody will ever believe it!'

'Mr. Buckingham,' said Ham in a very low voice, 'I believe it!'

CHAPTER NINE

The disaster with 'sound' was soon forgotten and business at the Bijou Dream was better than ever. Maurie, Lou and Ham shared a room in a boardinghouse three blocks up Main Street from their theater. Back in Harrisburg, Solomon hired a butcher to help him in the shop and managed to get down to York several times each week to watch his boys work and take them some food from their mother's kitchen so they wouldn't lose too much weight.

Solomon seriously thought of selling his shop and moving the family down to York so he could be with the boys full time and save the poor old horse the long trip. As a man who had made several major changes already in his life, he secretly envied his sons, getting into this promising new business, and wondered if it could be for him too. He could always open another butcher shop there, but this exciting new thing of moving pictures appealed to him. It was something to think about, but he knew that Esther and the girls would be unhappy about leaving the big wooden house and all their friends. Maybe the boys could find a new place in Harrisburg, move all the seats, the electric Kinetoscope and the cases of film and find a good location someplace on Grant Avenue. After all, Harrisburg was the state capital, and where there were so many more people, there had to be a bigger audience for those crazy jumping shadows. Maurie, the businessman, would see that right away and know that there was more money to be made in the larger city. He would mention it to the boys on his next trip to York. In the meantime he began to look around Harrisburg for possible locations.

Very late one night in their boardinghouse room, Ham stirred and cried out in his sleep. Again it was the familiar old dream of fire engines racing around corners and tearing down the streets. As always in this recurring dream, he held the reins tightly in both hands and shouted orders at the galloping horses. He had run this scene so many times on the

91

Kinetoscope and dreamed it so often that it had become difficult to tell reality from fantasy. Now when he half heard the clanging bells and the familiar pounding of horse hooves coming from the street outside their room, he lay on his bed with his eyes shut, still on his dream ride and half wondering how all those realistic new sound effects had been added. Had Leslie Buckingham brought back a new Alleffects machine?

Lou and Maurie jumped out of their beds and ran barefoot over to the windows looking down on Main Street.

'Fire! There's fire! Get up, Ham! You can smell the smoke – it's right near us!' Lou shouted across the room at Ham, who rolled over in bed as he maneuvered the sweating team and cracked a whip over their lathered flanks. He sat up suddenly when Maurie shouted loudly at him to come to the window.

The three boys leaned out as far as they could, trying to see down the street, as another engine thundered by, spurting steam and sparks almost up in their faces. Maurie first saw the glow of flames reflected on buildings far down the street, and at once he knew what must be burning.

'The theater ... our Bijou Dream ... it's on fire!' Maurie said to his brothers, almost disbelieving his own words.

They raced into their clothes, down the stairs and out into the street to join the crowd of people running toward the dreadful excitement. The entire building erupted flames, smoke and sparks, and where the firemen pumped water through their hoses into the inferno, columns of steam rose in the night air and there were loud hissing noises. It was a small structure, but it made a large fire, and only good luck, hard work and the strong backs of the firemen and volunteers kept it from spreading through the entire block. When at last the roof collapsed in its final agony, and the only upright thing left was one charred wall, it was all over and the Bijou Dream and three adjoining shops were a heap of wet ashes and smoking debris.

The three boys waited for the rubble to cool and then searched through as much as they could, but all that was left of the wonderful electric Kinetoscope was some misshapen metal, a puddle of melted glass and a heap of warped reels that had once held the magic shadows. Beneath a ruined wall they found the twisted piano frame, its scattered keys spat out like teeth as it died in the flames.

As they sadly walked back to their room, the sun was

coming up, vainly trying to get through the smoky haze covering the city.

'Lou, Maurie, let's pack our stuff right now and walk down the road to meet Poppa before he gets to where the theater burned down,' Ham said. 'We'll break the news to him, then we can all go back home to Harrisburg in time for lunch with Momma and the girls.'

Solomon was surprised to find his three boys standing by the road later that morning as he entered York. He reined in his horse to pick them up.

'Boys, you look terrible! What happened?'

'Poppa – the Bijou Dream – it burned to the ground ... everything's lost!'

Solomon looked stunned. 'A calamity, maybe ... but you're wrong. Everything isn't lost. You all still have health and energy. For a while you will rest and, if you feel like it, help me in the shop. Later we will think of what tomorrow brings.'

True, nobody had been hurt – not on the outside, only deep down where it didn't show – and the flaming blue sign with its lovely golden letters – BIJOU DREAM – came crashing to earth only in wounded memory.

Obsession with unhappy events is not for the young. A month passed, then another, with the boys speaking less and less often of their loss. With the approach of another spring, central Pennsylvania threw off its last layers of slush, snow and heavy winter clothing and turned its face toward the sun, which grew in warmth. Although they kept busy helping Solomon in the shop and Maurie went back on the road again selling for Armour, neither Ham nor Lou could let their dream come completely to an end, locked up in a case at home or resting in a heap of ashes down in York. Like their bodies, their minds seldom were still.

Once in a while Lou would open up the case bequeathed them by Birnbaum and the boys would dust, polish and oil the lovely piece of machinery. It was almost like anointing the dead, for without film the little Kinetoscope was just a collection of useless metal and glass.

One afternoon both boys were sweeping out Solomon's shop when they heard hammering coming from the street. A man was fastening a poster to the streetlamp that stood on the curb right in front, and curiosity drew the boys through the door to read the boldly printed words.

93

' "The World Famous Hale's Tours Are Coming to the Harrisburg Fair Ground! From Triumphs in St. Louis, Chicago, Youngstown and . . ." What's that word?' Ham asked his brother.

'I think it says "Skuh-neck-taddy" but I'm not sure. I'm sure glad we don't live wherever it is. I could never remember how to spell it, or say it, either,' Lou answered.

'Say – aren't you the boys who had the nickelodeon down the street about six months ago?' the poster man asked the boys.

'Yep, we're the ones,' said Ham proudly. 'We had another nickelodeon with a wonderful electric Kinetoscope down in York, but one night – '

'You boys go and see Chief Hale right away,' the man said. 'He's looking for guys who know something about film projectors; and if you want jobs with the Tours, get over to the Fair Grounds fast! He needs some operators right now!' He turned and went down the street to tack up more posters.

The boys ran back to their father inside the shop.

'Poppa, you're going to have to do without us for a few hours. Something real important is happening. Can we take the horse and wagon?' Without waiting for an answer, they turned and were out the front door and on their way to the stable. Twenty-five minutes later Lou and Ham were walking up to the temporary offices of Hale's Tours at the Harrisburg Fair Grounds.

George C. Hale was a real Chief, who for years had headed the renowned Kansas City Fire Department. Chief Hale put his department on the map when he took crack teams of firefighters to the great Louisiana Purchase Exhibition in St. Louis in 1904, where they used the most modern methods to put out staged fires in record time. Their pumpers, hook and ladder and rescue wagons, all were the latest and best equipment in the entire world and were pulled at breakneck speed by the finest teams of fire horses ever seen.

The St. Louis International Exhibition was memorable for many reasons. There the very first hot dog sandwich was eaten, and the first ice cream cones appeared to melt in a million happy mouths. The first publicly dispensed glass of iced tea showed up along with the ice cream cones to make the Missouri summer heat almost bearable.

Quite as important as Chief George Hale's exhibition of modern fire-fighting was his exposure to the brand-new medium of motion pictures. They had a primitive debut there, and at once Hale realized their immense potential. After the exhibition he teamed up with an inventor, William Keefe, who had dreamed up the strange combination of a motion picture projector with a railroad parlor car with a big white screen set up in the back. For the most part this new marriage of film and rail would use only one screen, but Keefe and Hale had ideas for grouping three projectors on a platform above the car, with screens not only at one end, but running down both sides to surround the viewer-travelers with the complete illusion of moving scenery all around them.

Chief Hale was overjoyed when Lou and Ham came to see him in his temporary offices at the Fair Grounds. In a few minutes of questions and answers he knew they could handle the special jobs he had waiting. Since anybody who had run a motion picture projector still was a rarity, he felt fortunate indeed to have found two highly qualified young men with so much practical experience.

He was a big friendly person who enjoyed entertaining and astounding people just as once he had loved the challenge of putting out fires, and dressed in a dark blue suit very much like the uniform worn with honor for many years in Kansas City. He took an immediate liking to the two Rabinowitz boys.

'Come with me, Lou, Ham . . . I want to show you how we run our operation and the way Hale's Tours is put together. So far it's only been seen in White City near Chicago and Idora Park outside Youngstown. Oh – we did have it in St. Louis awhile too, and a young fellow named Sam Warner came to see me, same as you did. Now he's my chief operator at Idora Park and later on he'll be coming here for a while. I want him to get acquainted with this new multiple projection system. I'm sure you'll get along well with him. He's a fine fellow, and you all should teach each other things about film projection.'

In a large field just outside the office shack a gang of roustabouts were hauling a big black canvas tent up side poles. After it was tied down, a specially built railroad parlor car was rolled up. It was in several sections, and the men assembled it carefully on a set of rails inside the tent.

'What you're now looking at, boys, is the perfect answer to traveling without any of the problems of travel. I hire cameramen to ride on platforms attached to the front of trains and shoot the most interesting and spectacular scenery all over the world. Sometimes we also get scenes from both sides of the train for this special three-projector

95

unit, which is the only one of its kind. That's why I've had to find extra projectionists, and you boys are a godsend. Ham, I think there may be a problem with you. You're kind of small and young, and I hate to think of you high up there on that platform in the air over the parlor car. I have another very important job for you here on the ground, which I'll explain later. Also, you can be the understudy for the three projectionists, so don't worry, you'll get your chance to run one of the machines later on when you're a little bigger.'

Not noticing Ham's dejection, Chief Hale went on to show them details of the almost authentic railroad car, which had been modified for maximum seating and for shipping around the country. The customers, called 'passengers,' entered the car through a small railroad station, then up steps and through a rear platform, to be welcomed aboard by a conductor complete with uniform, railroad watch, ticket punch and nearly unintelligible voice. Hale pointed over to the man who would act as the conductor, and the boys listened to him practice his spiel off to one side of the big dark tent.

'Ladeez an' Genn'men ... Welcome to the Marvelous Hale's Tours! Be seated, pleeze ... This car will leave Harrisburg Station in five minutes to cross the Great Plains. Sit still and do not move around the car. Watch for the herds of wild buffalo we will soon pass and the prairies and the savage bands of Red Indians. Do not panic, as you are perfectly safe in this wonderful Hale's Tour parlor car. A young man selling delectable refreshments will shortly pass among you. Have your tickets ready pleeze!'

Hale took the boys all through the car, where workmen had almost finished bolting down the rows of red plush seats. He was proud of the authentic interior, the cut glass window edging and crystal lamps, and told them how well the Tour was being received wherever it had shown. Even now several new locations were being set and equipment was being constructed and purchased for other amusement parks and fairgrounds.

'Some very bright people are interested in buying exclusive rights to different areas across the country, and once we have this one running here in Harrisburg several of them will visit us from New York and Chicago. I'm counting on you boys to help make a good impression on them. Now let's go outside the car and I'll show you, Ham, what your job is going to be.'

They stepped off the rear platform, walked over to the side of the car and squatted down to see several mechanics tightening a wide canvas and leather belt that ran on wheels and rollers from one end of the car to the other. It was studded with metal bars and springs that struck against bumpers fixed to the underside to make loud sounds, like a real train moving at high speed. An electric motor drove the big belt, and when the mechanics completed the installation and greased the rollers it all ran with a wonderfully realistic clickety-clack, clackety-click.

Over to one side a plumber and his helper tightened up pipe joints and adjusted jets aimed from the ground up at the big car windows. They checked a steam generator hidden behind a canvas screen, and great clouds of vapor poured up from the jets when they opened the controls. The boys were tremendously impressed by all this wondrous make-believe, which they knew must seem very real from inside the parlor car.

'Ham, you saw that big belt running beneath the car and those steam jets? Your main job is to see that they all start working when you hear the conductor yell "All aboard!" Keep the belt wheels greased and your fingers away from everything. Then run over and open the steam jets, but don't get in front of them and get yourself scalded. After you've done all that and the conductor pushes the cue light for the three projectors up there on the high platform, your really important job begins. Grab one of those long poles you see over there and set it on one of those apple boxes. Stick the end of the pole under the car, and be sure the three other boys who will be back here helping you do the same thing at all four corners of the car. When you see the pictures come on the screens you begin to rock the car – not too much at first, since it's only getting under way. After a minute you can rock the car more and more, and keep it up until the pictures stop. Drop the pole and run over to shut off the belt-drive motor and have one of the other boys turn off the steam generator . . . and that's all there is to it.'

Ham was in a daze. He thought of all the things he would have to do, then asked, 'Chief Hale, wouldn't it just be easier and safer to let me go right up on the platform now and run a projector? After all, I've already done that, and I won't get scalded or lose any fingers . . .'

'Later on, Ham . . . soon as you're a little older and bigger. What I want you to do is very important – in fact, the name of your new job is going to be chief rocker boy, so you're going to be a Chief, just like me. You run everything down here on the ground, tell the three other boys helping you what to do. Remember, it's important you all keep down low so the people inside the car don't see you. After all, they're supposed to be moving in a train at about fifty or sixty miles an hour, and seeing some kids scooting around would really cause havoc!'

Ham frowned. The fancy title didn't impress him one bit, but he brightened when Chief Hale added some hope for the future.

'Tell you what. As I already promised, if any of the fellows up top gets sick or drunk or slips off the platform, you climb right up and take over his machine. All right?'

Ham nodded with a little smile and hoped it wouldn't be his brother who got sick or slipped.

The Chief continued, 'Lou, I want you to take over the projector on top left. It will be in position in another hour, and my assistant, who will run the other side machine, will show you where it's different from the one you ran in your own place. That young man I told you about from Youngstown, Sam Warner, will be here tomorrow morning and take over the third machine. You both stick around the rest of the day and watch everything. We'll have a complete rehearsal all day Friday and open Saturday noon. Meantime, learn all you can, get plenty of sleep at night and be ready to get this Tour on the road!'

The rehearsal went off beautifully. Sam Warner came in early that morning, and he and the boys hit it off right away. They had the same interests, loved this exciting new business and showed each other all kinds of short-cuts in operating the big electric arc Kinetoscope projectors. They raced around the high platform as though there were no dangers at all, and Ham, seeing how surefooted and at ease his brother and the two others were, despaired of ever getting to go up top himself.

On Saturday the Tour began for real – or for what looked so real that it could fool an old railroader. The people lined up for blocks down the Fair Ground Pike, bought their tickets and entered the parlor car by way of the rear platform. Thirty at a time found seats on the comfortable plush chairs and settled back as the conductor shouted words nobody could understand.

A candy butcher followed the ticket-punching conductor down the aisle, and soon mouths were stuffed with popcorn, peanuts and soda pop. The passengers looked out the big parlor-car windows into the darkness of the surrounding black tent. A piercing steam whistle made them jump, a blast of steam beaded the windows and then came the mournful tolling of the locomotive bell. From beneath the car came a loud metallic rumble, from up front a chuff-chuffing sound. The entire car gently bounced up and down, jerked and swayed as the noises underneath grew louder.

'Good Lord! We're leaving Harrisburg!' said a woman, rising from her seat and grabbing her husband's arm. 'I've got soup and stew simmering on the stove! If we aren't back in time, dinner will be ruined!'

'Sit down, Martha,' replied her embarrassed husband. 'It's only a ride and we aren't going anyplace! Your soup is safe, so sit down and relax!' She sat down in nervous apprehension, which her husband secretly shared.

They must be pulling out of the station now, as the windows on either side and at the rear observation platform slowly lit up to reveal a bright scene stretching far into the distance all around them. The steel rails, shining in the bright summer sun, rolled out to vanish in the distance and they were crossing the Great Plains of America.

High up on the scaffold over the car, Lou adjusted the focus of the wide-angle lens, which threw an immense image on the long white seamless screen hung on the right wall of the black tent. The powerful electric arc brought everything out in clear focus from corner to corner. Across the platform another young man about Lou's age checked his projector, which threw its greatly magnified image of the prairie on the left screen. Sam Warner looked over and smiled at Lou.

'Hey – this is simply great! It has it all over the Idora Park stuff I've been running. Lou, check your focus. Those buffalo are fuzzier than they should be!'

'Thanks, Sam,' Lou called back. They could make all the noise they wanted up on the platform because the sound effects belt underneath the car was rolling at high speed now, steam was jetting on the windows every now and then and the inside of the tent was sheer bedlam.

Lou took a few minutes now and then to look down from the platform and see how Ham was doing. The kid was racing from the steam generator to the jets, then to the big pole on the box and heaving on it to help bounce the car up and down and sideways. Now and then he shouted orders at the three other boys, who listened to him because he seemed to know what he was doing. Lou shook his head and called over to Sam, 'Be careful of my kid brother when you get down to the ground. He's sore as a boil 'cause Chief Hale wouldn't let him up here to run a machine, so keep out of his way 'cause I think he might just swing that rocker pole and clip you one – by accident, of course!'

Sam laughed loudly. 'You can't tell me anything about kid brothers. I've got one, too, back in Youngstown . . . His name is Jack and he's a tough little kid too. He and Ham should get on great together, if they don't beat the hell out of each other!' Lou saw the Indians were out of focus and got them sharp again so they would scare the passengers down below.

The rocking, swaying parlor car never left the black tent, but the three wide screens surrounding its sides and rear showed great overlapping shadow images of vast prairies, panicking herds of buffalo and the steel rails reeling out from beneath the observation platform in back and vanishing in the distance. War parties of mounted Indians came close enough for their unheard shouts of defiance to be clearly seen, and some frightened passengers, who had read too many Buffalo Bill Cody stories, ducked beneath the windows, fully expecting arrows to fly into the train. Excitedly they gulped down popcorn, soda and peanuts until the aisles were littered with bags and empty bottles. Their heads swung from one side of the car to the other and their nervous jaws never once stopped moving.

Ham leaned on the end of the long pole and kept as low as he could in the dark underneath the busy screen. He shouted over at the other boy on his side, urging him to move faster and not make him do all the work on this side of the car. What a lazy one he had there! Later on he would suggest to the Chief that they get somebody who was big and fat and could really get things bouncing. He dropped the pole when the steam jet stopped and ran over to the generator to open the valve some more and get the cloud of vapor moving faster. Back to look under the car and see that the big sound belt was doing its job. No problem there. It was making such a racket that he couldn't hear Lou yelling down at him.

'Ham . . . kid! Keep your damn head down! The passengers inside are going to see you and think you're one of the Indians who got knocked on his ass off a horse. Get down . . . keep close to the ground and out of sight!'

He heard just the last part, stepped back and looked up at his brother in the flickering light.

'For Pete's sake, Lou . . . Get me up there and out of the dirt! I wanna run one of those projectors. I know all about them. Please ask Chief Hale . . . please!'

The train whistle blasted and drowned out both voices. There was a final flicker of light on the right side and the big screen went from the prairie scene to blackness, quickly followed by the other two machines. The entire place was without light. The conductor threw switches inside the car and the dome, and wall lamps came on as he bellowed to the passengers that the trip had been successfully concluded.

'I am pleased to tell you, ladies and gentlemen, our great locomotive hit only three buffalo and no Indians. There will be another trip in fifteen minutes, and I will now pass down the center aisle selling tickets for the next Hale's Tour. Pike's Peak – a glorious ride up the mountain and a thrilling run down again at a speed you will never forget . . . Please have your money ready. The young man with soda, popcorn and peanuts will follow immediately behind me.'

The first week went off beautifully. The car rocked and rolled right on cue and the steam hissed where it was supposed to while the sound-effects belt roared and the scenery passed the parlor car filled with its loads of astonished, thrilled and overjoyed passengers. Each night Ham counted his fingers and found them all present and unsteamed. He kept the belt greased and soon got used to the terrible racket it made – but always he looked up at the three projectionists on the high platform and wished he could be up there too. He bossed the other three boys around, and that was about the only pleasure he seemed to be getting, along with the pay, which for the first time in his life made it unnecessary for him to shake money from his sister Ruth's piggy bank when he wanted to buy something.

It was hot inside the unventilated black tent, and all the boys lost weight along with the rivers of sweat pouring off their bodies. The black tent fabric held the summer temperature even higher than it was outside, and the arc lights gave off so much heat that everybody was constantly thirsty and running out of the tent whenever possible between shows. Ham and his assistant rocker boys carried cans of cold water up ladders to the three projectionists, and once Ham lugged in some buckets of cool foaming beer from a stand across the Pike.

'Young man!' Chief Hale yelled when he saw what was in the buckets. 'Absolutely nothing goes up on the platform that might cause our projectionists to walk off the side! Water is all right – beer is for people with their feet on the ground!' He winked. 'Son, I know how much you want to get up there

. . . but please don't try to work your way up that way!'

'Chief, how could you even think I'd carry beer up there for such a reason!' Ham protested, wondering why he hadn't thought of the idea himself. From then on it was only water and lemonade.

The Great Plains of America were rewound on their reels and the next Tour up Pike's Peak was ready to leave the Harrisburg Fair Grounds station. The thrilled audience paid their money and bought more to stuff their stomachs with en route. When the car started to rock and the big screens came to life, they were carried through Hell's Gate to the foot of the cog railway and straight up the famed Pike's Peak then all the way down through Black Canyon. It was over in less than eight minutes, but every instant would live in each passenger's memory along with the lurching, rattling, bone-shaking parlor-car ride inside Chief Hale's big black tent.

Solomon, Esther and the girls took the twenty-minute ride out to the Fair Grounds on a Sunday afternoon. Solomon handed the conductor the passes he had received from his sons and they were seated next to the large observation windows. At once Solomon began a conversation with other passengers on the car, most of them friends or acquaintances.

'Over our heads is my son, Lou, who is in charge of running the projection machines that make the moving pictures we are going to see out there.' He waved a hand to indicate the great darkness outside. 'Also my other son, Ham, has something to do with what is going to happen, and . . . '

Before he could continue, the conductor hurried down the aisle toward the loud voice about to give away all the mysteries.

'Please, mister, please!' the conductor whispered in Solomon's ear. 'Be quiet and enjoy yourself, but stop telling secrets! Now sit back, mister take this bag of peanuts, some popcorn and cherry soda, compliments of Chief Hale. Fill up your mouth and please be quiet. Enjoy the Tour, but keep to yourself what your sons are doing!'

Solomon dug into the popcorn, put the bottle of soda to his lips and thanked the conductor as he passed the peanuts to Esther and the girls. A shame he couldn't share his inside knowledge with all his friends, but a secret is a secret so he looked out of the window to see what was happening. The darkness gradually gave way to the dazzling brightness of the Great Plains rushing past, and steam suddenly clouded the windows. The car itself seemed to come to life with a swinging and lurching motion and the rattle and roar of wheels clicking on the rails. The passengers swung their heads from side to side, then looked out to where the roadbed and rails seemed to pour out from beneath the car and vanish into infinity.

The Indian war party came alongside on their pinto ponies and Solomon pressed his nose to the glass to look into their threatening eyes. He again filled his mouth with popcorn and washed it down with cherry soda. Half rising from his seat he could see far out to the distant horizon and then he looked down to catch a sudden sight of a familiar figure.

'Look, Momma, it's Chaim! See him running around right outside with the big stick. He's stopping right there under our window! Hello . . . hello . . . Chaim! Solomon rapped loudly on the glass with his ring but nothing could be heard over the rattle and roar from the sound-effects belt passing beneath them.

'Momma, girls! Look at Chaim outside moving the whole train all by himself. What a boy!'

Suddenly Solomon sat down and clutched at his stomach. He groaned and doubled over.

'Oh, oh! Such an ache . . . Momma, stop the train.'

The rocking of the car, the scenery flashing by, the excitement of Indians and buffalo and then seeing his son racing around outside had all come together to collide with the popcorn, peanuts and soda and the proud father was violently trainsick. Solomon weakly excused himself and tottered down the narrow rocking aisle to the entrance platform. A nauseated rush took him through the station into the bright sunshine of the Fairground Pike just in time to be publicly sick all over the sidewalk from the wonderful realism his two bright sons had brought to Harrisburg, Pennsylvania.

CHAPTER TEN

'Meet Adolph Zukor from New York City, Lou. I want you to show him around and answer all his questions,' Chief Hale said as he caught up with his young chief projectionist, who was about to climb up to the high platform.

'Mr. Zukor and his partner, William Brady the stage producer, are going to take over one of our Tours and open it in New York City. I want you to show him how we do everything here. Stay with Lou as long as you wish, Mr. Zukor, and ask him anything. He knows all there is to know about our technical operations, so don't be bashful.'

The visitor was anything but bashful. He followed Lou right up the ladder, over the catwalk and to the high platform to watch all the action. Lou was impressed with the fine manners, attractive accent and stylish clothing of the young recent immigrant, whose questions showed he had a sharp and practical mind. Zukor sat on a box near Lou and complimented him and the others on their skill with the involved machines that turned illusion into reality, or something very close to it.

'This really is astounding! Even outside the parlor car up on this platform we seem to be rushing through space. One thing, though, I cannot comprehend,' he shouted at Lou over the machine and train noises. 'How do you stand the heat up here and all that dreadful racket?'

'What did you just say, Mr. Zukor?' Lou shouted, unheard by his guest.

'Never mind,' Zukor shouted back. 'Later we'll talk, when the show is ended.' The Tour came to a conclusion, and while Lou and the other projectionists threaded up for the next run and rewounded the trip just taken, the visitor went over to the other projector on the opposite side of the platform and introduced himself to Sam Warner.

'This is a much bigger setup, Mr. Zukor, than what I've been running at Idora Park ... that's near Youngstown, about two hundred miles west of here. All the other Tours just use a single projector, and some of them are right inside the car itself and projector over the heads of the passengers, but it's real cramped and they never get the tremendous scenic effects we have here. You really should try to do it this way in New York if you can.'

'I would like to but our space is much too limited. I'm afraid we will have to stay with the standard single machine. We have a fine location on Union Square and Broadway, right in the middle of Manhattan. It should attract many people who have never been on a train but read about them all the time. It is amazing how few people who live in New York ever travel across the East River or the Hudson! Now we can give them trips without travelling, and it may be the only way some of them will ever see America. A pity . . . such a great, wonderful country, and everybody should see all they can of it so they would appreciate it more.'

The next Tour began, and Zukor again sat on a box while they went over the Rockies, passed through orange groves in California and saw the Pacific Ocean, then to Niagara Falls and the Grand Canyon of the Colorado all in one short afternoon.

'My heartfelt thanks, Mr. Rabinowitz and Mr. Warner . . . Lou, Sam . . . You have shown me great courtesy, and also something I know will be highly successful in New York. I am impatient now to return and get the unit in operation. If you gentlemen come to New York I want you to visit me on Union Square. Perhaps one day you might want to work with my company . . . but of course I would not take you away from Chief Hale . . . unless, that is, you should like to join me. I leave that to you.' He handed Lou and Sam his card and started to climb down the ladder to the ground. Carefully he descended one rung at a time, watching each move of his shining black wing-tip shoes and trying to avoid getting any wrinkles in the fine dark suit, which set him off from all the others backstage in their drab work clothes. As he placed his left and then his right foot down on the ground, a pair of much smaller feet ran right over them and the bright shoes were bright no more. In spite of his anger, Zukor managed to sound polite.

'Hey – young man, at least you should apologize!'

Lou followed him down, looked over and smiled. 'You've just met my kid brother. Ham, come back here! Say hello to Adolph Zukor. You ran right over his shoes. He's in this business too, and if you apologize maybe he'll let you rock his Tour car in New York City!'

Ham skidded to a halt, dropped the long rocker pole he was carrying and walked back, putting on his widest smile.

'Gee, Mr. Zukor, I didn't even see you. They got me rushing around here doing so much that sometimes I guess I miss being polite. Excuse me, please. Your shoes are about the only polished ones we've seen back here for a long time. Here, let me wipe them off . . .'

Zukor couldn't help liking the boy and pulled out his white pocket handkerchief, which he flipped across his shoes.

'Never mind, young man. I like to see busy people and this looks like a very good business because of hard workers like you and your brother. I'm glad I shall be a part of this, and please remember, when you both come to New York, come to our penny arcade on Broadway and Union Square and be my guests. It is like a great amusement park in the middle of the city. Soon we will have a Hale's Tour there, and if you ever need jobs, you know where you can find me.' The courtly young man bowed and left the dark tent certain he would meet the Rabinowitz brothers again someday.

Another week came and went, and another bright young man, only a year or two in America, dropped by to visit. Bursting with ideas, energy and a heavy German accent, echoed by the three rotund cousins accompanying him, he came to Hale's Tours to see this very different kind of a motion picture show. Young Carl Laemmle, whose round cherubic face concealed the shrewd mind of a creative business genius, was deeply impressed. He remained for quite some time to negotiate rights to use a Hale's Tour unit with its library of exciting scenic films. Laemmle ran several other film operations and was about to take on the Edison Film Trust, as he felt their monopoly and its restrictions were strangling the growth and independence of the infant industry in its crib. Chief Hale gave him the usual tour, then turned him over to Lou and Ham, who showed Laemmle and his entourage the illusion machines and the bouncing parlor car with its surrounding giant screens. When he had seen it all and gone into Chief Hale's office to sign his deal, he again stopped outside between shows where the boys all had come down for fresh air and a bite of lunch.

'Chentelmen . . . My thanks are to you all. We shall no doubt see of each odder much more . . . May I make an introduction to my cousins, all only last veek here from Chermany.'

He ran through each relative's name, and the round bodies gave polite precise bows. Then they were off to catch the afternoon train to Chicago and on to New York, where Laemmle would meet with his lawyers to draw up battle plans against the Film Trust forces. Here was a dynamic young man in a dynamic young industry, and Lou and Ham were deeply impressed. Lou grabbed his brother's arm, squeezing it as he spoke.

'This business just has to go places – and the way to do it right is to have our own operation. We can only get so far working for somebody else. Zukor and Laemmle are smart fellows and they know their way around. We've got to figure how to be our own bosses the way they both are and own something that can grow!'

Ham listened but his mind was on more than just business.

'Lou, did you see how Laemmle and Adolph Zukor were dressed? The derbies, those spats and shiny shoes . . . Golly . . . spats! Suits with vests and gold watch chains. That's what I want, and if we have our own place again I can sing and dance . . . Jeez! Chief Hale has me stuck down here on the ground bouncing the car and greasing that damn noise belt! I wanna be up on top and out in front! I wanna meet people and have them meet me and do big things!'

'All right, Mr. Spats,' said Lou with a laugh. 'Begin by doing something big right now. Put your box over there, stick your pole under the car and start rocking it. Think of all the people inside the car you'll be impressing!' And up the ladder went Lou to await the buzzer from the conductor and again start rolling the projection machine to take them all up Pike's Peak.

Just like the shadows of steel rails pouring out beneath the parlor car and all the scenery going past the windows, the season too moved on. Soon it was time to close the Harrisburg Fairgrounds and move the thrills, exhibits and rides to where better weather would make it possible to prolong profits and pleasure. Chief Hale made a proposition to the boys.

'Ham, Lou . . . how would you like to move with the Tour down to Montgomery, Alabama, for a couple of months?' he asked them one afternoon as a cold wind whipped down the Pike and clouds scudded across the sun, throwing great dark shadows. 'My advance man has gotten us a fine spot in Athletic Park right outside Montgomery, and after that we've got another unit set to open at Ponce de Leon Park near Atlanta.

107

I'll get things started in Montgomery, then turn the operation over to both of you to manage so I can move on. I think you're ready to handle things.'

'Chief, you've got a deal!' Lou said for both of them. 'First, though, we've got to tell our folks . . . but they'll think it's great!' He paused a moment, looked over at Ham and added, 'Do you think they will?'

'Montgomery, Alabama!' Momma shouted that evening from her kitchen. 'Where is that? Can you still live here and go each day to there like the Fairgrounds?'

'No, Momma,' Lou answered. 'It's a couple hundred miles from Harrisburg. I don't know how far for sure, but it's a wonderful opportunity for us both. Chief Hale will see we get a good place to stay and –'

'Boys,' Solomon interrupted, 'it sounds like a very good thing for you. That man knows his business. If he says you can run things, then you can! Let's see, Lou – you're twenty years old now, and you're going to have to watch out for your brother. He may only be fourteen . . . no, he's nearer fifteen now, but I think he knows more than most boys older than that – much more.' He cleared his throat a couple of times, looked over at Momma and the two girls and vainly tried to send them a signal to leave the hall and go back into the kitchen. They were all eyes and ears but completely missed his imploring gestures.

'Ham . . . Chaim, my son. Sometimes fathers have to talk with their growing sons about certain things when they are going to leave home and go out into the world . . . to places far away like Montgomery and maybe Atlanta and – '

Ham's face crinkled into a smile.

'Oh – you want to tell me about the kind of girls I'm gonna meet and how I should be careful not to catch anything from them! I know all about that, Poppa.'

Poppa didn't know he knew and stammered in anguish as again he looked to Momma, Ruth and Miriam, who finally caught his signal and heard Ham's response. They turned and ran back into the other room, pulling the hall door shut behind them.

Solomon slowly walked to the front staircase and sat down on the second step. He took a deep breath and then gestured toward Ham and went on speaking in a very hesitant voice.

'Sit here with me, Chaim . . . er, Ham. Very soon you will be fifteen. Already you have responsibilities taking you away

108

from your home to Montgomery and other places. My son, one day you will be a father yourself and . . .' He paused to struggle with his thoughts. The boy sat quietly on the step and looked up into his father's face.

'Chaim . . . my boy. What I'm saying to you is . . . er . . . well, ah . . . let us put it this way. There are certain things a man must know that it is better to learn from talking about – and remember later – than to find out from experience when maybe it is too late.'

Ham moved up one step to sit closer to his father, and in a voice filled with assurance he said, 'All right, Poppa. Now just what is it you want to know?'

CHAPTER ELEVEN

Adolph Zukor opened his Hale's Tours unit at 41 Union Square in the heart of Manhattan, and it was a great success – for the first two months. Nobody is more fickle than a customer who has paid out his good money for entertainment, and the average New Yorker is the most fickle of all. The tough, sophisticated city looked on trains only as transportation or an investment – not as entertainment. Everyday life in the Big City was filled with so much excitement and constant struggle that the Tours, tame by comparison, could hardly compete. What people wanted, and what Adolph Zukor and Bill Brady gave them, was comedy, drama and the human condition reflected in shadows on a screen. Out went all the expensive Hale's Tour equipment, and the imitation railroad station and car became Zukor's Comedy Theater on Union Square.

Programs were changed every few days, and the people once again flocked in to be entertained. Now that the long narrow parlor car interior had been scrapped, and with it the feeling of close confinement that bothered so many people, there was room for more seats and more profits. Audiences wanted action, things they could laugh at or cry over. If you wanted to travel on a train, buy a ticket and 'Go west, young man!' Hale's Tours were an idea whose time had come and now was going.

Small production companies were springing up all over to supply the new needs of movie patrons and theater owners. The power of the Film Trust was waning as it fell out of step with the times and was outdistanced by creative independent producers and their little companies turning out what the people wanted to see. Carl Laemmle was meeting with success in leading the battle against the power of the Trust, and soon it would be completely wiped out.

Although Hale's Tours did not survive, it managed to establish some of the very first film exchanges throughout the country and abroad. These exchanges served more than five hundred different Tour units during the peak of their popularity. The physical problems in getting films out to the units, exchanging, repairing and switching them around so each print could be run over and over, until it wore out, brought about an inventory and billing system that became vital to the whole business. An entire new industry, serving as middleman between production and exhibition, came into being – the film exchanges – and their real beginnings in great part were with Hale's Tours; without the growing need of the extensive Tour operations, their arrival and development would have been long delayed or come about quite differently. Gradually the exchange system brought some order into the chaotic operations of this vital new infant industry. At first it was a simple matter of buying films outright from individual producers and selling them to the theaters, but because of constant changes in product output and demand, new forms of leasing by the reel or length were worked out.

It was Maurie who most benefited. Completely fed up with shuttling around the south-central states selling meat products for Armour, he stopped off for a visit with his brothers at the Hale's Tours in Atlanta. Chief Hale had been greatly impressed by the young man's sales experience and his serious approach to business. He sensed that everything Maurie had learned and practiced selling lard, hides and meat could easily be adapted to the growing film exchange business, which needed men with experience and drive. The Chief introduced Maurie to his southern area sales manager, who was equally impressed, and very soon a notice of thanks and farewell was on its way to Armour. Maurie first travelled to Kansas City and the Tours' central film exchange to learn more about his new career, and quickly found it was enough like what he had been doing for Armour to make him feel confident and comfortable. He was soon sent on to Denver to open a new film exchange for the Rocky Mountain area.

Hale's Tours were closing down one by one as business for this special form of entertainment dropped off, but there was still plenty of business for film exchanges in meeting the growing need for comedies and dramatic films. The five- to ten-minute show had grown into half-hour and hour-long presentations, and the profits grew right along with the expanded running time.

Ham and Lou found themselves out of jobs after the unit they managed folded and their parlor car gave its last rock,

111

rattle and roll. Chief Hale auctioned off the projection equipment to several theater owners who were expanding their operations. There was a friendly parting with the Chief, who returned to Kansas City to live out his life with pleasant memories of fires extinguished, dream trains set rolling all over the world and the bright young men he had started in an exciting new business.

Maurie was working late on Saturday evening in the Denver film exchange when he looked up to see two very familiar faces. He jumped up from his desk and ran around to hug Lou and Ham.

'You have no idea how glad I am to see you! You couldn't have picked a better time to come here. Something real big is happening ... I'm sorry the Tours have been folding, but maybe it's for the best . . . at least it could work out that way for us.'

He stood back and looked at the two boys again.

'Good Lord! You aren't little kids I can shove around anymore ... You're both real grown-up and got meat on your bones. Well – let's sit down and I'll tell you about this situation.'

'Wait a minute,' Lou said. 'Whose name is that on the door ... "Maurie Robbins" – somebody you got working for you?'

'I'll bet I know who he is,' Ham interrupted. 'He's you, Maurie, isn't he?'

'Yeah, that's right, it's me – but, fellows, please don't write anything about that to Momma or Poppa yet. I'll break it to them later on. You see, it took me so damn long to sign my name on contracts for film sales, and everything here has to be done in such a hurry that . . . well, one day Rabinowitz got caught in the clock and came out Robbins. Nobody complained, so that's the way it's been ever since. How about you boys using it too? You're perfectly welcome, I got no patents on it . . .'

'All right. After all, I changed Chaim to Ham and you made Maurie out of Moishe. I'll bet Lou would like to save time signing his name too. From now on, far as I'm concerned, it's Maurie, Lou and Ham Robbins,' Ham said with a big smile, hoping their parents wouldn't mind too much ... but that new name, Robbins, it really did have a good feel to it.

'There's great future in film distribution and you're coming into it with me. I've raised enough money to buy out the old Hale's Tours Exchange for this entire territory, so it's all

112

mine – and now it's going to be ours! The Tours are going out of the picture, but more and more regular theaters are opening up, and they need product and dependable distributors. The Robbins brothers are in business – let's go out and have a drink to our new beginning!'

Maurie knew his way around Denver and the best places to celebrate. He grabbed his hat, turned down the lights and pushed the boys out of the exchange and out into the street.

'Come on, fellows. I know just the spot to go, and tomorrow we can sleep until noon 'cause we're our own bosses from now on! You don't know what a great time can be until you've had it in Denver!'

Ham woke up the next day in a strange bed with a strange brunette. He sat up slowly and looked over at the thick mass of dark hair spread out over the pillow next to his. He let his eyes move on down to the sleeping face and all the curves lying there beside him. He shook his head, trying to bring the fuzzy images back into focus, but it wasn't quite as easy as twisting a Kinetoscope lens. He remembered sitting at the dinner table in a big hotel dining room putting away the biggest steak he had ever seen, washed down with a schooner of beer that could be lifted only with both hands. Maurie, who seemed to know everybody in the room, motioned to several very good-looking girls, who came over and joined them at their table. They looked as though they had been waiting all evening for this invitation.

The rest of the night was like a wonderful cross-country sequence from one of the Tour films, but instead of the parlor car doing the bucking and rocking, he was doing it himself with this wildly cooperative girl in a big hotel bed. It certainly beat the railroad car and those shadow illusions! The rocker boy had just become a rocker man.

Ham got up, slipped into his clothes, then softly closed the door to the hotel room behind him and left the sleeping girl, stopping at the desk to pay for the room. He walked in the bright morning sunshine to the film exchange, where his brothers sat behind a big table covered with sheets of figures and lists of available films.

'Welcome to Denver, kid!' Maurie said, looking up with a smile almost as broad as the one Ham was wearing.

'How do you like the Rockies?' added Lou.

Before Ham could think of an answer, Maurie was off again, pointing down at the sheets on the table, and the two

113

younger boys drew closer as he explained the workings of the film exchange system.

'It's a new business and a good one. More theaters are opening all the time, and the owners and their customers want program changes every week, sometimes twice a week. That means lots of work for us in getting film from producers and their representatives and from other exchange areas, inspecting them for any damage and fixing them so they go out of here in good shape. We have to get advertising sheets or posters to go with each show, and then we have to keep a record of exact dates and billings. We have to watch the theater people like hawks so they don't use the one print they're paying for in more than one theater. They're real sharp and have a cute trick called bicycling where the same picture is run in two or more theaters besides the one that's paying for it. The distributor, that's us, winds up getting gypped. You have to be real fast on your feet in this business, and you both should be perfect for it. Also, it helps if you can toss your weight around now and then. You'll find these guys respect you more when you back up a deal with a kick in the ass when they have it coming.'

'You mean they use bicycles here in Denver on all these hills to get film around to the theaters?' Ham asked.

'Nah, that's just slang. I told you what it means. You can do it with a rickshaw, an automobile or a motorcycle . . . just so it doesn't get done to us. And it won't be if we keep our eyes open and don't get too trusting. There may be some honest men in this business, but they're few and far between – everybody has his tricks.

'One thing you always have to remember,' Maurie went on, 'is that this film we are dealing with is a lot more than just entertainment or merchandise we lease or sell to theaters. It's an explosive! If you think back to what Birnbaum told us back in Harrisburg when we ran our first film and what we saw happen to our Bijou Dream in York, you know what I'm talking about. This stuff can go off if there's a flame anyplace near it. A big part of our job is watching the people we have working for us to make sure nobody gets careless. We could be out of business in five minutes or less the way that stuff burns – and there's too much involved to take risks.'

'How come they let us operate a film exchange here with so many other buildings around? Aren't they afraid a fire could start in our place and wipe out a few blocks?' Lou asked.

'This is such a new business that the fire department has

just begun to get after the exchange to build as fireproof as possible,' Maurie told him. 'Real soon they are going to force us to move out of built-up areas like this and go where we're not such a risk to our neighbors. Next week all the other film exchange operators are meeting with us and we are going to get together on setting up something like they have in a few other cities. They call it Film Row – and with luck, and a fast way out of the building if some dummy drops his lit pipe, we should be able to make it work and not go up in smoke.'

'Gee,' Ham said sadly, 'here we are now only three short blocks from the hotel with all those girls and now we have to move out to the sticks! What a rotten break.'

'Yeah,' Lou replied to his downcast brother as he let go a laugh, 'but it's the kind of rotten break that's going to keep us alive and in business. The girls will like you better if none of you gets singed or burned off!'

Denver was everything Maurie said it would be and the entire territory was a wonderful market for films that the Robbins Brothers Exchange brought into the area and distributed to the many theaters that had come into being. In a few months the boys knew they had dug themselves a gold mine, even though now it was a long ride for Ham to the hotel and its pleasures. Ham and Lou might have been content, but Maurie was always looking around for new places to spread out. Denver and the Rocky Mountain area plus surrounding states was just fine, but there were limits. Maurie saw beyond them, and what he saw was San Francisco, California.

'Fellows, have you ever heard of the Panama Pacific International Exposition?' Maurie asked both boys one night after a busy day that had left them worn out.

'Yeah, I read about it in the papers . . . something big in San Francisco celebrating the opening of the Panama Canal . . . is that it?' answered Lou, who digested several newspapers each morning with his breakfast.

'Right,' said Maurie, 'and that is where we've got to open an office just as soon as possible. I got a letter from an old friend of mine, Al Lichtman, and he wrote that the town is filling up with people from all over the world. Lots of theaters have opened and some stage houses have converted to film. They need product and there aren't enough exchanges there to supply them. It's our chance, and we have to move right away! The Exposition has just opened and we should have an

115

exchange in operation as soon as possible. My idea is for you two boys to get there right away and check around for locations, and I'll ship film to you from here. Al Lichtman can help you out, he's a good friend and knows the ropes. How does this idea hit you both?'

Ham was overjoyed and almost jumped up and down in excitement as though rocking another parlor car.

'Great! I've heard lots about San Francisco. Denver is fine, but how long can you look at mountains? That Bay is something – and I hear the dames are just terrific, too!'

'Easy, Ham,' Lou said, grabbing the younger man and getting him to quiet down. 'This is going to be a business trip, remember. Maybe some fun on the side . . . but let's keep our mind on distributing our films and not just our energies!'

'Now from what I've learned,' Maurie continued, 'there are several theaters opening up inside the Exposition grounds, and you can find out if they need any kind of special films. Also, there are several new theaters on Market Street and all the streets leading into it downtown. It's an opportunity to get there at the right time with something they are going to need. You've shown me you can take care of yourselves and you know the film exchange business – in fact, you learned a lot faster than I ever thought you would. You go a week from today, so get over to the hotel, Ham, and start saying good-bye to the girls. I'll bet a bunch of them show up on Market Street or on the Tenderloin in San Francisco right after you get there. One thing more – keep track of every cent you spend, and take it easy. Until we have it coming in there the way we've had it here, you spend as little as possible. We're all agreed, then – some of that gold in the Golden Gate is going to come to us. Fellows, we're really on the way!'

A few more nights on the town and then both of the boys were on the train, cases of film sealed in fireproof crates up forward in the baggage car and a list of requirements for a film exchange folded away in their pockets, with the wads of greenbacks they would need strapped around their waists in bulging money belts.

Ham was the only one with misgivings. He had learned on the trip to Denver months before that real trains made him sick to his stomach with their constant rocking and bouncing. He would much rather walk to San Francisco, but he gritted his teeth, ate sparingly and tried to keep his mind on the scenery. It was so strange to see it in full color and always in perfect focus. He shook his head in wonder as he looked out the train window at the magnificent Rockies and then the Sierras. He certainly had to admit there still were some things that God did much better than man!

CHAPTER TWELVE

Like nearly everyone who had come before or would follow, Ham and Lou fell madly in love with the fabled city on the hills overlooking the magnificent Bay. When they stepped off the train from Denver early in the morning, they found themselves in a city bursting with vitality and life. Crowds of new arrivals from every state, nation and continent were drawn here by the great Exposition. All paths led to the Tower of Jewels, which symbolized the Panama Canal, the eight magnificent Palaces dedicated to the achievements and hopes of mankind and, of course, to the Zone, which was the center of joy and merriment. So far as Ham was concerned, the Zone *was* the Exposition, and it would be some time before he got around to the Palaces and monuments celebrating man's less flamboyant achievements. The showmen and showmanship of the Zone were what made his blood run faster, and to him, this was life!

All the hotels were crowded with visitors to the city, and new construction had not caught up with housing demands even nine years after the great earthquake and fire of 1906. Lou and Ham had their baggage and the film crates put in storage and went right to the Independent Film Exchange on Taylor Street, where Maurie had told them to look for his old friend Al Lichtman, who had come to San Francisco the year before.

'Lou, Ham . . . It's great to meet you fellows! Maurie wrote you were coming and told me you were going to set up an exchange. Anything I can do to help you, ask and it's done! Now let me introduce you around Film Row and show you the greatest city in the whole world!' In just over a year Al Lichtman had become as proud of his city as any native son, and loved to show it off.

'Come on, I'm taking the rest of the day and all of the night off. First I'll get you into some rooms over where I stay, and then I'm going to take you every place there is in San Francisco to go!' Al grabbed his hat, slammed the office door and took them to a pleasant rooming house not far from the film exchange. The landlady, Mrs. Feinstein, was happy to rent them a room and bath of their own, and now they had a place to call home. Next Ham insisted they go to a men's clothing store down the street, where he bought his very first derby hat, a pair of spats, kid gloves and a fancy cravat. Only half a day in town, he already felt himself to be a San Franciscan. Lou and Al stood back and gave low whistles when they looked him over. The kid had style – even if it was rather on the flashy side.

'Lou,' Ham said in a conspiratorial voice, 'when we send Maurie our expense report, all this stuff I'm buying is "business equipment" I use in selling. What he doesn't know won't hurt us!'

'Where did you learn so much so fast?' asked Al. 'Later on you can buy yourself more "equipment," but right now we're going to catch a cable car and see the town!'

They rode up and down the hills, past the lovely old wooden houses with their ornate scrollwork spared by quake and flames, still standing as reminders of the past. North Beach, then the Embarcadero and a taxi ride up Russian Hill to see the magnificent fog-softened panorama of the city and its Bay spread out all around them. Off in the distance toward the Golden Gate they saw the blurred silhouette of the Panama Pacific International Exposition, its glowing lights promising good things to come. The mournful monotony of foghorns sounded a sad tone, but the boys' spirits were high up at the other end of the scale.

'Fellows, have you ever eaten a fresh-caught lobster that's steamed right in front of you? You've got a real treat coming. We're going to Fisherman's Wharf!'

Ham loved every moment, except the squeal the doomed creature made when it hit the boiling water. For such an ugly animal it sure tasted wonderful! So maybe it wasn't kosher, but what Momma and Poppa didn't know wouldn't hurt them. 'And this is what is called the Tenderloin,' Al said as they rolled through the notorious district. 'I understand before the fire it was lots bigger, but there's still plenty here to see.' Ham almost fell out of the taxi window, especially when he saw the lovely ladies standing in doorways or leaning out of their open windows to welcome the newcomers. Denver was never like this!

'Al, Lou . . . let me off right here! This is the part of San

Francisco I want to see up close! You both go on and I'll meet you back at the rooming house in four or five hours ... I've got to look over some very interesting "business equipment"!' His eyes were almost popping from their sockets.

'Hold on, kid. There's plenty of time later for the Tenderloin. Al's got more of the city to show us. The girls will still be here – so get back in the cab and be patient!' said Lou, wondering if his brother had been making a joke or a promise.

Chinese New Year was months away, but the boys celebrated ahead of time in a wonderful restaurant decorated with prancing porcelain dragons just off Grant Avenue. Within an hour they knew the difference between chow mein, won ton, chop suey, moo goo gai pan and a dozen other exotic dishes new to their palates. When the long happy meal ended, Ham broke open his fortune cookie, half expecting the message inside to read 'Bad Son Eats Pork and Keeps Secret from his Momma and Poppa – Shame!' The room was dark, so nobody saw the guilty look as Ham read what was really on the slip. It was routine, but appropriate: 'You Have Make Change for Better.'

'Now there's a fortune I can agree with!' Ham said. He ate the broken cookie pieces off all their plates, washing them down with hot green tea. They left the restaurant and Chinatown.

Al guided them across traffic-jammed Market Street, where the parallel tracks of many competing streetcar companies reached almost from curb to curb. Legitimate stage and movie theaters of all sizes lined the street in between the shops and office buildings. At once the boys could see why this was going to be such a great market for what they had come here to sell. Theaters were springing up all over the city and on down the peninsula. They could see the thousands and thousands of people crowding around them and knew that nearly every one of them would be going to the movies. For a little while, though, before their film exchange was opened, they could still relax and enjoy life in this fabled city. It was a happy time in San Francisco, which entertained a whole world destined soon to tear so much of itself apart in the war years to come.

Nothing Ham Robbins had ever seen in Harrisburg or even the wilder parts of Montgomery, Atlanta or Denver had quite prepared him for this vision standing only an arm's length away in the dim light. A hidden flute trilled and a tambour

120

drum softly beat out rhythms of the East. The air was filled with the heavy-soft lushness of Oriental incense.

Her name was Stella, and except for a filmy veil and the swirling mane of jet black hair sweeping down her shoulders she was completely nude. A full bosom, unfettered and almost entirely revealed, slowly rose and fell. The sound of a seductive sigh seemed to come from the half-open mouth, and her perfect red lips glistened with a promise. Deep brown eyes, half hidden by long black lashes, looked intently at the well-dressed young man who stood in frozen silence only a few feet away as though in worship before a goddess. Her breasts moved again, up – then down. The young man stepped even closer to see all he possibly could of the bare flesh behind the veil as it rose, then descended.

Now he stood much closer to Stella, who breathed even more passionately than before. He could almost reach out and touch this magnificent female whose glorious body seemed a passionate invitation. He stopped, looked closely to better see all he could in the bad light of what could have been a sultan's seraglio, then he stepped back, gave a raucous laugh and turned to his brother, who stood just behind him.

'This dame's a phony, Lou, a real phony. She isn't breathing at all. It's done with some kind of a pump stuck there inside her chest. Come here and look for yourself, but don't get hit in the eye with one of those lovely things. It's the old con, and we've been taken for a dime each!' Ham said, still laughing as he stepped aside. He went over to the left of the lifelike, almost perfect painted figure, where he saw a drape, which he pulled aside. There was an opening in the canvas wall and he stuck his head through. Sure enough, there on the back of the painting, which he could see by leaning far forward, was some kind of a flat balloon or bladder attached right up where that heaving bosom must be. A long tube ran down to a bellows being worked by a little boy who looked about the same age as Ham back when he first helped his brothers load meat on the delivery wagon.

A big, husky man, his outraged anger matching his size, ran over from the far side of the room and grabbed Ham by the shoulder. The two young men were rushed out of the exhibit and told to stay the hell away.

'I ought to have you tossed off the Exposition grounds, you young squirts! You got no right to expose Stella and peek around at her behind like that! She's the hit of the whole Zone and . . .' He fizzled out as Ham interrupted with a laugh.

'Take it easy, friend. We're all in the same business – fooling people. I just wanted to see how you were doing it. All right – so the kid in back breathes for her. Don't worry, we'll keep your big secret, and you can keep our dimes. . . we're even!' He and Lou were still laughing as they walked away from the side door back to the middle of the great street running through the Zone. Ham looked back with appreciation at the flashy front, gleaming mirrors, banners and decorations on the front of the imitation harem with all the gaudy signs proclaiming, STELLA! SHE LIVES – SHE BREATHES! ADULTS ONLY. TEN CENTS.

'Now that's a come-on done up right. What a damn shame she's only paint and soft lights. I'll bet she could put on a real show in bed. I'd sure love to pump those bellows!' Ham said, smiling at his brother, who wiped some dust from his tan shoes.

'We got our dime's worth, Ham. She wasn't too bad to look at, was she . . . even if that lovely set of lungs was as phony as her hair. Well, that's how it goes, but the people love it.'

What Ham had most on his mind was the crowd jammed inside and the line out front waiting to plunk down their dimes and stand in the bad light, inhaling stale incense and hot air in front of a painting that breathed. The rubes would bunch up and stare, listening enraptured to a second-rate Indian flute and drum and not getting so much as a cobra in a basket. Old Phineas Barnum was right, Ham thought. A sucker and his roll are soon parted. Stick something up on a fancy stage, lower the lights, strike up the band, hang up a sign and they'll happily beg to be taken. It was a lesson he would later put to good use.

The boys slowly walked down the Zone Road of the Panama Pacific International Exposition. Several times they had to move aside and let the bicycle-driven wheeled wicker chairs roll past with their loads of affluent fairgoers with money to spend and shoe leather to save. As they walked, the two boys were captivated by the magnificence of the Exposition, which celebrated the opening, only the year before, of the Panama Canal.

It was fifteen years into the twentieth century, and Europe had entered the turmoil and destruction of a war more devastating than any that had gone before. An entire way of life was threatened with extinction – but here in San Francisco a part of that soon-to-vanish world, and a glimpse of the one that everyone hoped might replace it, was on glorious display, a fairyland of dreams and promise standing on reclaimed land, most of which only a few short months before had been deep beneath the waters of the Bay.

Actually, the Exposition had been planned long before the first ships passed through the locks from Atlantic to Pacific. The leaders and movers of San Francisco, proud of their reborn city, talked of showing it to the rest of the earth. A phoenix risen from the ashes.

As they turned a corner, Ham stepped directly in front of one of the pedal-propelled chairs, which contained a pair of lovely young girls, one blonde, the other brunette. The man in the back who worked the pedals jammed on his brakes and both girls bent sharply forward, their broad-brimmed hats sliding down over their eyes as the chair skidded to a halt. They recovered themselves, lifted the hats so they could see and looked at the boys with apologetic smiles. The blonde spoke after taking a deep breath.

'Oh – I'm so sorry we frightened you . . . but . . .'

She never finished, as the man in back got the pedals working. As the chair scraped past Ham he gave out a loud whoop. The pretty blonde turned to her brunette companion and pointed back, saying something he could not hear. For a moment he stood there, then dusted himself off and looked after the girls, who had both leaned out around the wide wicker seat and were waving back as they wheeled off down the Main Pike Road.

'Lou – what a pair of cuties! Did you see them? . . . The blonde, that's the one I'd go for. I don't think I ever had a date with a real blonde. Oh, there was one night in Montgomery, but I think she was only a temporary one. I'll never know.'

All the walking and chair dodging had made them thirsty and hungry, so they stopped for schooners of steam beer at a big outdoor saloon. Next they went to a stand selling the recently invented ice cream cones, which had become the rage of the Exposition. They ate two each, strawberry and chocolate, then picked up some mustard-soaked knockwurst wrapped in big squishy buns, and very soon they both had genuine Panama Pacific stomach aches, which had them searching in agony for the nearest men's rest room. In spite of the loudly proclaimed advances in art, science and industry being demonstrated and proudly displayed here beside the Bay, the designers and planners had as usual neglected certain basic and vital human functions. It was a very close

123

race with disaster until at last, at the British Empire Exhibit in the Palace of Machinery, they found a row of booths containing the latest models put out by Thomas Crapper, Ltd., benefactors of mankind and Purveyor to Their Majesties. After a while they departed with sincere appreciation of British machinery and ingenuity, but absolutely no appetite for the rare and wonderful foods of the world on dislay all around them.

'Oh . . . I just remembered something! We were invited out for dinner tonight by Mrs. Feinstein, our landlady, and her husband! I'll bet you forgot too!' Lou said in shock.

'I wish you hadn't remembered,' moaned Ham. 'I'm still kind of sick from what we just ate. I won't be able to touch a mouthful.'

'I know you, kid,' his brother replied. 'If it's dead and on a plate, you'll eat it! Come on, we'll have to see the rest of the Exposition another time. We're gonna splurge and get one of those rolling chairs to the gate, then hop a cab back to our place. We'll just make it . . . come on! Hurry!'

At last they found an unoccupied chair, but the ride to the gate took some time because of the crowds of people on every street. From the rolling chair they transferred to a taxi at the main gate, and within fifteen minutes, after a high-speed trip up and down the hills they had made it back to their room in time to clean up, change clothes and join the Feinsteins, who were ready to leave.

Not too far from their rooming house was the Granada Hotel, a venerable survivor of pre-earthquake days. This had become the temporary residence of Benjamin Morrison, a well-known attorney, and his family while their apartment house on California Street was being rebuilt. The passing of time and the disaster of 1906 had speeded up the ageing process of the lovely old apartment house, which was owned by Benjamin's mother-in-law, Hannah Friedkin, who lived on the top floor. Reluctantly she decided that only a major overhaul could restore the structure. Benjamin Morrison was a widower whose young wife, Belle Friedkin, had been a great beauty from one of the oldest Jewish families in San Francisco. Her family had arrived not long after the great Gold Rush of '49 and with admirable foresight decided the real gold was to be mined right here in the city, not far away above Sacramento. Accordingly, they established a city lottery, which quickly prospered and became for them like the mother lode itself. When the earthquake leveled much of the

124

city, to reveal strange and unpleasant politics and politicians flushed out by fire and devastation, the city lottery became a casualty of a new morality that sprang up with the post-disaster rebuilding. The flames seemed to have purified much of the city, and some people were certain the quake and fire had been God's punishment for the town's loose ways. Many had called it Sodom on the Pacific, and it nearly met a similar fate. The city lottery was one of the ruins that was not rebuilt. Soon new vices would replace this mild diversion, but fortunately Benjamin Morrison had his own profession and need not depend upon what was forever gone.

So it was on this lovely Sunday evening that attorney Morrison sat at his regular table surrounded by his family in the big dining room of the Granada Hotel as the Feinsteins and two young gentlemen guests entered and were taken across the room to a table. Morrison looked over and nodded to his two old friends and clients, then spoke to his mother-in-law before she could ask him who he saw.

'That's Bess and Harold Feinstein. I think you met them with me at the Crocker reception New Year's Eve.'

No, she didn't recall them, but his two daughters became suddenly animated and looked over at the party just being seated. The ones catching their attention were, of course, the two smartly dressed young men who accompanied the Feinsteins. The girls followed them with their eyes until they were lost to view, and then they returned full interest to their rich desserts, paying no attention to Grossmutter Friedkin, who scolded them for indulging themselves with such fattening stuff.

'Lou, did you see those two girls across the room! I'm absolutely positive they're the same blonde and brunette whose chair nearly ran over me . . . Look!' Ham whispered to his brother. Lou rose enough to get a better view, then sat down and agreed that they seemed to be the very same girls.

Ham continued, 'Maybe we ought to go over and apologize for nearly ruining their ride . . . huh, Lou, think we should?'

Their host, Harold Feinstein, could not help overhearing.

'Those are Benjamin Morrison's daughters. I've known them since they were little girls. Ben's my lawyer, and I'll be happy to introduce you both to him and his family.'

Ham suddenly was quite flustered and without thinking ran his fingers through his hair, undoing in a moment all his earlier labors with comb, brush and pomade.

'Uh – wait a minute, Mr. Feinstein. We shouldn't just

barge over there . . . I mean . . . well – my hair is all messed up and I'll be right back. Excuse me a minute!' Ham said, and, keeping well to the far wall, he hoped out of sight of the Morrison table, he left the dining room. The bell captain directed him to the men's lounge, and in a few minutes he returned, hair again slicked down, necktie in a perfectly centered knot and black shoes gleaming. He crossed from the door to the Feinstein table, where Lou sat scowling up at him as the Feinsteins shook their heads sadly.

'What's the matter? Did something happen?' Ham asked.

Lou gestured across the dining room. 'That's the matter! What did you do, go out for a haircut, shampoo and shoeshine?'

Ham turned to look across the wide room. The Morrison table was empty. Only crumpled napkins and the remnants of the rich dessert remained. The blonde was gone, and so was the brunette.

'For God's sake, Ham!' said Lou in despair. 'Next time keep your damn fingers out of your hair!'

Another week passed, and again the Feinsteins asked their three young boarders to the Granada Hotel for dinner. Al Lichtman was also invited but was called back to his office to repair some botched-up contracts and had to beg off. This time the party arrived only a few minutes after Benjamin Morrison and his daughters and mother-in-law were seated at the usual family table. Harold Feinstein whispered something to the captain, who ushered them to a table next to that of the Morrisons, and introductions took place immediately.

The brunette's name was Betty, and her dark hair flowed down over the shoulders of her long-sleeved white dress trimmed with pink ribbon. Her sister, Irene, was the blonde. Her dress matched her sister's, but the ribbons were blue. Both girls were smiling as the boys were introduced, and Irene was first to speak.

'We've already met! How could we be strangers to anybody we nearly ran over with a chair!'

Betty was about to speak, but the sudden loud clearing of her grandmother's throat was a command for silence. Hannah Friedkin was not at all as pleased as the two girls she had brought up ever since their mother died when they were still little children. She was the product of a strict Berlin upbringing, the language, morality and manners in her home were *echt Deutsch* and she was far more Grossmutter than

Grandmother. Above all she had always sought to protect her girls from this very type of person she now perceived standing before her table. Deep inside she sensed they were not of her world – the tight little community of Old German-Jewish families ever on guard against encroaching outsiders, Jew or Gentile.

These young men seemed well enough behaved in spite of the garish pattern and cut of their suits and the impossible pointed black shoes with outrageous spats better worn by older and more mature men. Their accents, *lieber Gott!* . . . their accents were the worst Midwest America. As Harold Feinstein gave their names and city of origin, Grossmutter Friedkin muttered the one word that best summed up her feelings: '*Ach!*'

She knew her girls were well brought up, and hoped they could handle themselves in any situation so as not to bring disgrace upon the family, but those spats, the striped suits and the slicked-down polished hair of the younger one . . . *Schrecklich!* Who knew what ideas such people had! No matter how prepared for life a young lady might be, along could come a . . . a Hamilton Robbins . . . and . . . He was talking to Irene now, so the grandmother cut off her inner conversation to listen.

'We tried seeing all we could of the Exposition in one day. Even took one of those rolling chairs,' said Ham, hoping this might be the start of a productive conversation.

'Did you frighten anybody with your chair the way we did with ours?' said blonde Irene.

'No – we weren't so lucky,' he replied, wanting to thank her for keeping things going in spite of that grandmother sitting there across the table. If looks could shove, both boys would be out on the street sitting on the cable car tracks right now. Lou tried to join in with a few words, but as usual Ham beat him to it.

'We're planning to go back to the Exposition again tomorrow and see all the things we missed. Could we ask you girls to be our guests for the day? We're friendly with Sid Grauman, whose father has a big show in the Zone . . . something about Chinatown, I think. Sid has passes waiting for us at the gate, and we'd love to have you come with us, if it's all right.'

Lou looked in awe at his younger brother. Where in the world had Ham picked up such a smooth line? The grandmother, glaring across the table at him, didn't slow him up for a second. The girl's father, smiling at them from his seat, must be on their side.

'The Graumans are wonderful people, very creative and doing well in this new movie theater business. I know all about them, since I'm their attorney, and if you boys have met young Sid, you've got a very interesting friend indeed,' Benjamin Morrison said. The boys thought his voice was the most comforting sound they could imagine.

'We would love to go with you,' said Irene, without even looking to her grandmother or father for permission. Betty nodded her acceptance at once.

Grossmutter Friedkin again said the only thing she could think of for such an occasion – it was repetitious, but it was exactly how she felt about girls who accepted invitations from people like these . . . these Midwest Galitzianers!

'Ach!'

Early the next morning Ham phoned Sid Grauman at his father's office. Sid was one of the many new friends he had met through Al Lichtman, and he reminded Sid that he had offered them Exposition passes and tickets to his father's show, A Night in Chinatown. Sid was happy to help them out.

'Fellows, I'll have four passes waiting in your name at the special entrance gate. You're as good as in. Just give them my name, and since you're bringing girls you want to impress, you've got to take them on the Panama Canal trip. It's the hit of the whole Exposition! I'll line up passes for that too so you won't have to stand in line all day. After you go through the special gate, come meet me at the Night in Chinatown show in the Zone. You can't miss it – just go to the noisiest place on the grounds with all the gongs and drums . . . and the dragons! Remember to introduce me to your girls. Did you say their father was Benjamin Morrison? He's my father's lawyer. Bet you didn't know that. Oh – you did . . . Well, I'll see you later.'

Because they were saving so much money not having to buy tickets, the boys ordered a taxicab in front of the Granada Hotel when they called for the girls that day. Their passes were waiting at the gate, and Ham and Lou felt quite important escorting Irene and Betty around the long lines of people and through the special entrance. The girls were even more impressed when they reached the Zone and A Night in Chinatown to find Sid Grauman waiting for them, his hair wildly flying in the Bay breeze.

'Lou, Ham . . . girls . . . I want you to meet an old pal of mine, a real San Franciscan who actually went through the quake and fire and lived to talk about it – and talk and talk . . .' Sid said as a small copy of Charlie Chaplin, complete with bamboo cane, floppy shoes, battered derby and rocking walk, came sauntering down the Zone Road toward them.

'Meet Mervyn LeRoy. His job is to drive the customers off the street and inside the show, then keep them from escaping. Merv, say something!'

There was only silence; then the little moustache pasted on the upper lip quivered and was followed by a hurt voice.

'Gee, Sid . . . You know Charlie Chaplin never talks! What are you trying to do, ruin my act?'

The boys all shook hands, then introduced the imitation Charlie to the two girls.

'You went through the earthquake and fire too,' Irene said to Mervyn. 'So did we.'

'We were very little girls then,' Betty quickly added.

'Say – we ought to start up a club,' Sid said to the three survivors. 'The "We Went Through the Earthquake and Fire Club." I'll bet you girls were just babies then. Merv here was already out selling papers, and I was working for my father at his Market Street Theater when it happened.'

'We weren't exactly babies . . . It was only nine years ago,' said Betty. 'I remember running out of the house with Daddy and Grossmutter and seeing all the bricks falling down and the big wide cracks opening up on the street right in front of our house. The noise it made! That's something I'll never forget . . . the deep rumbling from somewhere deep down in the earth. We ran all the way to the stable to get our carriage, and Daddy and some men hitched up the horse, who was as frightened as we were. He reared and whinnied, and we had a dreadful time getting to the ferryboats and we had to leave our beautiful horse standing there on the Embarcadero. I wonder what ever happened to him. For days we watched the city burning from across the Bay in Oakland. It was simply dreadful!'

'No matter how young you are, things like that stay in your memory all your life,' Irene added. 'But look at how beautiful San Francisco is now. All of that seems like a terrible dream we had long ago.'

Mervyn just couldn't keep quiet about his quake and fire days.

'You girls were lucky. My mom and I got stranded on the wrong side of Van Ness and couldn't get through the rubble to the Bay and catch a boat. We got picked up by an army wagon and they took us to the Presidio, where we lived in a tent for nearly two months before we could get back to where we used to live – only it had become a big pile of junk.'

'Hey, hold it! That's enough history for now!' said Sid, interrupting Mervyn in the middle of his story about life in a Presidio tent. 'You kids still have to take the Canal trip, and then you can come back here in time to see our Chinatown show. After that we all can adjourn to our Survivors' Club meeting down the Zone to that terrific new ride they call the Earthquake. It's the biggest shimmy in the world and should make all us old settlers feel right at home!'

Thanks to Sid, the foursome were taken around the long lines waiting in front of the Panama Canal trip and passed through a small side door to the embarkation area. They all climbed up a gangway leading to a double tier of seats mounted on a flag-draped flatcar set on railroad tracks. The four of them sat in the front row, and very soon all forty-six places were filled and the passengers were told to pick up the handsets hanging beside each seat. These were connected by long flexible tubes to forty-six Edison phonograph machines standing on a long low table that ran all the way down one side of the car. Five or six men dressed as sailors quickly moved down the line of phonographs, turning the crank on each to tighten the motor spring. Each needle was set precisely on a cue mark, which was the same on each record.

A brass band had been playing ever since they boarded the car, and now it blared out a triumphant blast of brass, then suddenly went dead silent. A loud ship's whistle sounded, and at that moment a long cord was pulled, starting the phonographs simultaneously. Each passenger, handset pressed to an ear, heard another brass band playing a scratchy fanfare as the big double doors in front slowly swung open and the flatcar moved forward on its tracks, pulled by a hidden cable. The music dropped in volume and then came the booming echolike voice of a man which became clearer as the noise of the opening doors stopped. The voice spoke into all forty-six ears, as though an unseen personal guide were sitting right there beside each and every one of them.

'Welcome aboard, Ladies and Gentlemen. You are now about to travel through the marvel of the age . . . the greatest feat of engineering in human history since the building of the pyramids! Welcome to the Panama Canal!' The car rolled out of the building, down a gently sloping ramp and on into an astounding five-acre model of the phenomenal passage between the Atlantic and Pacific Oceans. Although the real Panama Canal in far-off Central America, thousands of miles away, took more than eight and a half hours to traverse with everything going right, here in the Zone on San Francisco Bay this miraculous feat would take but twenty-three astounding minutes – which was exactly as long as the special-length phonographs ran. From Colón on the Caribbean side through three sets of double locks, Gatun Lake, the Gaillard Cut, past the Madden Dam, finally leaving the Canal near Balboa and coming out into the Pacific, the flatcar travelled in reduced scale over the very same path opened only the year before to the ships and commerce of the world.

Every detail had been reproduced in miniature and each passenger on the rolling platform received the exact same verbal description of whatever they all were seeing at that very moment. Along with the guiding voice they could also hear the sounds of the Canal itself: donkey engines chugging as they pulled their loads up the inclines, the gush and swirl of water entering or leaving the locks, crashing noises of metal as the massive gates opened and closed, and always the whistles, bells and shouting.

Ham was absolutely enraptured, not only by the blonde at his side with the handset pressed to her lovely ear, but also by the technical marvel that imparted so much information to so many people at the same time – plus the fact that it could all be done over and over again.

'This is terrific! We tried working out something in our theater with sound and a movie projector a while ago, but it was a terrible flop . . . nothing like this!' Ham said to the two girls, who were much too interested in the sights and sounds to hear half of what he was saying.

The twenty-three wonderful minutes seemed to have passed in twenty-three seconds and the sailors reboarded the car, politely asking the passengers to disembark. They then rewound the long line of phonographs, put different records on each machine and reset the needles on their cue marks so the seats now could be reversed and the car take on a new load for the return trip through the Canal, from Balboa to Colón. The brass band struck up a forgettable something called 'The Panama Canal March,' and Ham stood over on the side of the loading platform to watch the lucky new forty-six passengers climb aboard and take their seats. He looked over at the hundreds and hundreds more, patiently standing

131

in line outside awaiting their turn.

'Will you look at that, Lou? All those people with all that money to spend and you just have to give them something they've been told they want – even if it's not the real thing – and they fight to make you rich! Listen, compared to this and what it could mean, Hale's Tours were penny ante!'

All the way to *A Night in Chinatown* Ham kept turning to look back at the long lines of people standing outside the Canal ride, and he almost walked right into the side of a long and friendly dragon prancing down the main Zone street. Sid Grauman ran out to introduce them to his young Chinese friends dancing beneath the happy fearsome creature, and then he took them inside the big building decorated with colorful Oriental banners to enjoy the great entertainment. Irene and Betty screamed as firecrackers exploded while gongs clanged and drums boomed.

'Relax, everybody!' Sid shouted above the din. 'Relax and enjoy yourselves . . . We just got rid of the last evil spirit in San Francisco!'

They loved the show and the delicious Cantonese food that went with it. By now Ham considered himself an expert on food of the Far East. In between dropping one chopstick or the other and eating all he could of the wonderful things spread out on their table, he kept wondering how late the Western Union telegraph office on the Exposition grounds stayed open. If he was lucky and the timing was right, he could still get off a telegram tonight to Denver telling Maurie to drop everything and meet them here as soon as possible. It was important for him to see the tremendous entertainment possibilities when realistic sound was properly combined with action. This was no Bijou Dream stuff, and finding some way to use it with imagination and daring could earn them all more money than they'd ever need!

Suddenly Ham dropped both chopsticks and laughed in the middle of his chow mein. Lou and the girls looked at him as though he had gone crazy. Maybe he had – imagine sending your brother in Denver a telegram at midnight to rush right out to San Francisco and take a trip through the Panama Canal! Crazy, that's what it was – absolutely crazy!

CHAPTER THIRTEEN

World history is a succession of actions followed by reactions. The shooting of an archduke in Sarajevo brought about an ultimatum, turning a national tantrum into an international catastrophe. From the firing of a student's pistol in an obscure Balkan city came a reaction turning Europe into two sets of warring nations tearing at each other's throats. Much of great and lasting value was lost forever, as well as some things that perhaps meant little in the grand scheme of life.

European motion picture production then led the entire world and was one of the first casualties of war. No longer were the small round tins full of entertainment and enlightenment shipped to the markets of the world. The effect was soon felt in the new film exchange that had just opened in San Francisco. Even though they were thousands of miles and an ocean away from the bloodshed and carnage, so many of the films they had depended on receiving were not made or rested in sunken ships that the small venture in far-off California lost its battle for survival, closing its doors less than six months after it had opened. Just as film once meant life to the old Bijou Dream, shutting it down when the supply was cut off, so did hope become hopelessness, and the Robbins Brothers Film Exchange, San Francisco branch, was no more.

Ham and Lou still knew how to operate projection machines, and there was increased need for their skill with the expansion of movies into converted legitimate theaters and those built just to show films. Sid Grauman's father sent them with his highest recommendations to the New Phoenix Theater on the busiest part of Market Street, and before even a week had passed they were in charge of the projection booth.

Even though their time was no longer all their own, the boys still managed to get over to the Granada Hotel now and then to see Irene and Betty. Ham especially enjoyed the

133

company of the blonde girl, who was so different from anyone he had ever known. Ideas of pursuing the romance had to be put off for a while, though, as he and Lou had to give almost every evening to the New Phoenix, but they still managed to be with the girls a few times each week. Ham worked out something with one of the theater doormen, who passed both girls through whenever there was an especially good film being shown. Ham would knock on the big glass viewing port and Irene, seated in one of the last few rows of the balcony, would turn around and wave up at him. It certainly was no way to carry on an intimate relationship, and they both knew things had to improve. Meanwhile Ham and Lou loaded the projectors, checked the focus and threw the image from one machine to the other.

It was a firm rule of management that no women were ever allowed up in the projection room. This was reason enough for Ham and Lou to invite the girls up to see the place where they worked.

'Irene, you see that film . . . it's called nitrate and it's made of the same stuff they make nitroglycerin from. One spark and wham!'

He should never have told them that. The girls were terribly upset. They didn't want any more fires in San Francisco; the one they had seen nine years before would last them all their lives. Before they could talk too much about the danger of an explosion, Betty saw the toilet sitting all by itself in the open projection room. She blushed, and Lou kicked himself for not thinking of covering it with a coat. Well, it was a part of nature and of being a projectionist; you couldn't take any time away from the machine – even for nature.

The girls were enthralled with the two big projectors and how easily the boys got them to switch the picture from one to the other when a reel ended.

'See those ports and the window I looked through at you up in the balcony?' Ham said. 'Well, there are big metal fire shields that slide down to cover them if there should be a rise in the temperature in here. Trouble is, it will keep the fire from the auditorium – but unless we can get out in a hurry, our goose and the rest of us is cooked!' This did little to make the girls feel happy about the boys' jobs.

'Isn't there anything else you can do?' Irene asked Ham over the racket of the projectors. 'Maybe you both should produce pictures yourselves, since you've told us they aren't sending any more from Europe. Wouldn't that be a good idea?'

'Hey . . . that's not a bad idea at all . . . in fact, Lou and I were talking about it, and it sure would get us out of this firetrap . . . but for a while we have to keep working here until we put together enough money to do something else.' Ham was very pleased that Irene had thought of this, and it was true that both boys had let it cross their minds at an earlier time . . . but now perhaps they might really do something about it. Right now, though, they had to smuggle both girls out of the projection booth without having the manager or his assistant see them. First though, Ham wrapped both arms around Irene and gave her a big kiss. It was something she had expected and hoped would happen. Betty was looking through the big port window at the movie down on the screen, and as the lovers on the larger-than-life screen hugged and kissed each other, she saw the same scene being repeated in the reflection coming off the glass. She turned around, pulling Lou with her, and laughed.

'Hey – you two ought to be in pictures!'

Ham and Irene unclinched. Irene blushed furiously while Ham took a big bow.

The manager could hear the voices and laughter up in the booth, although he did not realize girls were there. He rapped on the metal door after his long climb and yelled, 'Shut up inside! They can hear you all the way to the Ferry Building!'

The girls stayed until the show ended, and when the theater was dark, Ham and Lou got them out through a side door and took them back to the Granada.

The days and nights went on. Reels and endless reels of film were threaded up, kept in focus and thrown over from one machine to the other. Both boys were getting sick of the monotonous job, working in the hot booth, sweating and filling themselves up with water from the jug sitting in the corner. When there was time and the urge hit them, as it was bound to nearly every half-hour, they could use the porcelain flush toilet set out in the open against the back wall, where it had embarrassed the girls during their visit. There was a hooded light hanging over the toilet, and many times Lou had to yell at Ham to get off the can and over to his projector so they could make a smooth throw-over at the end of one reel and the start of another. Looking up from his newspaper as he sat there cozy and comfortable, Ham shouted back, 'Lou,

135

can't you do it without me? I'm real busy. Just stand between the machines and reach over for both the dowser handles . . . and . . .'

His brother shouted back so loudly that the manager sighed and sent his assistant off on another long hike up to the balcony.

'Kid,' replied Lou above the noise of the projectors, 'if you think anybody can do that without help, you're fulla crap!'

'Why do you think I'm sitting here!' answered Ham in an equally loud voice as the assistant manager pounded on the door, pleading for some silence inside. He would have fired them both then and there, but good projectionists were hard to find. In spite of their noise and attitude, these fellows knew their business. If only they'd shut up now and then.

But day after day and night after night running the short one-reelers, then the two- and five-reel pictures, and the growing length and improvement in production were giving them new ideas. More and more they were positive they were stuck in the wrong end of the business. With no product to sell, distribution was out for now. The Exhibition was getting on their nerves: the noise, the monotony and being cooped up in a tiny room – and small pay for that. Ever since Irene had brought it out in the open when she was in the booth, they had kept thinking about production – the one part of the picture business they hadn't yet tried.

'Lou, there's a fellow in town we know, Billie Gibson, who works in that equipment rental office near our old film exchange. He can get us a camera and whatever else we'll need. Let's get out of this damn booth and make some movies ourselves that somebody else can sweat over showing to people. The money's going to be in production, not up in a place like this, jumping from one machine to another, then to the crapper, and finally staggering home when you can't keep your eyes open to focus the lens. There's got to be a better way to make a living. At least we'd be out in the open air and meet people!'

'I'm with you, Ham. Production is what we should get into, but don't you have to put together some kind of a story so you know what you're going to shoot? Maybe you're a writer, too. You sure have a way with words, the way you talked to Irene and Betty's father and grandmother. You're such a smooth talker, I'll bet you're a smooth writer, too . . . if you ever learn how to spell!'

Ham laughed as they switched machines and checked focus.

'Since when do you think most of the junk we run here was ever written down on paper? Look, we've both been out and watched movies being shot all around Golden Gate Park and even out at the Cliff House on the beach. It isn't all that tough. All we need is enough dough for film and a camera with somebody to work it and a few guys to help out . . . borrow a car and then convince some people they want to be in a movie . . . then we go to it!'

For a while they played it safe and held on to their projectionist jobs while taking their regular day off plus a few more using the alibi of a mutual illness. The manager was suspicious since they kept reporting sick together, but he managed to find replacements and the show went on, even though it was more out of focus than usual.

Since they were going to shoot their very first movie in San Francisco, they made use of the most obvious and picturesque prop in the whole city – the little cable cars climbing up and down the steep hills, crammed with residents on the way to and from work and tourists experiencing the very special thrill only this ride through the spectacular city could give them. Ham and Lou had some friends working in vaudeville down the street from the New Phoenix who were eager to see how they would look on a big screen, and they were willing to work a day or two for a free meal and the fun of it.

Early one morning, soon after the last of the fog had blown out to sea, a baggy-pants comic named Eddie Muldoon pursued a tall blonde girl from a parked car, almost catching up with her at the cable car stop. She was really his off-stage wife and worked with him in their outstanding acrobatic knockabout act at the Orpheum Vaudeville Theater. He ran after her from the curb to where the Powell Street cable car had come to a stop, and they both jumped aboard as it took off and was pulled up the hill. An open Reo automobile carrying a Pathé movie camera on a tied-down tripod pulled out of a side street and moved directly behind the climbing cable car.

Billie Gibson, another new friend of Ham and Lou's, stood up on the back flooring and leaned over to look through the camera viewfinder, with his hand resting on the crank. Right beside him stood the director himself, Ham Robbins, who was about to shout instructions at the two actors who had just climbed aboard the moving set. Lou was at the wheel and kept the Reo about fifteen feet behind the cable car as it swung up and over the first hill. The young cameraman worked downtown for a photographic equipment rental company and made extra money on the side from things 'borrowed' from his employer. The camera and tripod were quite unofficially out on this job. Now he started turning the crank and Ham shouted directions at the two actors, who worked just as hard here in the daylight as they did at night on the downtown Orpheum stage.

Eddie chased the girl from one side of the cable car to the other, then out onto the rear platform, just ahead of the pursuing Reo. The puzzled cable car gripman shouted at them to sit down and stop acting like a couple of lunatics. He was so busy clutching the massive cable grip handle, which passed down through the car into a slot between the tracks where it grabbed the moving cable, that he never looked back to see the automobile just behind with the strange black box on a tripod and the other lunatic turning a crank in its side. The gripman twisted his head around, clanged his bell in a weird tempo, not seeing the other madman standing in the rear of the automobile yelling insanely at the top of his voice at the idiots who were about to climb up the side ladder to the top of his car for God alone knew what reason! The gripman was used to bad days, but he knew this was going to be the worst!

Up front in the cable car the conductor heard the frenzied ringing of the bell and knew something must be terribly wrong. As soon as the car topped the hill the gripman released his handle, and they coasted to a stop as the brake blocks took hold. The Reo jammed to a stop just in time to avoid slamming into the rear of the cable car. The camera tipped forward and almost went through the windshield, but was saved by the young man with the crank, who wrapped his arms around it in a hug of desperation. The two actors jumped down from the car roof and ran over to the Reo, which sped around the stalled cable car, then down the hill, leaving the gripman and his conductor standing out in the street staring after them while the passengers craned their necks trying to see what was causing all this madness.

The crowded Reo drove on to the next stop, pulling up behind another unsuspecting cable car, which was taking on passengers. The actors again took places on the moving set, and the chase up and down the hills resumed, with the girl, who had grown up in a large family of tumblers and married an acrobat, climbing the side ladder up to the very top of the moving cable car, with the crazed pursuer grabbing at her while she hung on to the metal roof supports. Behind all this

138

melodrama on the cable car top was spread the magnificent scenery of San Francisco, its hills, picturesque buildings and the incomparable Bay, which would make this modest little chase movie a very big picture indeed!

The gripman on this car now heard the clattering feet above his head and leaned out as far as he could to see what was going on up on his roof. He could not see the two crazies being photographed by the camera in the automobile following and was utterly mystified. It couldn't be seagulls unless they were wearing heavy hobnail boots! He clanged his bell with a questioning note but got nothing in answer, so he kept leaning out as he hung on grimly to his grip lever. The camera kept on grinding as the couple went back and forth on the roof and the background scenery changed from uniquely beautiful to merely magnificent and the pedestrians they passed stood openmouthed on the sidewalks and looked at the scene in amazement. Some of the cable car passengers rose from their seats, aware something strange was happening, and tried to look up top. When one of them looked back and saw the camera following them in the Reo, they all began to wave their hands and shout.

'Hey! Take my picture, mister!'

'Wait till I comb my hair . . . I look a mess . . . Why didn't you let us know we were in the movies!'

'My God, don't make a picture of me . . . my wife thinks I'm in Milwaukee!'

It was fast, exciting stuff, but reasonably safe as the cable car was moving rather sedately, and only the extreme slant and pitch of the Powell-Hyde Line at this point made it appear dangerous.

A policeman stood on the corner as they passed Filbert Street and began the climb up the next hill. He blew on his whistle and began a footrace to catch up with the mad parade. The cable car, the lunatics on the roof and the automobile carrying a strange black box stuck on some sticks followed the car, and two very odd-looking grown men were standing up on the back seat waving their arms and yelling. It was obvious something illegal was going on that needed immediate police attention. He ran after them, legs working and whistle blasting, but, being quite overweight, out of condition from years of slow walking on his beat and pinching snacks from every food stand he passed, the policeman was no match for the procession. Soon he was left, red-faced and gasping, with hardly enough wind left to blow his whistle.

139

Finally the troubled cable car reached the end of its route at North Beach and came to a stop as the grip was lifted from the underground cable and the brakes took hold. They were only a few blocks from Fisherman's Wharf, and Eddie and his wife quickly came down from the roof. For a moment they were hidden by the Reo, which pulled around to pick them up and take off toward the Bay. After a few blocks they pulled into a side street, where Lou parked. They put the camera and tripod on the sidewalk and began filming a continuation of the chase with the sudden entry of a third character – the hero. Since all that was needed was a reasonably good-looking fleet-footed male, Ham cast himself in the role. The cameraman shouted when he had the crank turning, and the hero grabbed the girl out of the villain's lecherous arms and dashed off with her toward the Wharf with its crowds of tourists and tradespeople.

The first take came off badly when Ham tripped over a small mongrel dog yapping at his heels and sprawled in the street. The girl bounced into a beautiful, professionally executed somersault, came easily to her feet and took a bow, utterly forgetting she was not performing on the Orpheum stage. They did it all over again and this time got it right, and the cameraman stopped turning the crank.

Lou helped Ham, the cameraman and Eddie carry the camera on its tripod into the middle of the Wharf area itself for the rest of the action, and when the pursuing villain was finally sent spinning over the edge of the pier into four feet of muddy water, they stopped shooting just as Muldoon's head came up through the layer of filth and the last of the film ran through the camera. Eddie spat out a mouthful of mud and screamed at Ham, 'Who the hell is going to pay for my ruined suit!'

'Eddie, you were wonderful! That was a great fall you took – it'll make the picture!' Ham called down at him, pushing back some tourists who were watching the moving picture being shot and restraining a sailor who had stripped off his shirt and was about to dive in for a rescue attempt.

'Never mind, we're shooting a movie. He's supposed to go in the water. Thanks anyhow. Eddie – you were great!'

'Forget the flattery . . . get me out of this stinking filthy water. This is a crazy way to get a free lunch! Now get me something to dry off with, and keep this damn seaweed I found in my pocket. I'll send you my cleaning bill. Next time you want to shoot a movie with me I want to see some kind of a written story so I know what the hell's going to happen!'

Lou and Ham joined the actors and cameraman as they walked back to the Reo. Under his breath Ham said to the dripping Muldoon, 'If there is a next time, Eddie, I hope I know ahead myself what the hell's going to happen. Excuse me for pushing you into the Bay . . . I just got carried away.'

'Movies – the hell with them. Vaudeville's the only way to make it and keep your health! This is the last time I get talked into being a movie actor!' Eddie grumbled as he blew his wet nose in a soaked handkerchief. His wife started to give him a comforting kiss but pulled back when she got a whiff of the Bay mud plastering his hair.

'Billie,' Lou asked the cameraman as they headed back toward the Orpheum, 'can you get this film developed and a print made right away?'

'Sure, I'll take the reels in tonight with some other stuff we're handling for a paying customer. I've got some pals at the lab and they'll put your film through on his order number and nobody will catch on. Tomorrow I'll pick up the negatives and prints, and late tomorrow night we can run it at my office after everybody has gone home and you're through working. It's going to need assembly and editing as well as some titles, and I'll help you out. After all, this could mean a whole new career for me. I'm sick of working in an office.'

'Great – you're a real friend, and if this thing sells we'll make some more right away,' said Lou with a big grin. 'Ham, let's send a telegram to Maurie and tell him to start selling a two-reel comedy . . . with the title . . . maybe something like . . . *Cable Car Mabel* . . . or *Frisco Follies* or – '

'That's enough titles!' interrupted Ham. 'First let's see if it comes out and how it goes together. Then, if we're satisfied, we send the telegram and let Maurie start selling.'

They dropped the vaudeville pair off at their stage door, slipping each a five-dollar bill with expressions of thanks and gratitude and instructions to send them the dry cleaning bill. The next stop before returning the borrowed Reo was at the equipment rental office, where they smuggled the camera and tripod back inside before they were missed.

The Robbins Brothers had become Motion Picture Producers.

CHAPTER FOURTEEN

'Young man, will you please help us get these gentlemen out of their cars and over there on the sidewalk,' a parade controller called to Ham and Lou, who stood beside a building entrance on Steuart, just off Market Street.

'Sure, glad to help,' Ham replied for them both, and went over to reach up for the arm of an elderly GAR Civil War veteran who very slowly stepped down from the vehicle onto the street. The boys helped a dozen of the old men in blue from their cars to the sidewalk, where they joined the growing crowd of fellow veterans awaiting the signal for their next move.

Ham carried a small metal box that contained the two-reel comedy Billie had helped them edit and title late at night during the past two weeks. Now it was about to be screened for some very special people.

They both stood on the cobblestone street, and Ham turned to speak to some of the GAR men milling around them.

'What's going on, Pop? Seems like quite a meeting.'

'Sonny, don't you read the papers. It's all over the *Examiner* and *Chronicle* front pages. We're having a real big parade right up Market Street, with us boys in blue leading the way!'

Another old man standing next to them spoke up.

'They damn well better have some wagons waiting for us by Montgomery Street – or even sooner. I'm not as young as I was back when we marched through Georgia in '64!'

'Who the hell is?' laughed the first veteran as he lit a long stogie, inhaled deeply and blew a cloud of smoke into the air.

Lou remembered reading about the big Preparedness Day parade that had been organized here to rival a similar one held on Fifth Avenue in New York just a few weeks before. America was officially neutral in the great war sweeping over most of Europe, but just beneath the surface appearance of a nation at peace there were strong currents and

142

violent actions designed to bring the country to the very brink. Labor was mostly for an enforced peace, strongly against militarism and any use of the militia in strikebreaking. A great many manufacturers were firmly behind all-out preparation for war, or at least for the full support of the Allied Powers. German-Americans, many still loyal to the Vaterland, decried any aid at all to its enemy, and the Irish in America saw any gesture toward Britain as another link in a chain they were determined to shatter.

San Francisco, already sorely beset with labor problems and growing anger between workers and employers, swirled with turmoil. Only a few nights before there had been a great meeting of workers in the Dreamland Rink protesting this Preparedness Day as jingoistic war talk. Speakers swore to disrupt the parade should it ever take place.

The San Francisco press was divided, with the *Bulletin* taking the workers' side while the *Examiner* and *Chronicle* saw anarchists in the shadows lighting torches to burn down the country. Emma Goldman and other radicals had come to town, and William Randolph Hearst saw red. The Pacific Coast Defense League and the Chamber of Commerce pressed for the parade, and with the final choice of July 22, a hot and sultry Saturday, an appointed committee made its plans, strung up its flags and banners and put out the call for marchers, thousands of them. Most of those preparing to parade were from the business community – financiers, merchants, employers and white-collar workers.

The governor of California arranged for something urgent to keep him in Sacramento. Mayor James Rolph, 'Sunny Jim,' was neither sunny nor enthusiastic, but the people who mattered in his city put pressure on His Honor and Preparedness Day was properly proclaimed. The mayor wanted as little as possible to do with it and appointed one Thornwell Mullally, who eagerly pursued the job as Grand Marshal of the parade. Because he commanded a civilian 'cavalry troop,' he was considered eminently qualified as a parade organizer. A committee of leading citizens of the community was put in charge under Mullally's direction, and now the business of bringing it all together was done. The Day of Preparedness and Defiance had arrived!

There was not enough room on the Embarcadero for the marching units all to assemble and then swing onto Market Street, so the different groups were assigned assembly areas as near the parade route as possible. Steuart Street, one block from the Ferry Building, was one of these centers for the gathering marchers. Here too was the building, right in the middle of the block between Mission and Market, where Billie had made arrangements for Ham and Lou to screen their two-reel comedy for their special audience. Because it was a Saturday, he was able to promote the room and the projection machine for free, just so long as the boys would run it themselves. Now they both stood on the sidewalk, looked at their pocket watches, at the gathering crowds on the street awaiting their marching orders, and wondered what had become of Benjamin Morrison, Grossmutter Friedkin, Betty and Irene, who already were half an hour late. Ham was getting worried. He was very eager to impress the girls and their grandmother with the film, and had special reasons for showing it to Benjamin Morrison for a purpose he felt was crucial to their entire future.

'Lou, will they still let us in the building? We were supposed to meet the Morrisons here at quarter to one and it's almost one-fifteen now. What could have happened?'

'Don't worry, kid. All the parade traffic must have held them up. I wish I had remembered about it ahead of time so we could have made it later today. Say – I can see a taxi turning off Morrison coming this way. I'll bet they're in it!'

The cab drove slowly through the crowds of waiting marchers, swollen by new arrivals of Spanish-American War veterans in dark blue shirts and khaki pants. A contingent of Sons of the American Revolution wandered down the street to join the others waiting for orders. At least a hundred American flags waved from the groups, but strangely there were no bands, and not one military unit from the Presidio or the Navy appeared for the columns to form and move toward their places in the marching line already slowly passing by on Market Street. The GAR veterans realized they must hurry to take their place of honor at the head of the parade, and moved as fast as their aged legs could carry them.

'I'm sorry we're late, but it took forever to find a street where the police would let us cross Market,' Benjamin Morrison said, paying the cab fare. He took his mother-in-law's arm while Lou and Ham helped the two girls down, and they all walked toward the building entrance. For a moment they stood in the middle of the sidewalk looking at the Civil War veterans in formation, backs stiffened as much as age and arthritis allowed, marking time, then slowly moving up

144

Steuart Street. The other groups fell in behind them, all trying to look somewhat military as they joked and laughed, old comrades in arms on a rare, hot and sun-drenched summer afternoon in San Francisco. It would be a memory for them all to cherish.

The explosion hit their ears with a sound like sudden thunder. A shock wave followed, and they gasped with terror at the unknown dreadful thing that happened only a hundred yards up Steuart Street from where they stood. It was impossible to see very much as a great cloud of black smoke billowed up and over the heads of the marching men. A mounted policeman was smashed into by something hurled out of the smoke and thrown heavily from his rearing horse onto the cobblestone street.

'Are you all right?' Ham shouted to Irene and her family. They all were stunned and frightened but showed no signs of injury and stood on the sidewalk gaping at the scene, which was obscured by dense clouds of swirling black smoke.

'Get in that building entrance and stay there until we get back! Now don't leave there and don't be frightened . . . we'll be right back. Come on, Lou – let's see what's happened!'

The Morrison family stepped quickly into the lobby while the boys ran toward the dense spreading smoke up the street. There was a moment of eerie silence following the explosion, but now it was broken sharply by a loud scream of pain, then another and another. The policeman's horse stopped rearing and madly turned to race down the street, hooves clattering on the cobblestones. Ham tripped over a figure lying on the sidewalk and stopped to see what he could do. The smoke drifted away and for an instant he thought he was back in the locker of his father's butcher shop. A human body, stripped of most of its clothing and both its legs, was sprawled out and great streams of blood ran over the sidewalk, dripping into the gutter.

They walked on through scattered groups of stunned marchers, many of whom were moaning and holding their heads, some sitting on the ground or blindly crawling away from the center of destruction. The mounted policeman who had been so violently unhorsed sat in the street splashed from head to foot with blood from the torn body that had smashed him to the pavement and now lay beside him. He was dazed and unable to rise to his feet. More bodies were down on the sidewalk and out in the street or up against the building walls. More than a hundred confused and horror-struck people began moving forward to see if there was anything they could do. Ham saw a city ambulance farther down Steuart Street toward Mission, where it had stopped only a few minutes before the blast to pick up one of the GAR veterans who had suffered a sudden heart spasm.

Still holding tightly to his film case, Ham ran out into the middle of Steuart Street and violently waved at the driver, who started his motor and pulled up as close as possible. Lou ran forward and he and Ham helped the attendants pull out folded stretchers, which they opened and set down on the sidewalk. A few police came running from Market Street, pushed through the onlookers and tried to do something for the wounded. Some of the marchers were beyond any help, and the old man, already lying in the ambulance, would join them later that day. At least forty-five people, possibly fifty, were badly injured and lay sprawled out on the street and sidewalk up against the building. It was strange how silent it had become again after the first screams and moans died out.

A big man with a detective badge pinned on his lapel came running up to Ham and grabbed him around the neck. He was shouting loudly, 'Drop it! Drop it, you son of a bitch anarchist!'

'Drop what?' Ham managed to say, utterly confused and quite frightened. He thought he would be choked to death.

'Drop that bomb, God damn you! You're not going to kill more people . . . you filthy scum!' yelled the detective into Ham's ear, which still rang from the explosion a few moments before.

'It's film . . . moving picture film . . . We're running it for some people in a screening room here on Steuart Street!' Ham managed to say, though it was almost impossible to speak with the policeman's arm cutting off his breath. He was terribly scared and squirmed trying to see his brother, who came running from the curb and pried off the detective's arm.

'Let go, let go of him! It's only film . . . Here, open it up and see for yourself!' Lou screamed and looked around at the growing crowd surrounding the three of them, moving in closer, thinking the bombers had just been caught. He was sure they were about to be torn apart limb from limb.

More police came running to push back the crowd and hold both boys while the detective foolishly grabbed the metal case from Ham, set it down on the ground, unsnapped the

146

latches and swung up the top. Sure enough, two shining cans – but they could be filled with powder, shrapnel and fuses, so the detective boldly twisted the covers off both tins and pulled out the reels of film. He stood up holding them, unspooled enough to make sure it was indeed film and then jammed it all back in the tins, which he replaced in the box. He slammed down the lid and handed it back to Ham.

'Damn it, I bet the real bombers got away scot-free while we were wasting time on you with this crap! I'm sorry I choked you . . . but, hell . . . look at what's just happened! Can't blame anybody for suspecting what you're carrying could be another bomb . . . Now get moving!'

They moved as fast as they could, looking back over their shoulders at the bodies still scattered in the street. Another ambulance pulled, and several open trucks came over from the Embarcadero to pick up the injured and begin the race to nearby Harbor Emergency Hospital, which quickly filled up with victims and the doctors trying to save them.

The last body Ham remembered seeing in the street was that of the old veteran who had marched with Sherman through Georgia. He lay sprawled out on his back, a widening pool of blood flowing from his shattered head. The cigar had fallen from his mouth but remained lit, and its tiny column of smoke rose to become part of the dirty cloud left by the terrible explosion. Later they would learn that the shrapnel-loaded bomb had killed nine marchers outright and gravely injured more than forty others.

Lou and Ham reached the Morrisons, who still stood in front of the building where they had left them.

'Boys,' said Benjamin Morrison, 'we had better see your film some other time. Come, let's try to find a taxi and get away from here and back to our hotel.'

They walked over to Mission Street and several blocks more to Folsom, where a cab finally stopped for them. The parade was still going up Market Street in spite of the bombing, so they had to drive several miles out of their way before reaching the Granada Hotel, where the girls' father invited them inside. They all felt deeply depressed from the horrible sights they had just seen and the dreadful mystery of it all. Ham felt a special, personal depression. Now he would have to wait some more to run their film for Benjamin Morrison – and he really had counted on his seeing it right away. A lot of hopes and plans were riding on that little comedy. Why in hell did those goddamn bombers pick that place and time to blow up the parade? What rotten luck!

'Who would do such a horrible thing to those poor people?' the Grossmutter said. '*Schrecklich! Schrecklich!*'

They all were still quite shaken, but Benjamin insisted they have some coffee, light pastry and conversation. It would do them good to speak of something else. He had gotten to know these two young men fairly well during the months they had been taking his daughters out, and he especially enjoyed the brash younger one. The older, more serious Lou impressed him too, but in a different way. This business they were thinking of getting into – he wanted to know more about it, much more.

'We can see your comedy another day. I know we all agree today is not a good day to laugh, but I do want to learn something about this movie production business you believe has such a good future.'

Lou brightened and spoke first.

'It's a really new kind of entertainment for the masses, maybe much more than that . . . like a way to educate lots of people and to communicate ideas besides just making them laugh and cry. Of course right now lots of it is terrible stuff and doesn't do a thing for anybody except – '

Ham interrupted him.

'Except make lots of money for whoever gets in early and stays with it – at least that's what we think. People want to be entertained . . . education I'm not too sure about . . . Look, we just saw something terrible on Market Street. The whole world is full of things like that. The war in Europe . . . people getting killed, families torn apart. All you read in the papers is bad news . . . So maybe it *is* an escape thing, but people have to get away from the real world now and then or a whole lot more of them would go crazy! Movies are one of those escapes. Maybe one day it will change, but right now that's how it is. This little two-reel comedy we shot in only one day should earn what it cost and be into good profits very soon. It's a start, and this could be a great business and earn plenty for anybody in it!' Ham was really wound up, surprising even Lou with all the words he poured out.

Benjamin Morrison too was greatly impressed, and as attorney and advisor for several successful San Francisco businessmen, he had watched new ventures take root, grow and prosper. He felt he well might be present at the birth of yet another enterprise that deserved support. With bright young men like these two, it stood a good chance of success.

148

He sat and listened as they explained to him how films were made and distributed. The problems of the exchanges in dealing with theater owners and the complex and unsatisfactory manner of collecting payments for showings were gone into briefly, all the devices where cheating was a way of life – the bicycling of prints, overcharges, holding back receipts and the lack of an honest customer count in the rare event that a percentage of the profits was involved. Both boys had ideas for surmounting some of these problems and would go into them later.

The power of the old Film Trust had just about vanished, thanks to Carl Laemmle and others like him, but still this film business had crazy problems. Very gradually the sprawling, unorganized, impossible combination of creativity and commerce was learning how to crawl, and soon it would rise up to its feet, stride forward and then run. Now was the time to get into it, and the production and distribution end was the most vital and could be the most profitable.

'There is something, though, we have to discuss,' Lou said. 'San Francisco is a wonderful city and the scenery is like nothing in the whole world, but for too many days of the year the fog or the rain makes it absolutely impossible to shoot very much out-of-doors. Going indoors to get out of the weather is too expensive for anybody getting started, what with the lighting and the sets you have to put up. We need sunshine and dependable weather so we can shoot films outside nearly all year long. Where we find that place is where we should set up production.'

'I've lived all my life in this city,' said Benjamin. 'For years anybody who is a real San Franciscan has had contempt for that other city, the one down in Southern California ... but ... '

'That's it! That's just the place I was going to talk about. That's where we have to go!' said Ham with excitement rising in his voice. 'There already are a bunch of picture makers down there and they've been shooting movies with hardly any problems ever since *The Squaw Man* was made nearly five years ago by De Mille and Sam Goldfish . . . I think he changed it to Goldwyn, for which I can't blame him . . . Los Angeles – that's the place where we have to go!'

'Don't forget Jesse Lasky,' Benjamin said. 'He's a very old friend of mine. We have had business dealings together here, and I have great faith in anything he undertakes. The others, his partners, De Mille and Goldwyn, I really don't know, but I

149

have great confidence in Jesse and trust him to make sound decisions.'

Irene and Betty sat wide-eyed and silent listening to all this. Irene's eyes never left Ham's face, and now and then he looked over at her and smiled. He wanted very much to impress this girl and to be alone with her instead of always with a crowd of people or the family. The Grossmutter sat stiff and Germanic, drinking strong coffee, keeping sharp eyes on her girls. Deep under her breath, heard only by herself, she muttered a very small '*Ach!*' She still was not at all certain she approved of these two young men, but had to admit they were bright and possibly might amount to something. Closing her eyes for a moment, she saw again in her mind the terrible sights they had just left on lower Market Street. She shuddered, and Irene reached over to take her hand. Ham looked down to see Irene's other hand resting by her side and quietly reached over to hold it as he and Lou went on talking with her father. At the touch of her hand he felt a warmth and excitement he could not define, and knew he wanted to hold it as long and as often as he could.

'Put together some cost estimates for me to show to certain of my clients. Find out about what it would cost you to go down to Los Angeles and learn all you can about production there and what films of various lengths are being made for the market. I'll give you a letter of introduction to Jesse Lasky, who I'm sure will give you whatever information he can to help you get started. Locate a temporary office and put together a budget for employees, any equipment you buy or rent and whatever else is required – the barest minimum, of course, to get under way. Before you leave we will sit down again and discuss more details and see how I can help you. I have money I might risk in such a venture, and several of my clients often come to me for investment advice. They all are looking for something out of the ordinary where they can earn a decent profit. This business of producing movies is anything but ordinary, I must say . . . extraordinary is more like it. I know they will be very interested. Next week please arrange another screening of your comedy for me and some people I will invite. Of course, there is always a risk in anything, and this could be money down the drain – but then, nothing ventured . . . '

'Nothing gained!' responded the boys in unison, and they all laughed at the unexpected choral effect. For a few moments they had forgotten the deep depression that had gripped them ever since leaving lower Market Street over an hour before. Ham especially felt a weight lifted from his shoulders and thought they had done a good job of properly impressing Benjamin Morrison, even though he had not yet viewed their little film. Another day, another screening – and this time, heaven willing, no bombs!

Ham leaned over toward Irene, whose hand he still held tightly, and whispered, 'Will you go out with me tomorrow, maybe a ride through Golden Gate Park?'

Irene had been listening to the conversation about making films in another city and realized that Ham might be leaving her soon. Suddenly she felt quite upset.

'Yes – yes . . . I want to be with you,' came her whispered reply, and she tightened her hold on his hand. She tried to conceal her emotions from Grossmutter Friedkin, but the old lady could easily read her face and was not pleased with the message she saw written there.

The boys left the hotel and were bumped into by several men rushing through the doors carrying stacks of newspaper extras. Great black and red headlines covered the front pages: ANARCHISTS BOMB PARADE! . . . MURDER ON MARKET STREET! . . . BLOOD IN THE STREETS . . . There were tightly packed columns describing the carnage in detail, with maps pinpointing the dreadful affair. Lou bought a copy of each paper, and they walked the blocks back to their rooming house reliving those terrible moments. Now San Francisco had something besides the earthquake and fire and the Exposition to talk about. Another tragedy, smaller perhaps than the disaster of nine years before, but certainly packed with almost equal drama and terror. Soon the newspapers would carry two names in their headlines and stories and the whole country would be asking if Tom Mooney and Warren K. Billings had indeed been at Market and Steuart on the hot sultry Saturday afternoon of July 22, 1916 . . . and if they had thrown the terrible bomb. It was something else that would divide the nation, but that would be in the future. Now the two young men folded their papers and went into their rooms. They had work to do, figures to put on paper, people to call upon in theaters, exchanges, laboratories and wherever there was information to get them moving into a new and exciting future.

Ham sat by the open window looking out at the lovely city as the sun began to set in a beautiful summer sky, entirely free of its usual fog.

'Damn it, Lou. Why can't the San Francisco weather be like this all the time! Los Angeles is nothing but a cow town and – '

'Turn it off, kid. We've got loads of work ahead of us. Stop mooning out the window. Now to get started – just how much real money did we lay out shooting that cable car comedy and how much did we learn doing that to cut corners the next time?'

They worked over their figures, now and then stopping to listen to the loud bells and horns of the police cars wildly careening up and down the steep hills of the city seeking anarchists, murderers and bomb throwers.

It was going to be a long and noisy night.

CHAPTER FIFTEEN

'Lou, is twenty years old too young to get married? I mean, when you're just getting started in something new, wouldn't it take your mind off the things you were planning?'

His brother looked across the table, pushed aside the papers on which they were working and reached over to slap Ham on the shoulder.

'Kid, don't tell me you're that serious about Irene! Hell, if you really love a girl then twenty or anything older is all right . . . but do you think you can afford marriage? I know you've saved up some money, but have you any idea what it costs to have your own family? I bet you'll both want children, and they don't come cheap . . . But really, the only person who can answer questions like that is you!'

'Lou, you know me. I've been around a lot of girls. Irene is something special . . . and, look, her father likes me . . . and you, too. If everything goes the way we hope, he and the men he talked about may finance us in producing pictures down in Los Angeles. Look how much more he would want to help out his son-in-law!'

Ham was not a complete mystery to Lou, but right now he wondered if he really knew his brother.

'Don't get involved if all you are thinking of is using somebody. All right . . . if it's love and you really are serious about the girl, marry her if she'll have you. But if what you're only thinking about is getting a meal ticket from her old man . . . well, that's not an honest reason at all.'

Ham gave him no answer.

The boys had been working nearly all night, and now the dim light over the hills showed the coming of another day. Their figures were not complete and more information would have to come from friends on Film Row and at the laboratory, but they both were much too tired to go any further now.

'I'm going to sleep a few hours,' said Ham in between yawns. 'I have a date with Irene around noon. We're going to

153

Golden Gate Park and she's fixing a picnic lunch. I'm borrowing a car from Sid Grauman, and maybe she and I can have a talk about something else besides making movies.'

'You mean you'll have a talk about making a move, is that it?' said Lou, still not certain he was judging his brother fairly, but feeling uneasy at the thoughts passing through his mind. He liked Irene and hoped that Ham would not do anything that someday might hurt them both. 'You'll be twenty-one soon and you should be able to make up your own mind about serious things like this. Now let's get some sleep. I'll set the alarm so you can make it over to the Granada in plenty of time. I hope you're thinking clearly when you dig into that picnic lunch she's fixing.'

The alarm jangled Ham awake at eleven-thirty, and he thought only ten minutes had passed since he dropped off to sleep. Lou still lay on his back, snoring lightly, and Ham got up, washed, shaved and dressed. He caught the nearest cable car, which let him off near the garage where he picked up Sid's automobile, then drove to the Granada Hotel. He entered the lobby just as Irene stepped out of the elevator followed by a bellboy carrying a large wicker basket. Ham crossed the room and looked at Irene, then at the basket, which he was sure held enough food for ten people.

'My gosh, is that all for us? You shouldn't have gone to such trouble just for a little picnic!'

Irene put out her hands, which Ham grasped, and he almost leaned forward to kiss her on the cheek, but for some reason never completed the move. Maybe later on when they were alone. He stepped back to look at Irene. She wore a big Italian straw hat of dark blue set back on her head to show a lovely oval-shaped face surrounded by a sweep of blonde hair that fell below her shoulders. Her white lace-trimmed dress was just short enough to let Ham appreciate her long smooth legs. Irene blushed slightly as she saw his eyes roaming from her face downward, but this was how boys were supposed to act – at least that's what it said in the books she kept hidden from Grossmutter. This afternoon would be much better than any book, she was sure.

'You look lovely, Irene. I'm so glad you accepted my invitation. I've looked forward to this, and Sid loaned me his auto so we can ride with the top down and enjoy the sunshine. Come on, our picnic starts when we get in the car!'

Ham dug up some change to tip the bellboy, who set the big basket down on the car floor in back, then they drove out of

154

California Street as he followed Irene's instructions until they could see the Presidio South Gate off to their right. Now they turned south and soon entered Golden Gate Park, a great green island set down in the middle of the city. When they reached a beautiful meadow, Irene told Ham to park the car under some trees. He picked up the basket and a folded blanket that Sid had thoughtfully left on the backseat, and they walked arm in arm over the lush grass to the gently sloping bank of Lloyd Lake, set like a piece of blue glass against the background of tall slender trees. It seemed impossible they were in the midst of a bustling city and not far off in some enchanted countryside. Irene had been here before and pointed out something across the small body of water.

'Do you see those marble columns and the stairs standing there all alone? They're called "Portals of the Past." Betty and I always come here with the family when we have a picnic. It's my favorite place in the whole park. They were brought here from the ruins of a lovely old house that was destroyed in the fire, and I think there's a sadness and beauty the way they reflect in the lake.'

'I really don't go for ruins myself – but that's a lovely one all right. I remember the ruin that happened to us when our Bijou Dream burned to the ground. That wasn't beautiful at all . . . plenty sad, though. Did I tell you how the nitrate film caught fire and what it did?'

'Yes, but you never did tell me what "Bijou Dream" meant. Was it something special?'

'Very special,' he said softly. 'It was only a nickelodeon . . . but it was ours. It meant something like "A Dream of Jewels," and it looked beautiful painted in gold with a bright blue background. It made a terrible ruin, though, nothing like those columns and stairs over there.'

He leaned over closer to Irene, put both arms around her body to draw her face closer to his. She had been waiting for this to happen and returned his kiss. Their first kiss was followed by another, even more passionate, and led to a third, which was even better.

'Wow! I'm not nitrate film – but you could sure make me explode!' burst from Ham when they pulled apart.

'Can't you ever think about anything except film?' Irene said, laughing and thinking of something herself that could never have been threaded up on a projection machine.

Ham sat back on the blanket and looked over at Irene. He

knew this was quite different from all the casual relationships he had had with girls over the past few months. What happened in Denver seemed a short lifetime ago, and while it was fun, this was different – very different. Yet there was a thought he could not get out of his mind. Lou had accused him of possibly using Irene to get closer to her father and Ham had been outraged by the idea, but now he wondered. It wasn't that he didn't care about Irene. He knew she felt close to him, and if maybe her father could help him . . . well, why not?

That old-fashioned idea of having a matchmaker set up financial arrangements the way they did when Poppa was a boy wasn't such a bad idea after all. Ham smiled at the thought of saving the matchmaker's fee since he was picking the bride himself! Another penny saved. He had given little thought to marriage until a month ago, when Maurice wrote from Harrisburg, where he had stopped off to visit the family on his way to New York and a new job. Suddenly Maurie again met, and this time fell in love with, Rose Kravetz, the pharmacist's daughter. Within a few weeks Lou and Ham had a sister-in-law. Now Maurie was a family man and working for a new film company called Famous Players, set up by the very same Adolph Zukor they had met when they were with Hale's Tours. Maurie went by to visit him, and the job quickly followed.

He kept writing with such pleasure about the joys and security of married life that he put his younger brother in a very receptive frame of mind. Irene was worried that some of the people passing on Transverse Drive might see them doing more than just having a picnic on the grass, but Ham grew more relaxed, and whenever she tried to say anything, he put an arm around her and shut off all objections with another kiss.

'Irene, why do you think they put Golden Gate Park where they did? It's here for people to do what we're doing . . . only I'll bet none of them ever had such wonderful roast beef sandwiches and chocolate cake eight inches thick while they were doing it. Did you make it yourself?'

She could boil wonderful water and burn beautiful toast, but kept that secret to herself and evaded a direct reply.

'Well, I did have a little help. I'm glad you liked everything, and I hope we can come here soon again . . . but if you go down to Los Angeles I'm afraid that can't be very often. I'm really going to miss you.'

He looked into her eyes, was silent for a moment, then took the plunge.

'Irene, listen . . . Why don't you come to Los Angeles with me? I mean, let's get married here before Lou and I leave San Francisco.' Now that he had said it, he couldn't help thinking about all the girls he hadn't met, but he had made his decision and that was that. Irene confirmed it for him before he could say another word.

'Yes – yes, Ham. I love you and I've been hoping you would ask me. Yes . . . I do want to marry you!' She threw her arms around him and covered his lips with hers.

They finally broke apart and caught their breath, and Ham sat back on the blanket. Now that he had said what had been far back in his mind, he pushed aside any second thoughts and began to think more clearly.

'Irene, you know we'll be leaving San Francisco and going down to Los Angeles. It means leaving all your family and making a new home down there with me . . . and I'm just starting out with Lou in this movie production business. It's going to be a tremendous change for you. Are you sure . . .'

'Of course I'm sure, Ham. I love you and I want to be with you wherever you are. That movie business sounds exciting. I know you'll do well making pictures, and I want to be there with you. I'm excited about the change and I love you!'

She pulled him close again and they kissed until they ran out of breath and had to come up for air.

'After going through the earthquake and fire here I am positive I could go through anything anywhere! Even Los Angeles and that movie business should be exciting, and with us there together – and maybe somebody else later on . . .'

Ham stopped whatever it was Irene was about to say. Somebody else later on! He swallowed and drew a deep breath. Well, why not? It would be another responsibility – but hell, why not. Then he heard a tiny voice deep inside saying 'Why?' and he wondered if he had thought this thing all the way through before he opened his big mouth. Too late now . . . it was done . . . he had asked her and she had answered, so he lost himself with her in another long kiss.

Irene no longer cared what people on Transverse Drive might be thinking of the young couple kissing and hugging on the blanket down by Lloyd Lake. Picnics are for acting the way people act at picnics, so who cares!

Ham suddenly remembered something and reached for his watch.

'I told Lou I'd be at the theater by four o'clock to help him. I'd rather stay here all day with you – but I promised him, so we'll have to hurry.'

They walked back across the soft carpet of meadow grass, stopping a moment to look back at the Portals of the Past, which still made a lovely reflected picture in the changing light.

'Someday we'll have to come back here. This just became my favorite part of Golden Gate Park too,' Ham said, and then they reached the car and left the park.

My God! he thought as they drove over to California Street. I've done it . . . I've done it! Now it was going to be up to her father to show how much he believed in a bright young man . . . his future son-in-law.

All the way back to the Granada Hotel, Irene held tightly to Ham's arm. She was bursting with excitement and could hardly wait to break the news to Betty and her father and grandmother.

'Maybe I should go in with you. Don't I have to ask your father's permission to marry you or something?'

'Don't be foolish. He's not that old-fashioned . . . but Grossmutter will be quite shocked. Don't mind her, though, she's really a dear, and she may say "Ach!" a few times, but that's all.'

Ham hoped it would be this simple. He wondered if his future father-in-law would approve. Perhaps if he delayed things now and had time to talk alone with Mr. Morrison. ·

'Don't you think maybe we ought to wait a few days before we tell them? Lou and I are quitting the theater job next week and haven't given them notice yet.' He had already taken the first step, and as they came closer to the hotel he became even more pleased with his proposal and what it could mean to his future, but he still wanted her father's blessing.

Irene seemed not to hear him. 'If we're going to be married here, I know my father will want the rabbi who married him and my mother,' she rambled on. 'He's a wonderful person and Betty and I both love him . . . you'll meet him soon and I know you'll like each other. Meantime there are so many plans to make for the wedding and –'

'Here we are,' Ham said as they pulled up in front of the Granada Hotel. 'I'll leave you off and come by later and then we can –'

'Oh, no. Come in with me right now and let's tell the family. Why keep it from them? You can be late for work. It won't even matter soon. Anyhow, Lou will be there, and he should be able to take care of everything.'

Ham only hoped Lou could take care of things. He could imagine him trying to operate both projectors and throw over from one to the other all by himself. Oh, well, they would be through with that miserable job soon enough. He did wish, though, that Lou were here with him right now to help handle the announcement to Irene's family, but it was something he had gotten into all by himself and he certainly could handle it – he hoped. There was just too much at stake to let either the opportunity or the girl get away. He left the car with the doorman and arm in arm they entered the hotel.

Rabbi Jacob Nieto had left instructions that he was not to be disturbed. An outspoken defender of human rights, especially those now of Tom Mooney and Warren K. Billings, the two radicals arrested as prime suspects in the Preparedness Day bombing, Rabbi Nieto believed the evidence against them was completely rigged and fraudulent. His opinion was shared by other community leaders, including Rudolph Spreckels, the banker, Fremont Older, editor of the *Bulletin*, and many who were positive the accused men were victims of hysteria and the vigilante thinking of repressive anti-labor forces. Whoever spoke on behalf of the accused men at once became the target of violent abuse in the *Examiner* and the *Chronicle*. Their mail was filled with obscenities, threats of mayhem and murder. While they all agreed the bombing was utterly senseless and indefensible, the police and prosecutors' apparently random choice of Mooney and Billings seemed just as criminal in its perversion of justice and the persecution of innocent men. A very tragic event was being used as a convenient device to bludgeon the rising influence of labor, and these two jailed men became their convenient scapegoats.

Because they had defied the power structure and most of the press, these few courageous men, Spreckels, Older and Rabbi Nieto, were attacked daily as defenders of destruction and apologists for anarchy. The rabbi certainly wanted no visitors this day as he sat alone in his large study preparing a sermon for the coming Sabbath. He looked up in annoyance as his assistant opened the door.

'Rabbi, please excuse me. Mr. Benjamin Morrison wants to speak with you about the wedding of his daughter. Since it was about something pleasant, I felt you wouldn't mind if I brought him to your office.'

'Send him in, by all means send him in! An old friend I can always see! Such a relief to talk about something besides that damnable bombing. A wedding . . . Ah – a serious matter – but a most happy one!'

The door again swung open and Benjamin Morrison strode into the room to embrace his old friend, who came across the room to meet him.

'Rabbi, how good to see you. I must say, I've been reading about you nearly every day. A miserable business the way Hearst and the *Chronicle* tear apart everybody who disagrees with them. Freedom of the press indeed! It's freedom for one point of view and the crushing of all others! Oh – did you know that my family and I were actually on Steuart Street that day and saw the bomb go off? It was dreadful, simply dreadful!'

The older man sighed deeply and shook his head.

'Ah, Ben, so much hatred and abuse of power and shedding of innocent blood,' said the rabbi. 'Yes, my name does seem to be in the papers much more than usual, and my cries for justice have made me many enemies. I am afraid the press is only a mirror of our mixed-up unhappy world. I despair every time I read the outbursts from either side. All these centuries of pain and suffering to build some kind of moral structure so mankind perhaps may live in peace, then we tear it all down. It seems all so futile, Ben. Let's speak of happier things. Your daughter, I've just been told, is to be married. *Mazel tov!* Now tell me more about the bride and her young man.'

'Irene, my younger girl, met this Hamilton Robbins about six or seven months ago,' said the attorney. 'A very bright and personable young fellow who no doubt will succeed in whatever he undertakes. Ham and his brother Lou have been here in San Francisco the better part of a year running their own film exchange and are now working as projection machine operators at the New Phoenix Theater. They are ambitious to get into the production end of the business. I saw a little comedy they made and recently ran for me, and I must say it was quite good. They feel there is an excellent future in this new business, and I agree with them from all I have read and heard. It is modern, exciting and could become quite profitable. I have even advised several clients to join with me as investors in a new company I am forming for them. Movies – er, motion pictures, I believe is the more acceptable term – should grow and expand, and they plan to produce films to meet this expected need.'

The rabbi's smile vanished into his beard.

'Those dreadful motion pictures! Yes, I have seen a few of them on Market Street and elsewhere, once even in their New Phoenix. They all seem to be aimed at the intellectual level of a chimpanzee! I hope and pray your young men will raise their sights and produce something fit for more educated and moral audiences. You have no idea the way those brutish audiences laughed at people on the screen being struck in their faces with cream pies, shot dead by desperadoes and assaulted by the most incredible villains! I certainly enjoy a good laugh, but I have serious doubts about anybody who finds humor in violence and pain done to others. See how this fits in with those newspapers howling for blood in appealing to the basest emotions! The terrible war ravaging Europe right now reflects that same lust for violence carried to its ultimate horror. I hope, Ben, you will exert some influence on your new son-in-law to employ these movies for a better purpose.'

'Jacob,' the visitor said to his friend, 'I can try, but I think the only thing interesting Hamilton – er, Ham – and his brothers for a while will be to get established and make money in this new business. Unfortunately, they must attract the kind of people who pay to see what you deplore. Let's hope one day it will change – but I fear the movie screen, just like those newspapers, is only another mirror of our crazy world. Meantime, Rabbi, we have a wedding to plan!'

'I still am curious,' said the older man, not changing the subject. 'What kind of person enters this moving picture business? I want to know because I believe one day it will have a tremendous influence over the way people think and act. It would be good to have some idea who may choose the direction it will take.'

Morrison thought a few moments before replying.

'Rabbi, as I told you, for a while I think the only thing interesting them and everyone in this business will be to survive with enough profit to produce more films. Ham Robbins has shown me he is bright, smart and resourceful. He is very likable, and he loves being the center of a group, especially if he can make them laugh. Our sad world can always use a laugh, but sometimes I feel he lacks an appreciation for the feelings of those who may be the targets of his humor – or wit. Perhaps that is the penalty one pays for seeking approval at any cost. He is still young, and only time will tell if he has been given the gift of compassion, something that comes only with maturity.'

161

'Ben, did you ever think of becoming a rabbi instead of a lawyer?'

'Certainly – but I prefer working with one person at a time instead of a whole congregation. About Ham, already I sense some of his methods will not meet with my approval, and I only hope he listens to me those times I may disagree with him. In this strange and fascinating business he and his brothers have entered, there seems to be another kind of morality that says, "If it works – it's right!" ' He paused, smiled at a thought and then continued, 'You know, Jacob, that's the case sometimes in my own profession too, and in most everything else these days. You see, my friend, I want the best for my girl, so perhaps I pick out every real or imagined flaw I see in the man she plans to marry. I must say, though, it is rather appealing how eager he is to be liked by everybody, but isn't there much more to a relationship than just being liked? I keep wondering if he isn't an opportunist who has cleverly maneuvered me into helping finance their venture. This, though, I am quite willing to do, because soon he will be family. So the boy is an opportunist, but that's no crime, now is it, Jacob?'

'Ben, we rabbis are always being asked questions like that, which can be answered a hundred different ways – so we really sound very wise and clever. It is man's nature to improve his condition whenever possible. Of course there is honest ambition, and then there is something we call opportunism – moving ahead at the expense of others without thought for their rights or feelings. The difference again touches something of which you spoke before – compassion. All of us are opportunists in one way or another. That's how we change our condition and move through life toward what we perceive as better things.' The rabbi paused, cleared his throat and continued. 'Now see here, Ben, he's not even married to your daughter yet – and already you're steering their lives! Let them find their own course. I know it is hard to see your child leave the nest, but they must live their own lives, and for them it begins with their wedding. Let us discuss that and put other things aside. Now just what kind of a wedding did you and your daughter have in mind . . . the full temple spectacular with a mob of ushers, bridesmaids and relatives with guests and enough flowers for the funeral of every member of the congregation – or did you have in mind something more refined and civilized? An intimate family affair right here in my study?'

The father of the bride thought a minute before speaking.

'Except for his brother, none of his family can be here for the ceremony. The father works and neither he nor the mother can leave. The older brother is just getting established in New York, and his two sisters must remain with the parents, so it seems we should have the intimate rabbi's-study wedding. I've had the pleasure of attending so many here, and I remember my very own you performed in this same room, Jacob. You have the gift to make it seem like a crowded temple during the high holidays. Let's have it right here. My daughter will agree, I am sure. She seems a little nervous anyhow about a big wedding. This way I can take all the money I might have spent on one of your "full temple spectaculars" with ushers, bridesmaids, flowers and all the relatives and friends and make a gift to the two young people to help them get a start. Thank you, Rabbi, for the appropriate advice I was positive you would give me!'

It was a very small and private ceremony held in Rabbi Nieto's study. The old man remembered the sadness at the funeral of the young mother of the lovely bride who now stood here before him. It had been so long ago, not really as years were counted, but so much had happened. The two little motherless girls had grown into lovely women. As for the groom and his brother, he knew only what Benjamin Morrison had told him. They seemed fine enough young men from what he could see at this meeting, though the style of their clothing and certain of the groom's mannerisms struck him as being a bit . . . well, *garish* was the best word he could think of. Something like this new moving picture business they were in. That was the word – garish – but as Ben had said, it held great promise, and perhaps so did this young man and his brother, the best man. Outer wrappings are not all that important, the rabbi mused. He hoped this girl he had known since she was an infant would find joy and a long and happy life with the man to whom he now joined her in holy wedlock according to the ancient rituals.

Ham stood up straight in his new dark suit and fought to keep the serious look on his face. Irene and her sister were on one side and Lou was on the other. The service seemed to go on and on, but he knew he could hold back his smile until it was ended. There was a tightening of muscles, tension crept up his back and his mind would not stay in this room. It had been a long time since Ham had been in a house of worship.

What free time he had before meeting Irene seemed to have been spent in other kinds of houses, including, of course, moving picture theaters. Now this ceremony was about to change the whole pattern of his life, but he scarcely heard the soft voice of the rabbi. He forced his eyes to focus and ears to listen, for an instant hearing the familiar Hebrew words he scarcely understood. He wondered if this old man with his impressive beard would go on with the wedding if he knew what thoughts were running through the groom's mind. Deep down, where he could not put it into words even to himself, he was certain that what he wanted was much more than this pretty blonde girl who stood beside him. It had to do with becoming part of a new family, a new life, in which he would be helped to reach goals he could now only imagine, and one day having the power to make everything happen his way.

'*Lieber Gott!* Did he have to make such a noise!' Grossmutter Friedkin said to Benjamin as the young groom's heel smashed down on the wineglass and Rabbi Nieto pronounced Irene and Hamilton Robbins man and wife.

A telegram from Poppa, Momma and the girls was waiting at the Granada Hotel. Ham read the message of congratulations from his place at the enlarged family table in the dining room, where only a few months before he had come to know the bright smiling girl who sat by his side wearing a wedding ring. Lou leaned over to read the message from their parents, and he laughed.

'All right, Ham. Now you can run your fingers through your hair all you want. You got the girl!'

'What's this about fingers and hair?' asked Grossmutter, and Lou had to tell everybody how Ham had messed up both his hair and the chance to meet Irene even earlier than he did.

The wedding cake was sliced and pieces were passed around with glasses of sparkling wine. The bell captain came in from the lobby with a special delivery letter for Ham and Lou addressed to them care of Benjamin Morrison at the Granada. It was from Maurie and Rose in New York. After sending their congratulations, along with regrets at not being with them on this happy day, Maurice passed along the good news that he had arranged for distribution of a series of two-reel comedies Lou and Ham would shoot down in Los Angeles. The little comedy they had made on the cable cars and around Fisherman's Wharf had been well received, and they were to get pictures into production as soon as possible.

'Listen to this!' Ham said, reading from the letter to everybody around the big table. 'Maurie says we're to go to the Christie Brothers Studios in Hollywood, where he's arranged for us to have an office. We're to get acquainted with other producers there and at other studios and companies in the neighborhood and see what they're doing – then do it better and for less money.' He looked around and smiled at Benjamin.

'Here's something else good. We're to have a honeymoon for four days, and Maurice is enclosing a check as a present to pay for a hotel room someplace on the way to Los Angeles.' He raised his head and pointed a finger at his brother.

'You're not involved in the honeymoon part, Lou. Maurie says you're to go right to Los Angeles and find places for all of us to stay after you have introduced yourself to Charles and Al Christie at their studio on Sunset Boulevard and Gower, where they'll give us an office. He wants you to send him a telegram when you get there and he will write with more instructions.' Ham paused and looked over at his father-in-law.

'This part of the letter is for you, Mr. Morrison. Maurice likes the company you've set up. He is deeply grateful for the faith you and the other investors have shown in us, and he feels you will be very pleased with the results. There's a good market for these comedies, and with the distribution contracts he has already made and is lining up, they ought to earn money for everybody.'

'Mr. Morrison,' Lou added as Ham finished reading the letter, 'I want to join Maurice and my brother here in thanking you and the others for your backing. I promise you we'll treat your money like it was our very own . . . I mean, we'll always remember how you all put your trust in us, and you will get back all your investment with dividends and interest. I promise you that for the three of us.'

The attorney was pleased. Now he would have something definite to tell his fellow investors, and very soon his bright son-in-law and his brother would be down in Hollywood making movies to make America laugh and pay good money to see. It had been a good day filled with good news.

Late that afternoon the honeymooners left San Francisco on the coast train with Lou, who continued on south to Los Angeles. They left him an hour and a half out of San

Francisco and checked into a lovely old hotel in Santa Cruz facing the Pacific Ocean. It was a rambling three-story wooden Victorian structure with great round cupolas, porches and bay windows looking out on a broad stretch of white sand. The management proudly advertised eight bridal suites on the top floor, each with its own balcony, and one of these was Maurie's gift to the newlywed couple.

Dinner in the softly lit hotel dining room was followed by a walk down the beach with stops along the way to empty shoes when they filled up with the fine white sand. Finally they pulled off their shoes and waded up to their ankles in the water, holding hands, and the waves gently rolled up the beach, then retreated to gather strength and return. The noise of breaking surf and the rustle of the sea wind were the only sounds, broken now and then by a discordant gull.

'Let's go up to our room, Irene,' said Ham, holding tightly to her hand and his shoes. Suddenly he felt her pull away from him, and the intake of her breath sounded like a little moan of fear. She broke away and moved ahead down the beach, away from the hotel. He stopped to pick up the shoes she had dropped on the damp sand and then caught up with her.

'Irene, where are you going? Our hotel's the other way. Come on, it's getting dark and cool. We should go back.'

He held her arm and in the fading light looked into her face. For a moment he thought the drops of moisture were from the sea spray, but then he saw tears were running down her cheeks, and he could feel her body trembling as he held her.

'Ham, I'm sorry . . . I'm so upset . . . and I'm scared. I've always dreamed of getting married and about my wedding night, and now that it's really happened, I'm afraid! Can you understand?' Her voice broke and she was silent for a moment, then drew a deep breath and went on.

'My sister and I have been so closed off and sheltered . . . Grossmutter brought us up so strictly and, well, maybe it's foolish . . . but I am . . . I am . . . ' Her voice faded.

He held tightly to her arm, then circled her waist to draw her closer. In a comforting voice he spoke to her.

'Don't be afraid or upset. You and I will have plenty of time to find out about each other. This is a big change in my life too, and even if I don't show it, I'm plenty nervous! It's natural for anyone to be frightened of the unknown, so just relax and we will take it easy, a little at a time. Come with me, and I promise nothing will happen until you're ready for it to happen. You're not the first girl who's been scared on her wedding night. Let me kiss you and we'll walk back.'

He held her close as the waves washed over their bare feet, and they returned down the beach to the imposing old hotel, which stared out at the sea through its windows like a very aged and unstylish lady, disapproving of the times in which it found itself, yet compelled to tolerate the intolerable.

They were back in their bridal suite, the little sitting room with its tiny balcony and the slightly larger bedroom adjoining it. Ham did not need to be told that Irene was a virgin, and a very frightened one. He wondered if he could cope with this situation. It always had been easy when the girl had experience to equal·or exceed his own. To be a bull in the bedroom now was out of the question, and he had no letter of instructions from Maurie or advice from Poppa to guide him. When he thought of strict old Grossmutter Friedkin bringing up Irene and her sister, he knew he must be patient, for it was going to take time to undo all that had been done. He hoped she would be a good and receptive pupil, because he had much to teach her.

They sat on their little balcony looking out at the breaking waves, almost invisible in the darkness. He took her back to the bed and lay down beside her, just able to see the outline of her figure in the dim light. His hand moved up to her cheek for a moment and then he got up on one elbow, leaning over to give her a reassuring kiss. She trembled. His hand moved down to cover a breast, where he let it rest. Irene seemed to shrink away from him, and he quickly pulled his hand away. He stared into the darkness and heard her sobbing beside him.

'Ham, I'm so sorry and ashamed . . . maybe I'm just not ready for this yet . . . please be patient. I know I will be all right, and I do love you. It's only that I'm frightened and . . . '

He softly kissed her, again held her hand and spoke.

'Don't be upset, please, Irene. We love each other and we're going to be together a long time. Maybe all of this has been just too sudden. There's no law that says everything has to go perfectly on a wedding night . . . there's lots of nights, and we have three more of them right here before we go on to Los Angeles. I know you'll fell more relaxed when you get used to having a husband. Come on,' he said, trying to cheer her up, 'let's sit out on our balcony awhile and watch this part of the world wake up.'

Wrapped warmly in a blanket and seated in the big chair,

which just held them both, they spent the night watching the stars flicker out as the sky slowly turned from black to pale pink, and they could almost see the long white line of breakers rolling up on the beach.

It was not yet light enough for Irene to see the little smile on Ham's face. Thankfully, she had no way of knowing that he had just composed a fadeout title for this balcony scene. 'Come the dawn – but not the groom!' Someday he might use it in one of his movie comedies – names and places changed, of course. At least, thank heavens, the night hadn't been a complete loss!

CHAPTER SIXTEEN

Lou had arranged a month-to-month rental of a little wood-frame bungalow on Lemon Grove Avenue, just off Van Ness. It was less than a twenty-minute walk from there to the Christie Brothers offices and studio on Sunset and Gower. To get from the bungalow to Santa Monica Boulevard, Ham and Lou had to cut through the Hollywood Cemetery, which occupied most of the adjoining block. It was not the happiest way to start a day and was rather dismal late at night when fog swirled around headstones and mausoleums and an owl hooted high up in the tower gate.

They raced through the sacred grounds like two characters in a chase scene from one of the comedies shot by the little movie companies clustered across the street from the cemetery. Rows of ramshackle wooden buildings fronting ugly warehouse structures stood in uneven lines on Santa Monica, continuing on around the corner and partway up Gower. The rambling buildings were filled with offices, and at the back the warehouses passed for stages. Each office bore an elegant-sounding company name, and these were the occupants of what had come to be known as Shoestring Alley, Busted Acres, the Poorhouse, or – most descriptive of all – Poverty Row.

'Lou, I never heard of most of these outfits . . . "Waldorf Productions," "Chadwick Pictures," "Magnificent Movies, Limited," "Goodwill Studios," "Yankee Doodle Dandy Films" . . . Hey, that one I like . . . "Bischoff Comedies," "Choice Productions," "Warner Features, Inc." There's a familiar one! I wonder if that could be the Sam Warner we knew from Hale's Tours?'

They stopped and tried the door, but it was locked and there was no response when they tapped on the window. Lou looked through a dusty window.

'Just a couple of beat-up desks and a whole lot of papers scattered around. The place is a mess! Look – here's a note stuck in the mail slot.'

He pulled out the piece of paper, which he unrolled and read aloud.

' "Shooting on Santa Monica Pier. Leave message. Be back late tonight." It's signed "Sam Warner" . . . Yep – he's the same one all right. Here's a P.S. he stuck on the bottom: "Jack – you were supposed to meet us at 7:00 A.M. not P.M. Left without you so have a good alibi ready. Sam." That's got to be the kid brother Sam told me was such a pain in the butt – same as you are sometimes. We'll come back another morning and say hello.'

They walked on toward Sunset Boulevard, passing several groups of men dressed in Western outfits, some of them looking as though they would be more at home on the range than waiting for casting calls on "Gower Gulch," where companies specializing in Westerns had their offices. No stage space here. All the great out-of-doors, California sunshine and versatile geography provided a free set where these frontier legends were ground out like so much celluloid salami.

'Hi, partner . . . Howdy, stranger . . . Any rustlers hereabouts?' said Ham, spreading early-morning cheer as they passed glum clusters of horseless cowhands waiting for cast calls that came slowly if at all. It was too late in the morning, most calls for extras and stunt men had already been made. Nobody else could be hired by some of the companies until they received checks from their distributors to meet their last payroll.

Ham looked at some of the despondent faces they passed. A few must really have once been cowhands who left ranches to come to this new spread. The legs of some were shaped like booted parentheses from the sides of long-gone cow ponies, and some of the gnarled hands seemed lost without a lariat. Several looked through narrowed eyes set in weathered faces as the two smartly dressed young men passed by on the sidewalk, stepping around the romantic relics seeking immortality and a few bucks making dreams live again. Some sat on the ground, backs up against building walls as they rolled Bull Durham into paper twists and lit up. Others in the sprawling groups must have spent all their savings on what they were told were genuine cowboy duds, tight high-heeled boots torturing their agonized city feet, Western accents made in Brooklyn and too-clean Stetsons worn at the wrong angle.

'What a rotten way to make a living,' said Lou in a low

voice to Ham as they worked their way through what looked like a long-lost posse. 'Hell, I know you need all kinds of people to make movies, but some of these poor guys look like they haven't worked or eaten for weeks. Remember that next time you think you want to be an actor!'

'They're not actors,' replied Ham, 'they're just atmosphere.' He saw a sign ahead on the corner building where Gower crossed Sunset. ' "Christie Brothers Studios" – about time we reached it. My feet are giving out. Don't worry about me ever becoming an actor . . . unless I'm the producer and the director too so nobody can fire me! Let's see what kind of office space the Christies are letting us use. I hope Maurie didn't promise to pay them any rent for this. He did say it was a friendship deal, didn't he?'

It definitely was a friendship deal. Al and Charlie Christie made them feel completely at home right away.

'Fellows,' said Charlie, 'just ask questions – follow us around and go out with our shooting companies when we're getting comedies in the can. Go with them right through the lab and titling, then final editing. That way you'll find out plenty in a hurry. I know you've already shot some stuff on your own, but things here are different – some worse, some better. When you're ready to go into production on your own, we'll help you line up crews and equipment, along with stages if you need them. I advise you to stick to the location stuff, though, if you want to cut down costs. If you want to stay on here, we'll work out a deal that won't break you, but if you'd rather find a place of your own, that's fine by me. Anything we can do to help we'll do . . . except we won't loan you any of our comics or our gag writers – and you better not try to steal any of them away from us! You'll have to find them for yourself.'

'Fair enough . . . and thanks to the Christie Brothers from the Robbins Brothers,' said Ham, who already was figuring how much more than they were being paid he should offer to anybody worth taking along with them when they left the Christies.

'Al, Charlie,' said Lou. 'Could you do us a real favor before we get too involved? We saw *The Birth of a Nation* last year in San Francisco and one of the people we've wanted to meet ever since is D. W. Griffith. We're sure not going to shoot anything like what he's been doing . . . well, not for a while, anyhow . . . but Mr. Griffith is someone we'd very much like to meet. He and his cameraman, Billy Bitzer, are kind of heroes to Ham and me . . . though there was plenty about *The Birth* we didn't like very much . . . all that propaganda and bias he stuck in . . . but the production part and the way they handled people and the battle scenes were absolutely magnificent! Those men are real picture makers, and if we could meet them and just watch them work for a day, I think it would be something we'd never forget. I heard he's shooting another big picture someplace near here.'

'Near here! It's all of two miles or so east of the very spot we're standing on right now . . . over where Sunset and Hollywood Boulevards run together. Believe me, just seeing the set he's put up is an experience! That Griffith, though . . . there's something damn strange about him, for all his talent. He's spending a fortune, his own money from *The Birth of a Nation*, plus loads more he's promoted . . . and believe it or not, he calls this new one by a crazy title, *The Mother and the Law* – imagine trying to set up advertising for something like that! So far as anybody knows, it has something to do with ancient Babylon. He doesn't even have a script, and nobody really knows what he's doing. Guess when you're a genius you can get away with things like that, but he's a nut about keeping things to himself. God help whoever has to help put it all together when he finishes shooting. There's a rumor he may change the title to *Intolerance*. Anything would be better than what he's calling it now. Sure . . . I can get you boys on the set. D.W.'s chief assistant, Joe Henabery is an old friend of ours. I'll get in touch with him tonight and make arrangements. Ham, you should take your wife when you go. You're right when you say this will be an experience to remember the rest of your lives. Don't get any big ideas, though. The things making real money now are the little comedies like the ones we shoot. Leave Babylon and the rest of the Bible to Griffith and those Italian producers and stick to the chases and the pratfalls!'

The Christies were right. It was something every visitor, participant and passerby would recall with wonderment for years: the colossal set reaching up into the sky, rows of tall wooden towers each holding larger-than-life seated plaster elephants with trunks curled up in the air, tremendous flights of stairs, fluted columns and elaborately decorated walls pierced by big gates all stretching back to reveal the royal palace of Belshazzar, ruler of Babylon and of the world. It was absolutely the most stupendous set that had ever been built for an American motion picture. Lou, Ham and Irene could see the towering structure as they were driven the few miles down Sunset Boulevard a few days later in the Christie Studios sedan. The car took them through the great mob of people standing in lines outside the Griffith studio gates and let them off, where they were picked up by a guide sent by Joe Henabery.

At once they were surrounded by a crowd of extras dressed as townspeople, priests, temple guards, dancers, musicians and various other citizens of ancient Bablyon. The extras stood in long lines leading to the wardrobe and make-up tents and filed past to have wigs put in place, veils adjusted, beards pasted on chins and cheeks and dabs of greasepaint applied. Men, women and yelling children stretched back hundreds of yards. Assistant directors shouted instructions through megaphones, moving the people along and telling them to assemble as quickly as possible in the great Temple Square and be ready for the first shot.

'Where is Mr. Griffith?' Ham asked their guide.

'He's someplace around . . . look for a crazy straw hat and he'll be under it. There he is – see him up there on the top of that flight of stairs?'

David Wark Griffith stood high above them all looking down at the confusion. He pulled scraps of paper from a pocket in his loose jacket and started reading one of them. He looked up at the cloudless sky, then down again at the gathering mob of Babylonians awaiting his orders. A heavyset man in a dark suit struggled up the stairs to stand beside him. Their guide told the visitors that was Harry Aitkin, a Griffith associate responsible for financial affairs. It was obvious even from a distance that Aitkin was in deep distress. He was puffing from his climb, his face a bright red, as he began waving his arms and talking to Griffith, who continued reading his notes, paying no attention at all to the keeper of the books. D.W. wore his familiar big floppy straw hat with the brim pulled up in front so he could see everything that happened in his Babylon. The mob poured into the Square as suddenly a slight breeze sprang up and quickly became a mild wind. The great set creaked and groaned, and Ham pulled Irene back in alarm, putting his arm over her shoulders when he saw some of the high walls billowing slightly as though made of plaster-coated canvas – which for the most part they were.

Griffith shouted through a megaphone over toward a large open-top tent: 'Bitzer . . . get ready! The people are all in

173

place! Start to go up when you hear the signal shot – the first shot! Do you hear me?'

A man came running around the high tent wall and climbed up the stairs to reach Griffith. They held a brief conversation, then the man ran back down the stairs to vanish behind the canvas. Now the assistant directors yelled again at the mobs of people who had surged into the Square and up the stairs. Helmeted soldiers holding spears and shields now lined the tops of the Temple walls, and the set was packed almost solid with the mob of extras. Griffith and his aides pushed their way down the steps through the crowd to the front of the set, where they stood only a few yards from the Robbins party. Lou and Ham could overhear the worried Harry Aitkin pleading and arguing with Griffith.

'How can you shoot this when you don't even have a written script? For God's sake, D.W., where's the money supposed to come from for all this? We'll run completely out in another week if we have no plans from you and know how much is going to be needed. Give us a schedule, or at least some kind of description of the scenes and how many people are in them . . . something to figure out our costs from. D.W., listen to me!'

Griffith kept his eyes on the mob, and it was as though the pleading man at his side did not exist. He spoke to Joe Henabery, who lifted up a big megaphone and bellowed for silence from the mob. The assistant directors echoed his call through their megaphones, and the voices died down as Griffith spoke in a very loud voice to all those assembled.

'Ladies – gentlemen . . . people of Babylon! You are subjects of a great nation and a great emperor! This is a day of celebration . . . you have just defeated the armies of Persia! You will stand in the positions where you are right now, and when you hear the sound of the second gunshot – I repeat, the second gunshot, not the first – you will cheer as loudly as you can! You will move around . . . but not too much, and then turn fully around to the great statue of Belshazzar over the main gate of the Temple, and you will bow . . . get down just as low as you can get . . . bow to Belshazzar, the mighty King of Kings of Babylon, who is your absolute monarch! You will do anything he tells you to do . . . the same way you will do anything I tell you to do. Remember – turn, cheer and bow on the second gunshot, and anybody who does it on the first one will never work in another picture of mine! Am I understood?'

174

From nearly two thousand throats came the ragged response: 'Yes, Mr. Griffith!'

'All right. Joe, tell Billy to have his crew ready with the winch, and on the first gunshot come up and start cranking.'

Lou, Ham and Irene stood almost hypnotized by all the magnificently organized confusion. The only sound now was that of the wind that sprang up again and swept over the set. It was something the natives of this region had accepted for generations, the warm Santa Anas that blew through the Los Angeles basin and drove away the smoke from fires burning in homes and on garbage dumps. Ham looked up in the air. He had never seen a sky of such intense clean and clear blue. Lord – it was good to be alive here and to be witness to such sights!

A gunshot made them jump. From behind the high canvas wall off to the side of the set a large gas-filled balloon slowly rose at the end of a rope tether. Suspended beneath it was a wicker basket in which stood a camera on its tripod and the famous Billy Bitzer, who had shot The Birth of a Nation. He made last-minute adjustments of focus with an assistant as they prepared to shoot the great Temple Square from high in the air to show the whole expanse jammed with more than two thousand people. Ham pointed with excitement at a woman in a cleared part of the Square. It was Constance Talmadge dressed as a noblewoman of the court and surrounded by fierce guards commanded by Elmo Lincoln. Another actress came over and stood quite near Irene. When she saw it was Lillian Gish, she nudged Ham and whispered that she could actually reach out and touch the leading lady of The Birth of a Nation. From then on Irene had trouble looking at all the action on the set.

The balloon swayed as it rose higher in the air. The wind again picked up and toyed with the big gasbag, making it swing and sway at the end of its rope. Bitzer and his assistant hung on to the side of the basket with one hand and clung tightly to the camera with the other. The wind blew harder, bringing a blast of heat from the distant desert. Joe Henabery fired another gunshot into the air, and the mob went into action. Hands went up; there was cheering and shouting. The great mob turned to bow to the statue of Belshazzar, which in turn bowed slightly from the wind buffeting the tower.

From the tethered balloon the assistant cameraman screamed through his megaphone as they were caught in the hot force of the Santa Ana and the gasbag swayed and gyrated like an upside-down pendulum. Bitzer tried to turn the camera crank as the assistant dropped his megaphone and began to vomit over the side of the basket. Several of the extras joined in the screaming as they were hit by his breakfast. Two more gunshots sounded, and the balloon was reeled down to its shelter . . . but it was too late. Now Bitzer was heaving over the side, and he let go of the top-heavy camera, which tipped and fell over the side to make a descent all by itself. A loud smashing noise could be heard as it hit the ground.

Harry Aitkin cried out in pain as he quickly computed the cost of the equipment that had just been destroyed and all the time and salaries lost on this crazy idea of Griffith and Bitzer's of shooting Belshazzar's palace from high up in the air. He put both his hands to his head, and Lou and Ham listened to him scream at the master moviemaker, 'D.W. That does it! Get rid of that damned balloon! If you don't plan ahead what you are going to shoot each day you will never finish this damned picture!' He turned and rushed off the set.

Griffith, Henabery and some aides ran over to the balloon and helped Bitzer and his assistant out of the basket. The assistant directors screamed through their megaphones at the mob, 'Lunch, everybody! Forty-five minutes . . . Don't mess your make-up or wardrobe. Be back on the set at twelve-thirty sharp! Now, men, watch your beards when you're eating! Ladies, don't get food on your veils! Children, damn it, quit running around!'

Lou, Ham and Irene were herded off the set by their guide, who took them to the gate and the waiting car.

'Well, what do you think of the movie business?' Lou asked his brother.

'Now I know what God must have gone through creating the Earth,' answered Ham, 'but He didn't have a budget or a schedule or Harry Aitkin nagging Him all the time . . . or do you think that was why there had to be a devil?'

'Whoever said we would remember watching D.W. Griffith shooting a scene for the rest of our lives sure wasn't fooling!' added Irene, and she wondered how she would ever be able to describe all this in a letter to her family up in sane San Francisco.

The driver let Lou and Ham off at the Christie Brothers offices, then took Irene to a grocery store and a butcher shop, where she bought some things for the first dinner she would cook in their little rented house. They had eaten out at a nearby café the first few nights, but she had been studying a cookbook given her by Grossmutter. The car took her around the Hollywood Cemetery, leaving her off at the bungalow on Lemon Grove. She made a light lunch for herself, then spent the next several hours in the tiny kitchen with the cookbook propped up and sweat running down her face as she opened a can of soup, boiled a piece of beef, cooked vegetables and hoped she had the right ingredients and quantities for the lemon pie that now baked in the oven. She laughed – a lemon pie for her first dinner in the house on Lemon Grove Avenue! She set the table for three, got out a tablecloth, napkins, plates and silverware, then sat down to reread the recipes and see if she had forgotten anything. After a quick bath and a change of clothes, she was ready when the door opened to let in Ham and Lou, still puffing from their evening run through the Hollywood Cemetery and eager for Irene's very first home-cooked meal.

She greeted them each with a kiss, a big one for Ham and a sisterly one for Lou. After they had washed up, she invited them to be seated at the dining room table, which almost filled the small room off the kitchen.

The boys looked down at the dark brown pieces of meat and the mushy green vegetables she set in front of them. The soup had been fairly tasty, if lukewarm and unseasoned, but neither had complained. Now, though, it was time to take their knives to the boiled beef and cut. After several minutes of determined sawing and hacking, Ham got through a small piece, which he put in his mouth. He chewed and chewed as Irene's face grew longer and longer.

'I don't know what I could have done wrong. I followed everything my grandmother told me in her letter. I must have made some terrible mistake! It's dreadful!' Big tears flowed down her cheeks.

'I'm taking both of you to Musso and Frank's for dinner as my guests so celebrate . . . uh . . . to celebrate our third night out for dinner. Let's go right now!' said Lou. 'Dry your eyes, Irene, we'll do this again real soon, and meantime you can find out from your grandma if the meat was supposed to be boiled or broiled. Come on, we've still got the whole evening ahead of us. Compared to Mr. Griffith's Babylonians, we haven't got a care in the world!'

Part Three

CHAPTER SEVENTEEN

'Not a care in the world . . . not a care in the whole damn fucking world.'

'What was that, Ham? Were you talking to me?' said the old actor seated on his left. Ham looked up from his glass and turned to the president of the George Spelvin Club.

'Uh, Monte . . . excuse me. I was thinking about the old days and I guess I started talking to myself. Can you believe it, forty-seven years ago I came here to Hollywood with my brother Lou and we worked right across the street from where we're all sitting now. The old Christie Studios over on Gower and Sunset. My wife and I had a little bungalow just past the Hollywood Cemetery the other side of Santa Monica Boulevard, and I was thinking about the first meal she ever cooked for Lou and me. Jeesus, almost half a century ago and I can still remember what she did to that poor piece of meat!'

The old actor chuckled. He went through his pockets and came up with a crushed pack of cigarettes, unfolded one and lit up. He spoke through a cloud of blue smoke.

'Gower Gulch. I haven't thought of those days for a long time. I sat on my ass on that hard sidewalk early every morning and waited for a chance to get myself killed for a buck a day, plus lunch. I was a punk kid off a New Hampshire farm and didn't even know how to ride, but I conned myself into thinking I could be a cowboy actor. Ham, you and I got here when it still was a hell of a lot of fun, even if we were hungry most of the time. At least you had some meat for your wife to cook. Some guys were luckier than others. Excuse me a few minutes, Ham.' He got up and left the table to find himself an uncrushed pack of cigarettes.

A large block of ice carved in the shape of an old-fashioned movie camera, complete with a cameraman wearing a rakish backward-turned cap, was wheeled between the tables. Under the hot lights the ice took on rounded edges, and by the time it made a journey around the big hall and reached the place cleared for it in front of the main table, the cameraman had melted down to a stoop-shouldered midget. A parade of waiters followed the ice sculpture, hopping about over the puddles it left on the floor as they handed out plates of dessert to the diners. Somebody on the planning committee with a sly sense of humor had chosen sherbet smothered with the most unloved of Hollywood fruits – raspberries. Liqueur was poured over the concoction, to be set aflame and complete the destruction before the molten mush was put on the tables.

I wonder if that crummy little bungalow is still there, Ham thought. Hell, I bet I could walk from here and over Gower through the cemetery, then to Lemon Grove in a half-hour or even less. Ha – who am I kidding? that was almost fifty years ago. I couldn't make it in an hour now ... if that. My God, was it that long ago we came here? I'll never forget that first meal of Irene's. Me up all night with a stomach ache and her crying her eyes out. Poor kid, she only wanted to give us a nice meal and everything turned out all wrong. Didn't everything turn out all wrong? Not just boiled beef, but all the other things too. All those roads to hell I paved with my good intentions ... and without too damn much help from anybody!

He shoved the dessert plate away and looked out at the crowd at the tables spread over the Palladium floor, eating as though the stuff set before them was good honest food and not plastic props, which was how it all had tasted to Ham. He took another drink, then popped some Mylantas into his mouth, washing them down with another quick drink. The Humanitarian of the Year sat all alone in the crowded hall, and he could not stop thinking of things that made him wish for some kind of antacid pills for his mind, which also seemed to be suffering from a kind of indigestion.

My dear family ... where the hell are they? Okay, so one of them is out of the country and probably still in no condition to be here or anyplace else. At least Jimmy is in town and should have had enough respect for me to have shown up tonight. Hell, what did I ever really give him to respect? And Nita ... dear sweet Nita ... my lovely loving star-crazy wife who insults me every time I see what she's turned into! Maurie and Lou at least have good alibis for not showing up ... they're dead ... safely dead ... and my sisters ... all gone. How they hated me ... everyone but dear, wonderful Lou. Why? Why did they all let me down? I only tried to do my damned best for everybody . . . my best what?

The music faded and the public address system boomed with the larger-than-life voice of Georgie Jessel pouring out of the wall speakers.

'For your pleasure, ladies and gentlemen, a great entertainer of whom we will be hearing much in the future. His energy is astounding, almost equaling mine – only I do it with vitamins and the encouragement of pretty girls, while Sammy Davis, Jr., does it with sheer talent and the kind of youthful vitality that keeps him going at top speed after the rest of us have fallen completely apart. Backing Sammy is the Will Mastin Trio . . . some of his *mishpocheh* . . . more proof that if you have any relatives with talent, better you should have them working with you than against you!'

Ham turned his head sharply toward Georgie and wondered if that crack was aimed at him after the business with Jimmy or if it was only an innocent remark. Very little around here was innocent anymore. He relaxed his suddenly tight jaws long enough to swallow another mouthful of Scotch, then listened to the words coming from the loudspeakers.

'Ladies and Gentlemen, Sammy Davis, Jr . . . and the Will Mastin Trio!'

The orchestra fanfared Sammy and his group onstage, where he took the microphone, still warm from Jessel's hot hand, and immediately captured the audience with his talent, flash, dash and bravado.

Another junior was on Ham's mind now, and he was again reminded that his son was not here at this celebration honoring his father. Another Hamilton Robbins . . . the next generation . . . born, when was it . . . 1917, when he and Irene were still living in that little bungalow. Thank God she had gotten over most of her fears about sex after their honeymoon disaster. Finally, after months had passed, she was almost relaxed enough to enjoy sleeping with him – but Grossmutter Friedkin never was completely banished from their bedroom. Well, something must have gone right, and after the proper time had passed, they had a baby boy. Irene didn't have too rough a time delivering him, but somehow their constrained sex episodes grew even less regular, and it was almost as though she blamed him for all the pain and inconvenience of having the baby. What in hell could he do? Several evenings when he worked late at the studio and there was an eager and willing woman available, why should he be a saint? Certainly Irene wasn't making him happy in that

183

department, and he managed to have some pleasure now and then without being caught.

Ham looked over at the Palladium stage, which jutted out from the opposite wall. He tried to pay some attention to the catchy lyrics and flying footwork. Sammy was belting out his song . . . dancing . . . a blur of sound and motion, the group behind him singing in tight unison as the little bundle of talent roved back and forth on the narrow stage.

The brassy music and amplified sound assaulted Ham's ears, but his mind was not here in the crowded Palladium with its musical sound and fury. His thoughts were three hundred yards, more or less, across busy Sunset Boulevard – inside a big ugly wooden barn of a building, a firetrap torn down maybe fifteen or twenty years ago to make room for an equally ugly but fireproof sound stage. He lifted the glass to his mouth for another drink, and through the clear amber liquid he saw the distorted scene far across the room. The dancer . . . mouthing unheard words . . . strutting . . . moving . . . moving . . . The lights flickered on and off, on and off, making him look for a few moments like a player in an old-fashioned movie. On . . . off . . . on and off . . . Dark and bright . . . black and white . . . It hurt Ham's eyes, and he closed them as tightly as he could to shut out the picture.

CHAPTER EIGHTEEN

'Cut . . . cut! Goddammit! What's happening to those lights? Who's watching the stinking kliegs! Eddie, run over to the office and get my brother Lou here as fast as you can. Either he finds us some lights that work or we sit here on our behinds and wait until the rain stops so we can go back on location!'

The cameraman came up from behind his viewfinder and spoke to Ham in a soothing Swedish-accented voice.

'Relax . . . relax, my friend. Most of the shot I already have. We can move to another angle and go right on with the scene once we have light. There is a natural cut.' The cameraman was a master of his craft, a calm diplomat who would last because he knew how to handle almost any situation with all kinds of people and keep his head. The man turning the camera crank had to be the coolest one on the set and not take out any frustrations on his machine, or later the projected action would run at crazy speeds. It was no wonder that most cameramen lived to a ripe old age, unless accidentally run over by a wild stagecoach, an out-of-control comic or a herd of stampeding extras.

Lou came on the run from their office. The set electrician showed him the klieg lights, which came on full power for a moment, then flickered fitfully. No adjustment of the carbon rods could give the steady light they must have to continue shooting. Rain poured down outside the big shed, drumming on the tin roof, and Gower Street was being turned into a muddy tributary of the Los Angeles River. Some of the water cascaded through an opening down into a vault carrying power lines to the shooting area, and soon the flickering kliegs and work lights went completely dead. The only light came through the sliding doors, along with the spreading puddles of water.

'That's it!' yelled Ham. 'Everybody take the rest of the day off and we'll get in touch with you by five-thirty tomorrow morning if we continue shooting . . . weather and electricity permitting. Don't show up unless we call you. Good night!'

Some power was still getting through to the rest of the studio, and they went to a tiny projection room where the film editor waited with a rough cut of the comedy they had just completed shooting a few days before. Most of it was passable stuff, with a high-speed chase in which a fat comic on a motorcycle pursued a thin comic driving a broken-down Model T Ford. They were rushing down a very familiar street – Larchmont Boulevard, not far at all from Poverty Row, and made to order for visual thrills. A long row of tall wooden poles had been set right in the middle of the wide street and carried power for streetcars. The chase scene weaved in and out, around and back again, with the cycle and car performing a crazy zigzag photographed by a camera mounted on a truck that kept directly behind the two madmen on wheels. The camera was being cranked at a slightly slower than normal speed to make everything dash across the screen at a super-fast rate when projected normally. The comics tore around every pole in the long line, missing some only by inches, causing the few pedestrians on the sidewalk to rush toward the houses for shelter.

A big moving van could be seen far ahead cutting across Larchmont on Second Street. It came closer, looming up dark and threatening, and its driver seemed in no hurry to clear the intersection. There was a slick mixture of oil and water on the pavement from the fine drizzle that had fallen earlier that morning, so when the drivers jammed on their brakes, they spun around and around, then slid up over the curb and sidewalk, missing two pedestrians and ending up on a lawn, where the wheels of the Ford were buried almost up to the hubcaps in the newly sprouted grass. The motorcycle left a deep circular trench before it flopped over on its side, and the camera car came to a jolting halt just in time to miss following the others over the sidewalk. The picture on the screen ran out as the frame tilted and a furious home owner could be clearly seen racing toward the camera, shaking his fist and mouthing what must have been outraged obscenities.

'And that little scene, my dear brother, cost us one hundred bucks to pay off the guy whose lawn we ruined,' said Ham as Lou let out a gasp and the lights were turned on in the projection room. 'What's worse, the bastard won't let us use his face in the picture unless we pay him another hundred. Said he'd sue us if we dare to show him. A damn shame – he's a natural actor. Did you see all that emotion on his kisser? What a shame to waste all that talent . . . but his dialogue could never be put on a title – and if there are any lip-readers in the audience, they're going to have some real shocks coming. We have all the show in the can except for the closing – shall I lay out the extra dough or do we reshoot the end?'

'We've already spent more than Maurie said we could on this little stinker and it still isn't finished. Better make the cut just before the guy comes on screen and we'll pick up a new ending when we go outside again. Hell, nobody ever sues anyone for making them famous! Forget what I said – go ahead and use everything the way you shot it and we'll take the chance that the bastard never goes to the movies,' Lou said, and they went out into the corridor. They walked to the dark stage and looked out into the rain. 'How's Irene and the baby? I haven't seen them all week.'

'Fine, just fine. Come on over tonight for dinner. Irene's been working hard on her cooking and she's pretty good at it now. Nothing like that night nearly two years ago when you saved everything taking us out to dinner. We eat all right now and I'm not losing too much weight. Trouble, though, is that I don't get home many nights for dinner, what with editing these films and getting them shipped off to Maurie. Say, I heard from Poppa by letter this morning. He's still angry at me for naming the kid after myself. Against Orthodox Jewish tradition . . . but what the hell. I like the name and so does Irene, and one day Ham junior will like it too – he better! Tradition . . . ha! It's just a bunch of narrow rules some old kockers put together long before we all were born to keep us from doing things that really don't matter.'

'You should have known Poppa would be upset when you named the baby after yourself. You're supposed to be dead before you give a baby your name. Why did you rush things?' said Lou with a wide smile.

Ham's jaw tightened. It was bad enough his parents had questioned his decision. Now his brother was butting in.

'Look, I did what I did! The subject's closed!' And so far as Ham was concerned, it was. He snapped his fingers. 'Oh . . . I thought it might be a good idea in a few weeks to take Irene and the baby to Harrisburg and visit Poppa and Momma and the girls on our way to see Maurie and Rose in New York. This comedy we're completing now winds up the series that Famous Artists is distributing, and we ought to meet and go

187

over what we're going to do next. You can keep things going here, and you remember Maurie wrote we might have a chance to do some war bond sales films for the government. We could do nicely with that kind of a contract, and so far neither of us is being breathed on heavily by the draft board . . . so perhaps we're safe.'

'Don't count on it,' said Lou. 'I'm single and they are using up the younger age groups, so maybe one day they'll get up to us over-twenty-nine-year-olds and I could get pulled in. You being married and a father ought to keep you out . . . but you never to know. Remember all that talk about getting the boys out of the trenches by Christmas? Well, here it is the middle of October and they're still in the trenches. I'm going over to visit the Hollywood Officer's Training Camp on Monday morning and see what's going on there. They put up a big tent on that twenty-acre meadow near Melrose and Western and turned the whole place into a training camp. Lots of guys we know from different picture companies and labs are reporting there, and after a six-week course some of them are getting commissioned as second looies. Hell, if I do have to go I should try to get into a photo outfit and do something I at least know something about. Those gold bars might go well with my complexion, and if they ever do get around to drafting married men and fathers, you could have the pleasure of saluting me.'

'God forbid!' said Ham, nervously wondering if it would ever come to that.

It never did come to that. Before another month had passed, an armistice was signed by the belligerent nations and the Hollywood draft board gave itself a victory and farewell party. The big tent off Western Avenue came down, and soon after that the training camp was subdivided into commercial and residential properties, which were quickly snapped up in the postwar real estate boom.

The films for war bond sales ended with the war, and now it was more important than ever for Ham to meet with Maurie, leaving Lou to finish editing the last comedy of their series. He and Irene packed their things, storing some furniture in a corner of one of the stages, and Lou drove them to the depot. The little house on Lemon Grove had been sold, so when they returned they would have to find another place to live. For four days now their home was on the transcontinental train that took them to Pittsburgh, where they transferred to another car for the short run to Harrisburg.

'A *shiksa* – she looks just like a blonde *shiksa*!' said Momma under her breath. 'I know she must have made our son name the baby after himself. He never would have done that himself!'

Irene smiled and kissed her parents-in-law and the two girls and wondered what they were saying about her. While she understood and spoke German, she was almost completely lost in Yiddish, but sensed that something was being said that she would rather not understand.

It was quite difficult for the grandparents and the two young aunts to tell just what the baby looked like. He was bawling from the moment they arrived, and bright red spots suddenly appeared all over his little body. His temperature shot up to nearly one hundred and four degrees, and a doctor was called the moment they reached the house. After one look at Hamilton Robbins, Jr., he notified the city health officer, who put the entire house under quarantine and posted red warning signs on all the doors.

'We're locked up in a ghetto!' complained Poppa in great disgust.

'Not quite,' said Momma. 'For just a little while we stay inside – then when the baby is well, down come the signs and we are back in the land of liberty again. You wouldn't want for the neighbors and their children to catch whatever he has, so don't complain, and let us enjoy our children and what health we still have.'

Solomon had to shout instructions through a window to his helper, who came by from the shop early each morning and was told what he should do that day. When evening came, he would slip the day's receipts under the front door to be counted. Solomon then went upstairs to see if there still were any red spots on the baby, then returned to shout more orders through the door. He was most unhappy, but sighed and hoped for a better tomorrow. Groceries were delivered to the house by one of the neighbor's boys, who scurried up the porch to the door, left the sacks of food, picked up the next day's order and money, then jammed it into a clean paper bag and ran down the street before any germs could rush out and catch him.

No school now for Ruth or Miriam and, worst of all, no synagogue for Poppa. The city's Department of Public Health and Sanitation made the rules now, and piety had to wait until the fever broke and there were no more red spots on Hamilton Robbins, Jr.

'Hamilton Robbins, Jr.! What a terrible thing to do!' said a disgusted Solomon to Esther in the privacy of their bedroom, in a voice easily heard in every upstairs room. 'The boy should have been named for his grandfather Nathan . . . *alav ha-sholom* . . . or maybe even for your father, Samuel.'

Irene could hear disjointed bits of the tirade down the hall and was able to understand some parts of it, but right now she had other problems on her mind. The strange kosher food was utterly foreign to her, and in trying to help Momma and the girls in the kitchen, she had unwittingly scrambled the meat dishes, knives, forks and spoons and implements used only for dairy food and was coldly invited out of the room. Crying, she went upstairs to sit beside the baby on the bed, joining him in his misery. His renewed wails filled the house in counterpoint to her softly muffled sobs.

Ham heard the concert and rushed to the bedroom. Once there, however, he felt quite lost trying to comfort the distraught Irene. It was clear even to him that she did not fit in with his family, and it was something she seemed unable to help. He did not know what to say or do. He knew that he too had become different from the others, but he could find no words to share with her. He sat by the open window looking in dull anger at the outside world going about its business while he was cooped up in the house. He had to do something, so he got up and went down the hall to be by himself in the room where he and Lou had once slept and dreamed of the future. He was sitting there on his old bed when he remembered the projection machine. Sure enough, after a half-hour of rummaging through closets and then up in the tiny attic, he found what he was looking for – a case with the markings FRAGILE – GLASS – HANDLE WITH CARE. He unsnapped the latch, swung up the lid and then reached down to softly caress the dulled copper and brass. A minute more to find a cloth and he wiped off the metal and the dulled projection lens.

If he could find any film, even some short lengths, he could show Irene how he and his brothers had gotten started . . . maybe even cheer her up. It was worth a search. High over his head in a narrow space Ham saw a long thin piece of painted wood resting on the roof beams. He reached up, turning it so he could read the faint golden words still visible on the faded blue background.

BIJOU DREAM. It had been there ever since . . . ever since they closed down that little store they had turned into a nickelodeon. Ham had thought it was gone forever . . . No, that was the other one, down in York – the one that burned to the ground in the fire. He would show it to Poppa and have him ship it to him out in California. Maybe one day when they had their own studio he would put things like this in a special place, kind of like a museum, a room full of things worth remembering.

Irene poked her head through the trapdoor.

'Irene . . . look what I found. Remember me telling you about our very first theater? This was the sign we painted . . . and here in this case is our first projection machine, an Edison Kinetoscope. My gosh . . . can you imagine all this has been sitting up here all these years!'

Her tears gone, she squeezed up beside Ham to look at the wonderful machine and admire the sign.

'Help me take all this down to our room. Poppa's got to ship it all out to us. I've got a wonderful idea about this stuff – I'll tell you about it later. Come on, start down and let me hand you the sign. Be careful!'

Ham returned to the far side of the attic and high up on a shelf found a small box filled with rolls of nitrate film. Thank heavens it had never caught fire. It might have burned the whole house down! He took the projector and box of film down the ladder to their bedroom. A bed sheet screen went up on the wall of the very same room where Birnbaum had slept before fleeing back to the Bronx, leaving them his treasured Kinetoscope. Irene went to see to the baby, who was sitting up watching his parents do strange things with a bed sheet and a mysterious box. He was alert and bright-eyed, and Irene felt his forehead. He seemed to be quite normal, and even in the poor light Irene could see the red spots were fading. Maybe they would be leaving this house soon. She hoped so, as she felt herself to be an outsider who would never be completely accepted by her husband's family.

'Kid, how'd you like to see a real old movie . . . a flicker?' Ham sat on the bed with his son and smiled at him. He was excited about finding a piece of his past, and the boy caught his enthusiasm. He jumped up and down on the bed and looked closely as Ham set the machine on its box. 'Now watch what I'm doing. Real soon after we get home I want to show you how this works and teach you how to operate projection machines and cameras. You can never learn too young. If you're going to be in business with me I want you to learn all you can about everything to do with it. Now watch me carefully . . . ' The little boy's eyes sparkled as he watched his father set the film in place and pull the head-end through the sprockets and gates. 'Come on, sit here beside me and watch everything I do. Irene, pull the curtains so it will be dark in here. We could use some blankets over the windows, but this ought to be dark enough to see the picture. Now both of you look at the screen.'

He finished pumping up pressure in the carbide lamp, lit the opening as the gas hissed out and began to turn the wood-handled crank just as he had done years ago in this room. He looked over at his son, who was transfixed, eyes fastened on the sheet, which suddenly had come alive with a street full of people, then the clouds of dust as the fire teams came closer and closer. The little boy cried out with joy and excitement and reached up for his father's hand. Ham looked down at his son while he kept turning the crank with his free hand. Irene smiled across at them both. He felt very close now to his son and his wife, here in this darkened room as they looked at shadows of the past. Maybe they could have more happy times like this together. The fire engines raced off the screen just as the old film shattered, and the projector light flooded the screen. The film cement had evaporated over the years, so that had to be the end of the show.

They pulled back the curtains and carefully swept up the pieces of film on the door. They boy pleaded for more, and Ham promised that when they returned to California the two of them would go to the studio and he would show him how movies were made. Then Ham reached out again to take his hand.

The next morning all the spots were gone and the doctor called the health department. Soon a man came by to remove the warning signs from the porch and the quarantine was over. Ham sent off a telegram to Maurie in New York that they were at last on the way. The whole family had a last meal in the kitchen. Irene still felt there was a distance from her husband's family that she could not bridge. Ham's usual good humor was obscured with impatience at their delay, and he blamed their little boy for keeping them there so long. He enjoyed visiting his parents and sisters, but he should have been in New York almost a week ago! Irene gave up trying to understand his attitude and the way he changed so quickly. In so many ways he was very self-centered, and she wondered if he could ever change.

Solomon, Esther and the girls stood on the porch waving good-bye as a taxi took Ham, Irene and their little boy up the street toward the depot.

'You know, Poppa,' said Esther, 'I couldn't understand everything she said, but I think she's a good person . . . even if maybe she does look a little like a *shiksa*. I can't help feeling a little sorry for her.'

'So do I, Momma, so do I,' Solomon replied. 'There is a strangeness about our son Chaim . . . a strangeness that will make unhappy anybody who loves him . . . or gives too much of themselves to him. He is not like you and me, or even like Maurie and Lou and the girls. With him there is always too much of what it is he wants, and never does he see the feelings of other people. I see them giving him love . . . always giving . . . and he is always taking . . . taking. Now that I can go again to the synagogue, I will pray for Chaim . . . that he gets *menshlichkeit* . . . a human feeling for other people . . . a compassion, the rabbi calls it. Getting, that is all right – but giving is more important. Our son will one day be a poor man – a pauper in the heart – unless he has what I do not see in him now – *menshlichkeit*.' They all turned and went back into the house.

CHAPTER NINETEEN

Ham shifted in the suddenly uncomfortable chair facing his older brother's desk. He was certain Maurie's loud voice could be heard outside the company offices on West Fourteenth Street.

'Something crazy happens to everybody in this damned business the minute they go to California! Soon as you cross the Rockies you think money grows on trees for us here in New York to ship out to you to spend as fast as it arrives! How in hell can we come out ahead if you get rid of it before we've even earned it and then keep on asking for more and more!'

'Now just a minute, Maurie. You sit back here working with those damn skimpy budgets you dream up with the thieving distributors, and no matter how hard we try, the cost of producing anything worthwhile has gone up and up. You don't go out into the streets the way we used to and pick up some friends and shoot a movie. The whole business has changed. Anybody who's good is asking for more dough, and one day soon there'll be some real tough unions out there in sunny California – then you'll see costs shoot up! You better get used to it now and start convincing the banks, distributors and theaters that films are going to be more expensive. They have to allow us bigger budgets or they better go into some other business before they're driven into it. You don't grind out pictures with machines . . . though I admit some of them do look like they came out of a salami stuffer. It takes people, time and talent to make movies – and more important than anything else is what you'll never find in schedules, scripts or budgets . . . blind luck!' His hands rested on the edge of the desk, and several times he slapped them down, making a sudden noise that got on Maurie's nerves more than the words he was listening to. He interrupted his brother.

'They're tightening up on me, Ham. I know the films are doing pretty well out in the theaters – somebody's making money with them – but distributors are all alike, and the

194

theater operators sometimes are even worse. We producers are all fair game, and they're out to get everything they can and the hell with us poor slobs busting our balls to shoot the films that earn them the money! I tell you, if we could only look at all the sets of books they keep we might come out ahead. As it is, they keep one set for their partners, another for distributors if they're forced into participation deals, and a set for the government where taxes are involved . . . and their very own set that nobody sees! We're just a little company now and we can't afford to audit all their books, and there just seems no way to check up on what pictures actually are bringing in at the box offices. Soon as we hire a checker to stand in front of a theater and count the people going in, the exhibitor pays him off and helps write his report. We're going to have to join together in some kind of an organization and fight all that, but for right now you and Lou are just going to have to hold the line on expenses . . . but still give us pictures that look like they cost something to make. There's a growing market for serious feature films along with the comedies we've been turning out. I'm negotiating with some stage actors here who've got reputations and have toured the country and see that movies are here to stay. They aren't looking down their noses the way they used to at this business, and soon I'll be sending several of them to you out at the studio. I'll let you know more about it later. I'm also tying up a few successful stage shows to make into films and approaching some directors with Broadway experience to put under contract. One of them will be out in a few weeks . . . his name is Buckingham. I saw a play he did, and he has the kind of class we're going to need in this growing market.'

'Buckingham . . . I remember that name . . . Is it Leslie Buckingham and is he from England?' asked Ham.

'Yeah, but he's been over here for a long time and he knows theater and what American audiences go for. I'm sure you and he will get along.'

'We already have!' Ham laughed, remembering the dreadful Alleffects fiasco so many years ago. He was glad to learn that the Britisher had survived, and looked forward to seeing the play he directed. It was something very successful running on Broadway written by a talented Irishman named George Bernard Shaw who wanted absolutely nothing to do with movies.

'I keep making him offers – he writes some wonderful stuff. Of course, most Americans are going to have trouble understanding some of it, but we could have it rewritten so it would go over here. I just can't figure, though, why this Shaw is so dead set against selling any of his plays for films . . . but that's how it is,' said Maurie, shrugging his shoulders. 'Say, how do you know this Leslie Buckingham? I don't remember him at all except for what he's done here around New York the last few years.'

'Don't you remember him coming to York just before the Bijou Dream burned down? That was when you and Lou went to Pittsburgh for that demonstration of Edison's sound machine, and when you returned I had poor Buckingham set up that Alleffects noise cabinet of his. My God, I'll never forget hitting the gong – or did I miss it? I turned the whole theater into a shambles! Well, as they say, that's show business, and when things start going too well you can figure you're in trouble. Now about this sudden attack of culture that's hit you. It means we can't do all our shooting on location or on a catch-as-catch-can basis. We're going to have to build sets . . . have lighting and everything else that goes with class. Comedies are one thing but this dramatic stuff is quite another. We're going to need some permanent stages and a back lot where we can control things better than out on the city streets. I've looked at some available space out in Edendale – that's just a few miles from where we are now on Gower and Sunset. Mack Sennett has his Keystone Studios there, and several other companies have opened up near him. I looked the place over and spotted a few warehouses we can take over with a building for office space. We can lease it with an option to buy later, and –'

'Fine . . . fine,' said Maurie. 'Tie it up if you can, but don't sign anything until I approve. How much it's going to cost is very important, but I guess we have to take that risk. Why is it whenever people go to California they lose all concept of how tough it is to earn a buck? You're all so damn good at spending it before we earn it . . . Do you know how much we owe the banks now? Never mind. You're right – we have to be willing to spend money to make money, and if we didn't take some risks you and Lou would still be in a projection booth and I'd be peddling lard and hides. You're right. We need stages and a back lot of our own, so go to it – but keep down all the costs as much as you can. Hey, are you listening to me?'

Ham wasn't listening at all. His mind was already back beside the blue Pacific, and he even felt some kind thoughts

196

toward his tightwad brother back here in New York who wanted good films for next to no money. Suddenly he heard some words coming from Maurie that brought him back to the little office in a sudden rush of anger.

'This may be none of my business . . . but I've been hearing some very disturbing things about you, Ham. It embarrasses me even to bring it up, but this is something that concerns our whole family and as your older brother I must talk to you. You have to realize you're being looked at – you're getting to be better known all the time – and if you pull anything in your personal life that's . . . well . . . tawdry . . . cheap . . . it is going to reflect on all of us.'

'What the hell are you talking about!' snapped Ham.

'I'm talking about women, that's what I'm talking about. You're a married man – happily, I would hope. You and Irene have a son, you have a position in the community, and what you are doing – thinking you are getting away with it . . . well, it looks terrible and it is terrible! I'm your older brother, and if I can't talk to you about this face-to-face and give you some good advice, who can?'

'You're right – it is none of your business!' shouted Ham. 'None of your goddamn business at all!' His face had gone a deeper red, and sweat stood out on his forehead. He knew exactly what Maurie was talking about, and it angered him to have been discovered and outraged him to be hauled before his brother's desk to be lectured as though he were a bad little boy. His mouth opened, but no words came out after the initial burst of rage.

'Look . . . a little playing around I can understand . . . Just so you keep it to yourself. I know all the temptations you must be exposed to out there. Lou is in the same place, but from him there's never a problem. You aren't being very clever. Lots of people have seen you late at night . . . I don't know where – I'm sure you know, though . . . and it looks wrong. It is wrong. Irene is no fool. She'll find out soon enough, and if she's anything like my Rose . . . well, terrible things will happen. I don't know why you have been doing this. You've got a family, and there's Poppa and Momma, who both would be sick if they ever heard about this!'

'There's nothing for them to hear, and I resent everything you're saying! All right – lecture me on spending too much money shooting pictures . . . even there you don't understand my problems . . . but my personal life is mine, so keep the hell out of it!'

197

He rose to his feet and turned, leaving Maurie's office without a handshake or a good-bye. Ham walked quickly down the narrow staircase with his fists clenched, his jaw tightly set and a blur of angry frustration in his eyes. He wanted to tell his brother how he felt . . . how problems in his relations with Irene had been increasing . . . and how was a strong virile man supposed to keep himself from getting interested in the beautiful and understanding women he ran into every day in this peculiar business they were in? They all wanted so much from him – roles in pictures, recognition . . . many things – and they were all so willing to give him some of the things he wanted . . . things he delighted in receiving. Love . . . affection . . . companionship . . . outlets for his sexual needs. All right, so it was all wrong, but damn it to hell, to be hauled up in front of Maurie like a schoolboy caught cheating in class, like a husband sleeping with . . . Who was the last one? . . . Oh, yes, of course – the cute actress who couldn't act worth a damn, but was Bernhardt in bed. He smiled remembering that wonderful audition late one night with her in his office when the studio was quiet and they were alone.

He took a cab to the Algonquin Hotel, paid the driver and went up to the room.

'Irene . . . where in hell is the kid? Is he packed? . . . Get our stuff together. We have to get out of here and catch the train tonight. We're going back to California!'

The kid was there all right. He was sitting down on the floor playing with one of his mother's long hairpins, and he thought it would be interesting to stick it into the little holes on the brass plate down where the wall and the floor came together. He stuck it in and there was a flash of light, a scream of pain and all the lights on their hotel floor went out.

'For God's sake, what did you let him do?' Ham shouted at Irene, who rushed over to pick up and comfort the screaming boy. He had a small burn on his hand, and Irene smeared on some ointment, which eased the pain and turned off his tears. The bellboy came for their luggage, and a hotel engineer, carrying a big flashlight, poked his head through the door to ask if they were having any electrical trouble in their room.

'Nah, nothing wrong here,' Ham said to the engineer as they left their room. He smiled tightly. 'What happened to the lights? Hasn't the hotel paid its electric bill?'

The little boy whimpered, and his father leaned down in the hall to speak to him in a very low voice.

'Shut up, you already caused enough trouble. Now keep your mouth closed until we get out of here or they might make me pay for whatever you did to their damn electricity!'

His son wiped away the tears with his sleeve and bit his lip, as the family took the elevator down to the lobby. Irene looked at Ham in disgust.

'Not a word of sympathy out of you. What kind of a father are you, anyhow!'

Ham still burned with anger at his confrontation with Maurie and said nothing in reply but looked straight ahead as they passed the floors and came to the lobby. Suddenly he reached down and squeezed his son's shoulder and spoke in almost a contrite voice to the boy.

'Kid, are you all right? I'm glad nothing worse happened. Don't you ever do anything like that again.'

The little boy looked up at his father with a hurt look on his face. Ham reached down and, without realizing it, grasped his son's burned hand. The boy let out a loud yelp of pain.

'Shut up! Quit making such a big thing out of nothing!' snapped Ham in an angry voice as the elevator door slid open and he strode across the lobby to pay their bill.

199

CHAPTER TWENTY

Edendale in the early twenties was a series of softly rolling green hills not far from the central Hollywood area. It was gradually changing from pleasant countryside as blocks of sprawling ugly buildings went up to house the new movie studios on the despoiled farmland. Trolley tracks ran on Allesandro Street, and it was easy to get here from anyplace in the growing metropolis of Los Angeles. Trees shaded the roads, which were used as backgrounds for many films shot by Mack Sennett's Keystone Company and other production organizations attracted to the almost rural area. Soon it grew less lovely as more sheds and squat wooden buildings sprang up and the groves of shade and fruit trees were uprooted to make room for the back lots, stages and homes needed by newcomers to the Golden State.

Ham, Irene and their son found a duplex apartment not far from Olive Hill on the outskirts of Hollywood, and the ride to the new Robbins' Feature Film Studios in Edendale took less than fifteen minutes by auto, twenty-five by trolley.

No matter how close Ham lived to his work, he was at the studio much more than at home. Several times he took his son with him to the studio, as he had promised when they were in Harrisburg, and he was overjoyed at the great interest the boy showed in the fascinating business of making movies. It was during these trolley rides that he felt especially close to his son, and he held his hand all the way as they walked the few blocks up to the studio gate and the stages, which all seemed to be set in the countryside rather than in the middle of a growing city.

'Now, kid, when we get to the studio I want you to keep out of the way and not get under anybody's feet. There's lots of people running around, and you watch what they do and how they do it. If they're shooting a crowd scene and you'd like to be in it, well, just get in front of the camera with the rest of the people and do everything the assistant director tells you to do. It's a good way to learn the business – but don't ever look into the camera. You know better than to do that. Just act natural, keep out of trouble and have a good time, then come to my office at noon and we'll have lunch together and you'll tell me everything you did and what you saw. By the way, let me know if you think anybody is just sitting around doing nothing!'

'All right, Poppa,' said the boy, and he was off to join the crowd scene and watch the movies being made.

Irene came to the studio several times to pick up Ham junior and stayed to watch her husband direct a few scenes. More and more they were shooting feature films, and Ham was supervising production operations for the entire studio. He hired directors to handle individual shows but knew everything that was going on. He knew who was working, who was not, who was hired and who was fired.

Left alone so much, Irene met several other women living nearby and struck up friendships that helped keep her busy while Ham worked at his studio. Most of her acquaintances had seen the strange people shooting movies out on the streets and chasing each other up and down the boulevards and hillsides.

'I cannot understand what a nice San Francisco girl like you is doing connected with these mad gypsies!' said Jennie Robinson, a new friend who lived in the other half of their duplex. 'I still haven't met your husband. I'm beginning to think he doesn't exist. Everybody in that movie business seems to work crazy hours. When does he ever get home to you and your little boy?'

Irene changed the subject. She wondered herself when Ham would spend some time at home like most of the other husbands in the neighborhood, but she knew he was working very hard and had much on his mind. Still, Ham junior needed a father. For some time after the incident in the New York hotel the boy remembered his father's stern disapproval and anger, which had left a deeper scar than the burn on his hand. While he looked forward to the happy times spent with his father going to the studio, there seemed to be less and less of this as Ham grew increasingly occupied with running production. Soon the wonderful trolley rides to the Edendale lot became only a memory as Ham busied himself making other people laugh, bringing entertainment to strangers in theaters, and he spent less time at home than ever.

Besides running the new studio, keeping track of the

money coming from New York and wondering where it went so fast, he still found himself deeply interested in personally casting the pictures being planned or produced at Edendale, and especially looked forward to the interviews and readings by young and attractive actresses. Usually Ham arranged for these casting sessions to take place late in the day after he had run all the dailies and finished conferences with writers, directors and editors. One burden he quickly grew to dislike was the tedious reading of all the stories either submitted by his own small but active story department or sent by Maurie from New York. Soon he worked out a system – each story, book, play or idea was condensed down to a single page or less so he could review it quickly and approve or turn down a purchase for development into a script. He was learning to listen to his gut reaction, and it usually seemed to work out right. Maurie, though, was driving him crazy, since he had hired his own home-office story editor and was bombarding him with salvos of material. He wished his older brother would stop reading so damn many books, listening to so many untalented people, going to all the new plays and being so charitable to new authors.

'What the hell are you trying to do to me, Maurie?' he pleaded on the long-distance phone. 'I only have one pair of eyes, and you're driving me into bifocals. Okay, if some of the stuff you sent me was really top grade, it might be worth your effort, but by the time the stuff gets here another company has it tied up if it's any good. Please, Maurie, don't read so much. Maurie . . . Maurie . . . are you listening to me? Shit! He hung up.' Ham looked at the dead telephone and slammed it down. 'Goddammit! If only I had a brother who was illiterate!'

Robbins International Pictures Corporation was the new name Maurie, Lou and Ham picked for their company when it was reorganized and went public late in 1925. They continued to release their pictures through outside distributors until Maurie worked out New York and Chicago bank financing to buy controlling stock in an established distribution company about to go out of business due to inept leadership that had not moved ahead since the days of the old Film Trust.

Maurie took Rose on a trip to visit their new distribution offices in fourteen cities from coast to coast, as well as four film exchanges they had acquired in Canada. Then they travelled down the coast from San Francisco to Los Angeles to be with Ham and Lou at the studio in Edendale. These were very good times for the film industry, and the Robbins brothers and their studio were riding the crest of prosperity. A modest annual program of features was being turned out and sold very well. Now that they were getting a fair count from their own film exchanges, more money stayed with the company to be invested in new product and transformed into profit.

Maurie was filled with good cheer and optimism by the time he and Rose reached Hollywood. It was not just the business that made him feel that way. Ham seemed to have gotten his personal life under control and appeared to be a good husband and father. Maybe he really had listened to everything his older brother had said to him that miserable day in the New York office. Maurie hoped so, and there should be no reason why the two of them shouldn't be the closest of friends as well as brothers.

'Ham, Lou ... I've visited every one of our new film exchanges here in the U.S. and Canada. We have excellent managers in most of them, and I took on a very bright young man from Famous Players to head our new distribution company. He knows everything about the tricks those momzers play in the theaters when they try to cheat the distributors, and from now on we'll get everything that's due us.'

'I see,' said Ham, smiling. 'If there's any stealing to be done, at least we'll be stealing from ourselves!'

'Don't call it stealing,' replied Maurie. 'Let's just say that Mike Hammersmith knows the ropes and how to keep our customers as honest as possible ... though they always manage to come up with some new tricks. You'll be meeting Mike very soon. He's coming here in a month after he covers all the key cities and plugs up the holes. I know you'll be impressed with him. He's a smart, conniving little bastard – but he's our bastard and he'll be conniving for us! We still have some problems, though. The company is climbing right to the top of the industry, along with Universal and the old Famous Players outfit – now they call it Paramount Pictures – Metro and all the others. The trouble is that we're expanding faster than our income and the money available to us. I'm going to try working out a relationship with some Californian banks instead of going to the same ones all the time in New York. We bring lots of money into the state, and the banks know that what's good for their territory is worth underwriting. I have a date tomorrow with Doc Giannini and next day with Motley Flint over at Security. They've led the way into film financing, and maybe we can do some business, since everybody is bullish on picture companies right now.'

'Fine, Maurie, just fine,' said Ham, lighting up a cigar, a habit he was trying to cultivate in spite of occasional nausea. 'Something's happening I'm sure you know about, Maurie. It's going to affect all of us. Sound pictures is rearing its ugly head again. Warner's has some kind of a deal brewing with Western Electric . . . or with something they call ERPI . . . a division they set up to develop new products. Anyhow, I learned they sent out some guy who I think must be a real anti-Semitic bastard and wouldn't answer the phone when I called or reply to any of my letters. I've been told he won't do business with anybody who changed their name from Rabinowitz to Robbins. It's hard to believe, but the real laugh is that he got steered over to Warner Brothers when some joker told him they originally were English *goyim*. So he went over there, and Sam Warner, who could pass for a Swede, went along with the gag and conned him into a deal. Just imagine, if only the Warners had kept their original name, whatever it was, or picked something a little more Jewish . . . like Robbins.'

The three brothers laughed, and Ham continued.

'Actually, it could break their whole company, because I hear they're trying to dig up lots of money to install equipment ERPI doesn't provide, soundproof some stage space, and they even have to finance sound equipment for key theaters all across the country when they release their first sound picture . . . if they ever do. Leave it to the theater people to want something new without having to put a penny into it. Maybe we ought to buy up some theaters of our own. That's where the real money is!'

Maurie had listened with deep interest. He inhaled some of the drifting cigar smoke, winced and blinked his eyes. 'I passed the Warner's studio coming here. It looks more like a Southern plantation stuck on Sunset Boulevard than a picture company. The story I heard is they only wanted to put in a radio broadcasting station, KFWB, and Harry Warner figured they'd save money that way, advertising their pictures. I can't blame him. Advertising costs are all out of line – radio, newspapers and magazines are getting impossible. You know, Harry and I should have gone into business together. We have the same respect for a buck and know how tough it is

204

to raise financing to keep you West Coast production geniuses happy.' He looked straight at Ham, who rolled his eyes up to the ceiling, awaiting the lecture that mercifully never came.

Maurie glared a moment at Ham, waved his hand to move the cigar smoke away from his face, then continued speaking.

'From ordering equipment for the radio station they got involved with somebody from Western Electric named Nathan Levinson who used to be a major in the Army Signal Corps. I guess their other man didn't know anybody with a Jewish name was even working for the company. Anyhow, this Levinson took Sam Warner back to their laboratories and showed him what they were doing with amplifiers and other things they'd developed for the Navy and Signal Corps during the war – and from such a *mishegoss* again comes sound movies!'

'Are they actually making talking pictures, or just talking about them?' asked Ham. 'I've tried to find out for sure, but they're keeping it a big secret right now.'

'They are and they aren't,' answered Lou. 'This girl I know who's Sam Warner's secretary's roommate said all they're really shooting and recording are a few one-reelers in a closed New York opera house late at night after the subways stop running. They've got a banjo player, a couple of singers, and to top it off, our old friend Will Hays, head of the Producers' Association. He's hailing the new miracle of sound as though there had never been any noise in the world before now! At least that speech will get past his censors. All they're doing here in Hollywood is just putting a music score and lots of loud sound effects into a silent picture called *Don Juan*. It's a costume adventure thing you already know about starring John Barrymore. A lot of good it will do him having that magnificent actor's voice nobody is even going to hear! They're having one hell of a time just getting him on the set each morning, but that's their problem and soon we'll have enough of our own. If sound pictures are successful this time around we had better get on the bandwagon or we'll be left out of the whole parade!'

'Sound pictures . . . Damn it, we went through all that way back with the Bijou Dream and it was no good then. It's a guaranteed flop . . . unless . . . unless . . . ' said Maurie.

'Unless what?' Ham asked his brother.

'Unless with his electric amplifier business you really can hear in every seat all the way to the back of the theater. If they've whipped the synchronization problem and the voices and music and effects all work together instead of against each other, then we may have an entirely new business on our hands. Lou, keep after your girl friend and find out everything happening at Warner's. Maybe we still can work something out. Possibly we could swing a deal with Western Electric, too, or with that miserable guy from ERPI – and if we changed our names to the Smith Brothers and coughed up a lot of dough, we might stand a chance. At least let's find out who else is developing sound pictures so we can deal with them. Ham, do you have any ideas?'

'Remember Leslie Buckingham? You were right to send him out here, Maurie. He's a damned good director and he has a good mind – knows what's going on. He and I have been talking about this very thing, sound pictures, and he knows plenty about it. Let's send him back east to find out even more and then we'll have something to go on before we make any expensive decisions. By then the Warners will either be in business or in bankruptcy. There's no big hurry. The pictures we're turning out now are doing pretty well. Costs are down, and from the figures you send me, Maurie, revenues are up. Hell, what good is it to produce sound pictures if the theater owners haven't got the equipment to show them? It's going to take time. Let's not rock the boat until we're more certain it's worth taking the risk – then we'll rock the hell out of it!'

Maurie thought a moment and frowned.

'You know something we have to think seriously about? These wooden stages we put up here at Edendale aren't soundproof at all. You can hear the damn trollies and autos passing by all the time. When somebody flushes a toilet in the wardrobe department you can hear it in all the projection rooms. Everything here will be completely obsolete if talking pictures are a success. Maybe we should all pray it's a big flop, or else I'll have to dig up more bankers and investors . . . maybe even issue more stock in the company so we can have more people to harass us at the annual meetings. I hate bringing in more partners, but that may be the only way we can afford to put sound into our pictures. We'll see . . . we have lots more to learn – and for now, that's enough business. Tell me, boys, what do you do with your nights out here in sin-soaked Hollywood?'

Ham looked quickly at Lou, shrugged his shoulders and answered.

'What we do is to go to Eddie Brandstatter's Montmartre

Café over on Hollywood Boulevard right near Highland and eat, dance, drink and look at each other until we get tired, and then we go home. I think it might bore you.'

'Come on,' said Maurie, suddenly filled with enthusiasm. 'Let's phone Irene and Rose to be ready. Lou, maybe you can get that girl who lives with Sam Warner's secretary. I'd like to ask her about a few things. We've done all we can today, boys, to change the industry and the world, so let's enjoy ourselves before maybe we enter a whole new business – that is, if we don't get our asses caught in the gate on the way!'

CHAPTER TWENTY-ONE

Irene sounded hysterical, and the telephone operator at the Hollywood Hotel had trouble understanding who she wanted to talk to at the unearthly hour of four o'clock in the morning.

'Please speak slowly, Mrs. Robbins. You want Mr. Robbins? Your husband isn't registered in the hotel. There is a Mr. and Mrs. Maurie Robbins here from New York – would they be –'

'Yes, yes. Get them for me . . . please! Right away!' came Irene's anguished voice over the headset to the girl in the hotel. The operator was used to hearing people in all stages of emotion and tried to comfort her as best she could while ringing Maurie's room.

'Yes . . . who is it? We're sound asleep – or were!' came Maurie's vastly annoyed voice on the phone, and he cursed softly to himself as he rubbed the shin he had just bruised on the heavy table leg in the dark room. 'Irene, why are you calling now? What's the matter?'

'Something terrible must have happened to Ham. Right after we got home from leaving you off at the hotel, he phoned the studio and told me there was some serious trouble there with a picture they had to finish and ship out tomorrow, and the cutter wanted him to come right over. He said he would only be gone a few hours. That was just after midnight – four hours ago. I think he was still a little dizzy from what he had to drink at the Montmartre, and I told him to call a taxi and not drive himself, but he said it was too important and left. I've been upset and terribly worried ever since, and I phoned the studio three times. Nobody's at the switchboard there at this hour. I called the direct office number and there was no answer, so then I phoned the emergency gate number and got the guard, who told me Ham never came to the studio at all and there are only a couple of watchmen there! Maurie, I'm worried sick. Maybe he had an accident on the way to the studio. He could be hurt and in a hospital or dead someplace and nobody's let me know!'

'Irene, get yourself some hot coffee or something and sit down and try to be calm. I'm positive nothing has happened to Ham, but I'll get on the phone and call the police and hospitals. If you want Rose to take a cab right over she can stay there and keep you company. She can be there in ten minutes.'

'No ... that won't be necessary,' came back the tense voice. 'My neighbor from downstairs is here with me, so I'm not alone. Thank Rose for me, though. It's just that I'm so terribly upset and Ham junior is awake and I think he has a fever and he's crying. Maurie ... I'm frightened at what might have happened to Ham!'

'He wasn't drunk when we left the Montmartre. I've seen him drink lots more than that and still be able to drive a car, so don't you worry. Get hold of yourself, and I'll do everything I can and call you back as soon as I find out anything. Now get something warm into your stomach ... maybe some tea ... then lie down and wait to hear from me. All right?'

She sobbed into the phone, and Maurie held the instrument away from his ear until she stopped. Then he listened to her promise to try to relax, begging him again to please do what he could – she was so terribly worried!

Maurie went over to his suitcase and pulled out a file. He searched through it and founded a list of names and telephone numbers. Running down the paper, he held a finger on one name and picked up the phone.

'Operator, Maurie Robbins in two two seven. I want Gladstone three five eight two. If there's no answer, let it ring. Somebody will take the call.'

The number rang and rang, and finally there was a loud crashing noise in the receiver, followed by a voice hoarsely swearing in some dark room.

'Who the hell is this calling! Goddammit, do you know what time it is?' came roaring out of the receiver.

Maurie spoke in a voice of ice.

'Is this Ed Garfield?'

'Yeah. Who the fuck is this!'

'Garfield, this is Maurie Robbins. For a man who's supposed to be head of publicity for our studio you have a very foul mouth! Now shut it up and listen to me!'

The heavy breathing on the other end of the line turned into a sudden gasp and was utterly silent.

'Part of your job is knowing where my brother Ham is at all times, so I'm sure you can find him even at this hour. He left his house around midnight, headed for the studio – so he said – but he never got there. I'm pretty damn sure you know where he is and who he's with. I want you to give me the phone number and the address, and I don't want any shit from you that you don't have it! I may fire you before the sun comes up – and if you want to save your job you better give me that information, and right now! It's possible later you may have to kill a story, keep it out of the papers and away from those damn nosy gossip columns – or you may have to call the police, the DA, hospitals or even the morgue. I want to be in touch with my brother, if he's alive, within three minutes!'

'Mr. Robbins . . . excuse me . . . I didn't recognize you . . . I was sound asleep . . . I . . . ' Garfield stammered into the phone, and found he was wetting his pajama pants, something he hadn't done for thirty-eight years.

'Cut the apology crap. Give me the number where I can reach Ham, and stop playing stupid!' Maurie demanded.

'Uh . . . sir . . . your brother told me it was absolutely confidential . . . only for emergencies . . . and I was never to give it to anybody! . . . But . . . but . . . '

'Garfield, this *is* an emergency and I don't give a damn what my brother told you. Give me that number and address now or you're out on your ass and I'll make sure you're unemployable in this business. All right – read it slowly to me!'

Maurie wrote it down as Garfield's defeated voice on the other end of the phone read it from a little card he pulled out of the hidden compartment in his wallet. His pants were soaked.

'Please . . . Mr Robbins . . . Please don't tell him I gave it to you!'

'For the record, Garfield, what's her name? I'm sure you know that, too.'

'God . . . your brother'll kill me for this! Her name is Jean Metcalfe . . . she's from New York. I think she's twenty-five years old. He's known her about seven months – he pays the rent on the apartment on Franklin, and I can tell you he's damn careful not to be seen alone with her in public. We have a man from my department who always goes along with them and everybody thinks he's her date . . . '

'A beard! Of all the childish ideas! Who does he think he's fooling? All right, Garfield, I'll keep you out of this and you keep your mouth shut about this call. There's not going to be a story in this – it's strictly private – and if you want to hang on to your job, you keep it that way! Understand me?'

Maurie hung up before the answer came over the wire.

Rose sat in the overstuffed chair across from Maurie and rocked back and forth. She spoke with misery in her voice.

'I can't understand it. He's absolutely crazy!'

'He's something all right – something rotten. I'm going to try to patch this up . . . though one day it's all going to come apart and cause a real disaster. Now don't you go and get hysterical too, Rose. There's nothing that can accomplish . . . This next phone call I'm going to make may cover things up for now or blow it completely apart. Be quiet and forget everything you've heard and are going to hear.' He looked at the number Garfield had given him and had the hotel operator place this call.

The sun was still well below the eastern horizon but the sky glowed and the rows of tall palm trees stood black against the purple Hollywood hills. Somewhere on Franklin Avenue in a dark second-floor apartment a telephone rang. It sounded again, a lonely noise disturbing the sleep of the couple sprawled out in the big mussed-up bed. It rang again, then again. The woman pulled herself slowly up and shook the hair out of her eyes. She got naked out of bed and unsteadily made her way across the room into the hall to where the telephone demanded attention. Her voice was blurred with sleep, but she managed to speak.

'Hello . . . Hello . . . Who is this?'

'This is Maurie Robbins, Miss Metcalfe. You know who I am. Put my brother on the phone – now!'

The woman dropped the phone with a crash on the hardwood floor, and several miles away Maurie jumped and swore as he clutched at his ringing ear. For a few minutes there was silence, and then Maurie could hear a shuffling sound as bare feet slowly came toward the telephone lying where it had been dropped.

'Maurie, how did you get this number?'

'Listen to me, you no-good little bastard! You have a wife and a son who think you're lying someplace dead – maybe you should be! Now you pull your pants up over your goddamn prick and get it and you home right now! On your way try to think up some half-assed excuse like being called to the film laboratory on account of a breakdown there and some important negative being ruined. You'll come up with

211

something, I'm sure. I'll back you up this time, though you don't deserve it. Irene is a good woman. She doesn't know about you and your fucking around – not yet. She's going to find out someday, though, and then I won't help you and nobody else will! I'm not doing this for you. . . I'm thinking of Momma and Poppa and the rest of the family. I may be as crazy as you are in some things, but I believe in family – even in lying through my teeth to keep it together if I have to – and I'm not going to stand by and let you destroy something I believe in!'

'Maurie, you have no damn business at all to –'

'I have all the business in the world. You do what I tell you right now or, God help me, I'll drive you out of our company . . . brother or no brother!'

There was absolute silence, only the humming of the phone line, and then came an intake of breath and a sound almost like a soft choking sob as Ham tried to speak to his brother.

'Maurie . . . Maurie . . . I only . . . Can't you . . . understand this . . . Try to . . . Everything isn't black and white . . . it's . . . '

'Quit the crap and get dressed!' snapped Maurie, ice back in his voice. 'Move your ass out of there, and I'll call the night supervisor at the lab to back up your story about the breakdown in negative developing. Be grateful that I even do that much for somebody who doesn't deserve it. This is the last time!'

'All right, Maurie . . . and thanks. I only wish you could feel what I've been going through and how I feel. I listened to you, I've been discreet. No more one-night stands . . . This is special. Why can't you talk to me without yelling or being so damn mad . . . '

'There's plenty to be mad about, Ham, and I don't think you listen to me even when I yell. Keep this up and one day you'll be all alone in the world wondering why everybody's left you or been driven away. By then it'll be too late and there won't be a damn soul who cares!'

He slammed down the phone and sat facing Rose, looking sadly at her in the growing light that came before the dawn and filtered through their windows facing Highland Avenue. They could hear a lonely trolley car coming closer, and a few autos coughed in the dawn as a new day began in the Land Where Anything Can Come True.

Before Maurie and Rose returned to New York he again met with several bankers and other sources of finance. As he had told his brothers, the money men here believed in the future of motion pictures, especially now that sound movies had been proven feasible and attractive to audiences seeking escape from the growing Depression. The short reels put out by Warner Brothers, along with the music and sound effects stuck into *Don Juan*, their converted silent movie, were packing audiences into limited engagements around the country. Certainly many risks were involved. The theaters were reluctant to put in the expensive new equipment, and then along came a whole new set of problems. Vitaphone, Warner's name for the sound process developed by Western Electric, used large clumsy Bakelite disk records that rotated on turntables synchronized by a flexible cable drive to the projection machines. If the needles were not placed on exactly the right spot, or if the oversize records warped from the heat of the projection room or film exchange, or if the needle jumped its groove, the sound went sour or out of sync and it was like the old Edison days all over again. It was a good start, though, and new methods came along quickly. Now the sound itself could be put right on the film along with the picture. A kind of light valve allowed an optical track to be printed down the side of the strip of picture frames, guaranteeing synchronization and ending all record warping forever. Voices sounded like voices, music like music.

Maurie was convinced by Lou, who had seen a demonstration at the Radio Corporation of America laboratories, that this sound-on-film was the course they should follow. William Fox controlled certain vital patents, and a legal fight was developing that would run on for years and years, making wealthy men of many lawyers. It became possible to sign a license agreement with RCA for this new improved method, and after several meetings with his brothers, Maurie pulled out his pen, signed more notes with the banks and then an agreement with RCA putting Robbins International Pictures Corporation into the new age of sound pictures.

'All right – so now we're in it ... with other people's money,' said Lou, 'but we can never shoot sound here in our Edendale studio. Every bit of noise from outside comes right through the walls and will ruin the takes. The back lot is a joke. Streetcars rattle by, and the trucks and autos on Alesandro Street make enough noise for a battle scene. It's just great for shooting silent films, but if we're going to make sound motion pictures, we'll have to do what the Warners did when they decided to pull out of their Sunset Boulevard place and move over to First National Studio in Burbank. Of course, they did soundproof a stage or two here in Hollywood, and shot Al Jolson in *The Jazz Singer*, but they had the same problems we've got, with noise and no space for a back lot. Soon they'll be completely moved out to Burbank. We've got enough money now to do something, thanks to you seeing the banks and working it out for us to issue more shares of stock, Maurie . . . but what exactly is our next move?'

Ham spoke before his older brother could say anything.

'I've gone over to the San Fernando Valley – past First National and a mile or two farther on, beyond Universal. There's an area called Encino where there's lots of space and next to no noise. We can get ourselves an option on three or four hundred acres, maybe more. I'll take the two of you there to see where we could put up a stage and office building, to start off. Then, if the pictures do what we think they will, we can expand.'

The San Fernando Valley was just over the Cahuenga Pass from Hollywood and it was almost like being in another world – a world of clear blue sky and clean air, though tending to be a bit hot in the summer, damp in winter. Ever since water, the lifeblood of this land, had been brought downstate into Southern California, this once dry flat land, set between the two ranges of low mountains, had bloomed with farms springing up as transplanted Midwesterners cultivated the newly irrigated soil. Most of it remained undeveloped, but gradually streets poked across the valley floor and little houses sprang up here and there, with centers of commerce beginning to appear – towns and cities of the future. Encino was one of these, and Ham showed Maurie and Lou the lovely rolling acres, dotted with live oaks and cut through with a wide dry wash that would flood during the welcome rains roaring down a very few days each year.

'You're right, Ham, this is made to order for us. We're out in the country but right near the city, the film labs, all our suppliers and the people who'll work here. There's plenty of space for stages, office buildings, whatever we need for storage and construction and a decent-size back lot. No wonder Carl Laemmle put Universal out here. I'll bet plenty of other studios will follow. You start looking for a buyer to take the Edendale place off our hands. I'll find out who owns this acreage here and what they want for it. We'll have to work through third parties, though. The minute those farmers know movie people are involved the bastards will raise the asking price a thousand percent. I'll convince them we're just interested in growing beans!'

One month after Warner's had opened *The Jazz Singer* at the Winter Garden Theatre in New York and sound pictures successfully took off and flew around the world, an announcement appeared in the trade papers that ground had been broken for the new Robbins International Studios in Encino. Ham and Maurie worked closely together during the planning and decision making, but there was a coolness between the brothers that even Irene could see, and she asked Rose if she knew what had happened.

'They're so busy and what they're doing now is so terribly important that maybe it's natural tension. I don't know, but once things are moving with the new studios, I'm sure you will see them relax,' Rose told her in a comforting voice. Knowing the real reason, she had very serious doubts about this.

A few pictures were completed in the Edendale studio, but the temporary sound system barely worked, due to the poor physical situation. The public was so taken with talkies that the almost constant background racket of passing trucks and trolleys did not bother them too much. Ham took his son to the old studio the last week before they moved out to the Valley. They walked around the crowded little stages and through the small back lot crammed with false-front streets. The boy, who was just past his ninth birthday, again felt close to his father, and he knew that this was the business he wanted to be in. Father and son stood looking at the once busy stages and turned at last to leave the lot. Ham junior looked up at his father.

'I want to work with you. Please let me come out to the new studio when I finish school. I know I can help you . . . please!'

They got into the shining new Pierce-Arrow that Ham had just bought, and as they rolled down the street back toward Hollywood, Ham answered him.

'Kid, first finish school, then go to college. You know, you'd be the first one in the whole family to do that. This is a tough business, and a good education won't hurt you. After you've worked a few summers at the new place and know your way around the lot, then you can decide if it's the life for you.'

'It will be – I know it will be,' the boy said. 'Please, let me start right now and not have to wait so long.'

'You've got other things to do first,' his father replied. 'I never did finish school, but I want you to. Let me see, did I get thrown out or did I leave on my own? I think it was around the third or fourth grade. I want you to do lots better than that! Hell, I can hire plenty of guys with fancy educations to work for me, but that doesn't prove much. Just do good in school . . . get older, and someday we'll talk about it again.'

The next morning the new owners took over the Edendale studio and began to level the stages and grade the land for blocks of houses they would sell to the new Californians flocking into the state. From now on Encino would be where Robbins International pictures would be made, and it was time for Ham and Irene to find a new place to live.

For the next few months they stayed in a suite at the Hollywood Hotel. Their son was enrolled in a boarding school near Glendora, where the overpowering smell of orange blossoms was almost unbearable during certain times of the year. The Pierce-Arrow was a lovely car, but to the boy it soon became a distressing symbol of car-sickness and sudden stops to throw up the boarding school food on the bumpy road between Hollywood and Glendora. Since he visited his parents only once a month, he managed to keep enough food down to put on weight and stay healthy. For years, though, he would get nauseated whenever he smelled orange blossoms.

Now Ham drove through the Cahuenga Pass early each morning to the new studio out in the Valley. He spent busy days and nights working on scripts with his assistants, supervising all the casting as usual, with many pleasant late readings and auditions with good-looking young actresses. Several times each day he and Lou would go outside their offices to watch the building of their new studio. One big stage went up along with an office building, and then another stage was started. The work stopped dead whenever a scene was being shot, and the workmen laid down their hammers whenever the warning bells rang. After the sound take was over, the bells clanged again and the men would get the nails moving as the big dump trucks raced once more down the wide roads being laid out in large neat squares.

Ham fumed at the delays, but nothing could be done unless the workers came in on weekends or lights were rigged for night work. Maurie refused to permit the extra money this would require.

'Our stupid brother only sees how to save pennies, while he lets the dollars roll away!' Ham complained to Lou as they watched the construction workers sitting idly by awaiting the sound of the bell telling them to go ahead and make noise.

'Ham, be fair. He got us the money to do all this in the first place, so don't get so damn upset. You seem to go out of your way to find things Maurie does to make you feel sore. Hell, it's only business, and we're doing pretty well at it with all the problems . . . so relax once in a while!'

Ham knew it wasn't only business. He knew exactly why Maurie was jumping on him so much and kept checking where he was, what he was doing and with whom. He stayed angry, but when the bell rang and the men started working again he managed a smile.

'As long as Maurie stays in New York and leaves us alone out here I'll be happy . . . but he's not made that way. Well, we're lucky to have a good man heading distribution – it certainly is an improvement doing it for ourselves, and Mike Hammersmith knows his business. He's arriving late today from Salt Lake City and we're having dinner together at Musso's. Can you be with us?'

'Just for dinner,' Lou answered, 'then I have to get back here to meet with some people from RCA and our sound department. They're not too happy about the plans for our recording and dubbing areas and the patch-panel locations. I'm learning a hell of a lot about sound from them and I better be back for our meeting here. Is Irene joining you for dinner?'

'No . . . it's strictly business and Irene would only be bored with it. A studio car is picking Mike up at the depot and bringing him right to dinner with me. We're going over all the grosses to see what pictures are doing well so we can plan the next group. He's trying to sell them even before we get them shot, and that way we can have money coming in to pay off the banks with something left over for product and profits. Paying off the banks is going to be a bitch – but that's more Maurie's problem than it is yours or mine.'

'Listen, where money is concerned it's a problem for all three of us,' said Lou. 'We've got lots of competition in this business right along with all our new debts – but we'll do all right. Everybody who's not in this business seems to want to be in it. They don't know that it's the roughest merry-go-round in the world. If we ever relax, even a little bit, we might miss catching the gold ring and get spilled off the damn thing onto our behinds!'

'Okay, Lou, have a good ride . . . grab yourself a ring, and maybe a girl, too, with a finger you can put it on. You're kind of old to be so single and so happy. I'm almost jealous of any guy who's a bachelor in this town,' said Ham with a wry laugh.

'I hear you've been having yourself a pretty good ride too . . . and not just on a merry-go-round. I can talk to you about this because I think a lot of you and we've been through a whole lot together. It worries me, Ham, when I see what I see and hear what I hear. Lots of other people know about it, too – and for your sake and Irene's, I hope she never knows.'

Ham went rigid and could feel a flush of anger rising, but he tried not to show it. He managed a tight laugh.

'I don't know what the hell you're talking about. You know how dizzy I get on merry-go-rounds – never touch the damn things!'

'Just who do you think you're kidding, Ham?' said Lou, looking directly at his brother. Ham shifted his eyes quickly up to the workers high above them on the cranes and scaffolds setting sections of the stage roof into position.

He was unusually quiet as they returned to the office building, answering Lou's question in a silent voice only he could hear. Who did he really think he was kidding . . . just who?

CHAPTER TWENTY-TWO

She stood naked in her bedroom staring into a full-length mirror. The long red hair, an inheritance from her father, flowed down to her shoulders and was all that she wore. The intense dark brown eyes sought out imperfections and could find none, though in better light perhaps some might appear. Her figure was slim, breasts not yet fully developed but each holding its promise of perfection, and the clear skin of her sleek body reflected the light with what she hoped was a sensual glow. Moving closer to the mirror, she parted her full red lips to show even white teeth, and then she frowned with a sudden anger.

'Those bitches! Those goddamned El Paso bitches! Acting as though I don't even exist!'

The doorknob turned with a little squeak and she reached out for her underthings, which were scattered on the bed.

'Just a minute, the door's locked. I'm getting dressed.'

'Nita, I wanted to ask if you would help your father in the store this afternoon before you go to the theater. I'm getting into bed . . . I don't feel very well.'

Nita pulled on her clothing, shook her long hair and spoke loudly enough to be heard through the closed door.

'Sure, Ma; I'll help out. You get into bed and stay there. I'm sorry you don't feel well. Don't worry, I'll help him out.'

The footsteps outside went down the hall and a door closed. Nita finished dressing, unlocked her door and looked in on her mother, Maria de Valle Rosenfeld, the Mexican wife of Jewish store owner Jacob Rosenfeld. A family almost isolated in a city, much of which shunned them because of age-old hates, prejudice and ignorance. Jake Rosenfeld had come to El Paso almost twenty years before, opened a women's wear store and did well enough to need sales help. When Maria de Valle came in looking for a job, he was impressed with her gentility, mastery of English and proud dark beauty. Some century past a conquistador must have begot her ancestors and imparted an inner sense of nobility, but here in El Paso she was just another Mexican, hemmed in by invisible Anglo walls. Jake was different – a Jew who came from oppressed generations, he looked at people for what they were. Blood lines, skin color and the other barriers some men build against insecurity were not a part of his thinking.

He looked at Maria and liked what he saw, and, as they both were young active people in the prime of life, he took her into his shop and eventually into his bed. She did quite well in both places. Business improved in spite of depression, which seemed to reach El Paso late and departed early. Maria's figure started to bloom soon after she told him she was pregnant with his child, and he was happy for them both. Jake had no real contacts with the small Jewish community and felt there would be rejection should he seek out the rabbi to marry them, and he saw less reason to go to a priest. Rather than face humiliation, he took Maria to a justice of the peace, where after worrying out the paperwork and a brief ceremony, they were married. What little family he had in New York City or Europe would probably never meet Maria de Valle Rosenfeld, and Jake couldn't care less. He was very happy, and even though the Anglos and Mexicans of El Paso pulled away from any close associations, just so long as they came into his shop and their women bought the clothes he sold, all was well. He was happy with Maria, and she found joy and peace, which she had thought existed only in the stories her grandmother told her years ago in Sonora.

In a while their little redheaded daughter was born, and then as the years passed Maria grew heavy and Nita seemed to become a radiant reflection of the slim clear-skinned girl her mother had been. Jake was deeply proud of his lovely daughter but was worried about the life she would lead here in a border town where race and religion seemed to bring them so much misery. Nita already had problems in school, with the Anglo children looking down on her while the few Mexicans in her class seemed mixed-up and hostile about where she fitted in, if at all. She was a calm, self-reliant child and easily accepted the decision of her parents to send her to a Catholic girls' school not too far from Jake's store. Maria felt her daughter would need the good education, inner strength and moral teachings later to survive in a world filled with rejection.

She enjoyed most of the schooling, the strict routine and

almost complete absence of hostile feelings, but as for the moral teachings and religious guidance, she might as well have stayed in the public school for all the interest they held for her. She was a wise little girl growing into an even wiser big girl, and she sensed the rejections, the pointless hates, and despised all of it, certain that one day she would escape to live a life like those of the happy people she saw in the movies and read about in fan magazines. The motion picture theater across town became a refuge of sweet escape from her world of bitter reality.

One of Nita's dreams was realized when she got herself a job as an usherette at the theater on weekend nights. It was fairly easy work, and the young assistant manager made it even easier after she allowed him to kiss and fondle her late one night after closing, in one of the wide upholstered loge seats near the back wall. She smiled when she walked home. The job was hers, and the pleasant experience in the big cushioned loge seat was almost as nice as watching them kiss up there on the screen. Best of all, she had found a place to get away from a sense of oppression and into another world of beauty, love and adventure. Shadows now – reality soon!

She was over seventeen and through with school. During the days she helped her father in his shop and waited on her mother, who grew weaker and weaker from some gnawing sickness that wasted her from a happy buxom woman to a pain-wracked wraith who one night quietly slipped out of life. In his sorrow, Jake was sure Maria's treatment as an outcast married to a Jew had embittered and shortened her life. His hope now was that Nita would have a better life and that it would be where she could live in happiness denied here. This was Nita's thinking too, though she rarely talked with her father about the dream of escape. The movies she saw every weekend held up a beautiful image, and she was determined to get away from El Paso and become a part of that lovely distant world.

Several weeks after her mother's funeral they sat up late and talked about Nita's future. Jake was deeply depressed over his loss, and his daughter felt she must avoid any mention of leaving him in the future. Losing Maria was something he had not adjusted to, and the thought of Nita going to another place was too much to bring up, but the time came at last when he surprised her and suggested it himself. Nita thought awhile before speaking.

'Do I want to leave here? . . . Yes – but now is not a good

time for me even to think of it. How could we afford to? I don't know how much it would cost to travel and then to stay someplace else and get started in a job.'

'Nita, I don't want you to be unhappy. You have a full life ahead of you. You're young, beautiful, and here in El Paso there are just too many boundaries you can never cross. Think about it. Maybe nothing can happen for a while yet . . . but when you do decide we will sit down again and work things out together.'

They let it rest at that. Nita saved her earnings from the movie theater and succeeded in talking the manager into having her work as an usherette more than just weekends. Thanks to a run of good pictures, her services were needed. The young assistant manager tried again to make time with her in the loge seat, but she kept him at arm's length and finally threatened to tell the manager that he was trying to rape her and he would get fired. Nita had a long sharp nail file and let him see it several times, letting him know that if necessary she would use it on more than her nails.

'Come near me again, you stupid son of a bitch, and I'll carve big pieces out of you with this! Understand?'

He laughed at her but he understood, and from then on she could keep her mind on ushering and earning money to spend on her dream.

The Anglo boys who came into the theater looked at Nita, and in the dark some tried to get familiar. She kept her distance from them, and her anger welled up that they saw her only as a thing to be sexually used. Their girls looked right through her as though she were unswept dirt on the floor. This was even worse to Nita than the sex cravings of the boys, which after all were a perverse kind of salute to her femaleness. But it would end . . . the day of departure was coming closer.

Jake had saved all the money he could, and Nita earned enough from the theater job to build up her savings account. He promised that when they had the price of a round trip to Los Angeles, plus enough for her to live there for at least three months, she would leave. Three months – long enough to see if the dream had any substance. He had deep worries, though, about his lovely girl going alone to California.

'Nita, I don't know anybody out there. I can't go with you. Where will you live, and how safe is it for you?'

'Pop, look,' she answered, 'I know you're worried, and I've been thinking about this for a long time. I've read all I can about Hollywood. Even those fan magazines have some good things in them besides all the junk. Just last month I read about a place there called the Studio Club that some women set up as a kind of refined boardinghouse for girls who come out to Hollywood and have no place to live. Lots of young actresses and other girls trying to bust into pictures or get some kind of studio work live there. It isn't a convent, but there's some supervision and the girls aren't alone or anything like that. I don't know much more about it, but you could write for information. It could be an answer for me, and then you wouldn't have to worry so much.'

'That sounds like a good idea,' her father said. 'I'll write, and if it can work out, then you can start to pack and get out of here real soon. Now don't build your hopes up too high. Maybe they're full . . . It might cost more than we can afford . . . We'll see.'

Within two weeks the Club replied, sending information that was just what Nita and Jake had hoped for, and he at once mailed a deposit and formal application, which was accepted. Now all that remained was for Nita de Valle to get on the train and say good-bye to El Paso, to her father and to Nita Rosenfeld.

The long white stucco building on Lodi Place, a few blocks south of Sunset Boulevard, was right in the heart of Hollywood. Nita moved into a cheerful small bedroom on the top floor and shared a bathroom with another girl. Older than Nita by nearly four years, Lorene Elliot was an easy, outgoing blonde who might be considered either buxom or large-boned. A popular and very cooperative girl, Lorene enjoyed life far too much to worry about any career that might interfere with the parties keeping her out nearly every night. Lorene was around the Studio Club only two or three evenings each week, and Nita wondered where she got the energy and enough money to pay for the room she used so infrequently. She had no regular job but now and then got extra work at one of the studios. Nita learned that the girl on the other side of the bathroom was given money by the men who took her to the parties and then to their rooms those nights Nita had the bathroom all to herself. Lorene was no romantic, and what mattered was having a good time, enjoying herself and the hell with tomorrow. Maybe some afternoons she felt sick from the drinking, rich food and bouncing on strange beds, but it was her youth to misspend – and there was always another party!

Two weeks after Nita's arrival, Lorene took her along to a studio on an extra call. She joined in the mob scene and hated every minute of it. The endless waiting for orders, the studio people looking at her as a faceless face in the crowd brought back memories of El Paso, the shoving of more experienced extras getting up front so their faces would be 'established' and they would get a call-back for another day of work. For a while Nita thought she was back in the lobby of the El Paso movie theater with the boys looking through her as though she had no meaning or existence of her own. Never again would she go after extra work – there were too many other things that paid off better, had a future and let her be her own person.

There were happy times, though, when Lorene took her along to a couple of the parties going on someplace every night. She met a half dozen of the smooth-talking, slick-haired young men who called themselves assistant directors, set dressers or assistant wardrobe designers. The ones who liked girls got as far with Nita as she permitted – which was usually a quick and cool turndown. Most didn't mind her rebuffs too much, as she was a nice piece of set dressing and they felt good being seen with a different girl still new to town. Nita didn't need the nail file now, as her voice could be just as sharp and threatening a weapon against unwanted advances. Those she rejected shrugged their well-tailored shoulders, figuring there would be another time to try harder. The ones who preferred boys for their serious attachments were kind of fun too, and after a while Nita felt comfortable in their non-threatening company.

Nearly a month after her arrival, two of the usual young men took Nita and Lorene to the Embassy Club, a brand-new night spot just opened by Eddie Brandstatter and much more exclusive than his busy Montmartre supper club next door. It was a place where movie stars and other celebrities could slip in through a side entrance and come up the stairs those nights they wanted private fun, without having to wade through the mob of fans and autograph collectors clustered around the Hollywood Boulevard entrance. The orchestra was there to be danced to, the food and drink were prepared by artists and the patrons existed to be gazed upon by each other as a never-ending floor show. Nita looked around and saw faces right out of her fan magazines – Clara Bow, Richard Barthelmess, Joan and Constance Bennett and Richard Dix, the Talmadge sisters, Norma and Constance,

224

with their husbands, and Lupe Velez . . . Nita was dizzy looking around the room at so many people she felt she knew personally. The young man with her pointed out Howard Hughes, who was producing and directing a big air epic, *Hell's Angels*, and he was with Billie Dove, a simply spectacular beauty. Hughes sat quietly beside her, never spoke and seemed to look quite lonely in the crowded room.

The two girls were taken to the dance floor by their interchangeable escorts, and as Nita moved from their table to the tightly packed little floor, she was nearly knocked off her feet by an elbow of one of the men dancing past her. She staggered and fell forward, losing balance on her high-heeled shoes, and would have fallen between the tables if the owner of the elbow had not quickly reached out to grab her arm and pull her up again. She wondered why the young man who was taking her to dance had so suddenly stepped back without making any effort to help. He just stood there, his mouth was open but no words came out, and he looked almost frightened.

'I'm terribly sorry, young lady. I didn't mean to bump into you. I was quite clumsy. Please excuse me!' said the man, one hand still holding her arm, the other around the waist of his partner, an unhappy-looking blonde.

'It's all right. Don't worry. Thanks for helping me stay on my feet,' answered Nita, smiling. Several couples came between them as he dropped her arm, and they were separated. She felt where he had gripped her and wondered if tomorrow it would be black and blue.

'Do you know who that was who just smacked into you?' the young man said, regaining his voice. He leaned in closely, whispering just loudly enough to be heard over the music. 'That was Ham Robbins – Hamilton J. Robbins – the guy who runs Robbins International Studios . . . really runs it!' They got out on the floor, and as they moved with the music the young man kept talking into her ear.

'That's the first time I ever heard a kind word or an apology for anything come out of his mouth. He's an absolute bastard to work for. I'll take Harry Cohn over at Columbia any time. At least with Cohn you always know just where you stand. He's a no-good bastard too, but he's proud of it and always tells you ahead of time he's going to screw you good on a deal – so when he does, you're not surprised! That Robbins, though, has delusions of niceness and lovability – you don't know you've been screwed until you shake your

225

head and it falls off. At heart he's only a prick trying to keep it a big secret!'

'Who's the sad-looking blonde dancing with him?' asked Nita.

'I think it's his wife, Irene Robbins. I've only seen them together a couple of times. Must be their anniversary or he lost a bet or something special tonight. Usually he's with some young sexpot broad along with a guy from the studio as the camouflage to make everything look kosher, but nobody's really fooled. For such a big success he sure is a prize foul-up in some departments!'

They danced a few more minutes, and every time Nita glanced over toward Ham Robbins she saw him looking at her. He was seated at a table with a large party of people who must have been from his studio. Whenever he spoke everyone else immediately shut up and listened to him, then laughed or nodded in obvious agreement. Right now, though, he was not talking; he was looking out at the dancers, at one in particular, and when she left the floor his eyes followed her all the way to the small table beside the entrance door. She felt a little embarrassed, knowing his eyes were on her, wondering what it would be like to know such a nice man who was also such a prick. He must be a very unhappy person – she could see it in his face. He seemed a little like that young Howard Hughes over at the other table, both of them all alone in the crowd, unhappy and solitary. She managed to look across the emptying dance floor at Ham's table and saw him stand up with the rest of his party, shake hands with Eddie Brandstatter and sign the bill before leading his group toward the entrance stairs, which went down to the side door and their waiting cars. He passed Nita's table, almost brushing against her, stopped and looked down full into her face. It suddenly was very quiet around her table.

'Good night, young lady. Sorry I bumped into you out there. Hope next time I won't be so damn clumsy,' and he was through the door and gone even before she could smile or say a word.

Next time, thought Nita. That sounds like a good idea. I wonder if there will be a next time . . . Her mind kept working, and she started suddenly at the loud voice from across the table.

'Hey, Nita! Come back to earth! He only bumped you – he didn't lay you! I'm surprised and shocked he even remembered or apologized,' said her young man. 'That was completely out of character.'

226

'Mike, besides shutting up for a while, will you do me a big favor?' Nita said, leaning over the table and speaking in a low voice so that only the young man could hear. 'Find out what parties Ham Robbins is going to this coming week and next weekend and fix it to take me with you to whatever ones you can get an invitation to. I'm sure you have enough influence and contacts to do something that simple. If anything good comes of what I've got in mind – well, it could do you some good too!'

Mike leaned far back in his chair and his face showed utter amazement.

'You're absolutely fantastic! You mean you actually want to know that guy? He's a real low-down pain in the ass, even if he is tops in this business. Well, Nita, it's your bed . . . make it or break it, baby. I can get Robbins' schedule through somebody I know in his publicity department and can get us invited to some of the things he'll be going to if it's at all possible. Remember, though, what you just said about helping me if he helps you . . . It's a deal!'

'Mike, you're a real friend. Now be a real quiet one, too, and don't go telling anybody about this.'

'I don't even know what you're talking about. You know, for a kid fresh out of El Paso, Nita, you sure have a fast head on those lovely shoulders. Now don't tie yourself up with any dates this coming week and be where I can reach you on the phone. There's a new outfit that is sponsoring some kind of award dinner party real soon. I'm sure Ham Robbins will be there, so wait to hear from me. When I move, I move fast!'

'Not half as fast as I plan to,' said Nita under her breath, unheard over the sudden blast from the Embassy Club orchestra as they both got up and went out to join Lorene and her partner in a last dance.

CHAPTER TWENTY-THREE

The pay phone in the upstairs hall of the Studio Club was ringing, and a girl dashed out of a door to answer.

'Nita de Valle? Wait a minute, I'll see if she's in her room.'

She went down the hall and poked her head into Nita's room, heard the shower running in the bathroom and pulled open the door, letting out a cloud of steam.

'Mike Russell for you on the phone, Nita!' she shouted over the noise of the water. 'Want me to get the message or tell him to call later?'

The shower was shut off and Nita came out from behind the curtain, dripping water all over the floor. She picked up a big towel and wrapped it around her wet body.

'No, no, tell him to wait a minute, I'll be right there!' she called after the girl, who already was on her way back to the phone. Nita wrapped a smaller towel around her soaking hair and walked down the hall, leaving a trail of water behind her on the linoleum floor. Upstairs was off limits to men, so modesty could be forgotten by the seminude girls who ran through the halls to get phone calls or visit each other's rooms. Nita stood in a puddle and picked up the phone with her wet hand, hoping she wouldn't be electrocuted, but taking the chance since she had waited for this call nearly a whole week.

'Mike, hello. No, it's all right – this call is much too important. I can always shower.' She listened as he gave her the news.

'We're in real luck,' she heard Mike say. 'Remember me telling you about that award dinner? Well, they're having their very first one next Thursday evening . . . that's on May the sixteenth at the Hollywood Roosevelt Hotel. It's formal, black tie. I managed to get us two tickets through that friend I told you about in the Robbins publicity department. He owes me something and I made him pay off. Anyhow, your friend Ham Robbins will be there, and so will you – if you want to be.'

228

'Want to be! I want to be – you know that! Thank you, Mike, you're a real pal . . . and –'

'A pal – is that all I am? Now look, Nita, couldn't we put it on a higher plane than that!' Mike said with a mock hurt tone in his voice.

'A pal is what you are, Mike . . . a real good one. Now what time will you pick me up here? Thank heavens I brought a formal dress from my father's shop.'

'Good for you. I've got to rent a tux . . . Oh, I just remembered another friend in Wardrobe at Columbia who can loan me a tuxedo and the trimmings for the night. Say – what kind of flowers you want for a corsage? I have a friend who –'

'Mike, orchids will be nice . . . and thank all your friends for me, please.'

'Okay, Nita. I'll be by at seven sharp next Thursday evening. Be out in front, because my pal never can find a place to park his cab in front of the Studio Club.'

'How many friends do you have, Mike?'

'You can never have enough of them in Hollywood, Nita. One I'd especially like to have, though, is somebody who's a good friend of Ham Robbins and who'll put in a good word with him for me. I'll be by for you Thursday . . . and leave room on your dress for the orchids, 'Bye, sweets.'

'Miss de Valle!' said the outraged house supervisor. 'Look at what you are doing to our hall! Now please put on something and mop up that water before it goes through the floor and stains the downstairs ceiling!'

Nita winked at the woman, turned from the phone, the towel flying open to show her lovely wet body, and then skipped down the hall back to her room.

The week seemed to crawl by, each day inching along like a leaden caterpillar. Nita put on, took off, then again put on the formal evening dress she had brought from her father's shop in El Paso. She had a good taste and it all showed, along with plenty of bare flesh. Shoes, though, were a problem, and she dashed up and down Hollywood Boulevard until she found exactly the right style in the wrong size and squeezed her feet into them, determined to suffer if necessary but to look as good as possible. Lorene stood back and applauded the result on Thursday as Nita completed putting on her make-up, straightened the seams on the precious silk stockings and combed out the long, fiery hair that fell to her shoulders.

'What a shame to waste all that on Mike. You look just gorgeous, Nita!'

229

'It's not all for Mike. I can't tell you who it's for, and maybe he won't even notice me, but I'm going into battle with every weapon I've got . . . and I think this is one I'll win!'

Mike agreed with Lorene. Nita was a knockout. The orchids were pinned to the shoulder of her long black dress, and her slender figure was enhanced by the perfect tight fit of the gown.

Even the cabdriver waiting in front of the Studio Club whistled with profound appreciation when he saw Nita come out of the door with Mike, who could say nothing to reprimand him because he was a friend and the cab was a gift, with his tip thrown in.

'Nita, meet Gus. Gus, this is Nita de Valle. What do you think?'

'Mike, you're lucky I gotta stay behind this wheel. I'd love to get my hands on that gorgeous creature . . . Oh, excuse me. Did I say something wrong?' Mike's friend asked from his seat in the front of the cab.

'Thank you, Gus . . . nothing wrong at all,' Nita said with a laugh. 'It's the nicest compliment I've received in the last five minutes!'

They reached the Roosevelt Hotel after inching up the long line of cars and Gus let them off directly across from the new Chinese Theatre Sid Grauman had recently opened. Mike pulled out their tickets to the first annual award dinner of the Academy of Motion Picture Arts and Sciences and they went up to the Blossom Room where they sat at a table with four other couples. Mike knew them all and introduced Nita to everyone. She was interested in the bland reactions of the four girls compared to the wide-eyed interest of the men, several of whom tried to get her name and phone number from Mike during the evening. She paid them a minimum of attention, her eyes busy looking around the ballroom, where most of the tables still remained empty. Just because the invitations stated the festivities would commence at 7:30 did not mean the guests would arrive on time. Most clocks in Hollywood were only meant to be approximate guides, and nobody who was anybody, or trying hard to be somebody, would arrive before others were already in their seats to be an audience to their grand entrances.

Mary Pickford and Douglas Fairbanks entered, and Doug looked at his wristwatch, muttering something in anger. As president of the Academy he at least had to be here on time. Soon others entered the ballroom, many of whom Nita remembered seeing at the Embassy Club. Richard Arlen, Betty Compton, Richard Dix, Nancy Carroll and Pola Negri all came through the door and were taken to their tables. Soon more crowds came into the room, pushing past the hotel guests and fans who came in from the Boulevard to see the celebrities. Ricardo Cortez, Bessie Love . . . Edmund Lowe and Lilyan Tashman, a tall blonde cracking jokes all the way to her table. Lowell Sherman, dark and unhappy that he had not even been nominated for recognition. The newlyweds Grant Withers and Loretta Young, with her sister Sally Blaine, and then both of the Beerys, Noah and Wallace. Monte Blue in front of Joan Crawford and then Charlie Bickford and Constance and Joan Bennett. Nita stood up to better see Warner Baxter, somebody she felt she knew personally from seeing him so many times on the El Paso screen. Her heart beat with excitement, but she appeared cool, calm and used to evenings like this. Various studio heads entered the Blossom Room – Mayer, Zanuck, Cohn, Schulberg – and then the officers and board members of the Academy proceeded to the main table – but the one man she most wanted to see had not arrived. The dinner began with a fanfare from the orchestra and clear terrapin soup from the kitchen.

'Mike,' Nita whispered into his ear, 'Mike, where's Ham Robbins? You told me he would be here – or did your friend give you the wrong information?'

'Don't worry, he'll be here. Look – there's Gloria Swanson! Let me tell you something about Robbins . . . he's notorious for always being late to everything. They've got a gag about him at his studio that he won't even be on time to his own funeral!'

'Oh, Mike – that's dreadful! That's . . . Oh – I see there – over by the door!'

Ham and Irene let the captain take them to their place over to one side of the long main officers' and directors' table, where the founders of the Academy sat in resplendent glory. Lou and a young lady followed, and two other couples made up the rest of the party. They passed the stand holding two rows of little gold statuettes, figures of a smooth-featured, muscular and sexless being gripping a long sword in both hands with the point stuck between its feet. Ham stopped to examine the figures and turned to his brother.

'Lou, look at those ugly little things. How did Will Hays ever let them get past his Code office? They aren't wearing a stitch of clothing – hell, they wouldn't even make good bookends! I'm just as glad our studio didn't receive a nomination to get one of those golden doorstops!'

'Come on, Ham. You know you're sore as hell we didn't get a nomination. You'd be the first to jump up here and grab one if it was offered, so don't shit me!' said Lou as they passed along to their table, which was set far back and directly in front of the orchestra. Ham saw the location and knew he would have a headache all evening, and he was angry his company had put up money to help the Academy get started. He came into the room angry and he stayed that way until he had had dinner and a few drinks.

Nita watched his progress across the room to his table with the stop for an examination of the awards. She hoped the orchestra would start to play so she could get Mike to take her out on the dance floor. The room held only about two hundred and seventy people, not quite half of them members of the new Academy of Motion Picture Arts and Sciences. Later on they would have to put this annual event into larger quarters – if it lasted. Tonight, though, was like a small child's first faltering step, and if it staggered now and then it was only because it was still learning its way.

Nita had never eaten squab before and thought it was a terrible thing to do to a chicken, but managed to consume all of it along with some lobster and the fruit supreme that topped off the dining part of the evening. Mike took her out to the floor, and this time nobody knocked her off her feet. They circled the dance area several times, and Nita was pleased to see the eyes of most of the men at the tables and on the dance floor looking at her with appreciation and, she hoped, lust. Somebody was speaking to her.

'Hello, young lady. Remember me?'

'Of course, Mr. Robbins. This is my friend Mike Russell. You must remember him from the night you and I bumped into each other at the Embassy Club. It's so nice to see you again.'

Nita felt quite cool, in charge of herself, and knew just what to say for the best effect, which she knew she was making. Ham Robbins introduced them both to his dancing partner, Bebe Daniels, and Nita was thrilled to meet another of the people she felt she already knew so well. The dancers pushed them apart, and as they moved across the floor Nita could see Ham still looking intently at her until other couples came between them. Suddenly her tight shoes hurt, and she asked Mike to take her back to their table. The music stopped and everybody was seated.

A blast came from the orchestra, making Ham cringe and put his hands over his ears. He damned whoever was in charge of table assignments – some bastard who'd never work for him! Douglas Fairbanks stood up and as the first president of the Academy told the audience about this new organization, founded only two years before, in 1927, by a group of industry leaders from all fields, anxious to gild the tarnished image of Hollywood and the movies. He spoke in glowing words of this art business that reached out to and influenced uncounted millions of people all over the world. There had been many reasons for the birth of the Academy of Motion Picture Arts and Sciences, and, as one of its mid-wives, Doug spoke about some of them, now.

It was a way to share ideas for the common good . . . to increase long-neglected prestige and status . . . a way to learn of the multitude of technical advances coming with such a tremendous rush: sound pictures, new lenses, film, cameras, lights and so much more. Talkies had plunged everything into confusion with different technical standards, ways of recording, frame measurements and presentation to audiences. Theaters had no idea what kind of equipment to install. There had to be some order in this chaos, sets of standards. Then too it became necessary for the creative end of the business to work with the Hays Office and the Motion Picture Code to fight the threats of uncontrolled censorship, which might constrain this special creative art form.

What had been perhaps the major reason for establishing the Academy was not even mentioned during this gala evening as it had become an increasing burden that would cost the organization many of its best members. The goal of many Academy founders had been to set up an organization to keep unions out of the industry, then, if that failed, to have a powerful base for negotiating the best deals possible. Soon conflicts of interest, friction and angry recrimination filled the heated air, and as quietly as possible, it was decided to abandon this sensitive field to the Producers' Association, which was quite welcome to all the headaches. It was one thing to give awards and exchange technical information, but quite another to be deeply involved in labor negotiations when so many members of the Academy could easily sit on either side of the bargaining table. This very hot potato was soon to be happily tossed into other hands.

Now it was time for the pleasant part, the bestowing of

certificates of honor and of the twelve Academy Awards, little gold statuettes that, like so much in this business of dreams, hopes and shadows, were not quite what they seemed. Made of an inexpensive metal and standing on lead-filled bases, they were only washed with the thinnest coating of gold. There was absolutely no element of surprise as to who would receive the awards, as this information had been given out many months earlier. Fairbanks explained how the nominations for Best Picture, Actor, Actress, Director, Writing and other exotic arts and crafts had been arrived at and the final winners chosen by a committee.

William De Mille, Cecil's serious brother, called the winners up to the table and Mary Pickford handed each of them a golden statuette. Best Picture for 1927–28 went to Paramount for the thrilling war film *Wings*, and Adoph Zukor walked forward with the producer, Lucien Hubbard, to accept the honor.

'Irene, did I ever tell you about the first time I met Adolph Zukor?' Ham leaned over to whisper in his wife's ear. He went on to tell her about that day at Hale's Tours. 'I ruined a pair of his shoes when I was working with Lou and was chief rocker boy ... what a title and what a job! He was a real smart dresser even then. I've got to talk to him later and see if he remembers coming down that ladder in the Chief's black tent. My God ... look at him now with that dumb little gold statue!' Ham tried not to let his jealousy show, but it managed to squeeze out into the open. One day he would make that same walk and take some of those dumb little things back to his studio!

It was announced that Emil Jannings, star of *The Last Command*, had already picked up his award a month earlier and taken it with him back to Germany. The lovely Janet Gaynor came forward to receive the award for Best Actress in her role in *Seventh Heaven* and then Frank Borzage and Lewis Milestone were jointly honored for Best Director of their two films, respectively *Seventh Heaven* and *Two Arabian Knights*. It had been too close to call, so they both took home awards. The rest of the statuettes went to writers, cinematographers, art directors and special effects engineers.

There had been brass fanfares for each of the winners, and Ham Robbins cringed at each blast of noise. Now it was relatively quiet again and a special award was bestowed on Charlie Chaplin, the Little Tramp, for his versatile genius in writing, directing, producing and acting in his film *The*

Circus. Unfortunately, he was not present, due to what De Mille politely referred to as an attack of cold feet, but he had sent a telegram of thanks and appreciation, which was read aloud to the Academy members. Last, another special statuette was presented to Warner Brothers for bringing about the sound picture revolution with their film starring Al Jolson, *The Jazz Singer*. The Warners joined Chaplin in his non-appearance, as they were vacationing in Europe, celebrating the success of their great gamble. The award was accepted for them by the oddly named but very talented Darryl Francis Zanuck, who held the golden figure on high as he returned in triumph to his table. The revolution had certainly been successful, as this was the only Academy Award year when only silent films would take home the gold.

Ham glumly sat watching the proceedings. Not once during the entire evening had there been even a mention of Robbins International Pictures. He swore this would never happen again ... that is, if this Academy thing lasted another year – something he strongly doubted. Any outfit that ignored some of the fine films he and his company were making deserved to go out of business! The hell with them! He listened to Mary Pickford introduce another speaker and then excused himself to go to the men's room.

Nita watched Ham leave and leaned over to Mike, quickly telling him her shoes were killing her and she wanted to go outside a few minutes to pull them off and get some life back in her toes. Mike murmured in sympathy, asked if he could rub her feet for her under the table but was sweetly turned down. Nita reached the ballroom entrance while Ham still stood there, looking one way, then the other for the location of the men's room. He saw her and smiled.

'Hello. Did all that bore you as much as it did me?'

'Not a bit. I found it very exciting ... something I'll remember for a long time,' answered Nita.

'You're excited – I'm bored. Let's go over there and sit out all the speeches. You're too pretty a girl to be stuck in that dark ballroom where nobody can see you.'

They crossed the hall to a group of couches set within a circle of large potted palms. He had completely forgotten his reason for leaving the room, and suddenly her shoes felt quite comfortable. They sat next to each other on one of the couches, and he half turned so he could face her.

'You know, I'd much rather talk to you than listen to them.'

'I'd like that,' Nita said. 'Did any of the awards surprise

you? I saw *Wings* last year and loved it . . . and Janet Gaynor in *Seventh Heaven* was wonderful, but I never heard of Emil Jannings. They all must be excellent to win the very first awards.'

Ham smiled, enjoying this experience of talking with somebody who was unimpressed with him and able to express herself without asking for something. Natural, unspoiled.

'Nita . . . I can call you by your first name . . . after all, we've met twice now, and the first time should have made a real impression on you . . . Didn't I really bowl you over?' They laughed together, and he went on. 'Those awards didn't surprise many people at all. You probably didn't know it, but they spilled the beans more than two months ago and gave out names of all the winners. That's terrible showmanship. No suspense at all. They should work it so the whole thing is a secret except for the nominations right up to the night they give out those gold paperweights. Nobody asked me for advice on how to handle it, but I'd sure do it differently.'

The drone of voices could hardly be heard where they sat, far down the outside hall. Ham suddenly felt utterly relaxed, and his headache seemed to have completely faded away.

'What do you do and why did you come to this crazy place?' asked Ham with a directness that surprised Nita.

She told him something of her life – not quite exactly all of it – and she turned her father into the owner of an El Paso department store. She had fled the Texas city to see life here, where she could know many kinds of people doing interesting things. Getting into the movies? Certainly something to think about – but really not for her.

'I like some of the people in this business – and it isn't really crazy at all. It's exciting . . . the center of the world, in a way. The things you do here are seen and heard all over, in every country, and you have such influence on everybody. I don't believe you even begin to realize how much you and what you are doing mean to so many millions of people!'

Ham enjoyed this girl. She told him about the day she was an extra and her feelings being in the faceless herd, being ordered around like cattle . . . the kinds of films she had seen and her dissatisfaction with so many of them not living up to their possibilities.

'What a wonderful thing motion pictures are . . . even more now with sound . . . and people like you should be leaders of the world . . . at least lead the thinking of the millions of people who see what you put on all the screens.'

236

He moved closer to her, that wonderful deep voice and flaming red hair arousing him so, making him desperately wish they were upstairs in one of the hotel bedrooms together instead of outside the ballroom. This wasn't one of those dithering dames who got on Ham's nerves with idle chatter. She entranced him – she was knowledgeable, she was lovely, and he wanted to know her much better. She knew how to listen, and when she spoke what she said was worth listening to. Her eyes – so bright and piercing – they could look right into a man's soul.

'I hate sounding like a punk just out of high school, but will you let me call you soon? It's been a miserable evening until we met out here, and I'd like to see you again.'

Nita knew exactly how Janet Gaynor must have felt when they gave her the Academy Award, but she let only a smile show on her face.

'I'm at the Studio Club . . . on Lodi Place, not very far from here. The phone is Hollywood thirteen fifty.'

'I've heard about that place – the Hollywood Convent. At least no other guys are going to get at you too easily!' said Ham, writing on a piece of paper he pulled from his pocket. He looked up to see Irene far down the room as she came out of the ballroom. She turned her head, looking toward the men's and women's rest room doors, and even from this distance Ham could detect the worried look on her face. He got to his feet, grateful for the row of potted plants that concealed them from Irene.

'Excuse me, Nita. I hate leaving but I better do what I came out for.' He reached down to take her hand, and held it a long moment before letting go. Irene had vanished into the ladies' powder room, and Ham crossed the hall to enter the men's room. Nita leaned back on the couch and reached down to pull off the shoes, which suddenly had gotten sizes too small, and let out a sigh of pure pleasure. A burst of applause came from inside the Blossom Room, and crowds of diners began to pour out through the entrance. Mike Russell pushed his way through the mass of people, finally locating Nita over on the couch.

'Say, you were right to get out of there when you did. They had some real dull speeches going right up to the end – thank heavens it's all over. How do you feel after seeing the Great Man from a distance?'

'Mike, my friend . . . it wasn't from a distance . . . it was a close-up, and I'll bet you an Academy Award's going to come from it . . . Maybe even one for you too!'

He laughed and looked down at Nita with admiration.

'The real award performance must have been going on out here, if I know you – and I'm beginning to. I wish I could have seen you at work. Come on, pull on your shoes and we'll try to find Gus and his cab out in that mob scene.'

She got up from the couch, and held the shoes in one hand and Mike's arm in the other as they walked down the wide flight of stairs, through the main lobby of the Roosevelt and out into the crush of fans and photographers on Hollywood Boulevard. Nita felt a run start up her silk stockings, but she didn't care. Her mind was filled with other things, about what had just happened and how long would it be until the bell started ringing in the hall outside her room. She and Mike looked for Gus, but he must have been stuck in the long line of cars down the Boulevard. They walked the few blocks to Musso and Frank's for coffee at a table filled with more of Mike's friends, and then he took her back to the Studio Club.

Nita lay awake the rest of the night and early morning wondering when the phone would ring. She was sure she would not have long to wait.

CHAPTER TWENTY-FOUR

Alla Nazimova, whose great purple eyes were surrounded by the palest of faces, was not the average screen star, if indeed there was such a thing. From Saint Petersburg in Old Russia she had come to the New York stage bringing a reputation as an actress of sensitivity and sensuality, both qualities highly valued by the silent screen and its broadly projected passions. Starring in *War Brides* for Lewis J. Selznick, she easily made the move to Hollywood, and followed that first triumph with a long series of films. Quickly she became the most fatal of femmes fatales. A remarkably shrewd lady, Alla invested her considerable earnings in a hotel-apartment that matched her startling personality.

The Garden of Allah, named only in part for herself, was in perfect tune with its place and time. Hollywood of the late and roaring twenties was filled with bright young people earning and spending bright young money, nearly all of which they invested in pleasure, sensation, forgetfulness and dreadful hangovers. The feeling of spacious public privacy, the inviting pool, the comfortable bungalows scattered among the trees and the many available beds of the Garden of Allah would in time make it home to many of the great creative minds of the world. Along with them would come a fine assortment of perverse geniuses bent on the slow happy suicide of prolonged orgies, endless drinking bouts, indiscriminate sex and every other pleasant and unpleasant vice conceived by the creative minds of men – and their women.

Lorene Elliot spent a good many of her nights in various beds and bungalows here at the Garden. The swimming pool was a convenient place to start a new day after a hard night, and there were always plenty of willing and handsome amateur lifeguards around if a girl got into the kind of trouble they could handle. This late morning she floated lazily on an inflated rubber mattress, alone for a change, while the man she had been with since yesterday sat by the pool incessantly talking business into a phone. She looked up at the drooping palm trees bordering the pool, the bright blue sky and a puffy cloud on a sightseeing trip. Lorene should have been happy, but the persistent thought of Nita wasting such a beautiful day in her lonely bedroom at the Studio Club waiting for a stupid phone call depressed her. There were so many better things to do, even if right now Lorene felt absolutely washed out and sore in most of her muscles from a long night spent with that guy haggling on his telephone. Damn phones . . . they usually brought bad news and that 'don't call us, we'll call you' crap.

Her air mattress bumped the side of the pool, and Lorene shoved with her foot until it floated over to the little island where musicians played for parties. She felt a little maudlin from her non-citrus breakfast drink, and would have cried a few tears but decided the hell with it – there was already too damn much water in the pool. Why make waves! She was angry that Nita made such a secret of the mysterious phone call she was waiting for, cooped up in that room of hers the last three days. The girl had been a fool ever since she came back to the Studio Club the night of the Academy Awards dinner with stars in her eyes and pains in her feet.

Nita had absolutely no idea her part-time bathroom-mate was so concerned about her. Sitting around the room began to be boring, so she made sure somebody would get her phone messages while she was gone and then took a streetcar over to Hollywood Boulevard. It was good to be out in the sunshine breathing fresh air for a change, and she slowly walked up the wide street until she came to B.H. Dyas and Company, a large department store at Vine. Nita looked in all the big windows, admired the styles and came to a door marked EMPLOYEES' ENTRANCE – EMPLOYMENT OFFICE FIRST FLOOR. Although Nita had more than enough money to last another two months, she thought that if she stayed past the time decided with her father, she should start learning what jobs outside the movie business were available.

The employment office was quite impressed. They could tell at once she had retail experience, plus the smartness and class they wanted in their expensive dress department. Immediately she was offered a saleslady's position with a good possibility of working up to assistant department head. The money they would pay was much more than she had expected, and after thinking it over for a moment, Nita told them she would be there when the store opened next morning.

240

As she came upstairs and down the hall toward her room at the Studio Club, the wall telephone rang, and she picked up the receiver.

'Is Miss Nita de Valle there, please?' came an unfamiliar male voice.

'This is Nita de Valle,' she said, and her heart suddenly seemed to double its beat.

'Miss de Valle, my name is Larry Gross. I'm calling for Mr. Robbins . . . uh, Hamilton Robbins. He would like to know if you could be with him this evening for dinner. It would have to be a bit late, at eight forty-five. I can call for you there at eight-fifteen. He asked me to apologize for the short notice,' said the voice in her ear.

Nita paused only a moment before replying.

'Thank you. Please tell Mr. Robbins I would love to be with him. I'll be down by the front door of the Studio Club at eight-fifteen. Do you know the address?'

'Certainly, Miss de Valle. I'll be in a light blue four-door Studebaker, so you'll know what to look for. Good-bye.'

The line went dead, but Nita kept the receiver tightly pressed to her ear nearly a whole minute after Larry Gross had hung up. She replaced it on the hook, then quickly walked to her room and pulled open the closet door. She looked at the clock on the table and saw it was already six. She had only two hours and fifteen minutes to decide what to wear, to shower, make-up and go down the stairs without tripping and be at the front door watching for a blue Studebaker. She would need every minute of it. She set her alarm to sound a warning at eight o'clock, and went right to work.

At precisely eight-fifteen Nita was looking out into the street through a large glass panel set in the front door. The Studebaker pulled up and stopped. A tall, rather nice-looking man got out and met Nita as she came through the door and to the sidewalk.

'Miss de Valle, I'm Larry Gross. We spoke on the phone earlier today. Would you please get in the car and we'll go to Mr. Robbins.' He paused a moment, then added, 'It's a pleasure to meet you in person.'

Larry meant it. The boss always had good taste in picking his women, and this time he had outdone himself. He gave another appreciative look at her as the chauffeur drove them down the street. She really was built like a brick sound stage – dressed like a princess in her powder-blue skirt, crisp white blouse and linen jacket and that wonderful red hair that glowed like fine vintage Burgundy. Larry remembered he wasn't paid to compliment Ham's women, although he could think whatever he wished about them. The money he received through the studio publicity department was for playing a role, being always discreet, available and trustworthy. He was very good at his job, which in part was to keep Ham's name and picture out of the papers and gossip columns so far as anything personal was concerned. Sometimes Larry thought of himself as an 'unpublicity' man.

They sat back in the comfortable seats as the chauffeur drove them east to Vine Street, made a left turn to cross Sunset and in a few blocks pulled to a halt in front of the Hollywood Brown Derby Restaurant. It had opened only a few months before and quickly became a favorite of the happy, hungry picture makers and the tourists they attracted. Nobody was happier or hungrier right now than Ham Robbins, who sat laughing in the large corner booth with Herb Somborn, founder and owner of the Derby and a former husband of Gloria Swanson, which practically made him a member of the film industry. Herb was telling Ham a new joke the talented and dissolute Wilson Mizner had just invented in this very same booth only an hour ago about J.L. Warner, the man who paid him to think up story ideas.

'Damn it, Herb, I'll bet Mizner tells you jokes about me to tell J.L. whenever he comes into your beanery!'

Ham looked up to see Nita and Larry walking toward them, guided by Chilius, the captain responsible for sorting out celebrities in all their gradations and seating them accordingly. Larry had taken Nita's arm as they entered the big room and held her so that to anybody watching it would appear he was her date, which was exactly what Larry Gross, The Beard, was paid to look like whenever Ham Robbins was in a public place with a woman not his wife.

It amused Nita, this transparent playacting by grown men, but she realized Ham's need for the farce and even managed a warm smile as Larry introduced his 'date' to Ham and Herb Somborn. Both men stood up to greet the young couple, and Herb, who knew much more about life than just running a restaurant, gravely winked at Ham.

'A very lovely young lady, Ham. Your friend Larry has a real eye for beauty. Why don't you put her into one of those pictures of yours? She doesn't need to know how to act – who really does around here? A girl that pretty should be seen! Enough compliments . . . Now if you're really hungry,

I just got in a shipment of blue-ribbon prime Kansas City beef that should keep you stuffed and satisfied for days. I'll have Chilius take your orders.' He turned and welcomed Bert Lytell and Grace Mencken, who came in with a large party for what was either a late dinner or an early supper. Norma Talmadge was with them, and her husband, film executive Joseph Schenck, bustled in and nodded recognition to Ham as he passed their booth.

Chilius leaned over and spoke in a low voice.

'You picked a quiet evening, Mr. Robbins. Not too many big names here, outside of the ones you just saw and yourselves, of course. Be here on a Friday or Sunday, or on a Wednesday, when everybody lets their cook off, and the place looks like a première at the Chinese. Be sure to phone me an hour ahead so I can have this booth reserved for you.'

Ham thanked the captain and slipped ten dollars into his hand. As Mike had told Nita a few nights before, you never could have too many friends in Hollywood, and the best ones to have were the influential captains in the night spots and popular eating houses. Chilius excused himself and rushed to the door to greet Lupe Velez, who loudly demanded something hot and Mexican and right away!

Nita slid along the soft leather circular couch of their booth, followed by Ham, who sat close beside her. Over on her other side sat Larry, close but not too close, his trained ears completely tuning out the conversation between the other two. The ability to be so close, yet far away and out of earshot, was one of several reasons he held his job.

'I hope you didn't mind my not coming by for you,' Ham said, moving closer to Nita. 'Sometimes Larry has to act for me in things like that, but from here on I take over. I'm sure you understand. I want to see you and be with you, and later on this evening we'll go someplace where we can continue that delightful conversation we started a few nights ago at the Roosevelt. Just what were we talking about?'

'I think I was telling you how to run your business, or something unimportant, wasn't I?' said Nita, and Ham laughed with her.

'Oh, yes . . . the importance of being Ham Robbins and the obligation to make movies to move the minds of millions. I remember. We have lots more to cover on that subject . . . but for right now what do you like on Herb's menu?'

She couldn't make up her mind when she saw all the pages of wonderful things, so she let Ham do the ordering. They started with the crisp crunchy green salad, went on to a small dish of the Derby's famed spaghetti with meat sauce and then came the Kansas City beef that Herb had recommended. It lived up to his advance praise, and finally there was a creamy cheesecake and cups of dark rich coffee. This all left Nita feeling she could never get up from the table and that if she did manage to, her skirt would burst open. Maybe later perhaps – but definitely not here in the Hollywood Brown Derby!

Ham talked to her throughout the meal, commenting on the food, the brief successful history of the Derby and about its founder and equally interesting clientele. He was pleased with the attentive way she listened to him and her intelligent comments when they went on to discuss the kinds of films being made. Nita impressed him every bit as much this evening as she had earlier in the week at the Academy Awards.

'We've just completed shooting a musical picture, one of the first like it we've done. I have to run it before it gets a final okay to go into post-production. How about coming out to the studio now and seeing it with me? I'd like your opinion. It would be nice to hear from somebody who'll be completely honest and tell me exactly what I want to hear.'

'If that's what you want, leave me out of it. I'm not a yes-man . . . I mean, a yes-woman. If it's good I'll tell you, and if it's something else . . . I'll tell you that too. Now do you still want to take me with you?'

'More than ever!' he replied. 'I was only kidding, I really want some criticism and you can help me with this thing I have to sit through. It's bad enough to pay the projectionists double time for working this late. Hell, they're entitled to it. I used to run those machines myself, and it can be damned monotonous after a while. I'd love to have you with me, and I promise to listen to everything you say – good or bad.' He signed the bill, adding a sizable tip for the waiter and captain, and then they got up to leave the dining room. At once Larry took Nita's arm and again held her close to him as Ham followed well at the back, stopping a moment to talk to Bert and Grace Lytell, who asked him about the beautiful girl at his table.

'I really don't know much about her. Bert. She's a date of Larry's. She's not in pictures . . . and don't you try to talk her into it. I'll have Larry pass along the nice things you said about her.'

He walked on and the Lytells smiled, playing out their supporting roles in Ham's charade, knowing all the lines in one of the oldest dramas of all time.

Nita and Larry stood out on Vine Street by the main door, waiting for Ham to come out and their car to be brought from the parking lot. Nita looked across the street at the big department store that faced her, its show windows still glowing and filled with displays. Electric lights high on the side of the building spelled out B. H. DYAS AND COMPANY, and Nita wondered if she would be there at eight-thirty tomorrow morning to begin her new job. She doubted it. Something much more interesting had come up. Ham joined them and all three got into the car, which drove over to Highland Avenue, then through the Pass out to the studio in Encino, where a uniformed guard saluted them through the gate.

The big car took them down the wide streets flanked with great square sound stages, shining white in the moonlight, finally swinging around to the block of projection rooms and the film editing area, where all the pictures eventually came together. The car halted at the foot of a metal staircase going up the side of the building, and Ham helped Nita out of the car. Larry remained in his seat and nodded a silent good-bye, and the car drove off after Nita and Ham started up the stairs. This was to be a very private screening indeed.

The little theater was furnished with a row of deep soft leather seats, each wide enough to hold two people, or one very fat one. All the controls for sound, lights and communication with the projection booth were set in a side table beside Ham's big chair. Nita could not help comparing these overstuffed kid leather couches with the shabby loge seats at the back of the El Paso theater where she had first enjoyed sex with the assistant manager and later had to fight him off. No matter what happened tonight, Nita had no plans to fight this man off – definitely not.

For two hours she sat in the dark beside Ham while he twiddled with the sound controls, talked over the intercom to the projectionist and made notes on a pad set under a dim light. The picture was just fair, and even in its present rough state was one of the most forgettable films Nita had ever seen, and she wondered how anybody would pay out good money to see it. Of course, Ham explained when it was over, it was still in an early stage – a very rough cut – there were terrible problems in ending it and he wanted her opinion . . . her woman's view.

'What was it supposed to be, Ham, a musical entertainment? It wasn't very musical and really not too entertaining. You want me to be honest and I hope I'm not hurting your

245

feelings, but the truth is that I thought it was just terrible!'

'You've settled it. I agree with you, but after spending so much money on it I didn't want to admit it. I'm having trouble with my brother in New York about what this thing cost – and there's going to be lots more screams coming from him before this is over. I was sold a bill of goods by the production supervisor and the director, who swore they could put the show in shape so it would turn out better than this. Metro is doing great with their musicals and our distribution department asked us for one right away. I got rushed into starting production, and I know I put the wrong people on it. Tomorrow I'm letting them all go and I'm bringing in a new cutter and the two of us will go over all the outtakes and the script clerk's notes to see if we can salvage something from this mess. It was all there in the script . . . the cast is as good as they can be with the material they were given, and the music has real possibilities. Maybe an added scene and a retake here and there . . . but it's like a suit of clothes that doesn't fit, even though the cloth is good. It has to be completely taken apart, refitted and then stuck together again – and then maybe thrown into the garbage can.'

Nita made several more comments she hoped would be helpful, and Ham wrote more notes on his pad. What she said made good sense, and perhaps everybody connected with this film had just gotten too close to it to perform the major surgery it needed. Sometimes a fresh, unspoiled, candid look by a stranger could work wonders. He read his notes again, folded them and slipped the papers into his pocket. Funny, he thought, all the years married to Irene and he couldn't remember when she had come to the studio with him to run a picture while it was still in work. Oh yes, back when they were younger in San Francisco with that crazy cable car comedy . . . a thousand years ago, it seemed. Maybe a few times on Poverty Row when they could barely afford to rent a projection room. He looked at his watch. It was past one-thirty in the morning. Irene must be asleep up north, where she had rushed a few days ago to be with her grandmother, whose old heart was acting up. Ham phoned the front gate to send his car to the projection room area and then got up and helped Nita out of the deep chair.

He kept his arm around her waist as she rose from the wide soft seat. She looked up into his eyes, and suddenly he pulled her close and their mouths came tightly together. Nita's arms met behind his back, drawing him even closer, and they stood

246

with their bodies tightly pressed in a passionate embrace. A long minute passed in the dimly lit projection room, and the operator up in the booth figured out what was happening on the other side of the wall without having to look through the port. He was an old hand who had worked many years for Robbins International, and he planned on making it to retirement without any problems, so he switched off the booth lights and quietly departed.

'Nita,' said Ham as they pulled apart, 'I've got something I want you to see. Say – that sounds terrible . . . What I meant to say was that I have some very special scenery I want you to look at. I'd like to make up for these two hours of miserable film I made you sit through with me.'

'Ham, I'm sure anything you show me is going to be special . . . and when you finish refitting that picture and sewing it all together again. I'm sure it will come out like that suit you were talking about. I'm ready, let's go.'

They went down the stairs to the waiting car. Nita quickly checked her lipstick in a small mirror and found it had survived. The chauffeur held the front door open as Ham help her into the car and went around to get behind the wheel. Larry Gross had vanished, and the chauffeur walked away into the dark, so it was obvious they were not going to a public place. Ham drove out of the studio and back to Hollywood through the Pass, which ran between the low mountains rising on either side. Only a lonely Pacific Electric red car kept them company as it rolled out of the Valley, picking up and dropping off its load of night people.

The Studebaker passed the dark, unseen Hollywood Bowl and continued to Franklin Avenue. In a few minutes Ham turned on to Beachwood Drive and the car began a gradual climb up toward the small range of mountains, which by day were such a beautiful backdrop for this part of the sprawling city. Far up ahead on the mountainside something glowed, and as the car rounded a corner, Nita could see looming closer the famous sign that until now she had seen only from a distance: HOLLYWOODLAND. Some of the light bulbs were missing or burned out, and the giant letters were blurred in the night, but she could feel almost an aura coming from the gigantic real estate advertising sign, which in another place might seem a monument to the despoilment of nature. Here, though, for some reason, it fitted in perfectly, like part of the mountain itself, which dominated a city built on dreams, hopes – and earthquake faults.

The car continued to climb until at last it came to a street with the improbable name of Detour Drive. Possibly named for a French real estate developer – or perhaps a warning originally painted on a rough sign by the road builders – it now was the permanent name of a charming little mountainside street that bravely poked its pavement into the hills a few hundred yards. Only a few houses had been built high up here, each perched on the steep slope in delightful isolation. Ham stopped the car, turning the front wheels against the curb in front of a little Spanish-style, tile-roofed bungalow that in the reflected light from the city far below seemed almost to be floating in the star-spotted sky.

There were no streetlights up here and it was too dark to make out details, but Ham obviously knew just where the key fitted into the front door and his hand then went directly to the light switch inside. Nita stood in the open door, the sudden light streaming around her and into the night. She had been asking herself all during the ride up the mountain if she really knew what she was doing, if she was right to be with this man . . . this married man. The head of a studio . . . a famous person. Almost without thinking she had the answer, which satisfied her. It was quite obvious that Ham was unhappy in his marriage but did little to change the direction it had taken. Affairs with other women might be his temporary answer – but it could be only temporary. Maybe that could be changed, and with it other things. She knew the risks of a relationship with a man like Ham Robbins – but felt that every risk was worth taking.

She took Ham's outstretched hand, letting him lead her into the house, through the hall and living room into the bedroom, where they stood in front of a large single-paned window looking down at the luminous city.

'Nita, this is my house . . . one of them. One day I'll tell you why I bought it. I want you to move in here . . . to live here. I want . . .'

He wanted her, it was that simple, and she did not need to hear him say it. He held her tightly and they kissed again. She stepped back, pulled off her jacket, loosened her skirt so it slid down around her slim hips to the floor, and then she removed everything else she wore. Ham paused only a moment, admiring her graceful movements, then began to throw his clothing over a chair in the corner, and quickly they were together on the big bed.

She lay flat on her back and he kneeled beside her, leaning over again to kiss her lips, then moving his head so that her right breast was at his mouth. He caressed it with his tongue, feeling the nipple grow larger, even as a part of his own body grew and rose up to meet her hand, which had reached down to hold it. He moved his head again and was over her other breast, kissing it softly, working his tongue over the sensitive nerve endings. She drew in her breath sharply and for a moment stopped moving her hand where it held him like a living, pulsating sheath.

Lips returned to lips, and as he opened his mouth, her tongue slipped inside. Now he lifted himself gently, molding their bodies close together, her tongue still inside his mouth as her hand released his penis to enable him to enter her. Moving, slowly moving together – then faster and faster until Nita brought him with her to a climax more powerful, more wonderful and prolonged than any he could remember in his entire life.

A little time of exhausted rapture, then once again the gentle rhythm of bodies one against the other in the indescribable insatiable friction of love. Faster ... ever faster ... moving together until he exploded inside again and again and she moaned in the ecstasy they shared.

Pale dawn sunlight streamed through the big window, bathing both naked bodies sprawled on the rumpled sheets in a glow of amber. Nita slowly came awake, stretched her arms as high as they would reach above her head, then lifted herself on an elbow to look down at the man beside her. She examined the relaxed face, wondering what dreams he might be having. Were they happy dreams? Was she in them? She knew she was happy, almost unbearably so if that was possible and that this house was where she would live for a while – not for always, though. Other ideas already were taking shape and form in her mind and, like everything else that had happened to her since last night, she would make all of them come true ... every one of them!

Nita was sure this man truly wanted her. She knew he had enjoyed her company these few hours they had been together, and she was positive there would be even greater joy to come in the intense physical relationship it was obvious he had arranged would have its beginnings early this morning in his little house in the sky.

Ham made her feel she was a very real person, desired, perhaps soon even to be loved. Nita would never again let herself be a nothing in the crowd, a faceless usherette in a dark theater. Life had started for her when she left El Paso, and she would never return. Ham Robbins was a man her every instinct told her she would make very happy. He needed her, and she was determined that nothing – nothing – would ever stop her from getting him and holding him.

Nita studied the face of the sleeping man.

'I wonder what sign he was born under,' she said to herself. 'When he wakes up I must ask him.'

CHAPTER TWENTY-FIVE

Ever since their marriage, Irene and Ham had lived in places belonging to other people: hotel rooms, rented apartments, a leased duplex, borrowed bungalows – nothing really theirs. Even now they were in a suite at the Ambassador Hotel, far across town on Wilshire Boulevard. With money rolling in and the increasing success of Robbins International Pictures, it was time to begin thinking of putting down their own roots.

Although Irene wanted them to have a home of their own, Ham felt unwilling to make a serious commitment until they had enough money to build a showplace, something much more than just a place to live. Now, with Nita set up in the little house he had secretly acquired in the Hollywood hills, he felt he should give Irene the home she wanted so much. After all, his mistress had a place, so why shouldn't his wife have one too?

In an unusual gesture, Ham suggested to Irene they go for a ride one Sunday afternoon and see if they could find a place for sale, or land where they could build their own home. He drove them in the Pierce-Arrow across town from Wilshire to Sunset Boulevard and then west toward the Pacific Ocean. They entered Beverly Hills, a city within the city, a lovely place filled with trees brought from all over the world. They stopped to look at some of the magnificent homes built on the rolling green hills, especially those behind the Beverly Hills Hotel . . . the Tom Mix estate . . . the Hellman mansion . . . a brief glimpse of fabulous Pickfair almost hidden by walls and gates, and the lovely Richard Barthelmess manor house.

Ham parked the car just off Sunset and they walked up to the pink stucco hotel, where they had lunch. Later he drove Irene up Benedict Canyon Drive, winding and twisting up the side streets until they came to Sierra View, then only a short little lane, where the view of the city spread out below was breathtaking. There was a small sign, hidden in the underbrush, giving the name of a realtor to phone for information, and by evening Ham and Irene had begun negotiations for the property that would become the site of their palatial new home.

They both shared in the planning, and Ham spent a great deal of time going over every detail from the basic floor plan of the house to the landscaping and design of the swimming pool, the tennis court and the combination party room and screening theater in the basement. This was going to be much more than a place in which to live – it was also to be a space for celebration, for parties that would proclaim and confirm Ham's place as a leader in the community and the industry.

During this wonderful time of planning and building, Ham and Irene enjoyed a warm feeling of closeness. Work with architects, contractors, interior decorators, landscape artists and craftsmen kept them joyfully frustrated and busy – even with all the usual problems they were bound to encounter when the desires of two people run into the practical realities of those who turn dreams into homes.

Ham left the actual construction to a well-known residential builder whose reputation had been made in San Marino, Pasadena, Hancock Park and now the far reaches of Beverly Hills. It was a very comfortable place, meant to be lived in and enjoyed. Rich in detail and appointments, slightly Spanish in tone, it all fitted together in a unity of white stucco walls, graceful arches and sloping red-tiled roof.

At last it was time for the traditional housewarming party, when friends were invited to admire – and rivals to seethe with envy. They filled the house – and their stomachs – and were extravagant with compliments to Ham and Irene on their magnificent new home and the gardens surrounding it. Irene's father and sister came down from San Francisco for the gala event, and after a wide-eyed tour, Betty took Irene off to one side in the library.

'How many of these people here do you actually know, Irene? I can't believe you and Ham have met them all! This house and all your grounds . . . It's more magnificent than I had ever dreamed. I know it took you almost a year to build, but I still can't believe it.' She shook her head as they went down to the basement screening room, which was crowded with guests.

'Please relax a little and enjoy yourself, Betty. Ham has done so well that it's only right that he has some of the things he always wanted. Come with me and I'll introduce you to

252

some of our guests. That man over there is Mike Hammersmith. He's head of distribution for Ham's company. He's interesting in a crude sort of way. Ham thinks he's absolutely the best of anybody in the business, but I've always thought there was something kind of . . . uh . . . "crooked" about him. Maybe that's what it takes to be the best.

'Mike, I'd like you to meet my sister, Betty Cohn, from San Francisco. She arrived this morning to help celebrate our housewarming. I'm sure you know her husband, Morris Cohn. He operates a chain of theaters in Northern California.'

Mike turned on the charm he reserved for theater owners and their wives.

'Mrs. Cohn, of course. We met in Seattle last year at the Pacific States Theater Owners' Convention. How is Morris? Is he here tonight with you?'

Betty started to answer, but suddenly Mike murmured an apology, turned and was on his way across the room, leaving both women standing there. Betty was just about to tell him that Morris was still in San Francisco meeting with other exhibitors planning a big lawsuit against the major distributors, including the one Mike worked for . . . but Hammersmith was deep in discussion now with Joe Schenck and his brother Nick, who had just come down the stairs into the screening room.

'That arrogant man!' said Betty to Ham, who joined the sisters in the midst of one of his shuttle trips across the room. 'I was just going to tell him about Morris, one of his good customers, and he walks away!'

'Betty, don't take it to heart,' said Ham, smiling broadly. 'Mike's a good guy . . . a little rough, but like most film distributors, he's under pressure almost all of the time and takes some understanding. I ought to know – I was in that end of the business myself, remember? Mike enjoys moving around, except in a courtroom whenever one of our good customers is suing us. Maybe he has to keep on the move and get out of town after he sells some of our pictures and they don't make the exhibitors rich. Personally, I'm happy to be in production and not in Mike's end of the business, or doing what your Morris does. Now if you'll excuse me, I'll move along and act like a host to our guests. Betty, make yourself at home. I hope you and your father can stay with us longer than just three days.' He walked on through the luxurious screening room, entered the bathroom, which ran the length of the basement, and poked his head into the card room, where the

Schenck brothers had just seated themselves with Mike Hammersmith and a few other men and were dealing out poker hands. Before the night was over, they each might rake in enough to build themselves a house like this one. He decided not to contribute to their building fund.

'Nick, Joe, boys . . . Sorry I have to keep things running outside with the party, or else I'd be in here teaching you pirates something about this game.'

'Ham, there's always room for you at your own table. Try to break loose later and we'll deal you in,' said Nick, looking up from the cards he held close to his unbuttoned vest.

'No chance, boys. You might have a run of your usual luck and I'd be paying for this house twice! I know you fellows. A scalp isn't enough . . . you want the rest of the hair off your victim's body too – plus his balls! Another time. Good luck, but not too much so you don't give the house a bad name. Here's my brother Lou. He has plenty of money, no wife or house to support, and he's ripe for the plucking. Lou, watch out for these *gonifs*. I'll send somebody in for your drink orders.'

He walked through the bar back into the magnificent screening room. Here in Southern California any kind of cellar or basement was unusual, and this room was unique. When buttons were pushed in a wall panel, a screen rose majestically from the floor, with sound speakers built into its frame. On the rear wall were paintings that slid on tracks to reveal ports to the projection room, the equal of any commercial theater booth. In this screening room Ham could run pictures in all stages of production, pictures and sound tracks separate or locked in synchronization. The editors, perhaps the director and a production associate, might be with him, and from the rough assemblage of film they ran would finally emerge a completed version of the picture. A music score, sound and optical effects and at last the magic of rerecording would complete the minor miracle. A preview in some near or distant theater so the public could cast its vote . . . changes made if necessary . . . and, if all had gone well, the laboratory got its order for release prints.

There were many guests at this housewarming who had their own projection rooms at home. They were the men who ran the studios, and such rooms, luxuries elsewhere, were among the tools of their unique trade. None of them would admit that what they had even approached this room, although many would swear the films they ran from their studios were far superior. Ham would be happy to debate them on this, but tonight he was the host and he was all smiles and charm. No arguments on this evening when he and Irene gave their very first party in their brand-new home.

Ham started up the stairs to the main entrance hall with its shining parquet floor leading off to the living room, over to the beautiful formal dining room on one side and the hall to the guest bedroom suite on the other. People still were driving up and entering the house, many walking through the sumptuous rooms on the first floor before coming down to the party-room basement. Ham was halfway up the stairs when he was confronted by Louella Parsons, who held tightly to her husband, Doc Martin. Of all the people in his house tonight, Louella was the one he least wanted to bump into on the stairs or anyplace else where escape was almost impossible.

'Ham, you and Irene have such a lovely place here. I hope you throw a lot of parties. It's a perfect place for me to get exclusive stories.'

One thing Ham never forgot was that Louella Parsons had a newspaper column to fill with anything she could find out about Hollywood and its inhabitants. He knew she was all newspaperwoman and let nothing stand in the way of something she wanted to print. He hoped that tonight she wasn't in a prying mood, and he tried to ease away before the questions started. He looked around for some excuse but paused too long, and the nasal voice started asking him something he dreaded.

'A little bird told me this isn't the only house you own, Ham. Isn't there something way up in the Hollywood hills . . . Spanish, too, I believe it is . . . and the same little bird told me there's something very lovely staying there . . . also Spanish, I believe.'

It was dark on the stairs, so Louella couldn't see the beads of sweat pop out all over Ham's forehead. He smiled and took her arm, wishing it were possible to trip her down the rest of the steps and get away with it. How in hell had she found out? Had Nita shot off her mouth to somebody? He must talk to her tonight – but first he had to say something to Louella right here and right now. He registered utter amazement and ignorance, managing somehow to control the panic that hit him in the gut like a badly digested meal.

'Louella, you know me better than to believe some bird, who must really be a vulture making up stories to get on your good side. You're much too intelligent to go for stuff like that. Now enjoy yourself and later I'll show you around the house. I'm sure you know everybody here. Take Doc and go down to the party.'

Ham grimaced as a sudden pain hit his midsection and he hoped it was still too dark for Louella to see his face clearly. She continued down the stairs with Doc, and Ham turned to go up to the reception hall. He managed a nod and word of greeting to Eddie Mannix of MGM as they passed on the stairs and the ache in his stomach grew worse as he slowly walked through the main hall, then began the climb up the sweeping circular staircase to the top floor and a private place where he could find refuge and relief.

Three-quarters of the way up he saw his son, in pajamas and robe and almost hidden by the railing. It was far past the boy's bedtime and he was not supposed to be out of his room. He had wanted to see all the people coming into their new house and had quietly been sitting here over an hour and a half watching all the guests enter the hall down below. Ham Robbins, Jr., was thirteen years old now and home from boarding school for a few weeks of vacation. He saw his father coming up the stairs and looked a little frightened at having been discovered.

'Dad, can I get dressed and go downstairs for a little while? I can't really see anything from up here and I can't get to sleep . . . please?'

'Kid, you should be in your room. Now go back there and don't argue with me. When you're older you can stay up and go to parties. Believe me, you're not missing too much, though maybe tonight is kind of special . . . the first party in our new house. If you promise to keep real quiet and get out of the way if anybody looks up here, or if your mother brings up visitors to show things off, it'll be all right to stay up for a while longer. Now don't make any noise. I gotta go to the can . . . something is giving me a terrible stomach ache . . . I'll see you later.'

He stepped around the boy, who continued to peer down, watching the maid and butler direct incoming guests downstairs to the party in the basement rooms. Somebody began playing the piano in the living room just off the main hall, and the boy tried to see who it was and wondered how long he would have to wait before he could stay up all night and go to parties.

Ham walked down the upstairs hall toward the master

bedroom suite, then turned into the side room that had been fitted out as a den and private office. There was also a steam room and space for a massage table, just like the one in the studio executive bungalow. In here the Greek masseur he had hired the year before got him to relax and helped him stay in good physical condition. The steam room and massage sessions had sort of tapered off since he moved Nita into the house up on Detour Drive. Now she took care of much of his relaxing and the Greek had some idle time on his hands.

When he thought of Nita his stomach ache returned with the pain of a sharp nail being driven into his stomach. He went into the bathroom adjoining the den-office, tightly closing the door behind him. Inside the large bathroom was another room, a very private place holding only the toilet, a bookcased wall with scripts and story treatments lined up on the shelves and a telephone set in a recess with a box and buttons to switch between lines. One of these buttons controlled access to a private line with no extensions. Lights did not glow in the rest of the house to show when it was in use. Ham pressed this button, dialed a number, then pulled down his pants and sat. The pain in his middle became almost bearable as he listened to the ringing tone and waited for an answer from the bedroom high up in the Hollywood hills. The phone rang . . . rang.

'Damn it to hell, Nita, answer it!' he said to his clenched hand holding the phone as pain again built up and he sucked in his breath.

'Hello . . . hello . . .' Her voice at last. He wished he could sound that calm.

'I've got to talk to you, Nita, and I can't get away from here. We're having this damned party and the place is full of people. But listen . . . somebody knows about us . . . about the house . . . about you . . .'

Nita's calm voice broke in on him. 'Ham, you sound so disturbed. Do you think I would have told this to anybody after you asked me not to? I swear to you on my mother's grave, nothing like that ever happened. I'm sure it's only some harmless gossip that Larry Gross in your publicity department can handle. You told me yourself he was very good at that. Please, Ham, you mustn't be so tense and upset. It's not good for you. There's no reason to get sick over harmless gossip.'

'Louella Parsons is no harmless gossip!' Ham shouted into the phone, his voice reverberating in the small room.

'Oh, my God! Louella Parsons! How could she know?'

'Nita, tell me, have you seen any little birds flying around the place? Less than half an hour ago Louella told me she had heard from one of them that I have that house in the hills with somebody very lovely living there. She certainly had that part of it right.'

He rid himself of what had been troubling his stomach . . . the physical part of it at least. Emotionally he still had a painful cramp, but he began to believe it could be handled.

'Listen, Nita, I may be making too much of this. After all, Louella depends on our studio for lots of story leads and favors and all kinds of legitimate material . . . and the papers running her column make plenty of money from all our advertising. Hell, they would never let her kill that golden goose! I know W. R. Hearst better than that. Nita, I have to get back to this damned party. My brother and his wife are due here about now. Sometime I have to tell you more about dear brother Maurie . . .' He paused, and his voice took on some warmth. 'I'm sorry I bothered you about this. It had me upset for a while, but I'm sure now it's something that can be controlled. I'm calling Larry Gross, who's very friendly with Louella's legman. He can usually kill anything like this before it hits the papers . . . if it ever would. I guess there's no cause to worry . . . not yet. I had to talk to you, Nita. I miss you so damn much. Maybe we can get together tomorrow night. I'll dream up an out-of-town sneak preview or something. Good night, dear. Get lots of sleep, and I'll phone you tomorrow from the studio around lunchtime.'

'Good night, Ham darling. Please relax now . . . put it all out of your mind and enjoy the party. Someday I'd love to see your house. You've told me so much about it, I almost feel I've been there already.'

The pain hit him once again and he hung up the phone after a final good-bye.

'My God!' he said aloud in the little room. 'Showing Nita around this house is one problem I couldn't handle right now. Damn it to hell! I'm all out of toilet paper. What kind of an upstairs maid did Irene hire who'd let something like this happen to me!'

Finally he left the bathroom, dignity restored and pants buttoned, and walked down the hall to the staircase, where he passed his son, who still sat there watching the few people remaining in the front hall.

'Dad, Uncle Maurie and Aunt Rose just came in. They're

258

downstairs with everybody else. Please, can't I go down just for a few minutes? I'll keep out of the way.'

'Damn it, no – go back to bed!' Ham shouted at the boy, who jumped up from the step, pulling back from the loud abusive voice and turning toward his room. Ham looked every bit as angry as he sounded, and just hearing that Maurie had arrived was enough to set him off. He heard the door to his son's bedroom close and clenched his fists in renewed anger as he descended the stairs to the front hall. He greeted a few late arrivals, then went downstairs to rejoin the party. By the time he reached the screening room his anger had subsided.

'Ham, where have you been?' shouted Maurie at his brother. 'We've missed you . . . why don't you drop in on your party! Rose, will you look at Ham? He looks absolutely terrible . . . so white in the face. What kind of Californian are you without a good tan? Now take us both on a trip through this house of yours I've already heard so much about. What I've already seen outside and in the front hall is beautiful. I'll bet you spent too damn much on it, like always. What the hell, just like I told you once . . . turn a guy loose out here and right away he goes nuts when it comes to spending money – his own or anybody else's. Well, it's yours to spend though, and . . . What's the matter – are you sick?'

Ham had gripped both hands around his middle, almost doubling over in sudden pain – the terrible sharp ache of returned burning anger. His brother had no right to humiliate him like this in front of his guests on this evening . . . on any evening . . . but that was Maurie, damn him, and he would never ever change. Damn him! Damn him to hell! He waited a few moments, then managed to speak.

'No. Something I ate or drank earlier. It's passed now. I feel better now. Come on, let's start over here with the bar. You can order anything you want to drink, Maurie . . . I'm paying.'

CHAPTER TWENTY-SIX

The back lot at Robbins International Studios covered nearly two thousand acres with permanent sets stretching far out behind the blocks of stages, administrative, technical and storage buildings. It was a crazy quilt of streets accurately reproduced in detail from all over the world or brought there from different places in time. A piece of Deadwood City, circa 1887, deserted now but needing only horses, extras and stunt men shooting each other off balconies and out of windows. Truckloads of loose dirt would be spread in the street early in the morning for oversized gas-driven fans to blow around so the cameraman could curse the realism fouling his delicate equipment as the actors chewed bits of the scenery. Farther on was a square out of old Sarajevo in the Balkans, where for a few hundred yards it looked as though Archduke Francis Ferdinand and his wife had just driven by in a carriage to keep their appointment with an assassin. A sharp turn right and it became a modern city block, interchangeably New York, Detroit, Chicago or Metropolis, U.S.A., needing only set dressing, actors, autos and drifting smoke to bring it alive. Another six hundred feet, as the camera dolly rolls, was a village high street in rural England with its shop windows emptied as though a horde of Yankee tourists had recently passed through.

At the very back of the back lot was the perfect replica of a small American town as it must have looked in 1910: a white clapboard city hall and library, the brick county courthouse, a school and church, with appropriate bell towers, and a row of small shops and offices that ran down both sides of a narrow tree-shaded street. Right in the middle of the block, between the hardware store and pharmacy, was a sparkling new nickelodeon. All the scene needed to complete the picture was *Saturday Evening Post* painted up top with Norman Rockwell's signature scrawled down in the corner.

This entire street had been designed and built for a feature film that was just about to begin shooting. The whole thing was made of weatherproof reinforced materials so it could remain standing, like all the other permanent back lot sets, for use as backgrounds in many pictures to be shot during the years to come. A new coat of paint, a change of trees and some set dressing would make it look like a hundred different American towns. The art director, whose creation it was, with liberal help from Rockwell, had every right to be proud of his achievement. He took all the drawings, plans, stills and blueprints of the small-town street to show to Ham, who took special interest in the permanent sets that were making his back lot the showplace of the industry. The art director was fortunate and had only to wait forty-five minutes instead of the usual hour and fifteen minutes Ham kept department heads sitting outside his office nearly every afternoon. The boss was anxious to see his newest street and personally opened the inner door to summon him inside.

'Fritz, it's perfect, just perfect. It's almost exactly like a few towns I've lived in myself. Beautiful!' Ham brought up one of the still pictures closer to his face and turned his desk lamp so the light fell on the shot, which he studied carefully. He pulled over the master blueprint and compared it with the spread-out renderings.

'That nickelodeon you stuck there in the row of stores . . . It seems just fine, Fritz, except no self-respecting nickelodeon owner would ever call his place The Budapest! Oh, I know what happened here. We've got that Hungarian director, Sandor Kurtiz . . . he's Mike Curtiz's cousin . . . spells it different . . . Maurie sent him here after he won some European film awards, and now we're putting him on a picture set in a small American town back in 1910. Well – drama is still drama whenever and wherever it happens, but if he louses it up he's on his way back to Budapest on the next boat. I want the name of that nickelodeon changed right away!'

He thought a minute, took a pencil and drew something on the blueprint.

'That's it . . . Gold letters on a nice light blue background. Put it right up here over the front and stick a sign on that column there saying 'Admission Five Cents.' My God . . . what's happened to admission prices! Now it costs at least a buck and a half to see a dog, and another fifty cents for some soggy popcorn! Get the sign painter out there right away. I want it to look like something that would fit in with the time period between 1905 and 1910. It's very important, Fritz, you keep this little name change between you, me and the painter for right now. Understand?'

The art director nodded.

'Sure, Mr. Robbins. I'll have it done within a few hours. Gold leaf is hard to work with and I hope there's no wind blowing out there, but I know exactly what you want.'

'Good. I'll be out there tomorrow at about lunchtime with my brother Lou. Tell the stills department I want a photographer there to get some shots when I show it to Lou. I'm going to give him a real surprise, and I want some pictures to put on the wall in the bungalow. We may set part of it aside to show the company history and to hold all the awards we're going to win from now on!'

Just before lunch the next day, Ham walked down the hall of the executive building to his brother's office. Lou's special interest was in the technical and physical operation of the studio, and he held the very important job of production manager, in addition to being a vice-president. He left nearly all of the creative end to Ham, and while they had an occasional disagreement, there was none of the friction and bitterness between them that always seemed to exist between Maurie and Ham. Lou was a relaxed person, liked to turn a serious problem into an easy laugh and work out solutions with people as people. He got on well with all employees, with the representatives of other companies and everybody else he contacted. Lou had great respect for technical and creative excellence and was genuinely liked by all the people with whom he worked. While Lou was accepted and respected without even trying to be, his younger brother seemed constantly on the defensive, always suspicious of others and, perhaps, without realizing it, encouraging their distrust of him.

Their sister Ruth had once told Lou that Ham wanted to be loved without ever being lovable, liked without trying to be likable. The image of bubbling good humor and joviality that he assumed and projected in public had the property common to most bubbles. It was all on the surface – tissue thin, quickly perishable and mostly for public display. Ham boasted that he had the ability to read the true character of others, yet he rarely faced himself head-on to read the most important character in all his life – himself. In spite of all this, the one who got along best with Ham was his brother Lou. Everything they had endured together on the rough road to success had helped to bring and hold them together.

'Ham, I'm due at the Producers' Association for a meeting on the new basic union agreements. We're having the usual problems with the Teamsters and IATSE and –'

'This will take less than half an hour, Lou. I have something out on the back lot I want you to see with me . . . something very special that should give you a tremendous kick!' Ham insisted.

'That sounds like you've bought a mule to star in a picture. Please, spare me animal actors! We have quite enough trouble with the human ones! All right, just for you I'll go . . . but I've got to leave by noon for the Association meeting.'

They got into the studio car, which drove them away from the executive building, past the sound department, around Editorial and through the New York street, then across the Western town and finally out to the farthest reaches of the back lot, where Ham had the driver park around the corner from the small-town street. They got out and walked, cutting through a little park where a greens department crew was putting in a hedge. Suddenly Lou came to a dead stop in the middle of the block and stared across at the line of store-fronts. He almost screamed at his brother.

'Ham . . . it's the Bijou Dream! What a shock – it's like bringing back the past!'

The waiting cameraman took pictures of the two happy men and posed them in front of the little nickelodeon, so very like yet unlike its namesake.

'Go on inside, Lou . . . go on . . . you have plenty of time,' said Ham, giving him a little shove. The two doors on either side of the glassed-in box office were swung wide open and they entered, almost expecting to see Poppa, Ruth and Maurie selling tickets. It was empty, though, and they were alone.

Most of the buildings on the back lot were only false fronts, but here and there some had real insides attached to their façades so that scenes could be shot with reality and economy. Actors could continue in a scene from an interior to the exterior or the other way around, and sometimes it saved time not having to pack up and move the company into one of the big stages on the other side of the lot. Whenever possible Ham insisted that a permanent set have several of these completed units. Thus, the reincarnated Bijou Dream was more than just a shell. It had a little lobby, a projection booth area and an abbreviated auditorium. Even several dozen benches were scattered around inside, and Lou laughed as they remembered how the undertaker and his son had rushed in to dump all the customers on the floor.

'It's not as neat as ours used to be. If I didn't have to leave for that damned meeting I'd put those benches in straight lines. I hate seeing it this way ... but after all, it's only a movie set, and the real one is gone forever, isn't it?'

'Not from our memories, Lou. Yeah, this is only a good imitation, but it sure does bring back those days. You know, we ought to throw a party out here some night, tie it in with the show we're shooting on this street. We can bring in the press ... all our stars and other people ... everybody dressed up the way we were back in 1910 or around then. Maybe we could even get some of those terrible old pictures we used to run ... "A Night of Nostalgia" – how's that for a nice title? It's the kind of story all the papers would go for. Maybe we could get Momma and Poppa and the girls to come out for it. Could you imagine Ruthie selling tickets again, then running down the aisle to the piano we'll put in down there by the screen ... and –'

'I know just what you're aiming at. You're planning to get down there in front of the screen and sing some of those terrible songs while I'm changing the reels!' Lou laughed.

'Since you suggested it ... it sounds like a perfect idea! I better start practicing right away. It's been a long time since I've sung anyplace but in the steam room and the shower ... duets with the Greek, who can't carry a tune!'

The car took them back to the executive building, and Lou's enthusiasm for the party increased as he thought up some ideas for using the nickelodeon setting and all the rest of the small-town street.

'Let's get a real Kinetoscope projector in the booth. I'll contact New York to dig out some of those old prints from the vaults. I know they have them, 'cause I was planning to turn them over to the Smithsonian for their new collection. Trouble with those old Kinetoscopes is the light output is so low. I'm sure the prop department can find us a machine, and I'll talk with the guys in electric and camera about putting in an incandescent lamp house so we can pump out a good bright picture for the big audience. We can't use a studio projector, since the speed ratio of sound is so different ... It'll work out fine. Ham, you've come up with a great idea, and we ought to have one hell of a good time with it!'

Within a week the studio had located an old projector that could handle the wonderful antique films New York shipped to the studio. A new, more powerful light source was added and a suitably out-of-tune upright piano was rolled up beside the screen. The benches were placed in neat lines and the publicity department went to work on the guest list and beat the drums in the trade and national press about the 'Night of Nostalgia' out on the back lot at the Robbins International Studios. Ham phoned Ruth and invited her and Miriam to come and sell tickets for a gag and play the old piano the way she used to. She laughed and turned him down on everything but being there. He begged her again to play the piano.

'No, absolutely no! I haven't played for years . . . Anyhow, I could never do it in front of all those talented people. Why don't you have a studio musician play? It will sound much better and . . . No, Ham. Please, forget it.' She and Miriam would be there, but Momma wasn't feeling at all well and Poppa hated to leave her even for one night. She had caught a mild case of pneumonia the winter before and had been in and out of the hospital ever since. Nothing serious right now, but she was still quite weak, and not as young as she used to be. Ruth would bring her husband, Abe Harris, who ran the Robbins Film Exchange in Pittsburgh, and Miriam and her husband, Larry Levine, an accountant, would make every effort to come back to the Bijou Dream.

'I can't believe it, Ham! After all these years to have our nickelodeon back in the family! It's a nice idea and we'll be there. Oh . . . how are Irene and Ham junior? I haven't heard from her in such a long time.'

'They're both fine. You'll see them when you come out.' That was all Ham had to say about his family. He waited for Ruth to ask him something else . . . and she did.

'Ham . . . please don't take offense. I'm your older sister, so I feel I can ask you this. Are you and Irene getting along? I feel there's something that's not right and . . . and I've heard . . .'

'What have you heard? And from who? From our dear brother Maurie! Listen, Ruth. My personal life is just that – personal! I appreciate your interest, but if you're about to lecture me, lay off!'

Ruth was shocked. Her brother had never spoken to her like this. She stammered a reply.

'Ham . . . don't be angry. All I want is for you and your family to be happy. If there's anything I can do to help you all to be that way, please . . .'

'There is something, Ruth. Leave me alone!' and he hung up

the phone on his sister – the first time he had ever done so in anger.

The invitations to the 'Night of Nostalgia' party went out. Acceptances came in quickly from the press, the stars and the various executives of other studios. Even a few selected agents were invited, although Ham agonized long over making them welcome on the lot. Caterers brought in their trucks, and a large tent was raised in the little park, filled with long tables and chairs for all the guests. Bars went into several of the storefronts, and the town pharmacy became a real soda fountain for the nondrinkers and the children who would be present. There was a run on wardrobe departments in all the studios and costumers for 1910 outfits, and Ham decided to let the make-up people paste a full moustache on his upper lip for the evening. A black derby, fawn spats and a pinstripe suit would put him right back into times long gone – only now he would be a man of thirty-seven, not a brat of thirteen.

'My God, not fire engines again!' yelled Lou at the screen. He was testing the old projection machine, and the picture it threw on the big white sheet was almost exactly like the one he remembered from the old days. The plans for the big party had been somewhat changed, typically enlarged. Now after having dinner across the street in the big tent, all the guests would come into the Bijou Dream and see some authentic old films; then there would be a special premiere of the newest picture about to be released by Robbins International. Two modern projectors were installed behind the façade of the pharmacy next door, and when the final fire engine had passed from the screen, the dividing wall would be pulled back to let the big sound projectors shoot their beams on the Bijou Dream screen. Ham was sure that when Maurie saw the cost of this rebuilding of the nickelodeon set he would scream, but it was for advertising and publicity, and everybody agreed it was a whale of a gimmick.

'Today you have to be different or be ignored!' was how Ham answered Maurie on the phone when he told him about it. At first Maurie wanted nothing to do with the whole idea, finally agreeing to take the train out the next day and arrive the morning of the party.

'And try not to bankrupt us in the meantime!' was how he closed the conversation. Ham shrugged as he finished talking, then turned to Lou.

'The same old Maurie. We're moving ahead because here in production we know where to spend money and how to

266

spend it, but he's screaming as though we were still in a nickel-and-dime business. This is playing for millions . . . and meantime all he does is to get me sore as hell!'

Lou calmed him down. He had become the most enthusiastic of all about the coming event and would be taking bows as the projectionist for the opening nickelodeon portion of the program.

'Ham, have you seen the set-up now in the Bijou? I'm going to spend some time there tonight going over the modifications we made in the old Kinetoscope projector so that when the time comes for the party in a few nights there won't be any problems. You want to come over with me this evening and see the way it's going?'

'Thanks, Lou, but I'm . . . uh . . . well, I'm running the recut final version of *Cinema Parade of 1931* up in Santa Barbara. Just the editor and I are going there. I don't want anybody else along and I'm keeping it real quiet. I made some cuts over the objections of the director . . . and the production associate I put on was also a shlemiel who was ruining the whole picture. Before I give it a final okay I want to see it without interference from either of them. I wish I could be with you tonight to see you run the old projector again . . . but, hell, I must have seen that a thousand or more times.'

'Yeah, but I never get tired of threading up one of those lovely things and watching the film move through and put that picture up there on the screen. No matter how much they improve them, I always love to get my hands on one of the genuine Kinetoscopes. It's kind of like reliving happy days from our past.'

'What's so unhappy about today, Lou?' Ham answered. 'You don't know when you're well off. You're an eligible bachelor and you could have any dame in this town. I can't figure why you'd waste a perfectly good evening with a hot Kinetoscope in a stuffy projection booth when you could spend it with a warm woman in a comfortable bed. You must be nuts!'

'I'm not the only nut in our family,' said Lou, smiling at his brother in a way that removed all criticism and barbs from his voice. He could see through Ham as though through plate glass, but took him for what he was without passing judgment. 'Go on to your "sneak preview," you sneak. It's in Santa Barbara this time, is it? You phony! Go on, don't keep the audience waiting.'

Ham kept up the fiction, threadbare as it had become,

knowing the film editor would take the print home with him that evening and return it to the studio the next morning, the tins unopened. He was paid to tell whatever story Ham told him to tell, and it was none of his business where the boss really went. Ham's preview would be up on Detour Drive, the audience was waiting . . . and there would only be two people present for what had become a rerun, not a preview . . . and most certainly no premiere! He would have dinner with Nita and spend a few hours with her in the hillside house looking down at the twinkling city and unwinding from his tensions before finally going home sometime before dawn.

Lou brought one of the studio projectionists along with him out to the Bijou Dream set after they both had dinner at a restaurant across the street from the studio. He was eager to get at the old machine and enjoy the thrill of making it light up and move. Soon they were far out on the back lot in the temporary booth, where a security guard threw on the power switches and Lou pulled off his coat, rolled up his sleeves and helped the two other men wrestle the heavy machine into position so it would throw its light in the right place. Finally it was all set and anchored to the floor so Lou could turn on the powerful light they had installed to get as bright an image as possible. The screen became a brilliant white square at the far end of the recreated nickelodeon, and Lou pulled the cover off the big round film tin.

'Phew! This is nitrate film . . . and it stinks! It must be an original. Most of them have turned into powder, but this one seems to be in good condition, except for the smell. I only wish we were working with safety film. I've always hated nitrate. Well . . . let's see if it'll bend without breaking.'

He pulled open the machine, put the reel up on the supply spindle and pulled a long strip of film down into the gate. The lamp housing was still hot from the test run, much hotter than the old carbide lamps had ever been. Lou was concentrating on getting the loop the right length around the pull-down claws, and when the tail end of the nitrate film touched the hot side of the machine he was caught by the billowing flame that almost seemed to gush out and cover his hands and chest as the explosive film ignited. He screamed in pain and the projectionist pulled him away, reaching for his jacket on the chair to throw over Lou's hair, which had begun to burn. The security guard raced to the fire alarm box, smashed the glass panel and pulled the alarm, then ran back into the booth to help. Suddenly the entire projection room area was a mass of flames, with bright red tongues of destruction running up the walls, licking at the thin wood panels and painted canvas. Lou was down on his knees, the projectionist half lifting and half carrying him as the ceiling caught fire. The guard reached their side and they worked their way through the black smoke and billowing flames as the whole top of the theater set collapsed around them. They were coughing and retching from the terrible black smoke that almost completely enveloped them. Pieces of the flaming set fell and for a moment pinned one of Lou's legs until the others pulled him free. Slowly they found the door to the outside, but only two of the men could still walk, and they carried their companion, whose clothing and hair gave off acrid smoke. The guard and the projectionist were gasping, drawing in great breaths of fresh air outside, but Lou did not move as they got him across the street and into the little park.

The wail of sirens came closer, and with a deep-throated roar the studio fire truck pulled up. Men jumped off and connected hoses to the standpipes, shooting streams of water into the burning row of shops and the nickelodeon. The entire sky over the studio reflected a pink glow, and the fire jumped over the pharmacy to the city hall and library, which quickly became twin infernos. The school tower caught and poked a finger of flame high into the night.

Chief Swenson of the studio fire department looked with horror at the badly burned man lying in the little park, then at the other two, who did not seem as severely injured. He shouted orders for more help, and soon some city fire units rolled in and Swenson and his reinforcements had the flames under control, dying down and finally turned into great white clouds of steam.

An ambulance raced up from St. Vincent's Hospital and another from City Service. A doctor arrived, sent the guard and projectionist off to the hospital in one ambulance, then, after looking at Lou, said he was to stay right there, that he would do what he could without the delay of getting him to the hospital.

The fire chief went to the telephone set in a box and called the studio operator. He asked her to call Ham Robbins' office. There was no answer.

'We've got to reach Mr. Robbins immediately!' Swenson yelled at the operator. 'Where is he?'

'I'll try his house,' she replied, and in a minute reported

back that he was out of town – at a preview in Santa Barbara. Nobody knew the name of the theater.

'Who would know that?' asked the frustrated chief.

'I'll contact Mr. Gross of the publicity department. He's supposed to know where Mr. Robbins is at all times.'

Larry Gross answered the phone in his apartment and at once knew what to do. He hung up and dialed a number.

Ham lay in the dark bedroom with Nita . . . slowly moving with her . . . sharing the deep sensuous feelings that had been building up and up for almost fifteen minutes now. Their act of love was about to come to its climactic passionate finale. He brought his body closer to hers, then away, and as he came toward her the metallic clangor of the phone bell made him jump. He tried to keep moving, listening for the next ring . . . and it came as he expected . . . then again and yet again. He rose up, heard Nita make a little moaning noise, her eyes closed, then opening in wide alarm as the bell rang almost in their ears.

'Nita . . . Nita . . . I . . . I . . . Damn it, the fucking phone's going off. What a terrible time . . . Oh . . . I can't stop . . . not now!'

The phone rang and rang. Ham paused. Nita waited for him to resume. He could feel himself shriveling and was angry at this raucous invasion of the bedroom.

'Ham . . . wait . . . it's a wrong number, I know it is . . . it'll stop,' Nita said in a soothing voice.

It did not stop. It rang and rang . . . and Ham got smaller and smaller with each ring, passion ebbing away like water in a tub when the plug is pulled. He lifted himself off Nita, swung around and put his bare feet down on the floor, grabbing his enemy, the ringing phone, by its plastic throat.

'Who is it! Gross! What the fuck! You –'

'Chief, I hate calling, but it's an emergency. There's been a fire on the back lot . . . in the small-town street . . . the row of shops . . . the nickelodeon set. Your brother Lou was out there with some other men. He was caught but they pulled him out. It's still burning, I think. It could spread and –'

'I'll be right there,' interrupted Ham, voice tense and strained. 'Get to the main gate and watch for me – and keep the damn press off the lot. Get moving. I'll be right there!'

Nita watched helplessly from the bed as he pulled on his clothing and told her in gasps what little he knew – that something terrible had happened. Lou was in a fire, he had to

270

get there right away. She nodded, got out of bed and stepped over to give him a soft kiss on the cheek.

'I'm sure your brother will be all right. You've told me what a wonderful person he is. God will take care of him. Ham . . . do you know when he was born . . . the year . . . the day?'

'Shit, right now I don't know where my shoes are! Don't ask me stupid questions like that! I'm sorry, I'm very upset . . . I'll phone you when I know what's happened.'

He ran out of the house and to his car. A screeching turn and he headed down Detour Drive and out of the Hollywood hills toward Cahuenga Pass and the studio in Encino.

There was a police barricade at the main gate and Larry Gross was waiting. He got into Ham's car and they raced through the back lot toward the larger cluster of fire trucks, their winking red lights and the rising cloud of white steam coming closer until Ham jammed on his brakes, jumping out of his car almost before it stopped moving. Chief Swenson rushed over and caught his arm. The studio doctor ran to his side. Chief Swenson spoke first.

'Mr. Robbins . . . I'm terribly sorry . . . Your brother is dead.'

Ham stood stock-still a moment, the flashing red lights turning the faces all around him into a scene out of hell.

He slowly walked over to the blanket-covered figure on the grass. Kneeling beside it, he pulled back the cover and saw the seared face . . . hair charred black . . . a frozen look of anguish fixed on the contorted lips.

Ham half lifted his brother, hugging him close. Sobs burst uncontrolled from his throat, and he could not hear Larry Gross ordering the studio security guards and city police and firemen to stand in a tight circle around the two brothers and block the press photographers from taking any pictures of the tragic scene. Ham looked up at the dark circle of backs all around him as he held his brother, clinging tightly to all that remained of Lou. Only a few days before they both had stood almost on this same spot happily posing for the camera . . . and now . . . now . . .

He looked up over the heads of the policemen and the others surrounding them, up to where the spotlights from the fire trucks were fixed on the still smoking front of the ruined nickelodeon. A sign was swinging at a crazy angle high in the air, its supports almost burned through where it was attached to the nearly destroyed building. Ham looked through his tears up at the once bright blue sign with the golden letters, again scarred by flames, as it tore loose and crashed down into the rubble. For one moment, just before it fell, he could see the two words – BIJOU DREAM – and he bowed his head and wept.

CHAPTER TWENTY-SEVEN

Nita read about the services to be held for Lou at the
Wilshire Boulevard Temple and looked at the pictures of
Ham's sad face staring at her from the newspapers. All his
family had gathered together, and for the first time Nita saw
what his parents, sisters and brother Maurie looked like. As
she read about the services, which were open to the public,
she decided to be there and phoned her friend Lorene, who
promised to come by for her. By now Lorene had also left the
Studio Club and was living with a director, but was about to
leave him for either a producer or a fairly well-known actor.
She had not yet made up her mind and was eager to ask
Nita's advice.

'Why go to the funeral of somebody you don't even know?'
she asked Nita as they drove in her little convertible down
Highland Boulevard to Wilshire. 'I hate funerals – I don't
even want to go to mine!'

'Lorene,' Nita answered, after a little laugh at her friend's
remark, 'I really feel something special about Lou Robbins.
He was about the only person in the whole family Ham really
loved, except of course his parents . . . and Lou loved and
understood him. That's something we both shared, so I feel
quite close to Lou in that sharing. We never did meet, but I
can't help thinking that we really knew each other very well
because we both felt so close to the same person. That's kind
of hard to explain, but I want very much to say good-bye to a
good friend I never met but know I will miss very much.'

'Sure, Nita. I can understand that,' Lorene said, not
believing a single word. Then she changed the subject.
'What's really happening between you and Ham and where
does it lead? How long is this kind of relationship you have
with him going to go on? After all, he's married, has a
kid – and he's a very important man in this business, who
can't afford to get in any trouble. It's not like shacking up
with some insurance salesman or even with an assistant

273

director, you know. Hell, you're still young, and you're not doing a thing for your life or future stuck up on the side of that mountain waiting for a telephone to ring. He doesn't seem to do much about changing the way things are, does he?'

Nita thought a while as they reached Normandy Boulevard and Lorene turned the car, looking for a parking space. As they got out and started walking toward the Temple, several blocks away, Nita answered.

'Deep down I hope it won't go on like this. Sure, I know better than anybody that Ham's married – but he's very happy, and I know that if I hadn't come along, somebody else would have. I've learned, without Ham telling me, that I'm not the first girl he's had sitting by a phone in a house somewhere. The difference is that I'm not satisfied at all to let it stay that way and I'm going to be the last girl he ever has waiting by a telephone somewhere for him to call.'

They came to the Boulevard and started to walk across. Nita was silent, and as they reached the center of the wide street she turned to Lorene and in a flat even voice said, 'I'm his mistress now – but I'm going to be his wife!'

Lorene stopped right in the middle of the pedestrian crossing as the signal changed and cars sounded their horns at the girls.

There was a kind of numb silence as they joined a group of somber people entering the front doors of the Temple and started up the marble stairs leading to the balcony. Lorene kept looking at Nita the whole way, still silent until they were halfway up, and when she spoke it was in a low and guarded voice.

'I'll bet you do it, too! I don't know how . . . but you'll do it. Make damn sure, though, that in getting him you don't lose sight of something very important to his family . . . Hell, I'm a fine one to talk about morality – maybe being here in a religious building drags it out of me – but the man's married, Nita. He has a wife, a son, a bunch of sisters and a brother . . . a father and mother. If they ever felt you came along and deliberately took . . . they would say "stole" . . . Ham away from his wife . . . well, I'm not the astrologer here. That's something you know more about than I ever will, but you better go over this with those planets of yours or you could wind up the big loser!'

'Lose what?' answered Nita in a small tense voice only Lorene could hear. 'Lose a little house up in the hills that isn't even mine? Don't worry . . . I've checked all my stars and planets, and what I'm thinking about right now has every chance to succeed . . . that doesn't bother me. Lorene, when this service is over you and I are taking a ride out to Beverly Hills. I want to see something there and I want you to see it with me . . . something that's going to be mine one day – along with Ham Robbins and everything else. I love him and I'm sure he loves me. Just because he hasn't shown the strength yet to make a new start and be happy the way he could be . . . with me . . . doesn't mean I should let things go on like this. I can give him some of the strength he needs and help him make the most important decision in his life – and he'll make it, believe me!'

They were shown to seats in the second row of the balcony far to the right side and sat looking down at the large auditorium, which was filling up with the many grieving friends of Lou Robbins. Every employee of Robbins International Studios was there, and a large group from the New York office, and soon nearly every seat was filled. The whole family – parents, sisters, brothers – all were off in a side room, out of sight of the rest of the mourners. Nita wished she could be there at this time to comfort Ham, who had just lost someone he loved. Not now, though – another time it would be very different, and Nita felt if ever there was another ordeal like this to face, she would be there to hold his hand and keep him strong. A lone male voice sang in sad melody, Rabbi Magnin stepped through a side door to stand beside the flower-covered casket that rested in front of the Ark, and with the solemn recitation of the Kaddish, the prayer for the dead, the service began.

In half an hour it all came to an end, the still unseen family departing through a rear door to enter a line of black limousines. Then the casket was put in a hearse and the procession drove off in a slow parade to Sinai Meadows and the private interment.

Lorene dabbed away her tears.

'He really must have been a wonderful man. The rabbi spoke so beautifully. I just don't know what to say . . . I've never been to a Jewish funeral . . . it was so full of meaning and so sad . . . from the heart. You know, I don't feel as bad as I thought I would . . . but I still don't like funerals.'

She stopped talking as they went down the stairs and looked at Nita.

'I can't figure it. You didn't cry at all. You're supposed to cry at funerals!'

'I did cry . . . deep inside where you couldn't see it. Now let's walk back to your car and take that ride to Beverly Hills.'

'This is great, we're just a couple of sightseeing tourists!' said Lorene a half-hour later as they turned north on Benedict Canyon and passed some of the lovely homes set far back on their plush green lawns. 'Say, I wonder who lives in that gorgeous house over there?'

'Please, Lorene, keep both hands on the wheel and your eyes on the road. It is gorgeous, but that isn't what we came here to see. Keep on this street to Tower Road, then when we reach Sierra View turn right.'

They followed the lovely street with its borders of manicured palm trees and gently curved up toward the hills. The palms soon gave way to tall pines and then to Italian cypress standing like green fingers beside the curbs.

'Where do the people here walk? I don't see a sidewalk anyplace!' Lorene said in wonder.

'They walk to their Rolls-Royces. Don't ask them to do more than that, Lorene,' Nita said.

'My Lord, half the people here must be gardeners and the other half tree surgeons!' contributed Lorene, holding the wheel tightly as they continued up the gentle slope passing many estates, most of which were invisible from the street. Only walls, gates and trees showed now as the girls drove past. Sierra View Drive came at last, and they turned to follow a high white stucco-covered wall that began far off in some trees and was broken several hundred yards farther on by a closed bronze gate that looked as though it belonged on a bank vault. Lorene slowed the car as they passed the towering portal, then moved on to where the wall turned a corner. They drove along this side street, coming to the end of the road higher up the hill. Here they could just see over the wall to where a large white house with a red-tiled roof stood on a hill of its own. A swimming pool, tennis court and beautiful gardens surrounded it. There was no sign of life inside the spacious estate until they saw a heavyset man come out of a little guardhouse beside the gate, peer up at the sky, spit on the lawn and then go back into his little house.

'Let me guess – who lives there?' said Lorene.

'One guess is all you get – but I'll bet you know the answer. It's Ham's . . . the place he finished building just this year,' said Nita, and her voice got quite serious. 'The question you should be asking, though, is who's going to be living there

276

with him one day. If you figure out the answer to that one, please keep it to yourself.'

'Don't worry, Nita. I won't go running to Louella or Hedda with the news, although they probably know all about you already. It's not something that can be kept a big secret when the man is as important as Ham Robbins.'

Nita's eyes widened as she rushed out a question.

'I suppose they do know, but how is it that nothing has shown up in either of their columns? It's exactly the kind of thing they love to print.'

'My dear not-so-innocent ex-virgin, you've got a hell of a lot to learn about the way things work in this town. Everybody who gets ahead has to have something on somebody. Since nearly all of them got where they are by screwing somebody in ways they don't want known, there are a lot more skeletons here than there are closets to hide them. The way I heard it put is that one man's pleasure is another man's pressure! That goes for the women who make it big out here too. You want to succeed? Then get out of the Hollywood hills and into the Beverly Hills. You've already told me that your plans include doing just that. The way you do it is to put someone who can help you get there into such a spot – through fear of being exposed or of being made to look like such a damn fool in public – that he'll put you right where you want to be . . . if it's worth it to get you off his back.'

Nita smiled before replying.

'The one place I'm not is on Ham's back, believe me!'

'There are a lot of different ways to please a man,' said her friend. 'Eventually, I'm sure, you'll try them all. You're clever enough, that much I know.' Lorene stopped talking and got the car moving, turning it in a tight circle at the end of the dead-end street. They started down the road, and their view of the estate vanished behind all the trees and the high wall, which they followed past the closed entrance to where they turned off Sierra View Drive. Nita turned her head to look again at the high bronze barrier as they passed, and in her mind she saw it sliding wide open to let her enter. Not today – not even tomorrow, perhaps . . . but soon, very soon.

It was Larry Gross who started events in motion that would lead Nita to fulfill her dream even sooner than she had hoped was possible. He phoned her two evenings after Lou's funeral, and she recognized his smooth voice at once.

'Miss de Valle, I'm calling for Mr. Robbins. He would like to have me call for you at eight this evening and take you to a place where you will have dinner with him. He asked me to tell you he cannot phone you himself, but he looks forward to seeing you later and he has missed you.'

Nita, who had not heard from Ham since the funeral, had been feeling quite depressed, and this call chased away the blues, leaving her happy and excited.

'Thank you, Larry. I'll be ready and waiting.'

As usual Larry was right on time for Nita, who watched for him through the front window and came out to meet his car, just as she had several months before when he first called for her at the Studio Club to take her to Ham on that first unforgettable evening. He held the door open until she got in the front seat, and then they drove off toward the Valley.

'Is Ham feeling any better now after that terrible tragedy? I felt dreadful about what happened to his brother. I've been so upset, and I haven't heard from him at all since it happened.'

'Well . . . he has been pretty upset himself ever since then, and his mother was quite ill when she was out here and that has him worried too. I think she had to go to the hospital when she got back to Harrisburg. You know, he was quite close to his brother Lou and the shock hasn't begun to wear off.' Larry slowed down to let a bus turn in front of them, and then he continued. 'All his family left town, which may be a help to him. For some reason that I don't know, he just clammed up around them and kept his feelings tightly bottled up. Mr. Robbins is a very different person around his family . . . always seems to be so angry about something but never comes out with what it is. At a sad time like this you'd think they would be close – but they weren't at all. I heard him arguing with his older brother, Maurie, and with his sister Ruth about something or other – really going at it hot and heavy, and they kept bringing up what his mother and father would think of him if they knew . . . whatever it was. He got real sore at both of them, and I never heard him talking about anything but business or unimportant small talk with them from then on.'

'That's a terrible strain on him after what he went through . . . finding his poor brother dead . . . and in such a horrible way!' said Nita, slowly shaking her head, her mind still trying to put together something that remained in bits and pieces. She could guess what the argument might have been about. Obviously Maurie and Ruth must know about her.

278

'I have the feeling that Mr. Robbins believes he doesn't have the respect from all his family he thinks he should have. That's really sad, because he's a very successful man and he should be a happy one too,' said Larry as they waited for a signal to change on Highland Avenue. 'You're giving him a great amount of that – happiness – the thing he needs so very much, Miss de Valle. I can see it, and I know he feels it too.'

'Thank you, Larry,' Nita said, staring straight ahead into the night as they came out of the Pass and started across the Valley, finally beginning a slow climb up the hill overlooking the city of Burbank. 'I hope you're right. Ham's a wonderful person and he deserves to be happy.' She continued on to herself, 'And he deserves me to make him that way. Not just now and then in a house that isn't his home – but for all of the time when we aren't a secret he has to share with Hedda and Louella until they decide the time has come to use what they know against him.'

The car stopped in front of a rambling Polynesian restaurant set high in the hills overlooking the Valley and Larry helped Nita out of the car, letting an attendant drive it off to the parking area. He led her inside the big noisy room, where a bright-shirted captain took them to a comfortable booth in front of a large window through which they could see the sparkling lights of the San Fernando Valley spread out like an electric ocean.

Larry ordered drinks, a plain cola and lime for himself and a mixture of pineapple juice, rum and coconut milk for Nita. They waited for Ham to arrive.

He came into the restaurant forty-five minutes later. His face was set in anger, and Nita could see how tightly he clenched his fists. There was bitter tension in his voice, and he fought to hold in unvoiced obscenities.

'My dear brother and his wife finally got themselves on the train and left town after I got a nonstop lecture from him that just about drove me crazy! Thank God my mother and father both went back home right after the funeral. I wouldn't want them ever to hear the kind of shit that Maurie dumped all over me! It's bad enough that my mother felt so sick she had to have a nurse travel back with her. I've been damned worried ever since Poppa phoned that she had to go to the hospital for a checkup when they arrived home. I still don't really know what's the matter with her ... There always seems to be something!'

279

He ordered a double Scotch and then continued, his anger coming out more and more.

'With all the problems I have, Maurie keeps hammering at me – criticizing me like when we still were little kids and he told me everything I did was all wrong! Waiter! Another drink for me. You want more, Nita . . . Larry? Another round for all of us. I was happy to get Maurie and Rose into a car and off to the station, and I'm so filled up with what he spilled all over me from his stinking mouth that I could – Ah! Good . . . here're the drinks.'

Nita looked closely at Ham's deeply disturbed face as he lifted his glass and drank deeply. She tried saying something to comfort him, but he was in too dark a mood, and the third and fourth drink plunged him in even deeper. Nita did not finish her glass but sat filled with concern about Ham as he looked out into the black night. The waiter brought them menus, and Ham dropped his to the floor.

'I'm drinking dinner tonight! You both order anything you want. I'm not hungry.'

Larry and Nita picked at some barbecued ribs and honey-soaked pieces of beef on long bamboo skewers. Neither of them ate very much. When they had finished, Larry slid far down the long upholstered seat so Ham and Nita could talk without being overheard.

'Ever since I can remember, Maurie has been finding fault with me. Sure, I know – the younger brother thing. Maybe I was kind of wild, but he went out of his way just as he does now to criticize me. We're supposed to be grown-up adults but he still treats me like little Chaim – the *pisher* – the kid who didn't finish the fourth grade because there were too many exciting things to do and learn in the world outside.' He stopped and looked down into his empty glass. 'Lou, though . . . Lou was so different from Maurie . . . understanding, taking me the way I was, not trying to make me into a copy of somebody else . . . of himself. Lou never took anything out on me. We got on so damn well, and now he's gone . . . he's gone.' He waved his empty glass at the waiter and ordered a refill. 'What I can't stand is that Maurie is always acting as though I'm just about to ruin his good name . . . and Poppa and Momma's . . . and the girls'. His good name . . . shit! He's stuffed tighter with morality than all the prophets in the Old Testament . . . my perfect brother and his perfect marriage and his good family name! Damn him!' His voice was starting to slur and the words tumbled over each other, but his anger was still clear.

Nita reached over to take his hand and spoke in a low, intense voice.

'Ham, he's still your brother and it's wrong for you to say such things about him. I'm sure he was terribly troubled about Lou and many other things . . . your mother being ill, and maybe he has other problems you don't even know about. It's a shame he has to take it all out on you, but . . .'

'We didn't pick each other to be brothers. The least he could do is to get it through his thick head that I'm me, I'm not him . . . and he's trying to squeeze me into his tight little mold. Screw it! I've worked hard all my life. I've done a lot of it my way. Little Chaim's grown up now, but his big brother still treats him like a *putz!* Then there's Irene . . . looking at me with those big wide accusing eyes of hers. Hell, it takes two to make a marriage miserable. Maybe I've done more than my share to louse up this one, I don't know . . . and my son . . . my son and heir . . . my descendant and the fruit of my loins! I only wish I knew how to be a better father – to be with him more and to listen when he talks to me. Whenever I'm with him something I can't explain happens. I feel I'm Maurie and he's little Chaim and I start finding fault . . . picking on him and doing to him just what's made me so damn angry my brother has done to me almost all my life. "The sins of the fathers shall be visited on the children." Maybe there should be a rewrite on that line so it comes out "the sins of the brothers . . ." '

He stopped a moment, and suddenly his eyes filled with moisture and he quickly looked away from Nita and out through the window, blinking the little tears out of the corners of his eyes and dabbing at them with a cocktail napkin.

'Ham darling, you're getting yourself so terribly upset. Why not wait until you can think it out better and maybe later on your family will –'

'Family . . . who needs a fucking family! They're all pains in the ass!' He angrily raised his glass and pieces of ice fell on the table and the liquid ran down his chin. The fire of his emotion quenched for an instant, he stared out the big picture window at the lights stretching far away in the blackness.

'Look at it out there . . . all those people . . . all those houses filled with families . . . all those brothers crapping on their brothers . . . all those fathers and their sons screwing up their lives! Here we sit on the top of a mountain – but we're really deep down in a fucking shitpool!'

The last of Ham's drink was gone and he looked down the table toward Larry, who kept his head turned away, trying not to hear any of the conversation.

'I've had enough to drink for dinner,' Ham said suddenly. 'Larry, pay the man and let's go. You'll have to drive us in my car. I know when I shouldn't be in back of the wheel, and I'm just loaded enough to get in trouble if I try. Leave your car here and figure out how to get it tomorrow.' He stood up, quite unsteady on his feet, and Nita helped him to the door as Larry called for the bill.

She helped him into the back of his car, then got in beside him. Ham hiccupped a few times, tried to focus his bleary eyes, then put his head on her shoulder and slept soundly all the way across the Valley, through the Pass and up the hill. Larry drove very carefully, and there was hardly a bump or swerve to disturb the sleeping Ham, although after a few miles Nita's shoulder felt numb from the weight of his head.

'I'll help you get him inside, then call a taxi to pick me up so I can leave his car here in the garage,' said Larry when they reached the house on Detour Drive.

'Isn't he expected at his home? Won't his wife be worried if he doesn't show up all night?' Nita asked Larry with concern in her voice.

'Not at all. She took her sister back to San Francisco last night on the train and won't be back until the day after tomorrow.'

'What about their son – won't he be . . .'

'Forget it. Junior's back at boarding school out near Glendora. Only the help are in the house, and they all know who pays their salaries, so they'll keep their mouths shut. Just let him sleep it off and tomorrow he should be able to make it on his own. If you run into any problem you have my number and can call me at any hour. Would you rather I stayed here and slept in the living room?'

'No, Larry,' Nita replied quickly. 'He'll be fine, and I promise to call you if he's not. Thank you and good night.'

The taxi Larry had called soon arrived and drove him down the hill. Nita undressed Ham and got him into bed. Soon she too was there, lying beside him and watching as he lay flat on his back, little snores coming from his open mouth. For a long hour she watched him in the dim bedroom light; then, without knowing just when, she slipped off into sleep.

It was still dark outside, and only a glow on the eastern

horizon gave advance notice of dawn. Nita was dreaming of a tall gate stretching high up in the sky set in a wall that seemed to go up through the clouds. She pushed and shoved but the gate would not open to let her pass through to whatever was on the other side. She could feel the strain as she vainly tried to move the massive barrier, finally letting go a deep sigh of anguish and frustration.

'Wha . . . what's that?' said Ham from across the bed. He was half awake and his hand went out to find who was there beside him making sleep noises. He found out quickly, and as he slowly awakened, his hand went down her body, fondling her breasts and then her flat stomach.

Nita's dream was wiped from her subconscious and she reached over to embrace Ham as they moved together on the soft, yielding mattress. He stroked her in her most sensitive parts until she gasped in passionate response and reached down to put her hand around his engorged penis. Something felt different about it, and even in her half-awake state she knew what it was: Ham was not wearing the rubber condom he always made sure was in place before entering her. So many times he had told Nita that he had all the children he wanted. He had had quite enough of big families when he was a little boy and the last thing he would ever do again was make any woman pregnant – even his wife!

She was sure the drinks had dulled his normal caution and he had completely forgotten what to him had been a necessity. Nita knew exactly what to do and let him come into her as he was – naked in all of his body – and as he slowly began to move up and down and in and out on top of her, she half closed her eyes, and, almost as though an image were being projected on the ceiling high up over Ham's moving shoulders, she could clearly see a tall bronze gate set in a long white wall as it silently began to roll wide open.

Her body was being violently shaken and she woke up with a sudden start. Ham stood over her in the bed, shaking her again and again, gently but firmly, until she was fully awake.

'Quick – did I put on a rubber before we got into bed last night? I woke up just now and couldn't find anything! That's something I'd never forget! Do you remember, Nita? Tell me!'

She rubbed the last sleep from her eyes, sat up and laughed.

'Relax, darling. There's nothing at all to worry about. I had to go to the bathroom during the night and I found it in the

283

bed, right here . . . all filled up with your wonderful sperm. What a mess! I picked it up and flushed it down the toilet, and by now I'll bet our children are having a swim somewhere off Malibu.'

'Thank heavens! I was worried I might have forgotten to put it on,' said Ham, greatly relieved.

Nita said nothing more. She smiled up at Ham, threw her arms around his hot sweaty body and pulled him down again on the bed, seeing the high white wall without any sign of a gate to keep her from going inside.

CHAPTER TWENTY-EIGHT

The voice on the phone sounded bright and happy.

'Nita, you've been cooped up in the house too damn long. How would you like to get out of town next week?'

'I'd love it, Ham . . . as long as it's with you.'

'Well, in a way it will be . . . but there are complications. I'm meeting with Mike Hammersmith in Palm Springs for a few days. We want to get away from the studio and talk about release dates and our future program without being interrupted. I've taken a bungalow at the Desert Inn and reserved a nice room for you very near it at the Palm Garden – right down the street. The problem is that Irene will be along and . . .'

'I'd be in the way,' Nita said at once. 'We better forget it. Maybe some other time.' She hoped her reply would only make him desire her more, and it did.

'No, no, Nita. I can work it out all right. I want you there. I have to hold some meetings with Mike, maybe just a few hours for the first couple of days, then I can get away now and then. Mike has lots of paperwork and doesn't need me the whole time – and Irene will be with his wife most of the time, so I can get away to see you. Anyhow, you need a change of scene, and God knows I do too!' There was silence for a while and then he spoke again. 'Nita, have you ever been to Palm Springs? It's only about a hundred miles or so from here and almost like being in another world. You'll love it!'

'I know I will, Ham . . . even if I can't be with you the whole time. Are you absolutely sure that I won't cause a problem? After all, it's not a big place there and –'

'Stop worrying. It will work out beautifully. I'm going to have Larry Gross drive you there and he'll stay at another place right near you. He will take you to dinner if I can't break away. The important thing is that the desert air and a change of scenery will be good for you. We'll manage to be together as much as possible during the four or five days we're there. Larry will be in touch, so start packing and we'll all be in Palm Springs the day after tomorrow.'

The ride was tedious, the road long, narrow and dusty. The final fifteen miles across the desert was like riding on a paved washboard between the little towns of Beaumont and Banning, winding past the San Jacinto Mountains, which stood like a great cyclorama behind the spa village of Palm Springs. The Aguascaliente Indian band had stumbled onto a very good thing with the hot springs, and the reputation of the health-giving waters was becoming known throughout Southern California. Ham had been there a few times in the past and let himself sit in a big tank filled with warm black mud, which then was washed off and followed by a long soak in the hot smelly mineral water bubbling fresh out of the earth. A husky young Indian massaged him, and he slept soundly for more than an hour. When he awakened it was as though years and worries had been washed away with the mud. He could not wait for another chance to return to the spa and the feeling he had had there, if for only a few hours, of rebirth.

Larry drove Nita to her bungalow at the Palm Garden. By the time they arrived she was nauseated from the motion of the car on the winding wavy road. Although Larry asked if she would like to see something of the little town before going to her room, she told him all she wanted was to make it to her bed before she threw up. She slept for hours until the phone beside her bed rang early in the evening waking her up.

'Miss de Valle. This is Larry Gross. Do you feel like some dinner?'

She felt only like going back to sleep until the room settled down or they built a road that was flat and not like riding on a roller coaster. She thanked Larry, turned off the light and drifted back into troubled dreams where big bronze gates were only partly open, not quite enough to let anyone through, and they seemed to be tightly jammed in their tracks. She awoke in sudden fright at the distant howl of a desert coyote.

Not far down Palm Canyon Road from where Nita lay listening to the desert noises, a studio driver delivered Ham and Irene to the Desert Inn, where Nelli Coffman, the owner-manager, welcomed them and saw that they were taken to their bungalow. The bellman spoke to Ham as he helped them move in.

'Mr. Robbins, your neighbor right across the pool is in your business – Darryl Zanuck and his wife. I'm sure you know them.'

'Certainly. I've known him ever since he was writing dialogue for Rin Tin Tin. Thanks, I'll give him a call later. Oh, it's very important I know when a Mr. Mike Hammersmith from New York checks into the Inn. He and his wife may arrive here tomorrow morning. There's another bungalow reserved for them, and I'd appreciate your telling the desk to call me the minute they arrive.' Ham went into the bathroom with his kit and in a moment came out again. Irene was unpacking a suitcase and looked up as he spoke to her.

'I forgot to bring my toothbrush, damn it! I'll get one in the lobby shop. You need anything while I'm there?'

'No, Ham. Let's just take it easy tonight. I'm exhausted from the ride here. Can't we eat in the hotel?'

'Sure,' he answered. 'I'll make sure we have a table. Maybe I'll call Darryl and Virginia and see if they'll join us tomorrow with Mike Hammersmith and his wife. I know a great place . . . tell you about it later.'

He walked around the pool to the main hotel building and went to a secluded pay phone, where he called Larry Gross, who told him Nita had become carsick on the ride and was staying in her room. Ham told Larry he would call him the next morning right after breakfast and then went to the desk and had the hotel operator connect him with the Zanuck bungalow.

'Darryl . . . hello. This is Ham Robbins. We just drove in and we're taking it easy tonight. I'm in the bungalow right across the pool from you. How about you and Virginia joining Irene and me for dinner tomorrow evening at Wertheimer's? Mike Hammersmith and his wife are coming in tomorrow and we can all try to bust the bank.'

'Great, just great,' said the voice on the other end of the phone. Darryl Francis Zanuck was the number two man at Warner Brothers studios. Ham liked him immensely, seeing something of himself in the dynamic little man. They shared a frustration in common. Darryl would always be the number two man in his company as long as he worked for Jack L. Warner, and often when he was with Ham he complained about the limits that bound him. Ham's problems with Maurie were somewhat different, but he could appreciate Darryl's feelings and sympathized with him. 'We'll meet here and drive there together . . . say at around eight o' clock. Is that all right?'

'That'll be perfect, Darryl. Give Virginia our love. See you tomorrow morning by the pool.'

'You won't see me near any pool,' said Darryl. 'I'm up at dawn and out on the desert on a horse. While you're still sleeping, I'll be riding down some jackrabbits!'

'Good luck. That's not my idea of relaxation, but have a good time and try to keep in one piece so we can get together later. 'Bye.' Ham hung up, then walked back to his bungalow after buying a new toothbrush in the lobby shop.

Darryl Zanuck had already brought his lathered horse back to the stables and was soaking in the Spa mineral baths by the time Ham and Irene were awake and having breakfast in their rooms.

'I'm going to walk around the Inn grounds while you finish dressing, Irene. Mike and his wife should be checking in around noon. I'll be back in a little while,' Ham said as he left the room and headed for the pay phone out front. He dialed the hotel where Larry Gross was staying and got his room.

'Miss de Valle is feeling much better, Mr. Robbins. I just spoke to her. She's waiting to hear from me, and I can take her to lunch if you're going to be busy.'

Ham thought a moment and told Larry that he would be tied up most of the day.

'Show her the town, Larry. Let her buy some stuff in the shops if she wants anything ... that is, anything within reason – I'll leave it to you. Oh yes, before I forget – I want you to phone Lew Wertheimer's place, The Dunes out near Cathedral City. Reserve a table for me this evening for dinner. I'll have six in my party ... say at eight-thirty, so we'll have plenty of time after for the casino. Larry, I want you to take Nita there for dinner too. She'll get a kick out of the place. Be sure your table isn't too close to mine. If she wants to go into the casino you stay with her and take care of the tab. Don't let her lose too much.'

'Sure, Mr. Robbins,' answered Gross. 'I'll take care of everything. You can reach me either here or at Miss de Valle's hotel if you want anything else done. Good-bye.'

Ham reentered the Desert Inn lobby just as Mike and Eileen Hammersmith were signing in, and he went with them to their rooms. They all spent the rest of the day around the pool, until suddenly the sun ducked behind a mountain and the early chill of the desert evening drove them back inside their warm bungalows.

Not many miles beyond Palm Springs was the grandly named settlement of Cathedral City, with its line of run-down stores and rows of shacks and shanties. One day it might become more than it was now, but the only object faintly resembling a cathedral was the great dark bulk of the mountain, which did have a look of awesome majesty in the growing dusk. Larry drove the car past the two long blocks making up Cathedral City and in a while came to a side road that bore no sign. He turned off the main highway and followed a narrow dirt road about a mile and a half toward a large date palm grove with strings of electric lights hung around its borders. Nita sat beside him looking up at the black sky and the diamond-bright stars, so clear and unlike what she was used to seeing back in the city. She could hear music coming from the cluster of palms even before she saw the large ranch-style building with the parking lot in front. An attendant took their car and they entered the place after Larry gave their names to a solidly built man standing on the porch. They were checked off on a reservation list and passed through a big heavy door to the captain, who took them into the dining room. The lights were low and a small orchestra played dance music for the few couples out on the floor and the others sitting at their tables eating dinner. A curly-haired man came to them and spoke to Larry.

'Mr. Gross, welcome to The Dunes. I'm Lew Wertheimer. I have a very nice table for Mr. Robbins and his party just across the main room. I'm sure he'll like it. If there's anything you want, just give me a call. Have a lucky evening . . . but not too lucky, please!' He nodded, smiled and left them to go through a large door set in the back of the room, where another man stood guard.

'What did he mean by "not too lucky"?' asked Nita.

'After we've had dinner I'll show you what's in back of that door Wertheimer just went through. Gambling is strictly illegal here in California, but there are a few places where they don't seem to have heard about that – and this is one of them. They don't mind the customers being lucky, just so they don't overdo it. Now, how about a drink of something?'

Nita was trying to snag the sugar cube from her champagne cocktail when she saw a group of people enter the dining room. Although the lights were low, she knew at once who they were. Ham crossed the room with Darryl and Mike, and their wives followed to the table far across the room where they all were seated. Nita was certain Ham had seen her, and she remembered Lew Wertheimer wishing her a lucky evening. The luck she most wanted was to be at the table across the room sitting beside Ham Robbins!

By the time they ordered their dinner most of the room had filled up. Nita recognized many of the same faces she had seen that night at the Embassy Club when Ham first ran into her. She was glad when Larry asked her to dance, hoping that once they were out on the floor she could get close to Ham's table and get a good look at everybody sitting there, especially at Irene. She smiled a little to herself at the alarm on Ham's face when he looked up and saw her dancing so close to his table. He continued his conversation with Darryl and Mike and tried to keep his eyes off the lovely dark girl dancing a few feet away from him. Several couples came between them and he breathed easily again as the music stopped and the dancers all returned to their tables. He was going to give Larry hell for letting her get so close to him when his wife was right there. He was grateful for the low light, which masked the flush on his face, and let Darryl talk while he regained his composure. Half listening, he heard Darryl complain about the problems he had at his studio and how he thought someday of moving on someplace else.

'Darryl, I know what's on your mind . . . but before you think of leaving Warner's, look around and find a place where you'll be the one running things,' advised Ham. 'Forget our place. I'd never let anybody come in who would be a possible threat to me – and you know it!'

'At least you're an honest man,' said Zanuck with a laugh and a flash of large irregular teeth under a scraggly moustache. 'You're right about that, Ham. We'd get along just fine for a little while and then it would be like me and J.L. all over again.'

'Have you ever thought of starting your own company? You have a great track record and there must be plenty of people who'd put their bets on you with hard cash. You should think about that . . . there's nothing like being your own boss in this business. Trust me to keep my mouth shut about this talk . . . Mike here will keep quiet too. I know J.L. wouldn't be happy at all if he thought anything like this was on your mind.'

'Thanks, Ham. I'd appreciate it if you did forget this ever came up. Now tell me, besides craps, slot machines and roulette, what else does Wertheimer serve guests in this place?'

Nita and Larry finished eating and he called for their check, signed it and then guided her between tables to the closed door in the far wall. She could see Ham and his group still eating, and made out the glowing tip of Zanuck's cigar as he waved it in the air to make some point in his animated conversation. The guard asked Larry for identification and pulled out a guest register for him to sign, and then the door was slowly swung open. As she left one room and entered the other, a chill ran up her back and for a quick moment she felt she had been here before, or someplace very like it. The door . . . the gate . . . that was it – and now it stood wide open for her to enter.

Back at the big round table in the dining room Zanuck knocked the long ash off his cigar and squinted through the haze of smoke at Ham.

'How about leaving an early call tomorrow morning and going horse-back riding with me out in the desert before it gets too hot? I've been riding a lot lately. It's great exercise and you use muscles you never knew you had. Some of us over at Warner's have put together a polo team. A terrific game!'

'Polo! Darryl, you're absolutely crazy!' said Ham, coughing a little from the cigar smoke. 'I haven't ridden a horse since my old man owned a broken-down nag who pulled our delivery wagon years ago in Harrisburg. No, thanks – life's tough enough just running a studio without playing polo too. I heard you were a little crazy, but playing polo – that's absolutely insane! Aren't you afraid they'll cancel your life insurance?'

'Ham, one day I'm taking you out to Hudkin's Ranch with me, right across the Los Angeles River from our lot, and you'll see how crazy I am. We have a team we call "Los Amigos," Mike Curtiz, Big Boy Williams . . . Lloyd Bacon and some other guys. J.L. himself plays, and not too badly. He loves the boots and helmet and waving that mallet around. Did you hear what Wilson Mizner said when he heard that? "From Poland to polo in one generation!" – and J.L. pays the bastard his salary. We're working on Hal Wallis and Henry Blanke, too, but they're holding out. You should see that mad Hungarian, Mike Curtiz, when he goes after the ball – you'd think it was a Budapest blonde! Look at this lump on my head he gave me the other day. I chased him all the way back to the stables and would have killed him if my horse wasn't so tired! You should take it up, Ham – it's a great way to relax and burn up any extra energy.'

'It's a great way to break your neck!' Ham replied. 'I need every bit of extra energy I can scrape together, Darryl, and there's not that much I can spare. I'll come out one day, though, just for laughs, to watch you guys doing your own pratfalls. Why don't you just hire some stunt doubles to do it for you? Come on, that's enough talk for tonight. Let's go into the casino, where the action is.'

They were quickly passed through the big door without having to sign the register. Wertheimer told the guard they were special guests who were not to be delayed and he was eager for them to get their chips on the tables. There was a subdued murmur in the large room where they now stood. No music, only human voices now and then raised in waves of excitement, then dropping down to subdued tones, like ripples on a well-mannered shore. Dice hit against each other with clicking sounds, bounced against padded barriers and came to rest showing their spotted faces. The spinning nervous rattle of a ball on the roulette wheel and polite requests of croupiers to place bets, the low clatter of chips being moved about on green cloth covered with red and black patterns all made their own special noises in the room. There was a harsher clash of silver dollars jangling as they hit tables, then a flurry of excited voices raised in prayer and exultation as little white cubes danced across the tables. Each game was like a small green island in the darkened room. Spotlights beamed down from the ceiling to pick out the players clustered around the action. There were four crap tables, two roulette wheels and a row of blackjack tables along one wall. It was a small room compared with those in the nearby Nirvana of Nevada, but it would do nicely and the wagering here was sufficient to speed up the most sluggish bloodstream. Here and there were cold-eyed, hard-faced men in black suits who watched every move at the tables. They initialed approval on checks, and when losses grew larger than credit could bear, they efficiently and courteously ushered the player out of the room and on his way, after securing his signature on an ironclad promissory note. Payment eventually would be forthcoming, as it was better than having a set of cracked leg bones and several weeks' vacation in the hospital.

Irene and the two other women moved to the blackjack tables, leaving the men to the frenzy of the crap games. Ham noticed Nita in the center of the room, feeding quarters to a hungry slot machine. He positioned himself at the middle crap table, not far from where she stood, and waited for her to notice. The sound of his voice caught Nita by surprise. She moved toward the busy table and stood at the side where the pass line faced her, directly opposite Ham. His raised hand shook the dice, which he tossed against the cushioned rail directly in front of where she was standing. Two single dots showed, and the stick man called out in a doleful tone, 'Snake eyes!' He flipped the dice to the next player as Ham's chips were whisked off the table. The dice passed on around as one player after another came up with losing combinations. Nita was completely mystified by the fast action and watched the table in fascination as the play worked its way around the table. Zanuck made one successful pass and then hit seven, and the dice went once again to Ham. He held them a moment in his hand, then turned to the stick man.

'I'd like that young lady across the table from me to roll for luck,' said Ham, and the stick man flicked a new pair of dice over to Nita, who picked them up, held them in the palm of her right hand and almost in panic turned to Larry Gross as Ham put a stack of chips down on the come line.

'What do I do with them? I've never even seen a crap game before!'

'Shake them up real good, then throw them out on the table against that far rail where Mr. Robbins is standing. Don't worry – the dice do all the work!' Larry answered in an excited yet calming voice.

She closed her fingers around the two cubes, shook them until they sounded like the teeth of a ghost-frightened man, then let them fly out over the green table all the way to where Ham stood grinning as a four and a three turned up. His stack of chips seemed to double in height all by itself, and the stick man flipped the dice back to Nita.

'Good girl!' Larry said. 'You couldn't have done better than that. Now try again!'

She did – and exactly the same thing happened. The chips grew higher in front of the smiling man across the table.

'What am I doing right?' Nita asked Larry.

'Everything! Don't ask questions, just roll the dice!' he answered.

Out they rolled, and a three and a one-spot showed.

'Oh – I've lost!' Nita said in sudden distress.

'No, no! Not at all! Now roll again, and if you get another four it's a pass – a winner!'

Rattle, click and roll and up came two dots on one of the dice and then the other die spun off all alone to mid-table, finally coming to rest and showing the same deuce; the pass was made. Ham's smile grew wider as his stacks of chips grew higher. He doubled his bet, and the box man called for another tray from the cashier.

It went on like this for nearly twenty-two minutes, with Nita rolling out pass after pass and Ham and the others betting him piling up more winnings. Lew Wertheimer was called from his office and stood by the stick man, sharing his worried look. People from all the other tables sensed what was happening and drifted over to watch the series of passes the pretty red-haired girl was throwing for Ham Robbins, and the babble of excited voices got louder with every throw of the dice.

Now Ham was being given the special square chips worth a thousand dollars, each, and he put half of his winnings into his pocket. He felt the streak had to end soon and he wasn't going to be wiped out if he could help it. He ran his gambling as he ran his studio, with a tight hand and complete control. Darryl and Mike kept picking up bets, and now at last when the dice were being rattled high in the air by the girl who had become the center of attention in the room, there was a moment of complete silence, broken only by the click of the cubes she tossed out across the table. They stopped directly in front of Irene Robbins, who had left her place at the black-jack table with all the others to watch the exciting happenings. The moment of silence before the dice stopped rolling was broken by Ham's voice.

'Young lady, you're very lucky for me!'

Nita answered quickly, looking up at him, into his eyes: 'I hope so . . . I hope so!' and then the dice stopped moving and came up boxcars – double six, a loser.

'Shit!' said somebody at the table, and the dealers pulled in all the chips and distributed some to the cynics who had bet against Nita. The stick man flipped the dice on to the next player in line, who asked for and received new dice for what he hoped would be a repeat of the lucky run.

'What did I do wrong?' Nita almost wailed at Larry, who was mopping the sweat off his forehead.

'Do wrong! Hell, you were nearly perfect! Do you realize the odds against holding the dice as long as you did? For a beginner you were strictly a miracle! I'm sure you made Mr. Robbins rich and happy!'

She felt much better about it and watched as the dice traveled around again to Ham. Irene stood beside him now, and as he picked up the dice she whispered in his ear, 'I can throw them every bit as good as that redhead!'

'All right,' Ham said, handing them to her, 'give it a try.' He reached down to put a stack of chips on the come line.

Irene shook the dice and let them fly to the middle of the table, where they staggered and came to rest with a one-spot and a deuce showing as the stick man sang his sad song, 'Craps!' He raked in all the chips with his wooden crook.

'Good night, Irene – good night!' said Ham. 'That ends the crap shooting for tonight.'

She turned away from the table, angry without quite knowing why, and Ham, laughing in spite of his sudden loss, looked across the table at Nita and very broadly winked at her. Then he turned and left the room with the others.

Nita's right arm ached all the way up to her shoulder from shaking the dice for so long. As she turned toward the door and pushed through the crowd, she noticed how terribly sensitive both her breasts felt, and knew in a flash what this must mean.

'This really is my lucky day!' Nita said to herself with a half-smile. 'I'll bet all the chips in this casino and every sign in the zodiac that I'm pregnant!'

Part Four

CHAPTER TWENTY-NINE

A man loomed up across the main table and captured Ham's attention with a loud rasping voice. He was one of the agents Ham remembered angrily barring from the studio lot years before when he turned a once satisfied actor into a money-hungry ingrate who walked out on a signed contract. Now this miserable prick ran one of the biggest and most powerful offices in town, and if you wanted to put together a decent package, get a name star, writer and director, you had to kiss his fat ass, wine and dine him and hope he might just happen to mention your production in passing to one of the precious clients whose careers he controlled . . . and whom you needed if you were to survive in this jungle. My God – what the business had come to!

'Ham, it's so wonderful to see you again. They couldn't have picked a more deserving person for this award. Congratulations. Give me a call – I'd love to have you for lunch real soon. Maybe I've got something or someone you want . . .'

'Yeah,' said Ham. 'Maybe you have . . . maybe you have.'

The head of the Biggest Agency in Town walked on, nodding to his many friends, enemies and clients in the audience, and Ham glared bitterly at his back.

Have me for lunch . . . Sure, he'd like to have my heart and my guts broiled and on a plate! I could hear the little shit laughing at me – son of a bitch! Who the hell let him in here!

He looked again out at the crowded main floor of the Palladium. There was not one face he really cared for. Look at all of them stuffing their guts, asking each other the time and wishing it was over. Look at the herds of cattle and flocks of sheep buying each other's tickets to each other's benefits and charities and all the phony-baloney affairs like this. 'I'll buy tickets to yours if you'll buy tickets to mine.' Tickets, tickets . . . who'll buy my tax-deductible tickets! Nobody really gave a damn anymore. It was all a big game, a lousy stinking farce. The awards given and taken, and it was a game played by egotistic status-hungry fools . . . the biggest game in town!

No . . . no . . . once there was another game in this town . . . nothing at all like this and all the other ones. That was a game you remember all your life with happiness and pleasure. Memories of the fun he and his son had all those wonderful days together at the Games – and Irene was part of it too. Those were the last good times he ever had with Irene and his son . . . at the greatest Games of all, more than thirty years ago. He closed his eyes and remembered.

More than seventy-five thousand spectators were on their feet in the Los Angeles Olympic Stadium, all shouting their outrage and anger at the judges who had just disqualified Mildred 'Babe' Didrikson because she had gone feet first over the five-foot, four-and-a-half-inch high-jump bar. No matter now that the rules would later be changed to permit her unorthodox style; this first week in August 1932 at the Tenth Olympic Games, Babe Didrikson had offended the judges and had to be satisfied with the silver medal for the event – a satisfaction not shared by the thousands of spectators.

'She was robbed by those nitpicking judges!' Ham shouted over at Zack Farmer, organizer of the Los Angeles Games, who was seated in a box directly in front with Louis B. Mayer, Irving Thalberg and Norma Shearer. Zack was red-faced with anger and spat a wad of tobacco into the aisle. An usher raced over to protest, saw who the spitter was, and kept right on running down the aisle steps, happy he had looked before he leaped.

Ham looked at his son who stood beside him. 'Kid, what do you think of the Olympics? Isn't it the biggest and best thing you ever saw!'

'Dad, it's just great. I really like being here with you! Can we come again tomorrow?'

• 'Not here. Tomorrow we're going over to the Riviera Polo Field. Darryl Zanuck invited us to the equestrian events there. That's just a fancy way to say they show off horses jumping and something else called "dressage," which I don't know a thing about. You and your mother are coming with me to Darryl's box at the Riviera Polo Field. How would you like it if we went up to the Will Rogers Ranch first for lunch?'

'I'd love it, Dad! I wish they had the Olympic Games every

year here in Los Angeles! It's the most exciting thing I've ever seen! It's bigger than any movie that was ever made!'

Ham smiled at his son. He had to admit he enjoyed being here with his boy. It was too damn bad he didn't find more time from work and the other things to spend more hours with him like this . . . to really be what a father should be. It gave him a real kick to see how much his son enjoyed the great sports spectacle and the excitement. Just watching him made Ham feel almost like a boy again himself. Of course, those dummies stealing the gold medal away from Babe Didrikson had spoiled part of the day, but hell – Babe could take care of herself and she'd win plenty of gold before this was over. Ham admired a woman like that – a woman who knew what she wanted and went after it.

'Look where she just threw the javelin!' yelled his son.

Zack Farmer turned to shout back at Ham, 'They won't take that away from her – that's a gold medal!'

The golden flame of the Olympic torch high over the peristyle blazed in the darkening sky as the thousands of people streamed out of the stadium toward the rows of yellow and red trollies and the lines of buses awaiting them or trudged off into the vast parking lots to search for their cars. Ham impulsively placed his arm over his son's shoulder as they came out of a stadium tunnel. The boy, now in his second year at Beverly Hills High School, was just fifteen years old and almost came up to his father's shoulder. He had Ham's gray eyes, and hair the same light blond as Irene's. As they emerged into the open and stood looking a moment for the location of their car, he turned to his father, a sudden serious look on his face.

'Dad, can I ask you something . . . something real important to me that I hope won't make you angry?' Ham took his arm and they moved on toward the line of chauffeur-driven cars waiting for their passengers.

Ham had a moment of upset about a question that hadn't even been asked yet. Did the kid know something he shouldn't know – and was he about to spring it on him now?

His son continued. 'I asked Mom and she wasn't too sure. Do you have a middle name? I know you have an initial, J, but does it really mean anything? Mom didn't know for sure.'

'It's only an initial, nothing more. I stuck it in there long ago just for looks . . . kind of to balance out the rest of my name. I made it up when I was a little younger than you are now. I wasn't crazy about the name my parents gave me. Any reason

301

you want to know?' said Ham with relief that the question had been a harmless one.

'I don't like being called "Junior" and some of the guys at school make fun of my name, Ham. Could I change it, Dad . . . please?'

Ham remembered why Chaim Rabinowitz had become Hamilton J. Robbins and he smiled, more in relief than in humor.

'Kid . . . er, Ham . . . or whatever you want to be called, I really don't mind. I had a problem something like that myself once. I'll tell you about it one day. You figure out a name you like and talk it over with your mother and me, and if we all like it, okay, you'll have a new first name. How about something that starts with the letter J – it kind of fits both our names anyhow, even if it's only an initial. John? Nope . . . Joseph . . . José? Come on – think up some names!'

They ran through nearly every name they could think of beginning with that letter, and even when they had reached Sierra View Drive had still not made a decision. It had been a happy day, and after his son had gone into the house to tell Irene about the wonderful time at the Olympic Games, Ham went on a short walk around the gardens.

There was a telephone in the garage, which Ham had installed a few months earlier. It was supposed to be for the help and was not a part of the house network, so he felt quite safe in using it for its real purpose – a way to call Nita without being overheard. He had not been with her for almost two weeks before the Olympics opened, although he phoned just as often as he could. He was busy every night with previews, late editing sessions or at meetings of the Film Industry Olympics Committee, but right now he felt a strong urge to talk with her. He made quite certain the chauffeur had left for his room and then let himself into the garage by a side door and went to the wall phone.

'Nita . . . I'm sorry I couldn't call earlier. We just got back from the Olympic Games. I took my son . . . we loved it . . . so exciting! The only bad thing was when they –'

'I heard it on my radio,' Nita said. 'That was a terrible shame about Babe Didrikson and the high jump – but she did all right after that. Ham . . . I've got to see you. There's something I want to talk about with you.'

'Can't we talk about it on the phone right now? This is a private line and nobody can hear us,' he said, wondering what was on her mind.

302

'No,' Nita said in a voice that seemed not to be as relaxed as usual. 'I'd much rather you came here so we could be together. It's been such a long time . . . I miss you.'

Ham thought a moment before answering.

'It's impossible tomorrow. I'm going to the Will Rogers Ranch for lunch, then to Riviera the rest of the day, and then we're going to a big dinner for the International Olympics Committee the Producers' Association is giving. I'll phone you sometime late in the day and do my damndest to be with you as soon as possible. I'm sorry, but that's the best I can do, Nita.'

'All right, but I want to see you and I'll wait for your call tomorrow. It's important we see each other, and I must talk with you. Good night, my love.' They both hung up, and Ham turned off the little light over the phone and left the garage in the dark so he could not be seen coming out the side door.

Ham had first met Will Rogers at a Motion Picture Relief Fund meeting, and the two men took an immediate liking to each other. This was not too surprising where Rogers was concerned, as he had long ago gone on record saying he liked everybody he had ever met. Ham had special reasons for being attracted to the shrewd Oklahoman, whose conquests included Broadway, Hollywood and all the newspapers carrying his penetrating comments on the American scene. As a frustrated performer, Ham secretly envied anyone who could get up in front of an audience, tweak its nose, gently boot idols in their behinds and toss the cool water of common sense and humor on the steaming flames of angry partisanship. The best quality of this remarkable man was his ability to come away from any confrontation and still be liked and admired by all present, regardless of race, creed or political idiocy. There was something about being accepted in spite of whatever was said to an audience, or to an individual, that Ham respected – because he sensed it was a talent he had never mastered.

'Will, I never met a man who didn't like you!' Ham said as he sat next to Rogers at the Fund meeting.

'You stole that remark right out of my mouth, Ham . . . but I reckon I don't mind. The way I said it was, "I never met a man I didn't like," and please don't twist it around 'cause I might get to believe it – then I'd be an egotist and have to go into politics like the rest of them. Worse yet – I might even get elected and spoil all the fun I'm having!'

'All right, Will. I'll quit misquoting you – but what I said still goes.'

Now, several months later, Ham was taking his family to a barbecue at the Will Rogers Ranch in the Santa Monica mountains. It was just before the Olympic equestrian events, which were being held right down Beverly Boulevard at the Riviera Polo Field. Ham, Irene and Ham junior, who was still trying to think of a new first name, all looked forward to seeing the famous ranch and its owner.

They could smell the beef being barbecued all the way up the hill, and as their car pulled around the Rogers polo field in front of the ranch house, there was another pungent odor – horses and their droppings. Most of Will Rogers' ranch had been carved out of the mountainside, and Will, who had never been completely at ease living in a city, again found his roots in this miniature gem of a ranch with a barn out back full of horses and a herd of calves waiting to be roped.

The three Rogers kids, Mary, Jimmy and Will junior, met them at the side door, introduced themselves and pointed out where the car should be parked. They took Ham, Irene and young Ham into the long rambling ranch house and through the big living room with its colorful Indian rugs, high beamed ceilings and the huge Texas steer head mounted over the stone fireplace. The sound of a mariachi band and many cheerful voices came through the open doors across the living room, and they all went on through the ranch house to join the crowd outside. Will hated to eat under a roof, and the big patio next to the house was set with long timber tables and benches for all the guests.

A crew of Mexican cooks and helpers turned sides of beef over the blazing chaparral, and great bowls of chili and heaps of enchiladas and refried beans were surrounded by platters of fresh fruit and bowls of punch. Since Prohibition was still the law of the land, beer and stronger stuff were not openly displayed but were available on request. Ham sat with his family at one of the long tables with Frank Capra and Clark Gable, who were deep in serious discussion and broke off to say hello. Ham was eager to meet Gable and hoped one day he could borrow him from MGM for a picture, but after Capra had introduced them, the entire conversation was about the problems he and Harry Cohn, head of Columbia Pictures, were having trying to do exactly that same thing.

'Clark, can't you talk some sense into L.B.? This picture

would be perfect for you – and he has nothing ready for you to do for a long time, or so I hear. Please, tell him you want to do it, and I know Harry will go for any deal that's reasonable.'

'You just don't know L.B., Frank. I don't think he knows what the word "reasonable" means. He's got writers working on that book *Mutiny on the Bounty* and I doubt you could spring me for anything before it's been shot . . . whenever that is!' He turned to Ham, who sat across the table, listening intently along with his son, who was fascinated by the conversation and the people doing the talking.

'Ham, you know L.B. Mayer,' Gable said. 'Do you think he'd loan me out with such a big picture in preparation?'

'Hell no!' Ham answered. 'One thing about L.B., what's his is his – and what's yours he's after! Maybe I'm being unkind . . . perhaps if Frank's picture could be shot and all wrapped up before the *Mutiny* show is ready . . . and I know they'll be writing that one for a long, long time . . . he might work something out . . . for Capra's arm and Cohn's leg! Frank, what's the film you and Harry have in mind for Clark?'

'Bob Riskin's adapted this comedy called *Night Bus*, and I think the screenplay is going to be absolutely terrific. We have our best woman star set to play opposite Clark, if we can get him . . . if L.B. frees him from his bondage. You know Claudette Colbert, and –'

'A comedy!' said Gable in alarm. 'I didn't realize we were talking about a comedy. I've never been in one. I'd be scared shitless! Frank, you better forget me for the part.'

Ham laughed at the star's upset reaction, then leaned forward and spoke with deep sincerity.

'Clark, I think a comedy would be absolutely great for a change. It could give you a brand-new career. Hell, I've shot more comedies than there are beans in this chili, and compared to dramatic shows they're a breeze. One thing though, Frank, that title *Night Bus* . . . it sounds like something you'd catch at a depot to get out of town. You should really think up something better than that. String together some catchy words that L.B. might like well enough to consider loaning Clark to you. How about a light, easy-to-remember title . . . something you know right away is a comedy?'

'We have another title in mind but Harry isn't too crazy about it – *It Happened One Night*. What do you think of that, Ham?'

There were several moments of silence to the spirited

accompaniment of the mariachi band. Ham toyed with his enchilada, pushed some beans under a soggy tortilla and looked over into the barbecue pit.

'God alone knows what kind of a title brings people into theaters, and He isn't telling us. That's a better one than the *Bus* thing . . . but maybe you should keep on thinking. I'm really not too enthused over *It Happened One Night* myself . . . but it's your picture and you should make whatever decisions Harry lets you make. I can only wish you luck, but, Frank, if the deal falls through and Columbia doesn't make it and the screenplay is as good as you say it is, maybe my company would take it off your hands. If the price is right we'd love to see it and help you out. See – there's always an answer to any problem!'

Capra almost choked on a taco but managed to sputter out a reply.

'That's no answer – that's only another problem! I happen to like *It Happened One Night*, and I'm getting Clark Gable in the male lead role if I have to slit my throat at high noon on Hollywood and Vine to swing the deal!'

'If I know L.B. Mayer, you may just have to do that,' said Ham in a less than comforting voice.

'What is it that makes all you studio heads such damned impossible bastards?' Gable asked Ham in his usual straightforward manner. 'I know it's a tough job, but does that mean you have to be worse than gorillas in a jungle?'

'Clark, you just hit it. It is a jungle, and only the tough gorillas survive . . . and sometimes other gorillas eat them. We're not in business to make but to take ideas, books, experiences, plays and whatever has happened or could happen to people that interests other people and get it all on film at what we hope is the right price. Then we try to show those reels of shadows to people who'll pay us back more money than it cost to get it into the cans. It's a business – but one with a big difference. What we're really selling is emotion, and the stakes are so damn high, the pressures and competition so fierce that your average Mr. Nice Guy falls flat on his ass or turns into a surviving tough bastard – another gorilla!'

'I know I ought to be grateful to Mayer after all he's done for me,' said Gable, his handsome face suddenly quite serious. 'After all, there's plenty of other guys he could have given those parts to at Metro – but I know that one of these days something's bound to come along from another studio

that could be good for me. If he makes a deal too damn difficult, then he hurts me and himself and his studio too in the
long run. Maybe Frank's picture is a possible smash hit, I
don't know, but if he let me do it then I'd be worth a hell of a
lot more later to MGM. Why does he make life so impossible
for everybody?'

'Because he's got an impossible job,' answered Ham. 'The
same job I have, and there's no book to tell you what's right
or wrong. One man runs things, one man makes the decisions
. . . although we all get shot at by our New York offices and
those damn second-guessers in distribution and in theaters.
We've got to be tough because we can't keep changing our
minds every minute. There's too much riding on what we're
doing, and the day this business starts to operate with decisions being made by committees is the day it's on its way
down the toilet.'

'Frank, please send me a copy of Riskin's screenplay as
soon as it's finished,' Gable said in a sure voice to Capra. 'I
feel like tangling with L.B. and I'll take your word this one is
worth a battle. I already told you, comedy frightens me . . .
but you're right. I ought to think of playing different kinds of
parts, and I hope this one will be worth my hitting the old man
so I can soften him up for you and Harry Cohn. That title,
though . . . Night Bus . . . it stinks. I kind of like It Happened
One Night, but I suppose you brains will give it some sappy
string of words that look good on a theater marquee and have
nothing to do with what's on the screen.'

'Clark, I promise you – we'll do right by you. Just get to L.B.
after you read the script, which I know you'll love, and leave
the rest up to us. If he insists I cut my throat to get you . . .
well, I have a big family and all those Sicilians will send me
their blood for a refill.'

Their host came over, a lariat twirling in his hand, and he
tossed the loop over Gable's head.

'Frank, you want this maverick for your picture? Just give
me a call and I'll rope him for you anytime! Now everybody
finish your grub and we'll go over to the polo field out front of
the ranch house. I've got some buses there to take us down to
Riviera so we can watch them show off their horseflesh!'

Ham and his family sat with Betty Rogers and the Rogers
children, and just before they reached Riviera, young Ham
leaned far over to where his parents were sitting and said in
a loud whisper, 'Jim – that's it! Maybe even Jimmy. How
about it, Mom, Dad . . . Please!'

'What's he talking about?' said the mystified Irene.

'A new first name – I forgot to tell you about it. He wants something else that's all his own . . . just like I did years ago myself. I told him to pick one out and talk it over with us. Now he's come up with something I suppose he just borrowed from his new friend Jimmy Rogers. I did suggest he try to find a name beginning with the letter J . . . How about it?' Ham said, laughing as he spoke to Irene.

She nodded her head and smiled broadly just as the bus stopped behind the clubhouse and the party started to leave.

'All right. I like "Ham junior," but I can see he might be happier with something different, and Jimmy sounds just fine. I approve, and I'll try to get used to it.'

'Hello, Jimmy Robbins . . . Welcome! Maybe we'll put a change-of-title notice in the trade papers,' said Ham.

'Oh, no!' his son gasped. 'I'll get word around myself, don't worry. I really like it. Jimmy . . . later on maybe James. Boy! Is this going to mix everybody up at school!'

Ham slapped his son affectionately on the back and put an arm around Irene's waist. They got to their reserved seats in Darryl Zanuck's box just as the Mexican National Equestrian Team trotted onto the green field and the band played lively music that had feet tapping and hooves clicking.

It had been a simply wonderful day, the happiest time Irene could remember having with Ham for years. He held her hand as they watched the magnificent jumpers clear the barriers, then later puzzled with him over the elegance of dressage, where horse and rider performed as though sharing a single body. It was almost like sitting with him on the meadow years ago in Golden Gate Park, and she half expected him to lean over and give her a big kiss. Suddenly he did just that, and she held even more tightly to his hand. She could see some of the old excitement in his eyes, and his hand went around her waist for a warm moment. Ham looked over at his son – the newly named Jimmy – who was happy to see his parents so happy. Suddenly one of the riders was spilled out of his saddle when his horse froze at a jump, and Irene gasped. The smartly uniformed rider got up to his feet and helped his horse find its footing, then remounted to try again.

'Thank goodness he wasn't hurt,' Irene said, and impulsively Ham leaned over to again plant a kiss on her cheek. There was something about watching horses sail over jumps that did things to him, or maybe it was the newfound pleasure at being with his family, relaxed, happy and far from the usual tensions.

The bright blue sky slowly darkened and turned into a lovely California sunset pink as the day finally came near an end and they drove back to Beverly Hills. Ham and Irene sat in the back of the car, still holding hands, while Jimmy excitedly chattered up front with the chauffeur about all the wonderful and exciting things that had happened with the horses and how Will Rogers had roped Clark Gable right in front of him at lunch!

When they reached the house on Sierra View, Ham and Irene had more than an hour before it was time to dress for the Producers' Association Olympic Dinner. They sent Jimmy off to the kitchen for his meal and went upstairs, where the warmth and closeness of the lovely day followed them into their bedroom.

With hardly a word passing between them, Ham made sure the bedroom door was locked, and then he and Irene removed all their clothes and got into bed. They made love more passionately than they had for longer than either of them could remember, and when it was done there was the fullness of a rich deep inner pleasure leaving them both in a dreamy peaceful mood they wished could last. It was a kind of intimacy neither ever remembered experiencing with the other before, and as Ham lay looking up at where the ceiling was hidden in the dark, he reached over and their hands met as they held on to each other.

Suddenly something he had completely forgotten came flying unbidden and unwelcome into his mind. Nita! He had said he would phone her. He said to himself, 'She'll just have to wait. I'm not calling her at all tonight. Maybe Irene and I have just found a new beginning. I don't know . . . but I feel close to her all over again and I enjoyed this lovemaking with her. We used to love each other so much, and I think it's going to be like that again . . . I hope so. Nita . . . well, this could mean an ending for Nita. I don't know if I want to give her up completely . . . I love being with her too and what's happening here might mean the finish of that . . . but I'm not going to think about it until tomorrow.' He leaned over and kissed Irene softly on the lobe of her ear. She put her arms around him again and gave him a long, lingering kiss as he heard the last little words deep down in his mind . . . 'Tomorrow . . . tomorrow is a long time from now . . . and suddenly I'm having a wonderful today!'

CHAPTER THIRTY

'I understand, Larry. The minute Mr. Robbins comes in or phones, I'll tell him his friend is trying to reach him. Sure, it's the very first message he'll get . . . I'll make certain.' Bob Silver pulled out a message pad and noted the information. As Ham Robbins' executive secretary, it was his business to get names and numbers of everybody calling, even if Ham never intended to get back to them. He knew this was different from the usual call and made a special notation up top where the boss could spot it first thing along with the telegrams from the home office and yesterday's grosses from all over the country. There was also a letter from Maurie having to do with family matters, so it too would be placed in the special attention file.

'When do you expect him in, Bob?' asked Larry.

'I'll only know that when he calls me or comes through the door. You've been around here long enough not to ask that question, Larry. He was at the Olympic Committee dinner the Producers' Association tossed last night at the Coconut Grove and I have no idea when he got home. He hasn't called in yet. Don't worry, he'll get your message about the "friend." ' Silver let out a sigh, then hung up the phone.

Bob had been in the office since eight o'clock that morning, checking wires from New York with the nationwide theater grosses, contract information from the New York legal office on talent, story purchases and options and some material for the coming labor negotiations with IATSE and the Teamsters. Five pages of one telegram covered purchases made for the studio property department at auctions on Lexington Avenue, and all this had to be broken down and sent to the department heads concerned. The grosses were for Ham's eyes only, being almost as confidential as grand jury proceedings.

Bob Silver told his assistant he would be down the hall in the barbershop but would be right back if Mr. Robbins arrived. Any phone calls could be transferred to the barber's

chair, and he carried along his notes so he could read them to
Ham if he called him there. Off he went to get his scalp rinsed
and his thinning hair trimmed. In twenty minutes or less he
would be back at his desk, continuing to organize the day,
which would shift into high gear when Ham drove through
the studio's main gate.

It was nearly eleven-thirty when Irene opened her eyes and
looked across the bed. She could hear the sound of her husband in the bathroom, the comfortable noises of teeth being
brushed, the spitting out of water and then the little belch
that echoed from the tiled walls. She got out of bed and pulled
the drapes back from the windows, looking out at the sun-
swept lawn. The house, on its gentle rise of ground, looked
down on the tennis court, the formal gardens over to one side
and the swimming pool, a turquoise oval, set down in a slight
hollow. Live oaks and pine trees accented the spaces
between flower beds, patches of lawn and the paths and
stone steps leading down to the lower parts of the estate.
The perfectly tended grass was interrupted by a sweeping
driveway of concrete and an arc of brick paving that circled
the lovely old Spanish fountain standing in front of the house.
The noises from the bathroom stopped, and Irene was aware
that Ham stood next to her at the window.

'Do you have to go to the studio? Can't you stay home
another few hours?' she asked him.

Ham put his arm around her waist, thought of the night
with her that had been like none he could ever remember . . .
the complete giving of herself . . . his eager acceptance and
the pleasure they found again and again in each other's body.
Why leave this wonderful rediscovery any sooner than he
had to? The studio could wait, and he felt like celebrating
their second honeymoon with a third one. Grossmutter had
finally been locked out of their bedroom after so damn many
years!

'Why no,' he told her. 'I don't have to rush back right away.
I may have some work to do late tonight, but what the hell . . .
it's too nice being with you to leave now.'

'There's something I want to surprise you with,' Irene said.
'Get dressed and meet me down by the front door in half an
hour.'

'A surprise? I think we've both already had some wonderful surprises, haven't we? We ought to surprise each other
more often from now on,' he said, holding both her hands in

311

his while she felt a blush and a warm happy feeling spread over her body. She kissed him on the lips, then quickly left the room and went down the hall to the stairs leading to the kitchen as he turned to go into his dressing room.

Ham pulled out something to wear, then reached for his telephone and called the office. Bob Silver had some routine messages for him, read the more important key city grosses from the New York wire, then told him Larry Gross had been calling with a message that his 'friend' wanted him to call her. Ham pulled on his pants, shrugged and told Bob to contact Larry Gross and relay the word that he would be calling later that day if he had the time.

'Mr. Robbins, there's a letter here from your brother about some personal family matters. Do you want me to read it to you?'

'Definitely not. Why spoil a perfectly good day? Leave it on my desk and I'll get around to it later when I get in. How's everything else going on there?'

His secretary assured him that every company was on schedule. So far there were no problems – but of course the day was young. All the shooting companies were breaking for lunch. The actors were acting, the directors were directing and the production department seemed reasonably pleased and happy about everything. Ham hung up after telling Bob he would be in the office in a few hours and that he was not to be disturbed unless there was an emergency – and there had better not be.

The half-hour had passed and Ham went down the sweeping half-circle of the main staircase to the reception hall and saw Irene standing beside the partly open front door. The butler was beside her and held a large wicker basket. Irene smiled at him, looking almost like a young girl.

'Ham, I'll bet you've completely forgotten what happened exactly sixteen years ago today!'

He stood beside her for a moment with a puzzled look on his face.

'Sixteen years ago ... that had to be in ... let's see ... 1916 and we were in San Francisco. That basket! Of course! We were on a picnic in Golden Gate Park!' He laughed and asked her, 'How did you ever remember that?'

'Some things you don't forget very easily, Ham. I thought we should celebrate the sixteenth anniversary of our first picnic by having another one right here in our own Golden Gate Park. Come on, I know the perfect spot, and I even have

312

a blanket to put on the grass.'

'That's a wonderful idea, Irene. Let me carry your basket the way I did that day in the park,' Ham said, and he took the wicker container from the butler. 'Now let's find this perfect spot of yours for our perfect picnic!'

They crossed the driveway and walked past the fountain and over to the wide lawn, climbing the gentle slope all the way to a lovely group of tall trees standing at the far end of the estate. Here they could sit on the blanket and look down at their house and everything that could be seen of Beverly Hills from high up here on Sierra View Drive.

'Remember how we sat beside Lloyd Lake in Golden Gate Park for our picnic?' Irene said as she put the food on plates and handed the cold bottle of rose wine and a corkscrew to Ham.

'One nice improvement over the view we had then is that here we get to look at our own house. This is our "Portals of the Present" instead of those earthquake ruins you told me were called "Portals of the Past." '

Repeating exactly what he had done sixteen years before, Ham pulled Irene to him and gave her a passionate kiss. As they finally pulled away from each other and started to eat the food, Ham saw some movement over to one side where the dead-end side road ran by the wall. A car had pulled up and stopped there, and he could just see its top over Irene's shoulder. Enough showed to make him quite certain whose car it was. He should know – it was the two-door yellow Ford he had bought the month before for Nita. Ham froze, the smile on his face gone. He gulped down a chunk of bread and swallowed half of his glass of wine, eyes still fixed on the car.

'What's the matter, dear?' said Irene, alarmed at the sudden change in her husband's face.

'Uh . . . nothing . . . nothing. I've got to have the gardeners order some trees set over there so sightseeing tourists aren't always snooping on us.' She turned a moment, saw the car, then looked back at him.

'Oh, so what!' Irene laughed. 'Let them see how happy we are. They'll go back to Kansas or Iowa or wherever they're from and tell all their friends what wild parties we throw out here in Hollywood! Mad picnics on the lawn in the middle of the week when all honest people are working!'

Ham slowly finished a sandwich, quietly drank his wine and let Irene do most of the talking. Now and then he looked far over at the upper portion of the Ford, several hundred yards away. His stomach seemed to squeeze into a tight knot, and he felt terribly angry about things he could not swallow as easily as the sandwich and other good things from the basket. Nobody had gotten out of the car and he was unable to make out any figure sitting inside, but it was there, and he chewed his food, which seemed to have lost all taste. Irene was disturbed at his sudden loss of enthusiasm, and they finished their little picnic almost in silence.

'What's bothering you, Ham? Tell me . . . you weren't this glum in Golden Gate Park. I don't remember what we ate then, but I do remember how we kissed. Now do that again . . . kiss me!'

He put down the food, leaned forward and put his lips on hers, but it was almost a mechanical action and there was no joy or passion about it. His eyes were closed and he tried to concentrate on what should have been a pleasant task, but his mind was over the wall where the car was parked and he fought to conceal his anger. Suddenly in the middle of their kiss he heard a motor start, the clash of gears, and he pulled away from Irene to look again toward the wall, where what he could see of the car moved away, then turned and was gone down the road past the long stucco boundary and the closed gates of the Robbins estate.

'Now you can relax . . . the tourists have left!' Irene said as Ham kept looking to where the car had been parked. But Ham did not relax. It was no use fooling herself, thought Irene. The whole mood had been broken. Golden Gate Park was sixteen long years ago, in 1916, and here they sat in 1932 and those damn gardeners had better plant a thick grove of bamboo and some Italian cypress to block the view of snooping strangers! How odd that such a little thing could affect Ham so much.

They rose to their feet, and Irene packed the picnic debris into the basket while Ham folded the blanket. Then they walked down the slope of the lawn toward their house.

'I'm sorry things went wrong, Ham. What was it?'

'Nothing, nothing. First those damn tourists – and then I was thinking about some trouble I'm having on this picture. It's something we can't seem to work out. I may have to stick around the studio late tonight . . . this is a hell of an hour to go to work . . . but honest, Irene, I did love your little surprise picnic. It was sweet of you to remember to the day when we had that one in San Francisco. Maybe sometime soon we can do it again. That spot under the trees is perfect. If I was shooting a picture and needed a place like that, well, with all our talent and dough we'd never be able to duplicate it in a studio stage. Don't worry, I won't ever let them use it for a picture location! I know what they would do to that nice lawn of ours. Did you ever see the mess a picture company makes when they shoot on location at somebody's house? This is strictly for us and nobody else. Say – what happened to . . . what's his new name? . . . our son – oh yes, Jimmy?'

'He went to the Olympic Games swimming events with some friends. You know that big stadium they put up just for the diving and swimming? I'm sure he'll be out there for the rest of the day.'

They reached the front of the house, and he stood with her until the butler came out for the basket and took it back to the kitchen. He kissed her, then walked over to the garage as she went back into the house. The chauffeur pulled out his car while he stood off to one side, where he saw the wall phone hanging inside. For a moment he hesitated; then, remembering it took longer than half an hour to drive from Beverly Hills back to Hollywood and up to Detour Drive, he swore under his breath and climbed into his car.

The first message he found on his desk was from Larry Gross referring to the call from his 'friend.' He wadded it into a tiny ball and tossed it into the wastebasket, then ripped open the envelope and pulled out Maurie's letter.

Dear Ham:

In just three months it will be fifty years since Momma and Poppa were married. A golden wedding anniversary is an important thing and I have been in touch with Ruth and Miriam about it. We agreed, as I am sure you will, that there should be a special party in Harrisburg for them. All the family who can be there should try to make it and . . .

The letter went on with more details about hotel rooms, a ballroom for the party itself and arranging for a camera and a sound crew from the studio to be there and preserve the event for the future. The date would be November 4, giving them all three months to prepare. Ruth would handle things there in Harrisburg, and at their parents' age, it shouldn't be a surprise party. Poppa would want to help, and they were going to let him and Momma do whatever they wanted to do.

Ham finished the letter. He realized it was the first communication, written, phoned or inferred, from Maurie he had

315

received in a long time that had not angered him. His brother was treating him like a brother, no fault finding, no recriminations. Maybe this was how it should be all the time. He called in Bob Silver and dictated a reply to Maurie. Although they would be speaking on the long-distance phone before the end of the week, like Maurie he preferred to have anything to do with the family in the form of a letter. He then dictated letters to both his sisters telling them how happy he and Irene would be to see them at the coming golden wedding anniversary and how good it would be to have all the family together again.

Now his day really began. A male star, under long-term contract, had sent in an ultimatum by way of his agent. He hated the script of his next picture. There was no way it could be rewritten so he would appear in it, and that was final. Ham first phoned the agent, who apologized for any problems and started to argue on behalf of his client, but found he was speaking into a dead phone after Ham slammed down the receiver. Ham then called in the head of the studio legal department and uttered a three-word directive.

'Suspend the bastard!'

The lawyer knew just where the suspension forms were in his files, and within an hour a registered letter was on its way putting the actor on suspension. He would have his way and not have to appear in the disputed picture – but every day and every hour of the time he stayed away from his assignment would be tacked on to the end of his contract. He might celebrate his own golden wedding anniversary still under contract to Robbins International!

Next came a session with the studio business manager, who had to explain why the company was spending so much more money on nails, lumber and concrete. He left the office with firm instructions to pass on to Set Construction that bent nails were to be straightened and reused, sets were to be left standing, repainted, repapered, re-dressed – and reused ... and that anybody who poured fresh concrete had better go out and look for another job someplace else!

Fred Simms, head of Publicity, brought in all his plans for the premiere of the musical *Dolls on Parade*, which would light up the sky in one month at Grauman's Chinese Theatre. Ray McClintock, head of studio Police and Security, was called in and told to start setting up traffic control with the Los Angeles police and planning the usual security for a premiere, where so many things could go wrong – and usually did.

Ham suddenly thought of something and called the head of the sound department.

'We're setting the *Dolls* premiere . . . Oh, you already know about it – good. Are you absolutely sure it will be ready on time? What! You need an extra three weeks? What the fuck for? What do you mean it won't come out of rerecording in time? Don't go blaming Music . . . tell them I want that track laid in and the show wrapped up by the end of this week and no excuses! Call me back when it's done – and it better be! The damn picture opens in one month at the Chinese!'

Next came a call to the film editor, who nervously told Ham the optical effects and titles had not been sent over from the labs and title house. He received an ultimatum – the picture was opening with or without titles . . . and there better be titles or by God an editor would be out on his ass!

Ham was outraged at the sloppy timetables and called in Bob Silver again, dictating a memo to every department head concerned. They were paper whips and he knew they would do the job. He was dealing with professionals – although sometimes they had to be backed up with a firing or two to show everybody he meant every word of every memo. When Leo Arnheim, his executive assistant, came in with scripts for approval, he heard Ham finishing the last of the new memos and shook his head in sympathy. That was all Ham needed to aggravate his anger.

'Damn it, Leo! Nothing ever gets done here unless I kick somebody's ass to get it done!' Ham complained. 'Those loafers all knew the picture was to be wrapped up by the end of this week and they've been sitting back on their lazy butts letting the time pass!' He paused, drew in a deep breath, then slammed both hands down hard on his desktop. 'Who in his right mind would ever want to run a studio!' He got to his feet and walked over to the picture window set in the far wall of his office. The sky was dark pink, slowly fading to black, and the streetlights flickered on to illuminate the studio. A long parade of giant lamps rolled by like a line of circus elephants, each holding the tail of the one in front and being towed by a tractor toward the gaping stage doors as rigging crews prepared the sets that had to be ready for shooting early next morning. Ham looked a moment, then swung around and called over to Arnheim.

'Leo, I want to run the first and fifth reels of *Dolls*. Call the

317

editor, Jim Fitzhugh. Tell him to set them up in my screening room in fifteen minutes . . . then I want to see all the dailies. After that have some food brought in. No . . . by that time I'll want to get the hell off the lot. I'll just have to get here early tomorrow and not sleep away half the day! Come on, by the time we get to the projection room they'll have the reels threaded up. Call them while I check something with Bob in the outside office.'

He stopped by his secretary's desk and picked up the sheaf of phone messages Bob held out to him. He fanned them out like a bridge hand and flipped one after the other back on the desk without comment. The last one he held for a moment. It was from Larry Gross with the same message he had already received. The 'friend' had to talk to him. Ham tossed it to Bob as he left the office and called back over his shoulder, 'Phone Gross. Tell him to stop bothering me with his damn messages. No . . . tell him to get in touch with the party and say that I'm still tied up. I'll try to make contact when I get through later. All right . . . you know where I'll be.'

Nearly four hours passed before Ham emerged from his personal screening room. During that time he ran and reran the problem reels of the musical film that was to have its premiere in a month. At last, after reediting several scenes, transposing a sequence here and moving another there, it was done and the editor went to his cutting room with the cans of film, a bundle of notes and a hard few days and nights of work to look forward to. The director would be on Ham's shit list for his repeated stupid errors, which had caused everybody so much trouble. Unless something else went wrong, the film should make it up to the booth at Grauman's Chinese in time for its night of glory. Ham was wrung out and could hardly sit through the eight reels of dailies that followed. He would gladly have skipped them, but it was vital that he personally review every foot of film shot in the studio. How else could he keep track of where the money was being spent and whether the scripts, so painfully concocted by expensive writers, were turning into anything worthwhile on the screen?

When he and Leo Arnheim reached the studio street, Ham saw Larry Gross waiting for him beside his car.

'Larry, you better not have any more of those messages for me! I'm so exhausted right now that all I want to do is crawl into bed and turn myself off!'

'I'm sorry, Mr. Robbins. I wouldn't bother you, but I

received more phone calls from Miss de Valle and I think something must be very wrong with her. She was crying . . . carrying on, and she sounded quite desperate. She said she had to see you as soon as possible, that she –'

'Damn it to hell! She knows how busy I am . . .' He started to say something else about already having seen Nita earlier that same day from a distance, but stopped before mentioning the sightseeing 'tourist' outside his walls.

'All right . . . all right. Give her a call. Tell her I'll stop by for a minute on my way home. I've been so busy I haven't had a chance to see her for over a week. Another half-hour before I get home won't kill me. Thanks, Larry. I'm sorry I make your job so tough, but that's the kind of job it is.'

Larry started to say something, but Ham was in his car and slamming the door. He drove out toward the main gate and off the lot. The familiar drive up into the Hollywood hills went quickly, and he turned off on Detour Drive, pulling up in front of the house as Nita pulled open the front door, letting yellow light spill out into the blackness.

'Ham . . . I've missed you so much . . . come in quickly!'

'What's the matter, Nita? Larry tells me you've been calling all day. I've been up to my neck in work and with those damn Olympics, so I couldn't get here before this. By the way – weren't you out driving earlier this afternoon . . . around Sierra View Drive?' he asked the girl, who held tightly to his arm.

'Oh – you saw me. I was so lonely and I missed you so very much, Ham. I didn't want to be seen. I stayed inside my car and I hope you didn't mind. Maybe I shouldn't have done it . . . and . . .'

'You're goddamn right you shouldn't have done it! Please don't go cruising around my place like that again, Nita!' For a moment he showed her his anger, but then quickly calmed down when he saw the hurt look in her eyes. 'I'm sorry. This has been one hell of a day for me . . . problems you couldn't begin to imagine at the studio. More idiots screwing things up, and unless I watch every move they make, they'll always make the wrong one. Now tell me . . . how are you?'

'All right, I guess . . . but there's something I've got to tell you and that's why I wanted to see you. Ham . . . I missed my period last month, and this one too . . . and my breasts have gotten bigger and very sensitive. Look . . . I'm getting a little tummy . . . only it isn't fat . . . and I went to a doctor last week and –'

319

'Now don't you go telling me you're pregnant, because I don't believe you! It's impossible – I used a rubber every time we –'

'Ham, listen to me, please. The doctor examined me and he said I'm definitely pregnant. It's your baby. I haven't slept with anyone else but you ... I swear it on my mother's grave!'

'What the hell are you saying, Nita? I don't believe it!'

'Ham darling ... please ... calm down and listen. The doctor is sure, and so am I.'

'Doctor ... What kind of a doctor did you go to? Did he know what the hell he was talking about?'

'Lorene took me to her gynecologist, who's very good, and he –'

'Lorene! You've gone all over town telling people you're knocked up! For Christ's sake, she took you to some quack who fed you a line of crap you believe. Does this Lorene happen to be a good friend of Hedda Hopper or Louella Parsons, too? At least you could have gotten to me and I would have set things up for an abortion ... in fact that's just what we're going to do ... even if I'm the last one to be told what's been going on around here!' He stopped a moment. His face had turned dark, and sweat appeared on his forehead. He sat down on the sofa, got up and began pacing back and forth. 'I wore a rubber every damn time. I know I did. If something happened anyhow, then you're getting an abortion just as soon as you can!'

'Ham darling, please sit down and stop being so excited.'

'I've got every right to get excited. Listen, Nita, I'm not going to have my life screwed up just because you say something went wrong with ... I did use a rubber, didn't I? You told me you found one all filled in the bed that night I got so loaded after we came here from the Valley. You did find it in the bed, didn't you? You told me you found it there, Nita! Did you?' His voice rose higher and higher, and his clenched fists shook.

She waited a minute before replying, vainly hoping he might calm down.

'The doctor said that maybe some of your sperm still got in me after the rubber came off ... that it is very possible to get pregnant that way. I don't remember exactly, but I was terribly surprised too. I was so sure it couldn't happen ... but it did! Ham, don't worry about one thing – the doctor doesn't know my real name. I made one up for him. And

320

Lorene is a good friend who can be absolutely trusted.'

Ham sat down heavily on the living room sofa. He looked up at Nita, who stood there in front of him, and no words came from his lips. At last, almost in desperation, he said, 'You're going to have an abortion! There's no way we can let –'

'No, Ham,' said Nita in a very firm voice. 'No abortion. For one thing, the doctor said it's too late for that. I'm nearly three months pregnant – and besides, I want our baby more than anything else in the world . . . except for only one other thing.'

'One other thing . . . what's that?' asked Ham in a voice he could hardly recognize as his own.

'You, my darling!' she answered, looking at him in a way that said much more than the three simple words ever could.

'Me! I'm a married man!'

'You can become a divorced one. You keep telling me how unhappy you are with your wife. Now, thanks to me, you've given her the perfect reason to divorce you . . . and, Ham, you'd better hurry. If everything goes the way it's supposed to, you'll be a father again in about six months from now.'

He could not think of anything to say as his mind raced through all the events of the day. What a hell of an ending this was! He would resolve it, though – in his way, and fast! What did this dame think she was going to pull on him! He remembered with sudden anguish how wonderful it had been in bed that morning with Irene and how they made so many exciting rediscoveries of each other . . . then the picnic in their own Golden Gate Park . . . his hopes that now there would be a new beginning for them. Yes, he had felt very close to Nita and she had brought him much happiness ever since they met, but a divorce? He wanted to get away and think about what Nita had just told him, talk with somebody else about all of this – but who could he talk to?

'My God, Nita, you don't know what you're asking. Be realistic. Irene's father is a lawyer, and if they want to make it tough, this could drag on for years. I'm not sure that I want to go through having my private life splashed over every damn headline in town!' He was thinking of the stories in the Harrisburg and New York papers and all the messages he would then be receiving from Maurie and his sisters . . . from all his family. Poppa, Momma . . . everybody remembering little Chaim the pisher . . . still going at it . . . bringing disgrace on all of them.

'Ham, I love you and I know you love me.' Nita came closer

to the silent man seated on the couch. 'We must have this baby and a happy life of our own. All right – so there will be some problems for a while, but eventually they'll come to an end. You've had problems before and you always faced them and worked them out. You can handle this, I'm sure of it, and I believe in you. You're a strong man and you need a better and a more loving wife than the one you have now – one who will make you truly happy the rest of your life!'

'Nita,' Ham finally said, lifting his head and looking into her eyes, 'tomorrow morning first thing, Larry Gross is taking you to another doctor. There must be some way to take care of this.'

'There is, darling,' she quickly answered. 'Tell your wife what has happened and that you want a divorce. Maybe you can talk her into going to Reno, and then we could be married before the baby is born.'

'Stop pushing me, Nita. Stop pushing me! Larry is taking you to a doctor tomorrow. He'll know who. If it's money you want, tell me how much and I'll give it to you.'

She burst into tears. 'Ham! That's a terrible thing even to suggest. I don't want any money from you!'

'Then just what the hell is it you do want, Nita?'

'I want you, Ham . . . I want you.' She sat down beside him and put her arm around his shoulder to draw him closer, and in her mind she could clearly see the image of a great pair of bronze gates set in a white wall as they slowly rolled wide open for her to enter.

He sat silently beside her, his face ashen; then he stood up and walked over to the window and looked out at the bright lights of the city far down the hill – and he too saw an image: the vivid mental picture of a lovely blue sign with bright golden letters high in the sky as it burst into flames, then fell crashing down into the rubble.

CHAPTER THIRTY-ONE

Ham left Nita and aimlessly drove himself west on Hollywood Boulevard past all the closed stores and buildings, staring straight ahead and seeing few of the other cars loose in the city at this hour. A police cruiser pulled alongside at La Brea and he looked almost blankly at the men in uniform as they noted his license plate number and checked it against their list of stolen cars. He moved ahead and the police pulled off in another direction. Now he was in the county strip and drove slowly, almost as though he were a passenger in his own car with somebody else at the wheel. Reaching Beverly Hills, he drove right past the Benedict Canyon intersection, where he should have turned to go to Sierra View Drive, and continued to follow the curves of Beverly Boulevard, which soon was to be renamed Sunset Boulevard. It was a road he traveled almost without design until he came out at the Palisades; then he drove down a steep hill coming out at the highway that ran between the beach and the high eroded cliffs.

The Pacific Ocean lay out there, black and nearly invisible, with only faint starglow reflected like tiny sparks off its restless surface. Ham parked and got out of his car, walking across the white sand toward the soft lapping sounds of low-tide surf. The dry sand became damp, and he stopped when his shoes sank down in the yielding wetness. He turned to walk back to where the sand became dry again and sat down, looking out to the faint line of white foam that rolled toward him from the ocean. The moon, hidden behind high fog banks, broke through some clear patches of sky, lighting the water enough for him to see waves forming offshore and slowly rolling up, almost to where he sat. His shoes were filled with the fine white sand, but he felt not even a grain of it. His mind was in another place, and for nearly an hour he did not move. When the waves reached up to where he sat and he felt the sand dampening all around him, he slowly rose to his feet and walked back to his car.

*   *   *

It was past three in the morning when Ham pulled up in front of his gates on Sierra View. He reached out to put a key in the box, turned it and watched the big bronze slabs silently roll aside on their oiled tracks. A light automatically went on to illuminate the entrance area, and the night-duty guard came running down the inside road, his flashlight beam bouncing ahead. He recognized Ham and stood off to one side as he drove up and stopped the car.

'Good morning, Bill. I'm going to take a little walk after I get this in the garage. I still feel wide awake, and it may help make me sleepy. Does it ever do that for you?'

'Oh, no, Mr. Robbins. I never get tired when I'm on duty,' the guard quickly answered, hoping nobody ever would catch him during his predawn siestas. 'Do you want my flashlight?'

'No thanks, there's one up in the garage and you'll be needing yours. Don't worry if you see me walking around the place for a while. I just don't feel like going to bed yet.'

Ham shifted into low, waved his hand and then drove up the long curving road to turn off toward the garage and away from the main house. He pressed a button on the door-lift box and, when it was clear, pulled inside. He saw the wall phone, and for a moment something that tasted vile and bitter rose up in his throat and he thought he might vomit in his car. He fought it back, got out and slowly walked from the garage, a flashlight gripped tightly in his hand.

The great lawn spread out like a manicured meadow. Ham stood on the road edge and with his flashlight saw a silver network of slime trails left by snails as they wandered across the grass. He stepped out on the soft turf, following the nearest of the tiny trails. At the end of the little glowing path he came upon a brown-shelled creature, its eyestalks retracting as the light hit them. Ham looked down at the snail, then lifted his foot and brought it squarely down with a tiny crunching noise.

'Goddamn gardeners ... letting something like this happen! I'll bet there's millions of these little shits eating up my whole lawn!'

He walked on, following another trail, and stalked the fleeing snail until it was sighted and crushed. Now Ham worked his way slowly back and forth on the big lawn, stopping only to lift his foot and bring it smashing down. His shoes soon grew damp from the wet grass as he followed the light beam, but he went on crushing the life out of the tiny trespassers, muttering an oath each time his foot came down on a shell.

'Little fuckers . . . bastards! I keep telling those idiot gardeners to do something, but if you don't do it yourself it doesn't get done! There . . . got you . . . you slimy little shit!'

He had covered almost all of the lawn and the imprint of his shoes crisscrossed the green battlefield, now littered with the oozing corpses of his enemies. Suddenly he felt as though a great foot had come crushing down on him, and all he wanted was to get into bed and lose himself in sleep. He crossed the driveway, wiped his shoes on the mat and silently let himself into the house.

Bob Silver had never before been quite this close to hysteria. For the second time in a week Ham had slept past eleven-thirty in the morning. He had left instructions he was not to be disturbed, but Bob called again and asked for Irene, who came to the phone.

'Mrs. Robbins, I absolutely must talk to your husband. It is very important and –'

'I don't know,' Irene answered. 'He left a message on the kitchen pad whenever it was he came in saying he wanted to sleep late, and he's still in bed. He must have taken something to relax, and he was sleeping so deeply that he frightened me and I had to listen very closely to even hear him breathe. I hate to disturb him. I know he worked terribly late and –'

'He'll be quite upset if you don't get him to the telephone, Mrs. Robbins,' the secretary said, his voice getting desperate. 'The vice-president of the United States is due here in about one hour for lunch and a tour of the studio. Mr. Robbins knows all about it. They met when the vice-president opened the Olympic Games and then later at the Producers' Dinner when we set the whole thing up. If Mr. Robbins isn't here it could be terribly embarrassing!'

'But he left such definite instructions about not being awakened, Bob.'

'Mrs. Robbins, in less than an hour from now Vice-President Curtis is driving onto the lot for lunch and a tour, and it's terribly important that your husband –'

'All right. I'll go up and get him on the phone. He must have completely forgotten. It's not like him at all. He worked so late, and I have no idea when he came home. I'll be right back.' Irene went upstairs, gently opened the bedroom door and walked over to the bed, where Ham lay on his back, his mouth open, and she was glad to hear the reassuring little snores.

'Ham ... Ham ... dear ...' she said, putting her hand softly on his shoulder. No response, and the snores continued. 'Ham ... please ... dear!' in a louder voice, and her hand shook him.

'Huh ... wha ... Irene!' His eyes creaked slowly open as though breaking a gluey seal, lower lip gripped by his teeth and voice slurred by whatever drug he had taken to relax. He lay there, sluggish, half conscious. 'Irene ... wha' time is it?' came through his dry lips in a furry voice.

'Almost noon, darling. Bob Silver is on the phone ... said it was very urgent he reach you, or I'd never have come in and disturbed you. Something about the vice-president coming to lunch and seeing the studio ... and you were supposed to know all about it and –'

'Dear God!' Ham moaned. 'I remember now. Why in hell did I ever let myself get sucked into that?' He struggled to sit up, swung his feet around onto the floor and like a man twice his age managed to coax his body into a standing position. 'Jesus H. Christ! I'm supposed to be standing at the gate to meet the old guy. Let me get on the phone.' He fumbled all around on the side table, finally located the telephone and pushed the glowing line button.

'Bob ... I completely forget about what's his name ... Curtis ... Can you have Fred Simms and his mob meet him at the gate, show him around the back lot? Get plenty of pictures and stall. I'll be there within an hour and go right to the executive dining room. Tell Fred to stretch things out as much as he can, and I'll have the front gate reach him the second I drive on the lot!' He slammed down the phone, dragged himself to the bathroom, turned on the light and looked at the haggard stranger in the mirror.

A voice spoke inside his mind ... and the words were his own ...

'Just what the hell is it you do want, Nita?'

And then her answer, striking him like a blow in the pit of his stomach ...

'I want you, Ham ... I want you ... Tell your wife what has happened ... a divorce ... Reno ... married before the baby is born ... I want you, Ham ... I want you ... you ... you ... I want ... want, want!'

Orders flashed out from the production department to hold off all lunch breaks for an hour so that the distinguished visitor could see the shooting companies at work. Fred Simms and his assistants expertly guided him all around the Western street, the New York street, the Midwest town and several of the stages where pictures were being shot. He was suitably impressed, flattered and photographed, and even allowed to hold a clapper slate on an unimportant scene. A security officer ran over to Fred and whispered that Mr. Robbins had just come on the lot, the tour was terminated and the Secret Service, publicity people and stills photographers piled into their cars and the studio bus to follow the vice-president and Simms off to the executive dining room.

Lunch was a great success, followed by a special tour of the Trophy Room in the bungalow, where Ham showed the visibly impressed visitor some of the tangible rewards received by the company and by him personally for excellence, or other reasons. There was a parade of the Oscars, plaques and certificates, with appropriate running comments from the genial host. This was the part of studio tours for very special guests that Ham most liked. He had a story for every award, and from time to time embroidered them with newly invented improvements that had Fred Simms covertly making notes for future publicity releases. At last it ended, and by four o'clock the procession had formed up in front of the executive bungalow, where Ham made a little farewell speech on the steps. The parade of limousines drove from the lot, taking the distinguished visitor off to a downtown meeting with the Merchants' and Manufacturers' Association, where he would give them President Herbert Hoover's message that the economy was getting back on a sound footing, the nation was in good reliable Republican hands and the Depression had bottomed out. Another four years under the Great Engineer and the nation would again achieve its preeminent position in a world blessed with a new and lasting prosperity.

Ham was back at his desk looking at the figures from New York, which indeed did show good returns on pictures being shown throughout the country and abroad. He knew, though, that this was one business that was not suffering as much as most others from the Great Depression that still afflicted the United States and the rest of the world. When an economy and its people were depressed, they sought some kind of escape, and movies were about the cheapest escape available . . . along with cigarettes and sex. Thank God, thought Ham, there's not much else for people to do with what little money they have left, and at least movies seem to be holding their own . . . but how long can it last?

He opened the mail folder that Bob Silver had set on his desk. A letter from the office of the governor of New York . . . Franklin Delano Roosevelt . . . a plea for support . . . contributions to the Democratic National Committee, with a note by that consummate politician Jim Farley . . . a request for cameras and technicians to cover his coming drive for the next presidency of the United States. Ham had met F.D.R. and was greatly impressed by the man, who had triumphed over such a terrible physical blow, sitting in a wheelchair as though it were a throne. Ham decided to write Maurie about throwing all possible support to help elect him. He had to be sort of clever about it, though, because Republicans also went to the movies and why antagonize any customers? Hell . . . it wouldn't hurt to have a good friend in the White House. He looked up from the folder just then to see Irene's picture, an eleven-by-fourteen, shot by the best man in their stills department. She looked right at him, her trusting eyes piercing through to his gut, which suddenly contracted as he thought of another woman up in the Hollywood hills . . . with the new life growing inside her body.

'Goddamn it!' Ham swore. 'Just when things seemed to be getting so much better with me and Irene, this had to happen. Maybe Nita's not even pregnant at all. I know I wore a rubber every time . . . every fucking time! She could be lying to me! What am I going to do? Who in hell can I even talk to about it? I'm not going to do a damn thing for a while . . . I'll wait and see . . . but how long can I wait?' He seemed to have no choice. Now other letters were there to be read, one from Ruth, another from Miriam – the excitement of the coming golden wedding celebration, their plans. Did he have any suggestions? 'Plans? What the hell plans can I make? I'm just going to have to stall as long as I can and try to think my way out of this. I'm damn sure not going to tell Irene about it now . . . not until after we get back from Harrisburg. Then . . . I'll see.'

Anger kept building up inside. Ham slapped the folder shut on the correspondence. He looked out the window at the beautiful blue sky, then back to the picture of Irene over on the side table . . . then down at his tightly clenched fists on the desktop. Suddenly there was a rasping buzz from his intercom box and Bob Silver's metallic voice came from the speaker.

'Mr. Robbins . . . Larry Gross is on the phone. Says he has a message. Will you talk with him?'

Ham's anger exploded, and he replied in a hard, strained voice.

'I'm not talking to him. I want you to get Fred Simms on your phone. Tell him to put through a closeout on Larry Gross. I don't want him around here anymore! He's to be the hell off the lot within one hour – understand me?'

Bob understood and clicked off. Ham looked at the polished wood intercom box as though it contained all his enemies and wondered why he felt no better for having lashed out at somebody who, after all, was only a messenger doing his duty. For a moment he nearly buzzed Silver to undo what had been done; then he pulled his hand away from the call button. He sat deep in his chair, stared out the far window as a fleecy cloud scudded by. It passed from his view just as a new thought came to his mind, and suddenly he knew who to call. The intercom button to the other office was pushed, and Bob answered.

'Get hold of Pops Johnson in the location department. Tell him it's important I see him right away!' said Ham, and he flipped off the talk switch.

The glowering bulldog-jawed autographed photograph of John Edgar Hoover, director of the Federal Bureau of Investigation, looked down from the wall on the silver-haired, heavy old man who reached deep into his desk drawer for a half-empty bottle of 86-proof Kentucky straight bourbon whiskey, which he poured with great care into a thick glass tumbler until it nearly slopped over the rim. Right now Frank 'Pops' Johnson, head of the Robbins International location department, felt every one of his nearly sixty-eight years. His ass was still dragging from the whirlwind trip around the lot with the vice-president. He had been overjoyed to see some old cronies from the Secret Service in the party, and his jaw still ached from all the talk about old friends back in Washington and out in the Baltimore police department – a place Pops well knew, having been its deputy chief, then chief for several years until he entered the FBI to work for J. Edgar. What wonderful memories were reawakened during those past couple of hours . . . and how glad he was now to be back here in his quiet comfortable office instead of running himself ragged chasing after people and checking security the way they had to. He'd had some damn good years in the Bureau, especially when he handled liaison between the FBI and the Secret Service, but this racket he was in now beat it all to pieces. Here he could sit calmly behind a desk and push the influence button, or know exactly the right person to do it for him. As head of the location department, it was his job to get things done wherever and however they needed doing. It could be a permit to tie up an entire lower Manhattan street for a picture company . . . stop all traffic on the Bay bridge to shoot a police chase scene up in San Francisco . . . divert three U.S. Navy destroyers or borrow an army division needed for background in a service picture . . . and he had all the right connections to do all that and more. Just a few phone calls to some of his good friends in Washington, New York, Sacramento or a dozen city halls or police departments – touch the proper nerve, twist the correct arm and promise whatever it was suitable to promise – and it was done. If he had not gone into high-level police and security work, Pops would have made a perfect Secretary of State. He dealt in people with power and instinctively knew how to get from them whatever was theirs to give that he needed for a picture . . . or something more personal. It could be a cavalry troop, exclusive use of the Washington Monument, the Statue of Liberty, the U.S. Marine Corps – or springing some company employees from a Seattle jail after a drunken Saturday night brawl on a distant location.

He still carried his old chopped-off .45 pistol in a belt holster and bragged about the permanent black-and-blue mark it had pressed into his behind. The rough tough years of bossing cops in Baltimore, then running around the country for J. Edgar Hoover had also left their permanent mark on this man, who had traded his youth for a pot belly, silver hair, a double chin and all the contacts and pressure points that made him the man to see when something impossible must be done. Above all, Pops Johnson was a man who could be absolutely, utterly and completely trusted. It was his life and the major tool of his trade. Ham knew this, and it was why the old man, past normal retirement age, was still downstairs behind a desk as head of the location department.

The phone rang and Pops took the message from Bob Silver upstairs in the Big Man's office. He looked sadly at the tumbler of bourbon, sighed and then twisted open the bottle cap. Very carefully, without so much as a shake of his hand, he poured all of the precious liquid back and rescrewed the cap. It would be in there waiting for him later. He pulled his solidly built two hundred and fifty pounds up from the high-backed, sway-bottomed chair, went out into the hall and then upstairs to the executive office area.

'Go right in, Pops. The Boss is expecting you,' said Bob Silver, and the older man pushed through the inner door.

'Pops . . . how are you? Did you enjoy our visitor today?' Ham came out from behind his desk and shook the old man's hand. 'Personally I found him a godawful bore . . . but then the whole damn administration's a bore and he fits right into it.'

Pops couldn't agree more. He had started working around Washington and Baltimore back when Woodrow Wilson was still president. Several times he had been called up to the White House by Mrs. Wilson and Colonel House after the president had gotten so deathly sick and they were practically running the country. He had performed many confidential jobs for them that were discreetly erased from his memory, and he had felt very uncomfortable ever since the wrong Hoover, Herbert instead of John Edgar, had taken things over. Nobody would be happier than Pops Johnson when the Democrats once again marched in triumph up Pennysylvania Avenue back to their old White House home.

From the serious look on Ham's face, Pops knew he hadn't been called up to discuss national politics, although that well might come up, as he was consulted on many things other than locations. Ham seemed terribly ill at ease, and Pops couldn't remember ever seeing him so nervous and jumpy. Charlie Curtis, dull as he might have been, couldn't have caused this mood!

'Frank . . . er . . . Pops . . . I have to talk to you about something that's so damn delicate and personal that it's vital anything we say here or may do later stays locked up inside your head. I don't have to tell you that, I know you too well, and I'd trust you with anything – anything. Excuse me for being so very upset about this . . . After I tell you what it's about I'm sure you'll understand.'

Motioning Pops to a comfortable chair, Ham sat down again behind the massive desk and began the story, including all the events leading up to Nita's pregnancy – or non-pregnancy. When he was finished, the expression on Pops' face remained unchanged. He wasn't the slightest bit shocked. This was an old story he had heard before from other men – and Ham was a man like any of them. The person he wanted to know much more about was the lady in the case, and Ham told him as much as he knew about Nita.

'What she's told me about her background seems to be legitimate. I had someone in El Paso check on her. What matters now is that she says she's knocked up and I'm the father. So far we're the only ones who know it. There's always the chance that if I don't give her what she wants she might possibly spill it all to our two dear friends Hedda and Louella, or to anybody who'll listen. I suppose I could handle it with a good lawyer, say Jerry Giesler . . . or just sweat it out . . . but for some very personal reasons having to do with my family, I don't want to see it come to that. Look, Pops, you know my older brother, Maurie . . . and, uh . . .' His voice drifted off.

'I know him well, Ham. I know him very well. I can just see him with that long finger of his pointed right at you, and I understand what you're up against there without knowing too much more. You haven't talked to me about other family relationships – your wife, your son. It's my business to listen and remember. Maybe you won't tell me a thing I don't already know, but don't worry, all this remains between the two of us. Does your wife know anything at all about what's happened?' asked the old man.

'Not a thing, so far as I know. She does know about some of the others before Nita . . . I admit I haven't been much of a husband. Yeah, it's possible she suspects I've paid the rent for one or two women . . . but the damndest thing is that just recently we've both started to work things out and are as close to having a good relationship as we've been since we were married sixteen years ago. Our kid doesn't know a damn thing about any of this, and I hope he never finds out. I admit I've been kind of a lousy father to him, but we've been getting closer too during the last few weeks and had some wonderful times together. I'd hate to have something like this come along now and spoil everything.'

'All right, Boss. Now I know the name of the lady. Tell me where she's living and anything else I should know.'

For more than a half-hour Ham told Pops all he could about the house in the hills and the girl who lived there . . . the yellow Ford . . . the friend named Lorene, the way he was told he was going to be a father in another six months.

'Has she made any payoff demands?' asked Pops, his policeman's senses alerted.

'No, not at all. I offered her money, anything she wanted, but her answer was . . . she said . . . uh . . .' Ham was flustered, turning beet-red as the embarrassment showed on his face. Finally he came out with the rest of it. 'What she said she wanted was . . . me . . . me! I was to tell my wife that I wanted a divorce, talk her into going to Reno for as fast a "treatment" as she could get . . . and then as soon as it was final and I was free, Nita wanted to become my wife!' Ham's voice got hoarse as he told Pops this last part, and he turned and twisted in his chair, cracking his knuckles and moving his feet beneath the desk in what was a seated dance of nerves.

'What do you know about her background before you met her? Was she a hooker, a streetwalker? Has she a record? What did she do in her hometown? El Paso, you said it was?'

Ham looked over Pops' head up into the blue sky outside his window. A lone airplane droned by, and Ham cursed it for the sound takes it must have ruined inside the stages.

'Uh . . . no . . . I'm pretty sure she was just a kid who lived there with her father . . . the mother was dead . . . and Nita told me she wasn't going anyplace there so she came to Hollywood. She didn't run away – her father helped her get here. She stayed at the Studio Club until I moved her into the house where she is now on Detour Drive. She never acted like a tramp – she was a very well-mannered young lady. I'm sure she wasn't a virgin, but that's nothing to hold against anybody, and she wasn't a whore. I wish I could come up with a simple solution and tell you she was a pro who was trying to frame me . . . but honest to God, Pops, I can't say that. Look – I'm a grown man, an adult, married, with a son . . . and because I haven't been completely happy at home – for reasons I won't go into – I get myself involved again . . . not for the first time, as I already told you, but this time, damn it, something new has been added – a baby! I just don't know what to do about it, and that's why I called you. What do you suggest, Pops?'

The old man sat there trying to look very wise, chewing on his lower lip and wishing this were a straightforward safe-cracking or armed robbery job, or even guarding the Boss and his family against some violent crackpot. This was the kind of problem he hated, a serious threat backed with dangerous reality.

'If only she was a hooker. How about scaring the shit out of her? I could have some boys drop in on her and –'

'No . . . no . . . absolutely nothing violent or harmful to her! Hell, Pops, I don't see a simple answer to this . . . that one definitely is out! If it was in some script we were shooting and ran into story-line problems, I'd haul in the writer and tell him to come up with a believable solution, even a few different versions of it, and get it to me the next morning. This isn't a script – it's for real and it's me who's playing one of the

333

starring roles! Damn it, I don't like it!'

Pops lowered his head and looked down at the thick carpet. His bushy eyebrows, like a shaggy white hedgerow across his forehead, suddenly rose, followed by his wise old eyes looking at Ham through wire-framed glasses.

'I have an idea . . . maybe worthless, but an idea we should talk out no matter how farfetched. You say your wife knows nothing at all about this?' Ham nodded, and Pops continued. 'You would have to figure that if you did sit down and spilled it all to her, everything, and if she did agree to give you a divorce, it would take one hell of a time to work out a property settlement and all the other damn things involved. You have to tell this de Valle girl . . . Nita . . . that there are all kinds of complicated legal arrangements to be negotiated for division of property, child care, tax audits and plenty more because of what you're worth. It's no big secret that you're well off, so she'll believe that part of your story . . . anyhow, it's the truth!' Pops cleared his throat, looked for a place to spit, then gulped and continued. 'So you've got to stall this Nita and let her think you're trying to work things out with your wife and how damn much time it's going to take.'

The buzzer sounded in Ham's intercom and he pushed up the lever, speaking into the hidden microphone.

'I don't care who the hell it is. I don't wany any messages or interruptions until I tell you I'm through!' He slammed down the lever and looked again at Pops, who patiently sat waiting.

'If she's really pregnant, and I'm always suspicious about these things,' continued Pops, 'she may resign herself to the fact that everything isn't going to work out fast and neat the way she wants it. Meanwhile, we do some work of our own. For a start, I want you to get me the name of the doctor she's been seeing. I have ways of getting into medical records without being found out and I can tell you pretty damn fast if she's pregnant or if she's shitting you.'

'I'll try to get it for you, Pops. She didn't use her own name and I don't think she'll tell me very much more than she already has,' said Ham in a depressed voice.

'Find out whatever you can about the doctor, and I'll check up on the girl friend, Lorene. There are ways I can learn things through other people and could even put a tail on Nita the next time she goes to see the doctor. Don't worry . . . whatever I do will never be traced back. Meantime you try to relax as much as you can and let me think about all of this.'

'Thanks, Pops. I'll talk to you this evening or in a day or so. I feel a little better already just being able to open up to some-body. Hell . . . it's terrible carrying around this kind of a load and keeping it all bottled up inside. That's almost as bad as the problem itself. One thing again, Pops . . . please, nothing violent or threatening with Nita. Do anything you think is necessary, but there is to be absolutely no strong-arm stuff! Spend whatever money you need and send me a confidential accounting. I don't have to tell you that this is something only you and I should know about.'

'Ham, there is somebody else who does know all about it,' said Pops, rising to his feet. Ham looked up at him in alarm. 'The young lady herself. If it all turns out the way she told you – and if you really are the father – it might not be too easy for us to keep her mouth shut if she ever wants to open it. Tell me once again, is there any chance at all for an abortion and a payoff? I know a place where no questions are asked and it's perfectly safe and sanitary. Terminating the young lady's pregnancy is something I could handle for you. All it would need is her okay . . . yours . . . and money!'

'Pops, that's the very first thing I asked her. There's no chance! She wants the baby. She told me it's too late for an abortion, even if she wanted it – and she refuses to be paid off. All she wants is what I already told you – me!'

Pops Johnson left the big office and walked past Bob Silver without saying a word. Once in the outside hall, he pulled out an old pipe, scarred and blackened from years of faithful service. He shoved it into a tobacco pouch, tamped it down, then struck a long wooden match and held the flame over the bowl. A few deep draws and the smoke billowed out, follow-ing him down the long corridor to the stairs and into his office at the other end of the building.

He headed for the leather easy chair by the window, dropped heavily into it with an old man's sigh and drew deeply on his pipe, exhaling until his head almost vanished in a white cloud. As the smoke drifted up to the ceiling, he took the pipe from his mouth and looked down into the bright red embers of the tobacco and then pounded his free hand on the side of his chair. The old man coughed from deep down in his chest and spat into the old-fashioned urn on the floor. In a quavering voice that betrayed every one of his years, he almost shouted up at the scowling photograph of his former boss, the director of the Federal Bureau of Investigation.

'Goddammit, John Edgar! With the whole FBI, I'll bet even you couldn't figure out the right answer to this one!'

CHAPTER THIRTY-TWO

There are few things more dangerous than driving a car when the mind of the man behind the wheel is on other things. Ham had several near accidents as he came over the Cahuenga Pass, and when he turned to cross the Pacific Electric tracks and got on Highland Boulevard, the oncoming Red Car on the Valley run was forced to squeal to a jolting halt to avoid a collision. He looked up at the looming red hulk of the big trolley, which could have pulverized him if the motorman had been less alert. Ham put his car in reverse and backed up to let the P.E. car haughtily rumble past. The drivers behind him angrily honked their horns and he continued on his way, finally pulling up in front of the little house on Detour Drive.

Although he had his own key to the house, Ham pressed the doorbell button and waited. There was a strange car parked in front, and Ham was concerned that Lorene or another of Nita's friends might be inside visiting her. He decided to risk being seen and stood a moment until she came to the door, reached out and kissed him.

'Whose car is that?' was the very first thing he said after he pulled himself loose.

'Darling, it's somebody you know very well, so don't worry. Come inside . . . I'm so happy to see you! Larry Gross dropped by to see how I was. He's in the living room,' she said, and Ham's heart leaped up in his throat as he remembered the message he had given Bob Silver to have Larry off the lot with his closeout check within an hour's time. He could taste the beginning of panic but managed to swallow it and went with her into the house. Larry was seated in one of the comfortable big chairs by the picture window with its sweeping view of the city, and he at once put down his coffee cup, rose to his feet and smiled at Ham as he entered the room with Nita.

'Hello, Mr. Robbins. It's so good to see you. How are you feeling?' came the soft, smooth voice.

'Uh . . . Larry . . . nice seeing you too.' Ham swore silently and wondered how long Gross had been here and what he had told Nita about being thrown off the lot. It was a time for game playing until he learned more about what was in Larry's mind and what might already have spilled out of it. He cleared his throat with a little cough, then went on. 'I've been thinking of you lately, Larry. I wondered if you might like to get into a broader field in public relations. The department on the lot has so damn many limitations for anyone with talent and ambition. What would you think of taking over one of our distribution zones and handling all their advertising and tie-ins with the theaters? It's along the line of what you've been doing at the studio, but there's much more chance to advance and use your imagination and –'

Larry broke in on Ham, his smile growing even wider. Ham wondered if he had arrived too late or just in time.

'Mr. Robbins, I'd love that! I really enjoy working for you at the studio . . . but you're right, it has its limits and not too much chance to move up in responsibility – or income. It isn't quite everything I had hoped for, and I'll certainly take you up on your offer. I really could use more income, and working in different parts of the country appeals to me.' Ham looked over at Nita. She had not stopped smiling, and now he knew for certain that Gross had told her nothing as yet about being tossed off the lot. He even used the present tense in talking about how he enjoyed working for him. Ham felt a surge of anger and fought to control it. He had been a damn fool to toss money and a good job to this blackmailing bastard. Wait – Gross hadn't asked him for anything . . . that was his own very clever idea! Maybe he was only visiting Nita the way she said and now Ham had gone and given him an entirely unnecessary gift – stupid son of a bitch that he was! Well – it was done.

'Larry, check with Bob Silver late tomorrow afternoon. He'll give you a letter of instructions and a check to cover your expenses in relocating. I know you'll do very well.' Then, reaching out with his hand, he added, 'Congratulations and good luck in your new job.'

His smile stayed firmly in place, and Larry congratulated himself on a bloodless victory. He had arrived only a few minutes before Ham and never dreamed things would turn out so well. Perhaps if he played his cards right, knowing everything he knew, he might come back someday for another visit with Mr. Hamilton J. Robbins. Perhaps he might

337

ask for another promotion or a raise in salary . . . or just a nice bonus. A final handshake between friends, a wave, and he was gone.

Ham stood back and looked at Nita. She was radiant. He looked down at her waist – hardly a change, perhaps a tiny bulge, but that could have come from a big lunch as much as from a small pregnancy. She threw her arms around him once again, smothered his lips with her kisses. He fought a moment for breath.

'Nita . . . take it easy! You'll knock me off my feet!'

'I hope so, my darling . . . I hope so! I love you and I'm glad you're here and we're alone.' She rubbed her body up against him, arms still around his neck, pulling him closer, moving slowly, with the silky noises of her dress sounding like the soft waves of the Pacific against the swelling front of his pants. He had not come here for this . . . but he felt all powers of resistance drain away, and soon he was moving his body with her as they stood in the middle of the room, arms locked around each other, lips pressed together, tongues touching. He pulled away and began to kiss her face as his hand moved down to softly caress her breasts. She pulled him toward the open door of the bedroom, but he stopped as they came into the darkened chamber.

'Nita, are you sure this is all right? Being pregnant . . . I don't want you to hurt yourself . . . or . . .'

'Don't worry, Ham darling. The doctor said I'm a very healthy girl and I can go right on doing healthy things – like this – for a while yet. Now stop talking and get out of your clothes!'

The doctor! That was why Ham had come here – to find out all he could about the doctor. Now look at what was happening to his good intentions! He felt all the stiffness suddenly go limp as he realized how easily he had been diverted from his purpose.

Nita looked down at where his penis was slowly deflating, making the front of his pants look like a flannel tent being struck.

'Darling, what's the matter? This never happened with us before. Come on . . . let's get into bed, and I'll make it grow big again and we'll make wonderful love!'

When it was over and he lay next to Nita, Ham stared up at the ceiling, passion spent and anger reborn. He had let himself get inveigled into this . . . Well, no regrets really, it had been wonderful – he needed to get rid of his tensions, and

338

there was joy in those moments when they both were the planets, the sun, the stars, and all else seemed to vanish.

Nita stirred, turned to face him, pressing her warm naked body against him, and she smiled into his face, only inches away.

'Are you absolutely sure, Nita, it's all right to do this? I know there can be problems . . . you being pregnant –'

'Ham, please don't think about that now. I told you, the doctor said I could do this for many more months. Isn't that wonderful for us both, darling!'

'Are you positive he's the best doctor you could get? After all, you really didn't know anything about him . . . there's so damn many things that . . .' He stopped as she shook her head. 'You must have the best doctor you can get for something like this! Let me have him checked out so you can be sure you're getting the best possible care. This is a terribly serious thing for you, and we'd both feel better if –'

'No, Ham, I'm perfectly satisfied with this doctor. I told you he doesn't know my real name – and of course he knows nothing at all about you. Let it stay that way. After all, I'm the one who's having the baby . . . and that's the way I want things to be.'

Ham wished he were alone right now so he could sigh, even shudder a bit, when he again realized that this indeed was the way things were going to be – unless Pops could put a tail on Nita on her next trip to this mysterious doctor and get into the records.

'All right, dear. If that's what you want . . . but I do wish you –'

'Ssh, Ham . . . Now hug me – hold me tight. You don't have to go for a while, do you? I've missed this for so long. I want you . . . I want you!'

She wanted – but Ham could not work himself back from the depression he felt building up in the pit of his stomach, flowing out to every other part of his body – especially to that formerly upstanding, lifelong friend who was so important at a time like this – and now was lying down on the job. After a bout of nonproductive caresses, finally she kissed him and smiled understandingly and they got up from the bed and dressed. Nita went with him to the door and before pulling it open gave him a good-bye hug and kiss. He left the house and got into his car, made a turn in the driveway and headed down the hill.

*   *   *

Ham pulled his car up to the main gate of the studio. It was closed during the night, but the security guard came out, recognized him and swung back the barrier. He rolled down his car window and spoke to the studio policeman.

'I'm going to be working awhile in the bungalow and may get some sleep there later. When the switchboard opens in the morning, give the operator a message for my secretary, Bob Silver. Tell him where I am and that I'm not to be disturbed until noon . . . and then he should give me a call there. Thanks.' He pulled his head back, acknowledged the wave from the guard and swung his car sharply around the nearest sound stage, went down the wide studio street, now empty of all life, and drove into the small private parking lot beside the executive bungalow. He left his car, slamming the door behind him, fumbled for the keys and let himself into the bungalow. There was a couch along one wall, wide enough for comfortable sitting, sleeping, or, when the opportunity was presented, for sex. He had spent time on the wide leather expanse doing all three, but now he was emotionally wrung out and all he wanted was to throw himself down, close his eyes and have this night come to an end.

He pulled off his shoes, removed his necktie and loosened his belt, then pulled up one of the sofa pillows and stretched out, looking over at the thin slits of light leaking through the venetian blinds across the room. He tried to relax, but there were too many things on his mind. He counted the lines of yellow light at the opposite window, found there were forty-six, recounted them and came to the same total. Then he turned his head toward the long oak table running across the opposite wall. The dim light coming into the room was reflected off the little golden men . . . the row of Oscars standing there like his troops awaiting orders or standing in review. He looked at them a few minutes, swung his feet around to the floor and sat up straight on the big sofa. His watch told him dawn was hours away, and his continuing anger made sleep a hard visitor to welcome. He remembered years ago counting sheep at times like this. Now he had no sheep to count – only Oscars – so he tried to recall the picture or achievement for which each of the statuettes had been given him or the studio. Memories of those magic nerve-wracking words: 'And the winner is . . .' Then the long happy walk down the aisle or between the dinner tables at the Coconut Grove not long ago when Will Rogers ran things and made even the losers laugh.

'One ... Best Art Direction, 1930 ... *The Girl from Brooklyn* ... what a stinker that was – but it made money ... Two ... something called *The Curse of the Catskills* ... did we really make that? Won an Oscar, lost a million. I remember firing everybody connected with it – then after it got the award I had to hire them back for double what I paid them before ... The picture business ... No wonder I can't sleep! There's number three ... Best Musical Score for a piece of crap ... *The Coed* ... when was that? Hell ... who cares! Mr. Four ... Cinematography – for another forgettable film. I remember when they were just called cameramen and there was none of that fancy crap language we're loaded down with now. Cinematography! Everybody has to have a fancy title now. This is foolish ... I'll never get to sleep counting Oscars!'

He switched on a floor lamp and the sudden glare reflected off walls that seemed to be hung almost solid with silver, bronze, gold and chrome. Plaques of honor and recognition from national, local and foreign governments, publications, centers of learning and citadels of ignorance. Ham lay on the couch, then propped himself up on an elbow and looked at the glorious jumble of the Trophy Room. There was the star-spangled red-white-and-blue American Legion Patriotic Recognition Award for some money-losing biographical film about George Washington that taught him never to make pictures about men wearing knee-pants. Next to it was the Eagle of San Juan (Fourth Class) of the Republic of San Marino, given for God knows what reason. The Isle of Man Exhibitors' Association Award – hell, he bet they only had one theater on the whole damn island! The Parent-Teacher's Gold Medal for some crummy kids' picture he had hated ... the Order of the Setting Sun, First Class, jammed up next to the Golden Bagel of the American Delicatessen Association. On and on went the engraved metal and polished carved wood, so tightly packed together on the wall that the original paneling could scarcely be seen.

Another entire wall was filled from carpet to ceiling with still photographs mounted under large glass panels. There seemed to be a picture of every celebrity who had ever visited Robbins International Studios, and every shot showed the smiling face and well-turned-out body of the man on the couch, whose multiple images looked down on the reclining figure.

Slowly he arose, swinging both feet down to the floor. Now

he crossed the room to a stack of large scrapbooks, each big enough to mount an uncut newspaper page. There were numbers embossed on the front of each book, and the one for 1932 was on top of the heap. Ham lifted off several of the books and grunted from their weight as he dropped them on the floor. Now the book for 1925 lay on top, and he opened it in the middle. There was a half-page newspaper cut of his own face staring into the harsh flashbulb light at some world premiere of an almost forgotten picture. Irene stood beside him, looking strange in a tight-fitting cloche hat, and a little boy won on the other side, holding tightly to his father's hand. He wondered why he had let go of that trusting hand so many times – pushing it away when his son reached out to him for love and companionship. Irene looked lovely, even in that ridiculous hat.

The scrapbooks and all the wall-hung awards were testimonials to success in the dog-eat-dog business of motion picture production, but hidden deep in his mind there was another room, littered with other trophies . . . the monuments to failure – as a son, a brother, husband, father and friend. He slammed the book shut and let it slide to the floor. This was no relaxed reading to make him feel like getting to sleep! Now he looked again around the room with its award-encrusted walls, the certificates, plaques, banners and proclamations – all those objects of pride and vanity he took such delight in showing to visitors. All he saw now were polished useless pieces of engraved metal, dusty banners, heaped scrapbooks of interest perhaps only to him and some future film historians who would use them to mock his achievements and resurrect his failures . . . the no-good fucking bastards!

There was a desk over in the corner, a beautiful thing made of ebony, where he had posed for the camera signing countless contracts and shaking innumerable hands. He saw a framed calendar standing on the desk and picked it up to see how much time was left until his parents' golden wedding anniversary. Not long now – and it hadn't taken long either for that damn sperm to find itself an egg . . . and for the cells to start dividing, then redivide over and over, each a special piece of life. Here would be an eye, there an ear . . . a mouth . . . arms, little grasping fingers . . . legs and tiny toes . . . growing every month . . . growing . . . growing . . . until nine months had passed and it was time to count the contractions . . . nine . . . ten . . . eleven . . . thirty-eight . . . forty . . . Here it comes! Tie the cord . . . slap its behind . . . sleep . . . sleep . . . sleep.

Ham fell back on the soft couch, slowly letting his body come to rest on the yielding surface, at last soundly asleep. Outside the first rays of the sun touched stage roofs and the top of the writers' building with its pale glow as daylight began to drive away the night. The early construction and rigging shifts checked in through the time gate and Robbins International Studios drew its first deep breath of the new day. Inside the Trophy Room, hidden away in the executive bungalow, the vice-president for production slept on, not to join the others at their labor until it was high noon.

At precisely twelve o'clock the phone rang and it was Bob Silver following the instructions he had received earlier that morning from the phone operator. Ham told him to wait, pulled himself up from the couch and went to the bathroom, where he relieved himself and splashed cold water on his face. Then he returned to the waiting phone.

'Bob, good morning. Get hold of Pops Johnson. Tell him I want to see him here in the Trophy Room in about ten minutes. You got that? I'm going to take a quick shower, so he can let himself into the room and wait for me. Remind me when I get to the office to call Mike Hammersmith in New York or wherever he is. I'll want to find out what film exchange district needs a new public relations and advertising man. I'm sending Larry Gross out into the field and I'll dictate a letter to you later about it. Gross will be coming by to pick it up, so don't let me forget – it's important. Also, have Accounting draw him a check for . . . uh . . . five thousand. Charge it to Publicity for Larry Gross's relocation expenses. It should be ready later today with the letter.'

Bob took it all down in his notebook, wondering what had happened since he had passed the word yesterday to get Gross off the lot within one hour. It was none of his business, although he could make a very good guess.

'I have it all, Mr. Robbins. I'll tell Pops to start right over, and later I'll remind you of the other things.'

'Bob, any messages for me – anything urgent?' asked Ham, starting to get out of his clothes.

'No, sir, only routine stuff. A call from title art for your okay on the main title and credits on –'

'Forget that. No calls from any of the family?' interrupted Ham, waiting while Bob searched his notes.

'Not a thing, Mr. Robbins. Shall I call you there if any come in before you get up here to the office?'

343

'No, don't call me at all while I'm here with Pops,' Ham answered. 'Later when we're done here I'll be up, and in the meantime have the commissary send over some coffee, some toast and a glass of orange juice. That's all I feel like having right now. I'm not very hungry.' He hung up and sat staring across the room at all the golden symbols of triumph.

Ham was drying himself outside the shower in the adjoining bathroom when he heard Pops Johnson unlocking the door. He wrapped a towel around his waist and went out into the other room. The old man greeted him, shocked at how tense and haggard Ham looked and the dispirited way he greeted him.

'Pops, she won't tell me a damn thing. All I got was what she said before – she's pregnant and that's that.' He went back into the bathroom, finished drying himself and began to dress, still talking through the door to the old man, who seated himself in one of the side chairs. 'I tried to get the name of her doctor, but I guess you'll have to find that out your own way and get into the records. I've done all I could, but I think from the way she acted and from what she said that a baby's on the way and no abortion or payoff is possible. Pops, I'm in real trouble.'

He came into the Trophy Room, fully dressed, and slumped down on the big couch that had been his bed. Pops looked at him and spoke in a quiet, confident voice.

'I already figured that might be the way it would go so I have somebody placed to follow her whenever she leaves the house and get names and addresses every place she goes. I figure putting a tap on her phone might be a good idea and –'

'No – no!' cut in Ham, upset showing on his face. 'Absolutely not! No taps – that's out!'

'Boss, this is only a suggestion. Something has to be done – and soon. You should sit down with your attorney and level with him. Get him started putting together a list of everything you would have to settle with your wife, with an estimated time schedule, if it goes to a separation and divorce. Property settlements, child support, insurance policy adjustments . . . the works. Your only hope is to have him complicate it so much that when Miss de Valle thinks of her own timetable she possibly might see the light and consider a payoff – though from what you've told me, I really don't know. If that doesn't work, we'll have to think of something else.'

Ham sighed and wondered who in the law firm handling

his personal and company matters was good at this kind of thing. He decided to call the senior partner, Nate Klein, a trustworthy man he respected. Nate could give him good advice and start things moving. If there was one thing a lawyer could do it was complicate things – and Nate was an excellent lawyer.

'Pops, I really don't have too many options. I'll have something put together to show Nita and hope to God it works, but I don't feel too confident. Let me know what your man learns about the doctor – and remember, no phone taps!'

The old man heaved himself out of the chair, nodded a good-bye and went out into the street, vainly trying to start a fire in his pipe bowl. Back in the bungalow, Ham phoned his secretary.

'Bob, get me Nate Klein at his law office downtown. If he's out, have him call me as soon as possible – got it? Okay. I'm not coming up just yet. I feel like taking a walk around the lot . . . need some exercise. All right, Bob, good-bye.'

He hung up, reached into the desk drawer and brought out a pair of dark glasses, then went to the bungalow door and down the three steps into the busy studio street, wishing it were not necessary to look pleasant and say hello to all the people he had to pass. Right now Ham Robbins hated everybody, but he wore a mask of good cheer with his dark glasses and waved, shook hands, asked and answered unimportant questions, finally breaking away from a group of production people and going on alone. He walked rapidly down the street and saw the vast cavern of Stage Three, its great doors wide open and the interior empty and inviting. He went up the ramp into the stage and wandered aimlessly around the deserted sets. Hands in his pockets, he tried to think of nothing that might upset him as he walked through the empty make-believe rooms, stripped memories of pictures made and gone . . .

At the far end of the stage Ham saw a large interior set that was designed to match parts of the permanent small-town street out on the back lot. Ham entered the open side of the old Western saloon set, walked past the ornately carved mahogany bar and went over to the glassless window, which looked out on a gigantic painted canvas cyclorama stretched in a taut half-circle completely filling the entire rear wall of the stage, from the timber floor up to the catwalks, chain-hung from roof beams, which would hold the big lamps when the set was rigged. It had been painted by fine artists whose mastery of perspective and color made it look so real that later, on the screen, the audience would believe without doubt there was a real street just outside. The work lights threw harsh shadows and bright glare on the canvas, and Ham looked through the window frame at an almost exact painted duplicate of the very same street where he and Lou had walked before the terrible fire that took his beloved brother from him. It was a street that now existed only on this giant cyclorama and on the construction plans being used to rebuild it from the ashes and rubble.

Ham stood and stared out at what once had been and was now no more. All the stores, the old hotel front . . . the general store and the little park where he and Lou had so happily posed for the photographer. In the middle of the row of buildings across the painted street he saw something that instantly brought tears to his eyes, blurring his vision. There was the little glassed-in box office, the two doors leading into the lobby . . . and hanging high up on the building front were the two golden lettered words on the blue background, exactly as he had drawn them for the art director.

He reached into his pocket for a handkerchief, dabbed at his eyes and looked for a long last time over at the sign, the past brought for a fleeting moment into the present . . . the sign that read, BIJOU DREAM. It was terribly hard to take his eyes from the scene as he wiped the moisture from his eyes. What had happened to all those dreams? . . . to all the golden hopes? Had he turned them all into painted deceptions to fool everybody – himself most of all? Where was his Bijou Dream . . . the Dream of Gems . . . an illusion . . . a crumbled vision. For a fleeting moment he hated himself for the years of cycloramas he had painted to serve his deceptions, for all the beards he hid behind for protection. He blew his nose in the handkerchief and once more looked intently for a last time at the little nickelodeon across the street.

'Hell, it's only paint and canvas . . . that's all it is. We paid plenty to make it look that good, like the real thing!' A moment more of looking out at the great curving canvas. 'People believe it. It looks real, and nothing else matters!'

Ham turned to leave the Western set, saw the far-off square of light coming through the open stage door and walked toward it. When he came out into the bright sunshine, he stopped and closed his eyes until he found his dark glasses and again hid behind them. One more look back into the empty stage and a little smile came to his face. A memory almost lost for years had just found him . . . the little old man in the shiny long coat and shapeless black hat . . . the straggly beard and those owl eyes squinting through thick glasses. Over all the studio noises Ham could almost hear the cracked old voice again . . . 'Be a Jew . . . Dream!' Then he turned and walked on to his office.

CHAPTER THIRTY-THREE

Several weeks passed, during which time Ham met for many hours with Nate Klein, who took a cool professional look at the situation. He decided to handle it himself rather than entrust so delicate a matter to any of his partners. Pops Johnson was right about the complications of a divorce should it become necessary. Nate sketched out a course of action that could take well over a year to become final, even if Irene fully cooperated, and that was far from certain. The documents worked up by the attorney filled his briefcase to overflowing, and Ham was horrified at the tremendous detail, the multitude of jointly owned assets to divide or dispose of – the setting up of trusts for Irene and their son. He told Nate Klein to put everything in a safe place until he had thought things out.

Getting into Nita's medical records was not such a simple matter. It took much longer than Pops Johnson had thought and required the arduous and discreet cultivation of a member of the doctor's office staff, who, for a few hundred dollars, was willing to furnish a complete copy of the medical file of a young woman known only to her doctor as Marie La Salle, a definitely pregnant unemployed screen extra. With no complications, she could expect a normal delivery sometime in March 1933. Name of father: Dean La Salle, sales manager for a hardware company.

The names and dates were burned into Ham's mind, and after several more consultations with Nate Klein, he decided to try Pops' strategy on Nita and confront her with the fact that a divorce would not be possible, if at all, until long after the birth of the child. It could not become final for perhaps another year, maybe even longer than that. There was every chance that there would be complications, and Irene could delay things for still another year, perhaps. Nita had to face the realities.

When he told her and showed a few of the documents, she

was quite upset, cried a little, then suddenly dried her tears and smiled up at him.

'I'll wait for you, Ham. I'm terribly sorry for the baby's sake and ours that we can't be married before it's born, but I can see now that won't be possible. I love you so much, and I know you'll do everything you can to speed things up.'

Ham tried to smile in return, but the shock of her words hit him like a slap in the face. Nita must really love him after all, but what could he do? Even if he loved her, and sometimes, when they were together like this, he thought perhaps he must, how could he go through with a divorce? Even if she were his one true love, could he risk losing everything for her?

When Ham left the little house on Detour Drive, he was more depressed than ever.

Maurie kept phoning and writing from New York about the coming golden wedding anniversary of their parents. Ruth and Miriam contributed plans and enthusiasm in their innumerable letters, and Ham dreaded the day when they would have something far less pleasant to communicate to him. He knew what their reactions would be. Chaim the *pisher* . . . getting his own way again . . . still chasing after something new . . . something different . . . bringing shame to the family. He never listened to anybody . . . did what he wanted to do . . . a brat . . . a miserable little . . .

'Damn it to hell!' Ham shouted to the empty room where he sat looking out the window at the studio activity. 'Here I am again letting my damn family write the whole script! This is no movie, it's my life, and when I find somebody whose company I enjoy, in and out of bed . . . who I realize that I do love . . . then why the hell do I still sit and listen like a little boy to the voices of my father and my brother and my sisters! Now I'm finding out what love can really be, and I let my dear family climb inside my head and spoil it all. I won't let them do it. Next thing they'll be climbing into bed with me and directing the scene the way they want it played! All right – so there's going to be a divorce, but I'll survive it, and so will they. I have to think about my own happiness and stop worrying about what the family wants. I'm already standing in too many shadows, and now I'm going out in the sunshine to live!'

He thought about telling Irene, then waiting for Maurie and all the others to hear about it. The great anger he felt made him bring both fists down on his desk so hard that the lamp jumped and shook and a stack of scripts fell over and dropped to the floor. Telling Irene was going to be the hard part, but it had to be done – and soon. God – if only he could leave town and turn it all over to the studio personnel department!

He signaled Bob on the intercom and told him to let Irene know he would be working late again and not to wait dinner. It was the same message he had sent her the night before and would be sending again the next day.

Life on Sierra View Drive still went on in spite of Ham's increased absences. All of Irene's hopes that she and her husband were about to make a new beginning, that their glorious day of lovemaking meant the start of a new life together, slowly faded away. The last midnight call from the studio had sounded as though it came from another person – a cold, secretive stranger. For a moment she thought it was Bob Silver or the projectionist in the booth, but it had been Ham and he sounded a million cold miles away. They shared the bedroom, and he did show up for dinner now and then, but he was still distant, his attitude strange and frightening because she could not understand it. Several times he started to speak to her about something, then broke off and went to other subjects, never finishing what she thought he really wanted to say. She tried and tried to get him to open up and talk to her about whatever it was that troubled him, but all she could see was the chasm between the two of them growing wider and wider. They were almost like strangers who happened to be married to each other through some accident. The only thing that changed was the passage of time as more and more weeks fell off the calendar. All of a sudden it was time for the golden wedding celebration of Solomon and Esther Robbins, whose loving family all came together to be with them once again in Harrisburg, Pennsylvania.

It was time for them to take the elevator down to the main ballroom and join the family and all their friends in honoring Momma and Poppa on their fiftieth wedding anniversary. It should have been a happy, wonderful time, but Irene could feel waves of tension and misery radiating from her husband, and she was deeply affected, fighting to hold back the unbidden tears that kept coming to her eyes. They had finished dressing and stood by the door, ready to leave the suite. Ham turned to her.

350

'Irene . . . I have to talk to you about something. I know this isn't a good time for it, but I cannot go on unless . . .' and he broke off, looking out into the empty hall, then slowly closed and locked the door behind them. They walked toward the elevator, and he tried to continue.

'Uh . . . it's nothing at all you've done . . . I . . . uh . . . Irene . . . I'm terribly unhappy. Here we are on our way to my parents' fiftieth anniversary, and you and I have only been married a little over sixteen years, and all this has been on my mind and being here for this party is forcing it out of me . . . and now I have to tell you . . . tell you . . .'

The elevator doors slid open and they stepped in. Ham looked at Irene in the dim light and tried to continue.

'I'm trying to tell you I don't want to go on . . . I want you to give me a . . .'

The elevator stopped, the doors silently sliding wide for Ruth and her husband, Abe Harris, who stepped in to join them. His sister was laughing and threw her arms around Ham, giving him a big kiss just as Abe leaned over to deliver a dignified peck on the cheek to Irene. They both were very happy, and Ruth babbled on about all the plans she and Miriam had made for the celebration. She stopped in the middle of a word, wondering at the strange way Irene looked at Ham all the way down to the ballroom floor, where the elevator stopped to let them out. It had been a brief trip, and Ruth realized she had been the only one speaking the entire time. What was going on with these two? Suddenly she knew – Irene had found out about Ham and that tramp he was keeping. Ham's secret was no secret to Maurie, who had discussed it in perplexed anger with both his sisters. Ruth clutched at her husband's arm, and he was shocked at the way her face suddenly changed from joy to sorrow. Irene walked beside Ham, looking intently at him all the way across the small lobby and into the ballroom where the family and friends waited, greeting one another, drinking at the bar, chattering, eager for the joyous evening to begin. Irene clutched at Ham's arm as they entered the main ballroom.

'Finish what you were saying in the elevator. You want me to give you . . . what?'

They came closer to the large family group, clustered around Momma and Poppa at the far end of the big room, exchanging kisses and congratulations. Friends were mixed in with all the relatives, and to Ham for a moment it looked very much like a crowd scene of dress extras in a very expensive picture. Irene clung to his arm, asking again and again, 'Give you what? Tell me! Tell me now!'

He whispered, hoping nobody but Irene would hear.

'Irene, for God's sake, wait until later. It'll keep. I can't talk about it now . . . not now!'

She looked at his face and instinctively knew what it was that he wanted. She pulled her arm away and they stood alone in the middle of the deserted dance floor.

'You want to leave me. Is that what you want to tell me?'

'Irene, later, please!' He threw his arms around Poppa, who had come forward to greet them.

'My boy . . . Ham . . . Irene . . . I'm so happy to see the two of you. Come now with me to Momma. It's so good to have all our children here. Your Jimmy is already over there with the rest of the children . . . he's been waiting for you too. I hope you all will have a wonderful time at our party!'

Irene looked over at their son. He was staying with several cousins in another room of the hotel and seemed to be having a good time with all the relatives he had just met for the first time. He raced over to throw his arms around his mother and give her a kiss, then reached to take his father's hand. How strangely silent and withdrawn they both were. He pulled back, suddenly afraid he had done something to make them angry at him. He stood there alone for a moment, looking at the sudden strangers who were his parents, and he wished he could leave the room and go someplace else. Jimmy stepped back, mumbled something, then slowly went back to his cousins across the room, looking back all the way at the two people facing each other all alone on the dance floor.

The orchestra finished tuning up and began to play some bright dance music, but Ham and Irene left the floor and went with the family and friends to the several long tables that ran down the middle of the room. Ruth and Miriam had spent months planning this evening, and there were place cards so that nobody would be lost or left out. Solomon and Esther sat side by side at the head of the wide table between the two others, rapidly filling up with family and friends. Their sons and daughters and the in-laws were all seated down either side of the center table, then came all the good friends from Harrisburg, from New York, California and so many cities from all over the country and from Canada. The grandchildren were down at the lower end of one of the tables.

There was animated conversation among everybody at the tables, Maurie calling over to others at the next table, replies flying back and the sisters talking with all their friends and to each other. Ruth, with a side look at her brother, leaned close to Miriam and whispered something, and then Miriam moved close to her husband, Larry Levine, telling him what her sister had just said. The smiles left their faces, then slowly returned when they quickly realized this night was so special that nothing, absolutely nothing, should be permitted to spoil it. Poppa was slapping Maurie on the back, and the rabbi got to his feet and signaled all to rise for the blessing.

A few moments with the ancient words and the mumbled amens and then the noises of all being seated once again. Maurie seized the opportunity to start off the evening with a toast to the couple they had all come here to honor. He rose to his feet and held a wineglass high in the air.

'Fifty beautiful years together. Fifty years as man and wife . . . as Momma and Poppa . . . Well, not quite all fifty years of that! After all, they were married nearly a whole year before I came along to bless the union.' There was laughter from everyone except Ham, who shot an angry look at his talkative brother, wondering if he knew something that must remain unknown. Maurie continued after a brief pause. 'Together all this time and still very much in love with each other! Please stand with me now and drink from your wine to Momma and Poppa . . . to Solomon and Esther . . . to our beloved parents on this their golden wedding anniversary!'

Maurie enjoyed making speeches. He was at his best when facing stock-holders at the annual meeting, his board of directors, the many charity groups he served – and tonight would be the very best of all. He looked out at the happy faces – looked at the tears streaming down the face of his sister-in-law, Irene . . . and the downcast dismal face of his brother, Chaim . . . Ham – and all the love in his voice seemed to turn to bitter gall and he quickly proposed the toast, joined the company in drinking the glass of wine and sat down, his happiness having turned into dull anger at what he knew must have happened.

The food was served, and all seated at the three long tables ate, drank and thoroughly enjoyed themselves – all except the two unhappy people, Irene and Ham. Maurie had gradually forced himself back into the spirit of the evening, while Ruth and Miriam thought only of making this the happiest night of their parents' lives. At last the five-tiered wedding cake was wheeled into the ballroom and the honored couple rose to their feet and stepped forward to observe the old American custom of cutting the first piece. Poppa turned to his sons and daughters, felt his wine and bellowed almost loud enough to be heard out in the lobby, 'My children . . . beloved family and friends . . . now you will see how good an old butcher can still be with a knife!'

He took the long swordlike blade and deftly split the entire cake in half without letting so much as a crumb or fragment of frosting fall to the floor. There were cheers from all the tables. The captain stepped forward with his men to cut smaller pieces and get them to all the places with the steaming cups of coffee and tea and the after-dinner liqueur.

'*Mazel tov!*' shouted Poppa's old friends from the synagogue, and more wine was poured into every glass. Music played, and Poppa took Momma out to the floor for an old-fashioned dance, vaguely remembered from another happy day fifty years before in a little Russian village that was no more. Slowly, very slowly, they circled the floor, relatives and friends smiling and softly keeping time with their hands, the old couple gently turning as they made the circle and then returned to their chairs. Momma was breathing very heavily and her face had changed from an almost normal pink to a ghastly white. She sat down, took a sip of water and waved her daughters away when they came rushing to her side. Dr. Schwartz, their old friend, had a terribly worried expression and came to stand next to Momma, taking her hand in his. She shook him away and spoke up in a voice they all could hear.

'Don't worry . . . I'm fine . . . Please, please . . . all of you enjoy yourselves!'

She was far from all right. She was sick, and only Poppa and Dr. Schwartz knew about it. Tonight it was to remain their secret – it was a night for their children, for their friends and all the family. Momma was sure it was the last time they would all be together, but that was something she said only to herself, not even to Poppa, and she laughed a little and waved everybody away.

Ham and Irene sat together while the others were dancing. He played with the piece of cake on his plate, uneaten and standing like a rebuke to him for everything he had done . . . and had not done. Irene looked over at the opposite wall of the room, silent, lips pressed tightly together, eyes glistening. He tried again to speak to her.

'Irene . . . I . . . please don't . . . Look, I have to go on to New York tomorrow night with Maurie for some very important meetings. You and Jimmy return home and I'll be back in about a week. Then you and I will sit down quietly and talk about what I started telling you in the elevator. This isn't the time and I just don't feel like saying anything more. It can wait . . . maybe we can work it out . . .' He rambled on a few minutes, saying things he knew he did not and could not mean, halfheartedly trying to reassure her so they at least could get through this evening, the happy celebration he almost had turned into a dreadful dead thing with his few words in the elevator. Irene got to her feet.

'Please tell your parents that I have a terrible headache and have gone to our room. Tomorrow Jimmy and I are taking the train back to Los Angeles and you can do whatever you want. I can't sit here with you another minute. I'm going to bed. Don't disturb me when you come up – if you do!' She turned from him and walked out of the ballroom toward the elevator.

Several weeks were to pass before Ham returned to California from New York. Most of his time was spent with Maurie and Mike Hammersmith in Distribution. Finally, the day before he was to return to the Coast, he was alone with his brother in the office. Maurie had said nothing about what he saw and heard at the golden wedding, but Ham knew he would have to talk with him now about what was happening. The time finally had come to get it out, and if Maurie didn't like it . . . well, that couldn't be helped.

'I'm sure you could tell that Irene and I are having a very difficult time . . . worse now than it's ever been. Maurie, I'm asking her for a divorce. It's something I have to do for my own –'

His brother exploded with outrage. He leaned forward, and his long thin finger waved in Ham's face, just as he expected it would.

'What legitimate reason do you have for dumping Irene – a woman who has loved you and been a good faithful wife and the mother of your son! God knows how she's been able to take all the crap she has from you! Yes . . . I could see it in her face at the party. I'm ashamed of you, brother or no brother, for the way you've acted. Tell me, you miserable no-good, what reasons can you possibly have for acting like the lowest kind of a –'

'Please, Maurie, please! I don't want to go into reasons with you. I'm terribly unhappy with Irene and this has been coming on for a long time. All right . . . I'll tell you. I've met somebody who loves me very much and who I love enough to be willing to go through all this with you and the rest of the family. I know it's terrible, the way you look at it, but it's my life and I have to live it my way. You can't influence me. This has been a decision I've had to make on my own. I don't want to hurt Irene or anyone else . . . but if I don't make a move I'll only hurt myself. I don't expect you to understand – you're happily married to your Rose and you're a very good father to your daughter. They're both lucky to have you for a husband and a father. I wish to God that I might have been a better husband to Irene and a more caring father to my son, but, Maurie, that's the way it is. Just because you and I are brothers doesn't mean we're exactly alike in every way. We aren't, and you'd be the first to admit that. All right, so there's never been a divorce in our family, but sometimes that's the only way out . . . the only solution to problems which have made two people completely miserable together when they might be happier apart. This is one of those times and situations, Maurie, and you must try to understand. Please try!'

Maurie looked at his brother with undisguised contempt and disgust.

'I understand . . . I understand all right! You've been whoring around for years. I know all about those houses and apartments you've leased or bought for the tramps you've kept – and now you want to throw out a good and faithful woman who's had to take all this shit from you – and you're asking me to understand! What the hell kind of a shmuck do you take me for?' He paused a moment, trying to get back some control over his emotions. Shrugging and slumping down in his chair, suddenly he looked years older. 'Do whatever you want. Advice from me is wasted on you. Try at least to act like a mensh . . . like a human being, if that is possible.' Maurie turned away and picked up a copy of Variety and ripped through the pages as the phone on his desk started ringing.

It was a call from their sister Ruth in Harrisburg, and her voice was distorted with anxiety.

'Maurie, Momma was just taken to the hospital in an ambulance. She's very, very sick . . . she has been for months and wouldn't let any of us know.' She broke down a moment, then went on. 'Maurie, is Ham with you?'

'Yes. He's right here.'

356

'Please get here as fast as you can. Poppa knew all about it and Momma made him and the doctor swear not to tell anybody so we wouldn't be upset at their golden wedding. They both knew it was going to be their last anniversary ... and they were so happy for all of us. What a terrible thing it must have been to keep such a secret! Come here fast as you can, and I hope and pray you won't be too late!'

They left on the train that evening, but when they reached the Harrisburg station early next morning, they saw Ruth, tears streaming down her face, holding tightly to her husband's arm, and they knew their mother was gone.

The next few days were a blur of condolence calls, telephone conversations from all over the country, the funeral, and the rabbi extolling a good woman and a faithful wife ... a blessing to all who knew her and whose lives she touched. Irene phoned Ham and in a tightly controlled voice, just short of tears, asked him to express her sympathy and sense of deep personal loss to Poppa and all the family. She was sorry not to be there at this time, but ... Ham had very little to say, and they hung up in a shared silence.

A telegram was delivered to Ham at his hotel, and he read it quickly before folding the yellow paper and sticking it in his inner pocket.

DEAREST: SYMPATHY TO YOU AND FAMILY ON YOUR GREAT LOSS. WISH I COULD HAVE KNOWN YOUR MOTHER. IF SHE WAS ANYTHING LIKE HER SON I KNOW I WOULD HAVE LOVED HER VERY MUCH. ALL MY LOVE. NITA

The day after the funeral the family returned to their homes: Maurie and Rose to New York, Miriam and Larry Levine to Pittsburgh, Ruth and Abe Harris to their Harrisburg house, Ham back to California. He sat in his drawing room watching the land rush by and wished the trip would go on forever. The train was right on time, and a studio car picked him up at the Pasadena station.

'Shall I take you home or to the studio, Mr. Robbins?' asked the driver.

Ham sat quietly in the backseat a few minutes before answering. The time had come to face reality.

'Home, take me home.'

Winter nights in Southern California can bring a damp and foggy chill that seeps under closed doors, around window frames and deep into the bones of the residents writing their lying letters to friends back on the Eastern Seaboard. Heating systems might be necessary only a few months of the year, but when the wet Pacific marine layer rolled in at night to mate with the snow-touched mountain winds, hundreds of thousands of forced-air heaters were turned on to make life in Los Angeles livable.

When Ham and Irene built their new house on Sierra View Drive, the central heating unit in the basement was one of the most important considerations. A vast network of tin ducts, blower fans, gas lines, thermostats, outlets and controls made certain there would be ideal temperature throughout the house on those dank and chilly nights and mornings never mentioned by the Chamber of Commerce or the All Year Club in their propaganda.

Besides carrying waves of comforting warm air, the large tin ducts also conveyed disturbing waves of sound from room to room and floor to floor throughout the house. When the metal baffles set in each heating vent outlet were left open, and if the forced-air fan motors were turned off, then the buzz of a vacuum machine, music from far-off radios, grumblings from the cook in the kitchen – and now sobs and cries from Irene Robbins and the pleading voice and sudden bursts of anger from her husband – traveled throughout the house.

Jimmy's room was in an upstairs wing far back in the mansion. If he went over near the heating outlet grille where the wall met the floor and pushed open the vent control plate, he could hear all the noises of the house and its occupants, especially those in the master bedroom suite sixty feet down the upstairs corridor and around a corner, where his mother lay sobbing on her bed.

He could make out his father's voice rising and falling over the background of weeping. Sometimes pleading dissonance, then sudden bursts of angry sound blustering with threats and frustration, growing louder and louder until Jimmy, terribly upset at what he heard, pushed down on the vent handle. The sounds were muffled, yet still came through, and he could make out the dreadful echoes of battle in the bedroom. He crossed over to the heater control set in his wall and turned it on as high as it would go. Far down in the basement a series of magnets closed and gas flowed through jets, to be set alight by pilot flames. In a few minutes the fan motors started up with their droning noise and sent heated air throughout the house. All the sound traveling through the ducts now was blurred and overpowered by the distant

358

impersonal machines as the temperature in the rooms began to climb. A door opened down the hall and a voice filled with anger echoed through the house. It was Ham, and he was shouting.

'Who in hell put on the heat! Goddammit, we're cooking in here!'

Indeed they were. Jimmy got up from his bed and switched off the heater control. Soon again he had to listen to the voices as they found their disturbing way into his room through the vent. Again a door down the hall opened, and was immediately slammed shut. There was the thud of feet on the thick hall carpet, a rushing down the great circle of stairs and the loud click of shoes crossing the parquet floor across the reception hall downstairs. The crashing sound of the heavy front door was like the last cannon shot on a field of battle. In a few minutes there came the roar of a car motor echoing from the garage, like the sound of a distant lion in its den ... then the clashing of gears violently shifted as Ham Robbins fled from his house, down the hill and through the great bronze gates, which slid aside to spew him into the night.

The muffled concert coming from the heater vent soon came to its conclusion in a diminishing burst of sobs, fading at last into silence so that the boy, standing all alone in his room, could hear only the pounding of his heart.

CHAPTER THIRTY-FOUR

Benjamin Morrison once again read the letter his daughter had received from Nate Klein, Ham's attorney. Irene's eyes were overflowing and her sister, Betty, sat beside her holding tightly to her hand. Irene spoke to her father in a voice hoarse with emotion.

'A divorce! Just like that he wants me to give him a divorce! He has this lawyer, this Nate Klein, write me a cold letter and I'm supposed to obey his command and let him have everything he wants, let him throw me out of his life so another woman can take my place!' She stopped speaking, her voice drowned in tears.

Her father looked up from the letter and spoke softly in a voice filled with compassion.

'Mr. Klein suggests you get an attorney to represent you and that they meet to discuss future action. Very simply, Ham is asking you to make the next move. He feels you have more than sufficient grounds to ask for a divorce and it really has been left up to you. I cannot act in this for you except as your father. The decision must be yours, Irene, and if it is to go ahead, I will help you get a good man with experience in divorce cases. I know you and Ham have been terribly unhappy for a while now, and you should think about this and everything else before coming to any decision. Whatever you decide, if you go ahead or not, you know I will stand behind you and help in any way I possibly can.'

Her father and Betty had immediately come down from San Francisco in response to her anguished phone call. Benjamin closely questioned his daughter, proving to himself that she indeed was the wronged party who, if she chose, had every right to sue for divorce.

'I'll be damned if I'll let anyone step in and take him away from me – if that's the real reason he wants his divorce!' said Irene, in a voice raised in the passion of her anger. 'I know there have been plenty of other women in the last few years, but he's always come back to me. I don't want a divorce, not after what we've been through together all of these years – from Poverty Row right on up to this lovely home we've built together. Things had been getting much better lately with us, or I thought they were . . . up to that time I was so upset at the wedding anniversary for his parents and wouldn't listen to what he had to tell me. I was wrong maybe to leave like that, but it was so sudden and at such a time! No – I definitely will not give up now just because he had this dreadful letter sent to me . . . not if he crawled here and begged me for a divorce! Never! I want you to tell him that right to his face for me! I would tell him myself, but I don't think I could talk to him at all right now. Maybe later, but now now.'

'If that's your decision, Irene, then I'll call Ham and tell him I want to see him in his office as soon as possible,' said Benjamin, and he went to the guest room, where he placed a call to Ham's office.

'Mr. Robbins will see you at five this afternoon, Mr. Morrison,' said Bob Silver, after Benjamin told him who was calling and he had checked with Ham on the intercom. Later in the day Bob met Irene's father at the main administration gate and brought him up to the office. After they shook hands, Ben spoke in his usual straightforward manner to Ham, who sat stunned behind his desk when he heard what the older man had come to say.

'What do you mean, she won't give me a divorce? She can't do this to me!' Ham shouted.

'I am here as Irene's father, not as her attorney, and I am telling you exactly what she asked me to tell you. She has agreed to nothing and you are assuming a condition that exists only in your own mind – something you wish was true but is not. You assume she will graciously submit to your demand and do exactly what you ask of her. This is not the case.' The old attorney looked into his son-in-law's eyes and saw how they darted back and forth, never returning his look, betraying the terrible anguish of a man in deep trouble. Benjamin suspected what that trouble very well might be. There must be a child, he thought, but was determined to keep that suspicion to himself for now.

Ham could not speak. He took a shooting script from the pile on a side table, riffled through it, then tossed it aside.

'There's nothing more I can discuss with you, Ham. Irene has no plans to give you a divorce and has asked me to

361

impress that fact most definitely on you. I suggest you think not only of yourself alone, but also of your son and of your wife and of making a serious effort with her, like a pair of adults, to work things out and, God willing, make a brand-new start together. I'm sure that's the way she wants it . . . and from what she told me, you felt that very same way yourself not very long ago.'

Ham stared past Ben's shoulder at the big window set in his office wall and without saying anything further got up from his desk, walked around his seated visitor and went to where he could stand and look out at the activity on the studio street.

Benjamin sat in the silent room, looking at Ham's back, then rose to his feet, said good-bye and left.

Late that afternoon when Jimmy returned from school and went up the stairs to his room, he heard the telephone ringing.

'Jimmy, hello . . . This is Bob Silver at your father's office. Could you come over to the studio tomorrow at twelve-thirty? Your father wants very much to see you, and you can stay here for lunch with him.'

The boy thought a moment before replying. He had a few afternoon classes, but this was much more important. He wanted to see his father, who he felt had been avoiding him ever since his return, but of course there must be problems he didn't know about. Yes, this definitely was more important than school.

'Sure I'll be there. Tell him I'm looking forward to seeing him . . . thanks.' He hung up and there was a smile on his face. There was the sound of the front door chime, and his grandfather came into the house and climbed the stairs. Jimmy left his room to say hello and give him a kiss, and was surprised to see how downcast the old man looked. Going back into his room, Jimmy could hear a murmur of voices coming from his mother's room . . . those voices traveling again through the heater ducts . . . and he could almost but not quite hear his grandfather, Aunt Betty and his mother talking in low distorted sounds, all the words indistinct, with the little sobbing noises he knew were from his mother coming intact through the long tin passageway.

Next afternoon Jimmy drove to the studio from school and went past all the familiar buildings and places where he remembered having such wonderful times and seeing so many exciting things. He passed the wardrobe building,

362

make-up and hairdressing, camera department, the still lab and the long row of cutting rooms with their squawking noises of sound tracks running backward, then forward again at high speed. Finally he parked beside the central executive building and went upstairs.

Bob Silver greeted him in his father's outer office. Bob had always liked Jimmy, and they had spent many hours talking while he waited to see his father, who kept him, like everybody else, always waiting . . . waiting.

The rasping noise of the intercom buzzer made him jump, and he heard his father's disembodied voice coming out of the little box on Bob's desk.

'Anybody there?'

'Yes, Mr. Robbins, your son,' said Bob, leaning over to speak softly into the hidden microphone. There was a brief humming sound and then, after a long pause, the voice again.

'Tell him to wait.'

Jimmy was used to this. It appeared to be part of the barrier his father seemed gradually to be putting up during this past year whenever his son came to see him at the studio during his summer vacation when he was working on the back lot. He had been so happy with the people out there who took the scripts, schedules, plans and budgets and turned all those pieces of paper into exciting, entertaining, happy and sad moving pictures seen by millions of people all over the world. Jimmy loved watching the miracles these wonderful people routinely performed as part of their jobs in his father's studio. Most of all he wanted to be part of it, to work with them and with his father – the makers of miracles, movie men, creators of shadows that lived a thousand lives. He listened to the people out on the lot, drank in all they said and watched everything they did. When he thought there was something that wasn't quite right and perhaps could be done better, he went to his father with ideas, suggestions, other ways to do them. Perhaps it seemed immature and sometimes even impractical, because he was not yet sixteen and had a while to go before he would take on the protective cynicism it seemed was necessary to survive in this business.

He saw things both good and bad, and wanted to share them with his father. Once he overheard several men in the metal shop out in the crafts construction building complaining bitterly about the hot-air hand dryers the studio manager had just put on the walls in the men's rooms in place of paper towel dispensers. The workers, grease embedded in

363

their hands, under fingernails and usually up to their elbows, swore at the front-office penny pinchers, then tore great wads of toilet paper out of the booths to get their hands properly dry. If they had had the nerve, some of them would have ripped the damn dryers right off the walls! Jimmy wanted to tell his father they should return the paper towels and how impossible it was with the blowers when your hands got as filthy as they did in the metal shop and other places on the back lot. Sure, it saved some money, but it wasted more time and tore tempers to shreds. He remembered waiting and waiting that time outside his father's office, finally getting inside late in the day and telling him about a problem he saw building up into an explosive situation. His father looked at him coldly for a moment, then spat out his terse reply.

'Forget it! Leave things like that up to the people who run the back lot. They know what they're doing, and you keep your nose out of the metal shop! They'll get used to the air dryers, and that's enough on that subject!'

Late in the summer the metalworkers and half of the mill walked off the job, greasy hands and all, in a wildcat strike, refusing to return until the paper towels went back on the walls. Days of work were lost, schedules ruined and tempers shredded from hours spent around the negotiating table. The union representatives wearily passed on their demands, and suddenly the blowers were off the walls and the paper towels back, along with clean hands and smiling faces coming out of all the metal shop men's rooms. The next time Ham saw Jimmy he glared angrily at him and at home that night bawled him out as though the whole damn mess had been his son's fault. He threatened to make up for the cost of replacing the hand dryers by docking money from Jimmy's small summer paycheck, but then he laughed and changed the subject. What a puzzling guy his old man could be!

Now Jimmy again was sitting outside his father's office, growing hungrier as more than an hour passed. It was a long time since breakfast, and again he looked at his watch. Off in the distance, behind the closed door, he heard a toilet flush and he knew his father had finished whatever he was doing and might be seeing him soon.

'Send him in!' came from the round hole in the squawk box, and Jimmy got up and went through the door.

Ham came around his desk and put out both hands, grasping Jimmy's right hand and smiling.

'Sit down, Jimmy. You look great. How's school? Sorry I

haven't had a chance to see you before now. I only got back from New York last week and I've been up to my neck in work here ever since. Uh . . . how's your mother?'

'She's all right . . . I guess. Of course, she's awfully upset and unhappy most of the time . . . and . . .' He fidgeted, stopping a moment to think of what to say. 'Grandpa and Aunt Betty are down visiting from San Francisco, and that's nice for her . . .' He wished he were in the gym doing hated push-ups or out on the field banging a drum instead of here with his father, who seemed so strangely anxious. The big desk was so much wider and higher than he remembered from his last visit. He looked over at the little table by the side wall, which had always held a lovely still picture of his mother and another of Jimmy proudly wearing his Boy Scout uniform. Now there was a stack of screenplays on the table and the pictures were gone.

Ham saw his son staring at the side table and gave a nervous cough, deciding to get started with what he had asked Jimmy to his office to hear.

'You know, of course, that your mother and I have separated.' The boy nodded; it was too obvious a statement even to answer. His father went on. 'Well, sometimes things like this happen and people who once were in love fall out of love and . . . uh . . .' Ham had read this scene, or many just like it, in dozens of scripts, but now when he was playing one of the leading parts in the scene himself, he was at a loss for dialogue that should have come so easily. 'Uh . . . Jimmy . . . our separation has absolutely nothing at all to do with you . . . and you must know we both love you very much – but your mother and I can't stay married and I want to talk to you about it because you're our son and . . . and . . .' Ham stopped and pulled the neatly folded white handkerchief out of his breast pocket and mopped his damp forehead. He stuffed it back, then spoke again. 'Excuse me, I've got to go to the bathroom.' He got up and quickly left the room, going through a door into a little hall behind his office, and entered his private retreat, pulling the door shut with a loud noise.

Five minutes passed, then ten. Jimmy still sat in the chair facing his father's desk and looked again over at the side table where he last saw the photographs of his mother and himself. He heard the toilet flush and then some water running in a sink. It went on for quite a while, then stopped, and all was silent for another ten minutes until his father slowly opened the door, came back into the office and again sat behind his desk, which seemed to Jimmy to have become a wide impassable mahogany wall.

'Your mother has just told me she will not give me a divorce,' said the man behind the desk in a strange voice that no longer sounded like his father's. 'There is no reason for her to ever think that I am coming back to her. Our marriage is over – done with – and I want you to go to her as soon as you get home and tell her that. Tell her I want her to divorce me, to start whatever has to be done and to do it right away! Jimmy, you've got to do this for me and for all of us or we all will be very unhappy!'

He looked at his father, tried to say something, but his voice quivered and his throat was so dry that words would not come. Finally he spoke in a voice so small and shaking that Ham could barely hear him.

'I can tell her that, I guess . . . but if she doesn't want a divorce, how can my telling her what you want change anything?'

Ham drew a deep breath and for a moment hated himself for what he was about to say – something he knew he should be so ashamed to use in a way that was inhumane, cruel and despicable – but that he felt was absolutely necessary: his final weapon.

'Jimmy, tell your mother that if she will not do what I ask, she will force me to sue her for a divorce, and if I have to do that she will come out much worse than if she had started it herself, as I have asked. Do you understand what I'm telling you? I have lawyers waiting right now to start this for me if she won't go ahead. God knows I don't want to do such a thing . . . but I swear I will if she makes it necessary!'

The boy listened to his father's strange cold voice, his eyes fixed on the face behind the barrier desk.

'Have you been listening to me, Jimmy?' Ham said in such a loud voice that he made his son start in alarm. 'If she won't give me a divorce, I'll go ahead and get one from her. I can't tell you what I will use against her in court if she forces me to! I don't want you ever to let her know I told you any of this, but I have plenty on her and I'll use every bit of it if she forces me to! Now you go home and tell her to stop playing games with me. I'll take good care of her financially – you too, of course. All I ask her to do is get started with a lawyer. Your grandfather can help her find a good man.' Ham stopped and looked at the horror reflected in his son's face. He had never seen such a look, and he hated himself for the terrible thing he had just done – the unforgivable lies invented in his desperation to force his boy into being an unwilling collaborator and convince Irene she must do what he wanted done.

'My God!' Ham said to himself. 'What have I turned into to make me do a fucking thing like this to my own kid! To frighten him into doing such a dirty rotten thing! What in hell have I become?'

He sat behind his desk in frozen silence as his son looked away, stood up and then without a word walked out of the room.

Ham had moved into the Hollywood Athletic Club on Sunset and Hudson the same night he rushed down the hill and away from Sierra View Drive. The Greek brought most of his clothes from the house to his new rooms in the Club tower, where it was only a short drive over the Pass to his studio – or up the hill to Detour Drive and Nita. He was quite careful to maintain appearances, and though he stayed many nights with Nita, so far as his associates and the gossip columns knew from available evidence, Ham Robbins lived as a celibate six floors above the swimming pool and gymnasium at the Athletic Club after his separation.

Jimmy said nothing to his mother about the dreadful afternoon he had spent with his father. He knew how terribly it would affect her. He did tell his grandfather, Benjamin, who was utterly disgusted with Ham's obvious tactics and lack of decency and the brutal way he had tried to use his son to get his way. He talked with Jimmy for more than an hour, let the boy unburden himself, and now he knew that Jimmy must tell his mother how desperate Ham had become and there was really no chance he would ever return to her. Meantime it would do no harm to let a few days pass so the boy could be more relaxed before the necessary heart-to-heart talk with Irene, who still must make the final decision.

With so much unhappiness and tension at home, Jimmy immersed himself in school activities, but often found himself thinking back to the dreadful things his father had told him would happen if his mother refused him a divorce. He sensed the terrible desperation driving his father all through that confrontation in his office. What Ham did not seem to have realized was that his son had a mind of his own. He did not believe his mother could possibly have done anything that his father could use to divorce her against her will. In spite of his youth and inexperience, he knew his father was telling him lies, and he felt crushed and betrayed. Was it another lie when his father told him all this had nothing to do with him and that both his parents loved him very much? He knew his mother did – but what kind of love was his father showing him? Would any father who cared at all for his son say such things, make such demands? He was beginning to believe his parents would be better off if they were divorced, even though this would mean an end to the kind of family security Jimmy had known for all of his years . . . but what kind of a family had it become? What security did it offer now?

At last he sat with his mother, grandfather and aunt and talked seriously from his heart as they listened to every word.

'Mom, I didn't tell you about being with my father in his office last week. I didn't want to upset you more, but I think you should know that he is so anxious for you to give him a divorce that he would do just about anything, and –'

Irene interrupted her son in an alarmed voice.

'Anything? He would do anything? What do you mean by that?'

'Uh . . . well, he told me he was never coming back to you, that you had to give him a divorce or he might do something to force you to do it . . . I don't know what.' He still would not tell her everything Ham had said to him. Perhaps it might not be necessary if he handled this carefully. He did not want her hurt any more. 'Mom . . . I know you don't want to believe this, but you and Dad would be much happier if you were divorced. I think it's the only way you ever can be happy again – someday, maybe not right away, but someday, I know. I hate seeing you so upset, and all I want is for you to be happy again. It's not easy but . . .' He stopped as Irene started to cry. Then suddenly she wiped her eyes, sat up straight and turned to her father.

'Poppa, Jimmy is absolutely right. I can see it clearly now. I've got to face things as they are, not the way I used to dream they'd be. Thank you, Jimmy. You've done more to make me happy today than you realize. Poppa,' she said, 'Poppa, help me to get a lawyer and let's get things started as soon as possible. After all, it's not the end of the world . . . it could even be the beginning of a whole new one!'

Soon the wheels began to turn and the ponderous machinery of the law started to grind out property settlements, trust agreements, insurance policies and trusts and the innumerable documents that, with a judge's approval, would ultimately in a year or so lead to the final decree of divorce. The law, the courts, attorneys and time could take care of *Robbins v. Robbins*, but it would take much more than that to soften or erase the memories of a son who saw his father, in one terrible afternoon, transform himself into his own most deadly enemy.

CHAPTER THIRTY-FIVE

Pops Johnson had excellent contacts with many unusual people and places, including the owner of a small private hospital specializing in obstetrics. It was located on a quiet street in the city of Long Beach, the fast-growing harbor community about twenty-five miles south of where Ham now lived in Hollywood. In this well-run establishment, just off Anaheim Boulevard, a woman or young girl could have her baby delivered in absolute privacy and complete safety. Birth certificates could be arranged to fit almost any circumstance without the true names of the parents or their real addresses ever appearing. Later on certain documents would be deposited in the proper files and the illegitimate made to appear completely legitimate.

Nita de Valle, under the name of Marie La Salle, was driven to this hospital a day and a half before her due date by her 'husband,' a trusted associate of Pops Johnson. In the car with them was a nurse, also screened and hired by Pops, who would stay with Nita and the baby for the next several months. Although she was nervous during the long ride, Nita felt comforted by the two kindly people, who remained with her until at last she fell asleep in her private room at the hospital. The man using the name of Dean La Salle appeared several times the next day with gifts and messages from the real father, who worried the hours away in his studio office or in his rooms high up in the Hollywood Athletic Club tower while he awaited the important news.

There was no chance that their baby, expected to be born in Long Beach, California, sometime this tenth day of March 1933, would ever be traced to its real father, who sat looking out a window in his tower room and suddenly wondered what in the name of God was happening to the building, which began to rock and sway back and forth. There was a crashing sound of glass breaking and the thudding of furniture hitting walls as he looked over at his bedside clock and saw it was

370

exactly 5:30 P.M. He heard a deep rumble that seemed to come from the center of the earth. At that very same moment a baby was being born twenty-five miles away in Long Beach, where hundreds of buildings were being shaken like rats in the jaws of giant terriers. One hundred and twenty people suddenly were dead or dying in the ruins and rubble of collapsed buildings, and thousands more were being injured as Ham Robbins clung with both hands to the window frame and the entire world seemed to shudder and heave beneath him.

The earth had a major convulsion, followed by several immediate after-shocks, just as Hamilton J. Robbins and Nita de Valle became the parents of a healthy seven-pound, four-ounce baby boy. The umbilical cord was cut and tied by a terrified doctor who could hardly stand on his feet as he leaned over the bucking, rocking delivery table under the mad swinging of an operating light that suddenly went dead. He tried to see what was coming out under the unsteady flashlight held by his OB nurse, who was too frightened and busy to faint. The clattering sounds of bricks crashing into the street outside, and the screams of terror in the hospital, completely drowned out the first little cries made by the tiny boy who had just entered the tossing, shaking, earthquaking world.

It took nearly eight long hours for the studio driver to get Ham and Pops Johnson to Long Beach. They tried following the usual Western Avenue route, but National Guard troops, U.S. Marines and police had thrown up barricades and were letting no one through. The streets were disfigured by warped trolley tracks, buckled chunks of pavement and the silent shapes of empty Pacific Electric cars. Everywhere there were heaps of rubble from demolished buildings, and dangling power lines showered sparks into the streets whenever they swung against metal.

Even though Pops used every bit of his considerable influence, waving several varieties of badge and throwing around top-level names in vain, they were forced to take strange side roads, many blocked with refugees fleeing the beach cities in fear of tidal waves that never came. The driver knew this area, but even he got lost time after time, and they had to ask frightened people for directions to the center of the earthquake – Long Beach.

'Thank heavens I've got a good man there with her,' said Pops. 'A real tough guy you can count on. He's the one who's playing the father role for ... er ... Mrs. La Salle ... and he's staying in a little hotel right across from the hospital. I'm sure he'll take care of her – so don't worry!'

It was perhaps better that neither Ham nor Pops knew that ever since five-thirty the evening before, the body of the man registered as Dean La Salle lay buried beneath tons of fallen brick walls outside the ruined hotel across the street from the small hospital, which suddenly was filled far beyond its capacity with victims of the quake disaster.

Except for cracks in its walls and water gushing from ruptured pipes, the hospital seemed to have ridden out the earthquake far better than most of the other structures on the block. Nita's private room now held twelve patients, crowded on beds, cots and mattresses set on the floor. She was very alert, free of pain, and held her baby as she looked at the doctors and nurses working on those needing help. Suddenly she heard a familiar voice coming closer and closer down the patient-jammed corridor, and she shouted with joy at Ham as he came through the door, followed by Pops Johnson. The baby awoke and cried until Nita comforted him and he went back to sleep. Nita gently handed the little boy to his father.

'Congratulations, darling! Meet your son. We've all been too busy ever since he was born to think of a name for him. Maybe you can.'

He looked down in wonder at the little face, laughed and proudly showed the baby to Pops, who leaned over for a closer look, smiled and congratulated both parents. The old man left the room to search the hosptial for Nita's nurse, whom he found helping with some patients in another room. The doctor, when they finally located him, was not too happy to release Nita and the baby so soon after birth, but since the conditions were decidedly unusual and the mother and child doing so well, he gave his reluctant approval. They found an empty wheelchair and took Nita and the baby very slowly and carefully down the staircase, since the elevator was jammed tightly in its shaft. Their driver brought the car up on the sidewalk and as close to the door as he could and helped them put Nita and the baby in the backseat with some supporting pillows. The nurse sat by her side holding the baby, while Ham was on the facing jump seat and Pops was up front.

After nearly four hours of very slow and cautious driving, they reached the house on Detour Drive, where Nita was put into her bed and the baby into the waiting crib, bought over two months ago. Ham fell heavily onto the living room couch and was sound asleep almost before his body came to rest.

Pops took a last look at the baby, another at Nita and the nurse, then went over to the couch where Ham slept. The old man looked down at his boss, shook his head and turned to leave, saying to himself as he walked toward the car, 'Can you beat it! The man spends millions for crummy stories to turn into movies, and here's a real lulu he's got going on right under his nose that wouldn't cost him a penny . . . or would it?'

He was still shaking his tired old head as he told the driver to take him back to the studio, and was sound asleep, loudly snoring on the backseat, before the car reached the bottom of the hill and turned toward Cahuenga Pass.

CHAPTER THIRTY-SIX

Irene wiped her eyes as the mover's van, loaded with everything she and Jimmy called their own, pulled around the circle, past the Spanish fountain, then down the hill on its way from Sierra View Drive to the apartment on Doheney Drive where they would live.

The attorneys had worked for months to hammer out the reams of documents that would lead to the final chapter. Jimmy's education and other expenses were provided for by Ham, and Irene surrendered all claim to the property on Sierra View after he set up an irrevocable trust to provide her with a monthly income and other benefits. While he was very unhappy at what all this had cost him, he had gone too far now to turn back.

A week after Irene's departure, Ham drove up to the estate, bringing with him a famed interior decorator, a one-time minor film star of indeterminate sex, who practically had an orgasm when he stood in the reception hall and saw the magnificent sweep of the great staircase and all the wonderful space he was determined to transform into a brilliant reputation for himself.

'I can't see a damn reason to change much of this,' Ham said to the dithering decorator. 'I spent a fortune to get it to look this good, and all I want you to do is replace the things Mrs. Robbins took with her. Today I want you to start looking it over, meet with Miss de Valle and then come up with some recommendations. I'm sure you know your business. The head set dresser in our studio property department spoke very highly of you.'

The decorator bowed his head in a little gesture of gratitude. The set dresser had damn well better speak highly of him, or he'd throw him right out on his ass and get himself a new boyfriend.

'Now I don't want anything too drastic. Nita . . . Miss de Valle . . . will sit down with you after you've seen everything, and later you can both tour the house and grounds so she can give you her suggestions. Let's walk around now, then go out and I'll show you the grounds so you'll get to know the whole place.' The butler went ahead to turn on lights, and soon the decorator was writing madly on his pad and writhing madly in his pants. This was even better than he thought it would be! He hoped that the Nita person would leave him alone and not destroy all the wonderful concepts he felt taking root. This man with him . . . well, he would have to get used to spending plenty of money if this dreadful house was to be rescued from being just another Beverly Hills Spanish klunker.

Nita had desperately wanted to be with them on this first tour, but Nate Klein strongly recommended she stay away from the estate until all documents were signed and in the hands of the court. No need to stir up Irene, as she could still roll boulders in the road or call the whole thing off . . . or at least create long delays. Nita must be patient . . . just a few more months.

'What you do after the final decree is your own business,' said the attorney to Ham. 'Until then it would be more prudent if the young lady stayed out of the public view with you – and kept away from the house. Above all, keep everything about the child strictly to yourselves. The fewer people who know he exists right now, the better. It could change a great many things if Mrs. Robbins knew facts and dates before the final decree was entered.' Ham sighed deeply, agreed with the lawyer and wondered whatever had possessed him to tell Nate Klein about the child in the first place. Sometimes he could be too damn honest!

He reluctantly broke the news to Nita that she could not yet visit the Beverly Hills house. After a while she stopped pleading like a deprived little girl, saw reason and agreed it was for the best.

'Look, Nita. I have an idea. It's not as good as being there yourself, but I can have one of our best still photographers from the studio take pictures of every room in the house . . . all the different angles, and plenty of the outside as well. You'll have a hundred or more prints to study with the decorator. I've got the original floor plans as it is now, and all that should be a big help. Remember, I only want a few changes to start with . . . nothing too fancy. It's a lovely house and we used the finest materials and furnishings, which should last a long, long time. Just replace what Irene took with her, maybe your bathroom and dressing room too if you want something all your own. I'm sure you'll love the the house just the way it is with those few changes. I can't even see why we need this decorator, but maybe he'll come up with some ideas that won't cost an arm and a leg.' He thought of something and smiled. 'One good thing about him, though – he's the kind of person a man can trust to be alone with his woman . . . right?'

Nita's eyes now were dry and her mind was active. She was going to change not only Ham's life, but his house – their house – as well. No need to go into details right now. She had already met a couple of times with the decorator and could tell they understood each other perfectly. This was not going to be just another Beverly Hills estate, it was going to be a jewel, a gem. The people who one day would fight for coveted invitations to the great parties they would give in their lovely house would be absolutely captivated by the beauty of everything they saw. As important as anything else in Nita's mind was the absolute necessity that the past be erased. There must be no trace that anyone named Irene Robbins or a boy named Jimmy had ever lived within those walls.

Several evenings later Nita waited impatiently for Ham to come home from the studio. She had something exciting to show him. It had taken almost a day of preparation and now it was laid out flat on the table, held down by books on each corner, as she listened for the sound of his key in the front door.

At last he came into the room, and she threw her arms around him to return his kiss. Still holding his hands, she pulled him over to the table and proudly showed him the big square of paper resting there, covered with lines, arcs, circles and marginal notes in her handwriting.

'Ham, look! The very first horoscope for our son. It proves that the name I picked for him is absolutely right. Now stop being so stubborn and say it . . . come on!'

'Donald!' Ham snorted.

Nita laughed at the face he made and the way he said the name.

'Say it again . . . slowly this time. Donald. It's a lovely old Gaelic name. See, I found it in this book. It means "prince of the universe." It's a wonderful name for our son.'

He took the small book from her hands, quickly read the short paragraph, then threw it down on the table.

'All right, I hope he likes it when he gets older and doesn't hate us for unloading it on him before he was old enough to object. I was never crazy about the original name my parents gave me and took another just as soon as I could. Well, I'll call him "Donny," or something like that.' Ham laughed as he leaned over to look at something Nita had written on one of the margins of the horoscope.

' "The Pisces Child ... February nineteenth to March twentieth is blessed with peace and tranquillity and enters a serene world, loved and loving ..." What kind of crap is that, Nita? Have you completely forgotten the exact date, day and time when our son was born? Friday, March tenth, at five forty-five P.M., right in the middle of one of the worst damn earthquakes ever! Tranquillity ... a serene world! Bull! You better shove those planets of yours in some other direction. Don't ever tell him he was born into any peace and tranquillity, for God's sake!' Ham thought a fleeting moment of all the other earthquakes and aftershocks that would knock everything apart if the baby's true date of birth ever became known. He was grateful Pops Johnson had done his cover-up work so well. Little chance their little Pisces would ever have to worry about that. He thought of something, and there was a sudden note of alarm in his voice.

'Nita, get rid of this damn horoscope. It has some dates on it we want to keep strictly to ourselves. You know why!' He took up the paper and tore it into small pieces, went into the bathroom and flushed it down the toilet. When he came back into the room, Nita was pouting, angry at the destruction of all her hard work.

'I only wish you'd realize that a horoscope is a serious matter. Our Donald is going to be a peaceful, happy person. If you hadn't thrown it away you would have read that he is going to be creative, artistic, giving and taking love from all around him. He's lucky to have been born under so many favorable signs, so you could at least be a little grateful ... please!'

'I still say it's a lot of bull ... I mean Taurus, if I know my signs,' Ham replied, a smile softening his sharp words. 'What I've brought you is a lot more important than all that, though. These are the still pictures, more than a hundred of them – every room in the house, and shots of the outside, too. Here, look them over!'

He spread out all the black-and-white prints on top of the table in front of Nita, then left her to go into the other room and play with his little Pisces son, who gurgled happily in his crib and drooled as he gently picked him up and held him close, with the nurse fussing around and wiping him off with a dry diaper.

Nita leaned over the pictures and looked carefully at each one under the strong light of a floor lamp she pulled over next to the table. She frowned at each print, and could not help sensing Irene in each of the lovely rooms she saw. Now Nita was more determined than ever to remake not only this house, but also the man who, like the house, would soon be completely hers.

The interior decorator, whose name was Sidney Jordan, met with Nita in her house several times each week. They studied the pictures of the house, and Sidney contemptuously tossed them aside.

'This was supposed to be a showplace? It looks more like a bankrupt Spanish furniture store! Could you convince Mr. Robbins that his studio should purchase this monstrous junk for the property department? I'm sure he wouldn't mind getting his money back plus a profit for what he was cheated out of. Once we're rid of these disasters, we could do the house the way it cries out to be done!' Sidney Jordan was not only a talented decorator, but a shrewd businessman – and he knew his customer. Later, when Nita made the suggestion to Ham, he thought it over, saw the merit in such a deal and sent a confidential memo to the head of the property department. Soon it was necessary to find nearly an acre of storage space at the studio for some very expensive set dressing that would appear in nearly every film turned out by Robbins International in the coming years. Later Ham received a sharp letter from Maurie, who recognized some of his brother's old furniture and wondered how it kept finding its way into their pictures. Ham crumpled the letter into a small ball and deftly tossed it across his office into a wastebasket. He was getting better lately at doing this with Maurie's letters.

Exact measurements were made of every room in the Sierra View house, and the decorator sent instructions to his agents in Europe. In France, England and Belgium antique wood panels and parquet floors were removed from great houses, manors and estates where they had been for centuries and carefully packed in numbered crates. After crossing the Atlantic Ocean and traversing the Panama Canal, they all arrived at the port of Long Beach, which had made an amazing recovery from the disastrous earthquake of the year before. Now they were loaded on trucks headed for Sierra View Drive.

Ham moved from the Hollywood Athletic Club into a bungalow behind the Beverly Hills Hotel, just off Benedict Canyon. In an adjoining bungalow, its entrance screened by a tall hedge, were registered a Mrs. Marie La Salle, her infant son and a nurse. Now Nita was less than a mile from the house on Sierra View Drive, but the repeated warnings of Ham's attorney grew in magnitude when he learned of her move. For a while longer Nita could only drive past the gate and watch as the trucks hauled out the old things and brought in the new. Very soon, after a few more months, she would follow those crates and cases through the bronze barriers in the wall, never again to be on the outside looking in. She already had waited almost a year and a half, and the rest of the time would pass quickly. In a few more months, if all went well, there would be the final decree . . . and then the beginning of their whole new life together.

CHAPTER THIRTY-SEVEN

'Dad, could I ask you a personal question?'

It was a month since Jimmy had graduated from high school, surrounded by his family, only his father conspicuous by his absence, with apologies from Bob Silver. It had hurt, but the promise that he could work at the studio for the summer made him feel a little less angry. Now he and his father sat alone in the projection room after the dailies had been run and it was time to leave. Ham did not answer as they got up from the comfortable chairs and started toward the door and the outside stairs leading to the street. It was quite dark outside, and the harsh glare from lights set high on the building threw shadows that made it difficult for the boy to see his father's face.

'Before you start with questions,' Ham said as they were halfway down the stairs, 'tomorrow morning as soon as you get into the production department tell Harry Saunders to have some decent lighting put on this building so some dark night I don't take a header and crack my skull.' They reached the street and his waiting car. 'All right, ask me your personal question – whatever it is.'

Jimmy, who now was as tall as his father, might have been able to look him in the eye, but Ham's face was still unseen in the shadows.

'Uh . . . Dad . . . I know a whole lot about what's been happening with you and Mom . . . the separation, the divorce and everything. I couldn't help hearing about . . . uh . . . about somebody else . . . and . . . uh . . .' His voice trailed off and was lost.

Ham was suddenly grateful the light was so bad that Jimmy could not see his face and whatever emotions it might reveal.

'Let's sit in my car, where we can be more comfortable instead of standing out here in the dark. You can finish asking me this question that's giving you so damn much trouble getting it out.' He opened the door on the far side and slid in behind the wheel. Jimmy got in to sit beside him on the front seat.

'Dad, I don't know just how to say it, but . . .'

'Say it. For God's sake, whatever it is, say it!' said Ham, desperately wishing he wouldn't.

'Well, I told you I know more than you may think I do about what's been happening with you and Mom . . . and about some other woman. I know that in another month or so your divorce will be final. What I want to ask you is if you're going to marry this woman. It's been so hard to talk to you about this and so many other things . . .'

'Did your mother put you to asking me that . . . that "personal" question?' Ham said, in a voice gone suddenly hard and angry.

Jimmy drew in his breath. He was nervous, and it showed in the way he spoke.

'No . . . no. It's my idea to ask you this and she doesn't know. I wanted to talk to you about it, Dad . . .'

'And just why in hell do you want to know?' Ham asked in the same tone he used when he saw a bad review of one of his pictures.

'Uh . . . well . . . I don't know how to put it. I know it's completely over between you and Mom. She realizes there's no chance you'll ever get together again . . . but honest, I'm real upset about things . . . about what I've heard . . . that you and this woman . . . Well, Mom learned about her from somebody and I couldn't help overhearing, and ever since I've wanted to talk to you about –'

'Her name's Nita. Go ahead, you can say it. She's a very nice person – and quit calling her "this woman." You're starting to sound like your mother!'

'I'm sorry, I really didn't know her name. I only wanted to ask if you're marrying her. You should be able to talk to me about that. I don't run to my mother and tell her anything like this – she's already upset enough. If we can't talk about something important like this – and not just about what's happening in the production department where I'm working, or how I did in school – about important personal things . . . like, well, like you not being at my graduation when I wanted you there so much and the time you were so awfully upset when you thought Mom wasn't going ahead with the divorce and then what you said to me in your office. It made me terribly unhappy and upset, and I've wanted to tell you that ever since. You've never let me get close enough, though,

until now. Even here it's hard to talk to you the way you . . .
the way you . . .'

Ham sat stiffly beside his son, half listening to his voice as
it again trailed off into silence. He held tightly to the car
wheel, wishing he had said a quick good night to the kid and
driven off – but like a damn fool he'd encouraged him to talk
and he had asked that goddamn question. Thank heavens he
hadn't asked him about the baby. What kind of answer would
he have given to that one? Ham looked through the windshield at the dark studio street, where pools of light splashed
on the pavement from lamps high up on stage roofs. He
thought a minute, then began to speak in a strained, slow
voice.

'No . . . no, I'm not marrying Nita. We're very good friends,
but I'm not going to marry her after my divorce from your
mother. Now I'll let you off at the parking lot. Go home and get
some sleep so you can get to work early and not fall asleep
during the production meeting. I'm late now for a . . . uh, for a
dinner meeting at the Producers' Association, so let's get
moving. Be sure you tell Harry about the lights on the stairs.
I'm glad we had a chance to have this good talk . . . we'll have
some more later on. I want you to tell me how things are going
in the production department, that's the heart of the whole
damn studio. Well – good night.'

Jimmy got out of the car and stood in the street as his father
drove off and around the corner of a stage toward the main
gate.

'Good talk – what good talk?' he said to himself, turning to
walk to his car, parked a few feet away. He started the motor
and soon followed his father out of the studio, all the time
wondering if he could believe a word he had heard. He
wished he could, but knew that much more than his father's
face had been left in shadow outside the projection room.

'And do you, Nita de Valle, take this man, Hamilton Robbins,
as your lawfully wedded husband, to have and to hold, in
sickness and in health, for better or for worse, until death do
you part?'

'I do.'

'Then, by virtue of the authority granted me by the State of
Nevada, and as Judge of the Municipal Court in the City of
Las Vegas, Clark County, I now pronounce you man and
wife!'

There was barely time for the groom and then the judge to

kiss the bride and for Ham to put a ring on her finger and for both of them to sign the marriage certificate. Pops Johnson, who was their witness, urged them to hurry with him to the studio car that waited outside the courthouse, and they all rushed to the station in time to meet the eastbound train that would take the two of them on to Chicago, then to New York. Pops, with all those good contacts of his, had phoned ahead to the judge, an old pal from his Department of Justice days, and everything had been ready and waiting when the studio car brought them into the fast-growing little city of Las Vegas. They had been hours and hours on the hot dusty road driving from Los Angeles, and Nita was grateful for the speed of the ceremony. When they got into their drawing room on the train, she flopped down on the wide seat and let out a sigh.

'Having a baby during an earthquake was easier than what we've been through since this morning, darling! But it's over now . . . and we're really married and we can sleep together!' She reached up to pull him down on top of her. 'I've never done it on a train,' Nita said into his ear. 'I understand it's absolutely wonderful!'

Ham smiled and answered with a knowing wink, 'Where did you ever hear such a thing? It's not wonderful at all – it's only terrific! Let's ring for the porter to make up our bed right now. I think we both could use some sleep after all that driving . . . Right?'

She laughed as he pressed the button for the porter.

'Sleep . . . who wants to sleep? We can do that any night.'

Ham realized they had eaten nothing since a quick stop hours and hours ago at a highway café, so when the porter came in and started pulling things together to make up their berths, they went forward to the dining car, where Pops had made complete arrangements through an old railroad friend to have champagne and a wedding dinner with flowers on the table waiting for them. Their first toast was to each other, the second to Pops Johnson, by now sound asleep back in a Las Vegas hotel with an early call at the desk so he and the driver could get back to the studio with the secret that only they, Louella Parsons, Hedda Hopper, and all of their eager readers would know by the next morning. The judge had rushed off to a phone just after the newlyweds left his chambers and given out the story, making certain his name was spelled correctly. It never hurt to be known when people came into town to get married, and what easier way was there to earn a few extra fees on the side?

Two hundred miles to the east of Las Vegas the train roared into the night, the wedding day at an end as they went beyond midnight, rocking in each other's embrace on the wide lower berth. Ham had been right – it wasn't wonderful, it was absolutely magnificent! The incessant vibration and movement of the railroad sleeping car as it rushed eastward on the steel rails made this a wedding night to remember. Somewhere in Colorado, as the train rolled on, they finally lay exhausted beside each other, and Ham spoke into Nita's ear, invisible in the darkness.

'Everybody should have their honeymoon on a train! Thank heavens for all that jouncing and bouncing – I was so damn exhausted that I needed all the help in moving my ass that I could get! Let's stay right in here for the rest of the trip!'

More than seven hundred and fifty miles west of where the train traveled on into early morning, Jimmy Robbins was awakened by a loud cry coming from his mother's bedroom. He quickly rushed through the apartment living room to Irene, who was sitting up in bed, sobbing uncontrollably, a handkerchief pressed to her eyes. He went to her side and put a hand on her shoulder.

'Mom, what's the matter? What happened?'

She could not answer him. Her whole body was shaking and she could not stop crying. The little radio beside her bed was on and the announcer was reading some news bulletins.

Jimmy leaned over and turned the radio off as Irene sobbed into the little piece of cloth, which soon was soaked through. What a fool she had been to hope one day she and Ham might work things out and come together again. A stupid foolish dream, which had just been exploded when she awoke before dawn, terribly depressed by events of the past few days, and found it difficult to get back to sleep. She turned on the radio just in time to hear a news bulletin that Ham Robbins, head of Robbins International Studios, had just been married in Las Vegas to Nita de Valle, and that the happy couple were on their way to a European honeymoon. Then followed some drivel about how suddenly it had happened, catching friends and business associates completely by surprise.

Irene sat up in bed and tears ran down her face. Jimmy anxiously sat beside her, not yet knowing what had happened.

'Mom, tell me, what's going on?'

384

'Your dear father has run off and married that woman who broke up our home and stole him away from me. It's already on the radio and it will be in the newspapers. My friends will all be laughing at me! Our divorce was final only two days ago and yesterday he sneaked off to Las Vegas and married that . . . that . . .' Her voice was lost in both hands as she covered her face and shook with sobs.

Jimmy still remembered the threats his father had made when he was afraid his mother might not go through with the divorce. Now he was terribly upset again to find he had been told a deliberate lie when he asked his father if he was going to marry . . . what was her name? . . . Nita. Perhaps he was afraid to tell the truth because Irene still could call off the divorce. Would it have made any difference if he had known the truth? Perhaps nothing would have been changed at all – but he had trusted his father, and he felt betrayed. Irene seemed to be calmer now, so Jimmy went into the kitchen and made them some hot tea, which he carried back to her bedroom. By now her eyes were dry, and they sat listening to radio music and watched the sun turn dawn into day.

'Ruth, your brother's on the front page of the *Harrisburg News!*' Abe Harris shouted into the breakfast room. 'He married some dame named Nita de Valle yesterday in Las Vegas. Ever hear of her?'

She raced over to grab the paper out of his hands and looked at the story.

'So that's her name. I knew he was keeping somebody, the damn fool. What a terrible thing to do to poor Irene. I didn't even know their divorce was final. My God, what will Maurie say when he hears this! He's given so much hell to Ham for playing around the way he has. I'll have to call Miriam right away!'

She started for the phone, but it rang before she reached it and she heard her sister's voice, pitched high with excitement, almost screaming into the phone. At last Ruth was able to speak.

'Yes, Miriam . . . yes . . . it's the one he's been keeping . . . Wasn't there another one before that? Yes, that's right . . . he's no good and before long he'll have another one! Imagine, our little brother Chaim . . . Hamilton, yet . . . a real fine gentleman. Hang up, Miriam! I've got to phone Maurie right now before he reads it in the paper and has an explosion. Abe

385

sends love. Good-bye, dear.' She rang off, then dialed the operator. 'Hello, I want Mr. Maurie Robbins, Great Neck, Long Island, New York. I'll wait.'

In a few moments her older brother came on the phone.

'Ruth, you just caught me leaving the house for the city.'

'Did you see the morning paper?' she asked at once.

'Morning paper? Yes . . . I just read the stock market. Why? Has something happened I should know about?'

'Our brother Ham married that woman he's been keeping. They went to Las Vegas and now they're on the way east. He'll probably be introducing you to the new bride by tomorrow evening!' Ruth said in anything but a comforting tone of voice.

'That miserable bastard! Dumping a good woman like Irene for that . . . that . . . I don't know what to call her! He's no good at all. My God – does Poppa know about it yet?'

'I'm sure not. He waits for the Yiddish paper to come from New York, and I'm sure there's nothing in it about this. He could hear from somebody, so I'll go right over and break it to him gently. He'll probably spend the rest of the day in *shul* praying or sitting *shivah*. Poor Irene . . . I really feel sad for her. I'm sure Jimmy must be upset too. Ham never told any of us he was getting married, even though we knew he was keeping a woman. That must be the same one he just married.' A few more moments of conversation, and they hung up.

Maurie shouted upstairs to his wife, 'Rose, pack up the bags again. We're going back to Miami Beach tonight. An extra vacation . . . I'll tell you about it later!'

'I'm sorry, your brother and Mrs. Robbins left yesterday for Florida. They expect to be away for two weeks.'

'Yesterday? I understood they had just returned from a vacation there. Was this business or something special?'

Maurie's secretary fumbled for a reply.

'Uh . . . they left rather suddenly and he didn't say. I can reach him for you if you wish. They're staying at –'

'Forget it!' Ham said. He was very angry now. Maurie had heard about the wedding, that was obvious, and rather than stay in town and have to meet his brother's new wife, he and Rose deliberately ran away. What a shit-heel of a brother! 'We're at the Waldorf for a couple of days, then Mrs. Robbins and I are taking the *Bremen* to Europe. I'll be coming to the office after lunch today. Transfer me to Mike Hammersmith's office.'

After congratulations and some general talk about film

grosses, Mike arranged to meet them at the '21' Club, then go with them to the office while Nita spent some money shopping on Fifth Avenue. Ham asked if Mike had any idea why Maurie had left town.

'Was it business or something else, Mike?'

'Search me. He just called to say he'd be away a week or two. That's kind of strange, because he and Rose just returned from a holiday last week and now they're off on another – and to the same place. Maybe he forgot his glasses or something.'

Ham listened, full of anger, but soon cooled down. He nearly blurted out something, but at the last moment figured it was none of Mike's business and the hell with it.

He took Nita the few blocks across town to the '21' Club, where Jack Kriendler, one of the owners, met them at the door. Mike Hammersmith had phoned ahead, and the best table in the downstairs bar was waiting for the couple, along with a chilled bottle of Dom Perignon sitting beside their table in a silver cooler. Nita was overwhelmed by all the attention she was getting, and she loved it – the crowds of Ham's friends coming over to congratulate them and be introduced to the bride, the captains, hordes of waiters and busboys, and Charlie Berns, Jack Kriendler's partner, making sure they had everything they wanted. The cork was popped, and a cheer went up from all the surrounding tables. Kriendler leaned over to whisper in Ham's ear.

'Is it okay if I let in a press photographer to grab a shot of the two of you? If not, tell me and he stays out.'

'Hell – why not? Nita's pretty as a picture . . . prettier than most of the models you've got here. She ought to be photographed – especially today!' Ham said, trying to be heard above the voices in the noisy room.

'How about putting her in some of your movies?' asked Charlie, and Nita laughed while she sampled the delicious prosciutto and melon.

'I should say not! That's one thing she definitely is not getting into. Posing here for a still or two is all right, but that's going to be it! I've got enough actresses giving me trouble at the studio without having one in my home, too!' Ham said with a laugh.

Two days later Ham and Nita sailed on the *Bremen* for a brief honeymoon in Europe. While they were gone, Mike Hammersmith was offered the vice-presidency of RKO Pictures, where the increase in salary and independence as international head of their distribution was too attractive to pass up. He conferred with Maurie Robbins, who returned to town as suddenly as he had left, and who agreed he should take the new job, reluctant as he was to see him go. Maurie tossed a farewell party at Sardi's, where he introduced the new head of distribution, Lennie Rhinehart, who had been Mike's assistant for a number of years. Ham cabled congratulations from Lake Como, where he and Nita were admiring the scenery and each other.

Unfortunately, Mike Hammersmith completely forgot to tell Lennie Rhinehart that Ham wanted a certain sales division public relations field man kept on, regardless of any other changes he might make. Thus, Larry Gross became the first casualty of a personnel cutback in the Salt Lake City film exchange. Larry knew he could get himself another job right away back in Hollywood, but he had a gut feeling that Ham Robbins was behind his axing, now that Miss Nita de Valle had become Mrs. Hamilton Robbins and their secret, or some of it, need no longer be secret. There were other things, though, and Larry knew them all – dates and places and times . . . and names. It wouldn't hurt at all to kick that miserable bastard in the balls, just for a farewell gesture. After he completed cleaning out his desk, Larry stuck a plain piece of paper and some carbons in the typewriter and looked up an address in Westchester. He would send the unsigned letter to his New York friend, who would remail it for him. One day he might need Ham Robbins again for something, and there was no need to knowingly create a long-term enemy when all he wanted was some short-term revenge. He finished typing the letter, then looked in one of the trade papers on his desk. A moment to check over dates on the wall calendar and he stuck the completed letter in his briefcase. The time to mail it would be later, when it would do its maximum damage. He could afford to be patient.

Ham and Nita could not move into the Sierra View house when they returned from Europe. The decorator, contractors and all their workmen had torn out nearly everything that had been in the house to make way for the rebuilding. While most of the exterior walls remained fairly intact, little else went unchanged. The final shipment of furniture for the living room, reception hall and formal dining room was deep in the hold of a freighter someplace between the southern tip of

Florida and Baja California, and the shipping agent swore it would arrive sooner or later.

'Nothing is lost, Mr. Robbins. We know it's at sea, but it's not possible to pinpoint just where.'

Ham swore in disgust and turned the whole mess over to Pops Johnson, who made a few phone calls, and like magic the ship turned up at the port of Long Beach and the crates began to emerge from the hold for the last part of their long journey.

Meanwhile, Nita, Ham and the baby moved into a furnished rental only a few blocks from the Sierra View estate. The dining room of this temporary residence became Nita's workroom, where she met nearly every day with the decorator, who set up his renderings of the new interiors and hung samples of fabric on chairs and over tables. Nita was ecstatic, picking this, rejecting that and laughing indulgently whenever Ham charged into the room to express indignation at what all this was going to cost.

'I remember telling you we were only going to replace the things Irene took with her and maybe put in a new bath and a dressing room for you with a big walk-in closet. Now look at what's happening! The wall panels were all right, and I almost broke even selling all my old stuff to the studio – but, Nita, what you and that oddball Sidney Jordan are doing is building a whole new house! The walls, roof and the grounds are the same . . . at least this afternoon they were. I'll bet you have plans for them too. Everything inside has been completely gutted! This is crazy! I get tied up and busy at the studio and you do this behind my back! I'll bet you figured out one hell of a horoscope on our dear decorator! Just what sign was that son of a bitch born under, the dollar sign?'

A properly run motion picture studio depends heavily upon schedules. There is a plan, a place and a time for everything that must take place from concept to release if a film budget is to have meaning and substance – and get back its cost, plus profit. Ham and Nita had a schedule of their own, which nothing could make come out right. There was the hard cold fact that one year after their marriage, their son, Donny, legally was nine months old – but biologically he was nearly two. It was a fiction that Ham insisted be kept. Even though he and Nita now were married and there should be no immediate question of illegitimacy, he could not abide the image of his brother's scorn, a brother who had refused to even meet

Nita when they stopped a few days in New York after their honeymoon. He would not face the veiled ridicule of his two sisters or the distress of his father, whose sad old eyes he could almost feel piercing right through him . . . little Chaim the *pisher* who had brought so much disgrace to all his family!

'So he's big for his age!' Ham said to Nita back in their leased house. 'Hell, my old man was a giant, a bull. Momma was a big woman. Donny's just like them!' They both watched with pleasure as the little boy confidently walked all around his room. He was large – very large for only nine months!

'We'll give him a birthday party and combine it with the housewarming when we move,' Nita said. 'After all, there should be no question about dates – it's all in the records, right there on his birth certificate. That's what Pops Johnson told us. You and I saw it ourselves, and I believe anything he says.'

'Yeah,' Ham answered with some worry in his voice, 'but I'm certain some people know the real dates, hard as we've tried to keep things quiet and change all the records. It still bothers me.' The worry vanished as he laughed and went on to say, 'I've just thought of something wonderful – and funny. Most people would love to lose a few years when they get to a certain age. Look at the wonderful gift we've given Donny – more than a whole year off his real age! I'll bet one day he won't complain about that.'

Jimmy could hear his mother talking on the phone when he came into the apartment. Irene was reading from an undated typewritten letter she had just received from New York. It had been written by somebody who had not signed his name. Jimmy tried not to listen, but Irene's voice filled the room and he could not avoid hearing something of what she said.

' ". . . and I feel you should know some facts about your former husband and the woman he married – and especially about their child. Perhaps you already know this – but if you do not, then you should. Over a year before your divorce from Ham Robbins was final, even before you brought any legal action, this woman had his child. What I write is not rumor or hearsay. I was in a position to know the complete truth and I feel you should know it too, even though now it may be too late to do anything. You will find no true record of the child's birth date, as somebody was able to plant false information in the official files. I have learned that money can buy almost anything – and Ham Robbins has used his wealth, power and arrogance to get whatever he wanted and crush whoever stood in his way." ' Irene paused a moment, then went on. ' "Someday I hope you will have an opportunity to meet with a man called Pops Johnson, who is the head of a department at your former husband's studio. He has all the answers to any questions you might ask – if he ever wants to give them. A day will come when he might want to talk to you, and if so it would be well worth your time. I wish you well, you deserve it after what that miserable man has done to you and so many other people. I regret I cannot sign this as being other than . . . A Friend." '

Irene was dry-eyed when she finished reading the letter and did not hear her son quietly go into his room and close the door. She put down the sheet of paper and listened as her father spoke to her.

'Irene, I see no good in opening any of this up again. Your divorce is final. The settlements that were made appear to be fair and were approved by the court. If Ham was honest in revealing all his assets for the division of property, nothing more can be done. If not, then that is quite another matter. Frankly, I feel a man of his type must keep secrets and lie when the truth would serve as well, and one day something may happen so the whole world will know the real person we know is hiding inside Ham Robbins. Meantime, put the letter away in a safe place and try to enjoy your life. Look at it as a new beginning. You have years and years ahead, and maybe you will marry again. Put all this behind you.'

'But if what this letter says is true, they had a child while he still was married to me!' said Irene, hoping her father would tell her something she could do.

'Irene, my dear, it isn't the first time and it won't be the last something like this has happened. It's too bad you didn't know about it before and have better proof than an anonymous letter before the divorce was final. Maybe then something might have been done, but now – well, just be glad you're rid of him.'

'I suppose you're right. How could I have been married so long to somebody I really didn't know?' she said, shaking her head in disbelief.

'You knew as much about him as he let you know. His problem may be that he doesn't really even know himself. I have a feeling his troubles aren't over but are probably just beginning. Irene, try to forget him – think of your own life

391

and your own happiness. That should come first, and he's no longer a part of it. Think of Jimmy, too. How is he?'

'All right. He's doing very well at the university. He sees his father at the studio now and then, and during the summer vacation when he works there he sees quite a lot of him, though I don't know if they ever have talks together. Jimmy doesn't tell me.'

'Encourage him to have a relationship with his father, that's how it should be,' Ben told her.

'What will happen when Ham tells Jimmy he wants him to come to the house and meet his . . . his stepmother?' The word came hard to Irene, and she could barely make herself say it. 'He may want him to see their child as well. So far I don't think his father has gotten up the nerve to say anything to him – at least Jimmy has said nothing to me about it. I feel certain, though, that one day it will happen, and I don't think I want my son to meet that . . . that . . . woman!'

'Irene, there are some things you cannot plan for your son. Remember, he's Ham's son too, as much as he is yours. Wait until his father asks him to come and meet them, if he ever does – then let Jimmy make his own decision. It's really not for you to –'

'I can't help it,' Irene answered, anger in every word. 'I know Ham is greatly at fault, but I place the real blame on her for deliberately taking my husband away from me. I don't want my son going to the house we both were thrown out of, to visit the woman responsible for destroying our family . . . breaking up our family. I cannot bear the thought of Jimmy seeing that child! Maybe someday I might change, but right now that's just how I feel. I couldn't stand it!' The tears flowed again, and her father waited patiently until she could listen to him.

'My dear, let some time pass before you make any final judgments. I'm always here for you to phone whenever you are troubled. Put things from the past back into the past and don't let them spoil any more of your life.' They said good-bye and hung up as Irene put a handkerchief up to her eyes.

Jimmy sat behind his closed door and could faintly hear his mother sobbing in the other room. He held a piece of paper in his hand and once again read the message he had been handed at the lobby desk before taking the elevator up to the apartment.

Mr. J. Robbins: Apt. 14-P – 5:32 P.M.:
Your father's office left message. Please
call. Wants to set time to see you late
tomorrow for important discussion.
Dianne: Operator #4

The message blurred as he brought his fingers tightly together and crushed it into a crumpled ball, which he threw beneath his bed. There was still time to get some homework started before dinner. That message would not be answered, not the next day, not the next week . . . maybe not ever!

Part Five

CHAPTER THIRTY-EIGHT

The Hollywood Humanitarian of the Year award dinner seemed to drag on and on. One long-winded speaker followed another and there seemed no escape for Ham, except into the deepest hiding places of his thoughts. If this had been a sequence in one of his films, he would have fired the director, edited it down to a quick montage and jump-cut to the closing title as soon as possible. He idly drummed his fingers on a plate and looked down at the puddled ruins of his dessert. Gesturing to a waiter for a fresh cup of coffee, he glanced out at the sea of faces, hoping to find one familiar one – that of his son. Jimmy could have shown up, he peevishly thought. He didn't owe him much, but he could have made an effort to be here tonight. When had he last seen him? Hell, why think of that now? He had tried, God knows he had tried, to get close to his son after he and Nita moved into their rebuilt home on Sierra View. That was the same summer Jimmie went to ROTC camp instead of working at the studio. When he finished playing soldiers he must have loafed away the rest of the summer until college started up again – at least, he never came near the studio.

Damn it! Ham thought. I tried to be a father. All those messages I sent and the phone calls Bob made for me. I never did get to tell him what was on my mind . . . the pressures on me. I wonder if I could ever have told him.

The fresh coffee arrived, just as bitter as the first cup, but holding enough heat to make it worth trying. It burned all the way down his throat, and he quenched the fire with cold Scotch.

The burning coffee made him remember burning memories . . . Nita telling him at last she had everything . . . well, nearly everything she had ever wanted . . . the man she loved, a beautiful son, a house like a palace . . . clothing, jewelry . . . but something was missing. She wanted to meet Jimmy, Ham's son, and was curious to know him better. For some reason Ham was not pushing things in that direction. Her husband must demand more from his son – demand that he come and meet his stepmother and half brother if there was to be hope for any kind of a relationship.

Even in the roaring electronic noise of the Palladium, Ham could hear Nita's voice as she kept up her harassment.

'It's nearly two years and I still haven't met your son! You haven't been strong enough with him, Ham. After all, the divorce and his leaving this house with his mother is all history now. I know he'll like Donny and I want them to meet. It isn't right that you let it go on this way! Do something about it, Ham. Get him to come here!'

How easy for her to command – and how hard for him to deliver. More notes, memos and phone calls went out, and when finally he saw Jimmy at the studio a few months later, neither of them said anything. Where were his guts, thought Ham, where were they when he needed them? He was getting sick and tired of the incessant way Nita harped on his getting Jimmy to the house to meet her. It was as though not being accepted by Ham's brother and sisters made her more insistent about this. He could not command them to change their attitudes – but his son was one person who should follow his father's orders!

'Damn it!' said Ham. He had knocked over the hot cup of coffee and it spilled out all over the tabletop. A waiter rushed over with a napkin, and he pulled his chair back while the damage was repaired. 'I'm lucky that missed going into my lap – it could have burned the bejesus out of my . . .' He stopped and looked suddenly down the length of the speaker's table. Somebody had just been introduced by Jessel and the echo of a name still came from the wall speakers. Ham felt a sudden pleasant kind of warmth, not from spilled coffee, but at hearing the name of Karen Lowell, a very beautiful vice-president of the Screen Actors Guild, who was standing up in response to Georgie's introduction.

She might have fallen right out of her extremely low-cut evening gown but for the dress designer and bra maker who had planned it to appear that way. Ham leaned forward as far as he could, narrowing his eyes to better see the woman standing at her place farther down the main table. He saw her in the glare of the spotlight and flashbulbs as each press photographer hoped he might be the one to catch a breast going public. No such luck, but Ham kept staring at her, letting the wonderful memories she brought rush back to him.

Hymie White, his East Coast talent scout, had spotted Karen Lowell as being the only good thing in a play that somehow got to Broadway one Friday evening and was mercifully put out of its misery by the critics before Saturday midnight. Photographs sent to the studio caught Ham in a good mood, and he approved a six-month contract with options.

She had the vitality of youth mixed with the kind of sensual innocence that Ham, who usually had been right over the years about such things, could tell would come across on the screen. The shining lips . . . the bright, soft, glowing redness of her hair . . . the body – oh, the body! A voice, low and vibrant, that spoke in promises. He ran her screen test in his screening room, then phoned Casting to get in touch with him the minute she checked in on the lot and then he buzzed the projectionist up in the booth.

'Mike, how many more reels of dailies?'

'The last two just came up from the lab, Mr. Robbins. About fifteen to twenty more minutes should do it,' came back through the squawk box.

'Okay, while that's on, rewind that New York test of Miss Lowell and then run it again for me.'

'Right, Chief,' said the projectionist, happy to have another good look at that terrific broad who was giving him one hell of a hard-on. He figured the Chief was getting the same message. During the rewind he called out of the booth to some assistant film editors hanging around to pick up their dailies and invited them into his hot little room to see through the viewing port what was turning the boss on. What a face and figure! They all crowded in and squeezed against the window.

A week passed and she arrived at the studio and was everything in person the screen had promised. Ham felt the old juices start to flow the moment the head of Casting brought her to his office. Within two minutes after introductions were completed, the two of them were alone in his big office.

'It says on your contract that your name is Karen Lowell. May I call you Karen, since we both work for the same company?'

'Why certainly, Mr. Robbins.'

'Please don't be so formal, Karen . . . my name's Ham.'

He could be utterly charming when he chose to be – and this was a time for charm. He reached out to take her hand and showed her to a comfortable chair.

'Your test showed a real talent, Karen. Hymie White saw you in that stinker of a show, said you were the only worthwhile one on the whole stage.'

She laughed – the full frank laugh of an assured young woman who enjoyed a compliment, yet knew it all was part of another play in another kind of theater.

'Thanks. The show really was horrible. How it ever made it to New York, I'll never know. I'm really surprised your nice Mr. White stayed through the first five minutes before I came on. It was good experience for me, though, even if it was only for two performances. It was my first real casting break, and luckily for me he did stay – at least long enough to make things happen so that now I'm here.'

That face, Ham thought. So young – and with such wise eyes. She makes the dames around here look like tired reruns we put together in Wardrobe and Make-up. Clara Bow? No. She's completely herself and nobody else, somebody special I want to know better. He found himself taking an interest in her that he rarely took in actors, who to him had always been just mobile surfaces for bouncing light into cameras, sound into microphones – and bait to lure audiences into theaters. She told him something of her background, how she had wanted to be an actress ever since she could walk and talk.

'Are you married, Karen? Excuse me for asking you, but that's the kind of question you're going to hear a lot. This is strange business and – '

'No, no . . .' She laughed, and Ham felt happy again just to hear the delightful sound. 'No, I've nearly gone down the aisle a few times, but, well . . . I wanted to concentrate on becoming as good an actress as I could be, and I wasn't ready to be tied down. Maybe one day . . . maybe after I've won an Oscar.' She laughed again, a deep throaty laugh. 'Maybe his name won't even be Oscar.'

It was Ham's turn to laugh.

'An Oscar?' You think that winning an Academy Award is the answer and when that's taken care of you've had everything? Hell – all that does is make you want more and more, and you get stuck on the craziest merry-go-round in the world. The only way you ever leave it is if somebody throws you off – or you jump and break your neck – or if the damn thing stops turning . . . which it never does! Don't wait for that, Karen, if what you're looking for is real happiness.'

He wondered where this sudden rush of insight and honesty was coming from. It was completely out of character. He looked at the beautiful smiling girl sitting across from him in his office. The light coming through the picture window had taken on the luminous glow of a California dusk. The things it did to her hair! He must be at least twenty to twenty-five years older than this girl. Ever since she came into the room it was as though a camera had gone into reverse and he was once more the virile and desiring man he had always been. This was how he had felt for a while with Irene, when she allowed it – and of course with Nita, who now and then got on his nerves with all her demands.

This girl, though, this lovely creature, so fresh and unspoiled . . . He wanted to know her better . . . much better.

'Karen, all your talk about winning an Oscar. Have you actually ever seen one of those gold bookends?'

'Only in the papers and magazines,' she admitted. 'They mean so much, though, coming from people in your own business telling you they think you're the best – the very best. There couldn't be a greater compliment than that. Maybe one day I might feel differently, but right now I'd rather hold an Oscar in my hand than just about anything else I can think of!'

Ham almost started to suggest there was something very much better than an Oscar she could hold in her lovely hand, but caught himself, swallowed a smile and said, 'Come on, you can do just that. In fact, you can hold two Oscars, one in each hand – and if you're real clever with your toes, you can even hold four of them!'

He took her arm with excitement suddenly mixed with a little guilt as he thought of Nita waiting for him at home. He put her out of his mind. He had never cheated on her, at least . . . not yet. He led Karen through the door and past his secretary in the outer office.

'Wait a minute for me in the hall, Karen,' Ham said to the young actress in a relaxed yet formal voice. 'I have to give Bob an important memo, then I'll be right with you.'

After she closed the door, Ham spoke in a low voice to his executive secretary.

'Bob, get Mrs. Robbins on the phone. Tell her I'm running a very important sneak preview in . . . in Oxnard. I don't think she knows where the hell that is. I'm eating dinner with the producer and editor on the way there. We may have to come back to the studio after we see the reactions and recut some sequences right away to get the print shipped in time for its release date . . . so I don't know how late I'll be . . . Okay?'

'Yes, Mr. Robbins. Okay,' said Bob Silver without the slightest change in his expression. It was the very first time the boss had pulled this on his second wife. Some things never change, but whatever the Chief did at his sneak previews was his own business. At least he had taste – she really was some dish!

Ham took Karen's arm and guided her out of the executive office building, down a dimly lit walk beside a long wall to a closed gate, which he unlocked. They went through and were walking on the main lot as he began telling her something about this place.

'It's big . . . damned big . . . maybe the largest studio in the industry. Twenty sound stages, and we're putting up a few more whenever my brother gets around to okaying the cost. I want to leave up all the expensive standing sets I can, but that takes more stage space then we have when everything's shooting. Hell, the bigger the business, the bigger the headaches! It isn't the kind of fun now that it used to be.'

'Very little is,' she said. 'Fun is different things as you grow and change. We can't always be little boys or girls with the pleasures of children all our lives. A big part of growing up is facing new experiences and appreciating them in different ways.'

Ham was concerned. This girl was a thinker – she was smart. He could never recall having a happy experience with people like that. The smart ones made him remember he had never gone past the fourth grade and that there were great gaps in his learning he wished he had filled years ago. Never mind that school-of-hard-knocks crap – there were plenty of things he really didn't know, although nobody would ever hear that from him!

They were at the bungalow near the end of the dark row of sprawling office buildings and empty dressing rooms standing across from a long line of silent sound stages.

There was a light on over the door of the little structure, which looked so oddly out of place beside all the large buildings. Ham pulled out some keys and unlocked the door. A studio security car slowly rolled past and the officer driving it deliberately turned his head away, noticing nothing as he went on around the corner, vanishing into the darkness.

'Now stand right here, Karen. Close your eyes, and don't open them until I tell you to.'

She followed his instructions, and he reached around the side of the open door for the light switches and pulled them all on.

'Step inside now . . . Open your eyes!'

She gasped in amazement, and he stood beside her like a proud little boy showing off his most prized possessions.

'What is this, Fort Knox or King Tut's tomb?' Karen exclaimed. She saw rows of bright golden figures standing on a long table. The walls of the room seemed a solid mass of silver, bronze, gold and chrome tributes.

Karen walked over to look at some of the intricate pieces of metal and then turned to another wall made up of hundreds of still photographs mounted behind glass panels reaching from floor to ceiling. They included pictures of every celebrity ever to visit the studio. Nearly every shot managed to show the smiling face and well-turned-out body of Ham Robbins shaking a hand, gripping a shoulder, hugging a waist or pointing a finger. It was all there, frozen flat for posterity. This was the Trophy Room, something like the great hall of a medieval castle with its array of captured banners, shields and lances, recalling battles won and enemies crushed.

She looked around once again at this pharaoh's treasure chamber. There on the table, surrounded by a semicircle of Oscars, was the prized Irving Thalberg Award for Best Producer of the Year. When Irving was still alive he was one of the few executives from another studio that Ham genuinely liked – because he had never worked on this lot and never would, so he was no threat. Irving was always welcome here; his boss, L. B. Mayer was definitely not. One emperor at a time in the throne room was quite enough, and that effectively kept out men like Harry Cohn, Selznick, Goldwyn, Jack L. Warner, Goetz, Schulberg and many others of like power and prestige – unless there was something or someone they had that Ham wanted badly enough: a star, a director, a story they couldn't whip but Robbins International could. Then there were the times it was impossible to avoid coming together due to an industry crisis. There seemed to be more and more of these recently.

A very fancy piece of enameled metal caught Karen's eye. The Order of the Aztec Eagle (Third Class) bestowed upon Ham by some exhibitors' outfit south of the border. Imagine that . . . Third Class . . . fine good neighbors they were! Then the long heavy table running almost the entire length of the room bearing the battalion of Academy Awards – the Oscars.

The blank-faced little golden men stood shoulder to shoulder, each on its ebony pedestal holding its long sword like an outrageous phallus. Ham stood in the middle of the room enjoying the reactions of the girl, who was utterly overwhelmed. Just as Hollywood long has had its yes-men, so too must there be such things as this yes-room, where a man facing deep doubts could come to be sure, absolutely sure, that here he would find the golden pot of absolute approval and acceptance sitting at the end of his very own private Technicolor rainbow.

Ham reached over to pick up two of the Academy Awards. They were damn heavy – the little bastards must be stuffed with lead!

'Here, take one Oscar for your right hand and another for the left one. Someday you'll get a dozen of them all your own.'

She took the weighted gold figures, held them tightly a moment, then brought each statuette up in front of her face, and two bright spots of reflected gold light shone on her cheeks. She leaned over and impulsively kissed Ham full on his lips.

'Thank you, Ham . . . thank you for letting me live this silly little girl's dream of mine. I really hope one day I will win my very own . . . and . . .'

Her hands opened and both Oscars fell to the carpeted floor, where they hit with soft thuds as Ham put his arms around her waist, drew her body close and kissed her with a passion he had felt building ever since he had first been alone with this beautiful golden girl. Suddenly, as he held her tightly against his body, he felt her hands fumble briefly with his fly, and then she was holding tightly to an award she was about to win even before she had ever appeared in a picture.

With one arm still around her, he managed to reach over to the wall switch and turn down the room light. Quickly, without a word she let him go, undressed herself and began to help him out of his clothes. She had every bit of the magnificent body she had promised through the thin dress that now was draped over the corner of the desk beside his pants. For a man with all his experience, he suddenly felt all fumbling thumbs, and he was grateful for her help in getting out of the last of his clothing.

The sexless little golden Oscars held their swords in gleaming hands and stood facing the couple, who were just as naked now as they were – but with only a single sword between them. Karen drew him closer, and slowly they lay down beside each other on the soft carpet, their bed, the floor of the Trophy Room.

He began stroking her breasts, feeling her nipples harden to his touch. Her hands started working their wonders, running down his spine, moving around to grip his penis, which had become ramrod stiff. They moved their bodies in a slow rhythm and kissed again and again, tongues darting in and out of each other's mouth like little pink eels finding pink caverns. He had almost forgotten sensations like these could exist!

She pulled away, moved her head up to kiss the lobe of his ear and then sat up and leaned over to take the most sensitive part of his throbbing body into her beautiful mouth and do beautiful things with it. He was humiliated that he came so fast, it happened without his willing it or wanting it to happen just yet. He looked up, just seeing the bright round heads of the Oscars looking down over the table . . . golden voyeurs, their blank faces laughing . . . laughing. He sensed that she too was smiling, then she stroked him again and again until once more he was ready gently to get on top as she rolled on her back, lovely legs spread wide, inviting him to enter paradise.

The lights of a security patrol car passed. A flashlight flickered over the shuttered windows and the officer on duty noted that the inside lights were out and all was well. Just how well he could not possibly have imagined as he drove on around the stage corner.

On the soft floor of the Trophy Room, Karen thrust her body up and up, moaning joyfully from the peaks of her pleasure. Both her arms stretched far out on the carpet to either side of their bodies and she touched the two fallen Oscars, which lay where they had been dropped an ecstasy ago. Her hands clutched them both again and again and she lifted the heavy little statuettes high in the air where she could look at them over Ham's sweating shoulders. The golden metal gleamed in the dim light coming through the nearly closed shutters.

Ham carefully raised himself, rolled over on his back and lay beside her on the floor. He looked up at the two Academy Awards she still held at arm's length above them and laughed, feeling a kind of relaxed happiness he had not known for a long time, and said the very first thing to come into his mind.

'. . . And the winners are . . .!'

She stood in the brilliant Palladium spotlight, looking every bit as lovely and desirable as he remembered her. A talented woman who had finally won her own Oscar and been nominated for three others, a bright, witty and intelligent person who had earned respect and admiration – not just because she was beautiful. Time indeed had been more than good to Karen, that astonishing hair, the fine body, the way she held her proud head. Imagine – now she was a power in the Screen Actors' Guild!

Ham put both hands flat on the table and leaned forward to better see her standing there, nodding her head slightly in response to the applause rippling through the audience. She turned, and there was a tender smile on her face as she looked directly at Ham. The spotlight kicked a bright golden gleam off the wide band she wore on a finger of her left hand, and Ham wondered if the lucky man's name had turned out to be Oscar. The light moved away, and she sat down and was lost to his view, with only the echoes of memory remaining.

He closed his eyes and heard another voice, an unpleasant one, the voice of Nita grown petulant . . . the question she had asked over and over until he could no longer bear to hear it.

'Ham! When is your son going to come here to our house and meet me? You've got to do something about it – now!'

CHAPTER THIRTY-NINE

'Nita, lay off, damn it, lay off! I already told you that Bob Silver reached Jimmy by phone yesterday and the kid is taking his final exams at college. He promised to come out to the studio and see me just as soon as they're finished, then I'll ask him to come here and meet you and Donny. In the meantime, please change the subject. You're starting to sound like a broken record!'

She lay on her side of the oversize bed looking at Ham, who sat up trying to read some story treatments. He was grateful all these submissions of books, ideas, plays and other crap had been boiled down to single-page outlines so he didn't have to wade through a billion words. All these condensed story lines were bad enough on his eyes and patience without having Nita butt in on his concentration. Because of her he had to start reading again from the beginning on this one for maybe the fifth time. The story department had sent him a whole sheaf of them, and as usual it was urgent they get his reaction right away since it could take months of negotiations if anything looked worthwhile. His mind kept wandering off the typed pages.

'I don't know why the kid fights me on this, Nita. It's long past time he did this for me . . . I mean for us.' He looked over to see her frown. She sat up in bed, the sheet and blanket sliding down to reveal her dark shoulders and the breasts of which she was so proud. Ham felt a stirring down beneath the pile of story outlines. Not now, he thought, not now. There's just too much to get done today and there's no time. A bunch of freeloaders were due for Sunday tennis in a few hours and he didn't want any extra aches in his back when he served the ball. Maybe later, after the game, the screening and the buffet, would come the dessert – up here in bed, with Nita doing the serving . . . that is, if he still felt like it.

'Your whole damn family acts as though I was some slut you picked up on the street! They ignore me, run away whenever

407

I come near. Your sisters pretend I don't exist! Your own son hasn't done a thing about coming here to meet me – and that brother of yours, that miserable Maurie, he despises me and doesn't even bother to hide the way he feels! Tell me, what did I ever do to them that they should all treat me worse than dirt? Tell me!'

Ham shook his head and tossed a synopsis on the floor. There was no picture in the damn thing, just a lot of words some writer had stuck together about a family breaking up. Why did they keep bothering him with those tired old story lines? He wanted his company to put out money-making entertainment, good solid happy stuff – musicals, comedies, believable fun with maybe a little serious drama here and there – nothing like this pile of junk. The story department kept shoving these depressing problem stories at him. People had enough problems of their own. They went to the movies to get away from their troubles. He had an idea.

'Nita, do you want to help me with something?' He hoped to get her on another subject that would keep her mind occupied and her mouth shut. 'Here, read some of these story treatments for me. Later on tell me what you think of them, and if you find any you think I ought to read, we'll talk about them. I'd like a woman's viewpoint for a change. I only look at them from my angle, and it's a race between going blind and going nuts from reading so much. You could be a big help to me.'

She felt flattered, not realizing he was only trying to get her busy and off his back.

'Of course I'll help you. I'll bet I'm as good a judge as anybody. Here, give me some of them to read right now.' After all the pictures she had seen in the El Paso theater and the movie magazines she read even now, she felt she knew as much as some of Ham's experts about what made a good movie.

Soon the only sound in the bedroom was an occasional rattle of paper as pages were turned. Ham felt more relaxed now that he thought Nita's mind was on something else – but it was not to be for long. Suddenly Nita put down the synopsis she was reading, looked over at Ham and spoke angrily.

'I want you to tell your son that it's time he got to know me and his brother. It's wrong for you not to insist more strongly on his coming here. You've got to do something about it – now! Enough time has passed and he's still not making a move. You're his father. Can't you tell him what you want him to do ... or are you going to let him keep running all over you!'

Ham wearily shook his head, looked at Nita, then threw back the bedcovers.

'I'll do whatever I can. Right now, though, I'm going to the toilet. I'll finish reading some of this stuff in there. I only wish it was on softer paper.'

He was halfway across the bedroom when Nita thought of more to say.

'I can't see why you aren't running the company! You've got more brains than Maurie. He doesn't know the first thing about production and how hard you have to work making pictures so he can be so rich and important! It's unfair for him to be the president of Robbins International! You should be, Ham, and if you don't do something about it one day ... well, you're absolutely – '

He stopped at the door, looked back and broke into her monologue.

'Let me go to the bathroom, Nita. I can only hold it in for so long! Please keep all your ideas about our company to yourself. I've got enough problems just running the studio without taking on the whole fucking company, too. I know Maurie's a pain in the ass – that may go along with being the president of any company. He takes plenty from everybody – the theater owners, distributors, the government, banks, the stockholders. You've never been to a stockholders' annual meeting. You can have that pleasure. It's like being the piece of meat they throw to the lions for lunch. Maurie's welcome to all of it! Someday when I haven't got a cramp, I'll tell you all about the great movie business, where if you aren't getting screwed you're getting sued! Now please get back to reading those treatments and let me go to the crapper before I do it right here on the carpet!'

'Mr. Robbins, I have your son on the phone. Yes, I'll tell him to hold.' Bob Silver flipped the line switch. 'Jimmy, your father will be right with you. How are things going at school?'

'All right, I hope. Final exams ended yesterday and I think I did okay, but you can never – '

His father's voice cut in.

'Hello, Jimmy. How are you? I know you've been busy with exams so I haven't called. How about coming out to the studio for lunch next week ... say Monday at noon?'

Jimmy hesitated. He had seen his father a few times since

his marriage to Nita, but they were inconclusive, restrained and uncomfortable meetings that led nowhere and were mercifully brief. He knew exactly why his father was calling – enough broad hints had been dropped during their other times together – but it wasn't just his lack of desire to see Nita that held him back. It was facing his father again after all that had happened – the utter lack of respect he had shown for his son's feelings. It also bothered him to have to visit the place that had been his home until he and his mother were shoved out. Either he would evade this once again, or it was time to try for a new beginning. The past could never be completely forgotten – but perhaps it shouldn't be remembered so damn often either. He had made his decision and now answered his father, trying to put warmth into his voice that he still didn't quite feel.

'Dad, I'd like that. I'm sorry we've only seen each other a couple of times this year, what with school and you being so busy or out of town.'

'Good, good,' said Ham, happy that his son sounded so friendly. He decided to take the next step right now and not bother with a Monday meeting at the studio. 'Jimmy, there's something I want to talk over with you. I'm sure you know what it is. Instead of coming out here on Monday, I'd like you to make it on Sunday at the house. We've both let so much slide along and it's time we tried to change things. It can only make everybody much happier and life a lot easier.'

'Dad, I know. Nobody really wants it to go on this way. It's taken a while, but maybe now's the time for me to meet . . . uh . . . to meet . . .' He stopped, tongue-tied at the thought of her name.

'Nita, her name is Nita,' gently reminded Ham.

'Yes, Nita. Well, I'd like to do what you asked and also I want to meet Donny.'

'Good. Be at the house next Sunday around eleven-thirty and we'll get together, then later after lunch we can play some tennis. I know you'll like Nita when you get to know her – and just wait until you see your cute little brother! I'm really very glad you're coming, Jimmy. I'll see you next Sunday,' said Ham, feeling quite happy as he said good-bye and hung up.

Back in the apartment on Doheney Drive, Jimmy went into the kitchen, where his mother was making lunch. He told her what he had decided to do.

'I hope it won't upset you, Mom, but I think the time has

410

come for me to meet ... uh ... my stepmother ... and the little boy. I know you aren't happy about it, and I can't really blame you, knowing what I do. Part of me doesn't want to meet either of them at all, but it's something I think I should do. I haven't been happy about my relationship with Dad, and it's been getting no better. This could help things a great deal, even if all that happens is that he stops nagging me so much to do it.'

Irene stood absolutely still in the middle of the kitchen. She bit her lip, but she listened to Jimmy and let him go on talking.

'I really want to work at the studio next summer. I love the business, and an important part of it is seeing my father out there. It can't be avoided, and I don't want it to be. I expect to see a lot of him, and there's no reason why we shouldn't get along. Anything will be an improvement over the way things are.'

Irene reached out to take hold of the table edge. Suddenly she felt dizzy and distressed, but it quickly passed. She was terribly unhappy at what her son was going to do, and was about to object when she recalled her father's words. Jimmy is Ham's son too. No, she would say nothing to stop him, but she felt anger and despair, which came out as she spoke.

'Jimmy, you'll have to make up your own mind about this, but I can never forgive your father or forget what he did. I can't help it. I will always hate that unspeakable miserable woman!' She managed to stop before the tears came and regained control of herself, turning to put some plates on the table. 'Just be careful of her, be very careful. Anybody who would do what she did, take a husband away from his wife, cannot be trusted. She would stop at nothing! All right – meet her, but remember what I've told you and be careful, very careful!'

'Look, Mom, all I'm going to do is say hello, and that'll be it. Nothing can ever change the way I feel about you, Mom, so don't worry, please! I honestly don't want very much to meet her at all, but it's only going to be for a little while, and it will keep Dad from bringing it up to me all of the time. That's all there's going to be to the whole thing.'

Irene couldn't help feeling as she did, and on Sunday morning pretended to sleep quite late. She could not bear to see her son leave the apartment at eleven to drive to the house where once she lived and for a while had been so happy. After she heard him leave she got out of bed and made up her mind to think of other things ... at least for a few hours.

411

Jimmy drove up to the familiar gates, pressed a button set on a polished brass plate and waited until a man he knew from the studio police department came out and recognized him. The heavy gates rolled aside so he could drive in. The grounds had hardly changed at all. There was the tennis court, just as he remembered it . . . the swimming pool, the gardens and the putting green. He went up the hill, pulled around the Spanish fountain, which had been set in front of the house in the middle of a wide circle, and for a moment sat in his car looking at where he had once lived. It was different, quite different. The entire front of the house had been rebuilt and no longer was a classic Spanish colonial. It was . . . different. Now there were columns and white statues and a kind of Greek style about it. The man who pulled open the front door hadn't changed, though. It was his father and he was smiling, his hand outstretched to greet his son as he got out of the car and came toward him.

'Jimmy, I'm so glad you're here. Come in. I want you to meet Nita.'

They entered the house, and there across the front hall, so very different from what he remembered, he could see a woman standing against the far wall. Coming into the dark room from the bright outside sunshine, he was unable at first to see her clearly.

'Nita, this is my son, Jimmy.'

Now his eyes were adjusting to the dim light and he could see her come toward him. Her hand was warm and soft, and he hoped she would not notice that his palm was sweating. She was a light-complexioned woman with deep red hair not quite reaching to her shoulders. He could see the alert brown eyes, the half-smile on her oval face, and he wondered how old she must be . . . in her twenties? Maybe – it was hard to tell. He was aware his father was staring at him with great intensity, and seemed about to say something just as Nita spoke.

'I've heard so many nice things about you from your father, Jimmy, and I've looked forward to meeting you. I do hope we will become good friends.'

He started to say he was glad to meet her too, but his father interrupted, a nervous quality in his voice, which seemed suddenly to have grown a bit hoarse.

'You've got to meet Donny right away, Jimmy. Wait until you see him. He's such a big boy now – real big for his age – and so bright. Come on, let's go up to his room.'

412

Jimmy saw the strange, almost angry look that came over Nita's face when his father said that about Donny. What was it? That he was big for his age? How could that have upset Nita so much? They went upstairs and down the hall toward a room he remembered well. The very same one that once had been his. Everything, though, was so different – the walls, furniture, lights ... the sounds of a child coming through the door ... Now it was Donny's room. Ham opened the door, and he ran to them as they came in, wrapping his arms tightly around his father's knees ... their father's knees. Jimmy looked around his old room. Now it was a little boy's nursery, and he found it hard to remember what it had looked like before.

'Donny, meet your big brother, Jimmy. Give him a hug and a big handshake,' their father said, and the little boy toddled over to Jimmy. Jimmy kneeled down so he could look in his eyes as he took the small hands in both his large ones. Yes, he certainly was a big boy – and a very good looking one, too.

'Hello, Donny. It's so nice to meet you.' He felt foolish, not quite knowing what to say, and was aware his father was standing there looking intently at them. Why did that trouble him so much? It was as though his father was waiting for him to do or say something wrong so he could criticize him in front of Nita and Donny. He looked again at the little boy. It was almost like seeing pictures of himself when he was about ... how old? ... three? Donny was nearly two, his father had told him, but he seemed older than that. His face, eyes, so much of him looked just as he did when he was little, and there was something about his mouth and eyes, so much like their father, who kept staring down at them so silently, so intently. It was fun, though, Jimmy thought, to be an only child and then suddenly to have a little brother like this ... well, a half brother, anyhow. It was a very nice feeling, and he hugged Donny, who hugged him back.

A wave of unexplained nausea and heat swept over Nita, who stood looking at them from beside the door. Ever since Ham's son had entered this house she had felt the increased building up of tension and a painful cramping of her stomach muscles. She had desperately tried to be warm, welcoming and nice, but there was something about Jimmy that she had to know immediately before he remained one more moment in her home. Ham had never told her certain important things, and now it was up to her to fill in the blanks. She swayed slightly, gripped a chair back and spoke in such an

413

unnaturally tight voice that Ham looked over in alarm.

'Donny is a Pisces. What is your sign, Jimmy?'

At first Jimmy did not understand what Nita had asked him. Pisces . . . oh, yes . . . He wasn't interested in that stuff, but remembered seeing something in a newspaper about it now and then.

'My sign?' he said and looked over at his father, whose face was clouded with sudden anger.

'You know,' said Nita, 'the sign you were born under – your astrological sign. Everybody has one. It's a very important part of your whole life. You really should know. Now tell me, when were you born?' She already knew most of the answer, but there were things she had to learn as quickly as possible.

'Oh, I see,' Jimmy said, although he really did not. 'Nineteen-seventeen, right here in Los Angeles. On the twenty-second of September. I really don't remember a thing about it, though I was right there at the time.' His feeble attempt at humor must have failed dismally, since Nita didn't change her strange look and his father now seemed to have no expression at all. Well, at least Donny had laughed.

'No, no,' Nita said in a harsh voice. 'The important part is the time of day you were born – the hour. When was that? Just when on September twenty-second were you born?' The nausea seemed to increase, and she felt a flash of heat that brought sweat to her forehead.

'Oh, I'm sorry. I didn't understand. Dad, didn't you tell me once it was eight-thirty in the morning? You and Mom had been up all night waiting for me to show up and . . .' He stopped and looked at Nita's face. Her jaw tightened, her lips were clenched between her sharp white teeth and a strange intensity came into her eyes that seemed almost to pierce him through. Something was troubling her deeply, and her mouth moved with unspoken words. Donny's face was that of a frightened little boy and he let go of Jimmy's hand and went over to his father, putting his arm around his knees. Nita had closed her eyes and there was absolute silence in the room.

After a few moments, Nita looked down at Jimmy, seated alone now in the middle of the room on the floor. The change in her face now was complete – a volcanic calm before the eruption – and then it came in a voice that flowed like lava.

'September . . . the twenty-second of September . . . 1917 at eight-thirty A.M.! Ham, you never told me your son was born then. You knew – you must have known. I could feel the

414

dreadful vibrations the minute he . . .' She stopped speaking and drew a deep breath, trying to control her outrage. 'You must have known our signs were in absolute conflict. It is something nobody can ever change. It can never be different!' A sharp look at the astounded boy sitting on the floor and she almost shouted, 'You and I will never get along!' That was all she said. The rest of it, all the complicated convoluted reasoning, remained in her mind. She had prepared so many charts and graphs in every possible combination over the past weeks, hoping that whatever vibrations she might receive when finally she met Jimmy would be good ones and cancel out any unfavorable factors. It was not to be. Again she was assailed by the turmoil of negative vibrations and feelings that had swirled around her ever since Jimmy had stepped into the house . . . into her house. The past was forcing itself back and had to be stopped before any terrible forces it unleashed could destroy all her hard-won gains. Never mind if she had been the one insisting Ham get him up here. She had to be with him, face-to-face, before she could be finally sure of something like this. She bit out her words.

'You are absolutely positive about that hour, the day, September, that you are on the cusp of Libra?'

Jimmy was completely puzzled at what this woman was saying to him and looked at his father for some kind of support. Ham stood silently with Donny, stricken and humiliated, his face drained to a pasty white.

'One thing I'm sure of is my birthday. I've never thought much about the hour or anything more, and I don't know a thing about . . . what did you say? Libra?'

Ham managed to speak at last, his voice made hoarse with anger and growing embarrassment.

'Nita, what's this stupid talk all about? What the hell difference does it make when Jimmy was born or the time of day? We were having a wonderful time here until you opened up with that zodiac crap of yours . . .' He stopped as Nita stared coldly at him, then she turned and walked out of the room, slamming the door. It was so unexpected, so unbelievable, that Ham could not react for a minute and stood with his mouth hanging open in the middle of a sentence. Then the humiliation and shock hit him as he watched Jimmy rise to his feet and without a word leave the room to go down the stairs and out to his car. Ham was unable to think of what to say. He pushed Donny away, and the child began to cry in a high little voice. Ham rushed down the stairs, trying to catch Jimmy before he drove off. He remembered wrenching the front door open, going outside and shouting after him as the motor started and the car moved off around the circle. What was it he called out? Something stupid . . . something shouted by a fool who had worked so hard and long to bring together his son and his wife – then watched as she deliberately destroyed in a moment the delicate bridge he had so painfully built between them. She was the one who had insisted on, had demanded this meeting, and then she had deliberately humiliated him in front of his son! What was it he had shouted as the car drove away? . . . Oh, yes, now it came back to him.

'Don't go . . . don't go! Come back and say-good-bye to your father! Say good-bye . . . good-bye . . .'

The memory burst out from the dark place where he had hidden it so many years ago. He had cried out for his son to come back, to forgive him, help him, somehow to try again. All he could do was stand helplessly in the driveway looking at where the car vanished around the curve. He heard it stop at the gates far down the hill, then roar out into the street.

Ham slowly turned to go back inside the house and was sure he saw the curtain moving in the small upstairs window over the front door. He knew then that Nita had been looking down as he stood calling out to his son, crying out from his wilderness – looking down and mocking him. For a moment more he stood outside his house, and for the very first time felt he was really beginning to know the woman he had married.

For the first summer in many years Jimmy did not work at the studio. He spent a few weeks at Fort Ord in Central California on maneuvers with his college ROTC unit, then drove down to San Diego with some friends whose family had a home on Coronado Island. Ham surprised himself by missing Jimmy around the studio that summer, but tried not to think of him because his next thoughts were always of his outrage at Nita when he had gone back into the house that day after Jimmy drove away. He remembered how he went upstairs and pulled open the bedroom door to find Nita hunched up over her table, astrological charts scattered in front of her. Without a word he walked over and swept up all the sheets and tore them into shreds, which he stuffed into a wastebasket. She looked up in shock as he walked out of the room, and that night, and for nearly the entire following week, they

416

slept in separate bedrooms. She came to him late one night where he slept in the guest room, and like a little girl begged his forgiveness, hugged and kissed him, and soon they were back in the same bedroom and in the same bed – though not to sleep for another few hours. Several times he meant to discuss what had happened during Jimmy's visit, but too much interfered and he kept putting it off. There was a sudden wildcat strike of lab technicians that snarled up all the production schedules, then a rash of suspicious fires where only quick work by the combined studio and city fire departments kept the whole back lot from becoming an inferno. Soon the zodiac episode slipped back in his memory and was stored in the attic of his mind among other unpleasant things someday to be cleaned out and carted away.

Early in September Bob Silver buzzed Ham to tell him that Jimmy was in the outer office. This time his son did not have to sit and wait.

'How are you? Did you have a good time this summer? How was it up at Fort Ord?' Ham piled up his questions and threw them out all at once.

'Easy, Dad, not so fast and furious. The answer is fine . . . yes . . . and rough. I enjoyed doing nothing down at Coronado, loafing on the beach and getting sunburned after running all over those hills for the ROTC. I feel just great and all ready to get back into the school grind again.'

Neither of them spoke for a few moments and Ham was rather nervous, but pleased his son had come to see him. It was Jimmy who finally broke in on the uncomfortable silence.

'I really enjoyed meeting Donny. How is he?'

'Absolutely wonderful,' Ham replied. 'He keeps asking for you. I hope you'll see him soon again.' They did not mention Nita, and Ham decided that for now it was just as well. He had an idea, and decided to take the initiative while Jimmy was here with him.

'How would you like to come up for tennis next Sunday afternoon?' I'm having some great players and I know you'll enjoy being there.' He did not tell Jimmy that Nita would be out of town all that week and perhaps the next one as well. Her father was seriously ill and she had gone to be with him in El Paso, much as she hated the thought of returning there, even for her father. There was absolutely no reason that Nita should have to know that Jimmy and his bad vibrations from the wrong side of the zodiac would be anywhere near the

417

house. Ham frankly did not expect Jimmy to accept his invitation and was pleased when he said he would be there.

'Forty-love!' said the tall man in the far court. He picked up a ball and walked to the baseline and in one smashing serve ended game, set and match.

'Bill, come here,' Ham shouted over at his guest, who made the victory look as though he easily could have won with either hand tied behind his back and no gut in his racket. He walked over to the sidelines where Ham and the others were sitting.

'Jimmy, meet Bill Tilden, one of the greatest tennis players in the whole world!'

His son was impressed and excited. Who hadn't heard of William Tilden, winner of more matches at Wimbledon than anybody could count! He had been thrilled watching the tall graceful man win game after game, and hoped he could learn something just watching this master of the sport. Only five years earlier, Tilden had turned professional after dominating amateur play all over the world. Getting him here was a personal triumph for Ham and Sandy Nichols, his unobtrusive tennis casting director. The courtside guest house was crowded with dozens of the Hollywood tennis crowd, all hoping they would have a chance at a game with Bill Tilden so they could talk about it to anybody who would listen.

For serious tennis they all went to the Pacific Southwest or to a select group of clubs scattered around town, but here at Ham's place the game was for fun, drinks, business talk, good food and letting the host win his games – then going up to the screening room for a new movie. Pancho Gonzales was a regular, and whenever Don Budge was in town he came by. On this lovely Sunday afternoon William T. Tilden, Jr., was immaculate as usual in his long white flannel trousers. He did not approve of the shorts worn by the other players; while his legs were as well proportioned as theirs, he came from a more formal time and place. Actually, he could have been in kilts, jodhpurs or knickers and still would have beaten the pants off anybody present when it came to tennis.

Ham had a sudden idea he hoped might improve his next match. He sent the Greek running up to his room to bring down a pair of long white flannel pants like the ones Tilden was wearing. He went into a dressing room next to the swimming pool and emerged in white-trousered glory to play doubles as Tilden's partner. The white-pants team won love

418

game, set and match from the overwhelmed competition on the other side of the net in their skimpy shorts.

'From now on, Bill, this is what I wear to play tennis!' said Ham, filled with pride and pleasure at their easy victory, secretly knowing he helped very little to bring it about, pants or no pants.

Jimmy sat on the sidelines all afternoon watching the others play as the shadows slowly lengthened across the court. He had his racket in and out of the press a dozen times, but never got a call. His sneakers were still as clean as when he had bought them a few days before, and he wondered if he would ever dirty them on the court. At last it was time for a final set, and Ham waved to his son to get out in the last doubles game with Sandy and another pair of players who also had been waiting all afternoon. Jimmy served, faulted, then double-faulted.

'Love-fifteen,' said Sandy. 'Take it easy, Jimmy . . . take it easy. Just swing relaxed.'

He swung, very relaxed, and the ball sailed over the high fence out into Sierra View Drive, where they could hear it bouncing against the cars parked in the street.

'I ought to take up basketball,' said Jimmy. He got ready for another serve, but now it was so late and dark that it was almost impossible to see the court lines.

'Someday your old man has to put lights up out here. We're never able to finish a game this time of year. I'm sorry, Jimmy,' said Sandy to his doubles partner. 'Maybe I could give you a few lessons. You have a good basic swing, you're young and there's no reason you couldn't become a pretty good tennis player. Look at your father – he really caught on fast.'

'Thanks, Sandy. I may take you up on that. I'll have some time before school starts and perhaps we could – '

Sandy was called over to the sideline by Ham, so he never heard the rest of what Jimmy had been saying.

'Hey, Sandy, I read in the morning paper that René Lacoste is coming to California. Find out if he'll be in L.A. and invite him here next Sunday. Okay, everybody – get something to eat, then we'll go up and run a film. Jimmy, have another hamburger and some root beer – or are you drinking real beer now that you're a college man? I hope you can come back next week, and this time I'll make sure you get to play.' Ham felt quite safe inviting him. Nita had phoned that morning to say she would be staying another week with her father and that he was improving but still weak.

'Jimmy,' he said to his son as he reached for a sandwich, 'when does school start up again? Any chance you'll still have time to work in the production department?'

'I'm afraid not, Dad. Only two more weeks are left and then back to the grind. I'll be a junior then and in two more years they'll turn me loose on the world. Maybe next summer I can come out, so hold my job open after I finish with the ROTC.'

Jimmy now felt so at ease with his father after this pleasant afternoon that he brought up what had been on his mind ever since his father invited him here.

'Dad, how is Nita? I'm terribly sorry she was so upset about that . . . that thing. You know I didn't pick the day or the time to get born and – '

'Uh . . . forget it.' interrupted his father in a very low voice. hoping nobody overheard them. 'Forget it. Hell, it's not your fault you were born on the cusp of something or other, whatever that means. If anybody's to blame at all, it was me and your mother.' He smiled a little at this, then changed the subject to something less upsetting as quickly as he could. He seemed to be unhappy only when one of the guests came over to ask how Nita's father was doing. Jimmy overheard Ham saying he was not too well and she was staying with him another week or more. So that was why his father asked him here! That was why there had been no bad vibrations to upset anybody.

The nurse brought Donny down to join them in the courtside guest house and he remembered Jimmy at once, giving him a big hug. The whole group walked through the softly lit gardens up to the basement screening room in the house and had a wonderful time talking back to a brand-new MGM comedy. This was something that could be done only when Ham screened pictures from other studios. Nobody in his right mind would dare to talk back to the screen if it was one of his films.

When he finally left to drive himself home, Jimmy felt elated at how close he had felt to his father all that wonderful afternoon and evening. If only it could be that way all the time. He hoped it could be and looked forward to the next weekend and another day with Ham, but he wondered how it would have been with Nita in the house and all of those crazy vibrations of his upsetting her.

Two days later Bob Silver phoned him at the apartment and he had his answer.

'Jimmy, your father asked me to tell you he'd rather you didn't come to the house for tennis next Sunday. He hopes you'll understand.' Being by nature a kindly person who hated having to do these things, he added, 'I'm very sorry.'

He understood perfectly. It was obvious that Nita's father was better now and she had returned. He could not help feeling hurt and angry that his hopes for an improved relationship with his father had proved so fragile. Maybe another time it would be different. They had much more to talk about and he would keep trying. In the meantime, he was going to start taking tennis lessons.

CHAPTER FORTY

Louis B. Mayer, the master of MGM, stood in back of his teed-up ball on the ninth hole at Hillcrest Country Club and looked down the three hundred and seventy-five yards of fairway toward the invisible green where the flag must be stirring in the gentle breeze. He gripped his driver tightly, stood with feet widespread, set the club head just behind the waiting ball and slowly lifted his weapon in a wide arc until the shaft touched the back of his pudgy neck. He held it there a frozen second as a too-familiar voice sounded off directly behind him.

'L.B., wait a minute! Are you sure that's your ball you're hitting? It looks just like mine. Did you go and pick it up again by mistake back on the eighth green?' Harpo Marx ran around to the immovable mogul, whose club seemed to be wrapped around his head. 'Here, let me make sure before you hit,' said Marx and he squatted down, picking the ball off the wooden tee and inspecting it closely. 'Nope. It's your chopped-up Maxfly. Go ahead, L.B. Finish your shot.' He replaced the ball, then scurried away to join the others standing behind Mayer, all trying to keep from bursting out with laughter.

'Harpo, so help me God, if you ever pull that on me again, there will be only three Marx Brothers in the rest of your movies!' Mayer was livid, and when he readdressed his ball and smashed furiously at it, the dimpled little sphere veered sharply to the right and sailed through a cluster of trees to land in the middle of the first fairway.

'L.B., we already played the first hole almost two hours ago! Are you shooting another one of your remakes?' said Ham Robbins to the red-faced Mayer, who once again had hit out of turn and was already walking off the tee in the general direction of his ball before any of the others had even teed off.

'Come back, Mr. Mayer!' shouted Freddie, one of their

caddies. 'The rest of the foursome hasn't driven yet!'

Harpo Marx started talking again. All morning he had carried on a constant stream of conversation, joking, commenting, needling the others. It was as though he were getting rid of all the noise bottled up whenever he was in character as the mad, mute, harp-playing genius. He was stuffed to his lips with unspoken sound, and now it flowed out like an undammed river of words.

'L.B., didn't you ever read the rules of golf? It says very clearly that the honor of hitting first goes to the player with the lowest score on the previous hole and when you come to the tee you wait until it's your turn and everybody else has – '

'Shut up, Harpo. For God's sake, shut up!' Mayer roared. 'Jolie, can't you get him to shut up when we're trying to play serious golf? You've known the little bastard longer than any of us. Tell him to shut up. He's ruining my whole game!'

Al Jolson teed up his ball, waggled his driver and tried to keep a straight face.

'Harpo, L.B. wants you to shut up, I want you to shut up and Ham Robbins wants you to shut up.' He looked over at the tall young man who was walking the round with them. 'I'm sure Jimmy Robbins wants you to shut up. So, Harpo, shut up!'

'Nobody ever wants to listen to good advice!' said the aggrieved Marx. 'The rules of golf are for the protection and pleasure of all of us. They're meant to – '

'Please, Harpo . . . please pretend you're on camera right now. Groucho has just goosed Margaret Dumont, Chico is untuning a piano and Zeppo is wherever Zeppo is. You're chasing a blonde through the set – and you're quiet! Not a goddamn word comes out of you!' Al Jolson said, then made a nearly flawless drive that went over two hundred and seventy yards straight down the fairway. 'See? See how it improves the game when you cooperate and it's quiet? Okay, Ham, you're on.'

Ham drove sharply off to the left side of the fairway, half up the slope of a steep hill bordering the flat dogleg approach to the green.

'Damn it! Why didn't you talk on my backswing. Harpo . . . then I'd have an excuse for that stinking drive. Come on, Jimmy, see how your father recovers from a bad lie and gets on the green in two.' They waited for Harpo to drive almost up to Jolson's ball and then father and son trudged off with their caddy and climbed the hill to where Ham's ball snuggled behind a tall tuft of grass. 'They cut away everything else, but this they left here just for me! Freddie, what club do I use now?' It was a good hundred and seventy-five yards to the pin, and the downhill shot would have been difficult for Bobby Jones. For Ham Robbins it was not difficult, it was impossible. His mid-iron shot dribbled down to the foot of the hill as he almost lost his balance and came tumbling after the poorly hit ball. Jimmy quickly reached out just in time to catch him.

'Why did you give up tennis, Dad? You were doing so well at it. Are you sure this is the right game for you?'

'Jimmy, I can do anything I set my mind to! I'm going to play golf just as well as I play tennis. Look, this club is something special. I joined a couple of years ago so I could get out here and relax with friends . . . and maybe do a little business while I'm having some fun and exercise. Besides, most of these guys only play golf, not tennis, and this is the only way we can get together and relax. It's easy to talk a deal with just a couple of people in between shots out here. Also, as you've already noticed, the food here is great. Once in a while I like to get away from my house with all those *fressers* who eat up my hamburgers and drink all my booze. We still have plenty of tennis, but I enjoy coming out here now and then.'

They reached his ball and he chipped it to the green, where it picked up speed and rolled well past the hole to the far side, went through the heavily grassed border and plopped over the edge into a sand trap, where it found a resting place in somebody's deep unraked heelprint.

'Bastards!' Ham said, 'Why don't they clean their mess instead of leaving it for me to get into!'

The others waited patiently on the green while Ham gingerly stepped into the trap, waited for Harpo to stop talking, then swung back with his sand wedge. He was about to complete his shot when several men burst out of the pro shop twenty yards off to the right of the green. They were shouting as loudly as they could.

'Bombs – bombs! They've just bombed Pearl Harbor! It's coming in on the radio!' Charley Lacey, the club pro, came out of the shop and joined the others yelling down at the golfers. 'Our whole fleet is blown up and sinking . . . it's horrible! My God! It's still going on . . . Come here, they're telling about it on the radio . . . hurry up!'

Jolson, Mayer, Marx and the caddies ran over to the shop.

424

Jimmy raced after them, and Ham was left all alone in the trap, still addressing his ball, which was almost buried in the soft sand. He was about to follow the others, but first took a hard swing at the ball, which exploded out of the trap in a cloud of sand, touched down on the edge of the green and rolled down a long straight line to the hole, where it vanished into the earth. Ham stood with his club still high in the air.

'I sank it! Right out of the trap into the cup! I got a par four!' he shouted, but there was nobody to hear him. Not a soul had seen his minor miracle. 'Oh, shit!' said Ham. 'Who'll ever believe me!' He extracted his feet from the sand, which had filled both this shoes, and walked with great discomfort across the green to the hole, where he recovered his ball. For a wistful moment he looked at it, the only witness to his great shot, then ruefully popped it into his pocket. He hobbled on to the pro shop, which was jammed with golfers, caddies and club employees. A radio blared loudly.

'Where the hell is Pearl Harbor?' Ham asked his son as they stood on the outskirts of the listening crowd.

'Hawaii, just outside Honolulu, I think. We're in a war, Dad. It finally happened!'

'You just missed a great shot, Jimmy,' said Ham. 'I blasted right out of the trap and into the cup – you should have seen it!' Nobody heard him over the excitement. It was so crowded now that they went up to the men's grill in the big white wooden clubhouse, where everybody sat around tables or leaned on the bar listening to the dreadful news flowing out of the radio speakers. Ham emptied his shoes into an ashtray and sat down. Now it was the news about Schofield Barracks ... then the word about Hickam Field being destroyed. They all looked at each other in horror.

'Try another station!' somebody shouted. 'This could be another of those damned radio dramas like that crazy SOB Orson Welles pulled with his Martian invasion a couple year ago!'

The bartender spun the dial but Pearl Harbor had been bombed and was burning on every radio station. This was no *War of the Worlds* – it was a war by imperial Japan, and soon by Nazi Germany, on the United States of America!

Ham sat at a big table with Jimmy and a dozen other men as they all listened to Royal Gundarson in Manila describing events as they happened. Behind his agonized voice could clearly be heard the dreadful sounds of explosions, sirens and the screaming and shouting of people thousands of miles

425

away across an ocean. The war was being brought halfway around the world into this room and hundreds upon thousands more, where horrified listeners sat and asked each other what tomorrow would bring.

'Come on, Jimmy, let's drive to the house. The chauffeur will follow with my car. I want to get away from here.'

Jimmy drove them through Beverly Hills, and it was one of the few times he could remember riding in a car when his father was not doing the driving. Very few people were on the streets, and when an ambulance screamed past them Ham looked nervously up at the sky to see if Japanese Zero planes were strafing the city. They listened to the car radio with its continuing stream of war and carnage. At last the car reached Sierra View, where the gate guard was standing out in the street, his radio in the little house blasting at full volume.

'Mr. Robbins, I've been watching for you. We phoned the club – they said you'd left. It's just terrible! Those damn – ' They heard no more as the car went through the open gates, swept up the drive toward the house and stopped in front of the fountain, where they got out. The front door swung open and Nita came outside to meet them. There was a look of intense worry on her face.

'Ham, have you been listening to the radio? It's horrible! I phoned all over the club trying to find you. I've been so upset!' She saw Jimmy for the first time and her eyes widened and there was a little gasp as she drew in her breath; then she managed to speak to him. 'Oh, Jimmy . . . hello . . . Uh . . . come in . . . please.' Donny and his nurse stood in the hall. The little boy was very excited from seeing everybody rush around the house during the past half-hour. He came running to his father and hugged him.

'Jimmy was with me at Hillcrest. We managed to get in nine holes before we heard the news. Say, you won't believe what I did on the last hole we played – but nobody saw me do it and I guess I might as well forget it ever happened.' They all went into the paneled library and sat on the overstuffed couches placed around the lovely fireplace in which there had never been a fire.

Nita was terribly ill at ease in Jimmy's presence, remembering the last time she had seen him in this house, almost two years before. She managed, though, to say something.

'Donny, do you remember your brother, Jimmy?' The little boy, who now wasn't so little anymore, might or might not have remembered him, but he came over again to hold his hand. The butler brought in some drinks, and Ham turned on the radio so they could listen to the horror still taking place across the Pacific. Now it was mostly in the Philippines, and there was a sudden announcement that in a few hours President Roosevelt would speak to the nation.

Nita felt more and more upset, finally saying she had a dreadful headache and was going upstairs to lie down. Jimmy saw the way she looked at him and wondered if those vibrations from the cusp of Libra were hitting her once again. He vividly remembered the last time they had been together in this house. Now Ham, Donny and Jimmy were alone in the room with the voice from the radio.

'Come on, let's go outside for a walk. I can't sit here anymore listening to this. I want to get out in the air!' Ham said and got to his feet, walking out of the room.

Jimmy held Donny's hand and they followed their father through the hall and front door out to the driveway. Ham led the way across the wide lawn, and they slowly walked up the slope toward the little clump of trees where the surrounding high wall made a turn around the property. Tall rows of Italian cypress shielded them from being seen by anyone passing on the outside road. Ham remembered this was the same spot where he and Irene once had their little picnic, the time he saw a car parked outside with somebody spying on him. Somebody? Nita! The three of them sat on the lush grass under a drooping willow, and Ham looked across the wide lawn at the house.

'Jimmy, what's going to happen to you now with your Reserve commission? They'll probably be calling you.'

'That's right, Dad. I'm still a second lieutenant, but last December I was transferred into the Signal Corps and I'm in the new GHQ Reserve Unit that Darry Zanuck heads. He's a lieutenant colonel now. We've got a lot of top professionals from the industry in our outfit. The Academy Research Council helped put it together for the Army, and Colonel Nate Levinson over at Warner Brothers worked it out, just like the units they have at the telephone companies. We're all Reservists who are specialists and can get things organized and moving right away. Whether they call us as individuals or as a unit, we're ready to set up motion picture production for the Army – training films, record stuff, newsreels, stills, combat footage – all that and a lot more. Remember, I told you about it when we were getting started about a year ago?

Tomorrow I'll phone Colonel Levinson and Zanuck's office to see what's going to happen with us now. I have a hunch we won't hear anything for a while.'

Donny pulled at Ham, and the three of them got up to their feet and aimlessly walked around the estate, past the tennis court, the swimming pool, putting green, through the gardens, and then back to the front of the house. Jimmy looked up at the windows, and for a moment he saw Nita's face peering down at them. She must have seen him look up, as she immediately pulled back her head and dropped the curtain. Jimmy wondered if she still had her headache.

They went back into the library and for a while listened to the radio. There was little change – except for the worse. Planes were burning on the ground, oil storage tanks had exploded and heavy black smoke and billowing flames filled the air over the sunken battleships that had become tombs for thousands of men.

Jimmy had phoned his mother earlier from the club, and now he called her again to make sure she was all right. He came back to his father in the library.

'I'd better leave. Mom's all alone and she's real upset about everything. I'll be at the studio tomorrow and tell you if I hear anything about being put on an alert or getting called to active duty.' His father reached out to tightly grasp his son's hand, and they went to the front door.

'Say good-bye to Nita for me. I hope she's feeling better,' he said, then got into his car and drove down the hill.

Jimmy had been right about not hearing anything official for a while, and even Colonel Levinson and Darryl Zanuck were still awaiting word from the Chief Signal Officer about the GHQ Reserve Unit. He was told to keep in touch and leave word if he went out of town. Meantime the lights of Los Angeles and other coastal cities and towns in California put on their own versions of nightly blackouts and the anti-aircraft artillery shot down some of their own barrage balloons and everybody thought the Japanese fleet was just offshore. The studio rushed some propaganda and war-background films into work, and soon it became impossible to find Japanese actors to play the enemy during the first hectic months of war. The casting directors were god at their jobs, and soon every Korean or Chinese actor who came looking for work and could fake a Japanese accent went before the cameras.

Like the great complicated mechanism it was, the nation

moved slowly but completely into the bloody conflict that began for it on that terrible day in December. Christmas was not at all merry, and New Year's Eve anything but happy as the draft went into full effect and the arsenal of democracy speeded its output of weapons of war and the trained men to operate them. It was late in March before Jimmy and several other Reservists in the Affiliated GHQ Unit received terse messages from the adjutant general's office. He was put on alert and a date was given him to report for extended active duty with the Signal Corps Training Films Production Laboratory at Fort Monmouth, New Jersey.

As the days passed into weeks and the weeks became months, the nation mobilized its forces – and Nita mobilized her anger and resentment. She still felt a deep personal affront at Jimmy's presence in her house, and it appeared to her as another infamous act on that Day of Infamy. She lashed out at her husband for 'sneaking' his son into the house while she was visiting her sick father, and then the news came from El Paso that he had suddenly died. She went into even deeper depression, made worse when she thought of Ham bringing Jimmy to their home again that day from the club. More and more she took her troubles, real and imagined, from her astrology charts down to the bar in the lower level of the house, where she found comfort more quickly in a bottle than in the stars.

When Ham insisted she accompany him to an industry dinner dance promoting the sale of war savings bonds, she remained in her room the entire afternoon bitterly complaining about his family.

'Why do they despise me so much? Look – I've done charts on all of them!' She held up a handful of papers and waved them at him. 'See how full of hate and evil they are! If only Maurie and your sisters would accept me, give me half a chance to show what a good wife I am and how happy I've made you! At least they could do that for their brother and make us all more like a real family instead of – '

Ham thought of how 'happy' she was making him at that moment and spoke up loudly over her angry voice.

'Listen, Nita, it's damn important for me to be at this thing tonight, and just as important for you to come with me. The heads of every studio will be showing up with their wives, if they have them, and you're going to be there with me. I refuse to take any more of this crap from you. Now please stop driving us both crazy with your astrological bullshit! You know it only tells you the things you want to hear. Move yourself! Let's get going!' He turned away from her, went into his dressing room and started to put on the dress shirt and tuxedo his butler had laid out.

Finally, in peevish fury, she dressed, put on her make-up and did what she could with her hair. Then she went downstairs to the bar, opened a bottle of gin and poured herself nearly a full glass. Ham came into the room just as she dropped her drink on the floor, and he winced at the loud noise of the shattering glass. Her unreasonable, almost childish act was a gesture of defiance, and all the way to the Biltmore Hotel her behavior and comments had him on edge. He was grateful for the thick glass between them and the chauffeur, which helped confine most of his humiliation to the rear of the car. He regretted insisting Nita come with him, and remained silent the entire trip.

There were a number of men in uniform at the Biltmore Bowl in downtown Los Angeles, where all the studios were holding the war bond dinner dance. Jimmy was among them, with the shining gold bars of a second lieutenant on his shoulders, crossed signal flags and torch on his lapels, and a lovely brunette named Pat on his arm. Tomorrow his war would begin, but tonight was a chance to have fun, meet old friends and remember things he might not see again for a long, long time.

He stood near the wide red-carpeted staircase leading down to the Bowl, talking with Pat, Leo Arnheim and Harry Saunders. There was only one subject on everybody's lips – the war, how it was going, how it might go and how long it would last.

Jimmy looked up and saw his father slowly coming down the wide staircase. Ham's face seemed set and grim; all the good humor he usually showed on such occasions had been left elsewhere. The woman whose arm he tightly held was having difficulties with her long black dress – and with the man at her side. Nita looked strange, there was a wildness in her eyes and it was obvious from Ham's tense and restrained manner that something was very wrong between them. As they came to the final step, Nita stumbled and might have fallen if Ham had not been holding her arm. A waiter passed carrying a tray loaded with drinks and she reached out to grab at one, almost upsetting the rest of the glasses and causing the waiter to swear under his breath. She downed the drink, then flashed an angry look at her husband, who pulled her along with him as they started to make their way across the room. Ham tried tossing off some kind of jovial remark to someone he passed, but the strained look on his face and his unnatural manner contradicted any pretense at gaiety.

Nita saw a young man wearing an army officer's uniform standing almost in the middle of the crowded room. As she came closer and realized who it was, she pulled her husband along, her eyes burning in a face suddenly contorted with rage as they approached her stepson – the only one in the whole family she could reach and hurt. All day her thoughts had been on the way Ham's family treated her. Maurie holding her in contempt, avoiding all contact, shunning her. The sisters she had never met, who wanted nothing to do with her, ignoring her very existence . . . the old father who had turned his back. She was the wife of their brother, the wife of his son! Her anger grew with each step closer to the one person in the whole family she could lash out at. The whole damned family that made her feel as though she was still the ostracized, outcast little girl growing up in El Paso . . . still little Nita Rosenfeld, the daughter of Jake Rosenfeld and his Mexican wife, Maria de Valle . . . locked up tight inside a ghetto of rejection and bigotry.

Nita stopped less than five feet from Jimmy, who had watched her approach. As Ham tried to say someting, she spoke out in a harsh sharp voice that knifed through the air.

'Stay away from my house! Stay away from my husband! Stay away from me!'

All around them the room went silent. Nearly everyone within earshot looked at her and at Ham and wondered what was going on. Leo Arnheim nervously stepped back, then quickly turned and headed for the bar and a drink. Harry Saunders followed him while Jimmy stood frozen to the spot, his puzzled date wondering who the strange woman in black was who had just acted so oddly. Nita broke away from Ham, whose face turned deep red. As she walked off into the crowd, they all pulled back in hushed silence to let her pass.

Ham was devastated, though he did his best to hide his feelings behind an imperfect smile. He had known that Jimmy would be here and that he was leaving the next day for the army, God alone knew for how long. Now Ham stood alone, stammering out half-words nobody could hear, and then he plunged off into the crowd to search for his vanished wife.

Jimmy watched him go, with not a word passing between father and son.

Inside the Biltmore Bowl, just beyond the crowded reception room, Abe Lyman's orchestra struck up some music and gradually everybody drifted to their tables or the dance floor. Jimmy and his date sat with some of the people he had worked with in the production department, and he saw nothing more of his father or Nita the rest of the uncomfortable evening.

The next morning he phoned his father's office and Bob Silver told him Ham was not in and was taking no calls at the house. He left a message saying good-bye.

Just before noon, Irene and a small group of friends drove Jimmy to the Pasadena railroad station, and soon he was on his way to Fort Monmouth and the other war.

432

CHAPTER FORTY-ONE

The steaming-hot mineral water came up to Ham's chin and he leaned back against the side of the big square tub to look across at his son, Captain Jimmy Robbins, Signal Photo Staff Officer, Headquarters, Ninth U.S. Army. He was exhausted from the past two days of non-stop activity and the long flight from New York to the European theater of operations. It was sheer luxury now to sit in the mineral baths at the Wiesbaden spa for their first real moment of rest since the trip began.

Ham was one of eighteen American film executives flown over to the ETO as guests of the War Department to be given a whirlwind tour of the American Zone in occupied Germany, two months after V-E Day. Even the army had a public relations department, although it went under a much more dignified name, and it was considered well worth the time, effort and expense to have these film industry leaders see where history had been made – and those who made it. The films these men had produced all through the years of war had contributed greatly to public and military morale, to education and the historic record, and it was hoped this trip would influence their future films as well.

Jimmy was at Ninth U.S. Army headquarters in Braunschweig, deep inside Germany, only a few hundred miles and a few hundred thousand Russian soldiers from the fallen enemy capital of Berlin. It was a time for the victorious armies to regroup and put the occupation into effect, and Jimmy was responsible for coordinating Signal Photo activities in the Ninth Army area. The 165th Signal Photographic Company had recently relieved the 167th, which had been through hard combat coverage right up to V-E Day and now was alerted for return to the United States. The Photo Company had units scattered throughout the army occupation zone, all busy covering civil affairs activities, the processing of great masses of Wehrmacht and SS troops, now prisoners of war, and they were photographing anything that might be useful as evidence in the coming War Crimes trials in Nuremberg. Their cameras shot countless stills and exposed motion picture footage of the hordes of displaced persons moving west, fleeing the Russian troops just across the Oder River. The Red Cross was constantly asking for special coverage of prisoner of war handling to send to their international headquarters in Switzerland, and the medical departments all needed photography of the treatment and evacuation of patients. One unit was on assignment with the Graves Registration people in their continuing grim work, and a sudden demand for pictorial surveys of war damage to German cities meant that the Army Air Force brought in some special air photo groups. There had to be meetings to mesh together the ground and air coverage for this complex mission. Every staff section needed pictures taken, and for a while it seemed busier than D-day.

At last things were organized and rolling along smoothly enough so that when Jimmy received a message from Twelfth Army Group headquarters in Wiesbaden that his father would be in a party of visiting film production executives, he took them up on their suggestion that he come back for a few days of special duty with a photo unit and handle the pictorial coverage. Three days later he was waiting on the Frankfurt airstrip with his camera crew, watching the big transport plane circle for a landing.

Ham, looking very military in his officer's uniform without insignia, was overjoyed to see Jimmy waiting for him on the field, and he proudly introduced him to the rest of the party, most of whom the young man already knew. Harry Cohn of Columbia, Eddie Mannix, an old friend from MGM, J.L. Warner and Bill Goetz, Jack Karp, B.B. Kahane and Y. Frank Freeman of Paramount and others, all eager to get out of the plane and stretch their cramped muscles after the long trip. Jimmy signaled their vehicles to line up at the foot of the plane ramp.

'Dad, we've got some staff cars to take everybody to the guest house where you'll be staying. I'm attached to your party on temporary duty while you're here and my unit is going to shoot a complete record showing everything you do and see. You'll all be getting dupe prints shipped to you later.' He paused a moment, then went on, carefully choosing his words. 'Uh . . . Dad, how's Nita? I'll bet Donny's a big boy now. Are they both well?'

'They're both just fine,' said Ham. 'Yes, he's grown a lot

since you saw him.' He seemed quite happy to be here with his son after such a long time apart.

'Oh, before I forget,' Ham said as they walked toward the cars. 'I had Bob Silver phone your mother just before we left. She's feeling wonderful and sends you her love. She's anxious to hear when you'll be coming home now that this is about over. I knew you'd want to hear that she's all right. By the way, I read someplace that she's going with somebody and there was a rumor she might get married again.'

'Mom's written me several times about somebody special she was seeing. I hope it happens. Thanks for letting her know you were going to see me. I hope I'll be back soon, but there's lots of work ahead. Ninth Army is being deactivated and I heard I'm being transferred to headquarters here in Frankfurt to help consolidate Signal Photo operations in the whole theater. I'll know more about that next week. Anyhow, the minute somebody puts me on travel orders, I'll be on my way home!'

After lunch in the officers' mess, they attended a special briefing given by Air Chief Marshal Tedder, the Deputy Supreme Allied Commander, and Major General Walter Bedell Smith, SHAEF Chief of Staff. It was held in the situation map room in the tremendous I. G. Farben building that had been taken over intact as headquarters. Suddenly there was a flurry of excitement at the far end of the briefing room and General Dwight Eisenhower, the Supreme Commander of Allied Forces, entered the chamber with several aides and was introduced to the party.

'Gentlemen, I know I speak for the Air Chief Marshal, for General Smith and my entire command when I thank you and all your associates for what the American motion picture industry has contributed to our successful war effort,' General Eisenhower said in a warm and friendly voice. 'Morale is as important on the fighting front as it is back home and wherever people have worked for our victory. The films for which you gentlemen have been responsible have been of more help than you can possibly imagine. Your contributions to the production of training films were also a major factor in rapidly turning our peacetime citizens into skilled soldiers, sailors and airmen able to successfully meet and conquer Hitler's forces. The film medium has preserved the great events in our struggle for freedom just now concluded, and by seeing them again on the screen in the future, perhaps we may learn from the past and never again have to experience the great tragedy of war. I hope you profit from the too-brief time you will be here with us. I have issued orders you are to see whatever you wish and members of my staff have been assigned to your group to be of all possible assistance. Again, gentlemen, thank you for all you have done and for coming here.'

Ham and Jimmy joined the others in rising to applaud the general as he went around the room, shaking hands, meeting everybody in the group, before leaving through the door behind the situation maps.

The next few days were a blur of activity. There was a trip through the underground vaults of the Reichsbank, which left everybody in an angry and depressed mood. They saw a strong room filled to the walls and ceiling with stacks of shabby suitcases and trunks. Several had been pried open to show their contents: gold wedding bands, gold teeth and dental plates, spectacle frames, gold bracelets and necklaces. This was just part of the loot that had been taken from one of the concentration camps to the east by fleeing SS troops. Elements of an American regiment had intercepted the parade of murderers as they fled the oncoming Russian armies, and their cargo of death was put in these vaults beneath the streets of Frankfurt while the black-uniformed SS men were rounded up and put in guarded stockades.

'How terrible! It's beyond comprehension!' Eddie Mannix said to Ham as they stood looking at the heaped-up pieces of gold. 'Each one of those rings, those teeth and bracelets . . . those were parts of people! How could men who called themselves civilized beings do that to other men and women . . . and to children!' Later that same day they drove past a mile-square enclosure jammed full of SS troops in their black uniforms, many still wearing the death's-head insignia. Each of the visitors from America looked through the wire mesh and knew what it was to hate.

Now another stop, this one on the outskirts of Frankfurt, where, in a rambling collection of half-shattered factories, thousands upon thousands of Polish, Rumanian, Hungarian and other East European displaced persons had been gathered. This collection point was under supervision of United Nations Relief and Rehabilitation, which had the almost impossible task of feeding, clothing, housing and caring for the medical needs of the former slave laborers, who for years had been forced to work for the Nazi war machine. Off to one side of the great sprawling refugee camp in a separate enclosure was a large group of Ukrainians. They all were deathly afraid they would be shipped back to Russia, their homeland, where they believed a terrible fate might be waiting because of their willing or unwilling help to the German enemy. Here was such an overwhelming collection of human misery that no motion picture, no matter how accurate, could ever begin to portray it. The visitors from California were deeply moved, and after they had walked around, trying to speak to some of the refugees, Ham took aside one of their United Nations guides, a husky red-haired Irishman from Londonderry, to ask him why there did not appear to be any Jews at all among these liberated hundreds of thousands. Had they indeed all been slaughtered in the death camps?

'I must tell you, sir, we are housing and feeding a few thousand Jews from all over Eastern Europe, some from here in Germany as well, but not at this center with the Poles or the others . . . the Rumanians and Hungarians. It is hard to believe,' the UN man said, raising his hands in a gesture of sad despair, 'many of these poor people you see here who were treated like filth by the Nazis, in most cases just as bad as they treated the Jews, still refuse to be housed in the same camp with them! We have had to place all the liberated Jews in another camp a few miles away from here for their own safety and protection. You would honestly think that after they had been on the other end of the whip, most of these people might possibly have acquired some understanding or at least a little compassion – but no . . . that's not what happened. Ignorance and bigotry die very hard. It is something I cannot figure out at all. I fear for the future of the world if this represents the thinking of our fellowmen.' He shook his head as they returned to their waiting line of cars. The last thing Ham remembered seeing there was an elderly Ukrainian couple looking out at him through the fence. He was shocked at how much they resembled his mother and father. He turned to look at them through the rear window until the car turned a corner leading back to the Autobahn and they all were lost to sight.

Things were a bit happier the next day when they boarded a luxurious riverboat for a cruise up the Rhine. They were told this had once been Hitler's yacht, but they all agreed somebody was twisting the truth to impress them. Göring's yacht, perhaps, but it seemed much too fancy for Hitler.

They cruised up the lovely Rhine, passing the Lorelei, the Rat Tower and the steep hillside vineyards. Soon the quiet little city of Bonn went by on their port side and they reached Cologne, where the ruined bridges blocked all further river traffic. A wide circle put them back on the return trip, and at noon they were served lunch on the top deck as they cruised by lovely old castles that looked just like very expensive movie sets waiting for a director to shout 'Action!' It was late afternoon when they arrived at Rüdesheim and disembarked, driving the short distance to Wiesbaden, the world-famous spa, where they soaked away their fatigue in the big tubs of hot mineral spring water.

Now, as Ham leaned back against the side of his tub, he looked over at Jimmy through the steam. He spoke in a voice so low that only his son could hear him.

'You know, seeing all this destruction, death and misery makes you really think about things. All those families broken up, scattered, losing their homes and maybe each other forever because some madman started a war and dragged the rest of the world into it. We're damned lucky compared to most everyone else! We haven't had armies or bombers blowing up our country – but you know, sometimes we do a pretty good job of it on ourselves, without help from anybody.'

Jimmy listened with deep interest to his father, whom he had never heard speak quite like this before. The War Department tour must really have opened his mind to the world much more than he knew or realized. He waited for Ham to continue, hoping he would get to some things even closer to both of them.

After a few minutes of silent soaking, Ham went on speaking.

'Look at us . . . There's no good reason for all the problems we've made for ourselves . . . and yet there they are . . . all the ruined cities inside each of us. We should all be so close . . . close and whole . . . my brother and my sisters and me . . . and you, Jimmy. This trip has shown me so much real trouble, such suffering and agony, that I just cannot see why we should go on the way we have when we have the power to do something about it . . . to bring changes . . . if we really want to.' He paused a moment, the steaming mineral water completely relaxing his mind and body.

'Dad, you know how I feel. More than anything else I want for us all to be close – to be a real family. I know the past has been filled with problems, some that couldn't be helped and some I guess we brought on ourselves. You're right in

438

comparing it in a way to the real tragedies we've seen here and the even worse things that went on during the war.'

'I hope you'll be home real soon, Jimmy, and I want you to know I'm going to do all I can from my side,' his father said from across the hot tub. 'That night ... well, Nita was terribly upset. She feels as though the whole family has rejected her, so she took it out on you. I'd have given anything if that hadn't happened. You've got to be understanding, and when you come home, go to see her and get to know her – be the nice warm person you are, and maybe she'll meet you more than halfway and return that same feeling to you. I know we want to be a real family, and if you'll help out, we might be able to make a new start. I'm positive we'll all be much happier.'

'I think so too, Dad, and I'll do my very best. You and I should be close to each other, not just now and then at the studio, but outside it, too. I'll do everything I can. You can count on me.'

'I'm sure of that,' said Ham just as a loud bell sounded to warn all the soakers they had been in the tubs long enough. They got out, dried off with big soft towels, then went into another room with rows of massage tables. For fifteen minutes they let the skilled masseurs pound and pummel them, and then, after showers, everybody dressed and they were on their way to the Frankfurt guest house for their last night before flying on.

Early next morning Jimmy saw his father and the rest of the party to the Frankfurt-am-Main airfield. As Ham was about to climb into their plane, he threw his arm over his son's shoulder.

'Take care of yourself, kid. You got through the whole damn war without getting shot, so don't take any chances now. Just get home safe, healthy ... and soon!'

'Don't worry, Dad. The only shooting involving me will be with a Speed Graphic or an Eyemo thirty-five-millimeter ... Now, before you and the rest of your gang get into the plane, I want you all to stand on the steps here while we get some final stills and movie coverage.' The pictures were made and there was just enough time for a last good-bye. 'Say hello to Nita and Donny for me ... and, Dad, would you please phone Mom when you get back and tell her you saw me and I'm just fine. I know she'll be very happy if you call. I hope I'll be seeing all of you real soon. Good-bye.'

Almost impulsively, Ham gave him a quick hug, then turned

and disappeared inside the plane. He waved through the little round window by his seat as the stairs were pulled away and the motors coughed into life. The big transport circled the field after taking off and vanished in the direction of Munich, where the filmmakers would spend a last day in Germany seeing the Eagle's Nest at Berchtesgaden, where Hitler had plotted his new world, only to bring it crashing down with him in flaming ruins.

It was almost unbelievable how fast things happened in the next month and a half. Suddenly Jimmy's replacement turned up in Frankfurt, and after a week spent in signing everything over to him, Jimmy drove in a long convoy up the Rhine valley to Cologne, then across the Netherlands and Belgium to Antwerp, where he went through the redeployment center, finally boarding one of the waiting troopships for the voyage home.

Fourteen days and three violent storms later, the Statue of Liberty welcomed him back to America. Jimmy made phone calls to Irene and then to Ham from New York and was pleased that his father sounded as happy to hear from him as his mother had been. Six more days passed before he stepped off the train in Los Angeles, where Irene picked him up, welcoming him with a hug, a kiss and a stop for a thick chocolate malted milk.

That same afternoon he was out at the studio in his father's office. The welcome Ham gave him seemed strangely restrained. There was little in his voice or manner that resembled the happy father he had spoken to on the phone less than a week before from New York.

'Why didn't you come right over to the house instead of waiting to see me here?' Ham said in a peevish voice that shocked his son, who stood, still in uniform, before the desk.

'Dad, I phoned there the minute I arrived and they said you had just left for the studio. I asked for Nita and was told she wasn't taking any calls, so then I phoned Bob Silver and told him I was coming out here to see you.' Jimmy wondered what had happened to cause such a radical change in his father's attitude.

'Nita hasn't been feeling very well,' said Ham in a still troubled voice. 'I think you had better wait awhile before you try to see her. I'll let you know when will be a good time for it. Meanwhile, welcome back and what are your plans? Are you going back to work right away or taking off for a while to get used to being a civilian again?'

440

'I've got more than forty-five days of accumulated leave piled up and I figured on just loafing, taking off for somewhere, Palm Springs maybe, or Las Vegas. I only want to relax and do absolutely nothing for a little while.'

'Good idea. When you're ready to go back to work we'll have a talk. I have some ideas I want to discuss with you,' said his father.

'Dad,' Jimmy said, 'this getting together with Nita . . . how would it be if I went right out to the house from here? After that good talk you and I had in Wiesbaden I can't see why our new beginning should have to wait even a day. How about it? I'd like to see her right now . . . today . . . and Donny, too.'

Ham twisted nervously in his chair. He tried for a moment to think of something to say but had great trouble putting any words together. He cleared his throat, opened and closed the trade papers on his desk and finally spoke.

'I can't tell you what you should do right now, but maybe you've got the right idea. You know how some women are. Nita's been terribly hurt by so many people and . . .' He was lost again, remembering all the futile hours he had spent talking to her ever since his return from the European trip and all the frustration she had put him through. 'Hell, go ahead . . . go to the house. I'll phone her you're on the way.' A smile suddenly appeared on his face and he got to his feet. 'Say, kid, you look absolutely great. I'm really happy to see you back. Now don't go and eat too much rich food and get fat. You don't want to be too big for your old clothes. Does anything still fit you?'

'Nope, I've grown the last few years in nearly every direction. Some stuff is all right, but I'm going to have to get a few suits and other things. All right, Dad, I'm going to the house right now and I'll talk to you later.'

It took Jimmy nearly forty-five minutes to reach Sierra View Drive and park his car beside the big bronze gates. He reached out to press the button on the speaker, which had been set within easy reach. The guard's voice came out of the box, rasping and metallic, and asked who was there.

'I'm Mr. Robbins's son, Jimmy Robbins. Mrs. Robbins is expecting me,' he said into the microphone grille. 'My father phoned that I was coming.'

'Please wait a moment.' The humming noise went dead and there was silence for nearly five minutes before it came back on. 'I'm sorry, Mrs. Robbins is not seeing anybody. Do you want to leave a message?'

'Never mind – there's no message,' said Jimmy, and he backed his car away from the closed gate and drove down Sierra View toward Sunset Boulevard and the apartment. He was very angry, angry because he felt so powerless to do anything about what had just happened. He could hear his father's words back in the Wiesbaden spa . . . 'When you're back home again . . . see Nita . . .' he had said. 'Get to know her . . . maybe she'll meet you more than halfway . . . if you help out we might make a new start.'

Jimmy gave a bitter little laugh. Get to know her, his father had told him. He certainly was getting to know her all right, but the thing that hurt most was that his father either didn't really care, or for some reason was so intimidated by Nita or so frightened about something that no change could ever come about, regardless of what he might have said back in Wiesbaden. He would give in to whatever it was Nita wanted. If Jimmy ever had to depend on his father for any help in working things out in this strange non-relationship with her, nothing would ever happen. It couldn't all be on account of her damned horoscope. There just had to be something else!

He drove to the apartment, and after a welcome-home dinner at a restaurant with his mother and some friends, he returned to his room and started packing. Early next morning he was on his way to Las Vegas by way of Palm Springs.

'I told you I had some ideas to talk over with you when you returned,' said Ham as they rode in a studio car to the sneak preview. Jimmy sat with his father, Bob Silver and the producer of the picture about to be previewed. In a following car was the director, the film editor, his assistant and the cans of film about to be put on public trial. They had just finished dinner in the executive dining room and now were on their way to the theater in nearby Glendale. Jimmy looked tanned and rested from his vacation, which had stretched into three weeks. Now he was ready to go back to work, and he listened carefully as his father spoke. So far there had been not a single word from Ham about Nita, and it was as though his earlier conversation and Jimmy's vain attempt to see her had never even happened.

'You know that production is only one leg of the tripod that holds up this business. The second is distribution, which gets the pictures we make out here to the theaters, advertising them and not letting them hold too damn much out on us when

442

they count the take. It's a worldwide operation and involves a lot of organization, planning and knowing what the hell you're doing when you deal with our customers, the theaters that show our films. Then the third leg of the tripod, exhibition, the theaters. In another business you'd call them the retailers. Our company never went into theater ownership in the big way Fox, Paramount and Warners did. We only have thirty-seven good houses in key cities, and sometimes I think they're more damn bother than they're worth. We're always in court defending lawsuits brought by other theater owners complaining about the way we buy our own films for our own theaters. We haven't heard the end of that yet by a long shot . . . or by a close-up, either. The Department of Justice is nosing around asking questions all the time, and one day everything is going to explode. Before that happens, though, my idea is for you to learn all you can about distribution and exhibition. I had to find out about it the hard way before it all got so big and we began to call it an industry. It's very important that you find out there's a whole lot more to the picture business than a studio and all this glamour crap. Without distribution the theaters wouldn't get the product – and without exhibition, we wouldn't get the dough to produce the pictures to distribute to the theaters. You see, it's a big circle and has to keep turning all the time or the whole business stops dead!'

Ham pulled out a long cigar and lit it up in a big cloud of blue smoke, making Jimmy cough. He was fascinated, as he had never before seen his father with a cigar; it must be something new. He wished his father would continue his interesting discussion about the industry and his future in it, but for a few minutes more he sat contemplating his glowing cigar tip. They drove down Brand Avenue, and a few blocks away there was a lone searchlight sweeping the sky to announce the feature film preview. Ham pulled his eyes away from the cigar tip and returned to the industry.

'You're still learning the business, Jimmy, and so far you've only been in one part of it. I spoke with your Uncle Maurie about this and he completely agrees with me. We both feel the best thing for you is to go to our home office in New York and work there with Lennie Rhinehart for a while. You know him, he's head of distribution, and he'll put you to work learning about that end of the business. Later on you'll go out to some of our film exchanges in different parts of the country and see what they do under different conditions.' He stopped a moment, looked down at his watch, then went on. 'Distribution . . . you know, that's what I was doing when I met your mother in San Francisco. Before that Maurie, Lou and I had our own film exchange in Denver.' The car came to a stoplight and Ham looked out at the traffic until they started moving again toward the preview beacon. He sounded a bit pensive as he continued. 'Those were good days – good in so many ways we didn't appreciate then. Life wasn't so damned complicated . . . But what the hell, here we are, today is today and yesterday's gone forever. Oh, we're finally at the theater. Come on, boys, let's see if this sow's ear we're running tonight can somehow be turned into a silk purse.'

Jimmy followed his father and the others into the theater and they filed into the roped-off preview section at the rear of the auditorium. The houselights were still up and most of the audience twisted around in their seats to see if anybody famous had come in. There was a buzz of conversation until the lights dimmed and the screen lit up to announce the preview. Ham sat between the film editor and Bob Silver, who held a large pad and flashlight so he could take down all Ham's comments during the running and make notes on audience reactions.

The picture ran for eighty-four minutes. It was not great, it was not terrible – it was in the mediocre middle, and no matter what was done, it would retain some resemblance to a sow's ear. Maybe next time, mused Ham, maybe next time a silk purse . . . but not this one. He quickly got up from his seat before the houselights came fully up and led the small procession of studio people across the lobby into the theater manager's office. Two ushers collected the previously distributed preview comment cards from members of the audience as they came out of the theater and took them into the meeting. Ham spread them out on the manager's desk, looked at a few of them and read aloud. The producer and director squirmed in misery at what they heard.

' "War was hell – this was worse . . ." "I want to enjoy myself when I go to the movies. Tonight you made me suffer!" "Bring back Dish Night, please." Those are just some of the more favorable ones,' said Ham as he shuffled through the cards. 'You want to hear a few more?' He didn't see the director shake his head in an unheard prayer for silence, so he went on reading from the cards. Suddenly he stopped, gathered up all the comments and dumped them in the wastebasket. 'Fuck 'em! There's enough in this picture we can save

444

with some recutting, changing the sequence of a few scenes ... absolutely no retakes, that's out ... and then when we cover most of the slow spots with final music and effects, it might help. All right, Bob, start reading the notes you took during the running.'

Bob Silver began a recitation, reel by reel, scene by scene, of changes, suggestions and audience reactions. Jimmy listened awhile from the back of the room, then quietly left the office and went into the lobby. His father really knew his business. A poor film like this really wasn't typical at all. Most of the pictures coming from the studio reflected Ham's instinctive gut feeling for what would sell, and he was right more often than he was wrong. He seemed intuitively to know who would be the right director, the best producer and the proper cast and when the script was ready to go. All that he knew, but there was something else about his father, something terribly incomplete. Jimmy couldn't explain it fully even to himself; maybe an explanation was unnecessary. His father was indeed a self-made man, a self-made success – and he seemed also to be a self-made failure in so much that was personal, private and important. Whenever Jimmy thought a door was opening to his father, it was suddenly slammed shut.

For a while he stood in the back of the theater while the newsreel came on, and he watched the exciting shots of returning ships loaded with arm-waving servicemen coming home from Europe. It was the very same scene in which he had played a part, maybe on one of those same ships, only a month before. The fireboats sprayed water in great arcs, whistles blasted and sirens screamed off lower Manhattan. The ships loaded with returning troops passed the Statue of Liberty as though she had been put there just for this purpose. How strange it was to be seeing it all over again. Soon he would be back in New York, and he knew exactly why his father had the idea he should go there to study distribution and exhibition. The home office, to put it simply, was about three thousand miles away from Sierra View Drive in Beverly Hills, California – and Nita Robbins. Maybe for a while it would be a good idea to study the other two legs of the tripod. Later there would be other talks with his father, and perhaps after time had passed there could be another visit to the gates in the wall on Sierra View to find out what the voice from the box would have to say, or if Mrs. Robbins was still not seeing anybody.

He went back into the lobby as the preview group came out of the manager's office and left the theater for the waiting studio cars out front. The editor and his assistant lugged the tins of film to the nearest car and locked them in the trunk. A small group of people from the preview audience still stood clustered in front of the theater, hoping to see some movie stars, and they peered at each face of the studio party as they came outside. A solitary and piercing voice came from the little group of onlookers.

'Max . . . you see anybody?'

The answer came back in a voice so filled with disgust that it made Ham want to spit out of the car into the crowd.

'Nah – they're nobody!'

The cars pulled away, and it was all Ham could do to keep the window up and his temper down. All the way back to the studio they were silent. Whatever could be said about the previewed picture was already said. Now it was up to the editor and the post-production people to salvage the wreckage. The producer slumped deep down in his seat. He was going to miss all those great meals in the executive dining room – but there were other studios and other dining rooms. Tomorrow he would start cooking up a new deal someplace for himself before the word got out on the stinker they ran tonight. The director was in the car following. He counted himself lucky not to have to listen to what he thought they must be saying about his work and how he had botched it up in spite of the best technicians the studio could provide and an adequate cast. Well, win a few, botch a few, and he could always go back to radio. The cars arrived at the studio and passed through the main auto gate.

'Good night, Dad. Thanks for dinner. I really enjoyed being with you. I even liked parts of that picture.' They got out of the car and Jimmy walked to the front of the bungalow with his father, and as soon as they were alone he spoke to him again. 'I'm sure you're right about the importance of distribution and the theaters . . . but the really interesting part of the whole business to me is the pictures you distribute and show. I think that end of the business is the most important. Everything I did in the army the last few years was really production work, and I think I did a darned good job of it. Dad, you were talking about the three tripod legs that make up the industry. Well, the studio and production is the one leg I know I'm better suited for than either of the others on that tripod. I feel I should be working here, because my whole

446

background is in this end and this is where I want to wind up.'

Ham stopped walking and turned toward his son. His face was in dark shadow, but Jimmy heard the sudden anger in his voice and knew it must also be on his face.

'Damn it! Everybody and his uncle wants to be a picture producer, work in a studio! I can buy and sell producers and all the other genius types I need here for a dime a dozen . . . or I could before those shitty agents moved in and took over! I want you to go back to our home office and learn something about the whole industry, not just one single part of it! Hell, any shmuck with a camera and enough money can make movies! What I want you to know is a hell of a lot more than just production. You have to know the market, what the customers will buy and won't buy and how we get them to take whatever we give them . . . and then see that we get back at least part of what's due us from the box office. That's distribution – and that's where you're starting!'

'Dad, I appreciate everything you're saying, but – '

'But my ass! Do what I tell you to do and stop giving me answers about production. You're not ready for that until you find out everything you can about distribution and exhibition!'

Why didn't his father come right out with it and tell him the real reason he wanted him out of town and more than three thousand miles away at the home office? Nita still must be giving him trouble and this was a simple answer. Where there was no solution, remove the problem, even if it meant all the way across the country. He cleared his throat, determined not to let it die so easily.

'Dad, I'd like to talk some more about it with you.'

'What the hell's to talk about!' answered Ham in continued anger. 'You know where New York is . . . you were there only last month, weren't you? I'll tell Bob Silver to get you a ticket east and line up a hotel room until you find something more permanent. The sooner you get there and check in with Lennie Rhinehart, the more time you'll have to learn about some very important things. Give me a phone call before you leave. Good night.' He went up the bungalow steps and vanished inside as the door swung shut behind him.

Jimmy stood alone on the dark street, filled with words left unspoken and shaking with frustration. One day his father must sit down him and listen . . . hear the things he had on his mind . . . and then open up and tell his son in all honesty why he did some of the things he did . . . really listen without slamming doors shut between them . . . but when would that be? He looked around at the long rows of sound stages, drew a deep breath, then walked on to the parking area to find his car and drive off the lot.

CHAPTER FORTY-TWO

Tommy Harris was one of thousands of good-looking young men who drifted into Hollywood seeking easy work, cash in his pocket and not too great a strain on his mind or body. There was an appealing boyishness about Tommy that many older women found irresistible. At first he seemed to be like a grown son to many of them, but then their maternal feelings usually turned delightfully incestuous. He soon found easy work at which he excelled, being a hired companion and occasional lover to lonely wealthy ladies. Nita first met him when Roberta Gould, one of the town's better and lonelier screenwriters, brought him as her escort to a party she and Ham gave at their house for Lennie Rhinehart and his new wife. The disturbingly good-looking young man stood off to one side, not terribly impressed with all the clever people, caring little for their constant industry chatter.

Nita walked over to the young man and introduced herself as the hostess. Soon she was taking him on a tour of the house, pleased to get away from the suddenly boring conversation of all the others. She liked his smile, the way he listened so closely to everything she said, making it all seem so important – and the wonderful movement of that six-foot-three-inch body. He looked like one of the Greek statues set out in the garden, only he was wearing a gray wool suit instead of a white marble fig leaf. Nita wondered how he would look with just a fig leaf . . . or without one. She found herself stripping Tommy with her eyes as she led him through the house, showing him paintings and other works of art that meant little to him. The only object he watched with any real interest was Nita herself, and their eyes met several times as they engaged each other in an unspoken dialogue, dialogue older even than the ancient figure of Buddha in the library or the antique Persian carpet in the formal dining room.

'I never thought I could hate one of my own parties in my own house,' said Nita. 'I can't wait for this one to end. My

husband invites people he sees all day up here so he can talk
business to them all night and I have to sit around listening to
them for hours. Even during the screenings downstairs they
never shut up. You wouldn't believe the things they say to the
screen . . . if it's a picture from some other studio. I've
decided that most of our guests are only here to do themselves some good, to get something they want from Ham.' She
felt a bit surprised to be confiding so quickly in this young
man she had just met, but it seemed so easy and natural. He
must have been born under a good sign.

'How can you be sure that isn't the real reason I'm here
too?' said Tommy, a smile appearing on his face.

'For one thing, you aren't in this crazy business . . . or are
you?' said Nita.

'I guess you could say I'm in entertainment. I take out
women who can't stand being alone. It's not a bad living. I've
got what they want and they've got what I want . . . money,
places to go . . . parties like this where I meet very interesting
and lovely people like you. It's harmless. They're old enough
to know what they're looking for . . . or at least hoping for . . .
and I provide it. We always understand each other perfectly
and nobody gets hurt. Of course, some of them are kind of
ugly, but I just see their beautiful hearts and they're all Miss
America. Sometimes they're married and the old man is out
of town, so they want to get out too. You could say I'm a kind
of specialized tour guide. I show them around, keep them
company, know how to order off a French menu, read a wine
list and keep up my end of the conversation.'

'And what else do you do for them?' Nita asked, looking
closely at his handsome face. He answered her directly, not
the slightest bit overawed by his lovely inquisitor.

'I show them the kind of time in bed they forgot ever
existed. I take them on a guided tour of my body and of
theirs. I give them back the part of their life they thought
was dead.'

Nita drew in her breath, surprised by his answer, and she
kept looking at him in silence. Only the sound of Ham's voice
coming from the other room could be heard as he talked
grosses, print costs and advertising with Lennie Rhinehart.

'Have I offended you, Mrs. Robbins?' he said, still smiling
at her.

'Offended me? I wouldn't say that at all. Please, my name
is Nita, don't be so formal.'

She looked around quickly to make certain they were alone

in the reception hall, then moved close to the young man and spoke in a low voice.

'It's been a long time since I've been on any kind of a tour, even a guided one. It sounds quite interesting. How could I reach you if I wanted to get more . . . uh . . . to get more travel information?'

He was not at all surprised by her direct approach, or was it indirect? This had happened too many times before. He wrote his number on a card and told her he lived in a little house borrowed from a friend who was in a New York play. It was just a few miles up Beverly Glen, a twisting, almost rural canyon road leading from Bel Air all the way over the Santa Monica mountains and down again to the San Fernando Valley.

'Where I live is quiet and isolated. I think you'd like it. Maybe in exchange for you taking me on this tour of your house you'll let me show you around mine.'

'Maybe,' said Nita, 'maybe . . . Now let's go downstairs to the bar so I can show you the rest of the place, then return you to the fortunate lady who brought you here.'

'Oh, Roberta Gould. I don't think I'd call her fortunate. I understand she's a very talented screenwriter, a nice person, too, but one of the most lonely and unhappy women I've ever met. Just about the only people she ever lets herself get to know are the ones she invents for her stories. She's been divorced I think four times, she told me, and she never even got to know any of the guys she married. When she's forced to go out, like tonight, she has to have a man along, so she gives me a call and I make a few bucks being a glorified baby-sitter. No sex, absolutely no sex with her – you have my word for that. She saves it all for her scripts. Somebody told me there's so damn much of it in the stuff she writes for your husband and other companies that it drives the Producers' Association absolutely nuts every time they get hold of one of her screenplays. To look at that nice, innocent-looking lady you'd never think she had such a wonderfully dirty mind!' They both laughed.

'Back to her you go, and don't you dare teach her any new tricks for her scripts. Ham has enough trouble with the Code and he keeps telling me how they ruin all his good sexy films. So that's the dear lady who writes all that "filth." I should get to know her much better – maybe she could teach me a few things.'

Tommy leaned over and whispered into her ear, 'Maybe I could too.'

They joined the rest of the party down in the basement

screening room, where they sat in the dark and watched the characters created by Roberta Gould playing out their twisted shadow lives in a film produced by Robbins International. Nobody talked back to the screen tonight, not with the Boss sitting there with the control box beside him and all the power of his position. Nita sat in the back row next to Tommy Harris on a soft leather couch set against the wall. In the darkness during the running of the film, as the scenes they watched risked the Code office's wrath with implied sensuality, Nita's hand slowly moved over to Tommy's lap and rested there. Almost at once she could feel him grow big and rise up as though he would burst through his pants to get at her. She pulled her hand away quickly before anything could happen that would be embarrassingly difficult to explain – or to clean up.

Less than two weeks after Nita had taken Tommy on the house tour, she sat in her dressing room and looked at the bored and frustrated image of herself in the mirror. It was past three o'clock in the morning and Ham lay in the bedroom sound asleep. He had come home very late for the third straight night, after working with the editors on a picture that was set to open at the Radio City Music Hall on Easter Sunday. This was one of the great showplaces of the world, and the prestige of having a preferred play date here was so vital to the company that Ham had personally taken over all post-production work himself.

'I'm sorry, Nita. I hate being away from you again, but this is too damn important to leave to anybody else. I've got to do it myself or it isn't going to be done the way I want it,' he had told her late that afternoon. 'I know you understand.'

'Oh, I understand, dear. You're the only one in the whole business who can put these things together. What I can't understand is how with all that money you spend hiring all those great brains, you can't seem to find anybody bright or clever enough to take some of the load off your shoulders and do it for you. After all, you've got a home, a wife and a child, and they don't see you more than a couple of times a week anymore. I want to complain to somebody about the way you're being overworked!'

'Complain to me then, dear. I'm the boss who gives all the orders. You're right, though. I have gotten too tied up here lately, but just be a little more patient, Nita. This should be wrapped up in a few more nights and then we'll catch up on everything together.' He waited for an answer but there was none, so he went on. 'Good, I'm glad you understand. I'll try not to make a habit of it, but there's just too much at stake on this one. I'll be home real late tonight . . . I mean real early tomorrow morning . . . and then I have to get back here around noon to run opticals and the credit titles before we go on with the re-editing. I promise you, another week should see it done.'

Nita frowned at her mirror image. Promises! She was sick of promises. It would be the same next week and the week after. Some new emergency at the studio would keep him from coming home to her. She thought of him lying there when she had awakened as he got into bed and immediately fell asleep. She had looked at him lying next to her in the wide bed and been unable to get back to sleep. There was a dim light in the bedroom and she could just make out the shape of his body and hear the light breathing from his half-open mouth. Just seeing him there made her restless, and she felt like doing something, going somewhere . . . getting out and releasing all her pent-up tensions – her sexual energy. Maybe if she had to meet a release date at the Radio City Music Hall, Ham might do something about it instead of leaving her all alone every day and most nights.

On impulse, she pulled open the drawer to her vanity. It was filled with a jumble of lipstick holders, eye shadow jars, brushes and tubes of ointment. She could just see the edge of a little white card sticking out from under a hand mirror. For a moment she looked down at it, remembered something and reached in to pull it out. She knew at once whose phone number and initials were scrawled in blue ink. That good-looking young man who lived somewhere up in Beverly Glen . . . what was his name? There were the initials above the phone number – T. H. . . . Tommy Harris. She went back into the bedroom to look at Ham, from whose mouth the little buzzing snores still came, and she felt a sudden excitement at thoughts set off in her mind by the little white card held tightly in her hand. She left the bedroom, closing the door without a sound, went down the stairs to the library and over to the telephone beside the sofa. It was just 3:45 on the ornate Napoleonic clock standing on the mantel, the worst of times to call anybody, unless it was an extreme emergency. She looked at the card and dialed.

'Nita? . . . Nita . . . Oh – that Nita! Hello, how are you? I wondered when you were going to give me a call,' said the voice in her ear.

'I hope you don't mind me waking you at such an hour,' she said in a very low voice.

'I can always sleep, Nita. I can't always talk to you.'

'Remember that tour you said you wanted to talk about with me? Are you still ... uh, are you still running your ... your travel agency?'

'Am I! I should say so. Are you considering a trip?' he said in his deep voice, making her feel warm all over with thoughts in the dark.

'Let's get together tomorrow afternoon ... that's today now ... say at one o'clock ... and we can talk about it,' Nita said to him. 'I'd like to know more about what your ... your agency has to offer. I can come to your office.'

'It's not easy to find for the first time. Suppose we meet someplace and I'll show you where it is.'

'Fine. Where will that be?' she said, her excitement increasing as she thought of all the wonderful trips she had missed lately.

'One long block up Beverly Glen as you turn right off of Sunset there's a little park. I'll be sitting on one of the benches there waiting for you at one o'clock. It's called De Neve Park and you've passed it a thousand times, I'll bet, without ever noticing it. My, er ... my office is about two miles or so from there. I'll leave my car at the park and drive with you up to where all the cruises start. How does that sound?'

'It sounds perfect. One o'clock ... that's just nine hours from right now. I'll be at the park. Good night, Mr. Cruise Director.'

'Good night, Mrs. Tourist,' he said, and they both hung up.

Nita awoke that morning just before her alarm went off at eleven-thirty. The bed beside her was empty as usual and she could see the dent left in the pillow by Ham, whose day had already started hours ago in his projection room.

She dressed, ate some breakfast as she read the morning paper and then told the maid she was meeting a friend, Bea Miller, in downtown Beverly Hills for some shopping and a late lunch. She would be home sometime between four and five. Almost on reckless impulse, and with the dizzy feeling of flirting with danger, she added, 'I might be home later than that, though. I nearly forgot, we're going to a travel agency for a while to discuss a world cruise Mrs. Miller is considering. I've never been on one of those. It might be fun sometime.'

She went out to her car, drove down the hill and waved at

the guard as she waited for the gates to roll aside. 'Bea Miller – where in hell did I dream up that name? Oh . . . I remember,' Nita said to herself as she watched the gates open to let her out into the street. 'I remember reading about her in the paper. Oh, Lord! She was killed in that terrible car accident last night on Wilshire Boulevard! I only hope that Ham didn't read about it. Why did I ever pick that name! I'm sure he won't think of it, he couldn't know her . . . and poor Bea won't ever tell on me.'

In a few minutes Nita was driving west on Sunset Boulevard, and just before reaching the Bel Air East Gate, she turned sharp right on Beverly Glen, quickly coming to the tiny park. She pulled over to stop her car on one of the side streets bordering it and left her motor running. A bright red little MG sports car was parked directly in front of her, and she knew it must belong to him. Tommy sat on one of the cast-iron benches, and as soon as he saw her jumped to his feet and came over to her car.

'Good morning. You certainly are prompt. For some reason I figured you for a half-hour-late lady. My apologies for misjudging you.' He opened the door and got in beside her. 'You can drop me back here later today and I'll pick up my car.'

'For some reason I figured you for a bright-red-MG guy – and no apologies!' said Nita with a laugh, and she circled the park, getting back again on Beverly Glen. 'Now give me the directions to this . . . this travel agency where you live – or do you call it your tour center?'

'It's just a nice little borrowed house about two miles up the canyon. Be real careful, it twists and curves all the way. I'll tell you when to turn left. It's a little side street called Scenario Lane.'

'You're kidding! Scenario Lane . . . I just can't get away from the picture business! Is it really called that?' Her tension drained away as she laughed at the name of the street.

'Yep. Some writer must have dreamed it up. Anyhow, it's quite isolated and nobody sees you come or go and there's no better place to start off on a cruise.' Tommy said, and he casually slid his hand over onto Nita's lap.

'Hey, stop that! I'm driving a car on a very dangerous street, so don't give me anything else to think about except finding this Scenario Lane of yours. Now be a good boy, Tommy!'

'All right, don't worry, Nita . . . when I'm good I'm very,

very good,' he answered, pulling his hand back, and in another few minutes the little street sign told them they had reached his street and she turned off the canyon road. The house was almost completely hidden against the steep hill by heavy trees, and she followed his instructions, driving her big Cadillac into a carport meant for an MG. Even though the sun was still high up in the sky, here in Beverly Glen with the cliffs looming up on each side, every thing was in deep shadow. He unlocked the door and stood aside to let her enter, then followed, pulling it tightly shut behind them.

Tommy flipped on the light switch and they stood in the small combination living room, dining area and den. A tiny kitchen was off to one side, and within five minutes he had shown her nearly everything there was to be seen. The bedroom he saved for last. It opened off the larger room and there was just enough room for an oversized double bed, which was neatly made up with a big quilt and comfortable-looking pillows. Tommy held the door open while Nita looked into the little room.

'And this is the main office where the real work gets done, you might call that my desk,' he said, indicating the big bed.

'Let's have something to drink and then we'll talk about that guided tour of our bodies you told me about at my house a few weeks ago.' Nita felt warm all over and there was a feeling of expectation she could almost taste.

'Why waste good time on a drink – unless you just happen to be thirsty.' Tommy said to her.

'What I'm thirsty for I'll bet you don't keep in your icebox or in a bottle,' Nita murmured, almost so low that he could not quite hear her. She peeled off the fleecy cashmere sweater that suddenly seemed much too warm for her, then kicked off her shoes.

He laughed.

'You're right, Nita. I'd never keep that in the icebox or anyplace else except right here in my pants. Come on, let's board my inner-spring cruise ship. This is going to be one trip that you're never going to forget!'

The hours passed like minutes. Nita had never been so utterly, so completely satisfied. Not even Ham's lovemaking made her feel like this, all the happy little explosions in every nerve as Tommy played on her body, slowly building her up to one indescribably glorious orgasm after another until at last she felt wonderfully drained and delightfully exhausted.

Then he started all over again, stroking her, kissing every sensitive part of her responsive body until the fireworks started going off again. She felt as though they were floating in a great soft sea where waves of passion carried them both up to a white linen beach to be rolled over and over, then pulled out again until the tides swept them back, crashing at last into the absolute calm that only this sweet rage of the heart, soul and mind could bring.

Nita and Tommy lay in close embrace and slept. Slowly she came awake, and for a few moments saw only the strange room and the naked stranger beside her. Her left arm felt dead from where the weight of his body had rested, and she sat up in a sudden panic. Then it all came back in a happy flood of memory and she laughed, the sound of her voice making him stir, then slowly open his eyes.

'Hello, tourist. Enjoy your trip?'

'I'd have to invent a whole new language to tell you how unbelievable it was! I had forgotten.' She looked across his body to see the little clock on the table. 'It's six-thirty! We've been in here over five hours. I've lost all track of time. The things we did with those hours! I did tell my maid I would be home before six. I better start back – not that Ham would ever miss me. He won't even know I've been out of the house, but I really should get home. Darling, you were the most wonderful thing that's happened to me that I can remember ... well, at least since ... Never mind, that happens to be none of your business!'

'Nita, if you ever feel like calling me again, I'm usually here every morning. Now that you know the way to Scenario Lane by yourself, a cruise now and then will do you lots of good. One thing, though – this is going to be strictly on a friendship basis ... a physical relationship and nothing more.

'That way nobody will be hurt. If you ever want to break things off for any reason, that will be all right and I'll understand. Incidentally, you gave me one hell of a great time yourself. You're someone to remember! Anytime you feel like another cruise, give me a call and we'll pull up anchor and sail. It's entirely up to you.'

She went into the bathroom, washed herself, then put on her bra and panties and came back into the bedroom, where he still lay naked on the bed. She walked over beside him, leaned far over and kissed the very tip of his penis.

'There, that's for friendship! How about tomorrow, same place, same time ... same cruise ... or is there some other

457

older lady you have to take on one of your guided tours or who needs a baby-sitter?'

'Hell no! Tomorrow's for you. Nita! I'll just pull on some clothes and you can drop me off at my car.'

Nita smiled and softly laughed to herself nearly all the way home. She thought of the two of them getting her Cadillac out of Tommy's carport. It had proved more of a problem getting it out than it was getting in and she had a long dent in the front right door to prove it, but so what! It was a small enough price to pay for such a wonderful adventure.

She felt so completely relaxed and happy that it was hard to keep her mind on driving. She arrived home and the gates slid open as the guard walked toward her, saying something she did not hear as she sped through and up the long drive and around the hill to the front of their house. She glanced at the dashboard clock and saw it was just ten minutes past seven. Her car came around the turn and she saw a big black studio limousine parked in the front circle with a company driver behind the wheel. Ham must be home. But why? He was supposed to have been at the studio all day and late into the night. She felt a wave of fear and guilt sweep over her at the sight of the studio car. Nita turned off her motor and quickly got out to run to the front door. The studio driver silently watched her pass.

'What happened? Where's Mr. Robbins?' Nita asked the butler, who opened the door as she fumbled with her keys.

Before he could answer, she heard Ham shouting down from the top of the stairs.

'Nita, where the hell have you been! I tried to reach you. I've got bad news. Poppa . . . he's dead! Maurie called me at the studio. He's on his way with Rose and Jimmy to Harrisburg from New York right now!'

'What happened . . . what happened to your father?' she said, running up the stairs to her husband, hoping her face would show only shocked concern and not guilt.

'Poppa was sitting with some friends a few hours ago playing pinochle and he just fell over. Not a word from him, nothing, no pain. Maurie said he just picked up his cards and he was gone. Ruth got there and called Miriam and Maurie, who reached me at the studio just an hour ago. I'm packing some things and I'll take a plane at eight-thirty to Philadelphia and stay there overnight. A car from our exchange will pick me up at the hotel and get me to Harrisburg before noon tomorrow. It's a shock to hear it like this, so unexpected. Poppa must have been close to eighty-five, so maybe we shouldn't be too surprised. He was in pretty good shape . . . "like a bull!" he used to say. Such a wonderful warm man . . . It's a blessing to go that way – so fast, no pain, no warning.' Ham thought of something that made him smile a little. 'I hope that last pinochle hand he drew was a winner. A man so good deserves to go happy.'

'Can I help you with anything?' asked Nita.

'No, everything's been taken care of. Did you see Pops Johnson waiting for me down in the living room? He came along to speed things up. He's an old pal of the head of American Airlines and knows everybody out at the airport. Pops is always good to have along at a time like this.'

Nita remembered Pops very well and the memory brought her a sudden headache. She had no desire to see the old man right now, and for some fearful reason, she was positive he could look into her eyes and know exactly where she had been all that day and just what she had been doing.

'Say hello to him for me. I'm completely exhausted from running around all those shops today. There were some sales and it took so much longer than I had planned . . . and it about wore me out.'

The butler took Ham's luggage out to the car and then stood by the open front door. Ham went over to Nita and kissed her good-bye.

'I'll be in Harrisburg for about two days. The funeral has to be held before the Sabbath, so it should be sometime tomorrow afternoon after I arrive. I'm going back to New York with Maurie for some meetings with our lawyers. There's a real nasty antitrust problem coming up soon with the government and our company's involved along with the other majors. They want to talk to me. Thank heavens I finished re-editing the film today just before Maurie phoned about Poppa. The editor can take care of the rest of it without me, so I can be away for a week, maybe more if necessary. I'll call you just as soon as I know how long it'll be.'

Nita bit her lip before she spoke.

'Please give my sympathy to your brother and your sisters. I know they don't like me at all – and your father didn't care much for me either – but at such a time we have to forget such things. I am truly sorry about your father, Ham.' She gave him a kiss and stood at the top of the stairs as he started to go down to the hall below. Suddenly he stopped halfway down and turned to face her.

'That woman the maid told me you were with all day . . . Bea Miller . . . Don't know her? I could swear I just saw her name in the newspaper, but I can't remember now what it was about.'

Nita's heart jumped and she swallowed a great mouthful of fear. Her hands gripped the wrought-iron balustrade so tightly that her knuckles turned white.

'She's just a friend of mine and I don't think you know her at all. I can't imagine her name being in the newspaper . . . she's nobody famous. Have a safe trip, dear. Call me just as soon as you can.' She gave a little wave, grateful he was down there on the stairs and not close enough to see how her lips were trembling and the great effort it took her to speak. She quickly stepped back into their bedroom to avoid being seen by Pops Johnson, who came out of the living room, where he had fallen sound asleep in the overstuffed easy chair while he waited for Ham.

Nita stood all alone in the dark bedroom and waited for her heart to stop pounding. She heard the car start up outside and drive away. Soon it was completely quiet and she went over to open a window and let in some of the cool night air. Far off in the hills a coyote howled, and Nita slammed the window shut.

CHAPTER FORTY-THREE

It was nearly eleven-thirty in the morning and the three of them sat in Poppa's old house in Harrisburg waiting for the car to bring Ham from the Philadelphia hotel where he had stayed overnight. Jimmy was nearest to the door, while Maurie and Rose sat in two of the comfortable chairs the boys had given Momma and Poppa with all the other furniture for their golden wedding anniversary, so many happy memories ago. Maurie looked once more around the room at the familiar surroundings, then spoke.

'Sometimes, Jimmy, I find it impossible to believe we had the same parents! Your father is so unlike the rest of us, my sisters, Lou and me. There are times his whole nature is so damn twisted that he's like a complete stranger. Every now and then I think of him as still being little Chaim – that spoiled brat who used to live in this house and never grew up. You know, he was Momma's favorite. We didn't have very much for a long time, but she would always see that her little boy got all he could eat, even if we didn't. She made excuses for him, kept Poppa from making him go to school like the rest of us when he made up his mind to be a permanent truant. I'm really amazed he ever learned to read and write!'

'Take my word for it, Uncle Maurie, he reads plenty, though usually it's the boiled-down stuff the story department sends him. He knows everything being considered for a picture and reads every version of every script, and all the breakdowns and budgets, too. As for writing, well, he has secretaries who type whatever he dictates. You shouldn't be too hard on him. Sometimes a self-education is even better than the store-bought one you get in school.'

'Hell, there's always some excuse for the youngest kid in a big family,' said Maurie. 'Maybe we might have squashed him if Momma didn't look out for him all the time. I don't know ... but the thing that troubles me most about your father is the man he's turned into. Maybe all that power he's had

461

running the studio is to blame, that on top of the spoiled brat hiding inside him. I tried to tell him things. Lou was always more kind to him, but we got no place. His sisters could have been born voiceless and he stone deaf for all the attention he gave to any advice from them. I know that with your mother he just went his own way after a while and didn't give a damn about her feelings – or yours.'

There was a sound from the street. Jimmy went to the door and pulled it open, but it was a messenger with telegrams of sympathy for the family and not the car with his father. He came back into the room and gave the messages to his uncle, then sat down again. Maurie went on.

'That woman he married just one day after the divorce from your mother. I think I understand her. She saw something she wanted and she pulled the oldest trick in the world to – '

Rose looked at Maurie in alarm and tried to shut him up. 'Why go into that? Be quiet, Maurie! What happened, happened. This is no time to bring up the past! We can't change anything now!'

He glared at Rose, anger building up beyond control. 'The oldest trick in the world! Don't ask me how I found out, but I did. You met their little boy, didn't you, Jimmy?'

'Yes, a few times,' he answered.

'Didn't you think he was pretty big for his age that first time you met him at your father's?' Maurie asked, ignoring signals from Rose, who vainly shook her head at him. 'Well, I'll bet you won't be surprised that his real age . . . his real birth date is all tied into my loving brother's fear the rest of his family would find out why he pushed so damned hard for a divorce from your mother and then, within twenty-four hours after it was final, married the mother of his child – already over a year and a half old when they rushed off to Las Vegas. He couldn't bring himself to sit down with me. I would have helped him somehow if only he had trusted . . . but no, he treated me then just the way he treats me now – as a blood-related enemy! I would have understood his problem. Hell, he wasn't the first or the only man in the world to, you should pardon the expression, screw himself into such a problem, but – '

'Maurie!' Be quiet! Already you've said too much!' Rose cried out, her voice raised in anger.

'It's okay, Aunt Rose,' Jimmy interrupted. 'I've known all about it for more than a year. My mother received an unsigned

462

letter from somebody who must have been very close to whatever happened. Mom didn't want me to know about it, and even now she has no idea I overheard her reading the letter to my grandfather in San Francisco. After a while, though, I felt that all the things I heard were from the past and that they shouldn't stand in the way of my relationship with my father, if I could help it. I felt we were drifting farther apart and I didn't want it to go on like that. I'm sorry, though, that Nita won't accept me. I've had a hard time with her – some strange business about the sign I was born under. It's too bad, because I like Donny and I really wish it were possible for the two of us to be more like real brothers. I've been an only child all my life, the same as he is with his parents, and it would have been nice for both of us . . . but I guess that can never happen. I'll bet the poor kid is going to have terrible problems with Nita as he grows up, and I'm sorry for him and what he's going to be facing later.'

'You're more understanding than I could ever be,' said Maurie. 'I hate saying this about your father, but he's become a real – '

Before he could say what his brother had become, a car stopped in front of the house. Jimmy again went to the door, and this time it was his father, who had arrived at last.

'Jimmy, how are you? You look great! Maurie . . . Rose . . . I'm sorry I couldn't get a direct connection to Harrisburg, but this was the best we could do. I was very upset about Poppa, but when you think of his age . . . Well, he had a good full life.' He shook hands with his brother and gave Rose a little kiss on the cheek. They both were unnaturally quiet and restrained in their greeting, but if he noticed, he said nothing.

'Where's Ruth and Miriam? I thought they'd be here with you.'

'No, we're all to meet at the Temple for the service, then go together to the cemetery,' Maurie told him. He looked at his watch. 'We better leave right now. We're supposed to be there by noon. It's so hurried, but at sundown the Sabbath begins and it all has to be done before then.'

Ham wondered about the continued silence of Maurie, Rose and Jimmy all the way to the services. He himself talked almost without stopping throughout the short drive, about Poppa, the blessing of how he went, the good life he had led, how loved he was and the great inspiration he had been to all his children. The car pulled to a halt in front of the Temple and Maurie looked his brother full in the face as he broke his silence.

463

'You're absolutely right, Ham. The wonderful thing about Poppa all his life was that he was a good influence and an inspiration to everybody . . . especially to his children. That's the most important duty of a father. We should all revere his memory. I only hope our children will have reason to remember us the same way we remember Poppa when our time comes.'

Ham sat next to Jimmy at the service and was unusually quiet the rest of the day. Later at the cemetery he said hardly a word, and only the prayer for the dead, the Kaddish, came from his lips as he stared at the plain wooden box that held all that was mortal of Solomon Rabinowitz.

'Ham, do we have any writers, actors or directors working for us you think might be Communists?' Maurie asked his brother three days after Poppa's funeral, when they were back in the New York office.

'Hell no – at least none that I know about. We keep a strictly unofficial list and exchange confidential information between studios. That's something, though, that can't get out. We've already gotten enough black eyes with all the investigations. You know old Pops Johnson, he used to work for J. Edgar Hoover at the FBI, well, he's in close touch with some organizations and has good contacts with the congressional committee investigators. We're doing everything we can to keep on top of things and so far nothing has touched our company, but we're still keeping on the alert. Why are you asking? I thought they finally were laying off us with that miserable investigation business.'

Maurie fiddled with some papers and looked up at Ham. 'They're not laying off at all. Someone close to the committee counsel sent me a copy of a confidential letter about an actress we have under contract. They don't come right out and accuse her, but there are very strong hints she's a pinko.' He looked down at the letter in his hands. 'Her name is Gina Gerrard – her real last name is Garibaldi. She's under contract, and her father edits an Italian Socialist newspaper right here in New York. He was an anti-Fascist years ago and escaped from Mussolini and came here. What this says is that the two of them were . . . uh . . . . "premature anti-Fascists" and quite possibly involved in the international Communist conspiracy. Anyhow, it's the girl they are complaining about since an informant told them we had her working for us at the studio now and they're asking what we plan to do about it. What do I tell them?'

'Right now, nothing. I'll send a confidential night letter to Pops and have him dig up whatever he can on her. I remember-okaying the deal. She's a very good-looking and talented girl. Came from a theater group here in New York or from some summer stock company, I think. I really didn't know she had changed her name.' He smiled and went on. 'We have that in common with her, haven't we? My Lord, do you suppose they're after anybody who changed their name? We could all be in big trouble!'

'Don't take it so damn lightly!' Maurie snapped. 'These people have great power. You remember those hearings in Washington not too long ago? I was worried sick you or I would get subpoenaed to appear in front of them. We did have a few very questionable people working for us then, I remember, and they could have given us plenty of trouble. They're all gone now, aren't they?'

'Yes, two writers and a director we dropped, but nobody ever proved anything to me one way or the other about them. A lot of rumors and innuendos and some nasty politics inside their Guilds. Actually, though, they were doing lousy jobs on their assignments and I'd have let them go regardless of the stuff Pops showed me on them. It seems they raised some money for the Spanish Republicans before the war. I still can't figure how that made them Commies, but we got complaints from some veterans' organization and a confidential bulletin from some guy who runs a big grocery chain back here somewhere, and they seem to have convinced enough people that – '

'Don't go into details, please! So far as we're concerned, there absolutely is no such thing as a blacklist. We could get hit with all kinds of lawsuits if it ever came out and could be proven. After all, there are laws against conspiracies even when you're on the right side. Who did you say kept our copy at the studio?'

'I already told you, Pops Johnson. An absolutely trustworthy man – an old FBI agent and a personal friend of John – '

Maurie quickly cut him off.

'Tell him to burn all our copies of any lists. I have information we would be in all kinds of trouble if it's ever shown such a thing as a blacklist really exists. Have him destroy it – but first keep some kind of a record of all the names on something else . . . make it in code or something. If he was in the FBI he should know how it's done. If not, let him run some of our old spy pictures and see the way they did it.' He smiled at his halfhearted attempt at humor, then frowned when he saw his brother did not join him. Damn him – he always wanted all the laughs! 'If the wrong people ever get their hands on it, then they won't know what they really have. Now about this Gina Gerrard. How could you have signed her knowing that her father was editor of a Socialist paper? That was a real stupid thing to do!'

'Maurie, this is the very first I ever heard about it. I get lost in politics when it becomes that complicated. Aren't Socialists anti-Communists too or have I got them mixed up with somebody else? Anyhow, the screen test of the girl really was good. She's only been in a few of our films and I just can't see how anybody could ever be infected with anti-Americanism from seeing her in a movie. Hell, she only reads the lines in her script and does whatever the director tells her to do. It's crazy!'

'It's serious, damn serious!' said Maurie. 'We wouldn't have gotten a letter like this unless it was. Now do us all a favor. Have Pops Johnson run a check on her, give her the benefit of the doubt – then get her the hell off our lot any way you can.'

'Maurie, that's a line right out of one of our old Western films where the sheriff tells the posse to give the son of a bitch a fair and square trial, then string him up on the nearest tree!'

'Don't make jokes about this, Ham! It's much too serious a matter.' He handed him the letter. 'Read this, then give it back to me before you leave. Now let's talk about something else . . . about those goddamn exhibitors' organizations running to the Department of Justice with complaints against us and the other theater-owning production companies. That could be more trouble for us than the Commies!'

Ham agreed, but as he looked down again at the letter his brother handed him, he was troubled by the flimsy evidence against the actress. The letter was full of half-accusations, rumors and innuendos, mostly aimed at her father and implying her guilt by association. He vaguely recalled her as being a very interesting young woman and thought that perhaps he should interview her for some other reason, one he would think up later, when he got back to the studio. There was no substitute for personal contact, and the more he remembered of Gina Garibaldi-Gerrard, the more attractive the idea became. He handed the letter back to his brother, who was phoning upstairs to their legal department. In a few minutes three somberly dressed men entered the office, and

466

one of them put a thick portfolio on Maurie's desk. It bore a prominent label. *The United States of America* v. *Paramount Pictures Corporation et al.*

'Ham, you know all these gentlemen. Look at the nice gift they've brought us. I don't know about you, but I'm changing my party registration from Democrat to Republican after his kick in the ass we're about to receive. The government wants us to dispose of every one of our theaters and just produce and distribute! Can you imagine how all the wolves will jump in and try to get our theaters dirt cheap because we're forced to sell!'

'What the hell is this?' said Ham, pulling the big portfolio over and reading the label. ' *"United States* v. *Paramount Pictures Corporation et al."* Aren't we even good enough to make the main title? *"Et al."* is a shitty way to treat a company like ours! Hell, I may switch to being a Republican too! Later on let me tell you about this bright young congressman named Dick Nixon who I got to know through Pops. He's a good friend of our industry, and if somebody like him had been in there pushing for us, maybe we wouldn't be taking it in the ass so damn often. He's honest, a real driver, and if enough people like us got behind him with some support, there's no telling where he might go. A man like that could change the direction our fine friends in the White House have been shoving us ... or should I say screwing us! Just make a note of his name, Maurie, so when they write you for contributions you'll remember. I already mentioned him to you before ... Nixon, Richard Nixon. I'm going to have Pops set up a meeting with him for me and I'll tell him you want to see him next time you're both in the same city. He's our kind of man!'

'That's good constructive thinking, Ham. Let's get on with the problems we've got dumped on us right now. These gentlemen from upstairs need some questions answered.'

Ham pulled a small pad out of his pocket and scribbled a reminder to himself. 'Gina Gerrard – have Bob set appointment immediately on return. Also Pops J. arrange R. Nixon meeting.'

'Now, Maurie,' said Lionel Levinson, chief counsel for Robbins International Pictures, 'I want to ask you and Ham some questions. We have to prepare an answer to the government's complaint as it affects our company. Try to remember whatever you can, but if you do not have an answer, please be as completely honest as though you were

467

under oath and tell me so. We need as accurate a record as possible since none of this is in any of our files or correspondence copies.'

'Go ahead,' said Maurie. 'If I don't have answers for you, I promise not to make up any. Who am I impressing?'

'Do either of you ever recall meeting with the heads of any other company, or with their agents or representatives, and coming to a "gentlemen's agreement" verbally on cutting up certain cities to protect your theaters? To hold back pictures from independent exhibitors, or to set rental figures at terms favorable to our company and theirs?' asked Levinson.

'That I can answer,' said Ham with a sudden broad smile. 'We could never have made a gentlemen's agreement with anybody on anything! Where this business is concerned, we're no gentlemen!'

'Goddammit, Ham!' yelled Maurie in outrage. 'This is no time for your stinking jokes! It's damn serious. We could lose all our theaters and you sit here playing for laughs from lawyers! We don't pay them to laugh! Now shut up and let me try to remember. Boys, please excuse my shmuck of a brother, who's been around too many half-assed comedy writers at the studio to be serious about these things. Now let me see, yes . . . maybe it was three years ago, just after we decided to build the flagship theater of our circuit in Harrisburg, our old hometown. I had a private lunch here in my office with Henry Roberts of International Films . . . and Charlie Fitzhugh of Majestic, along with the heads of our distribution and theater divisions. We discussed all those things and came to an agreement . . . nothing in writing. Ham, you remember me telling you something about our arrangement before I committed our company to starting construction on the new theater, don't you? I told you it couldn't be put in writing, for obvious reasons – but I know I told you.'

'I don't remember anything except the name of our theater in Harrisburg.' replied Ham. To himself he said, 'How could I ever forget that! My God, I hope we don't lose the Bijou Dream again!'

CONFIDENTIAL INTEROFFICE MEMO
TO: H. Robbins. Personal Delivery
FROM: F. Johnson, Location Dept. & Special Projects
SUBJECT: *Gina Gerrard* (Real name: Angela Garibaldi)

Subject age – 24. Signed to six-month contract with options. Address – Hampshire Apartments, 3-D, 1707 N.

Hampshire, Hollywood, California. Phone GL4-7808. Education: Public schools, New York City, Borough of Queens; Barnard College, N.Y.C., Drama Major; summer stock, Ivoryton, Conn., Lake George, N.Y.; Crosstown Little Theatre, N.Y.C.

Subject seen by our Eastern Talent Dept. scout. Requested screen test - approved. Term contract signed. Has had minor roles in three films. Consensus of associates and studio drama coach - she has excellent talent, good looks, wears clothing very well and can handle better roles than have been assigned.

Family background: Mother, deceased; Father, Angelo Garibaldi, distant descendant of Giuseppe Garibaldi, mid-19th-century Italian patriot. Emigrated to U.S. 1936, fugitive from Fascist government. Well-known journalist. Edited Socialist newspaper in Rome until shut down by government and his life threatened. Now edits Italian-language Socialist weekly newspaper with offices on Varick Street, N.Y.C. Was subject of FBI check. Results not available. No action taken. Gave full support to U.S. during war. No negative information other than Socialist background, which appears moderate in nature. No evidence of Communist connections or sympathies. One daughter, Angela Garibaldi, actress. Known professionally as Gina Gerrard. End of Memo.

F. Johnson

Several glossy eight-by-ten photo prints were attached. They showed a long-haired blonde whose oval face coolly looked into Ham's eyes and made him impatient to meet the original. She was due in his office about now. The light flashed on his intercom and he looked at his watch. He like prompt women.

'Miss Gerrard is here, Mr. Robbins.'

'Please send her in, Bob,' he replied.

She was far lovelier than any of her photos, which Ham slipped back into the folder and put in a drawer. Her straight honey-blonde hair just touched her shoulders, and she was exactly his height, making it easy to look directly into her hazel eyes and then see the smile playing on her lips. No camera could capture the depths he knew must lie behind those wonderful eyes. She was not glamorous like the mass-produced starlets they stamped out over in Make-up, Hairdressing and Wardrobe. This girl's beauty was completely genuine. She came forward to meet him with self-assurance in her entire manner, and he put out his hand to take hers in greeting. She spoke first.

'Mr. Robbins, I've looked forward to meeting you. I want to thank you for all the nice things you said to the casting department about my test and the pictures I've been in. I really have enjoyed working for your company.'

Her well-modulated voice had delightful music to it, youth, vitality, warmth. He wished she would go on speaking.

'Miss Gerrard . . . Gina, I like to know everybody we've signed, and I must apologize for not meeting you long before now. I just returned from a trip to our New York office, and while I was there your name was brought to my attention several times. I realized I had never met you – so now that oversight has been taken care of, and it really is my pleasure. Please sit down.'

She was dressed very simply in a light jacket, matching skirt and silk blouse. Her make-up was understated and the real girl who showed through needed no artificial enhancement. Ham let his eyes drink in everything, the swell of her breasts, the narrow waist and slim hips leading down to a pair of legs to remember. He had to remind himself why he had summoned her.

'Uh – you were born in Italy, I understand. Your accent . . . you don't have any!'

'Oh, no. I've been here in America with my father almost all my life. Maybe I should have a Queens accent, but I guess I lost it in college. Have you ever been there?' she asked.

'To college? No, that's something I missed. I did make it to the fourth grade, though.'

'I meant have you ever been to Queens?' Gina asked with a cute tilt of her head and a laugh that seemed to tinkle.

'Queens – you mean that place across the river from Manhattan? No, I honestly have to admit I've missed that pleasure,' said Ham, feeling relaxed and completely at ease with this interesting girl. 'From meeting you, I can tell that from Queens come queens.'

'Oh, nothing like that . . . but thanks all the same. You haven't missed too much, though, although it was a nice place to live. You know, my father and I were only a few blocks from a movie studio there. Actually, it was in the part of Queens called Astoria. Before the war it was Paramount Studios and it went all the way back to silent film days. I visited it many times and secretly hoped someday I might be

470

in movies myself . . . and now look where I am!'

'Paramount Astoria . . . of course. I know a lot about it,' said Ham. 'During the war it was taken over by the Army Signal Corps and my son, Jimmy, was stationed there for a few months before he went overseas. Just think, perhaps your paths crossed.'

Gina was delighted with this warm, friendly man. He seemed so unlike what she had expected from the things people had told her. Knowing something of his difficult reputation, she remained more than a little wary, in spite of his pleasant manner. He didn't seem to be an obvious woman-chaser, but then, they had just met. If there was any chasing, she would be charming but firm in resisting his advances. Gina felt that if she got ahead in this business it was going to be entirely on her own and she wanted no help from anybody if the price was a roll in the hay.

'Are you busy this evening?' he suddenly asked her. The chase had started, even if no hunting horns sounded in the quiet office.

She looked at him, secretly amused. He certainly was direct and aggressive, even with his nice low-key approach. She guessed he had to be like that to get to the top and hang on in running a place like this studio. Gina decided she might as well tell him the whole story and not play any games. Better to stop things right away before he got any wrong ideas. It might be just an innocent invitation, but then there was a very good reason for her to turn him down and he better hear it now.

'I'm terribly sorry. I have a dinner date with somebody.' He started to speak, but she continued before he could say a word. 'My fiancé is here from New York and we're – '

'Fiancé!' Ham said, and she could have laughed at the sudden confusion on his face. 'I didn't know you were engaged.'

Ham had absolutely no memory of a fiancé in the memo from Pops Johnson. The old man must be slipping. What a damn shame – it would have been very nice to know her better, much better. If only he were ten years younger – and single.

'Congratulations. I had no idea,' he stammered.

'We're keeping it very quiet for another month, but thanks for your good wishes.'

'What does the fortunate young man do? Is he also an actor?' Ham asked, his interest rapidly lessening as he found himself suddenly eager to get back to reading some story treatments. What a shame she was involved . . . but then, so was he.

'He's an attorney. We met while I was going to college and he had just graduated from Fordham Law School. He's quite brilliant. The Department of Justice grabbed him right after he passed his bar examinations and he's in the New York office of the antitrust division. I'm so lucky he had to come out here for a few weeks to take some depositions on a case he's assigned to. He said it had something to do with Paramount. I'm glad it's another company and not yours, since I work here too. From what little he's told me, it sounds fascinating. I'd love to have you meet him. I think you'd like each other.'

'Yes, I can imagine it's very fascinating,' said Ham, a chill wave sweeping up from the base of his spine all the way out to the tips of his fingers. He certainly had no intention of meeting any antitrust lawyer without a formal invitation first being served on him. 'Well, good-bye, Miss Gerrard. It's been delightful to meet you. As I said, I try to know everybody working here and I'm sorry we never met before now.' He was up on his feet, shook her hand and saw her to his office door. Gina smiled at him so sweetly that he could almost hear his heart crack – but he stepped back into his office and pulled the door closed, reluctantly shutting off the sight of that beautiful behind as she walked away from him.

'Damn it! I almost wish she had been a Communist instead of this!' he growled, then went to his desk and phoned Casting.

'Ed, there's a contract player named Gina Gerrard with one month to go on her deal. Have a check drawn paying her off in full. Send it with a letter saying we're not exercising our option and release her as of now. Clear it with Legal first thing tomorrow. Thanks.'

He pulled the still pictures and memo out of the folder and sadly looked for a last time at the lovely face before dropping everything into the wastebasket. For a moment he stared across the room and out the picture window at the cloud-filled sky; then he pressed a button to call his secretary.

Bob, I want a confidential telegram on Maurie's desk tomorrow morning. Here, take it down and see it goes right out on the night line.'

REFERENCE GINA GERRARD. HAVE DROPPED HER EFFECTIVE TODAY. INFORM THAT PARTY OUR COMPANY BELIEVES IN AMERICA AND WILL NEVER KNOWINGLY EMPLOY ITS ENEMIES. LOVE TO ROSE. REGARDS: HAM.

CHAPTER FORTY-FOUR

'Her father's a lawyer! Millions of girls in the country and you find yourself a lawyer's daughter!' Ham's voice seeped around the earpiece of the phone, and Jimmy hoped the girl standing so close would not hear him.

'Dad, I know you're going to love her. Here, let me put her on the phone right now. Dad, this is Joanna.'

Ham was still a bit stunned by the sudden call from Jimmy in New York telling him he was engaged to, of all things, the daughter of an attorney! New York was crammed full of doctors, dentists, engineers, advertising executives and people in every other imaginable profession, with thousands of marriageable daughters, and his shnook son had to – He heard the girl's voice.

'Hello, Mr. Robbins.'

'Er . . . hello . . . uh . . . congratulations, Joanna. This is quite a surprise for me. I had no idea . . . uh . . . I look forward to meeting you,' he said with all the enthusiasm he could manage on such short notice.

'Thank you. Jimmy's told me so much about you. I'm looking forward to meeting you too. Will you be coming to New York soon?'

'I usually get back every other month. Maybe in four or five weeks from now I'll be there again,' Ham replied.

'Good,' said Joanna. 'We're planning a short engagement and we're looking forward to your being at our wedding. No plans have been made yet, but it will definitely be when you're in New York.'

Ham remembered Jimmy telling him about some girl he had been seeing lately, but as usual he had had too damn much on his mind to pay much attention.

'Send me some pictures. I like to know what people look like before I meet them. That comes from being in this business, where we always get screen tests of everybody,' said Ham, trying for a laugh. She took him seriously and promised that they would get some pictures to him, and then she said good-bye and put Jimmy back on the line.

'Dad, I can't wait for you to meet Joanna. I know you'll really like her, and her parents are just wonderful. I know you'll like them too.'

'What kind of a lawyer is the father?' asked Ham, hoping this one wasn't with the government, involved with entertainment law or something equally disturbing.

'He's with an important office with a whole string of names I can't remember. I think they handle mostly tax cases. He knows about you but says you've never met each other. His name is Irving Steinman and as soon as you get here you'll meet him and Joanna's mother.'

Ham was cautious. So Steinman knew about him. He wondered what and how much. Well, there were lots of lawyers, too damn many, and as long as he stayed far away, perhaps it didn't matter what he knew. Anyway, he was going to be in the family soon, and Ham would have to make the best of it.

'Good. Have you told your mother yet?'

'Of course. I just hung up from talking to her before I called you. I only asked Joanna to marry me a few hours ago, and we wanted you and Mom to know right away.'

'I figure on being in New York for some meetings with Maurie in about one month,' Ham said to his son. He thought of something, paused a moment and decided to go on. 'By the way, Nita and Donny are back there right now, at the Waldorf Towers.' He stopped speaking to think about what he could say next. Hell, why not see if Nita was ready for a change in her relationship with Jimmy now that something really pleasant like this was happening. Who could tell? She just might be in the mood for that new beginning they had once talked about so long ago. He went on. 'Why don't you both drop by there tomorrow morning? I think she'd like to meet Joanna. Donny is fifteen now, you know, and his mother's putting him into a boys' school near London. They're flying over later this week, so there's plenty of time to see them. I'm not too crazy about him going to school so damn far away, but Nita thinks it would be good for him to soak up culture, get a change of scenery and see that there's more to the world than Beverly Hills. Maybe you both could stop by the hotel and say hello?' He ended in what sounded like a hopeful question, a completely different approach for him where Nita was concerned, and to Jimmy the change was refreshing and hopeful. He decided they would visit her that same

474

afternoon, then said good-bye to his father and turned to Joanna.

'We're going over to the Waldorf now and perhaps you'll meet Nita and Donny. I've already told you something about that situation and perhaps it can still be changed for the better. I've always hoped so, and right now is a wonderful opportunity to give it a try. From then on it will all be up to Nita.'

Within an hour they both were at the desk of the Waldorf Towers and called up to Nita's rooms. She answered the phone herself, and when Jimmy told her who was calling, and that he wanted to come up and have her and Donny meet his fiancée, she did not reply for several moments. He could hear her heavy breathing in the telephone, and at last when she spoke, it was slowly and in a strained, throaty voice.

'We just returned to the room from shopping and I was about to shower and change. Could you come back in . . . say in about one hour from now?' There were no congratulations on his coming wedding. He told her that they would be back, then hung up.

After an hour of window-shopping on Madison Avenue, Jimmy and Joanna returned to the reception desk and were told that Mrs. Robbins and her son had gone out and left no message when they would return or where they could be reached. Jimmy turned to Joanna and shrugged his shoulders. They had their answer. There was just so much anybody could do.

'Come on, Joanna, let's go back to Abercrombie's. I'd like to look at some of their rifles and pistols.'

'Jimmy, don't be upset. You did the right thing. I hope your father comes to our wedding, and if she doesn't want to be there, that's her loss. Come on, back to Abercrombie's, but no rifles or pistols. Didn't you get enough shooting during the war?'

'All the shooting I did was with cameras, but I learned enough about guns never to want one around. I just enjoy looking at the beautiful workmanship. I've got an even better idea. Let's go to Willoughby's and look at cameras. That's all they sell, and they're lots safer than guns.'

'I have an even better idea,' said Joanna, with a little laugh. 'Let's walk over to Fifth Avenue and go through Bergdorf Goodman. You're not supposed to look at the wedding gown ahead of time, but it would be fun to see some of the other things they have.'

'Are you sure that's safer than guns and pistols?' Jimmy said, then gave her such a big hug and kiss that the Waldorf doorman and several waiting cabdrivers all smiled with approval. They crossed Park Avenue, his arm around her waist, and walked crosstown toward Fifth Avenue.

The time had come for both their parents to join them in the traditional first dance. Irene scarcely remembered how well Ham danced, it had been so many years since he last held her and they moved to music together. They circled the floor, and the three hundred and fifty wedding guests watched them pass Joanna and Jimmy and the bride's parents, the only other couples now on the dance floor here in the Plaza Hotel ballroom. Ham spoke softly to Irene.

'I'm really happy for the kid. Joanna seems to be a very nice girl – and a beautiful one, too. I hope they have a good life together.' Irene and Ham watched as their son and new daughter-in-law moved past them, laughing and calling out to the bridesmaids and ushers to join in the dancing.

'Jimmy's a fine young man and I'm glad you both are getting along so well,' said Irene. 'You really should know him much better.'

They circled the floor once more, and Ham saw a very angry look coming from Maurie as they danced past where he sat at a large table with Rose and other members of the family. Ham casually spun Irene around, thoroughly enjoying the five or six minutes of dancing with her before her husband cut in and they both moved off into the growing crowd of guests coming out to the floor.

Irene was quite relaxed now, feeling so much better than she had the evening before, when Ham first came into the room for the dinner she gave at the Plaza for both families and the wedding party. He had just arrived from Los Angeles and seemed quite lighthearted and happy. Jimmy told his mother that Nita still was in Europe with Donny and had not replied to the invitation he and Joanna sent to her London hotel. Although they really had not expected a reply, they felt it was only right to send the invitation.

Ham was quite happy to be with the families at this time of celebration and ceremony and almost seemed again to be the same man Irene had known so many years and heartaches ago. Though perhaps he should have offered to share in giving this pre-wedding party, he made no move to do so and enjoyed being a happy guest. Irene was a bit hesitant when the time came to introduce him to her husband, Charles Silverman, a senior partner in a downtown Los Angeles brokerage house, to whom she had been very happily married now for nearly a year. Ham was quite gracious, offered belated congratulations and made small talk while Irene stood between them, feeling rather strange standing there with the two men in her life. Everything had gone smoothly and now it was the following late afternoon, the wedding vows had been exchanged, the wineglass crushed under Jimmy's heel, and all eyes were on the couples out on the dance floor.

Ham worked his way past several tables, stopping to say hello to friends, being introduced to members of the bride's family and easing himself ever closer to the bar, where he finally stood, alone, watching the party over the rim of a full glass, which he emptied, then ordered refilled.

'And where's your wife? Shouldn't Nita be here at this happy time with you?' It was his dear sister Ruth and he wished she would shut up. He wearily put his glass down on the bar and answered.

'She's in London with Donny, getting him started in school. You know she'd be here if she wasn't out of town. I don't think she'll be back for another few weeks.' He stopped a moment, then with a little bitterness in his voice said, 'Thanks though for your concern, Ruth.'

'Still the little Chaim, aren't you?' she said. 'Still telling yourself stories you don't even believe. Well, what the hell, it's your life and she's your wife and –'

Ham turned on his heel and walked out of the ballroom, asking the way to the nearest men's room. Nobody watching would suspect he was seething with anger at Ruth and her unnecessary remarks. Anything to spoil the little pleasure he was having. She was as bad as Maurie! Maybe she was drunk – she'd never spoken to him quite like that before. That was it – his dear sister was loaded. Drunk or sober, she was getting as bad as Maurie. Maybe he should have stayed in California or gone over to Hawaii to look at that lovely little house on the Kona coast he thought of buying. Hell no, it was right here he wanted to be! With Nita off in London he felt almost completely free to do absolutely anything he wanted to do. His work was keeping him away from home and from Nita more and more lately, and there was something bothering him about her, something he couldn't quite put his finger on. A whole lot of changes, some subtle, some not. She would be laughing and singing without any reason when he suddenly

477

came upon her. Other things made him wonder, and if he didn't think he knew her so well, he would have sworn there was somebody else.

He stood in front of a urinal and finished what he had gone in there to do, then zipped up his pants and went over to a long row of sinks. The attendant ran a bowl of warm water and Ham plunged both hands beneath the surface, letting them stay there, feeling the fingers relax, the hands lose their tension. He looked up to see himself in the mirror set behind the sink, and he did not like the sight of the haggard man who stared back at him. Something was happening with Nita and he had to know for certain what it was. Little things she said, and did not say . . . things she did, and did not do. He thought of something that was very different about her lately – now she almost never talked about astrology and no longer seemed to waste hours drawing up those endless stupid horoscope charts of hers. She was just too damn happy, and he could think of no good reason for her to be like that. There had to be another man involved!

He pulled his hands out of the warm water and the attendant handed him a big linen towel.

When I get back, Ham thought, wiping the water off his hands, I think I'll have a talk with Pops Johnson. Who else can I talk this over with but him? He'll have ways of finding out if Nita is up to anything. Either I've got something to be suspicious about or I haven't. I smell smoke, and someplace there's a fire.

He reached deep into his change pocket and fished out the only coins he could find, a dime and a nickel. Handing them to the eager attendant, he quickly walked out of the men's room, leaving the man staring down at the coins in disgust.

Part Six

CHAPTER FORTY-FIVE

Ham's urgent need to rid himself of accumulated liquids made it necessary for him to find the Palladium men's room as soon as possible – wherever it might be in this big barn of a building. His table now was in the dark, and the audience sat suffering through a tired pair of comics, so he could slip out and find relief without being missed. Charlie Freeman spotted him moving against the rear wall and raced between tables, catching up just as Ham was leaving the main room.

'Mr. Robbins, is there something I can do for you?' he asked, breathless from his run.

'Yeah, help me find the men's room right away. The rest I can do for myself.' They walked on through the darkened outer room, finally locating the door to the men's lounge and toilets. Charlie pulled it open and stood there waiting.

'For God's sake, Charlie. Leave me alone – at least let me piss in peace!' Ham growled. Freeman let the door close behind him and unhappily started his return trip to the auditorium.

After he was finished and had breathed several sighs of relief, Ham was in no hurry to return to the dark room and the dull comics. He stood facing the mirrors lined up over the sinks and saw that same haggard man staring back at him, that face he remembered from another mirror ... when was it? Oh, yes, more than seventeen years ago in New York ... the night Jimmy married Joanna. He had such a great time that evening until dear sister Ruth opened her big mouth to remind him of Nita and all his growing suspicions about her.

When he returned to the studio he had called Pops Johnson, who sat and listened to him, nodded his old head and lit up his pipe. Ham could hear him speaking over the years.

'You've got to go on as though you suspected nothing, Ham.

Leave it to me, and if there's anything to it, you'll get a full report. You know, there could be nothing at all to this except what's going on in your head – but in any case, you should know one way or the other. Meantime, try to relax and leave it all to me.'

'I wish I could, Pops,' he remembered saying. 'I wish I could. I don't want to keep thinking that Nita's cheating on me – but somehow I think you're going to find one hell of a fire hiding beneath all the smoke I've been smelling lately.'

The image of the old man faded away and Ham returned to his seat at the main table. The entertainers were still on, and he wondered when they would get to the damn award part so everybody could get out of here and go home, or wherever they went. That talk he had so long ago with Pops kept coming back, and even now, seventeen long years later, he could remember exactly what they had discovered was happening in a little house far up Beverly Glen on a street with the unbelievable name of Scenario Lane.

The young man lay flat on his back and watched through half-open eyes as Nita took his penis deep into her mouth. Her head began to move up and down, slowly at first, then faster and faster. He reached down to put his hands on either side of her head, pushing back the long red hair. As she moved even more quickly, he arched his back, every muscle in tense spasm, and his hands kept pushing her head down hard as he came into her with great spurts and a long passionate moan that suddenly turned into a loud scream of agony.

'Stop it – stop! You're biting me! Stop, for God's sake, Nita! What are you doing? Is that something you picked up in Europe?'

He frantically shoved her across the bed, sat up and turned on the bedside lamp to look down at the throbbing, bleeding pride of his loins.

'Stop yelling. I only scratched you a little. You're such a baby!' Nita said, sitting up on the bed beside him. She laughed at his dramatics. What a dreadful act he was pulling, playing for her pity and sympathy from such a little scratch on his prick. She ran her tongue casually over her front teeth and was vaguely disappointed at not finding even the slightest taste of blood.

'Stop shouting, Tommy, stop it! You're going to give me a headache. Here,' she said, reaching over to the side of the bed for a piece of Kleenex, 'wipe yourself off with this, and if you can get it nice and big again, maybe we'll do some more. Here, let me kiss the poor thing and make it all well again.'

'The hell you will, you little cannibal!' he said, one hand tenderly cradling his rapidly deflating organ. 'I'm not letting you chew on me anymore!' He managed a little laugh now; the pain was going away and she was right about it being only a little scratch, although some blood still oozed a bit when he squeezed. It would be a long time before he could coax himself once more up to battle station, and he looked down again in self-pity at the shrunken victim.

Nita leaned back, smiling at the wounded warrior by her side.

'You'd think I was Moby Dick the whale and that was Captain What'shisname's leg! Shall I tie on a tourniquet or rush you off to the nearest hospital emergency room?'

'You're a damned strange woman, Nita. I think you actually enjoyed my suffering just now, such as it was. It does feel a little better now, and many thanks for all your sympathy.' He took his hand away from his penis and then looked closely at the woman lying beside him. 'Nita, do you realize the terrible chances you take coming here? Does your husband have any idea what you're doing? Doesn't he ever wonder where you go all those evenings or whenever we have a matinee? He's not just anybody, he's one of the biggest guys in town. Whoever runs a studio like he does is big – and powerful. Aren't you even a little afraid of what would happen if he found us out? I'll bet there would be some real bloodshed then!'

'My dear husband is too busy with his damn studio to remember he has me sitting around the house,' she replied, her smile gone. 'Most of the time he comes home late at night when I'm already asleep, and usually he's gone before I wake up. Sometimes the only way I know he's been home is from the dirty underwear, the wrinkled shirt and used socks I find on his dressing room floor. Oh, it's wonderful being married to the successful head of a movie company! He's too busy running his fucking studio to be home fucking me!' She pulled Tommy over for a deep kiss. 'Come on, we're just getting started.'

'Nita, promise me you'll keep your sharp little teeth away from me. I'm scared to go to the toilet now after what you just did. As for letting you have another nibble on my weenie, no thanks! That's it for tonight. I've completely lost the urge. Let's get some clothes on.' He got off the bed and reached over for his shorts. She stretched out her arms, gave a deep satisfied yawn and studied him as he started to dress.

'Tommy, all the time I've known you and still you haven't answered my question.'

'Which one haven't I answered, Nita?' He pulled on his undershirt, tucked it into his shorts and stood where the dim light made him appear even more handsome and desirable.

'You still haven't told me the day and the year you were born . . . or the time of day, if you know it. I'd love to find out.'

He interrupted with a deep laugh.

'What in hell for? I don't want any birthday presents . . . just a few relaxed afternoons and evenings like the ones we have now are enough for me. That's what we both agreed it was going to be. Nothing serious, strictly for the fun, the physical part of it, so when we say good-bye it will be without hearts and flowers. I told you that's how I wanted it and you agreed. Now you want to know when I was born, and the next thing you'll toss me a birthday party and invite your husband to help blow out the candles – and me. I'd get a lot more bitten off than just my prick, believe me. It could even ruin my whole Hollywood career, my dear Nita.'

She disliked the mockery in his voice but pretended not to notice. Watching him get dressed made delicious little shivers run up and down her back. Before he pulled on his tight-fitting pants, he stood under the floor lamp and again closely inspected the little scratch, blotted it with the tissue and looked over at her with a shake of his handsome head.

'Damn it, the skin really is broken. I have some iodine in the bathroom, but that would hurt almost as much as having another mouthful of your sharp teeth in me. I'll wash if off with soap and hope I don't pick up an infection. Maybe I ought to put on a Band-Aid . . . no, it wouldn't stay on very long. For a while, Nita dear, you and I are going to keep our love-making on a strictly conversational basis until this is all healed up.' He went into the bathroom and she swung her legs over the side of the bed, got up and started dressing. Band-Aid or no Band-Aid, she would be here again tomorrow. It was just too wonderful to let a day go by without it.

The man was a professional in a team of professionals. His job was to follow the big car in front, to keep tight on its tail without ruffling its feathers. When he came to the Beverly Glen turnoff, he managed to get through the intersection as the light changed to red. Half a block up ahead he could just make out the dark shadow of the Cadillac racing past De Neve Park and up into the hills where the little houses clung like shingled leeches to the steep slopes on either side. He was quite relaxed, but every time he drove up this twisting canyon he wondered what it would be like if some stupid bastard flipped a lit cigarette out of a car window into all that dry brush by the side of the road.

'Couldn't get me to live up here . . . gotta be absolutely nuts to take such chances,' he muttered, spinning the wheel sharply to circle a station wagon that loomed out of a side road, threatening to cut him off from the Cadillac he was trailing. He watched the names of the streets reflected from his headlights as they flashed by; very soon his relief man would take over. A mile and a half north of Sunset he reached Fernbush Lane and slowed down, pulling off the main road to watch as the second car in his team came out of the side street where it had been parked, motor idling, and took up the tail. He turned the car, killed the motor and lights, then reached for a cigarette and checked his watch.

Ten minutes later he started the car and drove up Beverly Glen to Scenario Lane and pulled far over off the road. His partner stood in the darkness to the side of the house; by now their subject would be inside, completely unaware of having been accompanied all the way from her house on Sierra View Drive to this little hideaway house in the hills. He reached down and pulled the camera out of its case and checked the multiflash holder. A gem of a camera, able to grab a whole series of flash shots that could be blown up big enough to make a pimple on an ass look like a crater on the moon. He hoped this job would be like most of them, so quick and stunning that the subjects would be startled stiff at being caught in the stream of light flashes while they were naked, screwing away in bed without a care in the world – until then. Usually it was easy to grab half a dozen pictures and be out the door before the first screams came, although once a guy had gotten really violent and came up with a pistol from under the pillow, but his aim was so thrown off by the flashbulb glare that all his shots went wild. Still, it wasn't the most relaxing job in the world. This one seemed to be going nicely so far. For more than a week they had been following the subject without being spotted, and now it was opening night. No more rehearsals. There was film in the camera, flashbulbs were all in place and it was time for the final move.

He left his car parked nose out for an easy getaway and moved over to join his partner, with the camera cradled in his right arm. Focus and exposure were preset, and the quick-change magazine was loaded with Tri-X film.

'Let's give them another ten minutes. It usually takes them that long before they're into serious banging,' he whispered to his partner.

'Okay. Fine, fine. Say, wasn't it a beautiful day? I finally got my tomato plants into the ground this morning. My wife's been nagging the hell out of me of to do this for weeks. You've never really tasted a tomato until you eat the ones you grow yourself. Some night when we're not on a job, I want you to come to the house and my wife'll give you a bowl of something called gazpacho. It's a cold Mexican soup she makes from our own tomatoes.'

'Gazpacho? That sounds more like a stomach cramp than a soup. How long we got now?'

The first man flashed the tiny penlight on his watch.

'Another three minutes. They should be at it by now. Let 'em have their fun another minute or two. You have the dupe keys?'

'We won't go through the front door this time. I was up yesterday when the guy was out and fixed a side window so we can get in without any trouble or noise. It takes us right into the little hall outside the bedroom, where they are now. You remember it from the floor plan we laid out. Easy to get in, easy way out. All right, another minute. Say, don't you have trouble growing anything in that crummy clay soil where you live? I can't even get a dandelion to come up where I am.'

'Nah, plenty of good steer manure, water twice a week and the tomatoes pop out faster than you can pick 'em. Okay, time to move.'

They slid up the window, which had been soaped in advance and made no noise. A little box had been left in position beneath the window and they used it to boost themselves up and then they were standing in the hall. A few steps to the door and the camera was raised up to eye level with a finger on the release. The second man kicked the door wide open. Flash! Flash! Another and another. The entire room was lit up by the bottled sunshine, and there, squatting on the

486

bed, with his great long stiff penis half in her mouth, was Mrs. Hamilton Robins astride the young man who lived in this house. Nita rose up in horror, came fully up to her knees, too stunned even to shield her nudity with her arms. Flash! Flash! The camera worked perfectly and the pictures were shot as though with a photographic machine gun. There was no better equipment in the whole world for this kind of job, and it was worth every cent it cost the company. The couple on the bed started moving fast now, but the two men spun around, slammed the door and were out through the window and back on the ground. The second one out pulled the window tightly shut and kicked the little box off into the bushes. They quickly walked to their cars and in a moment were on their way down Beverly Glen headed back to Sunset. All the preparations and rehearsals had paid off. It was an easy job, so neat that it had been a pleasure.

Half an hour later they met in the darkroom and slid the six exposed negatives into a developing tank, waited for ten minutes, put them through a wash and hype fixing bath. After they had been washed and dried in a forced-air box, they went into the enlarger for several sets of eight-by-ten glossy prints.

'Hey, look, you can even see her tonsils in this one!' said the first man. He slid the prints into a large envelope. 'Come on, let's go to the office and type up the reports.'

Later that same night he quietly returned alone to the darkroom and made up another set of prints and a duplicate report for a private client who had paid in advance for any information concerning Ham Robbins. As he put the thick envelope in a mailbox at midnight he wondered what use Larry Gross would have for this stuff. Maybe the slimy bastard was writing a story for one of those scandal rags about the time he was a beard for Ham Robbins.

It was more than an hour before Nita could stop sobbing. Tommy had chased after the shadows he dimly saw standing in the doorway, but in the bright afterglare of the flashes all he could see were glowing blobs and he kept running into the walls. When he did make it out of the front door into the street, pulling the door shut – and automatically locked – behind him, he heard the two cars roar off into the darkness. Suddenly he realized he was standing there completely naked, and although it was a balmy night, he felt as though he has been caught nude in a blizzard.

'Nita, let me in. Please! I'm locked outside!' He rapped on the bedroom window again and again. 'Nita, please! I think you bit me again! I'm bleeding and I'm freezing my ass off!'

But Nita did not answer. She had run into the bathroom and slammed the door behind her. Tommy went all around the house trying to force open a window, finally smashing one and painfully boosting himself into the house. He searched all through the place, finally coming to the bathroom, where Nita at last opened the door. She came out to sit beside him on the rumpled bed. She was still weeping, shaking and terribly frightened.

'Who was it . . . who would do such a dreadful thing?' she said, over and over.

'Do you think your husband knows about us?' he asked.

'I'm positive he doesn't,' Nita answered. 'How could he have found out? He's been away from the house nearly every day since I got back from London, more than a month ago. Last week he flew to New York for the annual stockholders' meeting and won't be back for three or four more days. He hasn't said one thing that sounds as though he had any suspicions. I have no idea who it could be.'

'Blackmailers! That's who it is! Blackmailers!' said Tommy, who had read enough detective novels to know a plot when he was in it. 'You just watch – they'll be getting in touch with you to tell you how much money they want for those negatives. There isn't a damn thing you can do until you hear from them. Do you have a lawyer you can trust, somebody your husband doesn't know?'

'No. I never needed a lawyer of my own. Ham always handles everything,' said Nita. 'I don't even know who to go to about something like this. Wouldn't the police help me out if I'm being blackmailed?'

'Police? Yeah. They'd help you out all right – right out to your husband and into the newspapers. This is something you have to keep quiet about unless you can find a tight-lipped mouthpiece. Let me ask around. I have some friends and can get some names without telling them who it's for. Do you have some money you can get your hands on right away if you have to come up with some dough for a lawyer?'

'Yes, I might be able to raise ten to fifteen thousand dollars in a hurry, maybe more if I sold some jewelry . . . but it won't be easy,' Nita said, her tears finally all dry. 'I'll meet you at noon tomorrow in the park and you tell me who to see. Now I want to get out of here and go home. Please come outside with me. I'm too scared to leave the house alone.'

She dressed and they went to her car and she drove back to Sierra View Drive, nearly sideswiping a Sunset Boulevard bus and another car, her mind was so far away in its deep and troubled thoughts. She was lucky, though, and made it to the gates, which slid open, letting her go up the long driveway to the house. It looked so cold and white in the moonlight, and for a while she sat outside in her car looking at the ghostly reflections on the wide front lawn and windows. There was a crisscrossing of snail-slime trails, and she would have to give the gardeners hell before Ham returned from New York. A deep breath and then she left the car, walked across the circular driveway and let herself into the house. It was Tuesday and Ham would not be back for three or four more days. She went through the hall and looked over at the telephone sitting on a table, wondering when it would ring and who would be on the other end.

'Don't be so frightened. I only want to help you,' the young lawyer said to Nita. He was a very alert and bright man named Norman Oliver Harris and he radiated a confidence that made her feel a little better after the first difficult minutes had passed. She told him the whole story after he assured her, then reassured her, that not a word passing between them would ever leave his office. He explained as to a child the lawyer-client relationship, which was almost a sacred one in the trust and confidence it held, and how she could be helped only if she opened up and told him everything in complete honesty.

It was one of the most terrible days of Nita's life but she managed to get it all out and now she waited, twisting her handkerchief into shreds, for him to tell her what to do.

'First of all, Mrs. . . . er . . . what did you say your name was?' Attorney Harris disliked clients who withheld information from him, especially their real names.

'Uh . . . my name? I already told you,' she said, squirming slightly in her chair, her voice betraying her as he shot a cold look of disbelief at her. She gulped, then began again. 'No – that wasn't my real name. I didn't want to tell it to you, but I guess you have to know.'

'Damn right, lady. I wouldn't represent you for an overtime parking ticket if you held anything back from me. Now just who are you?' he snapped at her.

'I'm the wife of Ham Robbins. My husband is head of Robbins International Studios. My name is Nita Robbins.'

His eyebrows rose a fraction of an inch, but otherwise he showed no reaction. He could understand now why this frightened woman had given him a phony name.

'Now we're in business. All I can tell you right now is to wait for the next move by whoever took those pictures. My feeling is that it's the kind of thing a husband might do if he was suspicious of his wife – but you tell me that doesn't seem to be the case here. Personally, I'd reserve judgment on that. It could be that he knows much more than you think he does – and then again he might know nothing at all, if what you've told me is absolutely true.' The lawyer paused a moment, then looked Nita squarely in the eye. 'Tell me, what is your relationship with your husband? Have you had sex with him recently and has he said anything during the past few months that sounds, well, different from his usual conversation?'

'He's away more and more, either working at the studio or on one of his trips to New York. Sometimes I go along, but I haven't the last few times. He's there now at an annual meeting. We did go to Hawaii last year for about three weeks and had a very good time, plenty of sex, but now he just seems too busy and leaves me alone more and more. He enjoyed himself so much while we were away that he thought of buying a house in Hawaii and going there for holidays or just to get away from work. Nothing's come of it, though. I don't have to tell you I have healthy sex drives and need it. We had very good relations sexually for a long time, but now with Ham staying away so much, it led me into this terrible thing and being photographed in bed that way with . . . with Mr. Harris, Tommy.' She shuddered and put her handkerchief up to her eyes. 'I don't know what it is. Sometimes my husband is completely withdrawn, there's no reaching him. Then he can be fine and we occasionally make love, but it's not the way it once was. I feel absolutely certain I've given him no reason to be suspicious, and I never felt I was being followed when I went to Beverly Glen. The whole thing is a terrible mystery to me.'

Norman Harris looked up from the notes he was taking as she spoke. He studied her face for a moment, then looked down to inspect his perfectly manicured nails.

'I hope you're right about that, for your sake, and that your husband has absolutely no suspicions, but it's something we

490

must take into consideration. There is another possibility, of course. It could be that the young man who sent you here to me – the one who's in the photographs with you, could possibly be involved in a blackmail scheme. Such things are not unheard of. I don't know him – he got you to me through a third party, a client of mine who's a screenwriter. Later on I want you to tell me everything you know about him so I can get a rundown and see if he would fit into setting you up for this. Other than that, all you can do now is the hardest thing of all – wait until somebody calls you.' He handed Nita his card. 'You are to phone me at this number immediately after you hear from anybody concerning those pictures, and I'll decide then how it's to be handled. Do you understand?'

She nodded.

'Now go home. Try to take it easy – and wait for a call. Once again, I promise you, absolutely nothing you have told me will ever leave this office. It won't be easy for you, but it's not hopeless and you're not alone in this. I'm here to help in any way I can. There are things that can be done if it's blackmail. Good-bye for now, Mrs. Robbins. Remember to call me when you hear anything, at any hour. If I need to reach you I'll leave a message at your house. My name will be Mr. Jones when I call, and if it is not possible for you to speak with me then, call me back as soon as you can.'

Nita put his card deep inside her purse and left the office.

'Nita – I'm back!'

It was Ham calling up to her from the front door. He had just driven home from the airport and she came downstairs to meet him. He gave her a hug and a kiss on the cheek and everything seemed perfectly normal. He smiled, told her how tiring a flight it had been, the delays in taking off and then later in locating his luggage and about the stuff they served on the plane that they called food.

'I'm completely beat! The stockholders took off on me and asked questions nobody could answer. Even Maurie couldn't handle them this time . . . but finally we voted and won everything we need for another year. Thank God they only have those damn things annually! I think I'll stay away from now on and let Maurie have all the pleasure. How about a bite to eat before I get into bed and catch up on some sleep? This damn day seems to have been going on for years!'

He looked closely at Nita. She had great circles under her eyes and seemed nervous.

491

'Nita, you look as though you haven't been getting enough sleep yourself. What have you been doing to get so tired? You've had plenty of time since you got back from Europe to take it easy and rest up. For a change, I'm not going to the studio tonight. Come to the breakfast room while I get a bite to eat, then let's both get a good night's sleep and I know we'll feel better tomorrow.'

For a long moment Nita felt terrified and hoped it did not show on her face. She mumbled something about not being able to sleep well and how having caught a little head cold made her feel miserable. In truth, she had not slept at all the past several nights, not since those damnable flashbulbs went off on that dreadful evening. Every day and every night she had been waiting for the phone to ring with the demands she dreaded – and each day passed without word. She had called the lawyer several times for reassurance, but there was very little he could say that he had not already told her when she was in his office.

Now she and Ham were in bed and he was already sound asleep. Nita lay across from him and stared with unseeing eyes up at the ceiling. After a while she left the bedroom and walked aimlessly through the downstairs rooms. It was almost midnight but she could not think of sleeping.

Suddenly the telephone rang, and she jumped as though somebody had just taken her picture again. She ran over to the phone on the library table to pick it up before it could ring again. A man's voice came through the earpiece, and at first she could not recognize who it was.

'Hello . . . hello. Is Mr. Robbins there?'

'Who is this?' she said in a very small voice.

'Oh, Mrs. Robbins. Hello. This is Pops Johnson. I hope I'm not disturbing you. Could I speak to Ham? Something came up I want to discuss with him.'

'He's sound asleep,' Nita told him. 'Can it wait?'

Pops apologized and in his usual hearty old politician's voice said, 'Certainly, Mrs. Robbins. Please don't disturb him. I'll see him tomorrow at the studio. It's nothing that can't wait until then. Good night, Mrs. Robbins. Pleasant dreams.'

He hung up, and for almost an hour Nita sat staring at the telephone, which she had placed on its side so it was not properly hung up. It lay there on the tabletop like a little dying thing, humming sounds coming out of its wide-open mouth. Soon the hum changed into a buzz-buzz, as though it were begging her to hang up and bring it back to life. She could not touch the instrument, and when she finally got up to roam through the house until dawn, the phone still lay there on its side, buzz-buzzing even when there was nobody in the room to hear its sad little cries for help.

CHAPTER FORTY-SIX

It was past noon when Nita awoke from a troubled sleep. The other side of the bed was empty and only the thrown-back covers showed she had not been alone for part of the long night. The phone light flashed and she quickly reached out to pick it up. A heavy male voice spoke, and she bit her lip in sudden terror. It was the dry cleaner asking about a late afternoon delivery, and with a shaking hand Nita transferred his call down to the kitchen. She dressed, had a very small breakfast and then sat down in the library across from the telephone, which obligingly rang with five or six calls, all inconsequential, unimportant and frustrating. There was no message from a blackmailer, no demands or threats, and as the hours passed, her tension increased. Once again she placed a call to the attorney, Norman Harris.

'I told you, Mrs. Robbins, there is nothing, absolutely nothing that can be done until you hear from whoever made those pictures and has the negatives. Now try to get hold of yourself, and if you do hear from anyone, tell him to contact me and that I am representing you. Assure him the police will not be brought in as long as it is handled on a direct basis just between us. I will keep you fully informed if I talk to anybody. Call me again if you feel you must, but really, there isn't a thing you can do until they make a move . . . so try, please try to take it easy.'

That's easy for him to say, thought Nita. So very easy. She walked again through the house, into all the familiar rooms she and Ham had rebuilt and furnished, and she remembered those photographs he had spread out before her on the big table that happy night when they began to remake the past into the present. Photographs! She shuddered.

Because it was Ham's first day back at work since his return from New York, Nita had expected him to remain at the studio very late that night. When she heard his car pull up in front of the house while it was still light outside, she was

494

surprised and a bit disturbed at his unexpected return. She came out into the hall to see him enter the house and start toward the stairs. He carried a large envelope under his arm and the look on his face was somber. Nita gripped the railing tightly and watched as he came up very slowly toward her, one step at a time; his progress seemed like a filmed slow-motion scene. Time was all out of proportion, and she could not take her eyes off the envelope held so tightly next to his heart. It had to be a story treatment, a screenplay . . . some contracts . . . it had to be!

Ham walked past her without saying a word, went through the door into their bedroom and over to the round table where she worked on her astrology charts. She followed him into the room and watched as he opened the envelope and spread out the six glossy eight-by-ten prints. Nita glanced quickly at them, saw what they were and turned away, a great sob welling up in her throat. Ham stood silently in the middle of their bedroom looking at her. She tried to speak to him.

'Listen to me, Ham . . . please listen! I love you . . . It was only because you were away so much . . . at the studio . . . then New York . . . always away all these last months. Those pictures . . . they mean nothing . . . I had no feeling for him . . . no feeling for that man . . . it was only a physical thing. Ham, you've got to believe me. You've got to understand! Listen to me!'

He went into his dressing room, pulled out his pajamas, took some toilet articles from the bathroom and then turned and spoke to her.

'I am sleeping in the guest room. I expect you to be out of this house when I return from the studio tomorrow night. Where you go is your own business. I don't want to see you!'

She ran over and tried to throw her arms around him, but he pushed her away, turned and left the room. Nita threw herself facedown on the bed, cried a few minutes, then suddenly sat up and reached for the telephone.

'Mr. Harris. This is Nita Robbins. I must see you right away! I've just found out who had those pictures taken and I have to talk to you!'

'You can tell me, Mrs. Robbins, tell me now who it was. I think I know just from hearing your voice. Was it your husband after all?' asked the lawyer.

'Yes,' she answered in a voice filled with hopelessness and

despair. 'Please, when can I see you? He came home from the studio with an envelope full of pictures and threw them down on the table in front of me without saying a word, then he told me to be out of the house by tomorrow evening.' Her teeth started to chatter and for a few minutes she almost lost control of herself. The man on the other end of the call waited, then spoke in a calm voice.

'I do not think you should meet me at my office right now, and it would be most unwise for me to rush over to your house. There are some things I must start doing immediately that you will understand later. You must try to get through tonight the best you can. Take a sedative and then first thing in the morning, nine o'clock, come to my office and we'll talk. Now don't worry. It really isn't the end of the world, as much as you may think it is right now. Something constructive can be done about this and I will help you any way I can. Dry your tears, take something to help you sleep and be here at my office in the morning. All right?'

'Can't you see me right now?' she pleaded.

'Listen to me, Mrs. Robbins. Trust me to do everything I can for you. Do not go to your husband tonight. Let him sleep, and maybe he will cool down a bit. Stay away from him – that is very important! There is absolutely nothing we can do tonight and I want you in my office tomorrow at nine. Do you have something to help you get to sleep? If not, I can arrange for a prescription to be delivered to you right away.'

She told him she had something and begged him to help her.

'Please, don't get yourself into thinking everything is over, because it most certainly is not. I've been doing a great deal of work on your problem ever since you came to see me and I assure you that nothing is final – no matter how it may seem to you. I'll spend all the time you want with you tomorrow and we will do something positive about this.'

She barely managed to reply with a feeble good night and hung up. He was sure something constructive could be done. How could she possibly be helped? She saw the picture-littered tabletop when she returned to her bedroom, and without looking at the images of the two naked frightened people shoved the prints back in the envelope and jammed it into the jewelry safe in her dressing room. Nita opened the door and walked down the hall to the guest room. She gently tried the knob but it was locked. She went downstairs and for a few hours resumed her nervous lonely walk through all of the rooms, down to the basement and bar, then upstairs again, and finally, when she could walk no more and her eyes were blurred from her tears, she again went to her bed and tried to get some rest. She remembered to set the little alarm clock on her night table for seven-thirty . . . only a few hours away. One last trip to the bathroom, where she found some sleeping pills and took enough to get her through what was left of the early morning.

Ham was surprised at first to find himself in the guest room bed next morning, then suddenly recalled with a wave of nausea what had happened the night before. He dressed and left the house without breakfast so he could avoid seeing Nita. It was important he get to the studio and bury himself in work to fill his mind and drive out the memory of those terrible photographs, that he had only glanced at quickly before he had stuffed them into the envelope and driven home. Ever since Pops Johnson handed him the reports and pictures the previous afternoon, Ham had felt a sense of deep depression. His self-pride had been so outraged, his ego so crushed that he found it impossible for a time to think clearly. After a while, when he had calmed down and was alone in his office, he reviewed the past few months of his life with Nita, admitting reluctantly to himself that perhaps she was right in saying he had left her alone too much lately. Indeed, she was a sexual animal and his thoughts were only of his own feelings, neglecting her when he should have been more sensitive to her needs. Still, to shack up like that with a nobody – or even a somebody – was an affront to him. Maybe, though, it was better the man was an unknown, otherwise it would have leaked to the press and then the phone would have rung from New York and from Harrisburg. He could almost hear Maurie's voice rasping over the long distance: 'See? I told you! I told you, shmuck, she was a worthless bitch! You got what you should have expected and just what you deserve!' Ham put his hands up to his ears to shut out the call that had not yet come – but surely would. God . . . how truth hurt!

He tried to read a story treatment, then a final budget, but nothing helped. He jumped nervously as the buzzer sounded.

'Yes? What is it?' he said into the box.

'Mr. Robbins,' said Bob Silver in the outer office, 'there's a gentleman at the main entrance who says he must see you immediately. His name is Norman Oliver Harris and he tells me he is an attorney for Mrs. Robbins. He says it's quite

497

urgent, and I'm holding him now on the phone.'

Ham felt rage sweep over him. It quickly ebbed, and he tried to think clearly.

'Go down and bring him up to the office . . . and Bob, keep all this to yourself.'

Eventually, Ham knew, he would have to see her attorney, but perhaps he should have his own lawyer with him too. No. He had gone through so damn much already with Nita, the baby, then the marriage and all the abuse he took from his family – and the gnawing guilt he sometimes felt eating away at him. He should listen to the man. Let him say his piece and give him no answers, just find out what he had come here to say that was so damn urgent – as though he didn't know. He was curious, too, wondering what this man he was about to meet would have to say in Nita's defense.

'Mr. Robbins. We haven't met before. My name is Norman Harris. I am an attorney with offices on North Roxbury in Beverly Hills. Your wife came to see me five days ago. She was terribly upset and believed she had become a victim of a blackmail plot. I must admit that I thought this to be a possibility too for a while. It was conceivable that a young man she had been familiar with might have lured her into a trap, but that no longer seems to have been the case. She called me last night after you spoke to her and then she came to my office early this morning. I do not have to tell you how terribly distraught she is and –'

Ham angrily interrupted the attorney.

'Distraught! Is that all she is! I'm a hell of a lot more than that! Here she's been screwing this guy – being familiar with him, as you cutely put it – for who knows how long, and she has the gall to have you tell me she's distraught because I found her out and have proof. If she thought blackmail was involved, why the hell didn't she go to the district attorney or to the police – or at least talk to me about it. She knew where I was all the time, and I would have helped her any way I could if it really had been blackmail! Well, it wasn't – and I don't buy a damned thing you're trying to sell me!'

'All right then, Mr. Robbins. Let's talk like mature men. Your wife has told me that for the past couple of months you've been so completely wrapped up in your work here at the studio that she's hardly seen you at all except very late at night when you come home to sleep – if she herself was still awake then. Your sexual relations with her have been at a

498

minimum during all this time. She is, as I am sure you knew even before you married her, a normal woman with normal . . . perhaps a bit more than normal . . . sex drives.'

Ham flinched at the implications in what the lawyer had just said and wondered just how much Nita had told this stranger. Probably everything. Well, what of it? The lawyer went on.

'In any case, she wasn't getting from you what she desperately needed. Forget the morality of it – think of it in a purely physical way from her viewpoint, if you possibly can. She met this man. There was no amorous attachment at all. He supplied something that was strictly of a physical nature and that she needed, something you had almost completely stopped providing. It is as simple – or as complicated – as that.'

'What in hell are you trying to do, make me the heavy in this?' said Ham, as he shouted in anger at Harris, who calmly sat back in his chair. He had handled cases far more difficult than this and he was not overawed by the exalted position of the man facing him. He had learned plenty about Mr. Hamilton Robbins since Nita first came to his office, and he would bring it all up if he had to. In the meantime, he would play his hand cautiously and give the angry man something to think about.

'Each of us makes our own guilts. That's something I can't do for you. I only ask now that you think of your wife's feelings during these past months you have neglected her and of the great strain she has been under because of that. Perhaps she sought relief in the wrong way – who's to judge that? But you – you of all people – should be more sympathetic and understanding and ask yourself what you would have done had your positions been reversed. You've done some playing around yourself, not only while you've been married to your present wife, but to the first Mrs. Robbins as well. Let's not go into morality here, just reality . . . the things you know are true.'

Images flooded Ham's mind. That of the actress he had laid that time in the Trophy Room. It wasn't all that long ago, and the memory was as bright as the Oscars that had looked down at them on the floor. This smart young lawyer had asked a good question, and Ham reached for an answer that would not come. He twisted in his chair remembering that early morning when he finally came home, wondering if Nita was still awake and suspecting anything. Memories of other women raced through his mind like the blurred images in chase scenes out of his old one-reel comedies. Suddenly he could see Maurie's angry face as he ripped him apart for his infidelities. Ham brought himself back from his quick trip to yesterday and glared at Nita's attorney across the desk. What was the old bromide about what's sauce for the goose? He certainly had had more than his share, and now he was pissed off because Nita had taken a generous helping for herself from the same dish.

He only half listened to the lawyer's voice, his thoughts again going back to that terrible night when Lou had died in the flames of the back lot imitation Bijou Dream. The years could not erase his feelings when Maurie finally ran him down in his apartment hideaway over on Franklin Avenue with some dame whose name he couldn't even recall now. Yeah, if there were stones to be cast, he was one hell of a good target, and this bright young bastard here must have plenty on him. Still, he couldn't just forgive and forget. Damn it, what did Nita want? He would make no quick decisions, but he did have an idea.

'Listen, Mr. Harris. Perhaps Nita really believes she had a good reason for what she did. Maybe I ought to think more about it, but I refuse to make any decisions until I've had more time to consider everything you've told me and what I have been thinking about since you came into my office. Tell her I need a week . . . no, make that two weeks. I want her away from me. I don't care where she goes, maybe Santa Barbara would be a good idea. It's too hot this time of year in Palm Springs. After I've had a chance to think things over, then maybe I'll talk to her again. No guarantees, though! I still believe I'm right, and that she should clear out of the house for good, but I'm a fair man and I need time to think.'

'That's fine, Mr. Robbins. I'll tell your wife right away and help her get located. If it's acceptable to you, I can continue to act as an intermediary between the two of you.'

'Sure, why not. At least it hasn't gotten into the papers. I don't want it to be blasted in those damn gossip columns, and there's no reason for anybody but us to know about this. I have more than enough enemies who would love to hit me with this if they knew. Tell Nita I still want her out of the house tonight. Let me know where she's going, and if I should want to get in touch, I'll call you. Two weeks, then, and I'll decide.'

Ham hated himself for not making a firm and final decision. He took Harris's card and watched the lawyer leave his office, then sat back in his chair, more angry now at himself than he had been at Nita. He poured a stiff drink of Scotch from the bottle he kept in the bottom desk drawer. Ham rarely drank in the middle of the day, but this was no ordinary day and he needed all the help he could get. He put the glass to his lips, tilted his head back and closed his eyes.

It was not two weeks but only six days later when Ham stood in Norman Harris's office and faced Nita. He had had enough time to think things over, especially after hearing what her lawyer had dredged up out of his past.

'Let him who is without sin cast the first . . . uh . . . cast the first picture?' he mused to himself. This was no time to play with words – it was a time for decisions. Decisions he would make alone and without any influence from anybody – except maybe the accusing images of Maurie, Ruth and Miriam . . . and the dim shadow figure of Poppa. The knowledge of his own transgressions lay like a rock in his stomach, and so now on the afternoon of the sixth day he stood facing Nita.

Her face was streaked with mascara as tears flowed their course, to be wiped away with a soaked handkerchief.

'Ham, listen . . . please listen. I love you. Don't throw it all away! After all we've been to each other and been through, you can't do that! I know what I did was terrible, but I'm a human being and I need human warmth and love. I swear on my mother's grave, I swear that man meant nothing to me. It was only physical. I was wrong, I know it, but you weren't with me when I wanted you, when I needed you so desperately!'

The lawyer slipped out of the room while Nita spoke to Ham, and neither of them saw him leave. Sobbing and crying in between her words, she tried to fasten some of the responsibility for what had happened on Ham himself. He tried to ignore her, thinking only of those six photographs, but he knew in his heart she was really right about his being away so much, and he grew so perturbed by his feelings and gnawing guilt that he walked to the door, intending to leave. Norman Harris stood just outside as the door opened and gently pushed Ham back into the office, following him and then closing the door behind them.

'Now, Mr. Robbins, I hoped I could remain outside and see if you both could talk this out like two grown-up adults. I'm afraid it isn't working out that way.'

'You're damned right it's not!' growled Ham, angry at having his exit blocked by this . . . this . . . lawyer.

'Sit down, Mr. Robbins. You too, Mrs. Robbins. Let's talk real straight, all three of us. I want to see this thing resolved without a permanent break. If you both will listen to me while I tell you a few things you may not want to hear, perhaps you both will leave this room a little more grown-up and better off than when you came in. Mr. Robbins . . . no doubt you believe you have grounds for a divorce. I won't dispute that, but there are some circumstances that would have to be part of any hearing, and you had better think about them right now before you make any final decision. First of all, you are not the only person who has access to private investigators. I have a pretty complete record on you over the past dozen or so years. Names, addresses, a whole list of the women in your life, besides your first and your present wives.'

Ham tried to control the outrage that showed plainly on his face, but he was cut off in the middle of a sputter by the attorney, who continued as though he were addressing a judge and jury.

'I have complete and absolute proof that my client, your wife, has never seen and will not see unless it becomes necessary. It shows that whatever your men caught her doing up in Beverly Glen can be more than matched by your activities off and on for some time. The file on you goes back quite far, and even now I am sure it could be brought right up to date with even more of your . . . uh . . . your adult escapades, shall we call them. I have no glossy eight-by-ten photographs of you in action with young ladies, Mr. Robbins, but I have other things just as good. Sworn affidavits from several of the women involved and from witnesses, including former employees of yours who were in positions to know exactly what you were doing, where you did it, when and with whom. In short, Mr. Robbins, you will not come before the court with very clean hands. Don't worry, there are many ways of introducing such evidence to make your wife the victim and you the victimizer.'

'You son of a bitch!' shouted Ham.

'My parentage is not a part of this case. Let me continue. I know a great deal about your entire family, Mr. Robbins. I have spent a very busy six days, I assure you, and have learned what your brother and both of your sisters have said privately, and not so privately, about this second marriage of yours. While none of that would be involved in your divorce, I mention it only because I know there is a matter of personal pride you seek to maintain . . . a respect you seek . . . and it would be seriously eroded by the comments they would most

502

certainly make not only to you, but also to those who would see to it they were made public. Think it over, Mr. Robbins,' continued Harris, 'think it over. I imply no threats or coercion, but I do indicate you have a clear choice. Proceed with a divorce against your wife, but be prepared to suffer a countersuit by her against you that can only blacken your name, hold you up to public ridicule and humiliation and depict you as a whoring womanizer, at the very least. Or take your wife back, realizing that she, like you, is a human being, with human needs and desires, sharing with you an ability to love and be loved. She wants a reconciliation, and you have already heard her tell you she loves you. Now it is up to you.' He stopped speaking and looked at the two of them sitting across from each other on the chairs facing him.

Ham balanced the choices before him. He looked down at the carpet and buried the tips of his shoes in the thick pile. He looked up at Nita, who was trying to repair the ravages to her smeared eye make-up. Even with the mess she had made of her face, she still looked pretty good. One thing, Ham thought, he always had damn good taste in his women . . . but what went on behind those pretty faces was what drove him absolutely crazy. Something else drove him crazy, too – that long poking finger of guilt and accusation attached to his brother Maurie, wagging under his nose, that voice he already could hear shouting, 'Shmuck! I told you so! See what you got yourself into because you wouldn't listen to me! You lie down with dogs and you get up with fleas!' Where in the hell did Maurie find all those shitty little sayings of his? He was full of them – and full of a lot of other things that Ham didn't ever want to hear from him or his sisters.

'Nita. Are you going back to Santa Barbara now?' he asked, in a voice so calm he surprised himself.

'Yes, I had planned to. I have a little suite at the Biltmore that Norman reserved for me, but I don't have to return. I can send for my things . . . and . . .'

He did not wait for her to say more. She was jumping the gun, all right. Well, why not?

'No . . . no. I need more time . . . more time to think and get over what we've been through. Follow me back to our house with your car and leave it there. I'll pick up some things and we'll both take a little vacation for three or four days up there. Maybe if we're together where it's quiet and we don't have this noisy young man talking to us we can think things over and perhaps work it out. I think we should give it a chance. How about you?'

She jumped up to her feet, a smile breaking through on her face for the first time in weeks.

'How about me! I love you – that's how it is about me!' and she threw her arms around him and kissed him full on the lips. Norman Harris was startled by the sudden turnaround. He reached into a pocket and pulled out a linen handkerchief to wipe his sweaty forehead. He was a pleased man, and happier than he would have admitted at not having to launch a very messy divorce case that would splatter everybody concerned with the kind of mud nobody could ever wipe completely away.

They all went to the door and Ham turned to face the lawyer.

'Young man, I want you on my side. When we return from this little vacation of ours, I'm making an appointment with you – only this time at my office. From what I saw of you in action today, I think you ought to handle my personal affairs. If you do half as well for me as you did just now for Nita, I'll be a very satisfied client. Good night, Mr. Harris . . . or can I call you Norman?'

'Please, always call me Norman . . . Ham.' They shook hands warmly and the door was closed.

Nita was suddenly radiant in the dim light of the hall as they waited for the elevator. Ham looked at her and asked a question.

'Just what sign was Norman Harris born under, Nita? I'll bet you have one hell of a chart on him – and from what I've seen, there certainly must have been no conflict with your sign . . . or have you given up all that damn nonsense?'

'Absolutely not! He's an Aries, on the cusp of –'

She was still talking her way around the zodiac when the elevator arrived.

The first few days in Santa Barbara passed and Ham felt more rested than he could remember feeling for months, but he was quite concerned about something that happened the very first night in the suite where Nita had been staying. Their trip up the coast was very pleasant and the blue Pacific stretched as far as the eye could see as they drove the ninety-five miles north, watching the sun set with an almost tropical glow. They arrived at the Biltmore just in time for dinner. The clerk was most impressed with the famous production executive moving in with his wife, who had been such a sad-looking sight all the past week she had been here. Now she looked so happy that he thought for a moment she was an entirely different woman. You could never tell with these Hollywood types.

Dinner, a walk around the illuminated gardens and then up to bed and then . . . nothing. Ham could not become aroused and lay naked for over an hour beside Nita while she stroked him, rubbed her body against him to help him have an erection. It was no use. He wanted . . . yet did not want her. Hoped . . . but had no hope, and finally, hours after they had turned off the light, they drifted off into troubled sleep. Nita had unfulfilled dreams, in which she threw her arms around someone who then vanished into smoke, and when she turned to find him again, clasping him once more in her arms, he melted each time into vapor.

Ham too was frustrated and lay sleepless for a while. Hell, he thought, I've been damned mad at her for over a week. I can't turn myself on and off like an electric light. Before he could think much more about it, he was asleep, joining Nita in uneasy slumber.

They explored Santa Barbara, visited the shops, played a little tennis, with Nita watching more than playing, and then they went on a beach picnic arranged by the hotel. Ham remembered other picnics, other years, and again that night was unable to do anything with Nita after they turned off the bedroom lights. Instead of remaining four days, he felt they had to get away from this place as soon as possible. He dreaded the thought of another night in bed here, fighting the deep feelings that had emasculated him, that made him feel less the man that he had been, a flabby imitation of himself. Another futile night in bed with Nita could not be faced. This hotel and the Pacific Ocean and beach outside kept reminding him of the first night of his first honeymoon . . . the one with Irene in Santa Cruz . . . in another hotel beside the ocean . . . how she had been unable to enjoy sex with him and the way he had worked to help her. Now he was the one who needed help.

They loaded the car and headed south after lunch. All during the drive Ham tried to figure out what had happened, and all he could think of was that his feeling went very much deeper than he had realized, that he could not so easily forgive Nita. His flabby impotence must be his unconscious revenge on her – and on himself. He looked quickly over to where she sat beside him on the wide front seat, her face terribly troubled as she sensed the dark things going on in his mind. Without voicing a word, they both were saying the same thing to themselves. What was going to become of them? Where were they going now?

They arrived at Sierra View Drive and passed through the gates. Ham told the butler who came out to unload the car to take his bags up to the guest room. For a while he wanted to sleep there, and perhaps they could work things out in time, but not all at once. It was too hard to turn anger into love so quickly, and he must make the transition slowly . . . if he could make it at all.

Nita ran up to the bedroom and threw herself down on the big double bed they once had shared, tears flowing down her cheeks, staining the silk coverlet. They were home.

Next morning Ham left the house early and went to his office, to find a letter waiting for him from Maurie. It was marked 'Confidential,' and Bob Silver had put it unopened inside Ham's folder for immediate attention. He ripped the envelope open, pulled out the single sheet of paper and started to read. In a moment his hand shook with fury, and the paper made a crackling noise as though it shared his outrage. His dear brother had written him a letter of congratulations, no less! Congratulations on finally wising up to the whore he had married and how it was never too late for him to make constructive changes in his life. Maurie went on to say how pleased he was that Ham at last had found out what a tramp Nita was, who would screw anybody, and what a terrible experience it must have been for him to learn about her the way he had. In time, though, he would be deeply grateful and thankful and . . . It went on and on, a tightly written page in Maurie's cramped hand. At least the son of a bitch had the good taste not to dictate it to some secretary to spread all through the home office!

He buzzed for Bob to come in and take a letter. He would get back at that no-good fucking bastard brother of his!

Dear Maurie:

I received your brotherly letter, the one marked 'Confidential,' and I thank you for your kind thoughts. You will, I am sure, be pleased to know that Nita and I both are in excellent health, thanks in part to our little vacation together the past few days up in Santa Barbara. A lovely place. You and Rose should try it someday – so much nicer than Palm Beach, but perhaps it is easier for you to

506

go to Florida than to come out here. Nita and I plan to fly to New York next week for my meetings with Distribution about future product. I also want to see some plays the story department has recommended for purchase. I hope you and Rose will join Nita and me for dinner while we are in the city. She joins with me in sending you both our love.

                                                    Your brother.

When Bob brought him the typed copy, Ham scrawled his signature much larger than normal at the bottom of the page and told him to have a messenger take it right out to the airport so it would be on Maurie's desk the next day.

Alone, Ham leaned far back in his chair, looking out at the piece of bright blue sky he could see over the sound stages, and only the walls of his office heard what he said.

'That should drive them down to Palm Beach! I wonder who in hell tipped Maurie off about Nita and me? The only other person in the whole company who could have known everything was Pops Johnson. There – that's the answer! It's got to be. It would be just like that old bastard to impress Maurie with how valuable he is to the company . . . and the family! I'd better have a good talk with Pops. He's getting too damned old for his job and ought to retire while he's still got some years left to enjoy. I'll personally handle it and let Nate Klein or Leo Arnheim fire him as soon as I'm out of town. I'm positive the old *kocker* shot off his mouth! Damn it to hell, who can you trust anymore!'

That night Ham was still so angry at his brother that when he arrived home from the studio he raced up the stairs and burst into the bedroom, where Nita lay on the bed, still wearing her robe.

'Ham, what happened? You look absolutely wild!'

'Stop talking, Nita,' he said in a loud voice. 'Get the hell out of your clothes. We're going to fuck until the sun comes up, and tomorrow night we're leaving for New York to pay my dear brother a visit. Hurry up – I can't wait!'

He was nearly all undressed, and Nita sat up on the bed, a wide smile driving the frown from her face. She pulled off her robe. She was wearing nothing underneath. He climbed into bed and their naked bodies thrust closely together. When the time came for him to enter her, Nita looked up at Ham's face in the dim light. She could hardly believe what she heard him saying in his angry voice as he drove down again and then again.

'You fucking bastard . . . Maurie . . . I wish you were here to see this . . . you son of a bitch!'

CHAPTER FORTY-SEVEN

Ham was wrong about his letter driving Maurie and Rose out of New York and back to Palm Beach. It was to Boca Raton. Maurie returned only when he received word from his secretary that Nita Robbins had gone on to London to visit Donny at his school. Now he sat in his office with his younger brother and said absolutely nothing about his letter to him or the reply that had sent him out of town so briefly.

Of course he kept an embarrassed silence about the dreadful still pictures and report some anonymous well-wisher had sent him and that could have been fact or fraud.

Ham was delighted at the acute discomfort Maurie found difficult to conceal, but something so important had been developing that it forced Maurie to return to New York as quickly as possible, and he was relieved that for a change it was not a personal matter. It was a different kind of disaster – television.

'You know of course that Jimmy has been in our Philadelphia film exchange the past couple of months, and I borrowed him a few weeks ago from Lennie Rhinehart to look into what RCA is doing in their Camden plant. We have good ties with them since we use their sound system. Because Jimmy was working just across the river from their factory and research center, he went there several times and phoned me about what he saw. I asked him to find out everything he could and we've spoken several times since then. Ham, that's the way things are going to go – television. There's going to be a theater in every home. If we don't want to be left out of it the way we were with sound when it first started, we'd better get off our asses and see where we fit in. All the television receivers in the world are worthless unless they have programs to receive, and we may still have a chance left to get in on the ground floor.'

'What else have you done about it?' Ham asked.

'Not a damned thing,' answered Maurie. 'I want you to

listen to Lennie Rhinehart so you'll understand what we're up against. I also asked Jimmy to come up from Philadelphia to have dinner with us so we can hear from him about his visits to RCA and Lennie can give you more details about our problems. Oh ... by the way, you've got congratulations coming to you. Jimmy's wife, Joanna, is pregnant. She called Rose yesterday to tell her and I got the news from him on the phone last night. Looks like you're going to be a grandfather!'

'Why the hell didn't he call me himself and let me know! I'm still his father, aren't I?' said Ham, bristling with anger and jealous that Maurie and Rose knew before he did.

'Relax,' said his brother. 'How could he reach you when you were someplace between here and the studio? They had just gotten the news themselves from the doctor, and he sent a message right away to your office. When you get back you'll find it buried somewhere on the top of your desk. If you'd act more like a father, maybe you'd have the close kind of relationship with him you should have. Anyhow, it's good news, so don't spoil it, and don't forget to congratulate him when he comes in.'

'Goddammit! Don't tell me what to say to my own son!' snapped Ham.

Maurie was tired of the whole conversation, which had begun in all innocence, but there still were a few more things he had to say.

'I won't tell you anything. You should know yourself what to say. Try not to sit there like a stranger instead of his father. You know, he's a fine young man and Joanna is a very good wife to him. You should be congratulating yourself that your son married such a nice girl and that they're giving you the blessing of a grandchild.'

'So my son married a nice girl! Go on, Maurie, say it . . . say what you're thinking about the woman I married! What did you call her in that shitty letter you wrote me? "That whore . . . a tramp." That was the kindest part of your letter. I'm damned sick and tired of your moralizing, your attacks and the way you pick on me!' Ham stood up, the muscles of his neck tightened, his face went red with anger and he moved toward his brother, who sat transfixed behind his desk. Maurie reached out toward a daggerlike envelope opener sitting on his blotter and with his right hand clutched it tightly. This madman coming at him might try to murder him – murder his own brother! He held the long, sharp paper cutter and his hand shook as though he were a senile old man.

The door burst open. It was Jimmy, who had just arrived from Penn Station. He quickly crossed the room and put out his hand to his father. Ham stood frozen, ignoring the intrusion.

'Dad, I'm so glad to see you. Did Uncle Maurie tell you the good news? I tried to reach you at your office. Joanna and I are pregnant – I mean Joanna's pregnant and I –' He stopped speaking and looked at his father, whose face showed his anger as he glared down at his ashen-faced older brother sitting far back in his chair. Maurie let something fall from his hand and it made a clattering metallic sound as it struck the floor.

'What's the matter, Uncle Maurie? Dad? Has something happened?' Jimmy asked, sudden concern in his voice.

'Nothing . . . nothing, Jimmy,' said Maurie, at last able to speak in a shaken voice before his younger brother, whose hands were clenched into fists and whose face was beet red, could say a word.

Ham finally managed to say something.

'Your uncle and I were having a little argument. You shouldn't have busted in on us without any warning.' Some of his tension ebbed, and he turned to face his son, thrusting out a hand in greeting. 'Congratulations on the baby. Give my love to Joanna, and I hope she has an easy time of it.'

'Thanks, Dad. One thing we both want to do as soon as we can is come out to California. Joanna's never been there, and Lennie wants me to see our exchanges in San Francisco and Los Angeles. We'd like it if the baby was born out there. Nothing's wrong at all with Philadelphia, it's a very nice place, but if you had a choice, wouldn't you pick California?' He gave a little laugh, noticed he was the only one to do so and went on. 'I'm glad you called me, Uncle Maurie, because I want you and Dad to hear more about what we discussed last week on the phone.'

More relaxed now, Ham sat down, and Jimmy took a seat beside him in front of Maurie's desk. His father began to speak, his voice almost normal again.

'Yeah, Maurie told me you had gone over to see the RCA plant in Camden. You want to know what we both were arguing about when you busted in here? Well, it was television. You may not realize it, but lots of our old customers, the theater circuit operators and independents, are going to raise absolute hell if we do anything at all in television. Crazy, isn't it? First they fuck us out of owning our own theaters, cause us to lose our whole circuit – including the Bijou Dream in Harrisburg, which was a stinking outrage – and now they're trying to keep us from finding new markets for our product. Try to explain that! Besides the usual crap about diverting pictures to TV that they want to run in their houses, they're threatening to go crying to the Department of Justice again. I'm sick of reading their bull about people wanting to be in crowds to see movies, wanting to get out of their houses for a change. Maybe they're right about that part – but I don't know and neither do they.'

'Remember the way they screamed when sound pictures came along,' said Maurie, 'Every time there's a new discovery, it seems there's always somebody it's going to hurt . . . or who thinks it will . . . and so they try their damndest to uninvent it.'

The secretary called to say that Lennie Rhinehart was coming in, and before he could do more than shake hands with Ham and say hello to Jimmy, Maurie announced that he was hungry and was taking them to Sardi's for dinner. In half an hour they were seated at a table after Ham had made the rounds, shaking hands, waving at old pals and cracking a few jokes that brought obligatory laughs. Finally he worked his way to their table and ordered a tall glass of Scotch on the rocks.

'Ham, you shouldn't drink that damned stuff before you eat. It'll ruin your stomach. Take it from an old ulcer man!' said Maurie, suddenly the solicitous brother.

'Ulcers? Hell, I don't get ulcers!' said Ham. 'I give them!' No laughs came from the table, and he sat down.

The waiter brought their orders and Lennie Rhinehart spoke in between the bluepoint oysters, which he gulped down like ugly oversized jelly beans.

'The exhibitors complain we're going into competition with them by making our pictures available for television, even the ones we released years ago that have been played out in theaters. They're not making any direct threats, mind you, but the message around the industry is that if we sell one frame of one feature to TV, forget selling anything to the theaters!'

'That's so much crap!' said Ham in disgust. 'The theaters have to show pictures. Who's going to make films for them, their ushers? They'll go out of business real fast if they shut down their sources. Hell, you can't keep a new business down. Wouldn't it be a nice thing if for a change we were the

512

ones to go to the government and scream there's a conspiracy against us!'

'Let's listen a minute to Jimmy,' said Maurie. 'I told you that I had him go through the RCA Camden plant, where they're already deep in the television business. What do you think about what you saw there, Jimmy?' Maurie asked.

'Well, Uncle Maurie, Dad, Lennie ... they're investing millions in it. The only thing that held them up for a while was getting some standards agreed to so that TV broadcasting throughout the country could be received on the sets that they and other manufacturers make. Something to do with the number of scanning lines. It's real technical. The head of RCA, David Sarnoff, was successful in having their system accepted by the Communications Commission, so they started up their assembly lines. I watched TV receivers pouring out of their plant and being shipped all over the United States. The screen size is kind of small right now, only about four or five inches across, but they told me that pretty soon they will be more than one foot across, maybe bigger as time passes and the cost of the big tube comes down. There are a lot of TV broadcasting stations being built, and they're working extra shifts to keep up with orders.'

'So what does all this have to do with us?' asked Ham.

'Just this, Dad. They must have programs to put on the air for all those receivers and transmitters. It's possible to do it with film, just the way radio depends so much on records or transcriptions instead of live broadcasts. That's where we come in. We should make new programs for television besides selling our old films, many of which are better than some of the things being made now. Maybe we could have some stations of our own, the same way we had theaters before the consent decree.' Jimmy was quite excited and his enthusiasm showed in every word.

Lennie shook his head.

'You can forget this company or any others who were defendants in the Paramount case ever getting the go-ahead to own television stations. I checked other major companies and we all agree the Department of Justice will fight tooth and nail against any production-distribution company getting into this television business, outside of providing program material. We're going to keep pushing, though, and perhaps we'll find a hole we can squeeze through. Here's a good laugh for you. I heard in confidence that some big theater owners are quietly shopping around for TV stations

513

and are going to get in before the big rush starts. How do you like that for talking out of both sides of their mouths!'

'In this business,' said Maurie, 'I believe anything.'

Still eagerly pursuing the idea, Jimmy turned to his father.

'Dad, our company must get into television! Maybe we can't do it right away, but other producers are going to make films for it, and they're telling any theater owners who threaten them to go to hell. As you said, exhibitors have to show pictures or close up shop, and while they talk big and make threats, I'll bet they never do anything about it. Our company should set up a special department to get started right away on planning so that we can get moving when the time comes – which could be very soon. That's the job I want to do, because I'm completely sold on what's coming in our future – and it's television! Please think it over, then let me find out everything I can and just where our company fits in. I know that we –'

'Forget it,' said Ham, cutting Jimmy off in the middle of his enthusiasm. 'All we need right now is to have some of the circuits and indies giving us more problems after what we've already been through. It's all right to keep me, your uncle and Lennie informed, but we're not going into television just yet. There's too much risk, and we're doing pretty damn well with what we're producing and selling right now. Even the stockholders aren't complaining, for a change.'

Maurie resented the way Ham took things over, making this statement without consulting him, but he had to agree they should be patient and not jump into this new thing just yet. Jimmy tried to get them back on the subject several times, but they dropped the whole discussion of television and began talking about future releases. Perhaps, thought Jimmy, tonight wasn't the time, but progress wasn't going to stand still and let them catch up in the late future. What he had seen at RCA was going to change the whole industry, and for a while he would have to be patient, learning all he could so one day he could help put their company on the winning side of the coming revolution. His father looked over at him.

'Jimmy. Quit staring out into space and eat your food before it gets cold!'

Maurie wiped his mouth, sipped his beer, then suddenly said something that surprised both Ham and Jimmy.

'I've been watching your son the past year while he's been working out of the home office and in the field. He's learned a hell of a lot about distribution and theaters. I want to be

514

honest with you, Ham. He should be out at the studio. He has a good creative mind, and while that's good in distribution too, I can tell you from what I've seen and felt that his heart really isn't in this end of the business – any more than yours would be, especially after all the time you've put into production. Jimmy would be of more value to the company and its future if he took what he already knows about theaters and distribution back to where you make the product. See how he is already looking into the future and sees the potential for us in television and how we must deal with it, whether the theater owners like it or not. Ham, I want Jimmy at the studio, where he'll do a good job for you and our company.'

Jimmy was overjoyed, but tried not to let it show on his face. He knew how much his father hated having Maurie push him and he was worried that it might work against him. Before Ham could gather his thoughts, Lennie spoke up in agreement.

'Your brother is absolutely right, Ham. Jimmy has done a good job here in New York and in the field. I've gotten excellent reports on him from every exchange manager wherever he's gone. I can hire plenty of people for distribution, but not one of them has your son's special background. I agree with Maurie that he belongs out there. With television coming along so fast, we should have somebody to keep us up to date so we know where we're going and can plan ahead. I doubt the government will let us buy into station ownership or the new networks developing from the existing radio nets, but there is absolutely no reason on earth why we shouldn't be one of the top suppliers of product for this coming new market. God alone knows how big it could become, and if we drag our feet we'll fall so far behind we might never catch up.'

Ham sliced another piece of steak, chewed it many more times than was necessary, then slowly swallowed. Maybe they were right, but they didn't know his problems with Nita. Ever since Santa Barbara, their sex life had slowly returned to normal, but other problems remained. She still harped on his family, on their hatred of her, and lately she had been pushing him to get rid of Maurie and make himself head of the company. He had about given up trying to keep her off the subject and she was deaf to all his explanations of the corporate setup and stock ownership. As for having Jimmy back at the studio, that would present some real trouble. Nita avoided the subject of Ham's son altogether. No, at this time, with their relationship on such tenuous ground, he did not

515

want to incur her wrath. He had to give some reasons for his opposition, so he grasped at arguments that seemed reasonable enough to give weight to what he said.

'You want my opinion? People like going to theaters ... they love being in crowds. Hell, your average working staff is fed up with sweating all day on the job, taking it in the ass from the boss. He comes home, cleans up, and if he's got the dough for tickets to a moving picture, he's not going to sit all evening in his own damn living room to look at it. He sees those same walls every night and he wants a change! He takes the old lady and the kids and they go out for a bite and then to the movies. It's a celebration and keeps his mind off the boring life he leads. And do you know how much those damn television receivers cost, just for a crummy black-and-white picture? Two thousand dollars and up! For forty-five cents a seat or less he can take himself and the whole family into a beautiful new world for an evening, see a great picture on a big screen, maybe in glorious Technicolor ... and with the kind of popcorn he doesn't get at home. You can't top that sitting on your butt in your own house squinting at a five-by-four-inch blur!'

Jimmy could keep silent no longer.

'Dad, do you remember the first pictures you ran in your nickelodeon? What was it you called it? The Bijou Dream. I've heard you talk often enough about it. Just compare those scratched-up jumpy images on that little screen to the films you make now. Don't close your mind just because something new has come along. Remember, you're one of the pioneers who took a new invention and made a whole new industry. Think of tomorrow! We've got to be there, and if something isn't done soon, there might be no future at all for Robbins International!'

'Who the hell writes your dialogue?' Ham asked his son, quite surprised at the sincerity with which Jimmy had presented his case. He had to admit the kid was using good sense, and secretly he was ashamed for fighting him for such a miserable reason – to keep Nita off his back. He felt like a hypocrite, using arguments he really didn't believe. Damn it, this was going to be one decision he was going to make for himself without Nita's elbow jamming into his ribs! Let her give him troubles later and he would deal with it then.

'Okay, kid, you want to set up a television department? Set it up,' he said. 'But don't spend any unnecessary money. You'll do it alone, and I don't want one line of publicity about it until we see how things go. You understand?' Privately he thought if he could keep it out of the trades, he might be able to keep it from Nita for a while, anyway.

'Sure, Dad, but we're going to have to spend some money now if we're going to make money later. I'm going to need some help, maybe just a secretary at first and an office, but certainly nothing that will cost a lot.'

'Use a secretary from the regular stenographic pool, but no fancy offices or gang of assistants. We have enough overloaded departments already. I want you to report directly to me or Leo Arnheim on everything, and I want it kept strictly confidential. All right, that takes care of television. Now let's get on to another subject. Lennie, do you think that you can get us a playdate at the Roxy next Christmas, or is it already booked?' He looked over at Jimmy for a moment. 'Didn't I tell you not to leave all that food on your plate? Especially steak that's costing your uncle five bucks for each of us!'

'Ham, take it easy,' Maurie said with a wide grin. 'This meal I'll charge to the company, so eat it or don't eat it, Jimmy. After all, it is for business, isn't it? You know, you're beginning to sound just like me, Ham.'

It was fortunate that in the noise of the dining room Maurie did not hear his brother's muttered reply.

'The last person I ever want to sound like is you!'

Jack Kriendler came to the front door of '21' when he heard that Ham Robbins was coming in with Lennie Rhinehart.

'How's your beautiful wife, Nita? Remember that great wedding lunch you had here? Be sure you give her my love. Now sit down and I'll have the boys bring you some real Scotch salmon I just got in.'

'Just make it Scotch on the rocks,' said Ham. A snap of Kriendler's fingers, the captain rushed over and in a moment a full glass was in Ham's hand. Suddenly a man started across the crowded downstairs barroom from a booth over on the other side. The waiters, customers, captains and busboys in his way all parted like the waters of the Red Sea to let him pass unhindered. Everybody followed him with their eyes, and there was a buzz from all the men leaning on the long bar. They all knew that face . . . the bulldog jaw, the tight hard body slowly going soft around the middle. It was the memorable figure of the Director of the Federal Bureau of Investigation, John Edgar Hoover. He crossed over to where Ham and Lennie were seated by the entrance door.

517

'Mr. Robbins, don't get up please. We met a few years ago in Washington when you and Pops Johnson, who used to be one of my boys, came by my office at the Bureau. It seems odd to call a tough old guy like Pops a boy, doesn't it? He's truly a fine man and a credit to the Bureau. It was a pleasure to work with him over the years and I hated to see him leave to go with your company. I'm sure you recall the matters we discussed when the two of you came to my office.'

Ham sensed all eyes in the room fastened on his table as he talked to the famous man. What in hell had he and Pops gone to the FBI about? Right now he couldn't remember a thing.

'Please, Mr. Hoover, join us for a drink. Here, there's plenty of room if we all slide over. We just left my brother, Maurie. I'm sorry he's not here with us now, he's a great admirer of yours.'

'Give him my warmest regards,' said the Director. 'I'll just have a cup of coffee, if you don't mind. My associate, Mr. Tolson, pointed you out to me, Mr. Robbins, and I am glad to have this opportunity to speak to you for a moment concerning something very disturbing which has been brought to my attention.'

Cold sweat gushed from Ham's armpits and he desperately wanted to go to the toilet, but he was tightly trapped here in the middle of the booth. He stared at the Director of the FBI with what he hoped was a relaxed look, but in reality was suppressed terror. His hand tightly clenched his glass, and it was fortunate that '21' served drinks in such thick-walled containers or it would have shattered and cut his palm. Something disturbing had come to the attention of the head of the FBI and he had come all the way across this room to tell him about it. My God, what did they have on him?

'It's about Pops Johnson, Ham. May I call you by your first name? I feel I know you well enough to do that,' said Hoover.

Ham was quite certain this man knew plenty about him . . . but just how much? He was worried, and swallowed most of his drink without tasting it.

'Word has reached me from my agent in charge of our Los Angeles Bureau office that for some reason Pops Johnson quite suddenly was kept from coming to work, actually locked out of his office, I understand. He was given no reason for this strange action and was almost forcibly ushered off the studio property. I'm certain you know nothing about this, because you would never be party to such shabby treatment of a truly loyal and wonderful man who is one of the finest Americans I have ever known.'

518

The Director stopped speaking and nodded to a passing friend. 'Uh, you know Judge Rafferty of the Federal Appeals Court, I'm sure. Judge, I'd like you to meet Mr. Ham Robbins from Hollywood. Be good to him if he ever appears before you.'

Ham covered his consternation with a feeble joke.

'A pleasure to meet you, your honor, but honestly, it never appealed to me to appear before a judge.'

The judge gave him a cold judicial look and left the table.

Hoover continued as though nothing had been said, his little eyes never leaving Ham's face, and he talked almost without seeming to move his mouth.

'In any case, I believe you should know that somebody in your studio is doing the company great harm in the manner this fine man has been treated. It happens I also heard about it from the United States Attorney in your area, another great friend of Pops'. You have no idea how many people love that old man and are incensed at what has happened in your absence. From what I know about you, it appears to be something you would never condone, and I am sure it will quickly be rectified. It's terrible how sometimes an underling takes advantage of the boss's absence to undermine things so very difficult to build, things like morale and a good public image. It is a problem not confined to private industry, let me assure you.' He drank the last of his coffee and rose to his feet. 'Please excuse me, Ham, I have to leave, but before I go I want you to meet my associate, Clyde Tolson.' He gestured to one of the several dark-suited men standing across the room. 'Come here, Clyde.' The big man moved over to their table, and Hoover introduced him to Ham and then to Lennie. Ham wondered if his sweating palm had been noticed as he gripped his hand.

'Mr. Tolson, it's a real pleasure to meet you,' he managed to say, and received a polite grunt in reply. The Director nodded, quickly shook hands and told Ham how pleased he was to have run across him at this fortunate time. He turned away and, engulfed in a swirl of dark-suited bodies, swept out of the room.

'What the hell was that all about?' asked Lennie.

'That was all about a telephone call I'm making the very first thing tomorrow morning to put Pops Johnson back to work. Lennie, you've just seen all the proof you'll ever need that who you know means a million times more than what you know. Right now I know that I need another drink – fast!'

519

CHAPTER FORTY-EIGHT

Jimmy and Joanna rented a small house in Westwood and looked for something more permanent, hoping they would find it and be moved in before the baby arrived. As they had more than seven months yet to go, there was no problem. Long before Joanna was wheeled into the delivery room at Cedars of Lebanon, she and Jimmy were living in their new home on Lindbrook Drive, not far from the UCLA campus.

Since Nita had stayed in London with Donny, Jimmy's return to the West Coast was pleasant and he saw a lot of his father. But eventually Nita returned to Beverly Hills and if she was aware that Jimmy was back at the studio, she made no mention of it to Ham for a while.

He was still in some conflict about setting up the new television department and expected Nita would bring it up to him. He did not have long to wait. She confronted him on a Friday evening in the hall between their rooms, holding a copy of the *Hollywood Reporter* like a battle flag and waving it angrily in his face. Her dark eyes flashed and there was a bite in her voice.

'You arranged all this while I was away and never told me. It's obvious you don't care how I feel. Maybe you think it's foolish, but I am not comfortable near your son, and now you have deliberately arranged it so that he lives practically next door. At least when he was in New York it was tolerable –'

'Nita, please shut up!' said Ham. 'Where he lives in Westwood is miles from our house, and anyhow I thought you had stopped all that astrology crap and your bad-vibrations bullshit!'

Obviously she had not, and she stormed into her bedroom, slamming the door behind her. Ham knew very well what was in the trade paper story. He had read it the day before in his office and was unhappy that it found its way into print. It was an almost meaningless story, a filler, saying merely that Robbins International had set up a new department headed by Jimmy Robbins, son of Ham Robbins, who had been in New York studying the new television medium. It went on to say that the company was exploring the possibilities of TV and there was nothing more definite than that. It was the kind of trade trivia that does little harm and less good. As soon as Ham read it he phoned Jimmy, who had no idea how it broke since he had been keeping everything under wraps as instructed. Obviously some of the wraps had worked loose, revealing a few facts underneath.

'Dad, I'm sorry it's out, but how long could we possibly keep it a secret we're serious about television? It would be easier to hide an elephant in the executive bungalow than to keep this quiet much longer. We should have released our own story and then it could have done us some good. As it is, what they ran is a waste and says almost nothing. It could spoil a well-planned future release we might have controlled and used for our benefit.'

'No more publicity, damn it! I told you I didn't want any more problems with the theater people!' Ham said, trying to hold his voice down so he was not heard in the outer office.

Jimmy was certain his father's real problem did not come from the theater operators but from Nita and nobody else. He decided not to let it bother him now. Too much important work was still ahead and the real TV sales job remained to be done on Ham. Early the next week Jimmy brought a copy of the Columbia Pictures Company annual report to lunch and showed it to his father as soon as he could get him alone. Television accounted for a very large proportion of Columbia's excellent profits, and Jimmy wanted to prove that they were on the right track.

'You don't have to tell me about it. I read those things myself. All right, so they're making money and maybe there's something to it. One thing, though, we hadn't considered. Columbia calls their television operation Screen Gems, and we should have a separate name and corporation for ours, too. That might keep the theater people off our necks when we show them our whole company isn't swinging over to their new competition. It should be a separate organization, under our control, so come up with a name and we'll have the legal department arrange things. I told you this would bring us a lot of new problems, but if we do it the way Columbia did, we may spare ourselves some trouble later.'

'You mean it won't be Robbins International Studios going

521

into television, but another company doing it and with a different name?' asked Jimmy.

'That's right. Harry and Jack Cohn are no fools and they were right to call their operation Screen Gems. We should do the very same thing, so get working on a name and don't bother me anymore for a while about television. Oh – something important. I don't want you to hire anybody, and you're only to use properties that we already own. Check with the story department and get a list from them. They must have a warehouseful of books, plays, scripts and story submissions we've been stuck with. Also you can adapt stories we've already made into features and released in the past. That way we won't be throwing money around and we'll still have something to sell.'

'Dad, there's something you have to know about the way television shows are sold,' said Jimmy, deeply concerned at the restraints his father was building around all his hopes and dreams. 'I did a lot of checking into this while I was in New York and I spoke with people in the advertising agencies. They all buy from sample films – from pilots. You have to shoot a segment or a single episode on film for each show you want to sell, otherwise they aren't interested. You know yourself how tough it is to decide if you want to buy a book or a play for pictures and you must read something that's submitted to you, even if it's only a short treatment. Please give me the go-ahead to spend some money for a few pilots when we find something we believe in. Otherwise we'll never sell anything. You must understand that's the way agencies buy for television and –'

'Don't give me arguments. I told you I wasn't crazy about us getting into this new business in the first place, and if it's going to cost us more money, then the hell with it. When our company comes out with an announcement that we're producing shows for television and the agencies all know it's Robbins International Studios making them, then they'll come knocking at our doors the same as they did at Columbia for Screen Gems.'

'I hope you're right, Dad, but that's not the way it's done,' Jimmy answered, realizing it was as though his father were trying to guarantee the new department would fail even before it drew a first deep breath. He knew that Nita was back in town, and he wondered if perhaps she had regained some of her old power over his father, doing all she could to again drive the son of his first wife out of the studio or thou-

522

sands of miles away. There must be reasons why Nita wanted to influence his father, and Jimmy could sense from the unreasonable restraints being put on him that pressure was being applied.

It was almost too much for Jimmy next morning when he read in the trade papers that Twentieth Century-Fox Films had entered television and committed itself to a healthy budget for a group of pilot films. He took copies of *Daily Variety* and the *Hollywood Reporter*, both of which ran first-page stories about Fox and its new TV activities, to Ham's office, but Bob Silver told him his father had several important appointments and was not available. After lunch he waited in the executive dining room an extra hour but learned his father had left the lot for a meeting at the Producers' Association and would not be returning to the studio. Finally he wrote an urgent interoffice memo to leave with Bob for his father about the Fox situation and with a red pencil circled several other trade paper stories about the boom in television commercial production. He noted this field as having great possibilities and asked if he could go after some of that business right away.

The next afternoon his phone rang, and it was Bob relaying a message.

'Your father is still busy, but he read your memo and the marked papers. He said to go on the way he planned it with you and forget what Fox is doing. He likes the idea about TV commercials and wants you to get us into that right away as well as continuing with series development.'

'Is that all he said?' asked Jimmy.

'That's the complete message. How are things going?' Bob said to him.

'The only good news right now is that we've got a name for the TV company. Encino Productions, in honor of this busy metropolis where our studio is located. Legal is clearing the name now and drawing up papers. The rest of the news is not as good as it could be. I borrowed an editor from the story department who's been digging through the files of material the company already owns, but it's slow going. Most of the stuff doesn't seem suitable for television – or for feature films either. There were some pretty good reasons originally for not producing most of it, but we're still trying to run something down that's usable. I only wish we weren't being forced to work under such limitations. I know we could develop original material, but we're not being given a chance. I've worked things out with the publicity department to borrow somebody from them part-time who's had experience with advertising agencies and knows something about TV sales and networks. I think you know him, Don Bergin. He handles the planting of stories and guest spots of our stars on radio and TV when they are in films going into national release. TV is such a new field that you can't find very many people who know much about it out here. We're trying hard and should come up with something soon. Instead of making pilot films the way Screen Gems does for Columbia and the ones Fox-TV has announced, we're putting together something called "presentation books." They sell Robbins International Studios with all its facilities, personnel and proven experience. Each one has some sample story outlines, a script or two and sketches in color from our art department to dress it up. It's a hell of a way to compete for business when we're approaching agencies that want something they can see on a screen, but what else can I do?'

Bob wouldn't voice an opinion, though he understood the frustration Jimmy must be going through.

'Well, just keep trying. I'm sure something will break soon. They're bound to be interested in anything we offer because it comes from this studio and we have a great reputation.'

'But not in television!' said Jimmy. 'It's a whole new ball game and the advertising agencies are the ones calling the shots. The only thing that impresses them is what they can put on a projection machine for their clients, and you can't do much with a presentation book, no matter how fancy you bind it or stuff it with scripts, sales pitches and our great reputation. How do you thread up a book and throw it on a screen? Bob, is there any chance at all my father can find time to sit down with me the next day or so, because I have to discuss this with him. I've put together five TV presentations and taken them to the West Coast offices of every top advertising agency buying shows for television. All I get are polite turndowns. Same thing in New York. They ask me to send them pilots, and I can't get an okay to shoot even one single frame of film! It's crazy. Here's a whole new market for product we could supply and I'm stopped cold. It's like being told to go out and break the record for the four-forty dash with your legs chained together!'

'Jimmy, your father is leaving later today for New York,' Bob told him. 'He'll be away about a week and a half. I've given him your messages, but he says to wait until he returns and then he'll get together with you. He's just too busy right now. I'm sorry.'

'So am I, Bob. Please make a note to remind him as soon as he's back. Say good-bye to him for me. Thanks.' He hung up the phone, dejected at the outcome of his futile talk, and then called Don Bergin's office in Publicity for an immediate meeting to discuss developments in his sales attempts with the New York agencies.

'Mr. Bergin left for New York on a special assignment, Mr. Robbins. He won't be back for at least a week. Is there any message?' said the department secretary.

Jimmy couldn't believe it. How could Bergin leave town without telling him?

'Yes, have him call me the minute he returns. We were supposed to have a very important meeting this afternoon. He should have called to let me know!'

'I'm sorry, but Mr. Simms phoned early this morning from the home office and told him to get there right away for something special he wanted him to do.' The connection with Publicity was broken and Jimmy sat back in his chair, unhappily looking at the stack of beautifully bound presentation books, all based on pictures that Robbins International had produced in the past, or that had come from the files and were worth another chance in this new medium. Sample scripts for episodes were included, along with pages of plot outlines and very well done color sketches of characters, key scenes and settings. So far these books had completely failed in their mission. Nobody wanted books, they wanted films – pilot films. The fact that it had been Robbins International Studios making the sales pitch had impressed not one account executive on Madison Avenue.

Suddenly an idea came to him. Suppose he took all of this material to one of the top talent and literary agencies right here in Hollywood, where they had plenty of experience selling shows to networks and advertising agencies? Jimmy decided to do some quiet investigating, and if it looked good, discuss it with Ham when he returned. He smiled, thinking of his father's reaction to having agents come into his office. 'Those goddamn leeches who bleed our company dry!' Those were the words he probably would hear when he brought up that idea. To have any of that miserable breed representing the studio in selling its TV would be a final irony. He could almost hear the bellowing noises of Ham when he thought of becoming the client of his enemies.

Nevertheless, it was worth a try. Nothing else was working.

Lennie Rhinehart was speaking about quite a sensitive subject to the three men in his office. The entry of Robbins International into television brought with it some serious problems that had to be faced now. Ham Robbins had just arrived in New York from the Coast, and also present was Fred Simms, head of Publicity and Advertising, who had been in town for over a week. Seated next to Simms was an overweight round-faced young man with curly-tight hair and deep-set eyes who was quite impressed at being in this room with these key men of the company and had visions of sharing their importance. Up to now his job had been promoting appearances of stars on radio and television to publicize films going into release, and because of this he had more practical experience with those two mediums than any of the others present.

Don Bergin had been working part-time with Jimmy Robbins in the new TV department at the studio, but that did not satisfy him. At every opportunity he worked on his boss, Fred Simms, until he finally convinced him, with his mastery of the jargon and the throwing around of names, that he was completely knowledgeable about television, the networks and the all-important agencies that made the real decisions. Simms had phoned him two days earlier to get here immediately and he sat, full of eager anticipation, awaiting developments.

Lennie was telling them about some highly confidential matters that would affect them all.

'You remember I told you a while ago, Ham, that some theater men I've known for many years have secretly been negotiating to get into TV. Well, our old friend, Harold Kosterman, who is head of Midwest Circuit, has very quietly bought up enough stock for himself and some associates in the World Television Network so that they now control it. In three days it will be announced that he's their new president and chairman of the board. Harold and I have worked on deals together for many years and he is quite anxious to talk business with us. We've held several very private meetings at his home in Westchester so nobody could spot us. He wants Robbins International to produce a series of hour-long TV shows for World, starting with a first group of twenty-six. If these go over, and there's no reason they won't, they will order another group of the same number to follow. They will pay all costs plus a guaranteed profit to be negotiated at meetings with people from both our offices who will work out actual figures. We let them broadcast – they call it telecast – these shows just once and then we can sell them again to World for a single rerun. After that we own the shows outright and can release them theatrically or in any way we want. The foreign theater and TV market would be pure profit and without limits.'

Don Bergin felt it was time to show off something of what he knew about television and spoke up with rehearsed authority in what he hoped would be an impressive sales pitch for himself.

'Some of the things they're doing in Europe – BBC especially and over on the Continent – are far ahead of anything here, technically speaking. You have no idea what a market it can develop into.'

Lennie waited impatiently for the loud young man from the studio to shut up, then he went on.

'We must be sure there's somebody out at the studio to handle this series we're going to make for World TV. Ham, you and I talked about your son, Jimmy, who already heads up the only TV department we've got. I thought that with his experience he could take this whole thing over, but you told me you wanted somebody else to run this particular operation.'

'That's right, Lennie,' said Ham, wishing his son's name had not been brought into the conversation with the others present. He thought out every word before he spoke. 'I don't want him involved in this at all. He's plenty busy now developing some series from properties we already own, and I'm afraid there's a problem selling them because he isn't getting them seen by the right people here who make the decisions at the advertising agencies. Before I left there he told me about another area in television that has great potential. Television commercials. One other major studio and several independents are already in it and doing rather well. We could turn a nice profit on them and also keep our stages and people busy in between feature production and these new TV series we're going to make. I'm going to let him take us into commercials, and I don't want him to be sidetracked by this World TV tie-in you're telling us about, Lennie. Bergin here has had studio experience and Fred Simms has convinced me he can handle it.'

Lennie started to say something but stopped. This wasn't

fair at all to Jimmy, he thought, but he would wait until later, when he and Ham were alone, and then he would bring it up. Ham continued to speak about the new department and the beginnings of planning.

'Fred has strongly recommended Bergin here to handle these shows. If you close the deal with Harold Kosterman, we'll set up a separate production unit headed by Bergin, who will report directly to me or Leo Arnheim at the studio.'

Lennie was still disturbed at the way things were going, but thought of something that might take some of the sting out of it later for Jimmy.

'I'm glad you mentioned TV commercials,' he said to the others. 'Harold told me he wanted to make this a complete package, shows and commercials, and he has some big companies lined up who are looking for something just like this to sponsor. They will buy the whole thing, shows and commercials . . . with their usual controls over their sales spots. If we tie all of this together, like a package deal, we can come out even more ahead. Commercials are going to be a big thing, and this can mean plenty of business for Jimmy's department. At least the theater people won't kick about us producing commercials, although you should see how many advertising films some of them run between pictures in their houses now. They're almost as bad as TV!'

'It's just like the old days when we used to sell peanuts, popcorn, soft drinks and silk stockings in the Bijou Dream,' commented Ham. 'Hell, if it makes us a buck, I'm all for it.'

Fred Simms and Don Bergin couldn't care less about the old days. Both of them were overjoyed at the way things were turning out right now and the way all their quiet advance work was paying off. Simms wanted to have his hand in the new TV production, which he believed one day would be more important than anything else the company was doing. If he personally could not head it, the man who did would be in his debt, and Fred Simms never forgot when anybody owed him anything. For a rather vacuous-looking man who drank far too much, Simms had the conniving devious mind of a successful press agent, and it never stopped working.

For a brief moment Bergin felt a small twinge of guilt about Jimmy and how he would feel about what had happened behind his back. He shrugged.

'That's the way a guy gets ahead in this business,' he said to himself. 'You've got to be in the right place at the right time and not be squeamish if you have to screw somebody to come out on top.' He was smiling as he and Fred Simms left the office to go downstairs and begin preparing a press release for the future when the new World Television series, produced by the special new production division at Robbins International Studios, would be trumpeted to the public.

Ham was left alone in the office with Lennie, who still had something he wanted to say.

'You know that Jimmy worked nearly a year for me here, then later out in the field in some of our exchanges. He impressed me with his knowledge of the business, especially production. He was the first one to bring television to our attention, and we talked about it many times. You remember that meeting with you and Maurie when he told us what RCA was doing. He certainly was right about what was going to happen, and maybe it's going to be the biggest thing in entertainment. It may be none of my business, Ham, but you did put him in charge of television and he has been working very hard at the studio on those series the last several months. I wonder if it's right to jump over his head like this and put his part-time assistant, that Bergin character, in charge of something I've already gotten for us with network time assured. Jimmy might take it as a personal slap in the –'

Ham did not wait for more to be said. From the sharp tone of his voice, Lennie could tell he was quite angry and knew he had made a mistake in bringing it up.

'Lennie, you were damned right. It is none of your business! I don't want Jimmy to have anything at all to do with this series. He'll do the commercials and that's all. I'm sorry I even let him take charge of our first TV effort and I'm disappointed in him for not getting anything sold yet. He hasn't done the kind of a job I expected.'

There was a hidden streak of decency in Lennie Rhinehart and now and then it broke surface in spite of his trying to shut himself up.

'Now, Ham, you're not being fair. I know a lot of what's going on at the studio and I've heard that for some reason you refused to let Jimmy shoot any pilots of the series he was developing for sale. Naturally the agencies wouldn't give us a tumble. I honestly think you should have let him shoot a few. I've learned enough already about TV to be convinced that's the only way shows get sold, even by a big-name studio like ours! This deal with Harold Kosterman and World TV is different because they are directly involved and own the time.

529

Otherwise you must have pilots. How could you expect Jimmy to make any deals?'

'I'm giving him one more month to get some sales with what he already has,' said Ham, ignoring what Lennie had said on Jimmy's behalf. 'If nothing has happened by then I may pull him out of TV entirely . . . at least the series part of it. Meantime he's getting us started in commercials, and we'll see how well he does with them.' The subject was closed.

'Quiet on the set! I want absolute silence and I mean from everybody!' shouted the assistant director into a public address microphone. He pressed the button that made bells go off on the outside stage walls and put red wigwag lights in movement. Now only the lone voice of the director could be heard in the vast stage as he said, 'Action!' and signaled the company grips to very slowly push the camera dolly forward on its long track.

'Closer . . . closer. All right, slow down a bit now . . . Watch your focus! God . . . oh, God! . . . Do it slowly . . . Come on, fellows, just ease up a little at a time . . . Now hold . . .' They were coming in on a very tight shot of the delicate scene, and the crew stood frozen on the set edges, staring enraptured as the lens of the Bell and Howell crept ever closer to the brightly lit scene. Every breath was held, and at last the director exhaled and broke the silence.

'Make me taste it . . . Good . . . Ahhhhh . . . More . . . more . . . Get it coming . . . Up a little . . . now down again . . . Come on, keep your mind on what you're doing . . . Let it all come out . . . All of it . . . More . . . Oh . . . Ohhhh . . . Oh *shit!* Cut! You stupid bastard! Haven't you ever poured beer out of a bottle into a glass, for Christ's sake?'

The actor's hand started to shake as he carefully held the cold bottle so its label faced the camera and the frothy liquid gushed into a bell-shaped glass. The foam had slopped all over the front of the glass, covering the beautifully hand-painted brand name, and it dripped from the table down to the highly polished floor. The storyboard showed a very neatly poured glass of beer, and what the agency demanded was exactly what they intended to get. This was take number twenty-eight and they already had gone through ten and a half cases of beer, what with rehearsals and spoiled takes, still without a perfect pour. A bright young man from the agency stepped forward. He wore a deep frown and a charcoal-black suit with tattersall vest, and there was desperation in his voice.

'The client demands a neatly poured glass! Look at our storyboard. Isn't there anybody here who can pour beer out of a bottle without having the shakes?' He glared with rage at the actor, a rugged manly outdoors type, who had been up partying most of the night before, drinking much stronger stuff than mild lager. 'Who in hell cast him for this part? he growled.

'You did!' said the disgusted director. 'You picked him from a casting call out of thirty-five men. You wanted a rugged cowpunched type – and that's what you got!'

'Rugged doesn't mean ragged!' snapped the angry agency representative, looking for somebody else to blame. 'This damn commercial has already gone over budget and schedule with these added takes and we're not paying one cent extra where it's not our fault. Now get somebody with a hairy arm who can pour beer without missing the glass and let's get this stinking close-up in the can!'

The casting department scurried around and within an hour had three sets of hairy arms on the set. A new case of Pacific Pride beer was broken open and two takes later the close-up was on its way to the lab with the rest of the first day's work.

Jimmy came on the set just in time for the wrap-up of the commercial and joined the company in finishing off the remaining three cases of beer. It tasted like cold soapy water, and he hoped it wouldn't corrode his stomach lining. He was extra polite to the agency man, praised the product as having a unique and memorable taste and assured him he would see that the studio absorbed any budget overruns. After all, this was the very first commercial the new department had shot and he wanted all the happy customers he could collect. The word had spread around all the agencies that Robbins International was in TV commercial production all the way, and the response had been even better than Jimmy hoped. Nobody ever called the new department by its legal name of Encino Productions. It was the TV Commercials Division of Robbins International Pictures, Inc., and Jimmy canceled the special letterheads that he had never wanted in the first place.

Ham retracted his order that there was to be a separate company and deep in his heart would have liked to retract having Jimmy here at the studio running the new department.

Nita still nagged at him now and then before he could shut her up, but he knew that Maurie had an eye on the new operation and liked the way things were going with Jimmy in charge. He would not stand for any changes right now. It had been Maurie's idea originally to put Jimmy back in the studio, and Ham was not quite ready to tangle with his brother over this, regardless of Nita.

Besides the completed group of beer commercials, there were two dozen one-minute spots and a dozen thirty-second ones introducing the new Ford Mercury. It helped that the studio had closed a deal with Ford to show their cars in several upcoming features, and the agency happily threw some TV spot business to the studio. By the next week there would be a group started for the new RCA color television sets, four different brands of beer, a General Mills cereal job plus a batch for Reynolds aluminum foil wrap. Jimmy had to add ten more people to his staff and was finally allowed to have air conditioning installed in their offices. He took over more space for the new people, and the TV commercial business hummed. All this made Ham feel very pleased when he returned from New York and looked at reports showing projected profits, and he had to admit to Jimmy that he was doing a fine job, though there would be no releases to the press saying this. Ham had trouble concealing his enthusiasm, but found he was secretly quite proud of what his son was accomplishing.

Don Bergin also came back to the studio, explaining to Jimmy that he could no longer be involved in his department as he now was on a special assignment for Fred Simms. Several quite experienced people phoned to inquire about job openings. and after interviewing them Jimmy took on a fulltime assistant who came from Cascade Productions, a leading independent commercial producer. Alan Pauley brought along some excellent clients, and with his remarkable experience and contacts, the business continued to grow. Ham approved the added overhead without complaint, so pleased was he with the way things were going. Soon there was a solid backlog of contracts for commercials, and one afternoon Jimmy managed to catch his father to tell him about a way to sell the TV series on which so much time and effort had been spent.

'Dad, give me just a few minutes to go over this with you. It's not at all like feature film distribution. Right now we need some experienced professionals to work on sales for us. You may not go for this approach, but please listen and think it over. We have all these series presentations but we have no pilots. The Stein-Rodney Organization has sold as much TV as anybody else here or in New York. Of course, it helps them as agents to put their clients to work and they take their commissions plus some extras, but the important thing is that they do get shows on the air. They have contacts with agencies, sponsors and networks they've developed over a long period of time. We don't have their knowledge, their contacts or the type of people who do this specialized kind of job. Maybe someday we can do our own selling, but for now we should consider turning over all our television series sales to an established organization, work out a commission deal and put our company into television series production!'

Ham listened quietly, thinking about his meeting in New York with Lennie and the others that was really going to put them into television, but he said nothing, though there was a little twinge of guilt at keeping it all a secret from his son. He thought for a minute. It wouldn't hurt to let Stein-Rodney have a crack at it. Maybe it was his guilt that influenced him. It certainly wasn't his past relationships with agents, because there it had always been more like mortal combat than business. He remembered once giving orders to have that very same agency barred from the lot, along with several others, but that lasted only until they came along with some clients he needed for a picture.

'You've got a good idea. Go ahead. Try the Stein-Rodney office. Those initials of theirs might be good luck for a change. I can remember the times I used to stick that "Standing Room Only" sign up in front of the Bijou Dream back in the old days. SRO . . . My God, you could run the worst crap in the world and still have lines of people around the block fighting to get in. Maybe television is the modern nickelodeon and we should really get into it all the way. Go ahead, contact Abe Stein over at SRO and set up a meeting right away. Don't promise anything more than their normal commission, and have them draw up an estimate of their sales costs. See what you can do, and have our legal department put together a contract or go over anything Stein-Rodney draws up. Bring it to me when it's ready to be signed. Now get going, and good luck.'

Jimmy was flabbergasted at the ease with which everything happened. He had come prepared for an argument from his father the moment he mentioned turning TV sales over to an

533

agency. The complete acceptance couldn't have surprised him more, and he left the office bursting with joy, eager to get things moving. Within three weeks a deal had been worked out with Stein-Rodney and the trade papers ran headlines that read, SRO AT ROBBINS INTERNATIONAL! OLD ENEMIES – NEW ALLIES!

The production meeting room was crowded with all the studio department heads and every production executive from the front office. Leo Arnheim had sent out a memo the day before that Ham Robbins wanted everybody there at five o'clock sharp to hear about something very important to each of them and to the entire company. Nobody could recall a meeting like this since the bond drives during the war and the NRA rallies years before. At least business was good, with three features being shot, four more in preparation and two in post-production, plus several groups of TV commercials taking up the slack. Nobody was more than normally nervous, but after they had waited until after five-thirty-five for Ham to enter, there was a noticeable buildup of tension in the room. Jimmy sat at the long table on the right side and discussed the next day's requirements for commercials being shot with several involved department heads.

The wide double doors swung open and Ham Robbins marched in followed by the small entourage of Leo Arnheim, Bob Silver with his notebook, and Harry Saunders, studio production manager. All conversations were cut off as though a sound man had twisted his volume control to zero. Ham had a well-fixed smile in place and cracked a few fast jokes with senior department heads at the front table. He glanced at the rear of the room and saw Pops Johnson. The old man now was assistant head of the location department, working under a younger man he had trained, but he was back at work and outwardly appeared to be happy. Ham's smile faded, and he was unusually serious the rest of the time he was in the room. A moment to clear his voice, a quick drink of water that Bob poured from the glass pitcher, then he spoke.

'We don't get together like this often enough, but I see no reason to keep you from your work unless it's something really important – and this is.' His face remained so serious the more nervous people in the room saw visions of pink slips flying out of the personnel department. 'You all know enough about television so I don't have to describe it to you. Right

534

now it isn't giving us too much trouble, but there are growing signs it could cut into theater grosses, and that would affect all of us. Well, for one reason or another, we've kept as far away from TV as possible. You all remember not long ago I ordered the property department and all art directors never to have a goddamn TV receiver showing in any of our pictures. I nearly fired one set dresser who slipped one into a living room scene. Well, I've grown more lenient and understanding lately. TV is a baby who's growing into a giant, and we want our share of the monster it's going to be. We're already doing a good job with commercials and hope we'll be selling some series through an agency that seems to know how it's done. You all read about that in the trades, so I'm not giving away any secrets.'

Ham paused. His voice seemed to be drying up, and he took another drink from the water glass, wishing it held something much stronger. He glanced over to where Jimmy sat, then quickly looked away. Well, enough stalling for now. A few more words and another couple of minutes and it would be out and over.

'Lennie Rhinehart, the head of Distribution, has worked out a big deal with the World Television Network for our company to produce twenty-six hours of television films, a complete series with commercials to be included. The deal was just signed this morning in New York and you'll read about it in the papers tomorrow. Up to now it's been confidential, but now you all have to know because we're setting up a whole new department here at the studio just to produce those twenty-six shows. Don Bergin, who up to now has been in our publicity department, will be the executive in charge of this entire project, and I expect you to cooperate as fully with him as you do with all our executives. We have a wonderful opportunity to break into television on one of the top networks once a week at the best available hour. There is no name for the series yet but . . .'

Jimmy sat in shocked silence. He could not believe what he had just heard his father say. He was the head of the television department of Robbins International Studios and now, after it was signed and sealed, done and delivered, he had to learn about it here at a meeting with all these people he worked with. He turned to look across the room at Don Bergin, his part-time assistant who so suddenly had been assigned to a special project and could no longer work with him. Bergin quickly looked away, avoiding Jimmy's eyes. His ruddy complexion seemed to go a shade pale. Ham's voice continued with more details.

'As I said, we are to provide the entire hour, including the commercials, which will be turned out by the department producing them now. They are doing an outstanding job and I know will continue to do it. Their commercials will be integrated into the hour-long shows for sponsors now being lined up by World TV. It is a tremendous break for all of us, and I expect you to do your very best to make Robbins International the top industry name in television production as it has been in theatrical films. Thank you. Now go to work.' He turned and quickly left the production meeting room, followed by Arnheim, Bob Silver, Harry Saunders and Don Bergin, who jumped out of his chair, racing through the door just before it swung shut.

Everybody got to their feet and began to leave the room. Jimmy remained seated, staring straight ahead. Pops Johnson came over from the rear of the room and sat down beside him.

'That was a rotten thing your father just did, Jimmy. It absolutely stinks! Everybody knows you brought this television thing here in the first place and you were the only one pushing it when it still was a dirty word around the place. Now when he's got something good he hands it to that loudmouth jerk to run. I know him and I'll bet he falls flat on his ass before they even get one hour of the twenty-six shot. I can't understand why he's letting somebody else handle this when you're the one who should be in charge. I can tell from your face this thing was as big a surprise to you as it was to the rest of us.'

The meeting room had emptied and they sat alone at the long table.

'Pops, I'm so damned angry about this that I feel like quitting and walking right out of the studio,' Jimmy said to the old man. 'You know, that might be exactly what he wants me to do. I'm sure you know who's been working on him.'

'I know, Jimmy. I know much more than you realize. Your father does miserable things like this now and then, and he's not the same guy I used to know, although there always seemed to be a mean streak in him. You know, he had me tossed off the lot for something I didn't even do – and he never gave me a hearing or a chance to ask him why. Somebody, I have no idea who, spilled some confidential information and I was handy to blame, so out I went. Sure, I got back, but that was only because I knew where some bodies were buried and had some very powerful friends who weren't frightened of him. I wish I could do something for you in this damn mess. One thing, though, I want you always to know I'm your friend, and if you ever want somebody to talk to, you know where my office is. I have a lot of spare time now that I'm not the department head anymore. Believe me, Jimmy, I know what you're going through, I really do.'

The feeling of outrage and shock had almost passed and Jimmy felt like standing up. He was still quite angry. Don Bergin could be expected to double-cross anybody to get ahead; that was the kind of person he was. What his father had done – the deliberate withholding of facts he was entitled to know as head of the TV department, the public humiliation in front of his fellow workers – and the terrible feeling that he had intentionally been betrayed by his own father left him shaken and depressed. He still felt like walking out of the studio, but before he did that he would tell his father just how he felt about what had been done and the shabby manner in which he had acted. He would make a serious try at getting this new series back in his department, where it rightfully belonged – and he would stay right here at Robbins International Studios. He was going to do the best job he could and not make it easy for anybody to shove him out. Nita was not going to have her way!

He stopped at a water cooler in the hall, filled a paper cup and drank it down, then went up the stairs and walked to the big black door at the end of the corridor. It bore chrome letters that read, HAMILTON ROBBINS – VICE-PRESIDENT – PRODUCTION, and he pushed it open. Only Bob Silver was in the long outer office, and he was on the phone. When he saw Jimmy enter, he hung up and quickly got to his feet, moving around his desk to come and meet him.

'Jimmy! I'm so glad you came up. I've been trying to reach you down in the meeting room but there was no answer. Joanna called. She wants you to get home immediately!'

'What's the matter? Is something wrong?' asked Jimmy in alarm. Joanna was in her ninth month. Even though the doctor had said everything was going well, things still could happen without warning.

'She said that the pains just started and she called the doctor right away. He told her to get to the hospital within an hour. Don't worry, though. It only began a few minutes ago and she said she's absolutely fine. She does want you to get home as soon as you can and to drive carefully. The baby will wait for you! Good luck, Jimmy, and give Joanna my best wishes. I hope it goes easily for both of you and for the baby. I've had two myself, and the father should enjoy it.'

Jimmy was already out the door and heard little of what Bob said at the last. He caught himself at the top of the stairs and ran back to the office, pulling the door open and calling in to Bob.

'I still have to talk to my father. After the baby's born and everything's all right, I'll phone you. It's very important that we get together as soon as possible. He'll know what it's about. Good-bye, Bob.' He left, still angry, but now he was more concerned about his wife and getting her to the hospital.

Four and a half hours later Joanna delivered a healthy baby girl, seven pounds, thirteen ounces. Name: Esther Robbins, for Ham's mother, Jimmy's grandmother. It was an easy delivery, although to Jimmy, sitting out in the fathers' waiting room, it seemed an eternity. The excitement of rushing home from the studio, then counting Joanna's pains all the way to the hospital and the admission procedure, came together, collided with his emotional upset over the television series disclosure, and he sat outside almost in collapse as he awaited the news. He felt better when the maternity nurse and then the doctor told him he was the father of a beautiful girl, and he immediately phoned Joanna's parents in New York. Then came a call to Irene and Charlie Silverman, who at once started over to the hospital. The next call was to his father's office, and he caught Bob just as he was about to leave.

'Jimmy, that's great . . . great. Congratulations to you both. Your father still hasn't checked with me and he's not home. I honestly don't know where he is, but I'll call the house again right now and leave a message.'

'No, please don't call there about this,' Jimmy said. 'Just leave a memo on his desk so he can see it tomorrow. I'm sure he'll get around to it then. Tell him his granddaughter has been named Esther, after his mother. He might like that. Thanks and good-bye, Bob.' He hung up the phone.

The nurse met him as he returned to the waiting room and handed him a sterile gown and cap, which he put on before going into the recovery room to see Joanna, pale and happy, lying in bed. He leaned over to give her a kiss.

'Congratulations, honey. You did a terrific job!'

'Thanks, dearest, but I couldn't have done it without you.

Have you seen the baby yet? I just got a quick look at her. She's darling, real red and wrinkled, but the doctor said she'll be beautiful in a few days.'

'Why not?' said Jimmy. 'She's got a beautiful mother! I called your parents and they send you their love. They're calling again tonight to your room downstairs. My mother and Charlie are on their way over right now and you'll see them later. I tried to reach my father, too, but he seems to have disappeared and Bob has no idea where he is. I left a message for him.'

Soon Joanna was wheeled down to her room on the maternity floor and Irene and Charlie arrived, to be met by Jimmy out in the hall. Irene kissed him and Charlie shook his hand in congratulations.

'I'm so glad Joanna had such an easy time,' said Irene. 'Jimmy, this must be the happiest day of your whole life!' she said, giving him another kiss, then going with her husband into the room to visit Joanna. Jimmy was left alone outside the door.

'Yeah, the happiest day of my whole life!' he said to himself. Then he smiled. 'Yes . . . yes, it is! Nothing can ever change that!' He walked down the long corridor and around the corner to the glass-walled nursery, where finally he saw the tiny red-faced little girl in the crowd of newborns. A sign was stuck on the basket holding her and it read, ROBBINS GIRL – 7 LB. 13 OZ.

'Hello, sweetheart,' Jimmy whispered, looking down at his daughter. 'Welcome to the world. I hope you enjoy it.'

CHAPTER FORTY-NINE

One week after Joanna and the baby came home from the hospital, Jimmy phoned Bob Silver to arrange an appointment with his father.

'He's all tied up the rest of the day. Call tomorrow and we'll see what we can work out.'

On Tuesday he tried again, but the message was the same. Delay, evasion, postponement. Late Wednesday he was in the upstairs corridor, leaving the legal department after reviewing some TV commercial contracts, and saw Ham at the far end of the hall as he opened his office door and headed for the barbershop, which was a few doors away behind an unmarked door. He hurried to catch up with him.

'Dad, I've been trying to see you. There's something I've got to discuss with you. It's quite important and –'

'All right – all right,' said Ham, licking his suddenly dry lips. He stepped into the barbershop and took off his jacket, which the manicurist hung on a rack. 'Sit down and talk to me here. I'm getting a haircut and shave, but my ears will be open if Hymie doesn't fill them with lather. I don't know if I can do much talking while he's shaving me, but sit down and go ahead anyhow. Go on . . . I'm listening.'

Hymie whipped a large white cloth around Ham's shoulders, then tilted the chair back after turning it around so that Ham's head was lined up with the shampoo sink. He turned on the water and got the hand spray going while the manicurist stuck her tray on the side of the chair and began to work on his nails.

'Uh, Dad . . . I don't think this is the best place for a discussion . . . too many other things . . .'

A voice came from the vicinity of the soaked scalp that Hymie was massaging with his strong well-trained hands.

'Speak up! I can't hear a damned thing you're saying to me! What is it that's so important?'

'About this television series for World. I want to discuss

540

something about it with you. You know I was put in charge of –'

The barber interrupted. He never listened to any voices other than his own and that of whomever he had in the chair.

'Mr. Robbins, do you want me to finish with a nice cold spray?'

'Yeah. I like a cold finale, closes the pores. Go ahead, Jimmy. Speak up! I still can't hear much of what you're saying. Now what was that about the commercials?'

'Dad, it wasn't about commercials. It was about –'

A thick terry cloth towel was wrapped around Ham's wet hair and ears as Hymie brought the chair back to an upright position. He whipped off the towel, massaged Ham's scalp, then reached for a soft dry cloth and kept working on the head of wet hair until it was only slightly damp. Jimmy kept quiet for a few minutes, knowing it would be impossible to get his father's attention until the rubbing stopped. Now Hymie reached for a hand-held dryer and switched it on, and a high-pitched whine filled the little room. The towel fell away from Ham's eyes and he looked over at his son sitting just a few feet away.

'For God's sake, speak up! I still can't hear a damn thing you're saying to me over this racket. What is it that's so important it can't wait until later?'

The high whine went on, becoming a nerve-wracking irritant. His father had a good head of hair and Hymie was making sure every single strand was dry before going on. It didn't need much trimming and Ham had wanted it shampooed first. The barber thought it was better to trim first and wash later, but Ham was stubborn and that was the way he wanted it and Hymie knew better than to argue. At last the dryer was snapped off, but as Jimmy again started to speak, the telephone rang. Hymie picked up the receiver, mumbled, 'Barbershop,' then handed it over to Ham.

'For you, Mr. Robbins. It's Bob.'

'Yeah, Bob. All right. Have it switched here . . . Hello, Lennie. How are you? Good. What's up?' There was a long pause as Ham listened while Hymie carefully snipped away at stray hairs that had grown a bit too full at the temples and on the nape on his neck. Ham grunted a few times, but kept listening to Lennie, a continent away, near midnight in New York. The barber reached down to unlock a cupboard. He brought out a small bottle of dark liquid, which he shook several times. He unscrewed the cap and applied a small

541

wad of cotton to the top, then very delicately touched up the gray hair on either side of Ham's head until everything was the same ageless dark brown once again. Jimmy thought the gray hair gave his father a kind of distinguished look, like some of the models they used as business executives in the TV commercials, but Ham thought otherwise. In another week there would be a general coloring of all his hair right to the roots, but for today just a touch-up would do. The manicurist switched over to his other hand and went to work with her cuticle snippers.

'Lennie, you tell them we're not going to spend any more on the hour shows. I don't give a damn if they're not happy. You know we signed new wage agreements last month, and now World TV is stalling on making it up to us. What do you mean, we don't have anything like that in our deal with them? Then damn it, we're going to spend less on each show to make it up! That Bergin shmuck I put in charge may know publicity, but he doesn't know shit about production! He's out as of this morning. Someone else will take over. I was suspicious of him the minute he opened his mouth in your office and shot off all that crap to show how much he knew! He's a blowhard who's all chutzpah and no brains! Okay – you tell your good friend Harold Kosterman at World that we have to renegotiate that part of our contract with them to make up these added costs – or else we will just cut back on everything, and nobody wants to do that!' Ham was getting angry, and the barber wished he would finish talking so he could comb his hair and trim his eyebrows.

Jimmy listened to the conversation with great interest. Everybody at the studio had known that Don Bergin was bungling the series. Pops Johnson had bet he wouldn't last through the first hour show, but somehow he'd managed to hang on through five of them. Now an envelope would arrive on his desk quoting an obscure clause in his contract and terminate his employment effective immediately with three months' salary. He would vanish this same morning as though he had never been. New locks would go on his office door and his name would be scraped off. Now Jimmy knew the time had come to go after something he should have been running from the beginning. He sat on the edge of his chair waiting for his father to hang up and the barber and manicurist to complete their work.

The call ended and Ham gave the phone to Hymie, who hung it up, snipped a final few hairs and whipped off the white cloth. He took a whisk broom to Ham's shoulders, and then his jacket went back on and Ham started for the door, seeming almost surprised to find Jimmy standing there beside him.

'Dad, can we go into your office and talk now? It's been impossible to speak to you here in the barbershop.'

Ham glanced impatiently at his wristwatch.

'I haven't any time now. There are people waiting for me in the projection room to run dailies. By the way, I saw Abe Stein at a dinner last night and he told me SRO was going to drop our account. They can't sell your series. See, you went about it all the wrong way. If they couldn't make a deal, then nobody could. I never should have allowed you to get us into it in the first place!'

They walked to Ham's office door, Jimmy deeply angered at his father's convenient amnesia about the forbidden pilot films. Jimmy knew SRO wasn't doing anything for them, and he knew why.

'Dad, it's damned unfair of you to say that! You know we should have had pilot films if we were going to make any sales. The agencies insisted on them. Over and over I asked your okay to make some and you turned me down every time. Television series just aren't sold without them and you refused even to let me shoot one frame of film. Now you're blaming me and my department for following your orders. It's almost as though you wanted me to fail! I'll bet Abe Stein told you the real reason SRO couldn't sell our shows was because they were forced to use those substitute presentation books while every other production company was shooting pilots and selling series. You nailed me into a box so I couldn't move!'

Ham was taken aback by his son's emphatic reply and his anger. The kid was really right, but that was something Ham would never admit to him, or to anybody else. Jimmy's anger upset him, stirring up old guilts, and he found it suddenly difficult to speak. He wished he could escape into his office and gripped the doorknob behind his back, trying to turn it in a sweaty hand. How dare the kid talk to him this way! He tried to clear his throat and say something to shut him up so he could get away, but Jimmy started speaking again and Ham felt the doorknob slip out of his grasp.

'Dad, that's not what I wanted to talk to you about. I want to take over the series we're making for World TV. I should have been handling it from the very start, since I was the head of our television department.'

543

Ham fumbled again with the door and got it open, then stood half in his outer office with one foot still in the corridor. Again he looked at his watch and raised his impatience up like a shield between them. This time he did not let Jimmy finish what he was saying. His voice came back and he almost shouted at his son.

'You've got a department to run and you're doing a pretty good job of it, except for those damn series we can't sell. Forget them. Lennie told me everybody likes the commercials you've been making for the World TV shows, in fact they're just about the best part of what we've shipped them so far.' Ham felt he could be generous with a small compliment. It eased some of the guilt that hit him when he saw how angry at him Jimmy was. Funny thing, he had never seen the kid so sore. What the hell, a few knocks would be good for him, toughen him up. 'Keep your mind on the commercials and the other deals you're lining up. The series for World are to be none of your concern. I already have somebody set to take them over starting tomorrow. I'm late now and we'll talk about it another time.' He backed into his office, leaving Jimmy alone in the hall, looking at the chrome letters on the black door that swung shut only inches from his face. The gleaming symbols were as chillingly unresponsive as the man whose name they spelled.

'It's unbelievable!' said Jimmy under his breath as he turned and started down the stairs. 'Here we are, both of us in the communications business, and he won't honestly communicate with me! It's almost like trying to talk to those damn letters on his door.'

More and more Nita avoided being seen in public. Ham continued to be absent many nights, and when he did come home he spent much of his time screening films or wandering around the grounds, a heavy walking stick in one hand and a flashlight in the other. It had become almost a ritual with him. After he ran pictures with producers or editors in his basement theater, whenever he wanted a change from the studio projection room, he would go on a snail-crushing walk under the night sky, talking cuts, revisions and rerecording with the other member of his lonely safari. One night it was the head of the music department, a talented man who had a wonderful feel for saving poorly done sequences with the magic of music. Phil Velasco was at ease on the podium facing a hundred and fifty musicians, but here on the spacious lawn of Ham Robbins' house, crisscrossing the silvery slime trails, he felt uncomfortable and depressed. Also, he could feel the damp coming through his thin shoes and knew he would be ruining takes with his sneezes on the music recording stage within a few days.

'Mr. Robbins, isn't that your wife looking at us from that window?' asked Phil, catching a glimpse of Nita peering out at them and the flash-light, which wove crazy patterns on the grass ahead of the two men. Ham turned toward the house, which the full moon lit up with a strange luminous glow. The yellow square of the window over the main door showed a thick silhouette that was unmistakably Nita. She must have gotten cramped up leaning over that damn round table of hers in the bedroom working on those fucking charts, thought Ham. Whose was she figuring out now?

'I met Mrs. Robbins for a moment in the hall before you arrived,' said the music man. 'She's quite a unique person, I must say. We'd never met before but she showed such an interest in me, even asked what month, year and hour I was born. It's so refreshing to run across somebody who is so aware of other people.'

'Oh, yes . . . an interesting woman. My wife is quite aware of other –' He stopped in mid-sentence as he spotted an exceptionally large snail. It must have been the father of the whole stinking tribe of gastropods decimating his beautiful lawns and rose garden. He moved in for the kill. The beam of light transfixed the creature for a blinding moment and then suddenly it became a shapeless glob of bubbling mucus stuck on the sole of Ham's shoe. He wiped most of it off, cursing the gardeners who permitted such things to happen.

'Phil, can you make a deal to have the London Symphony score this film for us? I know we have as good musicians right at our studio, but we've piled up some frozen pounds sterling in England and they won't let us take it out. We have to spend it there and maybe we can get rid of some of it scoring this film. This picture needs all the help we can give it.'

Velasco nodded, thought a moment, then spoke.

'It could be worked out. Of course the boys over at Local forty-seven will scream bloody murder if we use foreign music behind a U.S. production, but we're giving them so much other work that maybe they won't be too rough on us.'

'Fuck 'em. The unions are shoving us around all the time. You should see how much more it costs each year to make a picture. Nobody ever asks for less or wants to keep it the same – they all want more and more. Hell, there's no such thing in this business now as loyalty or pride in the product. They want all they can squeeze out of us – actors, the back lot unions, musicians, the writers ... they're about the worst! Everybody! There ought to be a union for people like me! I'd love to go out on strike and picket somebody!' His voice took on a sharp point of anger, which he directed at the next unfortunate snail he spotted at the end of his flashlight beam, crushing it deep into the grass.

Phil Velasco faced the house, trying not to watch the slaughter on the lawn. He saw the window suddenly empty of its shape as the curtains were drawn. It was a very strange night and Phil almost thought he could hear strains of *A Night on Bald Mountain* being played by an invisible orchestra, but it was only the buzz of insects and the muffled wail of an ambulance in a hidden canyon. At last Ham said good night and the musician went to his automobile, happy to leave this strange place and the man whose shoes were coated with the slime of dead enemies.

Ham went into the house and up the stairs. Nita stood waiting for him outside her bedroom door. There was tension in her voice.

'Get rid of that man! Get rid of him! He's all wrong, all wrong. Come in here and see what I've learned about Phil Velasco. You'll never believe your eyes. His chart is in chaotic contradiction to yours and you must –'

'Oh, shut up! He's already left and I've worked with the man for years without any problems. Just take your damn chart and shove it where the stars and planets don't shine!' He spoke in such anger that Nita was frightened and for a moment kept quiet. Soon, though, she had to speak again, and picked a subject she thought would be safe – the one person they both hated.

'Ham, I had a dream last night about your brother Maurie. It was a wonderful dream and I must tell you all about it.'

'Don't unload any of your fucking dreams on me,' he snapped. 'What the hell could be wonderful dreaming about Maurie, for God's sake! If it isn't your idiotic horoscopes, it's your stupid dreams!'

She waited for his rage to pass. In a moment he would calm down and want to know what she had dreamed about his dear brother. She could always count on Ham's curiosity. Sure enough, two minutes later he spoke in a reasonably calm voice.

'All right, Nita. Tell me about your dream.'

She smiled, took him by the hand and led him into the bedroom, where they sat on the long chaise just inside the door. She knew better right now than to take him any closer than this to the bed.

'It was so real and clear that it didn't seem to be a dream at all. Maurie suddenly decided he wanted to retire and he sold you all his stock in the company and you took over and became president. It was a wonderful dream, Ham. Why can't you make it come true? You know I've always said you should be the one running the company and not have to take all that constant punishment from your brother. He's getting old and he should retire. You have so many good years ahead of you, and they should be happy ones without the heartaches and problems he's given you. Isn't there anything you can do to make that dream of mine come true?'

Ham looked into his wife's eyes. They still had that quality of seeming to pierce deep into a man's brain and see his naked thoughts. He looked over her shoulder to get away from those eyes and saw the big table, still littered with charts and reference books, the paraphernalia of astrology.

'What do all those messages from outer space tell you about this, Nita?' he asked, not too unkindly. She really might be trying to help him, even with those crazy horoscopes of hers. Lately she had some odd people coming by to advise and instruct her, and now they seemed more complicated than ever. He still couldn't understand how intelligent grown-ups went for all that crap. Still, maybe there might be something to it after so many centuries.

'The stars and planets tell only the truth if you are willing to listen,' said Nita. 'They all say the same thing to me about you. Soon, when Pluto comes to a conjunction of your Sun, and Saturn trines your mid-heaven, things will come about to make you head of the company, and your brother, your enemy and mine, will have lost his power to oppose you or to speak against you.'

Ham snorted in disbelief.

'You don't know Maurie. The only thing that will ever shut him up about me will be his funeral, and even then he'll find some way to haunt me, the bastard!'

'Ham, now you're the one talking nonsense. Please come over to the table. I didn't do this alone. I had help from some of the finest minds here in town, people who have had years and years of experience in these things. Everything on these

547

charts is in complete agreement with what I've told you, and they all reflect my dream.'

'Damn it, Nita! Have you been discussing this with a bunch of strangers? Have you been blabbing about our company and me and my brother to outsiders? I don't like that! Even if they had the keys to the universe, you have no right to talk about things like that with anybody! You know how rumors get started by these experts just to get themselves noticed. With all their years of experience, they'll still shoot off their fucking mouths. Watch how fast your charts and all your stargazing gossip grow wings and fly to Maurie! If there ever was a chance for him to leave the company and for me to take it over, that really would kill it!' He slammed his hand down on the table, sending charts to the floor.

'Ham, please stop worrying. These are the most trust-worthy astrologers in Southern California. They know many things much more earth-shattering and important than who is going to run some movie company . . . and they keep it all to themselves. Please believe me! I pay them well and they know enough to be quiet about what we work out on our charts.'

'Tell me, Nita, are these experts of yours very rich?'

'I don't think so. Comfortable perhaps, but I'm sure they're not rich,' she replied.

'So if they know everything from their direct line to all those stars and planets out there, how come they don't know what stocks are going up . . . the price of diamonds next year . . . where to buy real estate . . . what long shots are going to pay off tomorrow at Santa Anita? Why are they just comfort-able and not filthy stinking rich with all that wonderful advance information they pull out of the zodiac? You put your faith in fakes, Nita, and what they feed you is shit . . . and fake shit at that!' He turned angrily away from her and left the bedroom, going down the corridor to the guest room where he now slept whenever he was home. A residue of snail slime came off his shoes and soiled the hall carpet.

Nita sat back on the chaise and laughed. She had replanted the thought in his head and would patiently wait for it to take root and bloom.

CHAPTER FIFTY

After nearly a year, television had made a very deep impression on theater box office receipts. Many people now remained in the comfort of their homes to view what passed for free entertainment, even though it was chopped up with commercial interruptions peddling everything from gadgets for unstopping sinks to pills for unstopping bowels. The noise of refrigerator doors opening and closing resounded throughout the land and hosannas were sung to nasal decongestants. It was the new age of the medicine show promising quick, quick relief from headache, hemorrhoid and heartburn, and the noisy world of the carnival pitchman moved into the living rooms of America.

TV commercial production prospered, and soon Jimmy convinced Ham that they should open sales offices in Chicago, Detroit and Pittsburgh to bring in more business along with that coming out of the New York office. The department was humming and Jimmy was too busy most of the time to think about the other television unit producing the series for World TV. Deep inside, though, he still remembered how he had been kept in the dark and shoved aside by the man who ran the studio.

His department had expanded a number of times and now he had several assistants and a staff of twenty people in what now was called the Commercial and Industrial Division. Alan Pauley was a great asset with his knowledge and contacts. He suggested they go after other potentially lucrative sources of business, corporations and other large organizations using motion pictures for advertising, training and public information. Industrial films, as they were generally known, were fast becoming a very active area, complementing the TV commercial side of the division. Jimmy planned to go after some government film contracts and convinced Ham they should open an office in Washington, D.C., staffed by somebody who knew government procurement procedures

549

and could get them business. The Departments of Defense, Agriculture, Interior, Commerce and many other branches of government all needed film and were untapped veins of gold. Pops Johnson strongly recommended a man named Frank Moreno, an old Washington hand who knew his way around all the right corridors and would see to it they won their share of bids. He was put on the payroll, opened up an office and quickly proved that he knew the way to the vaults.

Jimmy came home every evening, happy to be with Joanna and little Esther, who now was nearly one year old and ready to walk around the house by herself. He repeatedly had invited his father to visit his granddaughter, and suddenly one Sunday afternoon, as Ham was about to leave Hillcrest after a game of golf, he impulsively phoned to say he was coming by and would like to join them for dinner. Jimmy and Joanna were overjoyed and quickly rearranged chairs and added a place at the table. Joanna was a very good cook, not overwhelmed by having a sudden extra mouth to feed.

Ham drove himself to their house in Westwood and had a very pleasant time with his granddaughter, son and daughter-in-law. He seemed to be quite at ease and enjoyed playing with Esther, but soon after dinner he glanced at his watch, nervously cleared his throat and said he had to leave.

'Dad, please come back soon. We loved having you here, and I know Esther was very happy to be with you,' said Jimmy. 'She's going to have her first birthday next month. Will you come to her party?'

'Uh . . . well, I'll try to make it. Let me check with you later,' his father answered, and then he was gone.

He never did check with them, and Jimmy could get no definite answer when he phoned the office a week later. The birthday went on as planned. They lit a single candle on the cake that Joanna carried to the table, where they both blew it out for Esther, who sat back and laughed.

'Happy birthday, Esther! Next year you're going to blow out the candles all by yourself without any help from us,' said Jimmy, picking up his little daughter and hugging her. 'Now, a big kiss for your Momma and one for me.' After both of them had been kissed, he put her back on the chair and threw his arms around Joanna, who stood smiling at them.

'Jimmy, the strangest thing happened this afternoon. A messenger delivered a big package for Esther. I opened it, and I want you to see who it's from.'

It was a large brown teddy bear with a bright red ribbon

tied around its neck. Fastened to the ribbon was a card on which had been written, 'To Esther from her Grandfather – Happy Birthday.' Jimmy recognized Bob Silver's handwriting.

'How much nicer it would have been if he had brought it here himself instead of doing it secondhand like this,' said Jimmy, holding the teddy bear and looking into its beady black eyes. Joanna took it from him and set it back on the chair beside the baby's bed.

'Look, Jimmy, your father's not easy to understand. He probably doesn't even understand himself. Just take him as he is and don't expect too much. I don't think he always means to be unkind, and I can even feel sorry for him. He certainly can't be a very happy person – and I'm sure he's a very lonely one. Look at what he's missing.' She picked up Esther, who remained sound asleep, held her for a moment in her arms, then let Jimmy take the beautiful child to tenderly hug for a moment. 'Isn't she sweet? What a shame that your father doesn't really know what a delightful grandchild he has, but that's his loss. That one visit should lead to others – but that will have to be up to him. Now clean up and come to the dining room. I've put together a terrific dinner for you. Pot roast and potato pancakes right out of your mother's recipe file. I hope it tastes as good as it looks.'

'It better,' said Jimmy, giving her another hug and a kiss. 'I'm starved!'

Ham Robbins was not with his granddaughter Esther for her first birthday but was having a secluded dinner alone with Lennie Rhinehart, who was quite excited about something he could not wait to tell him. Room service brought the entire meal to Lennie's suite at the Beverly Hills Hotel, where they could speak without any danger of being overheard. There was a bright glint in Lennie's eyes as he spoke, and his voice seemed higher-pitched than usual.

'I had to get out here right away, Ham. I stopped off in Salt Lake City yesterday morning and spent most of the day at our film exchange talking on the phone to Harold Kosterman in New York. He sends you his regards. Harold came to me more than a month ago with something so big that I couldn't discuss it with you on the phone through the studio switchboard or even put it into a letter. It all came together earlier this week and that's why I'm here. Harold has brought together a group of people who want to buy the controlling interest in our company. They are ready to offer you and

Maurie, and anybody else in your family holding stock, a price that will be twenty-five dollars a share above the market. It must be kept absolutely quiet since this particular group is actively seeking a production-distribution company like ours. If a deal with us should fall through, they wouldn't want it to be known publicly and alert any other company.'

Ham felt his heart skip a beat. He hadn't thought of leaving the business just yet, but maybe this would give him a chance to relax for a while, then start something he could run himself without interference – without Maurie, to be more specific. He leaned forward and spoke to Lennie in a very low and intense voice, as if he were afraid someone might overhear him.

'Maurie might go for it. He's been talking a lot about retiring and enjoying life. To be honest with you, Lennie, I'm not quite ready for that yet, I mean retiring. Sure, I want to have some good times – and I enjoy running the studio. That's my life, and most of the time things are all right, even with Maurie sticking his long nose into things and getting me sore as hell now and then. He's the only thing I really don't like about the way things are now. The money they're offering sounds all right and I'm sure my sisters would be happy to sell, but I don't know . . .'

'Ham, all these people are familiar with you and everything you've done,' said Lennie. 'They know Maurie too, but it's you they want to work with. Maurie they can do without. That's the next part of their proposition – and this must be kept in absolute confidence for now. You'll see why after I tell you more about it. They want you and Maurie and the rest of your family to sell all your stock to them at this special price. That will give them the control they need. You'll have to work it out with Maurie and the others so they all agree to sell at the same time. Meantime Harold and his group will execute a confidential letter to you that will never enter the record. In it they will agree to let you, and nobody else, buy back one-half of all the stock you sold them at whatever is the market price at the time, which should give you a very nice profit. It would happen within two weeks after the official sale and relinquishing of company control by Maurie and you. At that time you would be announced as the new president and chairman of the board of Robbins International Pictures . . . and we go on from there. These people want you to run things. The group is to have several directors on the new board and a vice-president for finance, just to keep an eye on things. I'm to be given some stock options and a contract for my continued services. That's it – that's the whole deal. Harold wants you to think it over, but not for longer than a month from now, and let him know through me if you go for it or not. If you do, he'll want to meet with you in New York.'

Ham thought a few minutes before replying.

'The question is how Maurie will react when and if I tell him about it. Sure, he talks a lot about retiring, but when it comes right down to it, he loves the prestige being the president of this company gives him and all those speeches he's asked to make at meetings where he's such a *macher*. Will he really want to give it up so fast? Hell, it won't hurt to feel him out about some group offering to buy us out at such a good price. I'll tell him about it and see how he reacts. Naturally, if he thought for a second I was going right back in and be president after he was out, he would turn the whole thing down, profit or no profit. The thing is not to let him know anything at all about that part. He already has it in for me about so damn many things that one more won't matter too much. Give me a few weeks to think it over and decide what to do and how to approach Maurie and my sisters if we go ahead. I really don't know what to tell you right now. I'd like to know, Lennie, who are these people with all this money that Harold has brought together who want to buy control of our company?'

'They're a group I'm sure you don't know. Very wealthy and powerful men who have big cattle and oil interests and operate out of Denver. They've been watching our company and they like what they see. Harold knows them from when he operated a theater circuit that had offices there. Say – didn't you and your brothers have a little film exchange in Denver years ago?'

'Yeah, but the only people in town I ever got to know well were in the film business, such as it was then. That was long before Harold came to town. Oh, yes, I also knew some of the hookers who worked the downtown beat and the hotels near our exchange. There was one terrific redhead, my first lay – and that's something you never forget! I've always had a soft spot in my heart for Denver and redheads ever since. I wonder, whatever became of her?'

'Ham, forget it. This is business.' Lennie laughed. 'Right now I want you to think about the proposal Harold has made for them. I'm not putting a damn thing on paper, and neither should you or anybody else. If you decide to go with it, come back to New York and I'll set up a meeting with Harold and some of his group. We can work out everything in my house up in Mamaroneck, where it will stay private. Meantime, think it over. I'm sure you can handle Maurie and your sisters without too many problems. After all, they'll be paid plenty for their shares, and there's no reason why Maurie shouldn't relax for the rest of his life and be happy he doesn't have to yell at you anymore.'

'You don't know Maurie,' said Ham. 'That's the one thing he'd really miss. I appreciate everything you've done, Lennie. I know it hasn't been easy to keep anything this big to yourself, and I promise to keep as quiet about it as you've been. If I decide not to go ahead, then nobody but us need ever know. We'll talk again about it within a few weeks and go into how the press releases should be handled if I do give Harold the go-ahead. Now let's forget about it the rest of tonight and run over to Dave Chasen's for some drinks and find some of the fellows for a few laughs!'

Maurie had never slept so well. He awoke as the sun came up over Long Island Sound and he went into the breakfast room, leaving Rose still sleeping soundly up in their bedroom. He stretched and yawned, then looked out the window at the sky as it grew bright with the new day, and then he listened to the music of birds singing in the trees bordering his lawn all the way down to the shore. Deep breaths of the fresh sea air pulled into his lungs made him almost feel like joining the birds in song, but it was better to let Rose sleep another hour of two without waking her with his off-key singing. He looked ahead to the kind of a day he had denied himself for much too long.

More than two weeks had passed now since his resignation as president and board chairman of Robbins International Pictures. There had been all kinds of testimonial dinners, including one given by the Association of Motion Picture Pioneers, which had been soaked with sentiment and memories. He had worked hard nearly all his life and at last he was going to enjoy himself and his family. No more going into the city five days a week and sitting down behind a desk to read overhead reports that drove him into a rage when he realized what his crazy brother was spending out there in California. Hell, maybe he had been a little too rough on Ham. He shouldn't always have treated him like little Chaim . . .

Chaim the *pisher*. He really had done a good job and he had to be fair in admitting that. So maybe he was stubborn, head-strong and difficult, a real miserable son of a bitch now and then . . . but maybe that's what it took to run a studio. It was no easy job, and only the real tough ones lasted very long in that golden jungle. After all, Mayer, Cohn, Goldwyn, Zukor and all the rest of them who had made it weren't always the easiest or nicest people in the world to get along with. With Ham, though, there was something else deep inside that Maurie could never quite figure out. Maybe his brother didn't understand that part of himself either. He let you get just so close, then it was almost as though he slammed a door shut in your face. Oh well, let him enjoy the rest of his life too, if that impossible woman he was married to would ever let him.

The air was so crisp and clean out here. Manhattan, only a dozen miles away across the East River, was like a faraway different country. Later in the day he and Rose would finish their packing, and then tomorrow morning they would fly down to the lovely house they had bought in Boca Raton. A season in the sun, maybe some visits to old friends in Miami Beach, and then just relax and enjoy themselves. He was a lucky man, forty-nine years married to the same woman and still in love. Just imagine, he thought, next year they would celebrate their golden wedding! Immediately his thoughts went back to that night of his parents' fiftieth anniversary and the dreadful scene that took place when Irene found out that Ham wanted to dump her.

'Oh, Lord,' said Maurie. 'If only I had some new words in my vocabulary for Nita. I'm sick of the old ones.'

He walked over to the breakfast table, where the cook put a glass of freshly squeezed orange juice in front of him along with his copy of the *New York Times*. Maurie drank the juice, wiped his lips and turned his attention to the heaped plate of scrambled eggs and strips of crisp bacon surrounding them. He glanced at the *Times*. Nothing spectacular on the front page caught his eye. Russia had declared the official end of war with Germany.

'About time they got around to that. The war's been over, let's see . . . nearly nine or ten years now. Ah . . . George Meany was made president of the newly merged AFL-CIO. Thank heavens I don't have to worry about deals with unions anymore or being a president,' he mused as he dug into the eggs, finished a half-cup of coffee and noted that President

555

Eisenhower had just appointed John M. Harlan to the Supreme Court.

'Ha . . . what the courts did to us when they drove us out of the theater business! That was the beginning of the end, and now this television is going to destroy what's left of the whole entertainment industry!' He read on, wiped his mouth and picked up some buttered toast. 'Juan Peron has resigned as the president of Argentina.' Maurie nodded his head and smiled. 'We have something in common, Juan. We've both resigned as presidents. His reasons I don't know, but for me all the old pleasures were fading. Let those Denver big shots find out that making films isn't like fattening cattle or drilling for oil. I'm happy to be out of it. From now on I'm enjoying my life with Rose.'

He turned to the business news and propped the paper up on the table. A headline leaped out at him: HAM ROBBINS RETURNS TO HIS OLD COMPANY AS PRESIDENT AND CHAIRMAN OF THE BOARD. The piece of toast fell into the coffee with a splash and slowly sank out of sight beneath the cream-thickened surface. Maurie gripped the paper with both hands and read aloud from the page.

' "It has been announced by Leonard M. Rhinehart, the acting president of Robbins International Pictures, Inc., that Hamilton J. Robbins will return to the company as its new president and chairman of the board. The company, founded many years ago by Robbins and his brothers, Maurie, who recently retired, and Lou, who died some years ago, has come under the control of a group of wealthy Colorado investors in a deal described in these pages last week. There have been many rumors as to who now would be the new chief executive of the company, and Rhinehart's statement today revealed that Hamilton J. Robbins, popularly known as Ham Robbins, will return to take over the positions formely held by his older brother, Maurie. "We were most fortunate," Rhinehart stated, "to convince Ham Robbins to reassume a position of leadership in the company. His knowledge of production and worldwide distribution is based on many years of invaluable experience. Although it was difficult to talk him into coming out of his brief retirement, which lasted all of two weeks, he finally consented to return to the company that he and his brothers founded." When reached at his newly reoccupied offices on the Encino lot, Robbins stated he had long looked forward to happy years of well-earned retirement, but that the opportunities offered to lead his old company were too tempting to refuse. "I still have many years left and have great plans for Robbins International. Nobody can really replace my brother Maurie, a great man and a credit to the entire industry. I am sure that under my administration and with our new board of directors, there will be an infusion of new –" " '

Maurie stood up so suddenly that his chair crashed over, making a clattering noise as it struck the hardwood floor. He crumpled the paper in his fists and walked out of the room into the hall. As he reached the stairs, he staggered slightly, put one hand out to the wall to steady himself and tripped on the first riser. He dropped the newspaper to the floor and shouted in a frightened voice as loudly as he could.

'Rose . . . Rose! Please, come here . . . *Rose!*'

Maurie seemed to strangle on the last word and put both hands up to his head as he fell down to his knees on the staircase. For a moment he straightened up, and then his eyes rolled up in his head, and with one hand blindly reaching out for the newel, he toppled backward, landing on the floor with a crash. The cook rushed from the breakfast room, where she had just picked up the fallen chair.

Rose sat up, suddenly fully awake in her bed, and reached out for her robe. She came running to the top of the stairs and looked down to see her husband stretched out flat on his back, his mouth hanging strangely open and his face a terrible gray. The cook was kneeling beside him, holding his hand and calling out to him.

'Mr. Robbins . . . Mr. Robbins . . . Are you all right?'

Rose came down the stairs two at a time, dropped to her knees beside Maurie and felt his wrist, then put her hand up to her face in horror. She screamed at the cook, 'Quick! Get to the telephone and call an ambulance! Hurry – hurry!'

In less than ten minutes two attendants had Maurie on a rolling stretcher, an oxygen mask clamped on his face, and he was boosted up into the ambulance that stood in the driveway with its motor running. Rose rushed in to kneel beside him, and she held his hand all the way to Manhasset General Hospital.

'Maurie, Maurie . . . What happened? Please, Maurie darling, say something to me!' Rose said over and over, trying desperately to see some sign of life in the ashen face of her stricken husband. She kept her other hand on his head to steady it as they rushed down the road, rocking from side to side, the siren wailing and the traffic pulling aside to let them pass.

557

Back at their house, where the front door remained wide open, the cook sat weeping in the front hall. On the floor by the staircase lay the crumpled pages from the *New York Times*. A fresh breeze from Long Island Sound came through the open door, caught the wadded-up newspaper and rolled it over to reveal more of the statement issued by the new President of Robbins International Pictures.

'I am proud of the history and traditions of this great company, but the past is prologue. The present is change, and the future belongs to those with the skill and daring to take risks. I should deeply have loved to join my brother in a well-earned happy retirement,' said Ham Robbins, 'but I have been convinced by the members of the board of directors that my place was here at the helm of our company. I know my brother Maurie shares my feeling that what has happened is for the ultimate good of . . .'

Again the soft breeze caught the crumpled newspaper, rolling it like a ball until it came to rest beside the wastebasket under the front hall table.

558

CHAPTER FIFTY-ONE

Maurie sat alone silently staring out his upstairs bedroom window at the lawn, which descended in a long gentle slope to the waters of Long Island Sound. The cerebral hemorrhage and the stroke that followed it had taken place almost between heartbeats, and eight months passed before he could be taken home from the hospital. Not even Rose could say for sure that he knew where or who he was, or could even recognize her. Only his eyes seemed to have any life, and they moved almost constantly from side to side as he sat propped up in his wheelchair with a blanket wrapped around his legs.

Maurie, who had survived so much, survived this too – though only the slow rise and fall of his shrunken chest and the confused little movements of his eyes showed that something resembling life was still hidden in this husk of a once strong and vital man. A male nurse was always with him, leaving only when Rose came into the room to sit beside her husband, talking as though he heard and understood her every word and might answer at any moment. She still could not believe that Maurie was sealed away from her. While such a thing might happen one day, now he sat beside her in his chair and she truly believed he could hear all the news she brought of friends, family and the world outside.

In the mornings, after the nurse had fed him breakfast, Rose opened the newspaper and read to Maurie what was happening in the theater and the art galleries and to all the pleasant people doing things. There was no conflict, no war, bloodshed or illness in the stories Rose read to her husband, and never anything about the motion picture industry in which he had spent so many of his vital productive years. The news Rose read to the man in the wheelchair consisted only of things she believed would not be disturbing if he heard and could understand.

Their daughter, Gail, and her husband visited them as often as they could with their two little children, who both

559

became frightened when they saw their silent grandfather staring out the window, never saying hello or hugging them the way he always had before. Ruth, Miriam and their husbands came to sit beside their silent brother, whose eyes moved slowly from one to another. The rest of his body remained motionless, and it was all they could do after a while to hold back their tears.

'Rose, in another two months you and Maurie will have been married to each other for fifty years,' said Ruth as they sat drinking coffee in the breakfast room. 'I know it's terribly hard to think now of having some kind of celebration, but for your sake and for Maurie's, you should have just family and some close friends here with you at that time. They all love you both so much and now especially they would want to be with you. Maurie may not be able to take part in anything, but it is an important milestone and it should be remembered.'

'No . . . no. My heart wouldn't be in it,' said Rose, shaking her head almost in anguish. 'How could we ever have a party, a celebration, with him sitting up there like that?'

'For that very reason, Rose. He is up there. He's not with Momma and Poppa and poor Lou. He's alive and he is your husband and the two of you will have been married for fifty years! Maybe something will get through to him. How do we really know if it does or doesn't? I feel sure he does know a great deal about things that are happening around him, but he has no way to tell us. Miriam and I will be here to help you and take the whole thing off your hands. It will be just for family and close friends, and one of us will always be with Maurie in his room. We should talk to the doctor about it and I'm sure he will agree it would be wonderful for your spirits, and for Maurie's too. Honestly, Rose, you should think about it. I love you both so much and I would never suggest anything that I didn't think was right for you to do.'

'We'd have to ask all of the family, wouldn't we?' asked Rose, an edge of bitterness and anger in her voice. 'There's one person I will not ask and will not see!'

'Rose, you cannot keep Ham away if he wants to come,' said Ruth. 'You and Maurie are both finer human beings than he could ever be, and you should invite him. There's a good chance he will send some kind of excuse and never show up. Somehow I believe he is suffering deeply about what happened, even though he may never tell anybody what's going on in his mind. Guilt has a way to get through the thickest of skins. He doesn't lead such a wonderful life, for all his suc-

560

cess. He's always away from his house, it seems. I don't blame him, and I refuse to discuss that impossible woman he's married to. I've heard that she's away for months at a time herself. She goes to someplace called the Willows in Ojai, near Santa Barbara, I understand. What she does there God alone knows or cares. Oh, yes, our dear brother is keeping somebody again. This time it's a twenty-four-year-old divorcee he's set up someplace on Sunset Boulevard. What did Ham say before he became such a success . . . 'I made my bed, now I'll have to lie out of it.' I could never understand why most of his jokes were so sad and unfunny.' Ruth reached out to take her sister-in-law's hand. 'Rose, I know it's hard, but please ask Ham to come. He may and he may not, but it's something you should do. Now let's talk about my idea of putting up a big tent outside so the party won't be inside the house, where there's a chance the noise might disturb Maurie.'

'No, Ruth. I don't think that under the circumstances it would be right to celebrate anything.'

'Nonsense. There's no better reason for a celebration than a golden wedding anniversary. How many of those can you have in a lifetime? The family and all your friends will want to be with the two of you. Let's leave it up to the doctor. Will you let us make plans if he says it's all right? Think of the wonderful time we had for Momma and Poppa years ago their fiftieth. It's only fair that you and Maurie have a party too. I'm sure he'll be aware of it and that it will make him very, very happy. Do it for him, Rose.'

'Well, if the doctor agrees, I might let you and Miriam help me do it,' she replied, still a bit reluctant. 'I keep feeling it might be too much for Maurie, but your idea of a tent on the other side of the house and just having one person at a time with him makes it sound better. The evenings here are lovely that time of year, and if we only invite family and close friends, say about a hundred people in all . . . no, it may come to a few dozen more than that . . . well, it would really be nice. We could use a few pleasant hours here after all the terrible things that have happened. Let's phone the doctor right now, and if he says it's all right, we can start working on the guest list and decide where to have them put the tent.' Rose grew excited as she spoke, and there was a smile on her face for the first time in many months.

They went to the telephone and Rose placed a call to the doctor. Ruth sat beside her, waiting for him to come to the phone. She felt positive there was going to be another golden wedding celebration in the family and that Maurie would know about it and be happy.

Tiny specks of airborne light flickered near the water's edge and the nurse held tightly to the hands of the little boy and girl who pulled her first in one direction and then in the other, trying to catch fireflies with their hands. The boy broke loose and ran all the way across the wide lawn, finally reaching out to clasp both hands around the flashing light of the tiny flying insect. The nurse dragged his sister over to him, very angry that he had gone so close to the water.

'Steven, don't you dare do that again! Your mother would be very upset. Now take my hand and we'll go back to the party.'

The little boy lifted his fingers and looked down at the tiny firefly. 'Look, he's turned off his light!'

'Young man, don't play with fireflies. Let the poor thing go. Now we'll all walk back to the house.'

He stuck his fist deep into a pocket, then reached up to take the nurse's hand. She looked up at the pink sky, then at the house sitting far up the sweeping lawn.

'Isn't that your grandfather up there looking at us?' she said to the children, trying to point without letting go of their hands.

'What's wrong with Grandpa?' asked the little girl. 'He just sits in his room all day and looks out the window and doesn't even talk to anyone. I don't want to see him anymore. He scares me.'

Their nurse shook her head and sighed.

'Children, your poor grandfather is . . . well . . . he hasn't been very well and he's resting. You see, he's an old man and he's very tired. You should go up and see him before you go home. Remember, this is a very special party. Your Grandma Rose and Grandpa Maurie have been married to each other for fifty years. Can you imagine that – fifty years! This is what is called their golden wedding anniversary, so when you see them, be sure you give them a big hug and a kiss and tell them how much you love them. That will make them both very happy.'

'I don't wanna kiss Grandpa. He scares me!' said the little boy as they went into the house.

Nearly all the guests had arrived while the late-afternoon sky was still bright. It was to be an early party and they all would be leaving before eleven o'clock, but while they were here, it was a time for restrained celebration. One or two at a time, members of the family and old friends went into the upstairs room to sit for a while beside the silent man in his wheelchair. Maurie did not seem to notice. No movement came from his body other than the slow measured breathing and the eyes sweeping from side to side.

Ruth gave him a kiss on his cheek, then Miriam came in to sit beside her stricken brother for fifteen minutes. Both their husbands took turns, then more old friends who had known Maurie in his good years and now. As some of them left the room, they put handkerchiefs to their eyes and wiped away tears. To see this once strong, vital and dynamic human being propped up in a mockery of life was more than several could endure, and they were deeply distressed at the terrible changes they saw in Maurie.

The nurse entered the room in between visitors, checked his patient, wheeled him into the bathroom when he thought it necessary, then rolled him back into the room again. A glass of juice was lifted to Maurie's lips, and he seemed to swallow more by reflex than by desire.

Jimmy and Joanna sat at a table with other family members in the big tent that had been set up on the far side of the house. A small orchestra played and a few couples danced on the portable floor spread out on the grass courtyard.

'Joanna, I almost wish Aunt Rose had decided not to have this party, but perhaps it's a good idea for her morale and his. I heard her say she was sure Uncle Maurie knew what was happening, even though he couldn't say a word to anybody. It must be terrible for the poor man being locked up inside his body like that, not able to communicate with anybody. Did you see his eyes? They almost seem to show he knows something is happening around him. That's the only part of him I guess he can move, and sometimes he looks so terribly frightened. Hell, I'd be frightened too . . . the poor man. Come on, let's dance. After all, how many people celebrate fifty years together, even if one of them can't join in everything. I guess we should try to have a good time for them.'

They went around the tent a few times and stopped to talk to some cousins, aunts, uncles and friends. Several men Jimmy had worked with in New York were there, and they stopped dancing while he introduced Joanna. Some of them were now retired, and they talked a little about the old days when Jimmy was learning all about the business. He saw Mike Hammersmith, now an old man, and took Joanna over to say hello.

'Mike, I want you to meet my wife. Joanna dear, this is Mike Hammersmith. He was the first head of Distribution when the company began years ago.'

'Hey, Jimmy, stop making me ready for the boneyard!' Mike laughed. He looked around the tent, which was filled with several dozen big round tables. 'Say, has that old man of yours shown up yet? He never was on time to anything I can remember for as long as I've known him.'

'No,' Jimmy said, feeling suddenly quite uneasy. 'I don't think he's going to be here tonight. He's been over in Europe the last couple of weeks. If he was coming at all, he'd be here by now.'

Mike looked shrewdly at the young man and wondered how much he really knew about his father and Maurie.

'Well, that may be, but he should try to get here regardless. After all, Maurie is his only living brother and he owes him something. Hell, let's not talk any more about that. This is supposed to be a happy time, a celebration. Forget I mentioned him. Now you both go on and have a good time. Real nice to meet you, Joanna. You're a very pretty girl. Hope I see you both again. G'bye.'

They danced a few more times around the floor. Suddenly Jimmy felt like going into the house to sit in the big empty living room. The tent seemed crowded, too warm and noisy as he thought of his father and about what had happened to his uncle upstairs in his wheelchair.

'Jimmy, I've been looking for you.' It was Aunt Ruth's husband, Abe Harris. He had been appointed schedule maker for family members and others visiting Maurie up in his room. So far things had gone quite smoothly, one person at a time sitting beside him, talking softly about the party, how well he looked and other fabrications they hoped might perhaps get through to give him some comfort.

'Would you go up and sit with your Uncle Maurie for about fifteen minutes? I know he'll be very happy to see you. He has always thought so much of you, Jimmy.'

'I was going to ask when I could go up to be with him. Joanna, stay here with Uncle Abe and Aunt Ruth and the others. Maybe you can look in on us in fifteen minutes when somebody else comes up to be with him. There shouldn't be too many people in his room at the same time.' He gave her a kiss and then went up the stairs to his uncle's room. Pulling the door open, he went inside to find old Pops Johnson from the studio sitting beside the wheelchair. He was chatting in his warm and friendly voice with the silent man, talking about some of the interesting places and people he and Maurie had known over all the years, memories that would not disturb the listener, if he heard at all. Pops looked up to see Jimmy crossing the room.

'Jimmy,' said the old man, rising to his feet and shaking hands, 'your uncle and I were just talking about the day President Coolidge came out to visit the studio with Mrs. Coolidge and how hard he tried to get a conversation going with him. You know, old Cal knew how to be a popular president – never say anything to anybody about anything! I know your uncle's enjoying himself and wants you to be with him now.' Pops came very close to the young man and his usual hearty voice dropped to a sad whisper. 'Damn it, Jimmy, I'm torn apart about this. What can I say? Try to keep him happy for a little while. Talk to him about anything – happy times from the past – and don't ever let him feel that he's alone. I don't know what else anyone can do.' He reached over to give Jimmy a friendly squeeze on the arm, looked back at his old friend and then quietly left, pulling the door shut so the distant music would not find its way into the room.

'Uncle Maurie, happy anniversary to you and Aunt Rose. Joanna is downstairs with her now enjoying your wonderful party and she'll be up later. They're cutting the cake soon and you'll get a slice of it.' He sat down beside his uncle, for a moment trying to think of things to say as he glanced at the ravaged face of the silent man. 'Can you see all those fireflies out on your lawn? We don't have anything like that in California. I wonder how they light up the way they do.'

The nurse let himself into the room, looked at Maurie and reached for a glass of water, holding it up to his patient's mouth, where it was swallowed almost automatically, and then he wiped a few drops off his chin. The nurse was a big, overly cheerful man, used to working with hopeless cases. Perhaps his constant state of cheer was a necessary defense against the misery with which he was usually surrounded.

'Mr. Robbins, let me turn your chair so you can look at your visitors instead of out the window all the time. Aren't you having a wonderful time at your anniversary party! Such a lovely family you've got. So many more are down there, all of them waiting to come up and be with you. It must be grand to

565

be married to the same woman so many years. Ah, my work makes it hard to be a married man . . . it does indeed. I don't seem able to stay with the same wife longer than two or three years. I'm on my fourth wife now. Can you believe it! I'll sure never make it to fifty years like you and your missus did!'

Jimmy wished the man would shut up, but then realized he had to keep up this chattering for himself, not for the patient. This kind of work must really get you talking to yourself after a while. He looked closely at his uncle. How terrible he looked! Those wide-open tragic eyes, staring straight at him. He sat rock-still and looked into Jimmy's eyes. What a terrible thing to happen to such a wonderful man. The nurse left the room and the two of them were alone.

It was very quiet; then a muffled noise of distant dance music came into the bedroom as the door swung open, then closed again, cutting off all outside sound. Jimmy turned to see who had come in. His breath almost stopped as he saw his father standing there across the wide bedroom, immaculate in his black tuxedo and white dress shirt with the little bow tie. A broad smile was fixed on his face, and for a moment he sounded like the departed nurse, inane conversation coming unasked from his lips.

'Maurie, congratulations to you and Rose! Fifty years! At last you caught up to Momma and Poppa!' He started across the room toward the motionless man in the wheelchair as Jimmy turned it so his uncle faced the visitor. Ham saw his son, nodded and spoke. 'Hello, Jimmy. I just saw Joanna as I came in. Uh . . . I had a lot of trouble getting here. I went from the airport to our apartment and changed, then drove here as fast as I could . . . I . . . uh . . .' He turned away from his son and looked at the man frozen in the wheelchair, that strange piece of furniture worn by his brother. He had not seen him since before Rose kept him from coming inside the hospital and he had to sit for hours cooped up in his car while they fought to save Maurie's life. My God, what Rose had put him through that day! Just now again she turned away from him when he arrived a few minutes ago. He tried to congratulate her and got a cold shoulder from her in front of all those people he knew downstairs. She'd get over it . . . or maybe she wouldn't. Hell, he still couldn't stay away when he was right here in New York, now could he?

The younger of the brothers stood in the middle of the room facing the paralyzed man in the wheelchair who could not say a single word to him. All those long-winded speeches he

566

had delivered to any audience that would sit still and listen vanished into the ears of time. Now he sat there struck dumb, his wide-open sad eyes fixed on the dapper man in the black tuxedo with the foolish little bow tie and the slicked-down, unnaturally dark hair.

Ham came closer, the smile still fastened to his lips, and looked into his brother's eyes. Jimmy watched them. There seemed no way for Maurie to escape from this man who was coming closer and closer to him. There was no way out, no place to hide from him . . . but there was one . . . the only one . . . and he took it. Slowly, very, very slowly, Maurie closed both his eyes and shut out the sight of the half-grinning man who came toward him, hand stuck out as though he wanted it grasped and shaken in greeting. Two little tears squeezed from beneath the tightly shut eyelids and crept down the sunken cheeks. The only movement on his entire face was that of the tears, followed by several more, passing around the corners of his mouth down to the tip of his chin, dripping off to fall on the blanket covering his spindle-thin legs. Maurie had triumphed. He had escaped his brother into a place where he could never be followed, secure at last within the decaying fortress of his body.

Jimmy looked up at his father, who so suddenly had been locked outside the closed gates of his brother's eyes. Ham's face went bright red, and he became so agitated that he dropped his outstretched arm and backed toward the closed door. His hands opened and closed, seemingly beyond his control, clasping and unclasping, until he thrust them deep in his pockets to hide them.

'Maurie . . . I . . . I want . . . please . . . Maurie!' He spoke without sense, mouth opening, closing, grasping for words he could not find. Now he moved backward, crablike, until his body struck the closed door and he pulled his hands from their pocket hiding places to wrench it open. He turned and ran down the stairs two at a time, past people who pulled aside to let him by. The front door was open and he rushed around the corner of the tent to the car park, where he tore open the door of his Rolls, clashed its gears and roared off into the night.

The little tears followed each other down Maurie's furrowed cheeks, and Jimmy reached over to take a thin nerveless hand, holding it and speaking in a very low voice.

'He's gone now, Uncle Maurie. He's gone.' All movement stopped on Maurie's face as the last tear reached his chin and dropped. Nothing more came from beneath the closed eyelids, and very soon they opened as Maurie again looked out into the room. Jimmy pulled out a handkerchief from his pocket and gently wiped his uncle's face, then sat for a while, holding the cold hand.

The silence of the room was broken when Maurie's daughter, Gail, arrived with a slice of anniversary cake and his two grandchildren, who still were a bit frightened of the stranger in the chair, but were trying their hardest to be brave. Gail took them over to sit beside her father as Jimmy let go of Maurie's hand, got up and left the room.

'Grandpa,' said the little boy, 'Grandpa, I've brought you a present for your . . . your anna-bersary.' He reached deep down into his pocket and pulled out something, held it a moment in his closed hand, then slowly opened it in front of his grandfather's face. A tiny firefly lay on his palm, its legs kicking in the air. It rolled itself over and opened its wings. There was a busy fluttering and then it rose, hovering almost directly in front of Maurie's open eyes. The little light flickered on and off, on and off, gaining strength and glowing brighter as the insect felt the fresh air coming through the window and the scent of other fireflies waiting outside in the dark. Maurie's eyes followed the flickering little light as it flew close to his face, then up and above his shoulder to fly through the window and far across the lawn to join with all the other twinkling little lights in the clear night air.

The eyes of the stricken man turned as far as they could to follow the tiny light. When it was lost, he closed them once again, this time not to escape, but to rest until he would need his eyes no more.

CHAPTER FIFTY-TWO

Jimmy was tired and depressed. He had just returned to the studio after a long hard week in Detroit trying to land the Ford Motor Company contract for a very important group of commercials. An entirely new line of cars was about to be introduced and whoever landed this deal would share in the glory. Now all he had to show for the months of effort with his team of art directors and production assistants was a collection of beautifully done storyboards, some sample reels of their best work and the decision of the agency to give the coveted job to a small Chicago commercial producer.

'They loved everything we showed them. Our storyboards and schedules went over great, and they kept telling us what a terrific job they knew we could do,' Jimmy told Harry Saunders after the daily production meeting. 'Still, somebody else had the inside track long before we flew back with all our best stuff to show them. What a waste! We weren't the only ones let down, though. Three or four other companies from here also showed up to make their pitch and we were all squeezed out together. Universal, MGM, Cascade and our shop all wanted to produce the very first television commercials introducing the new Edsel. It would have been a real feather in our caps. Hell, you can't win 'em all . . . and anyhow, who wears caps here in Southern California, with or without feathers?'

'Better luck next time,' said Harry as he gathered up his schedules and breakdown sheets for the next day's shooting. 'Did you get a look at their new car? Nobody seems to know anything at all about it. The Edsel is the best-kept secret since D-day!'

'Yeah, here are some stills I just happened to pick up at the agency office. Very hush-hush. I'm not supposed to have them. What do you think of that weird front they stuck on it that looks like a horse collar and that odd set of flaps or something on the tail?'

'It looks exactly like my old La Salle,' grunted the studio production manager. 'Edsel . . . what a strange name for a car. I wonder how it will go over. Well, that's their problem. We've still got plenty of commercials to shoot with the Buick, Pontiac and Goodyear spots, plus the new line of RCA receivers and those World Series inserts for Gillette. Say, I have to get around to your set more often when you're shooting those shampoo spots. It must be wonderful when the girls drop their towels. You never heard so many back lot guys begging me for assignments to those jobs!'

'Harry, you're too young to be such a dirty old man! Come over tomorrow to Stage Three. We're doing some laxatives and underarm deodorants for McMillin Drugs and I'll see that you get lots of samples.'

'What happened to all the beer? Aren't we doing any more of them? Those are the kind of samples I'd like to pick up,' said the production man.

'Budweiser the end of next week, Pabst and Schlitz to follow. Keep in touch and we'll keep you in beer. Say, what went on around here while I was in Detroit chasing after the elusive Edsel with my gang?'

'Nothing too much. The real action's been over in France, where we're shooting that Versailles epic near Paris. Your father took a plane there the day before yesterday. Nothing was given out to the press and we're not supposed to talk about it.'

'Bob Silver told me he left the studio for a week or two,' said Jimmy. 'I figured something was cooking over there. I wouldn't have minded that trip myself. Last time I saw Paris was during the war, and we tore through the place too fast to see very much of it. I've got to tell him about the Detroit thing and the thirty-eight hundred bucks we'll have to write off for what the whole sales pitch cost us. Bob only said that he was out of town.'

'Out of town is right. You know we're shooting that super-epic just outside Paris, or we were until last week. It's already run way over budget and schedule and your old man's hopping mad. Everything went wrong when they got to the last big sequence in the Hall of Mirrors at Versailles. We had special permission from the French government to shoot right in the real place and the whole company moved in with lights and equipment and all the usual crap. The actors playing President Wilson, Lloyd George and Clemenceau all showed up in their wardrobe and make-up with more than four hundred extras and bit players – plus that lovely lady star who causes me nothing but indigestion. So what happens? The cameraman had never seen the inside of Versailles before and nobody ever told him the Hall of Mirrors was actually lined with real mirrors. Can you believe that! Anyhow, they finally got to the part of the film where the Allies show up with their delegations to sign the peace treaty ending World War One – and they can't light the set! All those damn mirrors kept bouncing light flares right back into the lens, and the cameraman refused to push a button until they had sprayed every single damn piece of glass in the room with wax to kill the glare. You can imagine what happened when the Ministry of Something or Other heard what we were doing to their precious mirrors! They had a second French Revolution and kicked the whole damn company right out of Versailles. They moved over to Joinville Studios, where the asshole producer took it on himself to order a reproduction of the Hall of Mirrors put up inside one of the stages, full scale and with about ten thousand waxed mirrors. You can imagine what your father said when he saw the revised schedule and the amended budget! He really blew up, and now he's gone there to take over the rest of the production himself. Meanwhile all those expensive actors are drawing salaries and sitting on their butts in Paris hotels, eating French food so when they start shooting again none of them will fit into their wardrobe!'

'It sounds like something right out of a horror film,' said Jimmy.

'To top it all,' Harry continued, 'the director left the most important sequence of the entire picture until last and used up every cover set, so now there's no place to go and they have to wait for the Versailles interior. The producer was someplace visiting the wine country and must have been well loaded with grape when he okayed everything without any approval from Ham. By this time he's having himself a breakdown on the Riviera.'

'And I thought I had problems losing the Edsel account,' said Jimmy with a wan smile.

The production secretary called in to tell Jimmy that Bob Silver wanted him on the phone right away.

'I've been trying to reach you all over the lot,' said Bob. 'I'm afraid I have some bad news.'

Had something happened to Joanna or little Esther? Jimmy's heart jumped, and he breathlessly waited for the rest.

'It's your Uncle Maurie. We just now got a call from New

York that he died about half an hour ago at his home. I'm terribly sorry, Jimmy.'

'Have you reached my father? He'll want to know right away.'

'Not yet,' answered Bob. 'Come up to the office. I'm putting through a call to Paris and you can talk to him there. I may reach him at his hotel, or Carl Feldman will know where he is. With the difference in time it may be hard to make connections, but I'll try. Come right up.'

Bob was speaking to the international long-distance operator when Jimmy reached the office and his call was put through to the George the Fifth Hotel. There was no answer in Ham's suite and the call was transferred to Carl Feldman's office. He was gone, but the night operator would try to reach him and tell him to call. Bob tried the studio in Joinville, but nobody there knew where Monsieur Robbins was. He had left the studio hours ago and early next morning the builders would be there to continue work on the Hall of Mirrors set. Bob repeatedly asked them to try to locate Ham and have him call, but nobody seemed to understand. He hung up, and at once the phone rang with Carl Feldman, now at his home in Paris, returning the call.

'This is Bob Silver, Mr. Feldman. I am calling from Mr. Robbins' office in California. Will you locate him please as quickly as you can and tell him that his brother Maurie just died. Yes . . . yes . . . he was very ill. Thank you, I'll tell the family for you. It's most important you get to him. No funeral arrangements have been made and I'm sure they will want to know when Mr. Robbins will arrive in New York. What? . . . You're not sure you know where he is? Try to find him right away, please, and phone me here as soon as you do. I just sent him a cablegram care of your office and it should be there soon. See that he gets it. Thank you . . . Yes, of course. All right, call me back. I'll be waiting. Good-bye.'

Jimmy placed a call to his Aunt Ruth in Harrisburg. She answered and told him she had just spoken to Rose a few minutes before. Maurie had passed away in his sleep with no pain, no suffering. His tired, worn-out heart just stopped and he was gone.

'Can you reach your father? He should be told. I'm sure that Rose will want him here with the rest of the family for the funeral. At times like this we all have to come together and not think about the past.'

'Any idea when it will take place?' he asked. 'Joanna and I will fly there tomorrow.'

572

'No. By the time you arrive the arrangements should all be made. Maurie and Rose belonged to Sinai Temple in New York, so I'm sure the services will be held there. Right now, though, not a thing has been definitely set. Please get word to your father as soon as you can.'

'Aunt Ruth, he's in Paris. We just phoned there and the office is getting word to him and then calling us back.'

'Tell him that the funeral can be held up a day or two until he flies back. I'm leaving in an hour with Abe, Miriam and Larry for New York and we'll be with Rose at King's Point. Call us there when you arrive and tell your father to be sure to get in touch with us there so the time and the day can be made final. Good-bye, Jimmy. Thank you for calling. It's really a blessing Maurie is gone. Now at last he's at peace, the poor man. Please keep trying to reach your father.'

Ham read the cablegram a second time. So Maurie was really gone. He felt almost nothing, remembering the last time he had seen his brother and how he had shut him out with his eyes. What a terrible night that had been! Maurie shut *him* out . . . for good . . . forever. He must have known damn well what he was doing and did it in the only way still left to him. It didn't matter anymore. The cable said nothing about a funeral or anything else other than the fact that his brother had died and he should call the New York office at once. Wasn't that just like Maurie. Snap a finger, crack the whip and blow a whistle and little Chaim would do whatever he was told to do. The hell with that. Those days were finished.

He looked over at the sleeping woman in the bed they had been sharing until the phone rang, calling him to the door for that damn cablegram. There was something very wonderful about French women . . . or was she a Rumanian? He wasn't quite certain. The hell with her nationality as long as she knew exactly what he wanted her to do in bed with him. She really did know, and he had never felt so relaxed – until this piece of paper came along calling him to the funeral of a brother who, even dead, was still trying to ruin his good times. Fuck it! Ham looked closely at the date on the cable. It had been sent at least two days before. He had purposely kept this little weekend side trip to himself, and wondered how in hell the Paris office had located him. His watch showed it was past eleven in the morning. There was a phone extension hanging on the bathroom wall beside the toilet and he sat down there after closing the door. The operator connected him with Carl Feldman, who was supposed to run their European film distribution, but instead seemed to be a very talented detective when it came to finding people who wanted to be lost.

'Carl! Didn't you get the message I wasn't to be disturbed until Monday, when I would be at the studio? Never mind . . . you found me and I got the news.'

'Ham, I thought you'd want to know right away about your brother. We got the cable for you night before last and it took me all this time to find you,' came the distressed voice over the phone. 'You should have left a number with me. Emergencies like this can happen, and I nearly went crazy trying to locate you!'

Ham sat in the bathroom and thought for a while before speaking.

'Outside of you, Carl, who else knows where I am?'

'Only the man I sent there with the cable for you. He's a trusted friend who's with the metropolitan police and he checked passport records at all the hotels and pensions around Paris. He had one hell of a time running you down but –'

'All right, all right. Congratulations to the both of you for finding me. Now I want you to completely forget that you did. Cable New York and tell them I'm someplace between Paris and the Belgian border with the director scouting locations for an added sequence we're going to shoot while they finish that damned set at Joinville. You have that? Now, Carl . . . I like you very much and I want you to keep right on running things for us here on the Continent. One of your best qualities is that you know how to keep your mouth shut and not ask personal questions. Also you don't remember things like finding me at this hotel in Fontainebleau. You understand what I'm saying?'

'Of course I do, Ham. I have no idea where in hell you are and I won't know until I hear from you on Monday. For God's sake, you've known me too many years to ever –'

'Now send that cable and tell them not to delay the funeral. Then I want you to hang up and forget we ever spoke. Goodbye, Carl.'

He hung up the phone and reached over to open the bathroom door. He could hear the woman in bed as she yawned, her voice musical even doing that. He had a sudden need for her again, but first, as long as he already was sitting here on the toilet, he might just as well use it.

'So you're gone, Maurie,' he said softly to himself, and suddenly gasped with pain as a deep cramp hit his bowels, almost doubling him over.

'Oh, my God! . . . Oh . . . Oh!' he moaned, and he wrapped both arms around his stomach. A low rumble echoed in the little tiled room and at once he felt relieved and managed to slowly sit upright again, free of pain and the burden that passed heavily from his body. At last he rose slowly to his feet and turned to look down a moment before reaching up to pull the chain.

'Good-bye, Maurie . . . good-bye.'

The woman in the bed made little noises of invitation, and Ham went over to where she waited for him.

CHAPTER FIFTY-THREE

She stood alone in her bedroom and peered through the cloud of cigarette smoke into a full-length mirror. Long reddish-brown hair straggled down to her shoulders and was all that she wore. The piercing brown eyes, set deep above the hollow cheeks, vainly sought signs of improvement and she turned on more light in the hope some might be revealed. Her figure was much too thin and too many bones showed beneath the tightly stretched skin. She coughed deeply as she stubbed out her cigarette, then lit up another and pushed aside the smelly, overcrowded ashtray.

Her breasts hung loose and flaccid and the most skilled life painter would have been hard pressed to duplicate the mottled skin colors of her body. She moved closer to the mirror and parted her lips to inspect her teeth, still sharp and shining. A frown wrinkled her ravaged face.

'Those stinking bastards! Two whole weeks in this health prison and I still look like ... like I did two weeks ago!'

The doorknob squeaked and she turned to yell at the unseen intruder.

'Keep the hell out of my room, damn it! I'm getting dressed. Can't you leave me alone at least five minutes?'

'Mrs. Robbins,' came a silky female voice through the door, 'it's time for our walk in the garden and then our breakfast after we've had our morning juice cocktail.'

Nita angrily pulled on her underthings, then wrapped herself in a shocking-pink housecoat that had a tiny drooping tree embroidered on the upper left pocket and the words 'The Willows' beneath it in flowing script. All those beautiful clothes of hers she had dragged up here and then they made her wear this ugly shmatte, as her father would have called it. A shapeless pink rag tent with buttons and a pocket!

'Just a minute, damn it! Just a minute. Cocktail! What a laugh. It tastes like milk of magnesia! How in the hell can anybody start their day on that stinking drink? You should serve it out of an enema bag!'

She tore open the door, and the slim young lady she had grown to hate stood out in the hall giving her the usual well-rehearsed smile.

'Aren't we cheerful this lovely morning. All right, Mrs. Robbins, let's see exactly what we weigh so we can keep our records right up to the minute.' She herded Nita over to the scales and waited for her to step up on the platform. The numbers were noted and went on the clipboard forms. The healthy young woman smiled her way to the door. 'Later today there's a special lecture for all you ladies by a nutrition and health expert from the University of California. You're all going to hear about calorie intake and creative breathing. After that you're going to –'

'After that I'm going to leave this damn place! What do I need to hear about breathing? I've been doing it for years without any advice from some damn expert! I was told before I came here that you had classes on astrology and gourmet dieting, and so far all you've done is walk me around a stupid garden, bore me with your dull lectures, feed me uncooked vegetables and dress me in this ugly thing. I look absolutely terrible in pink!'

The young lady never lost her smile.

'Let's put on our shoes now and join the other ladies in the garden. Our protein cocktail is waiting for us there, and then the delightful walk in the glorious morning sunshine before we have our breakfast.'

'You sound like a bad trailer for a worse movie,' said Nita. 'Did you actually ever try to drink a glass of that junk? This morning we think we might throw up!' She tried to keep up with the athletic girl walking beside her down the long corridor, taking one long stride to her hurried two.

'Mrs. Robbins, a positive attitude is a very important part of your program at the Willows. You must only think of –'

'Shit!' replied Nita, terminating the conversation.

'I distinctly recall when we spoke on the phone before I left New York, Mr. Robbins, you promised me a poolside bungalow at the Bel Air Hotel. I also specified a Thunderbird convertible to be picked up at the airport on arrival. Now I find that I've been stuck away in a small room at the end of a long dark upstairs hall and the car you delivered to me is a very ordinary Mercury – hardtop with four doors! If this indicates

577

the kind of cooperation your company is going to give my agency, we may very much regret that you received a contract from us to shoot this group of commercials for our client!'

Jimmy stood in the Bel Air Hotel lobby and let him spill it all out. This one really wasn't too bad. Usually they flew into town hinting at a willing starlet to go with the car, but this young assistant account executive, sent out from New York by the agency to ride herd on the Royal aluminum foil commercials, seemed quite uninterested in girls. The hotel room could easily be switched and the car sent back to Transportation for an exchange.

'Any special color on the car?' asked Jimmy.

'French blue.'

Uh-oh-this one was going to be trouble . . . but that all went with producing television commercials. After you landed the contracts, then your real problems began.

'Okay, it'll be taken care of. We'd better get moving. They're all ready to shoot spot number one as soon as we get on the set. This is where the little girl is on the swing hanging from the tall tree. The seat of the swing is made out of a wide strip of your aluminum foil. We pick her up high in the air moving in and out of frame, then freeze the image for voice-overs.'

'Make sure she's wearing underpants and that everything's covered. My office would raise absolute hell if anything shows that shouldn't!'

'Don't worry,' said Jimmy with a patient shrug. You heard everything shooting commercials. 'The kid's only five years old. What's to see?'

'Don't joke about it!' said the serious young man. 'They're very touchy about some things. The network could even refuse to run the spot and my ass would really be in a sling, and I don't mean an aluminum foil one! Just be sure she's covered from all angles. Maybe she ought to wear slacks. I'll check her wardrobe before we shoot, and I'll want to see a complete rehearsal through the camera.'

'Okay, but take a hint from me. The cameraman on this job doesn't like anybody to look through his finder except the director and the operator. Once he accidentally bumped into an agency account executive who stuck his head into the camera and the poor guy lost his top front tooth on the rack-over knob.' Jimmy enjoyed passing along this kind of information and figured that within an hour or two the director and rest of the crew would have the New Yorker cowed and compliant. They were very good at sticking sharp needles into junior executives from Madison Avenue who lived in walk-up cold water flats and rode to work on the IRT and then came to California armed with temporary authority, insisting on poolside at the Bel Air and French blue Thunderbirds.

The director welcomed them to the set. He was a rough, tough man who had cut his teeth on hard-riding Western films. These commercials weren't as exciting, but they meant money in his bank account and food on the table, and the hell with winning Academy Awards.

'Jimmy, we're all set to go. We got the little girl ready. Plenty of pads off camera to catch her if the damn aluminum foil seat splits. Her mother's signed the release and there's standby nurse here on set from First Aid.'

'Sounds fine, Eric. I want you to meet Fred Alberts of the Haynes Bradley Agency. This is their account and he's here for the usual agency supervision. I know he'll be pleased with the way you get their storyboards on film,' said Jimmy, trying to meet any problems before they got started.

'Don't you worry, young man,' said the director, 'I've shot hundreds of these fuckers. You have any comments, bring them right to me. Okay, stick the kid on the swing and let's have a run-through for Mr. Alberts here. Wait a minute! Is that skinny strip of aluminum foil supposed to hold the girl while she's swinging? It'll never work. She'll go down right on her little ass!'

The prop man came running over from his wagon.

'Don't worry . . . don't worry,' he said with his usual professional pride. 'I thought of that and put a piece of real tough nylon netting in between the two pieces of foil. It's hidden so you'll never pick it up with the camera, and I guarantee that swing seat could hold an elephant. The little girl can swing on it until she's ready to play character parts!'

The agency man was horrified.

'We're trying to show how strong our aluminum foil is and you're planning to fake the whole thing!' he wailed.

Jimmy took him aside with the director.

'Look, all we're getting across is an idea, a kind of symbolic presentation of product strength. It's right off the storyboard your agency laid out. Now if you want the girl to swing on a plain sheet of unreinforced foil, we'll shoot it that way and there won't be any cheating. Of course, she'll bust right

579

through and we'll never get the take in the can. That means we'll go over schedule, the budget will be blown sky-high and your office will ask who screwed things up. Naturally I'll have to send them a copy of our report, which will show that you made us do it differently from the way we had it planned. Nobody will ever see the nylon netting between the pieces of foil and we'll have the shot in one or two takes. What do you want?'

The assistant account executive thought for a moment. This was his very first trip to California for the agency and after New York he thought he could really get to like it out here.

'Shoot it your way, but don't tell me how you get the effect. I just want to be amazed and happy.'

Jimmy relaxed. The guy was going to work out all right after all. He let them start the spot run-through, and when the little girl was swinging wildly back and forth, her behind intact and firmly in place on the foil seat, he went to an outside phone and called Transportation.

'Chuck, remember that Mercury loaner we sent back early today from the ad agency guy? Do everything you can to find him a Thunderbird. He'd like it to be colored French blue. Thanks, I knew I could count on you.' He hung up, whistled at a passing pigeon, then went back to the stage.

Ham Robbins sat all by himself at a far corner table of the '21' Club bar. It was one of the few places where he could feel comfortable, but right now he was a very upset man. Only an hour earlier he had driven back from a visit with Rose in the house at King's Point on Long Island. She received him in a cold, polite and distant manner. There were no accusations, but he could sense her unspoken words. All his excuses for not being at his brother's funeral weeks before, the whole sorry mess about the way he became president and board chairman after his betrayal of Maurie when they had had an agreement to sell their stock and retire – he knew what she was thinking, and all through the unpleasant half-hour he spent with her he waited for the unsaid to be said. Her silence was worse than any accusation or denunciation could have been. Ham sat facing Rose in the big living room and tried to make harmless conversation, but kept coming back to the same subject.

'Rose, it was terrible to find that cable after I returned to Paris and then learn the funeral had taken place the day

580

before. Of course you couldn't hold it off any longer. It was the only time during my entire trip I was where I couldn't be reached. I should have let the Paris office know where they could find me, but we ran into a terrible emergency. We had to find some locations in a big hurry to pick up shooting on a picture that was stalled and I was way out in the countryside with the director and production people. We just never expected that –'

Rose looked into his eyes and he knew that she saw all his lies.

'Ham, why keep going over it? That's all I've heard from you ever since you arrived. It was unfortunate, it couldn't be helped, so let's not talk about it anymore. Poor Maurie is at peace now and there's nothing else we can say. Now tell me, how is your younger son, Donny? I'm sure you must have seen him while you were in Europe. Is he still working in the London theater? He must have such an exciting life.'

Ham was grateful Rose had changed the subject, but he wished she had asked him about somebody else. He had seen Donny all right on his trip and it was a most unhappy and uncomfortable meeting for both of them. He had to give some kind of answer to Rose, even a lying one.

'Oh, Donny . . . yes . . . er . . . he's still in stage design or something like that. I tried to talk him into working in our London office, but for some reason all he wants is to be in the creative end. You know how headstrong and stubborn young people can be. I don't think he wants anything at all to do with the motion picture business.' It was an answer, but only part of an answer and the rest he would keep sealed in his troubled mind.

'Just so he's happy and healthy,' said Rose. 'That's about all we can wish for our children. What do you think of your lovely little grandchild, Esther? It was so nice of Jimmy and Joanna to name her for Momma, wasn't it?'

If only Rose would get the hell on subjects other than his children and grandchild. He did not want to admit to her he had seen Esther only that one time he went to Jimmy and Joanna's home. For reasons he had hidden so deeply he almost forgot they existed, he felt the old guilts rising like bile, and again he wished Rose would talk about something else. She sat waiting for his answer, so he had to say something.

'Uh . . . she's fine . . . a lovely little girl . . .' Quickly he rushed on to a more comfortable topic, the best one of all:

getting the hell away from here as quickly as he could. 'Rose, I hate to leave, but I have to meet some people in New York tonight. I'm flying back to the Coast tomorrow morning and this is the last chance I'll have to talk to them. I did want to see you, though, and tell you personally how terrible I feel about Maurie and missing the service. If only they could have located me a day or two earlier, but it's too late for that now.'

'Yes, Ham, it's too late for many things. Thank you again for coming here to see me,' said Rose. 'You know, your brother may have been hard on you these last years and you were quite sensitive about him, but deep down he had feelings of real love for you, just as he did for Lou and your sisters. I wish you could have heard how distressed he was at the way things were going. It's a shame you never let yourself get to really know him . . . but like so much else, it's too late for all that now.'

He got up, eager to be on his way. This kind of talk disturbed him and he could not wait to get into his car and begin the drive back to New York. He gave his sister-in-law a little kiss on the cheek, held her hand for a moment, then left the house.

Two hours later he was still quite depressed, although now his stomach was filled with one of Jack and Charlie's steaks and a tumbler of their good Ballantine Scotch. People kept coming over to talk with him and he got rid of them as quickly as he decently could. The last thing he felt like tonight was to be surrounded by these damn leeches, all of whom he knew wanted something out of him. It was well past midnight now, and the bar was half full of people who had come in after the Broadway theaters let out. They stood around the bar and filled some of the tables and chattered about the music and the acting, all the mindless talk of people determined to stretch out a good evening before confronting their dull tomorrows.

'Captain, let me have my check, please,' said Ham as he pulled out his gold money clip, which held a wad of large-denomination bills. Lennie often told him he was crazy to carry so much cash around with him, but it was a habit he had no desire to break. There had been too many years when he had almost nothing to carry around, not even a money clip. He liked the security the wad gave him nestling against his chest down inside his breast pocket. Wallets were a pain, spilling out junk half the time and making unsightly lumps in his beautifully tailored suits. Most places he just signed the bill, but tonight he needed change for the papers he planned to pick up on his way back to the Waldorf Towers. He paid his bill, tipped the captain and waiter, then went to the front room. Mack helped him into his topcoat and pulled open the front door to let him out into the street.

'Do you have your car, Mr. Robbins, or should I signal for a cab?' he asked.

'No thanks, Mack. I left my car at the garage and I feel like taking a little walk. I'm only going a few blocks crosstown and the exercise may help me sleep. Tomorrow I'm flying back to California, and I always have trouble with the time change. See you on my next trip. Please say good-bye to Jack and tell him I'm sorry I missed him. Good night.'

Ham stood in the cool night air on Fifty-second Street, looked up at the narrow strip of black sky between the tall buildings and took a deep breath. It was pleasant with so many cars off the street at this late hour, and the city smelled almost good. This was the best time for a walk, a few relaxed minutes to clear some of the crap of his mind after that visit with Rose. There was something about the way she kept looking at him the whole time with those sad eyes of hers. He tried to blot out the sudden memory of his brother and the way his eyes had closed that night to shut him out forever. He walked over to the corner of Fifth Avenue just as the light changed to green, crossed and continued on toward Madison.

The two men were jammed into the little space between building walls, crowded with stacks of filled garbage cans that would be collected the next morning. They lit up cigarettes and wondered if they should take the subway home now instead of waiting here for a prospect to show up. So far it had been an almost completely wasted evening. Just as they had spotted an old man shuffling along with a black satchel, which could have been stuffed with diamonds or dirty laundry, along came a police cruiser and they had to pull back behind the piled-up garbage cans. Bad luck for them but a break for the old man, who went on unaware that he had nearly become a statistic. If nothing happened in the next fifteen minutes they would leave and roll some drunks in the subway on their way home.

'Put down your cigarette. There's a guy all by himself walking up the street toward us. Looks well dressed from what I can see. Let's give him a quick going-over, then call it a night.'

Ham walked very slowly, his mind on Donny. He was

worried about what had happened to him over the last few years. All right, so he did fine for a while in that English school Nita insisted he go to . . . but somehow he found the wrong friends . . . wispy fellows who never went near the playing fields and were more at home designing scenery and costumes for theaters and pageants. Designers . . . for God's sake! He had too damn many designers flitting around the studio without having one for a son! A panicked call from the London office told him the school was about to toss Donny out on his ear for smoking something that wasn't tobacco and the irate father flew right over to set things straight. Suddenly, Donny just walked away from the school and moved into a Soho flat with a couple of other misfits, all of them studying stage and costume design. Ham was angry all over again, just remembering it, although several years had passed since Nita's son had taken off on his own. Ham tried at times not to think of Donny as being his son too, and even when he cut off all money, it seemed to make absolutely no difference. Ham's connections with the government were of no help. His son had done nothing to get him deported, and a kindly official, who looked and sounded like C. Aubrey Smith, suggested to Ham that he leave the young man alone and let him find himself.

'Find himself,' Ham said aloud, as he walked up the street. He found himself, all right . . . shut up in a very expensive sanatorium outside London where Ham secretly had placed him for the treatment of a drug habit and assorted psychological ills that drove him to the brink of suicide. He visited his son on this last trip and found him locked away and completely uncommunicative. What was it Rose said to him earlier today about Donny?' 'Just so long as he's happy and healthy . . . that's all we can wish for our children.' He stopped walking long enough to spit some of his bitterness into the gutter. Then Rose had to go and ask what he thought of his granddaughter Esther, named for his mother who mercifully had not lived to see all these terrible things. A wave of guilt washed over him as he remembered the times Jimmy had asked him to visit Esther and how he avoided all contact except for that once. Just who had been cut off from whom?

Ham continued up the street, walking from one pool of soft light coming from the overhead lamps on to the next one, toward his hotel straight across Park Avenue. What a fucking farce it was. What was it that kept him from seeing his only grandchild and having some kind of a relationship with

Jimmy, who had wanted him as much as Donny rejected him? How had he become an actor in this stinking script? Was it still the image of dear Nita always at his side, whispering in a voice only he could hear ... dates ... places ... times? Was it the chorus of Maurie and Irene accusing him of the wanton destruction of his first marriage? Or was it the voice of his own conscience, that miserable censor he despised and defied? He shook his head and walked on toward the lights of Park Avenue.

'Mister. Stop where you are. Nothing'll happen to you if you keep your mouth shut and do what we tell you!'

The strange rough voice confused him. He had been miles and years away and was startled when two shapeless figures shoved up against him and he was dragged into the space between two buildings. It was dark and terribly crowded, with a pyramid of filled garbage cans towering over their heads. A moment of struggle and then one of the shapes wrapped an arm around his neck and pulled him almost off his feet. Ham tried to shout for help but his voice was choked off by the pressure on his throat. He struggled again, and his topcoat was yanked up over his head. He could feel strange hands tearing off his wristwatch and thrusting into his pockets, pulling things out, taking them away – the money clip, his glasses, even his cigars and his neatly folded handkerchief. He was trapped like an animal inside his own coat, which was tightly held over his head and arms. He kept trying to cry out, but the strangled noises he made were muffled by the heavy cloth wrapped around his face. Suddenly he was struck so hard on the side of his head that everything flared red and black and there were great bursts of light he could see even through his closed eyes. Another blow to the back of his knees and he fell heavily to the ground, groaning in agony from the terrible pain. He reached up and tried to pull the coat away from his head to see who was doing these terrible things to him. Before he could free himself from the entangling coat, a heavy shoe caught him just behind his left ear, and the shock rolled him over against the stacked garbage cans, where his body made a loud clanging noise. He had never known such pain. Another kick to his head and he almost lost consciousness. Suddenly both men kneeled down to hold him still. A police car came slowly down the street, the officers inside chatting with each other, eyes fixed straight ahead, and not aware of anything unusual happening between the two buildings where a man was about to be left alone in the dark, bleeding from his mouth and ears, his last fragment of memory a final smashing blow to the side of his head. As Ham Robbins sank down and down into a bottomless pit of blackness, one of the cans spilled over on its side to empty garbage all over his unconscious body.

It was nearly dawn when two Department of Sanitation workers came by to empty the cans stacked between the walls of the two buildings. At first they thought the figure that lay sprawled with only his legs showing was a passed-out drunk; then, after a closer look, one of them ran to Madison Avenue, where he found a foot patrolman.

'Jesus! Look at what some bastard did to this poor son of a bitch! Doesn't that make you want to puke!' said the intern to his driver as they gently put the unconscious man on a stretcher and carried him to their ambulance.

'Find any identification?' asked the policeman, making notes on his pad and holding back the few curious spectators who had come running when they heard the ambulance roll to a stop behind the Sanitation truck.

'Not a damn thing,' said the doctor. 'He's cleaned out. Well dressed, looks like a prosperous type and a setup for this kind of thing. We better hurry. There's almost no pulse and he might not make it.' The doors were pulled shut and the siren screamed again as they swerved into the crosstown traffic. The policeman got the people moving again, then walked to the nearest blue-box phone to call in his report.

'Unidentified white male. Sixty to sixty-five. Got the shit kicked out of him. Well dressed and pockets stripped clean. Nothing left showing name or address. Location between Madison and Park on Fifty-second. Yeah, he's in the meat wagon right now on the way to Roosevelt Emergency. Nope, not a witness and no idea when it happened ... maybe between midnight and six-thirty. Okay.'

The men from Sanitation loaded the rest of the garbage into their collection truck. One can had spilled all over the alley, and they grumbled about the mess but cleared it away with their shovels and drove on to their next pickup.

CHAPTER FIFTY-FOUR

Flight Three, American Airlines, departed from New York nonstop for Los Angeles on schedule, with only one passenger failing to claim his reserved First Class space. Since this particular no-show was a rather prominent individual who always called if he switched flights or canceled, he rated special concern. Just before takeoff, the airline phoned his office, but they knew nothing. The secretary was surprised he was not at the airport and placed a call to his apartment. There was no answer, and she called the manager's desk. Perhaps he had slept late or had forgotten about his flight. An assistant manager was sent up to the apartment, and he opened the door with his passkey, looked through all the rooms and then phoned downstairs.

'All of Mr. Robbins' things are still here in his suite. His luggage is in a closet and it's not packed. Maybe he stayed out with friends. The bed hasn't been slept in and the maid hasn't worked this floor yet today.' The Towers manager was noted for his tact and passed the message along to Ham's office. So he spent the night with a friend and missed his plane. That was his privilege.

'I'll tell him to call you as soon as he comes back,' he said to the secretary and hung up.

The girl then phoned Rose Robbins at King's Point. Yes, Ham had been with her for nearly an hour the day before, during the evening. He said he had had an important meeting with some people in New York and it was his last chance to see them before flying back to California the next day. No, he did not tell her whom he was seeing or where he would be. Now the secretray called Fred Simms, who was in the New York office all that week. He usually knew where the boss could be located.

'I have no idea. He told me he would only be in town until noon and wasn't seeing me until we met on the Coast next week. Are you sure he was booked for that flight?'

587

'Yes. He didn't go to his Towers apartment at all last night. Nobody seems to know where he is and the plane took off without him. What should I do?'

Fred told her to sit tight and he would come right up. She got out Ham's phone book for New York, and together they began to call every place he might possibly be. Finally Fred reached '21' and learned that Ham had eaten a late dinner there all alone the night before. Mack came to the phone and repeated everything that happened when he offered to call a taxi and Ham insisted on walking across town to the Towers.

'What time was it then, Mack?' Simms asked him.

'We were beginning to empty the place. Ham was among the last guests having dinner in the bar, the usual steak and Scotch and I forget what dessert –'

'Skip the menu. What time did he leave?'

'I'm sure it was close to twelve-thirty, going on twelve forty-five. He sat here all alone for over two hours, looked kind of strange the whole time. He kept shooing people away from his table. I never saw Ham like that before. Usually he likes company, but last night he just wanted to be left alone. Yeah, twelve-thirty it was. We started closing up about an hour later. Is something the matter?'

'Mack, keep quiet about this. Ham was supposed to fly back to L.A. earlier today. He never showed up at the airport. We sent a car to the Towers in plenty of time to get him to the airline, but the driver called in that he wasn't at his place. We figured he went there on his own by cab or a friend drove him. Now we know he never was in his apartment at all and his stuff is still there. I phoned all over town before I got you. Mack, I'm getting real worried.'

'Let me get in touch with a friend of mine over at the precinct. Ham could have had an accident or something while he was walking alone across town. He seemed to be okay when he left here, but we better check. I'm going to call somebody who will know what to do. Wait right there, and as soon as I have some information I'll be back to you.'

He phoned the precinct and the lieutenant put him on hold for a few minutes.

'Mack, we may have your man. They picked up an unidentified beating victim very early this morning not too far from your place between Madison and Park. He had the shit kicked out of him. I checked Roosevelt Hospital and he's still in Emergency. It could be your missing party. No ID on him, and he's not doing very well.'

'My God, it might be Ham Robbins! They're looking all over for him. Thanks, Lieutenant. I'll get word to his office and tell them to hurry over to Roosevelt Emergency. I appreciate your help – and I sure hope it's somebody else and not Ham!'

Fred Simms and one of his assistants immediately phoned the hospital but could not get much information. The harried voice in Emergency told them to hold and put on a police investigator who was going over the clothing found on the unidentified victim.

'They're still operating on him. Skull fracture and pressure on the brain. Looks pretty bad. No, we didn't find a thing to identify him except there's a label in his coat. "J. Press. New Haven and New York." Would that be something your man would be wearing?'

'Could be,' Fred Simms said excitedly. 'He bought things there. I know, I went with him a couple of times. We're coming right over. Who do we ask for?'

'Sergeant Levine. I'll be watching for you at Reception. It's on Fifty-eighth and Ninth Avenue. Hurry up.'

Ten minutes later Fred Simms arrived at Roosevelt with Al Weston of his office, and the sergeant took them around to Emergency. The patient was still on the table and they were shown the blood-spattered topcoat, suit and shirt. Fred winced as he recognized his boss's clothing.

'When can I see him?' he asked, now sure that he would be able to make a positive identification. He was taken for a moment into the operating room and looked at the man on the table, who was surrounded by doctors, nurses and technicians. He had only a glimpse of the pale face under all the towels and sheeting, but he knew. It was Ham Robbins, and he looked as though he would be dead at any moment.

'Get me to a phone, Sergeant. I have to call California right away!' He was taken to a little office the sergeant used for his work, and on the way they passed a reporter Fred knew from the *Daily News*. Now it would be all over town, and he would have to phone the studio immediately, before they heard.

Bob Silver answered the phone in Ham's outer office at the studio.

'Fred, hello . . . you sound excited. What's up? Oh, no! Where? At Roosevelt Hospital? How does it look? Oh, Lord! I hope not. Phone his New York doctor and have him get right over. His name is Lawrence Wilson and the secretary in Mr. Robbins' office there knows where to reach him. I'll call Mrs.

589

Robbins right now. She's someplace near Santa Barbara. I'll stay by the phone. Nothing in the papers yet, is there? You think you saw somebody from the *Daily News?* Damn it. Now they'll blow it all over the place. I'll call the family right now so they won't hear it from somebody else and get a shock. Thanks, Fred. I hope it comes out all right for him. Call me just as soon as there's anything. 'Bye.'

Bob hung up the phone and shook his head, trying to think of how to reach Nita. He had an idea. Ham's personal attorney did work for her too. He would know how to reach Nita, since he kept in close touch with her. He called Norman Harris and told him what had happened. Harris was shocked and thought a minute before saying anything.

'Bob, let me call Mrs. Robbins. She's at a place called the Willows in Ojai. She'll want to fly right back to Los Angeles and then to New York. I may go with her, since she'll be in no condition to travel alone. If something should happen with Ham . . . well, I should be around since I've been doing work for both of them and can help out. I'll phone you back after I reach her. Meantime, get us plane tickets on several flights out later today.'

Bob knew what Norman Harris was up to. He was going to be right on hand if Ham should die and protect the widow . . . and, incidentally, himself. He had been working with Ham for months on his new will, which had been rewritten several times. Bob was sure the bright young man would move right in on Nita and take things over. He had heard plenty about Harris, Esquire. Well, the hell with it. It really was none of his business, but he could not help feeling concerned.

'Mrs. Robbins, will you please come with me,' said the tall slim slave mistress. Nita painfully arose from her seat on the padded floor of the yoga class, where fifteen women were locked in the lotus position. She moaned as her aching knees straightened out, and then she hobbled after the girl into the outside hall. 'There's a Mr. Norman Harris on the phone for you in the reception office. He said it's very important. Please come with me.'

'Nita, I have bad news,' was how he began, and then he went on to tell her the few details Bob Silver had given him. Nita almost dropped the phone and raised a hand up to her mouth to hold back a moan.

'What a terrible thing! What is going to happen now? Is he still alive? I must get to him. Please help me, Norman.'

'Nita, I'm arranging for a chartered plane to fly me to Santa Barbara in about one hour. I'll meet you at the airport and we'll go right back to Los Angeles and catch a New York plane. We can go right to the hospital. Now try to take it easy. They have the finest doctors working on him, and if there's any chance at all, he's sure to pull through. In one hour, at the Santa Barbara airport, Nita.'

'Is it in the newspapers yet? Has anybody told his son?'

'No, Nita. It hasn't broken anyplace yet . . . but it will any minute. I don't think his son knows yet. Bob may have called him, I have no idea.'

'I don't want his son to be anywhere near him. There's something about him being near his father that creates terrible vibrations, and we have to do all we can to help Ham. Keep him away, Norman – keep Jimmy away!'

'I'll try, Nita, but I don't know if that will be possible,' the lawyer said to her.

'Make it possible!' She showed surprising firmness in her voice, and quickly plans began to be made and to fall in place. Dress, pack, kiss this dump good-bye and have them drive her to the Santa Barbara airport. It was only eight-thirty in the morning. She could be in New York before late afternoon, and with Ham right after that.

Jimmy had worked quite late on the new group of Chevrolet commercials, which were right up against an air-time deadline. It was well past three in the morning when he told the film editor to go home and they pulled the plug on the Moviola. Joanna let him sleep the next day until nearly eleven, and he was still bleary-eyed when he went to the bathroom and started to shave. There was a little radio on the shelf and he switched on the news. The warm lather felt good, and he drew the razor down the side of his face. The radio voice completed a commercial and then the alert buzzer was sounded for something of special interest. The announcer came back on, cheerfully dispensing his doleful tidings.

'A report just in from New York City. The famous motion picture mogul Ham Robbins, head of Robbins International Pictures, was assaulted on a midtown Manhattan street sometime during the night. He was found early today lying between two buildings, unconscious and bleeding. It is believed his skull was fractured by repeated blows and he was rushed to the –'

591

Jimmy dropped his razor in the sink and looked at the radio as though he might see the man talking to him. The voice went on.

'Robbins was unidentified for several hours and is now undergoing surgery at Roosevelt Hospital. Further news will follow jusι as soon as –'

He wiped away the lather and rushed out to find Joanna to tell her what he had heard. His father's office phone extension was busy and the operator put him on hold. He looked up the private direct number and dialed. It rang and rang, and he was about to hang up when Bob Silver came on, already hoarse from talking to so many people.

'Bob, I just heard on the radio about my father. Is there anything else you've heard? Is he alive?'

'Jimmy, we just got word a few minutes ago when the *Times* called us. Nobody knows much more than the fact he was beaten and left on the street. He's alive, but just barely, and they've been operating for several hours. I don't know anything more to tell you. We're all terribly upset. I'm trying to reach Fred Simms in New York right now. Call me back in half an hour and I should have more information.' He hung up before Jimmy could say anything more.

'Joanna, I'm going right out to the studio. Of all days for me to sleep late! I would have been at the studio hours ago any other day. I'll phone you from there as soon as I find out more. We may have to fly to New York later today. I don't know yet, but stay near a phone and wait for my call.'

No more news came through for hours. Ham was hanging on to life. The surgery was over and now the doctors were waiting to see if he would survive. Nita and Norman Harris flew to New York and drove to Roosevelt Hospital, where Fred Simms was waiting. He took her to the surgeon and to Ham's doctor. They explained the seriousness of the injuries to Ham's skull and how they thought the pressure on his brain now had been relieved. It was a matter of waiting and hoping . . . and praying. They had done all they could for now. Nita looked around the sprawling hospital, at all the people coming and going, and asked to be taken away from the newspaper reporters and photographers who pressed in, asked questions, tried to shoot pictures. Fred had some of his men form a cordon to help her into a side room.

'Shouldn't we have some specialists called in?' Nita asked Dr. Wilson.

'Mrs. Robbins, Roosevelt Emergency is one of the best

places in the world for Ham to be right now. They get many cases like this and their trauma team knows exactly what to do. If it had happened to me, this is where I'd want to be taken. As soon as he shows improvement and can be moved, we'll put him in a private room and continue round-the-clock observation and treatment. Right now, though, it's a matter of seeing if he survives. I'm afraid that hasn't been decided and you'll have to brace yourself for a wait. It could be hours or even days before we know if he will live.'

'Can I see him soon?' asked Nita.

'I don't think so. You will just as soon as possible. For a while after he comes off the table he must be under constant care, and there are people with him watching all his vital signs. It would be upsetting for you to see him right now. Please sit down and try to save your strength. It's going to be a long haul.'

Norman Harris leaned over and spoke in a low whisper so she alone could hear.

'Jimmy is on the phone from Los Angeles. Do you want to speak to him?'

'No, I do not!' she said in a loud voice that made the lawyer jump back. 'Keep him away from here. I don't want him anywhere near his father! It might cause his death! Who else has phoned?'

He looked at his notes.

'Well, Bob Silver, of course, some reporters and the trade papers and Harold Kosterman. A call from somebody at the White House. I talked to all of them and told them what I could. There's a whole list of others, but I won't bother you with any of them now. Bob Silver did ask if you would call him as soon as you could.'

'Get him for me right now.'

Bob was sitting in his office, waiting for the phone to ring. Jimmy came in from his office and sat on the wide couch across from Bob's desk. Leo Arnheim was beside him and Pops Johnson and Harry Saunders kept looking in to ask for news.

When the phone rang, Bob picked it up and spoke in such a low voice that Jimmy could not hear what he said. He looked up now and then and a frown appeared on his face. He seemed to be struggling to answer something being asked by the distant voice. Whenever Jimmy caught his eye, he quickly looked away. Now he could hear some of the words coming from Bob.

593

'I see . . . yes, I understand. Then you want me to tell him . . . All right. Yes, of course, Mrs. Robbins . . .'

Jimmy was alerted. It was Nita and she must be calling from the hospital. He wanted to ask her about his father. He got to his feet and crossed over to Bob's desk. He tried to catch his attention, but Bob looked down at his desk blotter and kept on talking in almost a whisper.

'Bob, is that Nita? Let me talk to her, please.'

The conversation continued as though he were not in the room. Bob did look up once, and his eyes were full of concern and there were sudden beads of sweat on his forehead.

'Yes . . . of course. Please do, we'll be right here waiting.' He hung up.

'Bob! I wanted to talk to her! You had no right to hang up like that. I asked you several times to let me talk to her!' said Jimmy, quite angry.

Bob was very upset and apologetic. 'Jimmy, she said she could not talk to you, that there was nothing she could tell you. Your father is alive, that's about all she knows right now. I'm sure that she heard you asking to talk to her and suddenly she just hung up. Jimmy, you know I wouldn't have this happen for all the world, but you see . . .'

'I see that I'm not finding out very much by being here,' Jimmy said. 'I'm flying to New York with my wife this afternoon. I should be there with my father.'

Now Bob seemed to be in a small panic. He jumped to his feet.

'Jimmy, don't go! Please don't! It won't help things one bit. Stay here and we'll get all the news to you as fast as we hear anything!'

'What the hell's going on?' said Jimmy. 'My father may be dead or dying and I'm not supposed to see him? I'm to sit here next to a phone waiting to hear from somebody who won't even talk to me? No thanks. We're leaving today!' He turned and went out of the office.

Bob slapped a hand to his forehead and looked over at Leo Arnheim, who still sat on the couch, wondering what this was all about.

'You know, Leo, sometimes I could take this damn job and shove it! That woman is absolutely impossible. You can't imagine what she told me on the phone just now. I was ashamed even to tell Jimmy. She's convinced that if he's in the same town as his father it could kill him – that their "signs are in conflict," whatever in hell that may mean! Can

594

you imagine that! The woman believes in that crap! No wonder the Boss has been seeing somebody else lately. The poor bastard . . . and now this happens to him!'

It was almost midnight when the taxi brought Jimmy and Joanna to Roosevelt Hospital after they left their bags off at the hotel. A guard at the Emergency entrance directed them around the corner to the main reception office. Nobody would tell them anything about Mr. Robbins. Jimmy explained he was the patient's son, but the tired lady behind the counter only shrugged her shoulders.

'Come back in the morning. We have instructions nobody sees him. Nobody gets any information. I'm sorry.'

He went to a phone and reached Fred Simms at his hotel in the West Sixties.

'Your father is doing all right, at least he's no worse. No, I can't even see him myself. I wish I could give you better news. In the morning when the doctor is there we'll learn more and tell you. Where are you staying?'

Jimmy gave him their phone number and room at the Gotham, then thought of something else to ask.

'Where is Mrs. Robbins? I know she's here and I'd like to speak with her.'

'Try their apartment at the Waldorf Towers. You could also try to reach your father's lawyer. His name is Norman Harris and he's at the Waldorf too. They were both at the hospital this afternoon and late tonight, so you must have missed them there. Sorry I can't tell you more, only that there's no change. I'll look for you tomorrow.'

After they returned to their hotel, Jimmy tried to reach Nita at the Towers apartment. The operator told him Mrs. Robbins had left a message she was not to be disturbed. He asked for Norman Harris and got the same reply, then hung up the phone and turned to Joanna.

'Either they really are asleep or all the wires from me to them have been cut. I don't know what more we can do tonight, so let's try to get some sleep and start in again tomorrow.'

The next morning Nita sat in a large side room at the hospital waiting for the doctor to come from the patient with news. She had managed to see Ham for a moment through the door, but found out nothing other than the fact he was still alive and unconscious. Now she sat waiting, thinking of new questions to ask the doctor, when she looked up to see Jimmy and his wife enter the room. She managed a stiff smile at Jimmy's introduction of Joanna.

'How do you do. I'm sorry we're meeting for the first time under these conditions.' What she did not say was that she was sorry she was meeting another Mrs. Robbins under any conditions. Her voice was almost as cold as her hand.

The attorney then introduced himself to Jimmy and Joanna, and for a while they all waited for something to happen.

Nita cleared her throat with a much louder than necessary noise. She sat in a corner chair, looking at all of them with her dark-rimmed eyes, and it was hard to know what she thought or felt. She did not move until the doctor came through the door, still in surgical gown and cap, pulled up a chair and began to speak.

'Mr. Robbins just now regained consciousness. He is quite disoriented, doesn't recall a thing that happened. From what we can tell, he is not in much pain, and we have him sedated. There appears to be no paralysis, but it still is too early to know what lasting effects, if any, will be present. We are moving him out of Intensive Care within a few days if he remains conscious and the slight improvement continues without complications. I think I can assure you that he will live. I couldn't say that until now. From here on it is a matter of watching and waiting. We do not know if there was any brain damage, but we will run tests to determine that as soon as possible. Meantime, I suggest you all get some rest and that we meet here tomorrow morning at the same time, after I have examined him again and have more to tell you.'

Twenty-four hours later Ham continued to be conscious and was growing more alert, taking an interest in his surroudings. The doctor allowed Nita to sit with him for a few minutes remaining in the room with her. Later she took him to one side and spoke in an intense low voice. The doctor listened, nodded his head and then returned with her to the visitors' room.

Jimmy rushed up and asked if he could see his father, and the doctor explained that the patient must rest now and could have no visitors. Nita sat by herself in a corner of the room, silently writing on a pad and looking into several books she fished out of her large bag. Now and then she called Fred Simms over, gave instructions in a low voice and sent him out to the hospital personnel offices to ask for birth dates and other important information concerning doctors and nurses assigned to her husband's case.

596

She was unapproachable, lost in the stars, and after some futile attempts to engage her in conversation, Jimmy and Joanna gave up and sat across the room from her. After several hours of this, they said good-bye and returned to their hotel. As soon as they had gone, Nita rose to her feet and went out to the nurses' station, from which she was taken to Ham's room for a long visit.

The week passed and Jimmy still had not seen his father, although he asked to do so repeatedly and was told it was best the patient see nobody other than his wife, and then for a few minutes at a time.

'Joanna,' he said late one night after yet another day had passed without seeing his father, 'I'm getting damned angry at the runaround I'm getting. After all, I am his son and I should be allowed to see him, if only for a few minutes. I know Nita is with him every day, and Mr. Harris let something slip yesterday about also seeing him. I'm being shut out, and it's wrong! We should go to the hospital very early tomorrow morning before they arrive and tell the doctor that I want to see my father now.'

They were in the visitors' room the next day before the others came in and Jimmy went to the desk, where he recognized one of the doctors. He was not the same one who had taken Nita in on her first visit.

'I'd like to see my father. We heard he was doing quite well and improving. My wife is with me and we –'

'Sure, no reason why not,' said the young doctor. 'Your mother and someone else have been in with him several times each day and he seems to enjoy seeing them. Come on, bring your wife – she may be able to go in after you. Don't stay more than a few minutes, though.'

When Jimmy opened the door and saw the pale and sunken face beneath the heavy bandages, he thought he had gone into the wrong room. Suddenly the eyes opened and his father looked at him. The hands lying on top of the sheet opened and closed and one of them feebly reached out toward him. Jimmy crossed the room and gently picked up his father's hand. He could feel it tighten slightly and hold him as something that resembled a smile appeared on Ham's face. They stood like that for a full minute until the nurse across the room broke the silence.

'He's doing so well now. I'm sure he's glad to see you. He speaks a little sometimes, and he's going to be fine.'

'Jimmy . . .' a cracked hoarse whisper came from the man

597

on the bed. It was a terrible strain for him even to say that, and his hand gripped even tighter. The doctor appeared.

'You had better leave now, Mr. Robbins. Just two minutes was all. Your wife can look in for a moment, if she'd like.' Jimmy started pulling away, but his father hung on to his hand.

'Stay . . . stay . . . Jimmy . . .' came from the cracked lips. Jimmy looked around at the doctor, who shook his head.

'That's wonderful, he does recognize you, but you really should leave now. He has to rest. Just your wife for a quick hello and then he can have no more visitors for a while. He mustn't overdo it.'

Jimmy gave his father's hand a gentle squeeze, leaned over and spoke softly. 'Dad, get well fast. We'll be back soon.' He left and Joanna came into the room, staying only a moment; after giving Ham a few encouraging words and patting his hand, she left the room and joined Jimmy in the hall.

They both walked toward the visitors' room, and as they approached the doors leading away from the Intensive Care area, they flew open and Nita appeared, followed closely by a nurse. She was walking rapidly and there was a dark look of anger on her face as she strode directly toward Jimmy and Joanna. Nita's hands were clenched into tight fists, and she seemed almost to run past them in the hall. They stood a moment as she passed.

'Nita, good morning. The doctor just said that —'

She was gone, the nurse trailing behind, through the doors and out of sight, leaving her anger like a black cloud hanging behind her. Jimmy and Joanna stood looking after them and then walked on to the visitors' room, where they sat alone for several hours.

None of the hospital staff came near them and all inquiries were met with silence. Finally they returned to their hotel, and just before they went to dinner their phone rang. It was Dr. Wilson and he sounded very ill at ease.

'Mr. Robbins, I understand you visited your father earlier today at the hospital.'

'That's right,' replied Jimmy, 'and he was quite happy to see me. He seems to be doing just fine. My wife looked in on him and he knew who she was. I feel quite relieved about him now after our visit.'

'Please listen closely to me,' said the doctor. 'Your father's temperature went up dangerously high right after you left and it would really be best if you did not see him for a while.

He must have absolute rest with nothing disturbing him. I hope you understand that –'

'Doctor, my little visit and that of my wife did not disturb my father. He really seemed quite happy to see us. He held my hand and said "Jimmy, stay" a couple of times to me. He even tried to smile a little. I certainly didn't disturb him, I can tell you that! The nurse was right there in the room and the doctor was in the hall with my wife and later with me when she went inside for a few moments. If his temperature went up after that, I am positive it had nothing to do with our visit. I came here all the way from Los Angeles to see my father and I intend to see him.'

'Mr. Robbins, please stay away from him. It is important for him to have complete rest at this time and see very few if any visitors. We're terribly afraid he might get pneumonia, and then there could be fatal complications. We don't want him exposed to any more people than necessary. For a while he cannot have any visitors.'

'I'll be at the hospital tomorrow morning,' replied Jimmy. 'I don't see why I should be kept from seeing my father if he is being visited by other members of the family or by an attorney.'

The doctor said good-bye in a heavy voice and hung up.

The next morning they were the first ones in the visitors' room. Nita and Norman Harris might have been in the hospital, but they did not come near Jimmy and Joanna. The whole day passed and they received no further word about either the patient or any possibility of seeing him. Finally, later that afternoon, they returned to their hotel. Jimmy had phoned his office earlier to check with his assistant at the studio on the progress of commercials in production. Everything was going well. A new group of important spots was set to shoot in two days and they all hoped he would be returning very soon. Clients were waiting to meet with him and there was great activity in the department. Everybody was happy to hear the good news about the way his father was improving.

When he phoned the doctor he was told that visitors were still not being permitted and that his father was doing well and would soon be moved to another room. Rather than come to the hospital and sit around all day, the doctor suggested, he should continue to phone for information.

'Doctor, I would like to see my father once again before we return to California. We may fly back tomorrow and I want to know if there is any chance at all that I can –'

'Definitely no. He must have complete rest. I told you before how his temperature shot up after your last visit. I am not saying it was directly associated with your seeing him, but it's something we cannot risk.'

'Cut out the crap, Doctor!' said Jimmy, furious at the way this man was being used as a messenger. 'You and I both know who's giving the orders where I'm concerned! Good-bye, Dr. Wilson!' He slammed the receiver down in disgust.

'Hello, Bob. Any news?'

Again Jimmy was calling Bob Silver, as he had every few days during the five months since his return to the studio. The news was almost always the same. Ham was greatly improved and regaining his strength. The doctor was pleased with his progress. If there were any new developments, he would hear.

Bob never answered one question that had been on Jimmy's mind for weeks. He had left a letter for his father and had written to him several times since telling him how the Commercial and Industrial Division was doing and sending on enclosures from Joanna and a childish scrawl from little Esther to the grandfather she had seen only once. He always asked his father how he felt, passed along all the good wishes from his friends and family and then waited for some kind of reply. As of yet there had been no response to any of his letters and his only contact was this secondhand one through Bob Silver. It was very upsetting, but there seemed to be nothing more he could do. When Ham returned to California he would see him and find out if his letters had been received. Right now he was too busy to spend much time thinking about it. His department was turning out new commercials, educational films and a documentary special for the 3M Company. It was good to be so busy that thoughts of the communications gap with his father were sometimes forgotten.

'Jimmy, good news – they hope your father can be flown back here and finish his recuperation at home. It may be in a few weeks from now,' said Bob, replying to Jimmy's inquiry one Monday morning.

'That's wonderful. Please let me know when he is due to arrive. I'll check with you again in a few days.'

Bob hung up the phone, looked at the desk clock and called Transportation.

'Have the car pick me up in front of the administration building right away. Thanks.'

They were passed through a special gate at Los Angeles

International Airport and went to a reserved parking space beside the terminal, where they parked to one side of the rolling stairs. Ham's doctor and Norman Harris stood there waiting, and when the plane taxied to a halt and the doors were swung open, they were the first aboard with an airline official. The rest of the passengers disembarked, and then the thin-faced gaunt man seated far back in the plane was helped into a wheelchair and rolled slowly to the exit and down a ramp. Nita and the nurse walked behind him, and she talked the whole time to the lawyer and Ham's secretary. She was in excellent spirits, happy they were almost home.

'He feels just wonderful! It's so good to be back again, isn't it, dear?' she asked the rolling patient, who kept his mouth tightly shut and said nothing. 'Bob,' Nita continued, 'you made sure the papers didn't know we were flying back? We don't want anything to get out for a while. Ham must have absolute peace and quiet without anybody bothering him.'

'No, Mrs. Robbins,' Bob replied. 'There's not a word in the press. We gave out a phony story to the trades that Mr. Robbins might return in a few weeks, but no date was set.' He looked down at the Boss as he was rolled across the concrete toward the waiting car. 'You look just fine, Mr. Robbins. We all were very worried about you. Welcome back.'

The man in the wheelchair nodded weakly. He did not want to open his mouth and speak until his front teeth were back in again. Those bastards really ruined his bridge, and a few of his real teeth, too. Damn them to hell! Well, that could all be fixed later, but in the meantime it killed him to look at himself in a mirror. He managed a few appreciative grunts and mumbles. Nita did most of the talking now, as she had for the last couple of months. Let her talk . . . let her talk. He would save his voice for later, and he would have plenty to say. His mood was black. He could not help thinking suddenly of his son, of Jimmy, who had flitted in and out of the hospital with his wife so many months ago and then vanished. Not one letter or phone call from his dear son, who had acted as though his father already was dead – and maybe that was what he really wanted. The hell with him!

Nita bustled about. She was clearly the person in charge. 'Good, I'm glad you could bring the car right up to the plane. I dreaded taking him through the buildings. Ham darling, you're nearly home again.' He lifted his head and tried to say something without having to open his mouth. Already he felt better being near his home and out of that damn hospital. As soon as his teeth were back in and he could get up on his feet without falling over, he would do everything on his own again. God, he was sick of having somebody take him to the toilet every time he needed to go. What absolute luxury it would be when he could take a crap for himself!

They eased him into the wide backseat of the car. Nita and the nurse sat beside him and Bob went up front with the driver. Norman Harris went off to pick up his car and then drove to the house on Sierra View. His mind was busy the entire time, working on the way things must go now that Ham was back and alive. Thanks to his coaching, Nita had worked hard at again being Mrs. Hamilton J. Robbins, and much more besides. She had devoted herself almost completely to his care during the tedious months of his recovery, and Ham seemed to have become almost entirely dependent upon her. Ham's self-esteem was at a very low ebb and there were many times he felt as badly beaten mentally as he had been physically between those buildings on Fifty-second Street.

The young attorney drove carefully, hoping to arrive at the house after Ham was put to bed so he could sit down quietly with Nita and review things. Now Nita had something to really keep her busy all her waking hours. He knew how much she would love her role of running the recovery, ordering Ham's meals, seeing he received his medicine, his physical therapy, took his trips to the bathroom. She would be watching him every damn minute, and heaven help the people around him if they neglected their patient. He had watched her briefly in New York and could see that she would never let him slip away from her again.

Yes, Norman Harris thought, Nita's time of exile had ended. She would strengthen her position during this crucial period and arrange for certain things to take place before Ham returned to the studio and his place as leader of the company. It would take time, but he had worked out a schedule with her and from now on everything was going to go her way . . . and, incidentally, his.

Not long after the last passenger had been wheelchaired off the plane, a stewardess from the New York-Los Angeles flight picked up her boy friend at the gate. It had been a good run, no real problems and some very interesting people aboard.

'You remember that big-shot movie mogul named Ham Robbins who was almost beaten to death about six months ago? Well, he was on my plane today. He still looked kind of beat up. After what happened to him, he's lucky to be alive. I suppose they're taking him home now, the poor guy.'

She received an extra kiss from her boy friend, who went to a pay phone and called his boss at the city desk of the *Los Angeles Times*.

'Bob! You told me he wasn't coming home for at least two more weeks! Now I read that he flew back yesterday afternoon. You must have known all about it even when I asked you on the phone. Why the hell was it necessary to feed me that bull!'

Jimmy was very angry and faced Bob Silver in his office, still holding the newspaper in which he had just read of Ham's return. Bob looked stricken. He swallowed a few times, wiped his forehead and tried to explain.

'I would have told you the whole story, Jimmy, if it had been up to me, but it wasn't. I was following instructions. I'm terribly sorry. I wish it was different . . . but –'

Jimmy did not let him finish.

'I'm going right up to the house now. If he's able to fly all the way across the country then he's able to see me! You should be ashamed to be a party to this, Bob! I went through it back in New York at the hospital, but then it was different. He really was near death, but now there's no legitimate reason I should be kept from seeing him.' He stormed out of the office and Bob reached for the phone. This was all a part of his damned job, hate it or not. Right now he hated it and he was disgusted with himself . . . but that also was a part of his job.

Jimmy stopped his car outside the closed gates on Sierra View Drive. He pressed the button on the speaker box. The metallic voice of the guard came through the little round opening.

'Yes, who is it?'

'I'm Mr. Robbins' son. I've come to see my father,' he said, speaking into the hidden microphone.

'Uh . . . just one minute, Mr. Robbins,' said the voice, and then the box went silent. In a few minutes the hum of the speaker came back on, followed by the disembodied voice. 'Your father is not having any visitors. Nobody's allowed in.'

'Can I see Mrs. Robbins?' Jimmy asked.

'She's resting and not seeing anybody either,' came from the box.

'I want to leave a message. Please let my father know I

603

came by to visit him. I just learned he was back in town and came right over. I'll return in a few hours to see him or Mrs. Robbins. Do you have that?'

'Yes. I'll give her your message.' Once again it went dead.

Jimmy looked at the silent box and then up at the closed gates. He got into his car, backed into the street and drove down the hill.

He did not feel like returning to the studio and was frustrated and angry that his father had been smuggled home and once again was locked away from him. He drove out Sunset Boulevard to the ocean, parked awhile and watched the sea gulls fighting over garbage on the beach.

Two hours later he was back at the gates.

'Mr. Robbins, I gave your message. No visitors are being permitted.' The gates remained tightly closed, and Jimmy stood beside his car looking up at the high bronze barriers.

'But I'm his son, I'm not just a visitor!' he said, wanting to shake the box until its speaker rattled. Not a sound came back in reply, only a hum, and then that too went dead and he knew the microphone was turned off. Suddenly it hummed back to life with a few last words.

'Sorry. No visitors.'

Jimmy looked at the box, then again at the closed gates. He returned to his car and followed the Boulevard back to his home in Westwood, where Joanna and Esther waited for him.

CHAPTER FIFTY-FIVE

The production department always added a full week and a half to the schedule of any film being shot during December. The Christmas and New Year's holidays made the twelfth month seem to have only two productive working weeks. The toughest assistant director could move a company only so fast when they heard the sound of reindeer bells and the splashing of eggnog. Distractions came with every present that was exchanged, and little parties sprang up in most of the offices, pulling people away from their jobs. The studio tried to discourage this, but there was little they could do against the pressure of tradition and the need for year-end release.

Los Angeles as usual was dreaming of a white Christmas but getting a wet one. The tractors sloshed through little lakes on the lot as they hauled tarpaulin-covered set units to the stages for final assembly. All exterior shooting was postponed and the companies moved inside to use their cover sets. Nothing could be taken for granted in this business. If it could possibly rain, it probably would, and there were almost always covered sets standing by for days like this.

Jimmy took a dry shortcut through the scenic crafts building. He had a company shooting a series of General Electric appliance spots on Stage Fifteen and another special in the works for Goodyear Tire. That one was completely bogged down. There was no such thing as a cover set for a state highway to shoot the car run-bys on location. He wheeled his bicycle from the stage, keeping well beneath the roof overhangs, and detoured through the big building on the way back to his office. His raincoat was buttoned high around his neck and a shapeless hat kept his hair from becoming soaked. The weather forecast at yesterday's production meeting had been for fair and dry, but as usual this time of year, the crazy atmospheric patterns over Southern California double-crossed everybody. He pedaled through the protected shortcut, leisurely rolling past the plaster shop, then the three-story-high cyclorama studio, where artists were painting a tremendous cityscape of some nonexistent metropolis. Looking up as he passed, he could have sworn the buildings on the huge canvas were real, while the men with their brushes and spray guns high on the platforms seemed to be what had been painted on the giant cyclorama. What worlds of magic were created in this building!

Over there were the prop makers, assembling furniture designed to collapse in a fight scene, so sturdy and solid-looking, but shattering harmlessly during a barroom brawl. Rows of thin candy bottles and large panes of something that photographed like glass stood on racks. Hit them with a fist or forehead and they safely powdered into nothingness.

His bicycle rolled past other shops in the sprawling complex: plumbers, painters and electricians. Tinsmiths, blacksmiths and gunsmiths. Workers in metals, liquids and plastics. Makers of miniatures and things larger than life. Here were gathered the people, skills and tools needed to run this incredible factory and bring alive the dreams of others. This was a business that was also an art, and Jimmy loved it all, everything in front of the cameras and all the wonders and wonder workers behind the lens making it happen.

One more area remained, the sign shop. Electric signs, neon signs, traveling-light signs, old-fashioned billboards and theater notices of every size, shape and description. Hanging high up on the wall was a lovely one, a carved wooden panel painted pale blue with ten golden letters spelling out the two words he had heard his father talk about for years. He looked up at it now as he rolled past and remembered what 'Bijou Dream' used to mean to his father and how nostalgic he became whenever it was mentioned. Those must have really been exciting days, when the two magic words hung in front of a nickelodeon and the people crowded in to sit on hard benches and see the flickering images.

The rain found a hole in the roof and a stream of water poured down into the sign shop. Several men rushed over to pull a long canvas banner away from the danger area. They ran past Jimmy, and he could clearly see the long streamer of heavy cloth as they hung it up on a rack. He suddenly gripped his hand brakes and skidded to a halt. What was it he saw painted on that banner? Bright red letters on a flashy yellow background.

YOU CAN'T KEEP A GOOD MAN DOWN
WELCOME BACK HAM ROBBINS!

He read it once again and rolled over to the shop boss.

'Joe, what's that banner for?'

'We got a rush order on it last night, Mr. Robbins. It has to be ready to go out front on January the second. Just try to get paint to dry in weather like this!' He stood back to admire the job. 'Looks pretty good, doesn't it? The Boss should be very happy to see the studio and that banner after all he went through. I'm glad he's all right again.'

Jimmy nodded and went on to the big sliding doors at the end of the building, which were opened wide enough to let his bicycle through. He splashed up the studio street, missed most of the puddles, and finally reached the main administration building. January 2 was only a few days away. The Christmas break had ended, then there were those few days when nobody did much work and suddenly it would be New Year's Eve and then a day later January 2 – and that banner would be hanging in front of the studio. Great! He had been kept from seeing his father at his house, but very soon now he would see him right here at the place where they both worked. Neither Bob Silver nor Nita could prevent that. Bob had taken him aside one day after lunch and asked him please not to go to the house again. Jimmy knew he was only carrying a message Nita had given him to deliver, and there seemed no reason then to make an issue of it. The time for that was coming closer . . . along with the new year.

He entered his office and pulled off his soaking raincoat and soggy hat, hoping he had not caught a cold.

'Any messages, Margie?' he called out to his secretary.

'Yes, Mr. Robbins. Bob Silver phoned half an hour ago. He wants you to call as soon as you get in.'

Jimmy went immediately to the phone and dialed the familiar extension.

'Bob, this is Jimmy. I just got in from the back lot. Great weather for making movies, isn't it?'

'Can you be in your father's office in half an hour, Jimmy?' asked Bob.

'Sure, I'll be there,' he answered, wondering if he should say anything about seeing the banner. First he would find out why he was wanted in his father's office. Maybe they wanted to wish him a happy New Year. Strange how downbeat Bob's voice had sounded. He left his office and arrived upstairs exactly a half-hour after hearing from Bob.

Two men were waiting for him inside the office as Bob took him through the inner door. He recognized one of them as Norman Harris, the attorney for his father and Nita who had been at the hospital in New York. The other man was Nate Klein, who handled legal matters for the studio. They were seated to the left of his father's big desk; the big high-backed chair behind it was empty, as it had been for many months. Both attorneys stood up and came forward to shake hands. A chair had been placed facing them, and Norman Harris indicated that Jimmy should be seated. He looked around to see Bob Silver take his seat directly behind him, and saw that he had brought along a dictation pad and held a pencil in his hand. Obviously he was here to make a record of whatever was going to happen.

Harris was the first to speak.

'Jimmy, I'm only here as an errand boy, a messenger. This is one of the most difficult things I have ever been asked to do and I feel very deeply about –'

Jimmy sat up very straight and cut in on the lawyer.

'Just a minute, hold it. What's this all about? Is this a business meeting, or is it something else?'

'I'm afraid it's something else,' said the errand boy. 'I have been instructed to tell you that you are to be off the lot by four o'clock this afternoon and that you will be given your regular salary for the next six months, and you are no longer associated with this studio.'

'What? By whose authority are you saying that? Are you an officer of Robbins International? Just where do you fit in this, Mr. Harris?' said Jimmy, shocked and incredulous.

'As I told you, Jimmy, I'm only a messenger . . . an errand boy your father has asked to tell you this. He wants you off the lot today, by four o'clock.'

'Why? For what reason? How can he do such a thing? . . . If he really did give you such a message. There has got to be a reason! Have I done a bad job with my department? Have I screwed things up? Is there any sane reason for this? I can't think of any!'

'Let's just say that your father will not return to the studio until you are off the lot,' said the attorney. 'It's that simple. I hate to be the one who has to tell you this, but somebody has to, and –'

'Then let my father tell me! I'm his son, and if there is some reason he wants me thrown out of here, then he is the only

608

one who is going to tell me! I work for him, Mr. Harris, I don't work for you. What you tell me means nothing. You are not an official of this company, and just because you happen to be sitting next to my father's desk doesn't mean you have the authority to fire me!'

Nate Klein leaned forward and handed Jimmy a typed sheet of paper.

'This is your resignation as vice-president of our company and executive in charge of the subsidiary producing television commercials and industrial films. Please read it and you will see where it requires your signature at the bottom.'

Jimmy looked at the company lawyer in amazement.

'Nate, that was well rehearsed, wasn't it? I'm not signing that or anything else. I've done absolutely nothing to deserve such treatment! If you want me to tear up your damned resignation, I'll be very happy to do that for you. Do you want it torn lengthwise or crosswise?' Jimmy's shock had turned into burning anger, and he almost reached out to rip the paper from Nate Klein's hand and tear it into shreds, but instead he gripped the arms of his chair. He looked around at Bob Silver, and sure enough, he was taking it all down in shorthand.

'Your father is emotionally involved, Jimmy, deeply so. He will not return to the studio or this office until you are off the lot. Those are the words I was given by him and –'

'By him and by who else, Mr. Harris?'

'By your father, the president of this company and the chairman of its board,' answered the attorney.

'Does he realize what he is doing? This studio is like a part of me. I've worked here on and off ever since we moved from Edendale. I think I've done a damn good job. My department is successful and earning plenty for the company. It has a great future!'

'He doesn't care about that,' said Harris. 'He wants you out of here today.'

'For what reason? You still haven't told me. Just what the hell have I done that he wants me to clear out with only a few hours' notice?'

'I told you. He's so emotionally involved that he just doesn't want you to be here when he comes back to the lot,' said the attorney in his calm courtroom voice.

'If that's the only reason, then he's still suffering from that terrible beating he took. It's a sick reason and impossible for me to believe. Listen – I was with my father for a few minutes when he was in the hospital in New York not long after he was operated on. That was all the time I was permitted, as I am sure you know. He was very glad to see me . . . he held on to my hand so tightly that it was hard to get away when the doctor told me I had to leave. He even said he wanted me to stay longer with him . . . I can still hear him saying it. That was the last time I saw him. I know now that his wife and you, Mr. Harris, visited him regularly, but I was never allowed near him. Bob Silver lied to me, and now he is sitting here taking all this down in shorthand, for God knows what reason. He told me my father wouldn't be back in town for another two weeks or more, when even then he knew damn well he was going right out to the airport to pick him up that same afternoon! When I read about it in the newspapers the next day, I went right up to the house and again I was kept away. I went there time after time and those gates always stayed shut. When I saw Nita at the hospital in New York, I was a gentleman to her then, as I believe I have always been, but it made no difference. Nothing I said or did seemed to make any impression.' He paused to catch his breath, and Norman Harris again spoke.

'There's nothing to be gained by prolonging this. You are to be off the lot tonight.' He rose to his feet, and Jimmy heard Bob Silver close the cover of his pad. Nate Klein still held the unsigned letter of resignation and left it on Ham's desk, glad to get rid of the distasteful thing. He and Bob left the room.

'Mr. Harris, could I have a few minutes alone with you?' asked Jimmy.

'Certainly,' the lawyer said.

'I'm going home now, but on January second, when the studio reopens, I am returning. I'm right in the middle of some very important groups of commercials and several special shows I fought very hard for us to produce. I'm not walking away from my work just because my father is . . . the way you put it . . . "emotionally involved." I think he needs more help, and he should try to get it as soon as possible so that he will be completely well again. You don't fire somebody just because of an emotional upset, at least that shouldn't be the only reason. I cannot accept it.'

'Jimmy, accept it. He's not going to change his mind. All you will do is make yourself and everybody else very unhappy. I've given you the message he asked me to deliver and that's all I can do. Good-bye.' He turned and left the office.

Tears of anger and frustration came to Jimmy's eyes and he wiped them away with his hand. He was all alone now in the room, but suddenly he saw someone else who had been there the whole time and was looking directly at him. On a side table, where he had never seen it before, stood a large still picture of Nita as she must have looked years earlier and fifty pounds lighter. The shining silver frame looked quite new, and he was positive that this set had just been re-dressed.

As he turned to leave his father's office, he could feel those intense dark eyes stabbing into his back, and he slammed the door shut.

New Year's Eve came and went. Jimmy paid little attention to the Rose Bowl game in Pasadena the next day, because his mind was on other things, and he was determined to return to the studio the following day.

Early the next morning he drove past the front of the administration building, where he saw several men hanging up the long banner over the main entrance. He drove on around to the auto gate, but as he turned to enter, two studio police stepped out in front of his car.

'Sorry, Mr. Robbins. We have orders to keep you from driving on the lot,' said the sergeant. 'Please put your car in reverse and clear the gate.'

'Who gave you orders to keep me out?' he asked, angry and upset, even though he had half expected something like this.

'We received our orders and we're following them. I'm terribly sorry, Mr. Robbins, I really am.'

No use starting an argument here. They were only doing their jobs. Jimmy drove around to the front of the studio again, passing the banner, which now was stretched over the main door.

They should have painted one for me too, Jimmy thought to himself. It could have read, 'Welcome Out!' He found a place to park his car far down the street in a passenger loading zone, and walked to the front of the building, where he passed under the banner and into the main reception room. Another pair of studio police awaited him there. Their dialogue repeated almost exactly what he had been told at the auto gate. Ray McClintock, the studio chief of police, and his captain stepped through the reception door and came over to Jimmy.

'I'm terribly sorry about this. It's the worst damn thing I've ever been ordered to do, but I have no choice, Jimmy. I'm here to make sure you leave the lot and to inform you we will collect all your personal things and send them to your house. I'd give anything not to have to do this and I'm very upset about it, more than I can tell you.' These men were both old friends, and he could see how they hated doing this dirty job.

'I don't hold it against you, Ray . . . or you either, Gene. Now that you've made your point and followed orders, how about the three of us going over to the drugstore across the street for a cup of coffee? I could really use it, and you both look as though you could too. Technically, that's not on the lot, is it?' The chief nodded, and they went to the drugstore.

Pops Johnson was seated all by himself at the counter. His face was unnaturally gray and he looked older than his years. Something seemed to have gone out of him, and he listlessly stirred a cup of coffee that over-flowed and spilled onto his lap. He did not seem to notice it.

'Pops, watch out, you'll get burned!' said Jimmy, going over to the old man.

'I've already been burned, Jimmy . . . burned right out of the studio! Can you imagine it! After all the years I've been here and all the things I did for your father and the company, I came to my office early today to help set up his welcome-back lunch and some bastard had changed all the locks! My name's even been scraped off the door, and I was told to pick up my check at the cashier's window! What a hell of a New Year's present. I heard you got bounced too, Jimmy. I'm terribly sorry. I have a very good idea why it happened to us, and we should get together for a private talk sometime soon. I can't believe it. All the things I did for him . . . some of them pretty damn miserable, too . . . and then this happens without any warning at all. I'm sure I know whose idea it was. I can't imagine your father letting himself get pushed around like this, but you really never know. He's been a pretty sick man for so many months. Funny things can happen when you're stretched out on your back for so long. There was a thing he had me do for him years ago up in Beverly Glen and it must have been remembered by somebody and her lawyer, who used it to have me thrown out. It happened before and this is almost like a rerun. I wonder if your old man knows about it – or if he even cares. This time I don't think I'll get back . . . and I really don't believe I want to. It's a hell of a world . . . a hell of a world!'

Jimmy sat on a stool next to Pops and Ray sat next to him, with the captain on the other side. Jimmy ordered coffee and Danish for all of them.

'We might as well have a going-away party. I don't know

what else there is we can say. It's a rotten way to end one year and start another.' He looked at the men seated beside him at the counter. They all had known each other for years and become good friends. He was sure that Ray McClintock and his men were almost as offended at what they had been ordered to do as he was at having it done to him. They drank their coffee in silence.

'Don't worry about any of the personal things in your office,' said Ray. 'I'll take care of getting it all together and over to your house with a written inventory. You don't know how terrible this makes me feel.'

'I understand, Ray. I'll check with you after you've dropped it off in case anything was overlooked. Don't forget the pictures and certificates on my walls. I may want to start a Trophy Room of my own one day.' He managed a smile, and Ray shrugged his broad shoulders.

'Thanks for the coffee, Jimmy. You were right, I did need it. I hope we'll meet again soon under happier conditions. I can't tell you how –'

'It's all right, Ray.' He turned to the old man at the counter. 'Pops, take care of yourself. In another week or so I'll give you a call and we'll get together. Oh, before I forget,' he said as he got off the stool, 'Ray, Gene, Pops – happy New Year.'

He walked the long block back to his car and found a ticket for parking in a loading zone stuck under the windshield wiper.

'This really is my day!' he said in disgust.

Jimmy got into his car to drive away from Robbins International Studios, and the last thing he could see was part of the bright banner stretched over the main entrance.

YOU CAN'T KEEP A GOOD MAN DOWN

CHAPTER FIFTY-SIX

It was midday and dull sunshine struggled through heavy layers of polluted air. The gleaming marble of a new mausoleum stood out in stark white contrast to the weathered gray of its crowded older neighbors.

He drove through the gates and parked his car inside the sacred grounds. For a few moments he stood and looked at the stone houses of the dead, then reached down into the car and very carefully lifted out a box wrapped in dull silver foil. A dozen white lilies thrust their heads out of the top and gracefully drooped over the side.

Slowly walking down the grass-bordered road toward the white mausoleum he could read the single word spelled out by the six bronze letters set over the entrance.

ROBBINS

Three steps led up to the column-flanked opening behind which were three polished marble slabs, only the center one bearing words deeply carved into its surface.

HAMILTON J. ROBBINS
SON – HUSBAND – FATHER

He kneeled down and set the silver box in front of the center slab, then thrust his hand deeply down into the mass of flowers to find what waited there.

Quickly he rose to his feet and walked back to the car at the cemetery gate. He turned and saw a very old man wearing a long shiny black coat and a round-topped hat who suddenly appeared.

The man at the car gasped, turned and ran down the road toward the old man whose face was almost concealed by his broad-brimmed hat and full beard. Words came from the hidden lips as he stood there, staring through bottle-thick glasses up at the bronze letters on the white marble wall.

'Be a Jew . . . Dream!'

614

'Rebbe . . . please! Come with me and pray for my family,' he said to the old man in a voice that was tense and urgent. He pointed far across the cemetery toward a small building made of weathered granite.

He gripped the old man's arm and dragged him across the road toward the distant mausoleum, looking back several times to make certain they were in the right place.

'Here, Rebbe . . . here is where you should pray. Pray for my family.' He pressed a contribution into the withered hand, then turned and left the old man in the long black coat staring after him, his eyes made owl-large by the thick lenses. He ran back to his car, opened the door and stepped inside.

He was almost through the cemetery gate when the heavy roar of the explosion reached him. Moments later a rain of small white marble fragments rattled down on the top of the car.

A dirty black cloud slowly rose high over the cemetery to become part of the pollution that bathed the city.

Ham awoke shaking and soaked in sweat. He sat up in bed, struggled to free himself from his damp sheets and almost ran to the bathroom, where he remained for nearly an hour before phoning his office.

All through the night he had had terrible dreams. The worst one was where he saw the crazy mixed-up image of a man carrying a strange-looking silver box filled with something that looked like lilies. White lilies – the flowers of the dead – things you take to a cemetery. He must have screamed in his sleep when he clearly saw his own name carved on a marble slab set in a little white building that stood someplace in a cemetery he had never seen. He strained to see who the man carrying the lilies was, but the figure was turned away and the face remained hidden and out of focus. Once he thought it was his brother Maurie, then for a moment it looked just like Poppa . . . then like his own son, Jimmy . . . and when at last he managed to look full into the man's face for an instant, it was as though he were staring into a mirror at the haggard image of himself. A hollow old voice sounded in his ears, terrifying him, and he heard it saying 'Be a Jew . . . Dream!' Dear God! What kind of dream was this?

It had ended in a tremendous explosion, and for a moment he thought he was again off Market Street in long-ago San Francisco the day of another bombing and he could almost

615

hear the little white stone fragments rattling down on something made of metal. The hollow old voice still sounded in his ears as he sat in the locked bathroom and called the office. Bob Silver caught it on the first ring.

'No, Mr. Robbins, there's nothing unusual at any of the studio gates.' Bob wondered why such a strange question had been asked. There were no picket lines, nobody was on strike and everything seemed peaceful and normal. He had an idea why the Boss was troubled, as he too had been terribly upset ever since that damned meeting with Jimmy and the two attorneys here in the office. He was thankful it was over, and he did not feel proud of his role in it.

'We're expecting you on the lot at twelve-thirty, Mr. Robbins. Come right to the executive bungalow. Something special has been arranged . . . just during the regular lunch hour. No, Mr. Robbins, there definitely is nothing going on at any of the studio gates. I'll have Ray McClintock check them before you arrive. No, there are no flowers that I know of on the dining room table, but I'll call Herman at the bungalow to make certain. Now take it easy, Mr. Robbins, and we'll see you in the dining room at twelve-thirty.'

The car carrying Ham swept through the main gate and brought him to the bungalow almost forty-five minutes late. He had the driver circle the entire lot and slow down at each gate so he could see for himself there was nothing unusual. Everybody in the dining room came to their feet and applauded as he entered. Ham held his hands high in the air, waving them as though he had just emerged victorious from an arena, which in a sense he had. Ham was back from as close to death as he could have been without making the complete one-way trip. He looked fairly fit, and even with the deep circles underneath his eyes and a somewhat haggard look, he did appear to be almost recovered from his ordeal. At least his voice was fully restored, and along with it much of the old wit.

In spite of the festive occasion, there was an almost perceptible layer of tension in the room. All the expected faces were there saying all the expected things. Ham found himself looking for a missing face, and for a moment his memory played him tricks and he wondered why Jimmy, his son and an executive of the company, was not here with the others to greet him. Where in hell was the kid? He missed him. Then it all rushed back and he remembered everything. The men standing around him later remarked to each other how pale he had suddenly gone and how for a moment he had trembled all over like a very old man.

Everyone present knew what had happened on the lot only two days before to Jimmy Robbins and Pops Johnson. Deep inside, most of them had a gnawing ever-present fear that something just like that could happen to any of them. The change of a lock, a call to the sign shop for the man with the razor blade, and zip – their names could be off the door, their keys useless and their precious parking space taken by a stranger. For now, though, it was 'Welcome back, Ham' and 'You look just great!'

John Wayne came over and stuck out his big hand.

'Get out on the tennis court again as soon as you can, Ham. It'll make you feel like a million bucks!'

'Thanks, Duke. It's good to see you here, thanks for coming.' He smiled, then sat down in his usual seat at the head of the table and raised his hand for attention. All the men were seated and the room was silent.

'Let's get this thing over in a hurry. I'm sorry to be late and for keeping you all away from your work. We don't pay you guys to eat and have good times, not even for an occasion as special as this!' Although Ham kept smiling, all the others knew there was an underlying edge to what he had just said. 'No speeches, just some food, and because I suppose it is special today, let's all have something to drink.'

Bottles of bourbon, rye and Scotch were taken from the locked cabinet and put on the table. This was almost unheard of, and it had to be a very special occasion for Ham to officially permit liquor during working hours. Leo Arnheim rose to his feet, a glass held high in his hand.

'Fellows, let's all stand up and drink to the return of the Boss. As it says outside on that banner, you can't keep a good man down, and those are words we all agree with. Welcome back, Ham ... and don't go walking alone on any dark streets.'

Ham stopped laughing. He did not like to be reminded of what had happened. Leo caught his look and could have bitten his tongue, but it was too late and he would have to get on to something else fast.

'How about a word or two for us, Ham? We really missed you and want you to know how good it is to have you back.'

There was a ripple of applause. Glasses were refilled and they all settled back for the word or two, which could easily stretch out to a thousand or more. Once the Boss started talking he usually took his own sweet time getting to the end title. Leo wound up the introduction, then reached out with his hand to help, but Ham rose to his feet unaided. He raised both arms high in the air once again as the others clapped their hands in dutiful applause.

The busboy bustled in from the kitchen carrying a square basket of white flowers just arrived from the publicity department. They were big round chrysanthemums, and Ham dropped his hands to his sides as he stared at them being put nearby on the table. He reached out for the side of the nearest chair and clung tightly to it. His eyes did not leave the basket of flowers and he looked at them almost in horror. A wave of dizziness swept over him and he gripped the chair even more tightly as the room seemed to spin and a bitter taste rose up in his throat. He shut his eyes as tightly as he could and the flowers and all else vanished from his sight. The pattering of hands coming together made a sound like distant surf, growing into louder and louder bursts of applause, the crashing of sound waves on a beach . . . breakers rolling up the white sand toward where he stood watching the ocean stretching out into infinity.

Very, very slowly he forced his eyes open . . .

Part Seven

CHAPTER FIFTY-SEVEN

'Ladies and Gentlemen. To present the first Hollywood Humanitarian of the Year Award to our guest of honor, may I introduce a man already well known to all of you, the president of the George Spelvin Club. A distinguished film pioneer, his involvement in our industry goes far back to those days when he waited with so many other hopefuls on Gower Gulch for an early-morning casting call. We all remember the glorious Westerns in which he was featured and the mobs of bank robbers and other wrong-doers he successfully cut off at the pass. Now the beloved leader of his fellow pioneers, he is here to honor the first recipient of this award. Ladies and gentlemen, the Old Sheriff himself . . . leader of a thousand posses . . . Monte Ross!'

The tall distinguished figure with his grizzled white hair and trimmed beard rose and waited for an end of the polite ripple of applause.

'Georgie, or should I call you Toastmaster General, distinguished guests, ladies and gentlemen,' said the old actor in the famed Western accent he had nurtured over the years. 'I have been asked by my outfit to bestow this very first Hollywood Humanitarian of the Year Award. The George Spelvin Club is a group of actors who have been here in this town for a combined total of more than eighteen hundred years. That sounds mighty impressive, and it is. Forty members, each with careers going back an average of forty-five years trying to get in front of cameras. Yep, it's a great business and Hollywood's a great place, even though I remember how I froze my behind on that cold Gower Gulch sidewalk waiting for the casting directors to invite me in. Lots has changed since then, but not the fascination and the excitement of this wonderful business of ours.'

Ham looked up at the speaker. He had to be one of those sad bedraggled men he and Lou used to walk past all those years ago on the way to the Christie brothers' studio when

621

life was so different and they all were so young. The old Western actor's voice boomed out again.

'Lots of people ask me who this George Spelvin fellow was, the one we named our club after. I can tell you more about old George than I can about what a humanitarian is. At least we know George Spelvin probably never existed, but his name has been used for years whenever one actor performs in two separate roles. So, you see, there really never was a George Spelvin, but we love and honor him for the good parts he's played and the work he's given so many actors. A humanitarian, on the other hand, is a very real person, deeply concerned with the needs of mankind and devoted to human welfare and all kinds of social reforms. Now I really don't know our guest of honor all that well . . . but . . .'

A raucous voice came from high up near the rafters.

'That's for damn sure!'

Laughter filled the big room, but the Old Sheriff went right on speaking his well-rehearsed lines.

'These seasoned veterans of our industry believe him to be the most qualified individual to receive such an honor. Mr. Robbins, Ham . . . would you please step forward and accept from me, on behalf of the George Spelvin Club, this beautiful plaque honoring you as the Hollywood Humanitarian of the Year.'

Ham shook his head to rid himself of the slight dizziness he had been feeling since his last drink. The room stopped spinning and he walked over to where Monte Ross held out the shining silver plaque set on a large piece of polished dark wood. He put out both hands to take the object, almost dropping it when the unexpected weight was transferred to him. It looked like silver, but it weighed like lead! The noise of polite applause built up modestly, not quite as loud as when greeting the Old Sheriff, but enough to assail his ears and make him wish this damn thing were done and over. Ham looked down at the bright metal, and the spotlight reflected off it into his eyes, forcing him to look away. Where the hell was he supposed to put it while he talked?

The podium was small, but he managed to rest the bulky thing there, holding it with one hand while fumbling in his pocket with the other. Where was that damn card? He scrabbled around inside, then switched hands so he could rummage through his other coat pocket. Ah, there it was, the card that guy from Publicity wrote up for him. Charlie Freeman, the bastard who must have invented this whole damn thing and conned him into it. He should have thrown him out of his office then, but it was too late for that now. He squinted into the glaring light that hit his eyes, bouncing again off the plaque and making it impossible for him to read the oversized typewritten words on the card.

'I had something here to read to you in thanks for this . . . this Humanitarian thing. Now I can't see a goddamn word of it!' He put up one hand to shield his eyes from the spotlight. 'For Christ's sake, can't somebody turn off that fucking thing! I'm going blind up here with that on me!' The spotlight snapped off. 'Now put up some houselights so I can see to read this stuff and look at your faces to see who doesn't laugh in the right places. If you all worked for me and didn't give the right reactions I could fire you, but since most of you don't, I'll have to take my chances.'

A few in the audience laughed, and the rest were not too sure he had meant it as a joke, but anything to break the tension was welcome. The wife of a distinguished banker leaned over to her husband and whispered in his ear, 'Does that vulgar man have to use such language?'

'My dear,' replied her husband, 'I'm quite sure he's doing his best to hold himself back – at least I hope so.'

'On this card, which I didn't write, so I'm not to blame for what it says, I'm supposed to thank the members of the George Spelvin Club for this award. Thank you. There, now that's taken care of. I'm very glad Monte Ross gave us the definition of "humanitarian." I was going to look it up in a dictionary or have our studio research department send me a page on just what the hell it meant, but I didn't have time or else I forgot. Anyhow, it's a big word and this is a big plaque. It could give me a hernia to carry out of here.' A pause for laughs while Ham reached down for a glass, any glass. He was in luck. It was Scotch, and he moistened his dry throat. The outer edges of the vast Palladium floor were still dark, and several tables of people seized the opportunity to get out before the speaker continued. Soon it was quiet again, and Ham looked down at the plaque.

He saw his face reflected in the bright silver surface. Strange how in this light he looked so much younger, maybe even a little like his son . . . like Jimmy. Quickly his eyes went around the hall, and he could see somebody far in back sneaking out of the place. The hell with them. He knew so many of those people out there staring up at him, shifting uneasily in their seats and waiting for him to go on. Let them sit awhile. He kept looking for somebody he could not find. The hell with him too. Another look down at the plaque, a change of angle, and now it was Maurie's face looking back at him, and his hand shook for a moment, the reflected image dancing crazily.

'Uh, what was I saying when I interrupted myself? Oh, yeah, this thing I'm holding. I'll try to find a good place to hang it where it won't pull down the wall. I'll sit there and look up at it and remember tonight. It'll remind me that I'm a humanitarian and shouldn't think of all the no-good sons of bitches I've known in this business. I'll try to forget all the double crosses I've gotten from so many loyal friends who screwed me when they thought they could get away with it and then screamed bloody murder when I did it to them!'

People at the main table and out front looked at each other. What was their guest of honor talking about? His mouth seemed to be running out of control, spilling old hates and angers into the open. Didn't he realize where he was and why he was here?

'I remember when it was still fun ... when you made movies and not goddamn motion pictures. When once there was a place called the Bijou Dream ...' He stopped talking, held tightly to the plaque and saw the bright blue-and-gold sign hanging in the dark, the dream, the unfulfilled hope of happiness in a place and a time when everything seemed right and good. A time gone with the flames that burned the Bijou Dream to the ground, that killed his brother Lou and so much else. A time that had come and gone and left him alone. He shook his head, trying to clear things out, then went on. 'We take a script, something a lot of people sweat and slave over until it's as good as they say it can be, then we try to put the best cast in it we can, we pick a director we hope will do the job ... then a cameraman and a crew and somebody called the producer who's supposed to watch things. Then we turn them all loose to spend and spend, to take all our plans, our hopes, our dreams ... our Bijou Dreams ... and turn them into money in the bank, or piles of shit stinking to the high heavens!'

Several groups of people got up from their tables and left the room. Ham was silent for a moment, looking at them but seeing other things.

'I was telling you a little about this crazy wonderful business, about the dreams and the risks. For every decision you make an enemy – or lose a friend. We've gotten soft! Soon there won't be any Harry Cohns, no more Warners or Laemmles. L. B. Mayer's only a memory, and one day there'll be no Zukor or Sam Goldwyn. Who in the hell remembers Tom Ince or even D. W. Griffith and Dick Rowland and all the rest of them who came out here when it still was Poverty Row and orange groves? Love them or hate them, still they had the guts and they had the pride and the vision and were willing to take the risks – to stand or fall. All of them knew what the public would pay to see, but most of all, they loved movies and moviemaking. Soon the real humanitarians will be moving in to take over the business . . . committees full of them. Blessed are the accountants, the lawyers and the agents, for they shall inherit the industry. Soon the only damn thing that will matter is going to be the deal and not the picture! This isn't just a business, and God knows it's not all an art either! Whatever happened to the love – and the pride!'

He stopped, reached down for the glass and remembered his own pride when he was shown a baby boy . . . the pride he once had felt at being the father of a boy, of another Ham Robbins, a whole new generation to carry on after he too was gone, even with that name of Jimmy he had picked up. The kid was doing all right and he had to give him credit. Deep down there still remained something he might call pride, but that would remain his secret. If only he had stood up to Nita's zodiac crap and thrown it and her out long ago, maybe he and his son might still be . . . No! Jimmy was far better off on his own than he ever could be with a Ham Robbins on his back. Already in some ways he was a greater success than his old man. He had a home filled with love, and the dream for Jimmy and Joanna and their little Esther was still possible – while his was ashes and rubble.

Ham's glass was empty and he slammed it down on the table.

'I don't see things improving, even with all the fucking changes everybody talks about. The hell with the business. Let's talk about the Hollywood Humanitarian of the Year. I know most of you sitting out there think I'm a real bastard and you hate my guts – but damn it, at least I've got guts! I know why most of you are here tonight. If this thing wasn't tax-deductible, or if the people you work for hadn't shoved your asses into those chairs, I'd be standing up here talking to myself! But you stuck it out this far and you're going to listen to me. I'm nearly through.'

The voice from the rafters flew down: 'Thank God!'

It was deathly silent except for the shuffle of feet on their way to the doors.

'I get the hint. Thank you.' He looked out at the thinning crowd, and suddenly his eyes filled with tears. Where the hell had they come from? Everything was blurred and he turned his head, hoping nobody had seen them. A quick wipe of the hand across his eyes, then he turned again to face the light. He held up a crumpled piece of paper. 'Now how in the hell could anybody have written this whole speech of mine on such a little card? Thank you again, George Spelvin, wherever and whoever you are, for choosing me as Hollywood Humanitarian of the Year.' He gripped the plaque with both hands and held it high in the air. 'I'll find a spot for this thing. I've got a room at the studio that's perfect for it. I'm all through now. Good night.' He sat down.

Georgie Jessel stood with his mouth hanging wide open, for the first time in memory rendered utterly speechless. There was the lonely sound of a few pairs of hands clapping, and Georgie rushed to the podium, where he gripped the microphone.

'Nobody can top that acceptance speech, or whatever it was. Thank you, Ham, for something different that we'll always remember.' He looked up and down the main table, trying to locate somebody, but saw only empty chairs. Georgie turned to those still remaining in the audience.

'We asked the Reverend George McLean of the First Community Church of Hollywood to pronounce the closing benediction, but I believe he must have left early.' He certainly had, along with several hundred others. Georgie desperately looked around the vast room. 'Is there a minister or a priest or rabbi in the house? A Christian Science practitioner? We really ought to wrap this up with a benediction. Are there any volunteers? Come on, somebody, it's your big chance to talk to God!' Not one soul raised a hand, so finally Georgie took it on himself.

'Bless this gathering . . . and all its survivors . . . uh, God . . . Oh, God! . . . Amen.'

Charlie Freeman rushed to Ham's side as soon as the houselights were all on. He had nearly wet his pants during his employer's rambling declamation. Now it was over and the perfect little gem of an acceptance speech he had worked so hard to compose lay crumpled on the floor.

'Mr. Robbins, can I take you to your car?'

Ham looked up at him. He sat all alone at the main table.

Everybody else had melted away like the snows of August.

'Freeman, do me a favor. Tomorrow morning when you go to the studio, stop by Personnel and tell them you've been fired. That'll save me a phone call. Now get the hell away from me. I can find my car without any help.'

George O'Neill and the blonde came up to him. George looked very worried, and he reached out to help Ham to his feet.

'You all right, Mr. Robbins?'

'Sure, sure. Let's get out of here. Where's the car?' They crossed the floor, the few people remaining all pulling back to let them pass, and at last came to the rear entrance. Ham carried the heavy plaque. He had been right, the damn thing could give him a hernia.

'George, take this before I rupture myself. Go on, get outside and wake up the driver.'

He stood in the waiting area with the blonde, not caring now who saw them together, while George scurried over to the long line of cars and waved his free hand. Ham and the girl went over and got into the backseat. The girl reached out to George.

'Can I see that? I couldn't tell what it looked like at all from where we were sitting. My God but it's heavy!'

She held the plaque on her lap as the car pulled out and circled to turn right on Sunset Boulevard. Her face was reflected from the polished surface, and she gasped in dismay.

'Hey! Why didn't you tell me my lipstick was all over my face!' She dug into her bag for a repair kit, then, using the plaque as a mirror, wiped off her lips and soon had them replaced. 'Ham, what will I do with this thing? It's going to make my lap all black and blue.'

'Dump it on the floor. The last thing I want is for your lap to get black and blue from anything but me,' he said.

The blonde giggled and eased the plaque down so it rested on its side against the car door. Ham looked at it a few times as they continued west on Sunset. He was silent all the way to Coldwater Canyon, and when the car pulled up in front of the little house on Lago Vista Drive, he reached down and lifted the plaque away from the door so George and the girl could leave the car. He spoke to her.

'I'm not coming in with you now. There's something I want to do first. Good night.'

She stood on the street in front of the house and there was

not enough light for the full effect of the pout she wasted on him. George nodded good night to the Boss, took her arm and propelled her to the door. He could tell this was a time Ham wanted to be alone. This girl, or another like her, would be available whenever Ham might need a companion.

'Let's go back to Sunset,' Ham said to the chauffeur. 'Take me out toward the ocean.'

They left Beverly Hills and in a while neared the west gate to Bel Air and the turn off to Beverly Glen Boulevard. Ham frowned as he read the street sign while they waited for the signal to change, bitter memories coming back, then sat quietly and watched the lights flash by. Again he spoke to the driver.

'Turn left when you get to Hilgard just before UCLA.' The car slowed down after making the turn and he said, 'Watch for Lindbrook . . . there it is . . . now turn there. Good. Stop in front of that house we're coming to. I'm not getting out – I'll tell you when to go on.'

The lights were off in Jimmy and Joanna's house, but Ham could see it clearly. There were no walls and no gates. It looked like a place where family and friends would always be welcome. How many times had he been asked to come here? Enough to remember the address, but why, except for that once, did he stay away? It didn't matter anymore, but he could not help thinking of what might have been if only he had allowed himself more than just that one visit to his son's home. Inside that house was a part of the only real legacy he would leave on earth after he was gone, his granddaughter Esther and her father and mother. Someplace outside London was another part of his legacy, but now he was not thinking of him. Maybe, he thought, maybe one day he might work things out with Jimmy, but he really didn't know and he would have to wait until some of the pressures eased up, if they ever did.

I wonder if it could have been different, Ham thought. Jimmy has so many of the things I lost or threw away . . . a family and a home filled with love and the kind of a life I might have had . . . instead of a room full of . . . these. He stretched out his foot to touch the plaque lying on the car floor. He was sure of one thing now. Jimmy was doing all right. He even had the beginnings of his own Trophy Room with that golden Emmy he was awarded just a week ago. Maybe Jimmy didn't need that kind of a room, but Ham remembered his feelings of pride as he watched his son on the television screen accepting the little statuette for the winning dramatic series he was producing over at Paramount-TV. Yeah, the kid was doing great and doing it all on his own. For him at least there was still a 'Bijou Dream' and part of it was right here on Lindbrook Drive.

'Okay, take me out to the studio,' he told the driver, and they went back to Sunset Boulevard and all the way to Hollywood, turning on Highland to go through the Pass into the Valley. Finally, just after midnight, they reached the studio main gate. The guard on duty was surprised to see Ham in the backseat and gave him a quick salute, waving him on inside the lot.

'Stop right in front of the executive bungalow,' he said to the driver, who circled the stages, went past the cutting rooms, Wardrobe and Make-up, coming to a halt in front of the little building.

'Leave the car here for me. You can take off now, thanks,' Ham said. He picked up the plaque and got out.

There was just enough light to find the keyhole, and Ham let himself into the outer hall, where an open arch led to the executive dining room on one side. Another locked door was opposite the arch, and he inserted his key and pulled the door open, reaching inside to turn on the lights.

He had never before failed to be comforted by this sight of the Trophy Room, with all the history and the memories hanging on its walls and standing on the tables. There was the pile of black scrapbooks, preserving the triumphs and pleasures of the past. The ranks of little golden Oscars, witnesses to so much that had happened in here, standing impassively on their ebony bases. All that hardware on the walls, the certificates, the flags and banners, the trophies of triumph and victory . . . the dust-collecting scrap iron of the past. His very own junkyard.

'Poppa, please don't sell Mr. Birnbaum's Kinetoscope for scrap . . . please! It's a wonderful machine. Lou and I know how to make it run and . . .'

How close it all had come to ending up in a real junkyard. Maybe it had. He walked into the room and looked at the pictures filling one wall. Not a single shot there of Maurie, none of Ruth and Miriam. No pictures of Jimmy, but so many of Lou, poor lost Lou. He stopped before a picture, the only one ever taken so many years ago of a little storefront in Harrisburg, Pennsylvania. He looked closely at the grainy enlargement of the old still. There was that first sign hanging up over the door, BIJOU DREAM . . . Be a Jew . . . Dream. Wasn't that what the nearly blind old man had said to them? Whatever happened to all the dreams? Gone, all gone like the burned sign . . . ashes and rubble. Worst of all, he knew now who set the fires to destroy the dream. It had been his own hand that held the match . . . but there was also another.

He looked for a picture of Nita, then remembered there were none of her in this room anymore. She was no trophy. She was nothing he wanted to remember. When he had heard about that 'antique' still picture of her in the fancy silver frame she had sent over to his office, he had Bob toss it into a closet. The face in that portrait was of another Nita, someone he had known years ago, another burned-down dream. He was still angry that she had had the gall to send it on her own to the studio only a few days before his return. It must have been her way of greeting Jimmy in his office when they held that damn meeting to throw the kid off the lot.

'Jimmy . . . Jimmy . . . If only we had tried harder to know each other. I think we really might have gotten along. I don't know why it all went so wrong . . . Oh, yes, I know, I know . . . and maybe you do too, and I hope someday maybe you can forgive me. I can't blame you, though, if you don't. Ah . . . fuck it! Let's hang this beautiful piece of tin up on a wall so I can come in here and look at it whenever I need a shot in the arm.'

He put the heavy plaque on a chair and looked at the wall-covering collection facing him. Something had to go. There wasn't enough room to hang up this new one unless he took another one down. Which one would it be? There – the Film Exhibitors of America award for something or other. It wouldn't be missed, and anyhow the lousy metal those damned cheapskates used was already turning yellow. He reached up and lifted it off its hook. The size was just right, and it went through the door into the massage room, where the Greek could throw it out tomorrow or take it home as a toy for his children.

He lifted the new plaque and set it in place on the hook. It needed to be straightened so it hung absolutely level, and then he stood back to look at it. The entire wall glistened and sparkled with recognition, glory, honors, accolades . . . and respect. Respect – the one thing he always had wanted from Maurie and from Ruth and Miriam . . . and from Poppa . . . from Jimmy . . . and from himself?

There it was, another one for the wall. He moved from the

center of the Trophy Room, closer to the bright new silver plaque, and again he read the engraved words on its shining surface:

Hollywood Humanitarian of the Year

—HAMILTON J. ROBBINS—

* * *

AN OUTSTANDING HUMAN BEING AND A CREDIT TO MANKIND AND THE MOTION PICTURE INDUSTRY HE HAS SERVED SO WELL

* * *

Given in Gratitude and Heartfelt Appreciation by the Members of the George Spelvin Club

Hollywood, California

A selection of bestsellers from SPHERE

FICTION

MONIMBO	Arnaud de Borchgrave and Robert Moss	£2.25 ☐
KING OF DIAMONDS	Carolyn Terry	£2.50 ☐
SPRING AT THE WINGED HORSE	Ted Willis	£1.95 ☐
TRINITY'S CHILD	William Prochnau	£2.50 ☐
THE SINISTER TWILIGHT	J. S. Forrester	£1.95 ☐

FILM & TV TIE-INS

SPROCKETT'S CHRISTMAS TALE	Louise Gikow	£1.75 ☐
THE DOOZER DISASTER	Michaela Muntean	£1.75 ☐
THE DUNE STORYBOOK	Joan D. Vinge	£2.50 ☐
ONCE UPON A TIME IN AMERICA	Lee Hays	£1.75 ☐
WEMBLEY FRAGGLE GETS THE STORY	Deborah Perlberg	£1.50 ☐

NON-FICTION

PRINCESS GRACE	Steven Englund	£2.50 ☐
BARRY FANTONI'S CHINESE HOROSCOPES		£1.95 ☐
THE COMPLETE HANDBOOK OF PREGNANCY	Wendy Rose-Neil	£5.95 ☐
WHO'S REALLY WHO	Compton Miller	£2.95 ☐
THE STOP SMOKING DIET	Jane Ogle	£1.50 ☐

All Sphere books are available at your local bookshop or newsagent, or can be ordered direct from the publisher. Just tick the titles you want and fill in the form below.

Name _____

Address _____

_____

Write to Sphere Books, Cash Sales Department, P.O. Box 11, Falmouth, Cornwall TR10 9EN

Please enclose a cheque or postal order to the value of the cover price plus:

UK: 55p for the first book, 22p for the second book and 14p for each additional book ordered to a maximum charge of £1.75.

OVERSEAS: £1.00 for the first book plus 25p per copy for each additional book.

BFPO & EIRE: 55p for the first book, 22p for the second book plus 14p per copy for the next 7 books, thereafter 8p per book.

Sphere Books reserve the right to show new retail prices on covers which may differ from those previously advertised in the text or elsewhere, and to increase postal rates in accordance with the PO.

Deutsch 2000

Eine Einführung in die moderne Umgangssprache

BAND 1

Arbeitsbuch

MAX HUEBER VERLAG

DEUTSCH 2000
Eine Einführung in die moderne Umgangssprache
Band 1
Arbeitsbuch
von Manfred Glück

ISBN 3–19–22.1180–6
3. Auflage 1975
© 1974 Max Hueber Verlag München
Textillustrationen: Ulrik Schramm, Feldafing
Bildnachweis: Sämtliche Fotos Bilderdienst Süddeutscher Verlag, München
Gesamtherstellung: Druckerei Ludwig Auer, Donauwörth
Printed in Germany

Inhaltsverzeichnis

Lektion 1

1. *Lesen Sie laut*

Fräulein Heim ist Sekretärin. Sie wohnt in Köln und sie arbeitet in Köln.
Frau Berg ist Verkäuferin. Sie wohnt in Berlin und sie arbeitet in Berlin.
Herr Weiß ist Student. Er wohnt in München und er studiert in München.

Und jetzt antworten Sie

a. Wer arbeitet in Köln?
b. Wer wohnt in Berlin?
c. Wer studiert in München?

2.

Wer ist das? –
... ... Fräulein Heim.
Wo wohnt sie? –
... ... Köln.

Was ist sie? –
Sie ist ... .
Und wo arbeitet sie? –
... ... Köln.

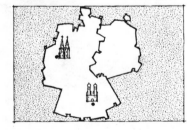

Wohnt Fräulein Heim in München? –
..., ...

4

Wer ist das? –

... ... Herr Weiß.

Wohnt Herr Weiß in München? –

..., ...

Was ist er? –

... ...

Und wo studiert er? –

... ...

Ist das Fräulein Heim? –

Nein, ... Frau Berg.

Wohnt ... in München? –

Nein, sie wohnt ... .

Was ist Frau Berg?

Ist sie Studentin? –

..., ...

Arbeitet sie in Berlin? –

..., ...

3.

a. Wo studiert Herr Weiß? – ... ... München.

b. Wo wohnt Fräulein Heim? – ... ... Köln.

c. Wo arbeitet Frau Berg? – ... ... Berlin.

5

4.

Was ist Herr Weiß?
Ist er Verkäufer? –
..., Herr Weiß ... .
Er ... in München.

Ist Fräulein Heim Studentin? –
Nein, ...
... arbeitet ... Köln.

Was ist Frau Berg?
Ist sie Sekretärin? –
Nein, ...

5.

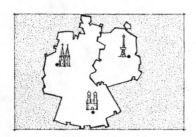

Wohnt Herr Weiß in Köln? –
Nein, ...
Wohnt Fräulein Heim in Berlin? –
Nein, ...
Wohnt Frau Berg in München? –
Nein, ...

6.

Wer ist das?

Lektion 2

1. *Lesen Sie laut*

Das ist das Studio A. Das ist der Quizmaster. Das ist die Ansagerin. Das ist das Team. Das ist der Reporter. Das ist die Verkäuferin. Das ist das Quizteam. Das ist der Student. Das ist die Sekretärin.

2.

Wer ist das? –
Das ist der . . . .
Er heißt . . . .

Und wer ist das? –
Das ist die . . . .
Sie heißt . . . .

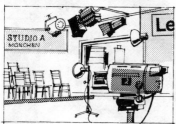

Was ist das? –
Das ist das . . . .
Es ist . . . .

3. der/er, die/sie, das/es

a. Das ist . . . Quizmaster.   . . . heißt Hans-Peter Sommerfeld.
b. Das ist . . . Ansagerin.   . . . ist im Studio A.

c. Das ist ... Reporter.   ... wohnt in Augsburg.

d. Das ist ... Studio A.   ... ist in München.

4. *Setzen Sie ein:* in/aus

a. Wo wohnen Sie? – Ich wohne ... München.

b. Woher sind Sie? – Ich bin ... Berlin.

c. Wo studieren Sie? – Ich studiere ... München.

d. Sind Sie aus Hamburg? – Ja, ich bin ... Hamburg, aber ich wohne ...
München.

5.

Herr Weiß, Fräulein Heim, Frau Berg und Herr Zinn sind heute im Studio.

Guten Abend.

Bitte sehr, wie heißen Sie? –

... ... Michael Weiß.

Was sind Sie von Beruf? –

... ...

Und wo wohnen Sie? –

... ...

Bitte, wie heißen Sie? –

... ... Ingrid Heim.

Was sind Sie von Beruf? –

... ...

Und woher sind Sie? –

... ... Köln.

Und wie heißen Sie? –

... ... Monika Berg.

Und was sind Sie von Beruf? –

... ...

Und woher sind Sie? Aus München? –

..., aber ... ... in Berlin.

Und wie heißen Sie, bitte? –
... ... ist Karl Zinn.
Ich bin von Beruf ... .
Und wo arbeiten Sie? –
... ... München,
aber ... ... Augsburg.

Vielen Dank, meine Damen und Herren. Sie sind ... das Quizteam.

6.

a. Sind Sie Herr Michael Weiß? – Ja, ich ... Michael Weiß.
b. Was ... Sie von Beruf? – Ich ... Student.
c. Sind Sie Fräulein Ingrid Heim? – Nein, ich ... Monika Berg.
d. ... Sie Sekretärin? – Nein, ich ... Verkäuferin.
e. Wo wohnen Sie? – Ich ... in Hamburg.
f. Wo arbeiten Sie? – Ich ... in Berlin.
g. Wo studieren Sie, Herr Weiß? – Ich ... in München.

7.

a. Wie heißt der Quizmaster? – Er ... ...
b. ... ... die Ansagerin? – Sie ... ...
c. ... ... der Reporter? – Er ... ...
d. ... ... die Sekretärin? – Sie ... ...

8.

a. Sind Sie Student? – Nein, ... Reporter.
b. Sind Sie Verkäuferin? – Nein, ... Sekretärin.
c. Sind Sie aus Hamburg? – Nein, ... Berlin.
d. Arbeiten Sie in Köln? – Nein, ... Augsburg.
e. Studieren Sie in München? – Ja, aber ... ... Hamburg.

9. *Antworten Sie*

a. Wie heißen Sie?
b. Woher sind Sie?
c. Was sind Sie von Beruf?
d. Wo arbeiten Sie?
e. Wo wohnen Sie?

Lektion 3

1. *Lesen Sie laut*

Das Quizteam ist im Studio A in München. Das Spiel beginnt. Herr Fischer kommt ins Studio. Zuerst fragen die Damen. Dann fragen die Herren. Herr Fischer antwortet. – Herr Fischer arbeitet nicht in München. Er arbeitet auch nicht in Augsburg. Er reist viel. Er reist oft ins Ausland, nach Afrika und nach Amerika, auch nach Südamerika. Er fliegt oft nach Brasilien. Aber er fliegt nicht allein. Er ist von Beruf Flugkapitän.

2.

Das Quiz beginnt.
Der Quizmaster und das Quizteam
. . . im Studio.
Der Quizmaster ruft:
. . . .

Herr Fischer . . . . . . Studio.
Der Quizmaster sagt:
. . . . . . Herr Peter Fischer. –
Guten Abend, ... –
. . . . . . bitte Platz.

Hier sind vier Herren.
Herr Zinn ist . . . . Herr Weiß ist . . . .
Herr Sommerfeld ist . . . . Herr Fischer
ist . . . .
Und wer ist die Dame? –
. . . . Sie ist . . . .

11

Und wer ist das? –
Das ist die . . . .
Wie heißt sie? –
. . . .
Und wo ist sie? –
. . . .

3.

a. Arbeiten Sie in München? – Nein, ich . . . nicht in München.
b. Wohnen Sie in Hamburg? – Nein, ich . . . nicht in Hamburg.
c. Sind Sie aus Berlin? – Ja, ich . . . aus Berlin.
d. Studieren Sie in Augsburg? – Nein, ich . . . in München.
e. Reisen Sie viel? – Ja, ich . . . viel.
f. Wohin fliegen Sie? – Ich . . . nach Südamerika.
g. Sind Sie Flugkapitän? – Ja, ich . . . Flugkapitän.

4. aus, im, ins, in, nach

a. Wohin fliegt Herr Fischer oft? – Er fliegt oft . . . Brasilien.
b. Wohin reist Herr Zinn oft? – Er reist oft . . . Ausland.
c. Wo studiert Herr Weiß? – Er studiert . . . München.
d. Wo arbeitet Frau Berg? – Sie arbeitet . . . Berlin.
e. Wo ist Herr Sommerfeld heute? – Er ist heute . . . Studio.
f. Woher ist Fräulein Heim? – Sie ist . . . Köln.
g. Und woher ist Frau Berg? – Sie ist . . . München, aber sie wohnt . . . Berlin.
h. Und wo wohnt Herr Zinn? – Er wohnt . . . Augsburg.

5. *Antworten Sie*

a. Was ist Herr Fischer? Ist er Tabakimporteur? –
Nein, ... Flugkapitän.
b. Was ist Herr Zinn? Ist er Student? –
Nein, ... Reporter.
c. Was ist Fräulein Heim? Ist sie Verkäuferin? –
Nein, ... Sekretärin.

d. Was ist Frau Berg? Ist sie Ansagerin? –
Nein, ... Verkäuferin.

6.

a. Rauchen Sie? – Nein, ich rauche ... .
b. Reisen Sie viel? – Nein, ich reise ... viel.
c. Arbeiten Sie in Köln? – Nein, ich arbeite ... in Köln.
d. Kommt Herr Sommerfeld heute ins Studio? – Nein, er kommt heute ...
ins Studio.

7. ja, aber / nein, aber

a. Ist Herr Fischer Tabakimporteur? – ..., ... er raucht Pfeife.
b. Arbeitet Herr Zinn in München? – ..., ... er wohnt in Augsburg.
c. Ist Herr Weiß aus Hamburg? – ..., ... er studiert in München.
d. Ist Herr Zinn Flugkapitän? – ..., ... er fliegt oft ins Ausland.

8. *Bitte, antworten Sie*

a. Rauchen Sie viel?
b. Rauchen Sie Pfeife?
c. Reisen Sie viel?
d. Reisen Sie oft ins Ausland?
e. Wohin reisen Sie?
f. Fliegen Sie auch nach Deutschland?
g. Arbeiten Sie viel?

Lektion 4

1. *Lesen Sie laut*

Hans und Eva Kaufmann wohnen in Nürnberg. Er ist Journalist und sie ist Lehrerin. Heute abend haben sie Gäste. Jetzt sind sie im Supermarkt. Sie brauchen noch ein Schwarzbrot und zwei Weißbrote, eine Dose Sardinen, ein Pfund Käse, drei Pfund Tomaten und eine Ananas. Sie brauchen aber keine Wurst mehr. Sie haben noch genug zu Hause. Sie haben auch noch genug Wein zu Hause, zwei Flaschen Rotwein und vier Flaschen Weißwein. Aber sie haben kein Bier mehr. Sie brauchen sechs Flaschen Bier. Hans kauft auch noch zwanzig Zigaretten und Tabak.

2.

Wer ist das ?–

… … … … .

… … … Nürnberg.

Was ist er von Beruf? –

… … … .

Und wer ist das? –

… … … … .

Wo wohnt sie? –

… … auch … … .

Und was ist sie von Beruf? –

… … … .

Wo sind Hans und Eva Kaufmann heute abend? –

Sie sind … … .

Sie haben … .

3. *Lesen Sie laut*

Sie, sie, sie

Das sind Hans und Eva Kaufmann.
Sie sind im Supermarkt.
Heute abend haben *sie* Gäste.

Das ist Frau Berg.
Sie ist Verkäuferin.
Sie ist aus München, aber
sie wohnt in Berlin.

Guten Abend, Herr Fischer.
Nehmen *Sie* bitte Platz.

Bitte sehr, wie heißen *Sie*?
Und was sind *Sie* von Beruf, Frau Berg?

Meine Damen und Herren, *Sie*
sind heute das Quizteam.

Und jetzt setzen Sie ein

a. Das ist Fräulein Schaumann. Heute abend ist ... im Studio.

b. Das ist Herr Zinn. ... ist Reporter. ... wohnt in Augsburg, aber ...
arbeitet in München.

c. Hier ist das Team. Zuerst fragt Frau Berg: Herr Fischer, reisen ... viel?

d. Fräulein Heim, was sind ... von Beruf?

e. Das ist Frau Berg. ... ist Verkäuferin und ... arbeitet in Berlin.

f. Das sind Hans und Eva Kaufmann. Heute haben ... Gäste.

g. Guten Abend, meine Damen und Herrn. Heute sehen ... das Quiz:
Was sind Sie?

4.

Was brauchen wir denn noch für heute abend?

Wir brauchen noch ... .

Wir brauchen noch ... ...

Wir brauchen ... ...

16

Wir brauchen ... ...

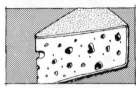

Wir brauchen auch ... ...

Und wir brauchen ... .

5. kein, keine, keinen

a. Wir haben ... Schwarzbrot mehr.
b. Wir haben ... Bier mehr.
c. Wir haben ... Rotwein mehr.
d. Wir haben ... Sardinen mehr.
e. Wir haben ... Käse mehr.
f. Wir haben ... Ananas mehr.

6. kein/nicht

a. Herr Fischer, arbeiten Sie in München? –
Nein, ich arbeite ... in München.
b. Reisen Sie allein? –
Nein, ich reise ... allein.
c. Brauchen wir noch Wurst? –
Nein, wir brauchen ... Wurst mehr.
d. Haben wir noch Bier zu Hause? –
Nein, wir haben ... Bier mehr zu Hause.
e. Brauchen wir noch Zigaretten? –
Nein, wir brauchen ... Zigaretten mehr.
f. Marion raucht ..., und Andreas raucht ... Zigaretten.

7. der, das, die

a. Was kostet ... Schwarzbrot?
b. Was kostet ... Käse?
c. Was kostet ... Ananas?
d. Was kostet ... Dose Sardinen?
e. Was kostet ... Rotwein?
f. Was kostet ... Pfund Tomaten?
g. Was kostet ... Bier?
h. Was kosten ... Tomaten?
i. Was kosten ... Zigaretten?
j. Was kostet ... Tabak?

8.

a. Frau Kaufmann, was brauchen Sie noch? –
... ... ein Schwarzbrot.
b. Brauchen Sie auch Käse? –
Ja, ... ein Pfund Käse.
c. Haben Sie noch genug Wurst? –
Ja, ... zu Hause.
d. Frau Berg, was kosten heute die Tomaten? –
Das Pfund Tomaten ... heute 70 Pfennig.
e. Und was kostet eine Ananas? –
Eine Ananas ... 6 Mark.

9. *Lesen Sie laut*

	DEUTSCHER SUPERMARKT
Das Weißbrot kostet	02,00
Das Schwarzbrot kostet	01,20
Das Pfund Tomaten kostet	00,70
Die Dose Sardinen kostet	01,60
Die Ananas kostet	06,00
Sechs Flaschen Bier kosten	03,00
Der Käse kostet	01,50
Was macht das?	
Das macht zusammen	16,00

18

Lektion 5

1. *Lesen Sie laut*

Herr Neumann hat Hunger und geht in ein Restaurant. Am Fenster sitzen zwei Herren. Er begrüßt sie. Herr Neumann nimmt Platz. Der Ober bringt die Speisekarte. Herr Kühn möchte eine Tomatensuppe und ein Beefsteak. Herr Schneider möchte einen Kalbsbraten und Herr Neumann möchte ein Kotelett. Aber es ist schon spät. Es gibt nur noch Wiener Schnitzel. Der Ober geht in die Küche und bestellt drei Schnitzel.

2. ein, eine, einen

a. Herr Neumann möchte . . . Tomatensuppe.

b. Herr Kühn nimmt . . . Beefsteak.

c. Frau Berg ißt . . . Kalbsbraten.

d. Herr Zinn bestellt . . . Wiener Schnitzel.

e. Herr Schneider trinkt . . . Apfelsaft.

f. Fräulein Schaumann möchte . . . Kaffee.

g. Herr Weiß bestellt . . . Bier.

h. Der Ober bringt . . . Rotwein.

i. Herr Kaufmann raucht . . . Zigarette.

j. Fräulein Heim kauft . . . Ananas.

k. Frau Kaufmann braucht . . . Dose Sardinen.

3. Wie spät ist es jetzt?

a. Es ist jetzt . . . .

b. Es ist schon . . . .

c. Jetzt ist es . . . .

19

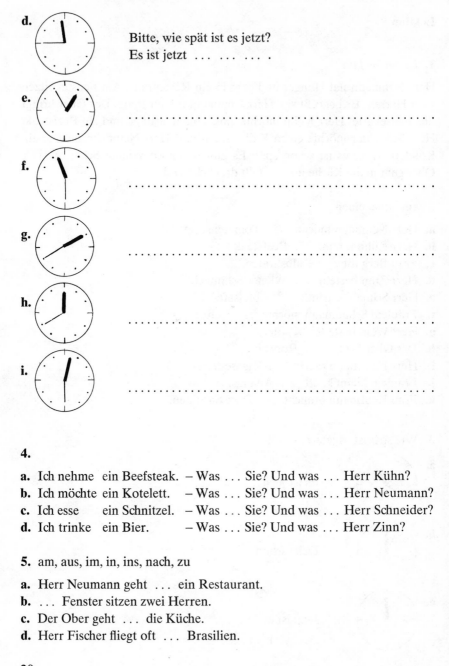

d. Bitte, wie spät ist es jetzt?
Es ist jetzt ... ...

e. ....

f. ....

g. ....

h. ....

i. ....

4.

a. Ich nehme ein Beefsteak. – Was ... Sie? Und was ... Herr Kühn?
b. Ich möchte ein Kotelett. – Was ... Sie? Und was ... Herr Neumann?
c. Ich esse ein Schnitzel. – Was ... Sie? Und was ... Herr Schneider?
d. Ich trinke ein Bier. – Was ... Sie? Und was ... Herr Zinn?

5. am, aus, im, in, ins, nach, zu

a. Herr Neumann geht ... ein Restaurant.
b. ... Fenster sitzen zwei Herren.
c. Der Ober geht ... die Küche.
d. Herr Fischer fliegt oft ... Brasilien.

20

e. Herr Zinn reist oft ... Ausland.

f. Herr Weiß studiert ... München.

g. Fräulein Schaumann ist ... Studio.

h. Woher ist Herr Weiß? – Er ist ... Hamburg.

i. Hans und Eva Kaufmann wohnen ... Nürnberg.

j. Heute abend sind sie ... Hause.

k. Jetzt sind sie ... Supermarkt.

6. was, wer, wie, wo, woher, wohin?

a. ... ist das?

b. ... arbeitet Herr Zinn?

c. ... heißt der Quizmaster?

d. ... studiert Herr Weiß?

e. ... ist Frau Berg von Beruf?

f. ... arbeitet sie?

g. ... ist sie – aus München?

h. Herr Fischer, ... fliegen Sie?

i. ... kauft er in Brasilien?

j. ... brauchen wir noch?

k. ... sind Sie heute abend?

7. der, das, die

Was kostet ... Tomatensuppe?	– Die Tomatensuppe kostet 00,80
.... Beefsteak?	– 05,40
.... Kotelett?	– 04,20
.... Wiener Schnitzel?	– 06,30
.... Kalbsbraten?	– 05,90
.... Apfelsaft?	– 00,70
.... Kaffee?	– 00,90
.... Bier?	– 01,10
Das macht zusammen	.....

Lektion 6

1. *Lesen Sie laut*

Herr Kaufmann ist Journalist. Er reist oft ins Ausland. Er fliegt oft nach England und Amerika. New York und London kennt er sehr gut. Aber heute ist er in Stuttgart, und Stuttgart kennt er nicht gut. Er möchte zum Fernsehstudio. Zuerst fährt er zum Hauptbahnhof. Dann fährt er zum Marktplatz und zum Rathaus. Dort fragt er einen Herrn, wie man zum Fernstehstudio kommt.

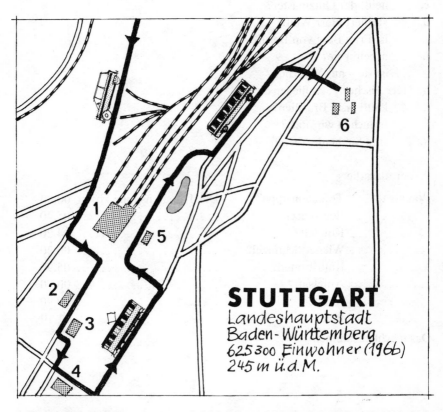

1 Hauptbahnhof, *2* Hauptpostamt, *3* Schloßplatz, *4* Marktplatz, *5* Omnibusbahnhof, *6* Fernsehstudio

2. Wie fährt Herr Kaufmann in Stuttgart?

a. zum Marktplatz
Zuerst fährt er immer ... . Dann fährt er nach ... zum Schloßplatz.
Von da ist der Marktplatz nicht mehr ... .

b. zum Fernsehstudio
Am Marktplatz nimmt Herr Kaufmann ... . Die hält am ... .
Dort nimmt er ... ... und fährt zum ... .

3. *Setzen Sie ein:* fährt, hält, ißt, nimmt, sieht

a. Der Quizmaster sagt:
Nehmen Sie bitte Platz.   – Herr Fischer ... Platz.

b. Der Student aus Nigeria sagt:
Fahren Sie zuerst zum Haupt-   – Herr Kaufmann ... zum Hauptbahnhof.   bahnhof.

c. Der Herr sagt:
Die Straßenbahn und der Bus   Aber er kennt Stuttgart nicht gut.
halten am Rathaus.   – Nur der Bus ... am Rathaus.

d. Sehen Sie die Kirche?   – Von dort ... man das Rathaus
und den Marktplatz.

e. Herr Schneider fragt:
Was essen Sie?   – Ich esse ein Beefsteak und Herr
Neumann ... einen Kalbsbraten.

4. *Jetzt antworten Sie*

a. Wohin möchten Sie?   –   ... ... Marktplatz.
b. Wo wohnen Sie?   –   ... ... Schloßplatz.
c. Wohin fahren Sie?   –   ... ... Fernsehturm.
d. Wohin gehen Sie?   –   ... ... Studio.

5. der, das, die

a. Entschuldigung, wo sitzt Herr Schneider? – ... sitzt dahinten am Fenster.
b. Bitte, wohin fährt der Bus? – ... fährt zum Rathaus.
c. Entschuldigen Sie, kennen Sie Fräulein Schaumann? – Tut mir leid, ...
kenne ich nicht.

d. Arbeitet Herr Zinn immer noch in Augsburg? – Nein, ... arbeitet jetzt in München.

e. Studiert Eva immer noch? – Nein, ... ist jetzt Lehrerin.

f. Entschuldigen Sie, wo ist das Rathaus? – ... ist am Marktplatz.

g. Entschuldigen Sie, wohnt hier Herr Weiß? – Ja, aber ... ist heute nicht zu Hause.

6. *Setzen Sie das richtige Wort ein:*

a. Bitte, wie komme ich ... Marktplatz?

b. Tut mir leid, ich kenne Stuttgart ... gut.

c. Ich nehme immer ... Bus, ... hält dahinten.

d. Die Straßenbahn hält ... Rathaus.

e. Fahren Sie ... diese Richtung.

f. Am Schloßplatz ist ... Kirche, ... dort sieht man das Rathaus.

7.

> Kaufen Sie Tabak? (in Brasilien)
> Kaufen Sie in Brasilien Tabak?

a. Er fliegt nach Stockholm. (oft)

b. Herr Kaufmann ist in Stuttgart. (heute)

c. Das macht sechzehn Mark. (zusammen)

d. Ich trinke einen Kaffee. (nachher)

e. Fahren Sie zum Hauptbahnhof! (zuerst)

f. Fliegen Sie nach Südamerika? (allein)

Lektion 7

1. *Lesen Sie laut*

Herr Fuchs ist ärgerlich. Sein Wagen ist kaputt. Seine Uhr steht. Sein Flugzeug geht um 9 Uhr 30. Er möchte sofort zum Flughafen fahren, aber sein Flugschein liegt im Büro. Es kommt keine Straßenbahn und kein Bus. Also geht er zu Fuß ins Büro, aber er hat nicht mehr viel Zeit.

2.

Herr Fuchs hat es . . . .
Sein Wagen ist . . . .
Was macht er?
Er geht . . . . . . ins Büro.

Herr Fuchs kommt ins Büro.
Was macht . . . Sekretärin?
. . . schreibt gerade . . . Brief.

Herr Fuchs sieht auf . . . Uhr, aber . . .
Uhr steht. Seine Sekretärin sieht auf . . .
Uhr und sagt: Es ist halb neun.

3. mein, meine, ihr, ihre

a. Fräulein Heim, wann geht mein Flugzeug? –
. . . Flugzeug geht um 9 Uhr 30.

b. Wann beginnt meine Besprechung? –
... Besprechung beginnt um 11 Uhr.

c. Wann kommt mein Taxi? –
... Taxi kommt sofort.

d. Wo ist mein Flugschein? –
... Flugschein liegt hier im Büro.

e. Wann geht meine Maschine? –
... Maschine geht um 9 Uhr 30.

f. Wo sind meine Papiere? –
... Papiere liegen hier.

4. Ihr, Ihre, Ihren

Im Restaurant sitzen drei Herren. Sie haben es eilig.

a. Herr Ober, wann bringen Sie meinen Kalbsbraten? –
Augenblick, ich bringe ... Kalbsbraten sofort.

b. Wann bringen Sie meine Tomatensuppe? –
..., ich bringe ... Tomatensuppe sofort.

c. Wann bringen Sie mein Schnitzel? –
..., ich bringe ... Schnitzel sofort.

d. Wann bringen Sie unser Bier? –
..., ich bringe ... Bier sofort.

e. Wann bringen Sie unseren Kaffee? –
..., ich bringe ... Kaffee sofort.

f. Wann bringen Sie unsere Schnitzel? –
..., erst bringe ich ... Getränke.

5.

Fräulein Heim hat heute nicht viel Zeit. Um zehn Uhr ... sie Herrn Baumann ... und ... die Besprechung ... 11 Uhr. Dann ... ... das Hotel Vier Jahreszeiten ... und ... einen Tisch ... 12 Uhr. Nachher ... sie die Werkstatt ....

Lektion 8

1. *Lesen Sie laut*

Fräulein Heim ruft die Werkstatt an. Sie möchte den Wagen zur Reparatur anmelden. Der Wagen hat eine Panne und steht am Hauptbahnhof. Jemand muß zum Hauptbahnhof fahren und den Wagen abschleppen. Aber Herr Meier kann jetzt niemand hinschicken. Es ist niemand frei.

2.

Fräulein Heim ruft die Werkstatt an.
Autohaus Neureuther, ...
... Firma Fuchs. Ich möchte einen Wagen ... ... anmelden. –
Augenblick, ich ... ... Werkstatt.

... ... Herr Meier. ... Heim.
Herr Meier, unser Wagen ... ... –
Wo steht denn Ihr Wagen? –
... ... Hauptbahnhof.

Was fehlt denn? – Das weiß ich nicht.
Ich glaube, sie ... ... abschleppen. –
Tut mir leid, das geht nicht.
Im Moment ist ... frei.
Wir haben heute ... ...

3.

a. Können Sie den Wagen heute nachmittag abschleppen? –
Ja, aber ... ... erst den Autoschlüssel herbringen.

b. Können wir morgen zusammen essen gehen? –
Ja, aber ich glaube, ... einen Tisch bestellen.

c. Können Sie morgen nach Frankfurt fliegen? –
Ja, aber ... ... sofort ein Ticket bestellen.

4. kann, muß

a. Können Sie heute den Kundendienst machen? –
Das ... ... jetzt nicht sagen. Ich ... erst nachsehen.

b. Können Sie morgen nachmittag ins Studio kommen? –
Tut mir leid, ich ... nach Hamburg fliegen.

c. Können Sie unsere Besprechung auf morgen verschieben? –
Das ... ... jetzt nicht sagen. Ich ... erst Herrn Fuchs fragen.

5. mich, ihn, Sie

a. Herr Fuchs ist jetzt nicht im Büro. Aber Sie können ... heute abend zu Hause anrufen.

b. Ich bin heute leider nicht frei. Können Sie ... morgen abholen?

c. Herr Fuchs ist heute nicht im Büro. Aber ich kann ... mit Fräulein Heim verbinden.

d. Mein Wagen ist kaputt und steht am Bahnhof.
Können ... ... abschleppen?

6.

> (Ich brauche heute keinen Wagen.)
> Herr Fuchs, brauchen Sie heute einen Wagen? –
> Nein, heute ... ... keinen Wagen.

a. (Sie sehen heute das Quiz.)
Guten Abend, meine Damen und Herren. Heute ... ...

b. (Kaufmanns haben heute abend Gäste.)
Sind Kaufmanns heute abend zu Hause? –
Ja, heute abend ... ...

c. (Mein Taxi kommt in einer Viertelstunde.)
Möchten Sie jetzt noch Kaffee trinken? –
Nein, danke, in einer Viertelstunde ... ...

28

d. (Die Maschine geht um 9 Uhr 30.)
Haben Sie es eilig? –
Ja, um 9 Uhr 30 ... ...
e. (Ich gehe morgen mit Herrn Baumann essen.)
Sind Sie morgen mittag im Büro?
Nein, morgen mittag ... ...
f. (Wir haben heute sehr viel Arbeit.)
Können Sie heute den Kundendienst machen? –
Tut mir leid, heute ... ...

7.

Um Viertel vor zwölf ruft Herr Weiß Fräulein Heim im Büro an. Er möchte mit Fräulein Heim essen gehen. Aber Fräulein Heim hat keine Zeit. Sie muß Herrn Baumann anrufen und die Besprechung verschieben. Sie muß im Hotel Vier Jahreszeiten einen Tisch bestellen. Sie muß den Wagen zur Reparatur anmelden. Dann muß sie den Schlüssel in die Werkstatt bringen und nachher muß sie noch fünf Briefe schreiben.

Antworten Sie für Fräulein Heim
Guten Tag, Fräulein Heim. Hier ist Michael Weiß. Wie geht's? –
. . . .
Haben Sie heute Zeit? Gehen wir zusammen essen? –
Tut mir leid, Herr Weiß, ... (viel Arbeit, keine Zeit)
Na gut, aber können wir nicht morgen zusammen essen gehen? –
Ja, das geht . . . . (vor elf Uhr anrufen)

Lektion 9

1. *Lesen Sie laut*

Herr Baumeister und sein Freund wollen in Österreich Urlaub machen. Sie fahren per Anhalter nach Salzburg. Dort wollen sie eine Woche bleiben. Sie wollen die Stadt besichtigen und ins Theater gehen. Herr Baumeister will dann in die Schweiz fahren, vielleicht nach Genf. Er möchte wieder mal Französisch sprechen. Sein Freund muß nach Wien weiterfahren. Er trifft dort seinen Bruder. Sie wollen zusammen nach Teheran fahren, auch per Anhalter.

2.

a. Wohin wollen Sie? –
   Ich ... nach Salzburg.
b. Wo wollen Sie Urlaub machen? –
   Wir ... in Österreich ... .
c. Wo wollen Sie studieren? –
   Ich ... in München ... .
d. Was macht Ihr Freund? –
   Er ... per Anhalter nach Teheran ... .
e. Warum machen Sie keinen Urlaub? –
   Ich ... nächstes Jahr ein Haus ... .
f. Warum stehen die zwei Studenten an der Autobahn? –
   Sie ... per Anhalter nach Salzburg ... .

30

3.

Guten Tag! ... ... mitnehmen? –
Wohin ... ...
... ... Salzburg.
Gut, ... Ihr Gepäck ... ...
auf den Rücksitz ... .
Mein Kofferraum ist ... .

Rauchen Sie?
Nein, danke. ... ...
Woher ... ... ? –
Ich ... aus Hamburg.
Mein Freund ist Perser. ... ... aus Te-
heran.

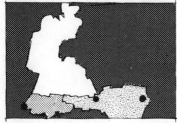

... ... in Österreich Urlaub machen? –
Ja. – ... ... eine Woche in Salzburg.
... ... die Stadt besichtigen und ins
Theater gehen.

4.

> Legen Sie Ihr Gepäck bitte auf den Rücksitz.
> Sie müssen Ihr Gepäck auf den Rücksitz legen.

a. Bestellen Sie bitte einen Tisch im Hotel Vier Jahreszeiten.
b. Rufen Sie bitte Herrn Baumann an.
c. Rufen Sie bitte die Taxizentrale an und bestellen Sie einen Wagen.
d. Verschieben Sie bitte unsere Besprechung auf morgen.
e. Fahren Sie in diese Richtung. Dann kommen Sie zum Hauptbahnhof.
f. Schicken Sie bitte sofort einen Wagen in die Ludwigsstraße.
g. Bringen Sie den Schlüssel bitte vor zwei Uhr in die Werkstatt.

5.

> Warum wollen Sie nicht in Köln arbeiten? –
> (Mein Freund arbeitet in München.)
> Weil mein Freund in München arbeitet.

a. Warum ist Fräulein Heim noch nicht im Büro?
Ihr Auto ist kaputt.
b. Warum will Herr Fuchs die Besprechung verschieben?
Er muß nach Frankfurt fliegen.
c. Warum brauchen wir noch Brot?
Wir haben heute abend Gäste.
d. Warum gibt es nur noch Wiener Schnitzel?
Es ist schon zwanzig vor drei.
e. Warum nehmen Sie nicht die Straßenbahn?
Ich habe es eilig.
f. Warum müssen Sie sparen?
Ich will nächstes Jahr ein Haus bauen.
g. Warum können Sie den Wagen nicht abschleppen?
Wir haben heute sehr viel Arbeit.
h. Warum können wir den Wagen nicht morgen holen?
Herr Fuchs braucht ihn spätestens morgen mittag.

6.

> Fräulein Heim ruft die Werkstatt an.
> Fräulein Heim muß die Werkstatt anrufen.

a. Herr Fuchs geht zu Fuß ins Büro.
Herr Fuchs muß . . . .
b. Ich melde heute meinen Wagen zur Reparatur an.
Ich möchte heute . . . .
c. Herr Meier schickt heute nachmittag jemand hin.
Herr Meier kann . . . .
d. Wir gehen heute abend ins Theater.
Wir möchten . . . .

e. Er macht nächstes Jahr überhaupt keinen Urlaub.

Er kann ....

f. Ich nehme Sie bis Salzburg mit.

Ich kann ....

g. Legen Sie Ihr Gepäck auf den Rücksitz.

Sie müssen Ihr Gepäck ....

h. Ich steige hier aus.

Ich will ....

7.

a. Er spricht Französisch.

Er möchte ....

b. Er trifft in Wien seinen Bruder.

Er will in Wien ....

c. Von hier sieht man den Fernsehturm.

Von hier kann man ....

d. Ich bin um 9 Uhr 30 in Frankfurt.

Ich muß um 9 Uhr 30 ....

e. Herr Sommerfeld ist um 11 Uhr im Studio.

Herr Sommerfeld muß um 11 Uhr ....

8. uns, mich, ihn

a. Ich möchte einen Wagen zur Reparatur anmelden.

Können Sie ... mit der Werkstatt verbinden?

b. Herr Baumann wartet seit einer Stunde.

Können Sie ... anrufen?

c. Ich brauche den Autoschlüssel.

Sie müssen ... herbringen.

d. Herr Weiß wohnt schon seit drei Monaten hier.

Kennen Sie ... ?

e. Herr Kaufmann kennt Nürnberg gut.

Fragen Sie ..., wo der Marktplatz ist.

f. Wir wollen nach Salzburg.

Können Sie ... mitnehmen?

g. Dort am Fenster sitzt Herr Sommerfeld.

Können Sie ... sehen?

9.

> Möchten Sie keinen Kaffee mehr? –
> (Ich muß um ein Uhr wieder im Büro sein.)
> Doch, aber ich muß um ein Uhr wieder im Büro sein.

a. Rauchen Sie überhaupt nicht? –
   (Ich rauche Pfeife.)
b. Können Sie den Kundendienst heute nicht machen? –
   (Im Moment ist niemand frei.)
c. Können Sie mich nicht mit Herrn Meier verbinden? –
   (Er spricht gerade.)
d. Können Sie unsere Besprechung nicht verschieben? –
   (Ich muß erst Herrn Baumann anrufen.)
e. Fliegt Herr Fuchs heute nicht nach Berlin?
   (Seine Maschine geht erst um drei Uhr.)

Anhalter werden besonders gerne mitgenommen, wenn sie Ausländer ...

... oder Akademiker sind.

Lektion 10

1. *Lesen Sie laut*

Herr und Frau Fuchs haben Besuch. Sie sitzen im Wohnzimmer und trinken Kaffee. Sie sprechen über ihre Kinder, über den nächsten Urlaub, über das Fernsehen und über den Sport. Herr Fuchs hat keine Zeit zum Lesen, weil er sich jeden Krimi ansieht. Früher hatte er viel Zeit zum Lesen und zum Wandern. Einmal ist er von München bis nach Innsbruck gewandert. Er hat Sport getrieben. Er hat zwei Instrumente gespielt. Im Sommer ist er durch ganz Europa gereist und im Winter ist er Ski gefahren. Aber früher war er nicht verheiratet. Er hatte keine Kinder, kein Haus, kein Auto – und keinen Fernseher.

2.

Das haben Sie früher alles gemacht?

> Hören Sie oft Beat? –
> Nein, jetzt nicht mehr. Früher habe ich oft Beat gehört. Aber früher hatte ich auch keinen Fernseher.

Hören Sie oft Beat? – (kein Fernseher)

Spielen Sie noch Gitarre? – (kein Beruf)

Spielen Sie jeden Tag Tennis? –
(keine Kinder)

Fahren Sie im Winter oft Ski? –
(nicht so viel Arbeit)

3.

Waren Sie schon einmal in Griechenland? –
Nein, ich war noch nie in Griechenland.

a. Waren Sie schon einmal in Salzburg? –
Nein, ... noch nie ... .
b. War Herr Fuchs gestern im Büro? –
Nein, gestern ... ... in Frankfurt.
c. Waren Ihre Söhne heute nachmittag im Kino? –
Nein, heute nachmittag ... ... zu Hause.
d. Waren Sie und Ihre Frau gestern abend nicht zu Hause? –
Nein, gestern abend ... ... im Kino.
e. War Eva heute in der Schule? –
Nein, ... in der Stadt.

4.

Kennen Sie Hamburg? –
Nein, ich war noch nie in Hamburg.

36

a. Kennt Herr Weiß Frankfurt? –
Nein, ...

b. Kennen Sie und Ihre Frau Wien? –
Ja, ... im Urlaub ... .

c. Kennt Ihre Tochter Griechenland? –
Ja, sie (und ihr Freund) ... letztes Jahr ... .

5.

a. Waren Sie gestern abend zu Hause? –
Ja, wir ... Besuch.

b. War Herr Fuchs heute mittag im Büro? –
Ja, ... viel Arbeit.

c. Hatten Sie früher ein Auto? –
Nein, ... ein Motorrad.

d. War Fräulein Schaumann heute im Studio? –
Nein, ... eine Besprechung.

6.

a. Wie geht es Herrn Kaufmann? –
Das weiß ich nicht. Ich habe ... schon lange nicht mehr gesehen.

b. Wie geht es Fräulein Heim? –
Das wissen wir nicht. Wir haben ... seit drei Wochen nicht mehr gesehen.

c. Und wie geht es Hans und Eva? –
Das weiß Thomas auch nicht. Er hat ... schon lange nicht mehr gesehen.

7.

Wir gehen zu Fuß. Wir haben kein Auto.
Wir sind zu Fuß gegangen, weil wir kein Auto hatten.

a. Wir fahren nicht nach Griechenland. Wir haben keinen Urlaub.

b. Er geht nicht ins Kino. Er hat kein Geld.

c. Sie bleibt zu Hause. Sie hat Gäste.

d. Herr Fuchs und Herr Baumann gehen essen. Sie haben Hunger.

e. Ich bleibe in München. Ich habe keinen Paß.

Sonntag, 7. Oktober

Deutsches Fernsehen

Die Krimi-Sensation ab 74: Horst Tappert als Inspektor Derrik!

).15 **Die Vorschau.** Hinwe⸱ das
Programm der Woch⸱
0.45 **ARD-Ratgeber**⸱
1.30 **Die Sendu**⸱
2.00 **Der in**⸱
2.45 **Woc**⸱
13.15 **Maga**⸱
14.15 **Wie**⸱
14.30 **Si**⸱

16.30

die ⸱ ⸱rforschung des
⸱abyrinths
⸱⸱ ⸱e (2., Erstsendung 12. 2.

⸱portschau

Weltspiegel. Auslandskorrespon-
denten berichten

19.30 **Die Sportschau**
20.00 **Tagesschau** mit Wetterkarte
⸱⸱.15 **Roulette in Rabat.** König Hassan
⸱ sein Regime. Autor: Gerhard

⸱⸱ll Mattei

„Auf falscher Spur"

Englischer Meister-Krimi

Zweites Deut⸱⸱⸱

9.45 **Jugoslavijo, dobar dan** (s/w)
10.30 **Vorschau**
11.00 **D**⸱
11.30
12.00

12.50 **Fr**⸱
13.00 **D**⸱
13.
14.
14.4⸱
15.10
15⸱

Ein großes
us Milten-
3 Mespel-

⸱rofessor
⸱renzen

Vⸯ
sch⸱

A.

⸱gramm

rikanischer Sp⸱⸱
1953 (Erstsendung am ⸱⸱⸱
he Vorschau)

17.00 **Die Sport-Reportage**
18.00 **⸱⸱eute**
18.05 **⸱ Sorgenkind**
18.7⸱
1⸱

⸱r katholischen

⸱hwarze⸱
⸱⸱her

Der neue Krimi

⸱⸱eg. **Deutsch** (28)
⸱ **Mathematik** (s/w). (2.)

entdecku⸱⸱
⸱chäologie

18.45 **Problem** Fortsc⸱⸱⸱
zum Umweltschutz (s⸱⸱ne Vorscl

⸱asser

Fallstud
⸱⸱⸱e Vorscl
⸱ nach

f. Herr Kühn fliegt nicht nach Hamburg. Er hat viel Arbeit.

g. Wir fahren per Anhalter. Wir haben kein Geld.

8.

> Spielen Sie heute nachmittag Tennis? –
> Nein, ich mache meine Hausaufgaben.
> Haben Sie gestern nachmittag Tennis gespielt? –
> Nein, ich habe meine Hausaufgaben gemacht.

a. Arbeitet Hans heute in der Werkstatt? –
Nein, er fährt in die Stadt.

b. Sehen Sie sich heute abend das Quiz an? –
Nein, ich lese einen Krimi.

c. Spielen Sie heute nachmittag Fußball? –
Nein, ich treffe meine Freundin.

9.

> Worüber sprechen Sie?
> Wofür interessieren Sie sich?

a. Herr Fuchs, wofür interessieren Sie sich? –
... ... nur für meinen Beruf.

b. Interessiert sich Fräulein Heim für ihre Arbeit? –
Nein, ... nur für ihren Chef.

c. Worüber sprechen Herr und Frau Kaufmann? –
Ach, ... schon wieder über ihr Haus.

d. Wofür interessiert sich Ihr Sohn? –
... ... nur für Autos.

10. *Antworten Sie*

> Nein, ich interessiere mich nicht für ... .
> Ja, ich interessiere mich sehr für ... .

a. Spielen Sie Fußball?

b. Gehen Sie oft ins Theater? (das Theater)

c. Lesen Sie Goethe?

d. Spielen Sie ein Instrument? (Musik)

e. Machen Ihre Kinder wenigstens die Hausaufgaben? (die Schule)

f. Spielt Thomas Fußball? (Sport)

g. Haben Sie gestern abend den Krimi gesehen? (Krimis)

„... aber heute haben wir
wirklich ein gutes Programm!"

11.

Er hat seine Tochter gesehen. (schon lange nicht mehr)
Er hat seine Tochter schon lange nicht mehr gesehen.

a. Unsere Jungen spielen Gitarre. (sehr gut)

b. Machen Ihre Söhne ihre Hausaufgaben? (wenigstens)

c. Meine Söhne sind durch ganz Europa gereist. (per Anhalter)

d. Ich war in Hamburg. (noch nie)

e. Ich mache das Abendessen. (schnell)

f. Wir haben sehr viel Arbeit. (heute)

g. Gibt es einen Krimi? (heute abend/im Fernsehen)

Lektion 11

1. *Lesen Sie laut*

Martina und Klaus haben Gäste zum Abendessen eingeladen. Martina
hat Wurst- und Käsebrote gemacht. Auch ein paar Salate hat sie gemacht.
Klaus hat den Wein auf den Balkon gestellt. Er hat das Bier in den Kühlschrank gelegt und er hat Zigaretten geholt. Jetzt sitzen Martina und Klaus
im Wohnzimmer und warten. Sie warten schon seit acht Uhr, aber ihre
Gäste kommen nicht. Sie können das nicht verstehen. Ihre Gäste haben
auch nicht angerufen. Aber sie haben die Einladung nicht vergessen. Sie
hatten eine Panne und sind zu Fuß zum nächsten Bahnhof gegangen.

2.

Hast du den Wein auf den Balkon ge-
stellt? –
Ja, der Wein ... auf dem Balkon.
Hast du das Bier in den Kühlschrank
gelegt? –
Ja, das Bier ... im Kühlschrank.

... ... die Salate gemacht? –
... ... auf dem Kühlschrank.
... ... die Biergläser gespült? –
Ja, sie ... auf dem Tisch.
... ... Zigaretten geholt? –
Ja, sie ... auf dem Hocker im Flur.

... du Brigitte und Werner eingeladen? –
Ja, ... sie gestern abend angerufen
und sie eingeladen.

3.

> Bist du fertig? –
> Ja, ich muß nur noch die Salate machen.

a. . . . . die Gläser auf den Tisch . . . .
b. . . . . das Bier in den Kühlschrank . . . .
c. . . . . ein paar belegte Brote . . . .
d. . . . . eine Platte . . . .
e. . . . . den Hocker auf den Flur . . . .

4.

> Peter kommt nicht.
> Sag mal, für wann hast du ihn eigentlich eingeladen?

a. Der Tisch ist nicht frei.
b. Der Wagen ist immer noch kaputt.
c. Das Taxi kommt nicht.

5.

Ihr Freund ruft Sie an und stellt ein paar Fragen.
Antworten Sie

> Warum hast du heute nicht Tennis gespielt? –
> Weil ich keine Zeit hatte.

a. Warum bist du nach Frankfurt geflogen?
b. Warum hast du die Einladung vergessen?
c. Warum hast du nicht angerufen?
d. Warum bist du zu Fuß ins Büro gegangen?
e. Warum bist du nicht mit dem Taxi gefahren?
f. Warum bist du jetzt ärgerlich?

6.

> Kannst du das Bier aus der Küche holen?
> Hol bitte das Bier aus der Küche!

a. Kannst du den Wein aus der Küche holen?

b. Kannst du das Bier in den Kühlschrank legen?

c. Kannst du eine Platte auflegen?

d. Kannst du den Wagen in die Werkstatt bringen?

e. Kannst du einen Augenblick am Apparat bleiben?

f. Kannst du heute um fünf Uhr den Wagen aus der Werkstatt holen?

g. Kannst du nachher die Zeitung ins Wohnzimmer bringen?

7.

Worauf freuen Sie sich?

a. Ich ... ... auf den Urlaub.

b. ... du ... auf das Konzert?

c. Er ... ... auf den Krimi.

d. Die Gäste ... ... auf das Abendessen.

e. Frau Berg, ... schon auf Ihren Urlaub in Griechenland?

f. Monika ... ... auf den Fernseher, aber Hans interessiert ... nur für Krimis.

g. Herr Neumann ... ... auf das Wiener Schnitzel.

8.

Wohin hast du die Wurst und den Käse gelegt?

....

Wo steht der Wein?

....

Wohin hast du meine Pfeife gelegt?

....

43

Woher kommst du jetzt?

. . . .

Wo steht dein Wagen?

. . . .

Wo war er den ganzen Tag?

. . . .

9. *Setzen Sie ein:* ich will, du willst usw.

a. Wie lange . . . . . wir denn noch warten?

b. Wo bleibt Brigitte nur? . . . . . du sie nicht mal anrufen?

c. Ruf doch Brigitte und Werner an und frage sie, wann sie kommen . . . . . .

d. . . . . . ihr heute abend zu uns kommen?

e. Warum . . . . . ihr denn schon gehen?

f. Wir . . . . . heute einmal früher zu Bett gehen.

g. Herr Schneider, ... Sie mit uns ins Kino gehen?

Lektion 12

1. *Lesen Sie laut*

Ein Gespräch am Telefon
„Hallo, Monika! Wo ist denn dein Bruder?"
„Thomas liegt im Bett und schläft. Er hat den ganzen Abend auf dich gewartet. Um zehn Uhr wollte er dich anrufen, aber es hat sich niemand ge-
meldet. Da hat er sich gedacht, du kommst doch nicht mehr und hat sich
im Fernsehen einen Krimi angesehen. Dann hat er eine Flasche Rotwein
getrunken und eine Schachtel Zigaretten geraucht. Weißt du, er hat sich ein
wenig geärgert, weil er doch heute mit dir ins Kino gehen wollte. Um halb
zwölf ist er dann ins Bett gegangen."
„Aha, und ich sitze seit zwei Stunden zu Hause und warte auf einen Anruf
von Thomas. Und vorher habe ich eine halbe Stunde vor dem Kino auf ihn
gewartet. Natürlich wollten wir heute zusammen ins Kino gehen. Aber wir
wollten uns doch vor dem Kino treffen. Aber das hat er wohl vergessen!"
„Das tut mir leid, Ingrid."
„Ist gut, Monika. Jetzt kann man nichts mehr machen. Aber sag Thomas,
morgen habe ich keine Zeit!"

2.

Klaus und Martina haben den ganzen
Abend auf ihre Gäste ... .
Um halb zehn haben sie ..., aber ...
... niemand ... . Da haben sie ..., sie
kommen nicht mehr und haben ... .

Aber Klaus und Martina konnten nicht
kommen. ... ... Unfall. Aber es
ist ihnen nichts ... . Sie sind nämlich
ganz langsam ... . Der Wagen vor
ihnen hat plötzlich ..., und sie sind
... .

3.

Früher mußte ich jeden Tag zehn Stunden arbeiten.

a. Früher ... ich jeden Tag eine Stunde Klavier spielen.
b. Warum ... du gestern abend zu Hause bleiben?
c. Werner ... seine Eltern zum Bahnhof bringen.
d. Das Auto war kaputt. Wir ... es abschleppen.
e. Wir hatten keine Zeit. Meine Eltern ... allein an den Tegernsee fahren.
f. Warum ... ihr schon um fünf Uhr in Wien sein?

4.

Warum konntest du nicht ins Kino gehen? –   Ich mußte meine Hausaufgaben machen.   Ich konnte nicht ins Kino gehen, weil ich meine Hausaufgaben machen mußte.

a. Warum konntest du in Salzburg nicht mehr Kaffee trinken? –
   Ich mußte um fünf Uhr in Wien sein.
b. Warum konntest du ihn nicht abholen? –
   Ich mußte mein Auto in die Werkstatt bringen.
c. Warum konntet ihr nicht zum Abendessen kommen? –
   Wir mußten unsere Gäste zum Flughafen bringen.
d. Warum konnten Sie gestern abend den Krimi nicht mehr ansehen? –
   Ich mußte heute morgen sehr früh im Büro sein.

5.

Warum hast du mich gestern abend nicht angerufen? –   Mein Telefon war kaputt.   Ich wollte dich gestern abend anrufen, aber mein Telefon war kaputt.

a. Warum habt ihr uns gestern abend nicht abgeholt? –
   Unser Auto hatte eine Panne.
b. Warum hat Thomas heute morgen nicht Tennis gespielt? –
   Monika hatte keine Zeit.

c. Warum sind Herr und Frau Kaufmann gestern nicht nach Österreich gefahren? –
Ihre Pässe waren nicht in Ordnung.

d. Warum hat Werner den Wagen nicht in die Werkstatt gebracht? –
Du hattest den Autoschlüssel.

e. Warum seid ihr nicht schon früher nach Hause gefahren? –
Wir haben am Tegernsee Freunde getroffen.

6.

> Wolltest du nicht mitfahren? –
> Doch, aber ich hatte Kopfschmerzen.
> Warum wolltest du nicht mitfahren? –
> Weil ich Kopfschmerzen hatte.

a. Wolltest du nicht in Berlin studieren? –
Doch, aber meine Freundin wohnt jetzt in München.

b. Wolltet ihr gestern abend nicht Fußball spielen? –
Doch, aber wir waren sehr müde.

c. Wollten sie nicht ins Kino gehen? –
Doch, aber im Fernsehen war ein Krimi.

7.

a. Weißt du, wo mein Paß ist?
... Paß liegt auf dem Tisch im Wohnzimmer.

b. Wissen Sie, wann meine Maschine ankommt?
... Maschine kommt um 17.35 Uhr an.

c. Weißt du noch, was mein Bruder gesagt hat?
... Bruder hat gesagt, er kommt morgen zurück.

d. Wißt ihr, wo unser Gepäck steht?
... Gepäck steht im Flur.

e. Wißt ihr noch, wo unser Wagen steht?
... Wagen steht doch in der Ludwigstraße.

f. Weißt du, was unsere Tickets kosten?
Ich glaube, ... Tickets kosten zusammen 460 Mark.

g. Weißt du, wo meine Pfeife liegt?
... Pfeife liegt auf dem Hocker im Flur.

8. *Setzen Sie ein:* bestellen, bringen, einladen, interessieren, kaufen, stellen, treffen, trinken, verpassen.

a. Peter hat deinen Vater schon nach Hause ... .
b. Thomas, hast du heute wieder deinen Zug ... ?
c. Gestern habe ich deine Freundin in der Stadt ... .
d. Wo hast du dein Auto ... ?
e. Ich habe dein Abendessen wieder in den Kühlschrank ... .
f. Warum hast du deinen Freund nicht ... ?
g. Wann habt ihr eure Tickets ... ?
h. Habt ihr euer Bier schon ... ?
i. Monika hat sich schon immer für deinen Bruder ... .

9.

> Wir haben gewartet. (den ganzen Abend)
> Wir haben den ganzen Abend gewartet.
> (*oder*: Den ganzen Abend haben wir gewartet.)

a. Wir haben den ganzen Abend gewartet. (auf euch)
b. Wir haben angerufen. (um halb zehn)
c. Wir konnten nicht kommen. (gestern/leider)
d. Meine Eltern sind gekommen. (heute morgen)
e. Wir wollten zurückfahren. (um fünf Uhr/nach dem Kaffeetrinken)

Lektion 13

1. *Lesen Sie laut*

Kaufmanns bekommen heute viel Besuch

„Sag mal, wieviel Personen sind wir eigentlich heute abend?"

„Claudia kommt mit ihrem Mann. Werner kommt mit seiner Freundin. Die kenne ich übrigens noch nicht. Monika wollte erst allein kommen. Ihr Mann mußte nämlich gestern nach Hamburg fahren. Aber sie hat mich heute morgen angerufen. Sie kommt mit ihrer Freundin. Herr Meier kommt mit seiner Frau. Er weiß aber noch nicht genau, wann er kommen kann. Wir sind also zusammen zehn Personen."

„Dann müssen wir im Wohnzimmer schnell ein wenig Platz machen."

2. ihr, ihre usw.

Fräulein Heim telefoniert mit ... Chef. Er hat nämlich ... Flugschein vergessen.

Herr Kaufmann geht mit ... Frau zum Einkaufen. Am Sonntag kommen nämlich ... Freunde aus Italien.

Thomas fährt mit ... Freund per Anhalter nach Salzburg.

Brigitte hat mit ... Mann und ... Eltern einen Ausflug an den Tegernsee gemacht. Dort haben sie auch ... Freunde getroffen.

Herr und Frau Fuchs sehen mit ... Gästen fern. Sie wollen nämlich nicht schon wieder über ... Kinder sprechen.

3. anrufen, bringen, gehen, kommen, sagen, vergessen, warten

a. Wir haben den ganzen Abend auf ihn ... .

b. Aber er ist mit seiner Freundin ins Kino ... .

c. Nachher hat er sie nach Hause ... .

d. Er hat erst um halb elf Uhr bei uns ... .

e. Da haben wir ihn gefragt, warum er nicht ... .

f. Aber er hat gar nichts ... .

g. Ich glaube, er hat unsere Einladung ... .

4. an, auf, aus, bei, gegen, im, in, ins, zum

a. Um elf Uhr klingelt ... Kaufmanns das Telefon.

b. Hans ist noch ... Bad.

c. Eva geht ... Wohnzimmer.

d. Hans will mit Peter ... Fußball.

e. Claudia und ihr Mann kommen ... Düsseldorf.

f. Claudia schläft ... unserem Schlafzimmer.

g. Bernd schläft ... Wohnzimmer.

h. Hol bitte die Luftmatratze ... dem Keller.

i. Meine Eltern wollten heute einen Ausflug ... den Tegernsee machen.

j. Am Sonntag spielt Bayern München ... Schalke 04.

50

5.

a. Morgen kommt Herr Kühn aus Düsseldorf. Fräulein Heim kann ... abholen.
b. Mein Wagen ist kaputt. Ich muß ... zur Reparatur anmelden.
c. Habt ihr morgen Zeit? Wir möchten ... zum Essen einladen.
d. Meine Eltern sind gestern zurückgefahren. Wir haben ... zum Bahnhof gebracht.
e. Tut mir leid, Peter. Ich wollte ... anrufen, aber du warst nicht zu Hause.
f. Kaufmanns sind wieder zurück. Wir haben ... gestern in der Stadt getroffen.

6.

a. Am Montag hatten wir Besuch. Claudia und ihr Mann waren bei ... .
b. Wollt ihr am Dienstag kommen? – Ja, gern. Wir waren schon lange nicht mehr bei ... .
c. Entschuldigen Sie, kann ich bei ... telefonieren?
d. Meiers wohnen jetzt in Augsburg. Wir waren am Mittwoch bei ..... .
e. Kennt ihr Kaufmanns? – Ja, wir spielen jede Woche mit ... Tennis.

7. *Setzen Sie ein:* Unfall, Gäste, Pech, Panne, Küche, Kundendienst, Urlaub, Hobbyraum

a. Am Samstag abend konnten wir nicht ins Kino gehen. Wir hatten nämlich ... .
b. Ich mußte mein Auto in die Werkstatt bringen. Ich hatte nämlich eine ... .
c. Kaufmanns wollten schon um fünf Uhr zu Hause sein. Aber sie hatten einen ... .
d. Wir wollten eigentlich bis nach Wien fahren. Aber wir hatten ... mit dem Auto.
e. Herr Meier konnte den ... nicht machen, weil er keine Zeit hatte.
f. Warum könnt ihr keinen ... machen? Habt ihr keine Zeit?
g. Am Sonntag habe ich den ganzen Abend in der ... gearbeitet.
h. Abends sitzt mein Mann die ganze Zeit im ... und hört Beat.

8. *Setzen Sie ein:* mich, dich, ihn, sie usw.

  a. Verbinden Sie . . . bitte mit Herrn Meier.

  b. Herr Kühn, meine Frau möchte . . . gern kennenlernen.

  c. Sag mal, kann ich . . . heute mittag treffen.

  d. Ist Peter wieder zurück? – Ja, ich habe . . . heute morgen in der Straßenbahn getroffen.

  e. Meine Brieftasche ist weg. – Heute morgen hast du . . . noch gehabt.

  f. Mein Wagen ist in der Werkstatt. – Wann bekommst du . . . wieder?

9. *Bitte, antworten Sie*

Was machen Sie am nächsten Sonntag?

  a. Machen Sie einen Ausflug?

  b. Gehen Sie zum Fußball?

  c. Spielen Sie selbst Fußball?

  d. Bleiben Sie heute abend zu Hause?

  e. Besuchen Sie Freunde oder bekommen Sie Besuch?

  f. Müssen Sie arbeiten, lesen Sie ein Buch oder machen Sie überhaupt
nichts?

10.

Am Samstagabend klingelt bei Ihnen das Telefon. Ein Freund ruft Sie an,
weil er mit Ihnen einen Ausflug machen möchte oder weil er Sie zum Kaffeetrinken einladen möchte. Was sagen Sie zu ihm?

  a. Tut mir leid, das geht nicht. Ich mache morgen schon einen Ausflug mit
meinen Eltern.

  b. Tut mir leid, ich habe keine Zeit. Ich muß arbeiten.

  c. Nein, ich gehe morgen mit Peter zum Fußball.

  d. Nein, ich möchte morgen zu Hause bleiben.

  e. Tut mir leid, das geht nicht. Wir bekommen morgen Besuch.

Lektion 14

1. *Lesen Sie laut*

Das ist gar nicht so einfach.

Manfred braucht Geld. Er möchte nämlich im Sommer nach Griechenland fahren. Zur Zeit arbeitet er im Hotel Hamburger Hof. Heute hatte er sehr viel Arbeit. Erst mußte er den Gästen im dritten Stock das Frühstück bringen. Dann mußte er dem Zimmermädchen helfen. Um zehn Uhr war im Konferenzzimmer eine Besprechung. Er mußte also in den zweiten Stock fahren und den Herren Kaffee, Saft und Whisky bringen. Mittags mußte er dem Ober im Restaurant helfen. Am Nachmittag mußte er zum Reisebüro gehen und Karten für die Stadtrundfahrt holen. Um fünf Uhr waren die Herren mit ihrer Besprechung fertig. Dann mußte er das Konferenzzimmer aufräumen. Beim Abendessen mußte er wieder im Restaurant helfen. Er war erst um elf Uhr zu Hause, und er war schrecklich müde.

2.

> Entschuldigen Sie, ich habe nicht verstanden.
> Wem soll ich helfen?
> (Der Ober im Restaurant braucht Sie.)
> Helfen Sie dem Ober im Restaurant.

a. Wem soll ich den Tee bringen? –
   (Die Dame von Zimmer sechs möchte ihren Tee.)
b. Wem soll ich den Brief schicken? –
   (Herr Zinn hat immer noch nicht geantwortet.)
c. Wem soll ich die Theaterkarten bringen? –
   (Die Gäste von Zimmer siebzehn haben Theaterkarten bestellt.)
d. Wem soll ich das sagen? –
   (Seine Sekretärin wollte es wissen.)
e. Wem soll ich die Tickets schicken? –
   (Mein Chef braucht sie spätestens bis morgen mittag.)
f. Wem soll ich helfen? –
   (Herr Meier braucht Sie in der Werkstatt.)

3.

Was soll ich machen?

a. Wohin ... ich den Schlüssel bringen?

b. Wo ... Fräulein Heim anrufen?

c. Warum ... ich zu Hause bleiben?

d. Wo ... du den Wagen abholen?

e. Wann ... die Arbeit fertig sein?

f. Herr Kühn, Sie ... in einer Viertelstunde zum Chef kommen.

g. Herr Meier spricht gerade. ... ich Sie mit seiner Sekretärin verbinden?

h. Kaufmanns haben heute abend keine Zeit. Wir ... morgen kommen.

4. bei, beim, vom, zu, zum

a. Herr Meier soll die Gäste ... Bahnhof bringen.

b. Wann soll Fräulein Schaumann ... Ihnen kommen?

c. Melden Sie sich bitte ... Ober im achten Stock.

d. Wir können ... meinem Bruder übernachten.

e. Kommt doch noch. Ihr könnt auch ... uns fernsehen.

f. Bestellen Sie meine Tickets bitte ... Reisebüro.

g. Ich habe Claudia ... Kaffee eingeladen.

5.

a. Weißt du, wann deine Eltern kommen? –
Nein, ich habe noch nicht mit ... gesprochen.

b. Kann Herr Zinn zu unserer Besprechung kommen? –
Das weiß ich nicht. Ich habe noch nicht mit ... telefoniert.

c. Weiß Ihr Chef, wann Sie nach Frankfurt fliegen? –
Nein, ich habe es ... noch nicht gesagt.

d. Ihre Frau ist am Apparat. Sie braucht den Autoschlüssel. –
Das verstehe ich nicht. Ich habe ihn ... heute morgen gegeben.

e. Die Dame am Fenster hat es eilig. Sie möchte ihr Frühstück. –
Ich weiß, ich bringe es ... sofort.

6. wem *oder* wen?

a. Mit ... sind Sie nach Salzburg gefahren?

b. Bei ... haben Sie die Karten geholt?

c. Herr Kühn ist nicht zu Hause. . . . soll ich jetzt anrufen?

d. Für . . . soll ich den Tisch reservieren?

e. Bei . . . hast du in Düsseldorf übernachtet?

f. Sie sind doch zu einer Besprechung nach London gefahren. . . . haben Sie dort getroffen?

g. . . . . hast du meine Beatplatten gegeben?

7. brauchen

a. Bis wann . . . ihr Chef den Wagen wieder?

b. Wir . . . drei Karten für die Stadtrundfahrt.

c. Kann ich heute das Auto haben? – Ja, ich . . . es nicht.

d. Thomas . . . ein Zelt für seine Griechenlandreise.

e. Hier ist dein Paß. . . . du ihn?

f. Ihr . . . kein Taxi. Wir können euch nach Hause bringen.

8.

a. Zimmer 13 ist im (1.) . . . Stock.

b. Zimmer 24 ist im (2.) . . . Stock.

c. Für Sie ist Zimmer 35 reserviert. Das ist im (3.) . . . Stock.

d. Das Restaurant ist im (15.) . . . Stock.

e. Die Herren im Konferenzzimmer haben noch eine Flasche Wein bestellt. Das ist schon die (6.) . . . Flasche.

9.

Der Chef ist ganz schön wütend.
Du solltest doch den Herren im Konferenzzimmer eine Flasche Whisky bringen.
Und wem hast du sie gebracht?

a. Du solltest doch der Dame von Zimmer sechs das Frühstück bringen. Und wem . . . .

b. Du solltest doch dem Ober im Restaurant helfen.

Und wem ... ...?

c. Du solltest doch den Empfangschef anrufen.

Und warum ... ...?

d. Du solltest doch zwanzig Theaterprogramme holen.

und warum ... ... nicht ...?

e. Du solltest doch das Konferenzzimmer aufräumen.

Und warum ... ...?

10.

Sie wissen: Herr Kaufmann ist Journalist. Er reist viel.

---

4. Januar/Rom

Am 4. Januar (= am vierten ersten) war er in Rom.

5.–11. Januar/Athen

Vom 5.–11. Januar (= vom fünften bis zum elften ersten) war er in Athen.

---

a. 3. Februar/Madrid

b. 7.–13. März/London

c. 9.–17. Mai/New York und San Francisco

d. 6. Juni/Kopenhagen

e. 8.–18. Juli/Stockholm und Helsinki

f. 9.–19. August/Südamerika

g. 14.–22. September/Türkei (!) und Persien

Lektion 15

1. *Lesen Sie laut*

Das Geburtstagsgeschenk

Am 16. September hat Renate Geburtstag. Aber Dieter weiß noch nicht, was er ihr schenken soll. Das ist auch gar nicht so einfach. Er weiß, Renate wünscht sich schon lange ein kleines Auto. Aber das kann er ihr natürlich nicht schenken, weil er nicht so viel Geld hat. In der Stadt hat Dieter eine schöne, schwarze Pelzjacke gesehen. Aber die war sehr teuer. Die kann er ihr vielleicht in zehn Jahren kaufen. Er hat sich auch eine braune Handtasche angesehen. Die war sehr schön und gar nicht teuer. Aber Dieter hat gedacht: „Vielleicht steht Renate Braun nicht" – und hat sie nicht gekauft.

Also, was soll er ihr schenken? Ein Buch, eine Platte oder eine goldene Uhr? – Oder einen Ring? Ja, der freut sie sicher. Dieter hat schon ein bißchen Geld gespart. Er muß nur noch ein paar Mal am Samstag im Supermarkt arbeiten, dann kann er ihr den Ring kaufen.

2.

Was wünscht sich Renate? Raten Sie mal.
Sie wünscht sich
a. ein . . . .
b. eine . . . .
c. einen . . . .

Was ist das?
Es ist . . . . Es ist . . . . Es ist nicht . . . .
Es ist nicht sehr . . . . Aber es ist auch
nicht . . . .
Es ist ein . . . .

3.

> Ich habe heute in der Stadt einen gelben Pullover gesehen.
> Aber er war nicht billig.

a. ein gelber Pullover – nicht billig
b. eine rote Handtasche – nicht schön
c. eine weiße Pelzjacke – ganz schön teuer
d. ein langes Kleid – sehr teuer

4.

a. billig, kaputt
  Thomas hat sich ein ... Motorrad gekauft.
  Leider war es ....
b. weiß, teuer
  Heute habe ich mir eine ... Handtasche gekauft.
  Sie war aber sehr ....
c. nett, verheiratet
  Monika hat gestern einen ... Mann kennengelernt.
  Leider war er schon ....
d. golden, billig
  Dieter hat Renate einen ... Ring mitgebracht.
  Ich glaube, der war nicht ....

5.

> Du wolltest doch schon immer einen gelben Pullover.
> Hier ist ein gelber Pullover.

a. Wünscht du dir nicht schon lange einen roten Sportwagen?
  Hier steht ... ...
b. Du wolltest doch schon immer ein kleines Zelt kaufen.
  Hier steht ... ...
c. Gestern haben wir einen schönen Ausflug gemacht.
  Ja, das war ... ...
d. Ich fahre nach Griechenland und brauche ein großes Zelt.
  Sehen Sie hier, das ist ... ...

e. Das Studio A braucht einen guten Reporter.

Ich glaube, Herr Zinn ist ... ...

f. Ich habe noch Hunger. Haben wir noch belegte Brote?

Ja, auf dem Kühlschrank liegt noch ein ... .

6. sich wünschen

a. Ich ... mir einen langen Urlaub.

b. Was ... du dir? – Ein schweres Motorrad.

c. Karin ... sich eine kleine Tochter.

d. Wir ... uns schon lange ein großes Klavier.

e. Ihr ... euch doch schon lange einen Fernseher.

f. Herr Baumann hat mich gefragt, was Sie sich zum Geburtstag ... .

g. Die Kinder ... sich einen Zug und einen kleinen Bahnhof.

7. mir, dir, ihm, ihr ... .

a. Sag mal, Peter, wer hat ... das gesagt?

b. Eva hatte sehr viel Arbeit. Aber Hans hat ... geholfen.

c. Andreas hat gestern seine Pfeife vergessen. Ich habe sie ... heute gebracht.

d. Fräulein Heim, haben Sie die Schlüssel? – Ja, Herr Fuchs hat sie ... gegeben.

e. Herr Fuchs, wer hat ... das gesagt?

f. Wir haben viel Platz. Warum habt ihr eure Kinder nicht zu ... geschickt?

g. Seine Eltern sind ärgerlich, weil er ... nicht geschrieben hat.

h. War Peter hier? – Nein, aber ich habe mit ... am Telefon gesprochen.

i. Renate hat sich eine weiße Handtasche gewünscht. Aber Dieter hat ... eine gelbe geschenkt.

8.

a. Auf Wiedersehen, Herr Fuchs! Ich wünsche ... eine gute Reise.

b. Hallo, Renate! Ich wünsche ... alles Gute zum Geburtstag.

c. Wo fliegt ihr hin? Nach New York? Da wünschen wir ... einen guten Flug.

d. Was, ihr fahrt per Anhalter nach Teheran? Da wünsche ... ich aber viel Glück.

9. viel *oder* viele?

a. Im August hatten wir sehr ... Arbeit.

b. Ich muß jetzt gehen. Ich habe heute nicht ... Zeit.

c. Wir haben noch ... Wünsche, aber leider haben wir nicht mehr ... Geld.

d. Ich war im Winter schon zwei Wochen beim Skifahren. Jetzt habe ich nicht mehr ... Urlaub.

e. Unsere Gäste haben ... Wein getrunken und ... belegte Brote gegessen.

f. Wir haben nicht ... Gepäck, wir sind mit dem Motorrad gekommen.

g. Es gibt noch ... Karten für das Konzert am Sonntag.

10. geben, treffen

a. Was ... es heute abend im Fernsehen?

b. Haben Sie rote Pullover? – Nein, im Augenblick ... es nur grüne.

c. Kennen Sie Herrn Kühn? – Ja, ich ... ihn samstags immer auf dem Fußballplatz.

d. Fräulein Heim, ... Sie die Schlüssel Herrn Meier.

e. Du hast doch jetzt ein Auto. Warum ... du dein Motorrad nicht deinem Bruder?

f. Kannst du das Buch bitte Thomas ...? Du ... ihn doch heute.

g. Fräulein Heim, haben Sie mein Ticket? – Nein, das habe ich Ihnen gestern ... .

h. Heute mittag habe ich deinen Bruder in der Stadt ... .

i. Fährst du mit an den Tegernsee? – Ja, wann ... ihr euch?

11.

Viele Deutsche kaufen sich ein Haus oder eine Ferienwohnung am Meer in Spanien. Möchten Sie ein Haus in Spanien?

a. Ja, aber dann brauche ich mehr Urlaub.

b. Nein, ich möchte ein Haus in Italien.

c. Nein, ich kaufe mir ein kleines Zelt, dann kann ich übernachten, wo ich will.

d. Ja, natürlich möchte ich ein Haus in Spanien, aber ich habe nicht so viel Geld.

e. In Deutschland habe ich nur eine Wohnung mit zwei Zimmern. Ich kann mir doch kein Haus in Spanien kaufen.

Ferienhäuser, Ferienwohnungen im Ausland

Gran Canaria

■ **Machen Sie mehr aus Ihrem Geld** ■ **Kaufen Sie eine Ferienwohnung in Spanien** ■ **An der Costa del Sol** ■ **Direkt am Meer**

Lektion 16

1. *Lesen Sie laut*

Vorübergehend geschlossen – Bin verreist

„Sagen Sie mal, was ist denn hier los? Was soll das heißen: Vorübergehend geschlossen – Bin verreist? Wie lange ist denn die Wirtschaft schon geschlossen? Vor vierzehn Tagen war ich noch mit meiner Frau und meinen Kindern hier und habe Kaffee getrunken und Kuchen gegessen."

„Ja wissen Sie denn nicht, Herr Neumann hat vor ein paar Tagen im Lotto gewonnen – eine Million!"

„Donnerwetter, und was macht er jetzt?"

„Tja, das weiß ich nicht genau. Gestern hat er dieses Schild geschrieben, hat sich ein Taxi bestellt und ist in die Stadt gefahren. Dort hat er erst eingekauft, ist dann in ein Reisebüro gegangen und hat sich ein paar Tickets gekauft. Dann ist er nach Hause gefahren, hat seine Koffer gepackt und hat mir den Hausschlüssel gebracht. Ich wollte Herrn Neumann noch zum Flughafen bringen, weil er so viel Gepäck hatte. Aber er hat sich wieder ein Taxi genommen und ist allein zum Flughafen gefahren. Und nun weiß ich natürlich nicht, wann er wieder kommt."

„Tja, dann muß ich wohl in der nächsten Zeit am Sonntag zu Hause Kaffee trinken."

2.

Wer war Fritz Neumann?

a. Fritz Neumann ... eine kleine Wirtschaft in der Nähe von Bremen.

b. Sonntags ... viele Spaziergänger zu ihm.

c. Sie ... bei ihm Kuchen und ... Kaffee.

d. Er ... seinen Gästen das Essen und die Getränke.

e. Herr Neumann ... nicht viel Geld, aber er ... ganz gut leben.

f. Weil er allein ..., ... er nie Urlaub machen.

g. Er ... jede Woche im Lotto. (spielen)

h. Eines Tages ... der Briefträger und ... :
Herr Neumann, ...

3.

> Er bestellte ein Taxi und fuhr in die Stadt.

a. am Marktplatz aussteigen – in ein Reisebüro gehen

b. die Gäste zum Bahnhof bringen – nachher ein Bier trinken

c. die Koffer packen – nach Berlin fahren

4.

> Wir wollten in einem billigen Restaurant essen.
> Wir aßen in einem billigen Restaurant.

a. Er wollte mir meinen Mantel bringen.

b. Ich wollte in die Stadt fahren und einkaufen.

c. Wir mußten jeden Tag um zehn Uhr ins Bett gehen.

d. Wir konnten erst nach dem Abendessen kommen.

e. Aus Wien wollte er seiner Freundin einen langen Brief schreiben.

5.

> Herr Neumann brachte seinen Gästen Kaffee und Kuchen.

a. Herr Fuchs kaufte ... Söhnen einen alten Volkswagen.

b. Herr Neumann schrieb ... Freunden aus New York eine Karte.

c. Warum gibst du ... Frau nicht das Auto?

d. Frau Kaufmann fährt mit ... Kindern in Urlaub.

e. Wir zeigten ... Gästen die Stadt.

f. Sie fuhren mit ... Eltern an den Tegernsee.

g. Dieter schenkt ... Freundinnen immer Ringe zum Geburtstag.

h. Thomas ist mit ... Mutter in die Stadt gefahren.

6. in einen/ein/eine

a. Am Flughafen stiegen wir ... ... Taxi.

b. Wir packten alles ... ... Koffer.

c. In Salzburg gingen Thomas und sein Freund ... ... Konzert.

d. Er ging zu Fuß zum Marktplatz, dort stieg er ... ... Straßenbahn.

e. In der Nähe von Bremen ging mein Auto kaputt und ich mußte es ...
... Werkstatt bringen.

f. Wir hatten Hunger und gingen ... ... kleine Wirtschaft.

g. Wir waren schon sehr müde, aber nach zwei Stunden kamen wir ... ...
kleine Stadt.

h. Dort gingen wir ... ... Postamt und riefen zu Hause an.

7.

Eines Tages kam ... ... und brachte ihm ...
... .

Er ging in ein Kaufhaus und kaufte zehn ...
und drei ... .

Er sagte zu dem Verkäufer: Ich brauche zwanzig
... und drei ... .

Weil Herr Neumann lange verreisen wollte, kaufte er auch zwölf ... ... und fünfundzwanzig ... .

Jetzt brauchte er nur noch fünf große ... und einen ... .

8.

> Viele Spaziergänger kamen zu ihm. (sonntags)
> Sonntags kamen viele Spaziergänger zu ihm.

a. Der Briefträger kam. (eines Tages)
b. Er bestellte ein Taxi und fuhr in die Stadt. (dann)
c. Er ging in ein Reisebüro. (nachmittags)
d. Er packte seine Koffer. (am nächsten Morgen)
e. Er kam wieder zurück. (nach sechs Monaten)
f. Ein neues Schild hing an der Tür. (am nächsten Tag)

Lektion 17

1. *Lesen Sie laut*

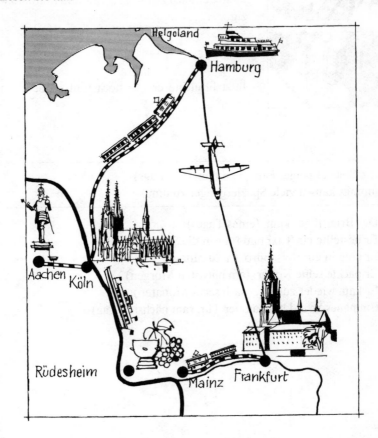

Herr Meier verbrachte dieses Jahr seinen Urlaub ohne Auto. Er fuhr mit seiner Familie mit dem Zug von Frankfurt nach Mainz. Von Mainz nach Köln machte er eine Dampferfahrt. In Rüdesheim unterbrach er die Dampferfahrt und blieb drei Tage dort. Er probierte auch den neuen Wein. In Köln besichtigte seine Frau mit den Kindern den Dom, und er fuhr für einen Tag nach Aachen. Dann fuhr er mit seiner Familie nach Hamburg weiter. Dort blieb er zwei Tage. Das reichte gerade für eine Hafenrundfahrt, das Museum in Altona und einen Bummel durch die Innenstadt.

66

Eigentlich wollte er mit seiner Familie noch für ein paar Tage nach Helgoland fahren. Aber dafür hatte er keine Zeit mehr. Er mußte nämlich am Montag wieder im Büro sein.

2.

a. Der neue Wein ist gut.
Haben Sie den ... Wein schon probiert?

b. Der neue Film von Visconti ist sehr interessant.
Haben Sie den ... Film von Visconti schon gesehen?

c. Die neue Sekretärin ist sehr nett.
Ich habe die ... Sekretärin noch nicht kennengelernt.

d. Das gelbe Kleid ist sehr schön.
Hast du das ... Kleid schon gesehen?

e. Der neue Volkswagen ist sehr schnell.
Haben Sie den ... Volkswagen schon bestellt?

f. Der goldene Ring ist wunderbar.
Ich habe diesen ... Ring in Amsterdam gekauft.

3.

Dafür hatten wir nicht genug Zeit.

a. nicht genug Zeit
Haben Sie auch einen Bummel durch die Innenstadt gemacht? –
Nein, ...

b. Geld
Sind Sie von Hamburg nach Hause geflogen? –
Nein, ...

c. Platz
Haben Sie die beiden Studenten mitgenommen? –
Nein, ...

d. Zeit
Ist dein Freund auch noch in die Schweiz gefahren? –
Nein, ...

e. Platz
Können Hans und Eva nicht bei uns übernachten? –
Nein, ...

4. Setzen Sie ein: besichtigen, bleiben, sich erholen, essen, gehen, gewinnen, unterbrechen, weiterfahren, regnen

a. In Hamburg haben wir das alte Rathaus ... .
b. Im Urlaub haben wir gar nichts ... . Wir haben uns nur ... .
c. In Köln haben sie die Dampferfahrt ... .
d. Warum seid ihr nicht noch ein paar Tage in Hamburg ... ?
e. In Salzburg hat es eine Woche lang ..., da sind wir nach Italien ... .
f. Sie können Herrn Meier leider nicht mehr sprechen, er ist nämlich schon nach Hause ... .
g. Herr Neumann hat jetzt einen teuren Sportwagen. Ich glaube, der hat im Lotto ... .
h. Haben Sie Hunger? – Nein, danke, ich habe schon im Flugzeug ... .
i. Nächste Woche ... wir in die Schweiz ... .

5.

> Wie geht es Herrn Kaufmann? – Das weiß ich nicht. Ich habe ihn schon lange nicht mehr gesehen.

a. Dieter – schon lange nicht mehr
b. Renate – seit drei Monaten
c. Herr und Frau Kühn – seit zwei Jahren
d. dein Bruder – seit meinem Geburtstag
e. deine Freundin – seit dem Urlaub

6. am, an, auf, aus, durch, im, in, ins, nach, von

a. Klaus ist eine Woche ... Salzburg geblieben.
b. Dann ist er per Anhalter ... Salzburg ... Wien gefahren.
c. Ich war ... Urlaub ... der Adria.
d. Thomas ist mit dem Motorrad ... ganz Griechenland gefahren.
e. Herr Meier war mit seiner Familie ... Rhein.
f. Meine Frau ist ... Altona ... Museum gegangen.
g. Unsere Freunde sind gestern ... Italien zurückgekommen.
h. Mein Mann wollte natürlich einen Abend ... der Reeperbahn verbringen.

7.

Wir sind gestern aus dem Urlaub zurückgekommen.

a. Herr Neumann – am Montag – aus Amerika
b. Mein Mann – heute nachmittag – aus Frankfurt
c. Herr Fischer – um neun Uhr – aus Berlin
d. Manfred – vor zwei Stunden – vom Reisebüro
e. Monika – erst um elf Uhr – aus der Stadt

8.

Frau Meier und Frau Berg treffen sich im Supermarkt.
Worüber sprechen sie? – Natürlich über den Urlaub.

„Na, Frau Meier, wohin fahren Sie dieses Jahr im Urlaub?"
„Tja, das ist gar nicht so einfach. Wir müssen dieses Jahr unseren Urlaub leider ohne Auto verbringen. Mein Mann hatte nämlich einen Unfall, und jetzt ist das Auto kaputt. Jetzt wollen wir eine kleine Rundreise durch die Bundesrepublik machen. Unsere Kinder sollen endlich einmal Deutschland kennenlernen."
„Und wie fahren Sie?"
„Von Frankfurt nach Mainz fahren wir mit dem Zug. Von Mainz fahren wir dann mit dem Dampfer weiter bis Köln. In Rüdesheim wollen wir die Dampferfahrt unterbrechen, und mein Mann will den neuen Wein probieren.
In Köln will ich mit den Kindern den Dom besichtigen. Mein Mann fährt für einen Tag nach Aachen und besucht einen Geschäftsfreund. Dann wollen wir noch nach Hamburg fahren. Dort machen wir natürlich eine Hafenrundfahrt und einen Bummel durch die Innenstadt. Mein Mann will auch einen Bummel auf der Reeperbahn machen, ohne Kinder natürlich. Von Hamburg fliegen wir dann nach Hause."
„Wie lange sind Sie denn da unterwegs?"
„Zwei Wochen. Mein Mann hat leider nur vierzehn Tage Urlaub."

Nach zwei Wochen treffen sich Frau Meier und Frau Kaufmann im Supermarkt. Worüber sprechen Sie? – Natürlich über den Urlaub.

„Na, Frau Meier, wo waren Sie dieses Jahr im Urlaub?"
Und nun erzählen Sie weiter.

9. Wie war das Wetter in Europa?

Es hat die ganze Zeit geregnet.
Es hat jeden Tag geregnet.
Ich hatte jeden Tag Regen.

Das Wetter war sehr schön.
Ich hatte jeden Tag Sonne.
Ich hatte wunderbares Wetter.

Das Wetter war gut, aber es hat ein paar Mal geregnet.
Das Wetter war nicht schlecht. Mal hat es geregnet, mal
hat die Sonne geschienen.

> Wo waren Sie im Urlaub? – Ich war in Spanien.
> Und wie war das Wetter? – Ich hatte jeden Tag Sonne.

a. Ich war mit meiner Familie in ... .
b. Wir waren in ... .
c. Herr Meier war im August in ... .
d. Brigitte war mit ihrem Freund in ... .
e. Thomas war mit seinem Freund in ... .
f. Kaufmanns waren mit Freunden in ... .
g. Andreas war mit seiner Frau in ... .
h. Wir waren mit unseren Kindern in ... .

Caravan-Urlaub

„Hoffentlich haben wir nichts vergessen…"

Urlaubsende

„Gott sei Dank – einer weniger …"

Lektion 18

1. *Lesen Sie laut*

„Du, sag mal, Dieter, weißt du ein Zimmer für mich?"

„Wieso, du hast doch ein Zimmer. Du wohnst doch bei deinen Eltern."

„Ja, das ist richtig. Aber ich möchte nicht mehr zu Hause wohnen. Weißt du, jedes Mal, wenn ich spät nach Hause komme, fragt meine Mutter: ‚Wo warst du denn so lange' und ‚Warum kommst du so spät?' Also, wie gesagt, ich brauche ein Zimmer."

„Und wieviel Miete kannst du bezahlen?"

„Na, sagen wir 130 Mark im Monat."

„Und wo soll es liegen?"

„Am besten in der Innenstadt. Du weißt doch, ich habe kein Auto und bin auf den Bus und die Straßenbahn angewiesen."

„Aha, und es soll 25 Quadratmeter groß sein, eine kleine Küche und einen Balkon haben, und die Vermieterin soll jeden Abend pünktlich um sieben das Abendessen bringen. Ganz wie zu Hause! Sag mal, liest du eigentlich nie die Anzeigen in der Zeitung? Weißt du nicht, daß so ein Zimmer heute 250 Mark kostet?"

Zu vermieten: Zimmer

Großes, möbliertes Zimmer zu vermieten an netten Herrn oder Studenten, DM 220,– Tel. 93 63 35, ab 16 Uhr	Nettes, ruhiges Zimmer, Nähe Universität, Küche, Bad, ab sofort zu vermieten, zu besichtigen am Samstag, 23. 7., Tel. 43 21 86
Ab 1. 8. komfortables Zimmer, eigenes WC und Bad, Balkon, 30 qm, Nähe Ludwigsstraße, 5 Min. zur U-Bahn. DM 280,– Tel. 23 76 91	**Viele Zimmer frei** 1-Bettzimmer ab DM 180,– 2-Bettzimmer ab DM 210,– Tel. 59 26 17 – 21

2.

Herr Neubauer geht zur Seefahrtschule. Er hat es mir erzählt.
Herr Neubauer hat mir erzählt, daß er zur Seefahrtschule geht.

a. Ich brauche meinen Wagen spätestens bis morgen mittag. Sagen Sie es Herrn Meier.

b. Herr Fuchs will nächstes Jahr ein Haus bauen. Er hat es heute im Büro erzählt.

c. Renate hat morgen Geburtstag. Dieter hat es vergessen.

d. Fräulein Schaumann kann nicht zu der Besprechung kommen. Herr Sommerfeld weiß es schon.

e. Du sollst dem Ober im Restaurant helfen. Der Chef hat es gesagt.

f. Thomas fährt mit einem Freund nach Griechenland. Monika hat es mir erzählt.

3.

> Interessieren Sie sich für das Zimmer?
> Schreiben Sie sofort, wenn Sie sich für das Zimmer interessieren.

a. Suchen Sie ein Zimmer?
Sie müssen die Anzeigen in der Zeitung lesen, ...

b. Soll ich Ihnen helfen?
Sagen Sie es, ...

c. Brauchen Sie Geld?
Schreiben Sie mir, ...

d. Kommen Sie nicht zu der Besprechung?
Rufen Sie Fräulein Heim an, ...

e. Wollt ihr mit uns an den Tegernsee fahren?
Ruft uns heute abend an, ...

f. Wollen Sie mit Herrn Baumann essen gehen?
Sie müssen einen Tisch bestellen, ...

4.

> Wie hoch ist der Fernsehturm?
> Wissen Sie, wie hoch der Fernsehturm ist?

a. Wie weit ist es bis zum Hauptbahnhof?

b. Wie teuer ist der neue Sportwagen?

c. Wie gut spielt Monika Tennis?

d. Wie oft fliegt Herr Fischer nach Brasilien?

e. Wie lange war Frau Berg in Berlin?

f. Wie oft fährt hier eine Straßenbahn?

g. Wie lang ist der Konferenztisch?

h. Wie hoch ist die Miete für seine Wohnung?

i. Wie spät ist es jetzt?

5. viele, wenige, alle

a. Bitte, schicken Sie ... Zuschriften an den Weserkurier.

b. Sie müssen sich sofort entscheiden, weil wir nur noch ... Zimmer haben.

c. Ich habe schon sehr ... Museen besichtigt.

d. Bitte, hält hier die Linie 17? – Ja, hier halten ... Linien.

e. Haben Sie auch ... wichtigen Geschäftsfreunde besucht?

f. Auf meiner Weltreise habe ich ... nette Leute kennengelernt.

g. Frau Meyerdierks bekam nur ... Zuschriften, weil in ihrem Haus Haustiere verboten sind.

6.

> Wer hat meine Platten mitgenommen?
>
> Weißt du, wer meine Platten mitgenommen hat?

a. Wer kann Herrn Neubauer nach Hause bringen?

Wissen Sie, ...

b. Wer hat die Karten für die Stadtrundfahrt bestellt?

Können Sie mir sagen, ...

c. Wer hat am Sonntag im Fußball gewonnen?

Kannst du mir sagen, ...

d. Wer fährt am Sonntag mit an den Tegernsee?

Herr Meier hat gefragt, ...

e. Wer geht heute abend mit ins Theater?

Monika möchte wissen, ...

f. Wer kann einen so teuren Sportwagen kaufen?

Ich möchte wissen, ...

g. Wer spielt am Samstag gegen Schalke 04?

Hast du gehört, ...

h. Wer interessiert sich für ein altes Akkordeon?

Wißt ihr, ...

i. Wer hat meine Luftmatratze kaputt gemacht?

Weißt du, ...

7. bis zum, bis zur

a. Können Sir mir sagen, wie weit es ..... Werkstatt ist?

b. Von meiner Wohnung ..... Schule sind es nur wenige Minuten.

c. Bitte, können Sie uns ..... Bahnhof mitnehmen?

d. Kann Herr Zinn ..... Straßenbahnhaltestelle mit Ihnen fahren?

e. Wir sind von der Innenstadt ..... Hafen zu Fuß gegangen.

f. Warum fahren Sie nicht mit dem Taxi ..... Marktplatz?

8. *Setzen Sie ein:* daß, wann, warum, wem, wenn, wer, wie, wo, wohin

a. Ich muß noch erwähnen, ... Herr Neumann nach seiner Weltreise kein Geld mehr hatte.

b. Manfred hat vergessen, ... er das Eis bringen sollte.

c. Herr Fuchs ruft Sie an, ... er nach Düsseldorf kommt.

d. Hat dir Monika erzählt, ... sie nicht nach Salzburg gefahren ist?

e. Hat Ihnen Herr Kühn auch erzählt, ... er früher jeden Tag Klavier gespielt hat?

f. Weißt du, ... das ganze Bier getrunken hat?

g. Ich kann dich unmöglich abholen, ... du schon um 17.15 Uhr ankommst.

h. Hans konnte mir auch nicht sagen, ... Eva gegangen ist.

i. Der Briefträger weiß sicher, ... Herr Weiß wohnt.

j. Leider haben Sie nicht erwähnt, ... hoch die Miete ist.

9. *Und hier wieder ein paar Fragen an Sie*

Wo wohnen Sie?

Haben Sie ein Zimmer oder wohnen Sie in einer Wohnung?

Wie groß ist Ihre Wohnung?

Wie viele Zimmer hat Ihre Wohnung?

Haben Sie ein Fahrrad, ein Motorrad, ein Auto, oder sind Sie auf öffentliche Verkehrsmittel angewiesen?

1. *Lesen Sie diese Anzeige*

Wohnen im Olympiapark– alles spricht dafür!

Eigentumswohnungen im olympischen Dorf in München

Hier kaufen Sie Eigentumswohnungen zu marktgerechten Preisen. Davon sollten Sie sich selbst überzeugen. Der Quadratmeterpreis beträgt je nach Komfort zwischen DM 1893,– und DM 1945,–. Vergleichen Sie diese Wohnungen mit anderen Objekten, dann werden auch Sie die Preise günstig finden. Es sind noch Wohnungen mit 3–6 Zimmern zu haben (zwischen 82 qm und 116 qm).

Wo wird Ihnen das sonst noch geboten –
■ nur 4 km zum Marienplatz – mit der U-Bahn brauchen Sie dafür 9 Minuten
■ beste Einkaufsmöglichkeiten im Olymp 1, der neuen Ladenstraße im olympischen Dorf, sowie im Olympia-Einkaufszentrum
■ große Grünflächen, Spielplätze und die olympischen Sportstätten vor der Haustür
■ Schulen, Kindergarten, Kirchen, Hotel, Restaurant, Ärztezentrum und Hallenbäder direkt im olympischen Dorf

Was müssen Sie wissen, wenn Sie im Olympiapark eine Eigentumswohnung kaufen wollen:

a. Wie groß sind die Wohnungen, die Sie dort kaufen können?
b. Wie viele Zimmer haben diese Wohnungen?
c. Liegen die Wohnungen im Olympischen Dorf verkehrsgünstig?
d. Wie viele Kilometer sind es bis zum Marienplatz?
e. Wie lange brauchen Sie dafür mit der U-Bahn?
f. Wo können Sie im Olympischen Dorf einkaufen?
g. Was gibt es noch alles im Olympischen Dorf?

2.

> Wissen Sie, wie hoch dieser Fernsehturm ist? –
> Ja, der ist fast so hoch wie der Eiffelturm.

a. Bitte, können Sie mir sagen, wie groß dieses Zeltdach ist? –
..... (elf Fußballplätze)

b. Haben Sie gehört, wie teuer dieser Sportwagen ist? –
..... (eine Eigentumswohnung)

c. Weißt du, wie alt dieses Restaurant ist? –
..... (das Rathaus)

d. Sag mal, wie gut spielt Monika eigentlich Tennis? –
..... (ihr Bruder)

e. Hat Ihnen Herr Meier auch schon erzählt, wie schnell sein neues Auto
fährt? –
..... (ein Sportwagen)

f. Hast du auf dem Stadtplan nachgesehen, wie weit es von unserem Hotel
in die Innenstadt ist? –
..... (zum Schloßpark)

3. *Setzen Sie ein:* größer, schöner usw.

a. Der grüne Pullover hier ist doch schön. Warum kaufst du dir nicht den
grünen? – Weil der gelbe hier ... ist.

b. Dieses Zimmer ist doch sehr groß. Warum nimmst du es nicht? – Weil
das bei Frau Meyerdierks noch ... ist.

c. Die Wohnungen in Augsburg sind ziemlich teuer. Warum kauft ihr nicht
eine in München? – Weil sie in München noch ... sind.

d. Dieses Buch hier ist sehr interessant. Warum liest du es nicht? – Weil
mein Krimi noch viel ... ist.

e. Dein Bruder spielt sehr schön Geige. Ja, aber früher hat er noch viel ...
gespielt.

4.

a. Das Empire State Building in New York ist sehr hoch. Das ist sicher das
... Gebäude der Welt. – Nein, das neue Bürohaus in Chicago ist noch
... als das Empire State Building.

b. Diese Wohnung ist sehr groß. Das ist sicher die ... Wohnung im ganzen Haus. –
Nein, die Wohnungen im Erdgeschoß sind noch ... als diese Wohnung.

c. Dieses Hotel ist sehr teuer. Das ist sicher das ... Hotel in Hamburg. –
Nein, das Hotel Vier Jahreszeiten ist noch ... als dieses Hotel.

d. Dieses Theater ist sehr schön. Das ist sicher das ... Theater in der Bundesrepublik. –
Nein, das neue Theater in Berlin ist noch ... als dieses Theater.

5.

a. Dieser Fersehturm ist 290 Meter hoch. Ich glaube, das ist der ... Turm der Bundesrepublik.

b. Dieses Zeltdach war wahnsinnig teuer. Ich glaube, das war das ... Dach der Welt.

c. Diese Handtasche ist sehr schön. Ich glaube, das ist die ... Handtasche, die ich je gesehen habe.

d. Dieses Fußballstadion ist sehr groß. Ich glaube, das ist das ... Stadion der Bundesrepublik.

6.

> Sehen Sie den Fernsehturm dort? Der steht im Olympiagelände.
> Der Fernsehturm, den Sie dort sehen, steht im Olympiagelände.

a. Sehen Sie die Straßenbahn dort. Die fährt zum Hauptbahnhof.

b. Das Zeltdach hat euch (doch) so gut gefallen. Das ist jetzt leider kaputt.

c. Gefällt Ihnen der goldene Ring? Der kostet 275 Mark.

d. Diese Anzeige stand im Weser-Kurier. Ich habe sie schon gelesen.

7.

> Warum dürfen Sie keine Reklame machen? – Das ist verboten.
> Ich darf keine Reklame machen, weil das verboten ist.

a. Warum darf Herr Neubauer keine Haustiere halten?

b. Warum darf man nach zehn Uhr nicht mehr Akkordeon spielen?

c. Warum dürfen Kinder nicht in der Fabrik arbeiten?

d. Warum dürfen wir hier nicht Fußball spielen?

e. Warum können Deutsche in der Schweiz keine Häuser mehr kaufen?

8.

> Der Fernsehturm liegt im Norden von München.

a. Wo liegt der Olympia-Park?

b. Wo liegt der Flughafen?

c. Wo liegt der Tierpark?

d. Wo liegt der Schloßpark?

e. Wo liegt das Atomei?

9.

> Warum haben Sie sich einen BMW gekauft? –
> Das hat mir Herr Baumann geraten.

a. Warum haben Sie sich eine Eigentumswohnung gekauft? –
Das hat ... Herr Kühn geraten.
b. Warum rauchst du nur noch fünf Zigaretten am Tag? –
Das hat ... der Arzt geraten.
c. Warum geht Herr Neubauer auf die Seemannsschule? –
Das hat ... sein Lehrer geraten.
d. Warum sind Kaufmanns an die Adria gefahren? –
Das hat ... Frau Weber geraten.
e. Warum hat Fräulein Heim im Hotel Vier Jahreszeiten übernachtet? –
Das hat ... Herr Fuchs geraten.

10. *Und hier noch ein paar Fragen, die Sie sicher beantworten können.*

a. Wie heißen die fünf größten Städte der Erde?
b. Wie heißt der höchste Berg* der Erde?
c. Wie heißt der längste Fluß* der Erde?
d. Wo steht das höchste Gebäude der Welt?
e. Was, glauben Sie, ist das schönste Gebäude der Welt?

---

* (Diese Wörter müssen Sie im Wörterbuch nachsehen!)

Lektion 20

1. *Lesen Sie laut*

Wer verdient schon, was er verdient? *oder* Was ist Gerechtigkeit?
Mit der Gerechtigkeit ist es so eine Sache. Die Leute, die mehr verdienen
als andere, glauben, daß es Gerechtigkeit gibt. Der Ober im Restaurant,
der sehr viel mehr verdienen kann als das Zimmermädchen, das die Betten
macht und die Zimmer aufräumt, glaubt, daß das gerecht ist. Der Flugkapitän, der 6000 oder 7000 Mark mehr verdient als der Lokomotivführer,
glaubt, daß das gerecht ist. Er glaubt das auch, weil er mehr Verantwortung
hat, und weil Fliegen gefährlicher ist als Zugfahren. Daß es Gerechtigkeit
gibt, glaubt auch der Millionär, der mit seiner Firma jedes Jahr ein paar
Millionen verdienen kann. Natürlich hat er mehr Verantwortung als der
Mann, der bei ihm in der Werkstatt arbeitet. Aber man muß doch fragen:
Stimmen die Verhältnisse?

2.

> Unsere Wohnung ist sehr klein. Nächstes Jahr brauchen wir eine größere
> Wohnung.

a. Sein Zimmer ist sehr teuer. Nächsten Monat will er ein ... Zimmer
suchen.

b. Mein Auto ist sehr langsam. Nächstes Jahr will ich mir ein ... Auto
kaufen.

c. Diese Diskussion war nicht sehr interessant. Ich habe schon ... Dis-
kussionen gehört.

d. Der Krimi gestern abend war gut. Ich habe schon oft ... Krimis gesehen.

e. Diese Handtasche ist sehr teuer. Ich möchte gern ... Handtaschen ansehen.

f. Dieser Ausflug war sehr kurz. Nächsten Sonntag wollen wir einen ...
Ausflug machen.

g. Das Wetter in Irland war nicht schlecht. Wir hatten schon oft ... Wetter
im Urlaub.

3.

> Eine Frau verdient weniger als ein Mann.
> Inge findet es nicht richtig, daß eine Frau weniger verdient als ein Mann.

a. Eine Frau muß mehr arbeiten als ein Mann.

b. Ein Lokführer hat weniger Urlaub als ein Flugkapitän.

c. Eine Ansagerin beim Fernsehen verdient mehr als ein Journalist, der jeden Tag zehn Stunden in seinem Büro arbeitet.

4. *Setzen Sie ein:* höher, mehr, langsamer, schneller, weniger

a. Wußten Sie, daß dieser Sportwagen ... gekostet hat als eine Eigentumswohnung?

b. Stimmt es, daß dieser Fernsehturm ... ist als der Eiffelturm?

c. Wußten Sie, daß sein Haus ... gekostet hat als eine Eigentumswohnung?

d. Wußten Sie, daß der neue Sportwagen von Herrn Maier ... fährt als ein Schnellzug?

e. Sie dürfen mir glauben, mein alter Volkswagen fährt ... als eine Straßenbahn.

5.

> Ein Zimmer mit 25 Quadratmetern kostet im Monat 180 Mark.
> Finden Sie es richtig, daß ein Zimmer mit 25 qm im Monat 180 Mark kostet?

a. Studenten müssen in den Ferien arbeiten.
Finden Sie es richtig, ...?

b. Nach zehn Uhr abends darf man nicht mehr Akkordeon spielen.
Findest du es richtig, ...?

c. In der Stadt darf man nur 50 Stundenkilometer fahren.
Es ist sicher richtig, ...

d. Das Rauchen in der Straßenbahn ist jetzt verboten.
Findet ihr das richtig, ...?

e. Das Flugzeug ist das sicherste Verkehrsmittel der Welt.
Stimmt es, ...?

6.

> Ich weiß, daß er kommt.
> Ich weiß nicht, ob er kommt.

a. Er hat geschrieben, daß er kommt.
b. Fräulein Heim hat gesagt, daß sie heute abend ins Konzert geht.
c. Ich weiß, daß das Empire State Building das höchste Gebäude der Welt ist.
d. Hier steht, daß das Verhältnis noch stimmt.
e. Ich weiß, daß die Lufthansa den Piloten höhere Gehälter zahlen will.
f. In der Anzeige steht, daß die Wohnung einen Balkon hat.

7.

> Wir müssen über dieses Problem diskutieren.
> Ich bin der Meinung, daß wir über dieses Problem diskutieren müssen.

a. Das ist eine Ungerechtigkeit.
Ich bin der Meinung, ...
b. Studenten sollen ein Gehalt bekommen.
Sind Sie der Meinung, ... ?
c. Beatmusik ist schrecklich.
Herr Fuchs ist der Meinung, ...
d. Die Lehrer sollen nicht soviel fragen.
Die Schüler sind der Meinung, ...

8.

> Weißt du, wann Herr Neumann heute abend kommt?
> Das kann ich dir nicht sagen. Ich weiß nicht einmal, ob er kommt.

a. Wißt ihr, wo Herr Weiß studiert hat?
b. Wissen Sie, wo Herr Neumann seine Wirtschaft hat?
c. Weißt du, wieviel Miete Herr Neubauer zahlt?
d. Weißt du, wie lange Kaufmanns bei uns übernachten wollen?
e. Wissen Sie, für wann Fräulein Heim einen Tisch bestellt hat?

9.

Ich habe gehört, daß sich Herr Neumann schon wieder ein neues Auto gekauft hat.
Ich möchte wissen, ob sich Herr Neumann schon wieder ein neues Auto gekauft hat.

a. Herr Zinn hat sein Büro jetzt in Augsburg.
   Ich habe gehört, ...

b. Kann Herr Baumann zu der Besprechung kommen?
   Herr Baumann wußte noch nicht, ...

c. Claudia macht mit ihrem Mann Urlaub an der Adria.
   Claudia hat geschrieben, ...

d. Thomas fährt im Sommer nach Griechenland.
   Peter hat mir erzählt, ...

e. Darf ich abends Akkordeon spielen.
   Bitte schreiben Sie mir, ...

f. Möchte Peter bei uns übernachten?
   Peter wollte eigentlich gestern abend anrufen, ...

10.

Ein Lokführer hat die Verantwortung für viele Menschen.
Aber er verdient weniger als eine Stewardeß.
Ein Lokführer hat die Verantwortung für viele Menschen.
Trotzdem verdient er weniger als eine Stewardeß.

a. Herr Fuchs sagt immer, daß die Krimis schlecht sind.
   Aber er sitzt jeden Tag vor dem Fernseher.

b. Dieter hat überhaupt kein Geld.
   Aber er hat Renate einen goldenen Ring gekauft.

c. Herr Zinn findet Beatmusik schrecklich.
   Aber er schenkt seinem Sohn eine Beatplatte zum Geburtstag.

d. Die Zahlen sind von 1969.
   Aber ich glaube, daß das Verhältnis noch stimmt.

e. Das Zimmer von Frau Meyerdierks ist sehr teuer.
   Aber sie hat viele Zuschriften bekommen.

11.

> Ich möchte einen Lokomotivführer mit einem Flugkapitän vergleichen. –
> Einen Lokomotivführer kann man nicht mit einem Flugkapitän vergleichen. –
> Warum kann man einen Lokomotivführer nicht mit einem Flugkapitän vergleichen?

a. ein Flug nach New York – eine Zugfahrt nach Hamburg
b. das neue Theater – ein Supermarkt
c. Schiller – Goethe

12.

> Peter soll nicht selbst nach Hause fahren. Er hat drei Gläser Bier getrunken.
> Ich bin dagegen, daß Peter selbst nach Hause fährt, weil er drei Gläser Bier getrunken hat.

a. Wir machen morgen einen Ausflug. Das Wetter ist sicher schön.
Ich bin dafür, ...
b. Meine Söhne sollen nicht jede Woche ins Kino gehen. Sie müssen für die Schule lernen.
Natürlich bin ich dagegen, ...
c. Seine Frau möchte einen neuen Kühlschrank kaufen. Der alte ist kaputt.
Natürlich ist er dafür, ...
d. Wir fahren mit dem Zug. Das Fliegen ist so teuer.
Ich bin dafür, ...

13. *Setzen Sie ein:* Einwohner, Gäste, Menschen, Leute, Personen

a. Das Olympische Stadion in München faßt 80 000 ... .
b. Stuttgart hatte 1966 etwa 625 000 ... .
c. Im Olympischen Dorf haben während der Spiele 12 000 ... gewohnt.
d. Herr Neumann hat auf seiner Weltreise viele, nette ... kennengelernt.
e. Der Empfangschef teilte allen ... mit, daß sie ihr Gepäck selbst zum Auto bringen müssen.

14. *Lesen Sie diese Anzeige der Lufthansa.*

Stewardessen-Report

für alle, die meinen, daß sie den Beruf Stewardeß besser kennen als eine Stewardeß. Über den Beruf Stewardeß ist schon viel gesagt und geschrieben worden. Tatsache bleibt: Stewardessen fliegen. Rechts sehen Sie den Flugplan von Karin Scheller, 26 Jahre alt, Stewardeß bei der Deutschen Lufthansa seit dem 1. Februar 1969.

Ihr Gehalt ist jetzt nach vier Jahren: DM 1857,– pro Monat. Die Kosten unterwegs bezahlt die Lufthansa. Was mußte sie für diesen Beruf mitbringen? Gute Englischkenntnisse, Kenntnisse in einer zweiten Fremdsprache. Alter, als sie bei uns anfing: 19 Jahre.

Möchten Sie noch mehr wissen über diesen Beruf? Dann fragen Sie doch bitte uns. Schreiben Sie an die

Deutsche Lufthansa
6 Frankfurt am Main, Flughafen

Flug-Einsatzplan		
1. März:	ab Frankfurt	20.20
2. März:	an Nairobi	04.05
3. März:	Aufenthalt Nairobi	
4. März:	ab Nairobi	04.55
	an Johannesburg	08.40
	ab Johannesburg	18.10
	an Nairobi	21.55
5. März:	Aufenthalt Nairobi	
6. März:	Aufenthalt Nairobi	
7. März:	Aufenthalt Nairobi	
8. März:	Aufenthalt Nairobi	
9. März:	ab Nairobi	22.55
10. März:	an Frankfurt	07.00
11. März:	Freier Tag (Frankfurt)	
12. März:	Freier Tag (Frankfurt)	
13. März:	ab Frankfurt	09.05
	Rom—München—Rom	
14. März:	ab Rom	16.05
	Düsseldorf—Hamburg—	
	München	20.55
15. März:	ab München	18.35
	Frankfurt—München	21.20
16. März:	ab München	10.40
	Belgrad—Sofia—	
	Belgrad—München—	
	Frankfurt	18.50
17. März:	Freier Tag (Frankfurt)	
18. März:	Freier Tag (Frankfurt)	
19. März:	Freier Tag (Frankfurt)	

Was meinen Sie?

a. Stimmt es, daß eine Stewardeß nur das Frühstück servieren muß?

b. Für Frauen gibt es wenige Berufe, die interessanter sind als Stewardeß. Stimmt das?

c. Eine Stewardeß kann die ganze Welt sehen und bekommt auch noch ein hohes Gehalt dafür.

d. Was macht eine Stewardeß, wenn sie älter ist als dreißig?

Lektion 21

1. *Lesen Sie laut*

JOHANNES BRAHMS
**Sonate für Violine und Klavier
Nr. 2 A-dur op. 100**
David Oistrach, Violine;
Anton Ginsburg, Lev Oborin, Klavier

LUDWIG VAN BEETHOVEN
**Die Violinsonaten Nr. 1 - 10
Gesamtausgabe**
Natalia Oistrach, Klavier

JOHANNES BRAHMS
**Konzert für Violine und Orchester
D-dur op. 77**
Großes Rundfunk-Sinfonieorchester
der UdSSR; Dirigent David Oistrach

IGOR OISTRACH
BERÜHMTE VIOLINKONZERTE
**Konzert für Violine und Orchester
D-dur op. 61 (Beethoven) · Konzert
für Violine und Orchester D-dur
op. 35 (Tschaikowsky)**
Sinfonieorchester der Moskauer
Staatlichen Philharmonie,
Wiener Symphoniker;
Dirigent David Oistrach

Also, das muß ich euch erzählen. Ich war doch am Freitagabend mit meinem Mann im Konzert. Es war das erste Mal seit zwei Jahren, daß wir wieder im Konzert waren. Früher sind wir ja öfter gegangen. Aber jetzt hat mein Mann immer soviel Arbeit, daß abends die Zeit gerade noch für die Zeitung und für ein wenig Fernsehen reicht.

Nun, wir hatten also zwei Karten für ein Konzert der Berliner Philharmoniker. Die Kleine Nachtmusik stand auch auf dem Programm. Die pfeift mein Mann immer, wenn er samstags in der Badewanne sitzt. Ich höre die Kleine Nachtmusik auch sehr gern, natürlich nicht, wenn sie mein Mann pfeift. Wir freuten uns also beide auf das Konzert. Vor der Pause stand moderne Musik auf dem Programm. Ich glaube, Henze oder Honegger. Ich finde diese Musik ja gräßlich. Aber mein Mann sagt immer: „Moderne Musik kann man nicht anhören wie die Kleine Nachtmusik. Moderne Musik muß man verstehen." – Ich denke da immer: „Warum pfeifst du nicht deine moderne Musik, wenn du in der Badewanne sitzt."

87

Na schön, wir sitzen also im Saal. Ich lese das Programm, weil ich doch endlich auch etwas von moderner Musik verstehen möchte. Mein Mann wartet, daß die Lichter ausgehen. ..... Die gehen aus, der Dirigent kommt herein. Das Publikum applaudiert. Der Dirigent hebt den Stab. Es geht los. Und was glaubt ihr, macht mein Mann? Nach zwei Minuten schließt er die Augen und macht sie nicht wieder auf, bis die beiden Stücke vorbei sind.

In der Pause sage ich zu ihm: „Du hast wohl die ganze Zeit geschlafen, aber moderne Musik ist ja so interessant." – „Nein", sagt er, „ich habe nachgedacht." Ich sage: „Worüber hast du denn nachgedacht?" – „Weißt du", sagt mein Mann und macht eine lange Pause, „ich sollte eigentlich mal eine Platte mit der Kleinen Nachtmusik kaufen."

Na, was sagt ihr dazu?

2. *Erzählen Sie diesen Konzertbesuch noch einmal von:*

„Na schön, wir sitzen also im Saal ....., *aber so:*

„Na schön, wir saßen also im Saal ....

3.

> Wir klingelten dreimal. Endlich machte er auf.
> Wir hatten schon dreimal geklingelt, als er endlich aufmachte.

a. Sie schleppten gerade die kaputten Autos ab. Da kam endlich die Polizei.

b. Das Publikum applaudierte schon lange. Endlich kam der Dirigent herein.

c. Herr Neubauer suchte sehr lange. Endlich fand er ein günstiges Zimmer.

d. Die Dame von Zimmer sechs klingelte dreimal. Endlich brachte der Ober das Frühstück.

4.

> Er kam nicht zu der Besprechung. Wir hatten ihn nicht eingeladen.
> Er kam nicht zu der Besprechung, weil wir ihn nicht eingeladen hatten.

a. Er konnte nicht ins Konzert gehen. Er hatte keine Karte mehr bekommen.

b. Wir konnten ihn nicht anrufen. Wir hatten seine Telefonnummer vergessen.

c. Er konnte nicht mehr Auto fahren. Er hatte zuviel getrunken.

d. Wir konnten leider nicht diskutieren. Nicht alle hatten das Buch gelesen.

5.

> Er saß im Zug. Plötzlich fiel ihm ein: Ich habe meinen Paß vergessen.
> Als er im Zug saß, fiel ihm plötzlich ein, daß er seinen Paß vergessen hatte.

a. Sie saß im Restaurant und hatte schon bestellt. Plötzlich fiel ihr ein: Ich habe mein Geld vergessen.

b. Sie saßen schon eine halbe Stunde im Kino. Plötzlich fiel ihnen ein: Wir haben ja Kaufmanns zum Abendessen eingeladen.

c. Wir waren schon lange im Hotel. (Da) fiel uns plötzlich ein: Wir haben unseren zweiten Koffer am Flughafen vergessen.

6.

> Er kann nicht kommen. Er ist nämlich nach Frankfurt geflogen.
> Er konnte nicht kommen, weil er nach Frankfurt geflogen war.

a. Herr Neumann macht eine Weltreise. Er hat nämlich im Lotto gewonnen.

b. Er fährt sehr langsam. Die Polizei hat ihn nämlich schon einmal verwarnt.

c. Renate hat es eilig. Sie hat sich nämlich mit Dieter verabredet.

d. Thomas kann sich nicht mehr erinnern, wo er Brigitte kennengelernt hat. Er hat nämlich voriges Jahr viele Mädchen kennengelernt.

7.

> Die Musiker stimmen ihre Instrumente. Herr Kreuzer liest das Programm.
> Während die Musiker ihre Instrumente stimmten, las Herr Kreuzer das Programm.

a. Das Publikum applaudiert. Herr Kreuzer sieht sich im Saal um.

b. Die Musiker spielen das erste Stück. Herr Kreuzer denkt an seine Steuererklärung.

c. Die Musiker spielen das zweite Stück. Herr Kreuzer schläft.

d. Die Musiker stimmen ihre Instrumente. Die Lichter gehen aus.

8.

> Herr Kreuzer las das Programm. Dann sah er sich im Saal um.
> Als Herr Kreuzer das Programm gelesen hatte, sah er sich im Saal um.

a. Die Lichter gingen aus. Herr Kreuzer schloß die Augen.

b. Die Musiker spielten das erste Stück. Da wollte Herr Kreuzer nach Hause gehen.

c. Es klingelte dreimal. Aber Herr Kreuzer trank noch schnell ein Glas Sekt.

d. Herr Kreuzer sah den Mann. Da wußte er, daß er ihn von der Universität her kannte.

e. Der Dirigent verbeugte sich dreimal. Herr Kreuzer wachte wieder auf.

9.

> Die Musiker spielten zwei moderne Stücke. Ich fand sie sehr interessant.
> Die Musiker spielten zwei moderne Stücke, die ich sehr interessant fand.

a. Meine Freunde diskutierten über ein interessantes Buch. Ich kannte es noch nicht.

b. Herr Fuchs erzählte von seinem Geschäftsfreund. Er hatte ihn in Aachen kennengelernt.

c. Herr Kreuzer hatte eine Eintrittskarte für ein Konzert. Er hatte es schon im Radio gehört.

d. An der Ecke wartete ein Taxi. Kaufmanns hatten es gerufen.

10.

> Das war die Dame von Zimmer sechs. Sie sollten ihr (doch) das Frühstück bringen.
> Das war die Dame von Zimmer sechs, der Sie das Frühstück bringen sollten.

a. Im Fernsehen spricht heute dieser gräßliche Politiker. Ich möchte ihm schon lange meine Meinung sagen.

b. Das ist Herr Zinn. Ihm gehört der rote Sportwagen.

c. Eben war Herr Schneider hier. Ich wollte ihm mein altes Motorrad verkaufen.

d. Vor der Tür wartet ein Mann. Du hast ihm einmal einen alten Anzug geschenkt.

11.

> Ich muß noch meine Steuererklärung machen.
> Woran denken Sie gerade? – An die Steuererklärung, die ich noch machen muß.

a. Ich habe im Urlaub ein hübsches Mädchen kennengelernt.

b. Ich habe gestern ein schönes Konzert gehört.

c. Ich möchte im Lotto eine Million gewinnen.

d. Dieser Betrüger hat mir neulich einen Gebrauchtwagen verkauft.

e. Ich habe diesen Herrn in der U-Bahn gesehen.

12. *Setzen Sie ein:* einfallen, geben, gehören, hören, kaufen, lesen, nachdenken, nachsehen, verkaufen, verstehen

a. Herr Kreuzer mußte lange ..., bis ihm der Name ... .

b. Ich weiß nicht, ob Herr Kühn morgen hier ist. Ich muß erst ... .

c. Dieses Problem kann man nur ..., wenn man dieses Buch ... hat.

d. Dieses alte Auto hat einmal meinem Bruder ... .

e. Ich habe in der Zeitung ..., daß es noch Karten für das Fußballspiel ... .

f. Wir haben von Kaufmanns ..., daß sie ihr Klavier ... wollen.

g. Weißt du, ob man für dieses Konzert noch Karten ... kann?

13. gut – besser

a. Wie fanden Sie den Krimi gestern? –
Ganz gut, aber den heute fand ich noch ... .
b. Wie findest du diesen Dirigenten? –
Sehr gut, aber Karajan ist ... .
c. Wie finden Sie mein grünes Kleid? –
Ganz schön, aber das rote stand Ihnen ... .

PAULANER ... das gute Bier aus München

1. *Hier sind ein paar Fragen, die Sie sicher beantworten können*

a. Wissen Sie, was ein Hobby ist?
b. Haben Sie ein Hobby?
c. Warum braucht man ein Hobby?
d. Treiben Sie Sport, sammeln Sie Briefmarken, fotografieren Sie oder spielen Sie Karten?

2. *Lesen Sie laut*

Herr Zinn ist Reporter. Heute fragte er einen Mann auf der Straße, ob er ein Hobby hat. Aber der wußte gar nicht, was ein Hobby ist. Der hatte auch gar keine Freizeit. Abends nach der Arbeit mußte er seinem Sohn bei den Hausaufgaben helfen. Dann mußte er mit seinem Hund spazierengehen. Wenn er mit dem Hund wieder nach Hause kam, mußte er den Rasen schneiden. Nach dem Abendessen saß er vor dem Fernseher oder er ging in eine kleine Wirtschaft in der Nähe. Am Samstag ging er mit seiner Frau zum Einkaufen und am Sonntag machte er mit seiner Familie einen Ausflug mit dem Auto. Er ging nicht ins Kino, er spielte nicht Karten. Er spielte auch kein Instrument. Er war in keinem Kegelklub und interessierte sich nicht für Fußball. Er las nie ein Buch. Er hörte keine Platten und er fotografierte nicht. Er trieb keinen Sport und sammelte keine Briefmarken. Als Herr Zinn sagte, daß doch jeder Mensch ein Hobby braucht, sagte er nur: Warum?

3.

> Erst muß Herr Meier den Rasen schneiden, dann muß er mit dem Hund spazierengehen.
> Wenn Herr Meier den Rasen geschnitten hat, muß er mit dem Hund spazierengehen.

a. Erst muß ich meinem Sohn bei den Hausaufgaben helfen, dann muß ich das Garagentor streichen.

b. Erst sehe ich mir den Krimi an. Dann möchte ich ein Buch lesen.

c. Erst muß ich einen Brief an Herrn Baumann schreiben, dann kann ich ins Kino gehen.

d. Erst muß Manfred das Konferenzzimmer aufräumen, dann muß er ins Reisebüro gehen.

4.

> Interessieren Sie sich für moderne Musik? Dann können Sie morgen mit mir ins Konzert gehen.
> Wenn Sie sich für moderne Musik interessieren, können Sie morgen mit mir ins Konzert gehen.

a. Kegeln Sie gern? Dann können Sie am Donnerstag mit mir in den Kegelklub gehen.

b. Interessieren Sie sich für Fußball? Dann müssen Sie sich das nächste Spiel von Hannover 96 ansehen.

c. Sie interessieren sich nur für Beethoven? Dann kann ich mit Ihnen natürlich nicht über Beat diskutieren.

5.

> Wir hatten schon die ganze Innenstadt besichtigt. Da fragte er: Wollt ihr noch das Deutsche Museum ansehen?
> Als wir schon die ganze Innenstadt besichtigt hatten, fragte er, ob wir noch das Deutsche Museum ansehen wollen.

a. Wir waren schon zwei Stunden zu Fuß gegangen. Da fragte uns ein Autofahrer: Soll ich Sie mitnehmen?
b. Er hatte schon zwei Stunden gewartet. Da kam sie und fragte: Bist du böse (ärgerlich)?
c. Sie hatte sich mit Dieter in einem Restaurant verabredet. Da kam Heinz und fragte: Willst du mit mir ins Kino gehen?

6.

> Haben Sie gestern abend den Krimi gesehen? –
> Nein, ich interessiere mich nicht für Krimis.

a. Ich brauche eine Briefmarke für einen Brief ins Ausland. –
Tut mir leid, wir verkaufen keine . . . .
b. Ich möchte einen Mantel. –
. . . gibt es im dritten Stock.
c. Verzeihung, ist hier noch ein Platz frei? –
Tut mir leid, hier sind alle . . . besetzt.
d. Haben Sie schon seine neueste Freundin gesehen? –
Nein, ich interessiere mich auch gar nicht für seine . . . .
e. Hast du einen Wunsch? –
O ja, ich habe sogar sehr viele . . . .

7.

> Können Sie mir sagen, ob es in dieser Gegend ein gutes Restaurant gibt?

a. ein gutes Restaurant
b. ein Fußballplatz
c. ein guter Kegelklub

d. billige Wohnungen
e. ein guter Wein

8.

> Der Kaffee in diesem Restaurant ist sehr gut. –
> Ja, aber früher war er noch besser.

a. Der Kuchen in diesem Restaurant ist sehr gut.
b. Die Mannschaft von Hannover 96 spielt sehr gut.
c. Herr Kühn verdient nicht viel. (!)

9. *Setzen Sie ein:* Ausbildung, Beruf, Freizeitbeschäftigung, Hobby, Verantwortung, Ungerechtigkeit

a. Herr Meier hat ein interessantes . . . . Er repariert alte Lokomotiven.
b. Dieter hat einen interessanten . . . . Er arbeitet in einem Forschungsreaktor.
c. Herr Zinn hat eine interessante . . . . Er baut kleine Flugzeuge.
d. Ein Lokomotivführer braucht eine lange . . . . Er hat nämlich eine große . . . . Aber er verdient wenig, und das ist eine große . . . .

9.

> Wenn ich abends nach Hause komme, fängt die Arbeit erst richtig an.
> Als ich abends nach Hause kam, fing die Arbeit erst richtig an.

a. Wenn ich meinem Sohn bei den Hausaufgaben geholfen habe, muß ich mit dem Hund spazierengehen.
b. Wenn ich das Garagentor gestrichen habe, muß ich den Zaun reparieren.
c. Wenn ich in München bin, besichtige ich den Olympia-Park.
d. Wenn deine Eltern kommen, fahren wir an den Tegernsee zum Kaffeetrinken.
e. Wenn Hannover 96 spielt, gehe ich natürlich hin.

Lektion 23

1. *Lesen Sie laut*

Ein Gespräch im Hotel

„Ich bin seit einer Woche in München. Ich habe schon das alte und das neue Rathaus gesehen. Ich habe die schönen Kirchen in der Innenstadt besichtigt. Ich war im Schloß Nymphenburg und im Olympiastadion. Was kann ich in München noch alles besichtigen?"

„Interessieren Sie sich für Technik? Dann gehen Sie doch mal ins Deutsche Museum. Dort können Sie die ältesten Flugzeuge besichtigen, zum Beispiel das Gleitflugzeug von Otto Lilienthal, aber auch die modernsten Düsentriebwerke. In der Automobil-Abteilung steht das älteste Auto der Welt, der berühmte Benz-Motorwagen von 1886. Es gibt dort aber auch die neuesten Modelle mit Wankelmotor. Wenn Sie sich nicht für Autos interessieren, können Sie sich natürlich auch die alten Eisenbahnen ansehen."

„Aha, das ist sehr interessant. Aber gibt es im Deutschen Museum eigentlich nur Fahrzeuge?"

„Nein, es gibt dort sehr viele Abteilungen. Zum Beispiel finden Sie da auch eine Abteilung mit alten Musikinstrumenten. Gitarren aus dem 17. Jahrhundert, Geigen aus dem 15. Jahrhundert und Klaviere aus der Zeit von Ludwig van Beethoven. Die müssen Sie sich ansehen."

„Ja, das mache ich. Wenn es heute nachmittag immer noch regnet, gehe ich ins Deutsche Museum."

2. *Nun erzählen Sie.* Was haben Sie im Deutschen Museum alles gesehen?

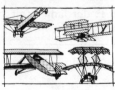 die ersten ...

 alte ...

 die ältesten ...

 die ersten ...

die modern-
sten ...

die erfolgreich-
sten ...

alte ...

alte ...

3. vor dem – vor der

a. Eine Touristengruppe steht mit ihrem Führer gerade ... ... ältesten Telefon.

b. Herr Meier steht mit seinem Sohn ... ... ersten Düsentriebwerk.

c. Wir standen lange Zeit ... ... Prunkwagen von Ludwig II.

d. Dieter steht mit seiner Freundin gerade ... ... alten Lokomotive.

4.

> Bitte, ich möchte gerne das älteste Flugzeug der Welt sehen. –
> Ich weiß nicht, ob wir das älteste haben. Aber in dieser Abteilung stehen viele alte Flugzeuge.

a. das älteste Musikinstrument	**d.** das älteste Fahrzeug
b. der teuerste Prunkwagen	**e.** die teuerste Geige
c. der schnellste Rennwagen	**f.** die älteste Uhr

5.

> In dieser Abteilung steht der berühmte Ford Modell T.
> Er war lange Zeit das erfolgreichste Auto der Welt.
> In dieser Abteilung steht der berühmte Ford Modell T, der lange Zeit das erfolgreichste Auto der Welt war.

a. Hier steht eine Junkers. Sie war lange Zeit die wichtigste Verkehrsmaschine der Lufthansa.

b. Dort fliegt eine Caravelle. Sie war lange Zeit das modernste Flugzeug der Welt.

c. In Stuttgart steht auch ein Fernsehturm. Er war lange Zeit das höchste Gebäude der Bundesrepublik.

d. Hier ist das Foto von unserer Fußballmannschaft. Ich wollte es dir schon lange zeigen.

e. In Rüdesheim haben wir den neuen Wein probiert. Er ist übrigens ausgezeichnet.

6.

> Gibt es in diesem Museum eigentlich nur deutsche Erzeugnisse?
> Ein Tourist möchte wissen, ob es in diesem Museum nur deutsche Erzeugnisse gibt.

a. Gibt es in dieser Abteilung eigentlich auch amerikanische Rennwagen?
Ein amerikanischer Tourist ....

b. Gibt es in diesem Museum eigentlich auch italienische Musikinstrumente?
Ein italienischer Tourist ....

c. Gibt es in diesem Supermarkt auch französischen Käse?
Ein Kunde ....

d. Fahrt ihr nächsten Sonntag wieder an den Tegernsee?
Thomas ....

e. Lesen Ihre Kinder eigentlich nur Krimis?
Die Lehrerin ....

7.

> Hier hängt eine Geige aus dem 18. Jahrhundert. Raten Sie mal, wieviel die gekostet hat. – Das kann ich nicht, ich weiß nicht einmal, was eine neue Geige kostet.

a. Hier steht ein Peugeot von 1904.

b. Dieser Fernseher ist von 1955.

c. Hier steht ein Klavier aus dem 18. Jahrhundert.

d. Hier steht ein Mercedes von 1938.

8.

> Ich finde dieses Buch sehr *langweilig.*
> Haben Sie keine *interessanteren* Bücher?

a. Ich finde dieses Zimmer sehr klein.
b. Dieses Auto ist viel zu alt.
c. Ich finde dieses Kleid sehr teuer.
d. Dieser Wagen ist mir zu langsam.
e. Ich finde diesen Wein nicht gut.
f. Diese Handtasche ist mir viel zu teuer.

9. *Lesen Sie diesen Bericht*

Erstes Motorrad mit Wankelmotor in Nürnberg vorgestellt

Die ersten Motorräder mit Wankelmotor kommen in den Straßenverkehr. „Wir haben einen Schritt in die Zukunft gemacht", sagte der Direktor der Nürnberger Herkules-Werke, der die ersten 50 „Herkules W 2000" an den Handel übergab. Der Preis für diese technische Neuheit ist 4100 DM.

Lektion 24

1. *Lesen Sie laut*

Urlaub mit oder ohne Auto?

Vor ein paar Tagen übernachteten Freunde aus Frankfurt bei uns. Sie kamen aus ihrem Urlaub in Jugoslawien. Früher sind sie jedes Jahr nach Italien gefahren, zuerst an den Gardasee und dann an die Adria. Den Stadtplan von Venedig kennen sie besser als den von Frankfurt. Sie waren mit dem Auto schon in Spanien, in Griechenland und in der Türkei. Aber von Deutschland kennen sie nur München, die Alpen und ein paar Städte am Rhein. Er muß manchmal nach Hamburg oder nach Hannover. Das ist alles. Aber dann fährt er mit dem Zug oder er fliegt. Er findet nämlich, daß der Verkehr auf den deutschen Straßen immer gefährlicher wird.

Dieses Jahr wollten sie ihren Urlaub in Deutschland verbringen, aber ohne Auto. Sie sind mit dem Zug von Frankfurt nach Mainz gefahren. Von dort haben sie eine Dampferfahrt nach Köln gemacht. Dann sind sie nach Hamburg weitergefahren. Von Hamburg sind sie wieder nach Hause geflogen. Unsere Freunde sagten, daß das sehr schön gewesen war. Aber sie sagten auch, daß sie so eine Reise nie wieder machen würden. Das heißt, sie würden natürlich sofort wieder durch Deutschland fahren, aber nicht ohne Auto. Erstens, weil eine Reise mit Bahn, Schiff und Flugzeug für zwei Personen ziemlich teuer ist, und zweitens, weil man immer das schwere Gepäck mitnehmen muß. Unterwegs sagten sie oft: „Wenn wir mit dem Auto unterwegs wären, würden wir jetzt anhalten und spazierengehen, und dann in einer kleinen Wirtschaft Kaffee trinken." Oder: „Wenn wir das Auto hätten, würden wir jetzt noch gerne hier bleiben und abends einen Stadtbummel machen." Aber das ging natürlich nicht. Sie mußten pünktlich zum Flughafen oder zum Bahnhof, weil sie die Tickets oder die Bahnkarten schon gekauft hatten. Und deshalb hatten sie es auch überall eilig.

Also, unsere Freunde sagten, sie würden nie wieder ohne Auto in den Urlaub fahren.

Was ist Ihre Meinung? – Soll man mit oder ohne Auto Urlaub machen?

Was machen Sie selbst? – Nehmen Sie das Auto oder reisen Sie mit Bahn, Schiff oder Flugzeug? – Buchen Sie Ihren Urlaub beim Reisebüro oder fahren Sie lieber per Anhalter?

2.

> Soll man die Flugzeuge abschaffen? –
> Ja, wenn ich Politiker wäre, würde ich die Flugzeuge abschaffen.

a. Soll man die Autos verbieten?
b. Soll man noch mehr Autobahnen bauen?
c. Soll man die Finanzämter abschaffen?
d. Soll man die Olympischen Spiele abschaffen?
e. Soll man in Europa die Währungen abschaffen?

3.

> Ich gebe meiner Tochter Geld, weil sie sich ein Kleid kaufen will.
> Ich gebe meiner Tochter Geld, damit sie sich ein Kleid kaufen kann.

a. Ich habe dieses Buch auch gelesen, weil wir darüber diskutieren wollen.
b. Manfred arbeitet in den Ferien in einer Autowerkstatt, weil er im Sommer nach Frankreich fahren will.
c. Thomas ist in einen Tennisklub gegangen, weil er jeden Tag Tennis spielen will.
d. Er hat seiner Tochter das Auto gegeben, weil sie einen Ausflug machen will.

4.

Spielen Sie im Lotto? Was würden Sie tun, wenn Sie 100 000 Mark gewinnen würden?

a. eine lange Reise machen?
b. eine teure Eigentumswohnung kaufen?
c. ein kleines Haus bauen?
d. für ein paar Jahre den Beruf aufgeben und nichts tun?
e. mit dem Geld einen neuen Beruf lernen?

Ich würde . . . .

Und was glauben Sie, würde Ihr Mann oder Ihre Frau, Ihr Freund oder Ihre Freundin tun?
Ich glaube, er/sie würde . . . .